Melvyn Bragg

Melvyn Bragg's first novel, *For Want of a Nail*, was published in 1965. Since then his novels have included *The Hired Man*, *A Time to Dance*, *Without a City Wall* and *The Maid of Buttermere*. He has also written non-fiction including *Speak for England*, an oral history of the 20th Century and *Rich: The Life of Richard Burton*.

Melvyn Bragg was born in 1939 and educated at Wigton's Nelson Tomlinson School and at Oxford where he read History. He has worked extensively in television and radio, and lives in London and Cumbria.

SCEPTRE

'I enjoyed – nay, loved – Bragg's magnum opus . . . a passionate love story set in deepest Dark Age Britain, *Credo* is part historical novel, part family saga. The action – and there is plenty of it, with lots of hair-raising battles, blood-spattered duels and pestilence – revolves around the extraordinary Bega, a young Irish princess. In the most bewitching way (she is beautiful, strong and royal to boot) Bega personifies the great, page-turning tension between the senses and the spirit – she is at once in love with Padric, a young prince; and determined to be a bride of Christ'
Catholic Herald

'A marvellous read . . . a magnificent effort'
Paul Johnson

'Fine, fascinating detail weaves the fabric of history in this outstanding romantic tragedy'
She (Australia)

'Very impressive . . . he has brought to terrible life the most deadly period of British history'
Financial Times

'The lure of this story is its aura of authenticity. The descriptions of people's lives and expectations are wholly credible and appealing . . . Bragg's scholarship is put to good use in this absorbing yarn'
The Brisbane Courier-Mail

'His depiction of life in this time, in all its brutality and savagery, reeks of authenticity. He is particularly good at conveying the physical sense of place . . . Many genuine historical personages move convincingly through Bragg's pages'
Sunday Independent (Ireland)

CREDO

MELVYN BRAGG

SCEPTRE

Extract from *A History of the English Church and People* by Bede, translated by Leo Sherley-Price and revised by R.E. Latham, published by Penguin Books Ltd, © Leo Sherley-Price, 1955, 1968.

'The Nine Herbs Charm' reproduced from *Anglo-Saxon Verse Charms, Maxims and Heroic Legends* by Louis J. Rodrigues, published by Anglo-Saxon Books, © Louis J. Rodrigues, 1992.

Riddles on pages 175 and 263 reproduced from *Old English Riddles from the Exeter Book* translated by Michael Alexander, published by Anvil Press Poetry, © Michael Alexander, 1980.

Extract from 'The Dream of the Rood' reproduced from *The Earliest English Poems*, translated and introduced by Michael Alexander, published by Penguin Books Ltd, © Michael Alexander, 1966, 1977, 1991.

First published in 1996 by Hodder and Stoughton
A division of Hodder Headline PLC
A Sceptre Paperback

10 9 8 7 6 5 4 3 2 1

A CIP catalogue record for this book is available
from the British Library

ISBN 0 340 66706 0

Typeset by Palimpsest Book Production Limited,
Polmont, Stirlingshire
Printed and bound in Great Britain by
Cox & Wyman Ltd, Reading, Berkshire

Hodder and Stoughton
A division of Hodder Headline PLC
338 Euston Road
London NW1 3BH

To the memory of my father
STANLEY BRAGG

To the memory of my father
STANLEY BRAGG

Another of the king's chief men signified his agreement with this prudent argument, and went on to say: 'Your Majesty, when we compare the present life of man on earth with that time of which we have no knowledge, it seems to me like the swift flight of a single sparrow through the banqueting-hall where you are sitting at dinner on a winter's day with your thegns and counsellors. In the midst there is a comforting fire to warm the hall; outside, the storms of winter rain or snow are raging. This sparrow flies swiftly in through one door of the hall, and out through another. While he is inside, he is safe from the winter storms; but after a few moments of comfort, he vanishes from sight into the wintry world from which he came. Even so, man appears on earth for a little while; but of what went before this life or of what follows, we know nothing. Therefore, if this new teaching has brought any more certain knowledge, it seems only right that we should follow it.'

Bede, *A History of the English Church and People*
Book II, Chapter 13

PROLOGUE

A.D. 647

e went up the mountain as God had commanded and it was there that the miracle happened.

Though only half the way through Lent, Donal felt that his fasting had already turned into starving.

The rocks, almost white under the clear, late-winter sun, glinted marble and granite. He tacked around them carefully to avoid scraping his bare shanks. The wasting monk went slowly, weakly, bowed with hunger and the burden of sin from three score years. The devils gave him no rest.

'Unto thee will I cry, O Lord my Rock. Be not silent to me, lest, if Thou be silent to me, I become like them that go down into the pit.' First he mumbled the words of the psalm in his heavily accented Latin and then he spoke them more firmly. Finally, growing fearful of the silence about him, he called them out. As he did so he stood still and surveyed the stony landscape as barren, he believed, as any wilderness in Israel. 'Save thy people and bless thine inheritance,' he spoke the last verse desperately. 'Feed them also and lift them up for ever.' Feed them. Feed me. If an eagle came now with cooked meat in its beak to drop into my mouth, as happened to St Brendan, would I eat? God help me, God forgive me, I would.

It was not a high mountain, few were in that part of the world, but his weakness made a cliff of every incline. He wanted to scratch the skin from his belly to distract that greedy sinful part of him from its malevolent aches and cries for food. The devils were in his belly, champing on his guts, screaming for meat.

Donal thought, as slowly he steered himself higher, of the heavenly feast with the angels which was promised God's chosen. Every sort of meat, game, beer, mead, bread. Just bread would do, a mouth blessed with fresh bread and then milk to soak it and pulp it and ease it down to that craving craven belly. The munch of fresh bread: for a moment the recollection of its smothering fragrance threatened to overwhelm him.

He rubbed the sweat from his brow on to his lips. They were parched and he could hear no sound of water. His legs were in pain: across his chest was a force clamped like a succubus.

It was a mistake to stop, even to pause. His devils raced into his resting mind, tempting him not only with food and drink but with the sins of the flesh he had never wholly conquered: of lust and envy. 'Unto thee will I cry, O Lord my Rock.'

He was near to sobbing, a frail old man, straggle-grey-haired, in commonest monk's robes, tattered and dirty, legs half numb but used to raw weather. He would never be rid of his sins, he thought. He would never sit at the right hand of God. Was it really God or the Devil himself who had sent him away from the household and up this bitter trackless mountain?

A picture of Christ in the wilderness went through his mind. The devil had urged Him to take all He saw before Him ... Donal put his hands over his eyes – had he seen Christ accept what the devil offered? That would never be forgiven; not by all the interventions of all the saints.

Suddenly he was at the top of the mountain and before him was a large rock slanted from the ground in such a way as to make a shelter from the rising wind. Donal lay there and trembled. All his limbs felt pinched and cramped. In this awesome and unvisited place, he felt at the edge of the world.

What worth was he? How could he be certain that the pit would not claim him and the fires and smokes of hell consume him for ever more? He plucked a stalk of the tough grass and sucked on it for the water. But was there not food in the grass? And was this not breaking his most holy promised fast, promised not only to Christ but to the memory of St Columbanus? Oh, it was all the devil's work. What hope had he, an insignificant creature on the outer edge of God's understanding, to expect the grace of a miracle? Why had he listened to a dream? What soil of sin was that? What a fool to let the devil tempt him into such vanity. Donal whimpered on helplessly, cold now and giddy with emptiness.

His poor thoughts scattered across his past as patternless as a handful of pebbles thrown carelessly into a lake. His mother had soothed his childhood sobbing with a song charmed by gods he had made her abandon. The Devil sent the song into his ear now, lulling and poisoning a spirit enfeebled by vanity. His mother had died unhappy with her new God, her son's God. She longed for the old ways. Donal put his hands over his ears but he could not keep her pagan song away. His will could not prevent sensual excitement gripping his flesh. He wanted to cry out as Christ had cried out on the cross but how could he dare? Merely a life spent in humblest obedience, how could he dare? Oh, little vain unworthy slave.

When he woke the sun was hot on his face. His limbs no longer ached. His belly felt full. There was a soft, warm entrancement in his mind.

She came towards him with the sun behind her, her robe ice-white streamered with gold, around her neck a golden torque, golden armlets along her white arms and, encircling her head, a ring of fine twisted white gold from which her black hair flowed down to her waist. In her hand before her she held what had looked at first like a small cross but, as she came closer, Donal saw it was simply a fragment of wood glistening in the sun.

'Donal,' she said, and the word of his name moved his spirit with a longing so deep that his eyes sparkled with tears. Her tone so silvery soft dispersed all his fears. 'Listen to me. Listen to every word and repeat none. See all that I am and tell none. Do all the things I say and question none. This—' she held forward the fragment of wood and Donal felt pushed back, as if a force were propelling him away '—this is the greatest treasure on earth. This is from the cross on which Our Lord suffered and on which He died before His glorious resurrection and ascent into heaven. God seeks out the humblest,' she smiled again and once more tears surged into Donal's eyes 'and sometimes those who think themselves wholly unworthy. But He sees into the soul of those whose struggle is hard and whose rewards are meagre, whose fears are so terrible and whose salvation they fear for ever in doubt. These are also true servants, Donal. These are God's secret messengers, unsuspected because so unassuming.' She held out the fragment. 'You are one of these.

'This is for you. It is for you to pass on. When you leave this mountain you will see a young girl, a virgin, a child. There will come a time when she will have great use for this gift of God. Its meaning will be revealed as her life lengthens. When I go you will find it beside your right hand. Take it up.' Once more she smiled and Donal's arms reached out to her, but she was gone.

He began to shiver. The sun fled from his face and seemed to flee from the sky itself as the clouds bundled across the lower heaven, lead-grey and turbulent. His limbs shook as if he were in a fit. He stood up and tried to slap and stamp himself warm. He remembered her final instruction and collapsed on to his knees and scrambled for the divine gift. Yes, there it was, lodged beside a small glittering marbled rock. No longer than his thumb, no wider than his smallest finger. 'Take it up,' she had said. 'Take it up.' His courage failed and then the memory of her smile fortified him. He held it in the palm of his hand, unable to think or act at all.

Eventually, after putting down the fragment, with difficulty Donal tore a square from the hem of his coarse habit. He reached out to regain it. His hand hovered and of its own volition made the sign of the cross. When he picked up the fragment, a burn of ice went through his body. He wrapped it up with all the care he could summon, reciting the psalm of David which had helped him up the mountain.

Hunger was gone. Thirst gone. All fear gone. He strode down towards the household, oblivious of the pellets of hail which his devils spitefully hurled on him. No devil could stop a miracle! They hurtled around him in vain. Donal moved quickly so that his heart would not burst. For if he paused at all, he knew that he would be overcome by the joy of the gift given him, he was certain, by the Mother of the Son of Almighty God. No, he would not talk of it. No, he would not mention Her. Yes, he would be humble dumb which was why he had been chosen.

But it had happened! And to him! To Donal, to the most unworthy and insignificant of the brothers and sisters in Christ. In this remotest of spots, he had been granted a Visitation, and he had proof. He chanted the *Magnificat* and came down the last fall of the slope like a deer. Her smile would be with him until his earthly death.

The little girl was at the gate of the compound, a distaff in her hand which looked too big for her, but which she handled skilfully. She was no more than six years old. Her thick, untidy, deep-red hair, uncut, scrambled down her back and all but obscured the rather tight, dark decisive face with the disturbingly pale blue eyes. Her large wolfhound – big enough for her to treat as a pony – snarled viciously but the little girl lightly slapped its jaws and silenced it. She was Bega, daughter of Cathal, princess of the household.

Donal put his hand tight around the cloth which bound the fragment and walked towards her, full of the power of God. In all the slaughter and plague, in all the famine and murders of this world, Bega, with your name which sounds like the giver of the honey of life, in all the torments which may come to you, God will be with you. Christ will be with you. He feared she might have second sight and charged himself not to let his guard drop. To give to Bega the fragment of the True Cross at the right time was now his mission on earth.

She smiled at grim-faced old Donal and let him take her hand and lead her through the gate.

BOOK ONE

❧❧❧❧

CONNACHTA,
WESTERN GALWAY,
IRELAND

❧❧❧❧

A.D. 657

CHAPTER ONE

Was this what a soul felt like, she wondered, as it sped from the body? The sense of speed shot through her like a streak of fear. There was no steady state of heaven, only a racing army of puff-white clouds; no earth, but the fathomless ocean pulsing no more than the thickness of an ox's skin beneath her.

The wind that came out of this great sea which went to the ends of the earth, the wind that came from the resting place of the night sun and the edge of creation itself, roared and slapped into their single square sail. It lifted the slight wicker-framed boat to the tops of the long waves, hurling them towards the shore.

If saints felt like this, Bega thought, then that might be a good reason for seeking out their arduous path. Cathleen, her childhood teacher, had often urged her to do this, and even Donal had hinted at it several times. But it was all much more simple than that, she reflected, as she held the side of the boat, the oars safely in, Congal the fisherman securely at the steering oar: it was something that made you want to sing in your eyes and your heart as well as in your throat and mouth. When white clouds broke, the winter sun hit the water, making the white crests glitter. It plumbed the ocean for deeper blues and greens. In this new world, Bega searched for the word to describe the agony of pleasure this speed, this ocean which faced the sunset, this great God of a wind gave her. Freedom. Yes, freedom. She smiled softly to herself: that was the truth of her feeling, the secret joy which possessed her so completely and made her helpless in its grip. It was her first time at sea.

Padric stood beside the mast, clasping it with one hand, ignoring the constraining looks of Congal. What force this fragile small boat had when combined with the powers through which God governed the world, he thought. This little boat, which could be carried by two and could carry six and now carried half that number plus a few glistering fish, still squirming for life in the bottom, slithering silver. This tiny craft multiplied by a hundred, a thousand, could fling an army on to an enemy shore so rapidly and so powerfully that the men would leap off and go into battle like giants. This is how the Germanic Tribes had fallen on his home country, Britain, Padric reflected.

As he stood full in the power of the boat's speed, he could imagine again – as so often haunted him – those pagan warriors skim from the eastern seas on to the long white strands of Northumbria which now they called their own and on across to Rheged on the Western shore where the last of the Britons, his father's people, Arthur's people, were now threatened with extinction.

Padric dreamed of defeating them, and of claiming back the whole of the island for those to whom it rightfully belonged. But his father had felt that he needed the strength of true Christianity and scholarship such as could now be found only in Ireland. He had lived there for some time and counted among his tasks the education of Princess Bega.

Now it was time to go home. He wanted to start the battle to restore the kingdom of Rheged which had existed before the Romans. The desire had been growing. In the sting of salt and the bucking of the ox-skin sealed boat as it flew for the shore, the force outside himself fired an equal force within himself and he felt sure.

The invaders would be thrown back. He, Padric of Rheged, would drive them back across the sea which had brought them unwelcome to seize a land not their own.

He turned and smiled at Bega, but her eyes were closed and he had to shout out her name to claim her attention. For a moment he caught the compelling image of this strong-featured young – woman, dark face upturned, calmly blissful, hair wild as the waves, lean body braced against the speed, spellbound, utterly unlike the childish mischief, the tease who had tagged his last two years. Padric was surprised to find her beautiful. He held out his hand.

Bega looked at Congal – could she stand? He shook his head but smiled. Padric stood above her, slim, even spare, lighter than her brothers, but taller, with long hair much redder than her own and almost as wild. Both were Celts, he British, she of the Irish strain. A sadness in repose lay within both of them as if they sensed that time was shortening for that ancient race.

He held out his hand once more and gave her a look which dared her and which he knew she would never refuse. Wedging her feet on the bottom of the hurtling boat she collected herself and then stood, swayed, and was all but flung overboard. The water and the sky seemed one, a shaft of hot sunlight blinded her eyes. Padric appeared dizzily through a tremble of mist. She reached out and was clasped by him, as he leaned to take her by the waist and haul her towards him, making her safe. He held her hand longer and more tightly than necessary and to her surprise she did not object. They stood together as the sea made its final rush for the shore and Congal steered them to a sandy sliver which took the boat as easily as a shell takes an oyster.

As they carried the boat up the wide deserted beach beyond the high tide mark, Bega saw at some distance old Donal hobbling towards them and prayed for forbearance. She wanted to hold on to this new exhilaration, this upsurge of new feeling. Donal always fussed her back to dusty practicalities. Padric too was still stirred by the thoughts and ambitions the great ride on the sea had reaffirmed in him. It was as if, for both, their bodies had gone ahead of their minds and hearts which were still skimming freely on the ocean and played no part in the mundane business of pulling the curragh up the rib-sanded shore.

'Would you like to sail the sea again?' he asked.

'Oh yes.' She did not look at him to keep close the excitement at that prospect. 'Oh yes,' she repeated softly.

'Would she make a sailor, Congal?'

The large, salt-scarred fisherman smiled and nodded at the two young princelings in front of him as he wound up his nets with care. Bega held the basket while Padric filled it with the fish they had caught.

'Imagine . . .' said Padric, and then trailed off. It was not time to talk about his ambitions and dreams. Besides, she was still a tease, her responses unpredictable. Although, at nineteen, he was three years older than she, it was the rather spoilt young woman who often assumed the superior role and had done since his arrival at her father's household.

Everyone had seen it as a game. Her father had encouraged it as he encouraged her in all her wilfulness. Her brothers were not displeased that this scholarly and war-hungry British prince should be so trussed up in invisible threads by their cunning Irish sister. None gave Padric credit for gallantry. None – not even Bega and Padric themselves – understood that the teasing might be an expression of something other which neither was yet ready to understand. Sometimes she had irritated and frustrated him so much that he had sworn to himself to have nothing more to do with this girl-woman, who challenged her brothers with the sword and contemptuously outscored them in the lessons Padric gave. But he was soon back with her, always a pace ahead but always at her heel.

'I would like to go on the sea again,' she said with unaccustomed earnestness. 'I would.'

She wanted to taste again the sensation that had swept through every cell in her body and made her feel more different and yet more *right*, more Bega than any experience she had ever had. Freedom. Where did that come from? Only in perfect service, surely? So what had she been serving?

'There could be a time,' said Padric, rather grandly, she thought. 'We'll see how you behave.'

He could be such a boy!

She picked out one of the juicier trout and threw it in his face. As often happened, he hesitated for the fraction of an instant before he reacted. But that dark face, the pale eyes warm yet always mocking, the defiance of the slender young body, made him laugh, however ruefully.

Yet in the boat there had been more than that. There had been a flicker of what he thought he recognised but she would not let take hold, like a spark from which the breeze will not allow the flame to settle on the tinder.

Behind Donal, near now, was Maeve, Bega's companion, a slave. Murcha, Bega's dog, big as a wolf, had galloped way ahead of them and snivelled a little at Bega's unusually subdued welcome.

'You must come home immediately,' Donal gasped out but even that short and urgent message was delivered with the adoration to which he had for so long subjected her. Bega had to respect Donal's age and his piety; as the humblest of all the monks he was given special dispensation. But sometimes his intimate conspiratorial overtures made her want to shake him. It was as if he wanted her to know that there was something unique between them but under no circumstances would he reveal it. She had challenged him on this more than once but he had turned tail on every occasion. It irritated her and she blamed herself for being so impatient with a holy old man who, as now, never failed in wanting to help her. She had become so used to being obeyed in her own world, so heady with the liberty given her by her autocratic father, that she could never fully control her restlessness with him and with many others in her father's iron-ruled household.

'Your father sent me because he could rely on my finding you wherever you were.' Donal now did a poor imitation of her father's voice. 'Donal will find Bega, he said, if she's stuck in the cleft of a rock in the middle of a forest in the kingdom of the furthest shore. He'll pry her out, his truffle, won't he? Put Bega down the smallest hole in Connachta, he says, and Donal will turn himself into the dog small enough to reach her. And he's right. Here I am. And Maeve to help you back on your way.'

Why was Maeve here? Donal's garrulity could be borne, his exaggeration was a matter of course, but the presence of Maeve was disturbing. Bega saw Padric smiling aimlessly at her and thrust the basket of fish into his arms more vigorously than necessary.

'What is the reason? Why must I return?'

'Maeve will tell you. I was told not to.' Donal was bent now, with severe old age, his meagre frame bowing over but at this point he executed a little jig which threatened to straighten him up. Bega's apprehension grew. 'Your father told me not to,' said Donal, 'and I never say what I am told not to say.' This boast seemed to afford the old man the most quicksilver private pleasure. He looked up after these words and his lips moved moistly in a silent prayer.

'Let me walk back with you then, Maeve,' said Bega.

Bega nodded to Donal, now bowing at her once again and watching her closely with eyes she could cheerfully have blackened. It was a small comfort to turn Maeve around from the gaze of Padric and, taking the plumper girl firmly by the arm, steer her towards the nunnery where they were lodging.

For a few deliberate moments Bega did not speak. She intuited what had happened. For a few moments longer she wanted to live without that knowledge being confirmed. Behind her the surge of the sea reminded her of how recently she had felt so unrestrained. She walked steadily but rather heavily, knowing for certain that the new world she had just discovered on that ocean would be for ever closed to her once she heard her fate.

'You look lovely, Maeve,' she said, to delay still further the execution of the sentence. 'You look as if you have benefited from my absence.'

Maeve blushed at the accuracy of it. With Bega gone from the household, she had flourished in a way she never could in the nipping, badgering presence of her mistress. Maeve wanted no mistress nor had she been born to have one. However kindly Bega tried to behave, she was no greater a princess than Maeve herself had been. Capture in a raid already turned into epic song had changed Maeve from mistress to slave: in name but not in the truth of it, she insisted.

'You are a real beauty, Maeve,' said Bega, briskly flattering the rather sulky young woman at her side. 'You are the woman our poets say is the ideal of Irish beauty.'

So she was. She had the thick, glowing black hair, long as Bega's (never cut since birth). But where Bega's was a tough and tangled briar of red-brown curls and straggles, a thicket of colours never to be tamed save into savage plaits, Maeve's sweep of velvet was as silken as the hair of the Virgin. Her complexion was marbled white, which no weather seemed to reach, no harsh sun or storm blemish, whereas Bega's colour was gypsy, white only in rage. The faint ruby foxglove cheeks of Maeve had earned the direct praise – in front of Bega – of Padric himself in one of his more foolish moods. Then there were blue eyes, not the faded distant mysterious washed blue of Bega but hard Celtic sea-blue eyes, shining out from under the black eyebrows in full knowledge of their beauty.

Bega had long since given up trying to convert Maeve into a friend. She still had some confidence in her as an ally. This particular encounter undermined that.

'There's an O'Neill wants to marry you,' said Maeve with some truculence. 'Not the son of the High King himself but of his brother. Soon he'll be king enough. Your father is very full of the pride of it.'

It was as Bega had anticipated and feared. Her father's insistence on searching out a dynastic marriage had resisted her fiercest arguments. Nevertheless she had secretly hoped he would never compel her.

And you, poor Maeve, thought Bega, would have welcomed it. Had the fortunes of war tilted the other way it would very likely have been you set to marry one of the greatest princes of Ireland.

'And you so much more fitted to it,' said Bega, pursuing her thought aloud.

'Fitted. For what now?' Maeve had good cause to be bitter. Her father and two older brothers were dead. There was no one to pay a ransom price for her release and she and everyone else knew it. Her best fate was not to be the wife, not even to be the acknowledged concubine – as Bega's mother had been – but a mistress, third in line and, unlike the concubine, with no rights. But for the turn of battle she could have been a queen.

'Say it,' Bega commanded her. 'Say it.' She scooped and took up a small piece of driftwood and hurled it surprisingly far, setting off her hound in full yelping pursuit.

But Maeve would not reply. Perhaps she does not know how much she hates me, Bega thought. I would rather she said it aloud than kept it a secret. Secrets are obstacles and they soon become invisible walls.

'I would rather you married him than I,' said Bega quietly. 'If we could exchange places I would sooner he took you than me.'

It is easy to say that, Maeve thought, hating Bega even more for articulating it. It is easy when you have a conquering father, a household growing in strength and a Prince of O'Neill riding to marry you.

They walked on in silence towards the still-distant knot of buildings which made up the tiny nunnery – God's final outpost braving the might of the Atlantic, which was the waterway to the edge of the world. Both young women knew that this marked a decisive change. With Bega gone, what would Maeve's role be?

'What is this news then?' Padric asked when he and Donal caught up with them. They were leading the horses which had been tethered near the boat.

Bega shook her head at Maeve who stayed silent.

Padric looked at the two women. One glanced away, her head lowering in seductive modesty, flirtatious submission. The other looked him in the eye, level it seemed, although she was far from being as tall as he. He felt aroused but by which one? By both? 'What does he know who has not been tempted?' – the words of Solomon came to Padric as he felt the disturbance of desire.

'I'll come back with you,' said Padric – Donal had told him they were to return in the morning – 'I've finished my work here and I want to talk to your father about releasing me.'

'So it is now you choose to go,' said Bega, angry with him for deserting her even though she had not told him of O'Neill. Why could he not see that she needed him?

'Now or soon.'

'Is Padric not to know, then?' Donal enquired.

'Am I to be the only one not to know?'

'Tell him,' Bega ordered Maeve and then flung herself on to her horse and kicked it too hard. She pulled sharply at the reins, causing it to buck, but her teeth flared as determinedly as those of the small stallion. No horse would throw her. She hand-whipped it along the hard sand and then inland to the home of nuns and a few monks where she had been taken by Padric to spend some weeks with Cathleen before the ailing old woman died.

Maeve told him brusquely as Padric stared after the galloping figure. Bega held the reins in one hand only, the other slapping the beast's haunches or pushing the hair out of her face so that it flew behind her like a cloak. Murcha streaked and zigzagged about the horse as if one run were not enough and it must follow several paths at the same time. Padric watched her until she became indistinguishable in the twilight. On the sea, he remembered acutely, she had been beautiful. He remembered the hard clasp of her hand still through his fingers.

'She is full of grace,' said Donal and Padric was surprised to find the unexpected remark so true to his own feelings.

CHAPTER TWO

In the guests' quarters Bega had been provided with a separate space, draped across with long woollen cloaks, making a snug cell. It was here that Bega flung herself on to her knees to pray with all her power to St Brigid, her chosen patron and heroine. Royal, as Bega was, holy, which Bega in her best moods longed to be, a ruler of her principality around Kildare and the equal of the virile chieftains who followed her word and kings who bowed down to her: Bega loved her intemperately. Now Brigid was one of the heavenly host able to transmit her powers to those whose prayers could reach her. Since learning as a child about Brigid from Cathleen, Bega had sensed a special bond with her and had clear proof that Brigid would listen to her prayers. Sometimes she dared to believe that she was being called by her.

When she was seven, thanks to St Brigid she had found her long-lost pet hen in a hole beside the torn roots of an oak tree. When she was nine, her father had given her the best of the three horses he had captured in a raid, preferring her over his sons – again thanks to Brigid. Her golden ring, inherited from her mother, had been stolen and only owing to the intercession of St Brigid had the thief been caught and mutilated and the ring returned, never to leave her finger since. While on the night of storms, when the walls had shaken and fallen, she and Cathleen had slept right through, guarded by St Brigid. But now she did not know what her prayers should say.

She was rigid in trained concentration but what was her request? The harder she screwed up her brow, the more clearly she saw Padric leaning out from the mast, holding out his hand, his red hair streaming, the white sail so taut behind him, smiling at her as she swayed dangerously on to her feet for that willingly unsupported moment before he caught her. Now he would go back across the sea to what he still called Britain.

She had never imagined he would go. He had come into her father's household soon after her thirteenth birthday, which her father had celebrated according to the instructions of a soothsayer whose word he listened to as keenly as to that of his poet or priest. Until then Bega had been a rather isolated child: simply the wrong gender for her stepbrothers, too sharp for any comfortable companion, too keen on dogs and her horse and the games of war as well as being so quick at learning – too uncomfortable and full of herself altogether.

Soon after that birthday, Padric had been enrolled as her tutor for part of his time. All but unconsciously he had become her friend, perhaps her only friend. Bega had simply claimed him.

The young man's background and manners and his dependency on her father meant that he was seen as no threat. In fact, Bega often seemed a threat to him. In mock spear and sword play – with wooden sticks – she would beat him mercilessly: unpunished, since he chose never to hurt her. If he failed to teach her something rapidly enough for her temperament, she would publicly scold him. She would demand he come with her out into the hills nearby – never very far, but places which she would not be allowed to navigate alone – and then torment him by hiding or deliberately baffling the path so that they got lost. She would enjoy his concern that they might not be back inside the fortified walls until after sunset.

They were like brother and sister, said her father, and in some circumstances a marriage would have been a possibility. But she was his only daughter and he had dynastic ambitions nearer home. Yet the family of Rheged was a great one, rightly claiming King Arthur as its noblest ancestor; and although it was on the retreat it could rise again.

Bega's father – who had ascended to kingship by force alone – had a regal and romantic view of history. Some kings were sent to rule and rule they would even if that rule were interrupted by the plagues of defeat and temporary overthrow. At one time, Bega had suspected the possibility of a marriage was crossing her father's mind, and she was confused. Padric's place in her life was as the person with whom she could do anything she wanted *and* the only person who would always give in to her. At times he seemed part of her. Better by far, she thought, not to introduce the notion of marriage which would have changed everything. He was her friend, her comrade, as her father and her brothers had comrades. She had steeled her thoughts against it and it had gone away.

Why had he said he wanted to be released now? And why were these thoughts rushing so madly through her mind when she was seeking to compose it to prepare herself to meet her father and formally respond to this unwelcome news?

Some power which she did not understand was making her mind ache. It was painful to think in a way so foreign to her background and training but like a loose thread which she could not pull out, the elusive pressure teased her beyond patience. Just as that strange sensation – freedom – had come to her on the sea, so this news, Padric's announcement of his departure and the slow sadness of Cathleen's lingering death acted on her mind in these unaccustomed surroundings to crystallise her deeper hopes and ambitions, to strengthen the slender longings of her adolescence. She did not want marriage! She wanted to be bold, alone, out in the world for God, fighting His battles against the heathen, carrying His torch throughout the dark world of ignorance and belief. Once formulated, the idea seemed inevitable. Yet she knew it had to be kept fast to herself. It was against her father's will and to set your face against the will of a father such as hers . . . But still, Bega consoled herself, she had a heavenly Father who would surely help her to pursue a path aimed at spreading His word. She smiled to herself at the vision of the adventures she could have and then, out of nowhere it seemed, the spell was utterly broken when she said, as if in prayer, 'I hate you, Padric.' And then she crossed herself and asked St Brigid to forgive her.

What would the man O'Neill look like?

Chaitline, whom they called Cathleen, stroked the young woman's hand and tried to soothe her.

'Your father will have taken care to look out for you,' she

said. 'You have always been his favourite, ever since your mother died.'

Cathleen was in the smallest of the cluster of beehive huts, the one designated as the hospital. It was only because of Cathleen and her illness that Bega had been able to make this first and sole move away from her father's household, a full day's ride from home. Cathleen was her father's aunt, and had mothered Bega since her real mother's death. A year or so previously she had asked permission to come to the nunnery and end her days in prayer. When Bega, fearing that Cathleen might die without giving her a blessing, had begged her father to let her go, he had capitulated. Padric would be a suitable guardian. Four of her father's best men provided the escort across the wild lands to the coast which faced that final sea where God took down the sun to the black world.

A single candle illuminated the tiny cabin. Cathleen lay on the low narrow frame of a wooden cot, flat on the board, wanting no comfort there. She wore the long gown common to all the women of the place: plain, close-woven with some simple spirals and other motifs worked in around the collar. Her hair was thin and coarse, grey. Her skin was fine, almost transparent, glistening over the prominent cheekbones and the large knuckles stained brown.

'I want to go into the world,' Bega whispered.

'Why is that, Bega?'

Because I just *do*, Bega thought, and knew that it would not answer. Outside she heard the sea and it excited her: she could see the miles of barren land and that thrilled her too. The very desolation of this holy place seemed to inspire her to go out and see what the world was.

'It's true that from a few, so few places as small and insignificant as this,' said Cathleen, telling Bega the story she loved to hear repeated, 'we have sent men who have kept alive the word of God and the works of Christ, from here across all the world. And some women,' she added, shyly.

As the wind grew louder outside the thatched hut and the sea nearby roared again and again at the shore, these tales of courage and learning, of high purpose, great journeys and ultimate dedication came haltingly from the older to the younger woman, calming the one in her weakness but fermenting the other in her turbulence.

The story the old woman told was bold and rich enough to match the heroic tales in the Bible. It was a story of scholarship and the devotion of saints who had continued to flourish in Ireland in ways unmatched elsewhere in the barbarised darkness following the end of the Roman Empire. It was as if the whole weight and future of the world's learning and Christian purpose were being tested by God Himself, and had come to depend on small and isolated communities, especially those in Ireland and those fed from Ireland. In the hands of Celtic scholars and some isolated few elsewhere, lay the transmission of those worlds of learning and faith and the power of knowledge. Cathleen feasted on that chosen few and knew that in Bega she had kindled a spirit which could also rise to this ultimate challenge.

She prayed that Bega would be called to God's work and, despite her father's decision, she told the girl now, as so often, that with God's help she could go out, alone, among the hordes of the heathen and take them the Word, suffering, if necessary, martyrdom and death for His sake.

When she listened to Cathleen, Bega wanted nothing more.

But how? How, when she had to marry an O'Neill and be bolted up in his household, kept fast and bound with those Irish warriors who loved fighting more than anything on earth? She needed to appear calm, for Cathleen's sake, but her feelings were extreme.

Yet it seemed to Bega that if she could continue to read, which had come so easily to her, and teach the words of the saints to the pagans, then that would be a life which would take every ounce of her strength. She wanted no less. She loved to see the shapes and strokes of line and turn them into words: she loved the idea of battling against enemies external and internal and all her will and spirit being consumed in that battle. She had dared suggest that to Padric on more than one occasion and he had not laughed at her.

'If you want enough what you say you long for, then pray that it will be granted,' said Cathleen, as she had said many times. 'Indeed, I know,' she emphasised, 'pray and it will be granted.'

Was Cathleen being merely kind or was this evidence of the gift of second-sight her father said had been given to the old woman? Bega was too hot in confusion to ask and, besides, Cathleen was tired.

It was unfair, Bega knew, to bring her own troubles to this

holy woman now preparing herself for her heavenly marriage. She ought to be helping Cathleen compose herself, but instead she could not contain her own selfish feelings.

She tried.

'Tell me again about St Columbanus,' she said, wanting to revisit the comforting tales. Cathleen in her childhood had met the great saint in his old age when he had returned to Ireland after a mission which had taken him to Gaul and Northern Italy. It was Cathleen who had interested Donal in St Columbanus and Donal's small hoard of his sayings provided the starting point for many of his largely unheeded monologues.

It was not so much his adventures which drew Bega in – St Brendan's fantastic voyage was far more seductive, with the white talking birds, the gryphon and the miraculous islands – as what Columbanus had said. It was his words which captured her. 'Even when we consume Christ through love, even when we devour Him through longing, we nevertheless wish to long for Him as if we were hungry.' Only such a profound and demanding longing could satisfy Bega and so far, she knew, she had failed to achieve or deserve it. Secretly, she admired his arrogance when he said 'When I believed anybody else, I almost became stupid'.

'"We ask You that we may know what we love",' quoted Cathleen. 'Do you ask, Bega? Do you know?'

The old woman was exhausted but Bega could not wrench herself from the candlelit containment of this place made sacred by the dying of such a holy being.

'And Padric?' said Cathleen, who had seen and noted the two of them entwined in games and teasing; seen how he quickened the girl and how she exasperated but beguiled him.

'He's to go back home!'

'Ah.' Cathleen nodded: the wound had been revealed. Not only was a stranger about to claim her, but the truest friend of her youth was leaving her. In this unhappy time, might not the spirit of God seize this child whom she thought would serve Him so well?

'Do you know what you love, Bega?'

Bega was silent and then shook her head. That was the truth of it.

'I will pray for you,' Cathleen said. 'And now you must go.'

Bega stood up, reluctantly and bowed her head as she went to the low door. Outside the wind rose higher, the sea's sound gave it a texture of impending terror. Bega suddenly realised something. How foolish of her! Foolish and selfish not to have realised it! She turned and took the two paces back to Cathleen, knelt and buried her head in the wasted chest of the fragile woman who had denied all life save that which she had been taught met with the will of God.

'I will never see you again,' Bega said, 'will I? Will I?'

Her old nurse stroked the great tangle of hair and ssshhhed her as she had done so often when Bega was a child.

'Will I?' Bega repeated, beginning to weep.

There was a pause and then Cathleen repeated the words of the great scholar and saint whom she had once been blessed to meet: 'We ask You that we may know what we love'.

Bega's tears could not be checked. So much, too much had happened: too much freedom and hope, with Padric on the sea, started, stopped too abruptly; this new sentence of marriage. Too much misery in the knowledge of her own longings and weakness. Now this certain loss, this end of one she had thought would always be there. She knew that she ought to recognise that Cathleen, like her mother, was about to enter the Heavenly Kingdom, but a stubborn resistance saw it only as loss, and she cried like a child.

'There, ssshhh,' said Cathleen, her voice low and sad now. 'God will bless you if you submit to His will.'

Bega walked out of the tiny hospital. The great unseasonably warm wind gusting in from the sea filled her cloak as it had so wonderfully filled the sail of the boat.

Instead of returning to her quarters, she walked some way towards the shore. The rush and suck, the lush retreating roar of water across pebble and sand pulled her. Clouds scurried across a half-moon and the light caught the waves; their endless flickering and movement mesmerised Bega.

She folded her arms across her breasts and shook her head into the warmth and mass of air. To be spun on the back of the wind, lifted high, halfway to heaven and let what come happen! The feeling she experienced now, of the forces taking her as one of them, fused with the fierce thrill of losing control, of freedom which had swept through her on the boat earlier in the day. Never in her life had she been allowed such liberty of mind and body. How could you live so that such a feeling was sustained? Such exhilaration, such happiness – despite Cathleen, despite O'Neill, despite the life bound in fate behind her – such happiness as she faced the broken black sound and sweep.

She wanted to be back on the sea with Padric. She wanted never to leave this empty place. She wanted to feel at such ease with the wind and the quiet souls of the saints balancing the warm darkness.

Was she blaspheming by thinking such thoughts? Whether she was or not, sensations of flight and floating, of whirling in the waves and spinning through scudding clouds continued to excite and even agitate her mind until, after some hours, a calm weariness came over her and she went back to her narrow cot for a snatched sleep before dawn, leaving, she felt, a hallowed place, full of nothing but the elements of life and the presence of God.

❦❦❦❦

Bega's father had sent four men. Padric arranged the column. He would be in the front with one of the men, followed by Bega and Maeve, then Donal with the pack pony carrying the gifts, including salted dolphin meat. The two other men brought up the rear. In single file on the more narrow tracks, he would lead. The dogs spread around the column like outriders.

All four men had swords. Padric's, a gift from his grandfather, Urien of Rheged, was exceptionally long and highly embossed. Bega had seen him practise with it and though her brothers were stronger, neither could match him for speed and precision. She had caught the thoughtful look on her father's face while watching Padric exercise with that long-bladed silver-hafted sword, envied by everyone who saw it.

The two women carried light spears. Donal refused all weapons – though he, like all the monks, knew how to handle instruments of war and was expected to take his place in any battle. But in his sanctified age, he preferred the simple armour of a cross.

Padric had scarcely been able to meet the gaze of either Maeve or Bega. But he had noticed that the latter was red-eyed and felt guilty for it. He had observed also that underneath the shoulder-clasped Irish cloak that all the women wore, and underneath her long woollen dress, she wore trousers, sensibly, for this long ride, unlike Maeve, who appeared fresh as dew, her eyes flitting away from him when he looked, causing his heart to jump in pursuit.

Bega had been the last to mount, called twice from the hut in which Cathleen lay dying. Padric was annoyed with her tardiness and impatient to be gone, but the sorry state of her face checked his tongue.

Soon they had pulled away from the nunnery. The sea, now a vast and sullen mass, almost black, flattened under the louring grey cloud which lifted in slow and ominous formation, was behind them. The hail began almost immediately, now at their backs, now smarting into their faces as the path twisted up towards the perilous stretch of bogland which had to be crossed. It was a land of large and awkward boulders, rolled there, Bega thought, as plausibly by the gods and dragons in the local pagan tales as by any Christian deity. It was a land of water in innumerable small loughs and pools, in cuts of the turf and suppurating from under the sodden earth.

Now and then a pair of turf-cutters could be seen. Four times she saw a wisp of woodsmoke. As the cloud lowered until it seemed to threaten to press them into the earth and the hail spat bitterly in their faces as if the devil were jeering at them for their faith, Bega withdrew into a state of abstraction, like a trance, following the rhythm of her horse.

Before she met O'Neill she had to have a plan. She catechised herself more severely the deeper the small column went into the land where tales of giants and goblins were still believed. They passed shiny lichened rocks, reeds slanted in the water like slender stakes driven into the ground to face the charge of the enemy and an occasional tree so bare and contorted it looked like a soul trapped in torment, a Judas tree. Perhaps it was. Cathleen never told the stories of those agonised Celtic monks here and in other wild spots who had failed their God.

Once only she saw a cluster of dwellings and those of the poorest sort, built of sticks and reeds, walled about with sods and thatched with rushes, grasses, flax, heather – whatever was available. The thatch was held down by large stones attached to ropes which looped over the low roof out of which came a dismal scurry of peat smoke.

What would life be without Padric? She tried to force her mind into his. At times she had been convinced she knew what he was thinking. But not now. She had to see his face, especially the eyes: now all she saw was the back, upright, the back of the head, glancing from side to side. He was playing the war leader, she thought, escorting a party through unsafe territory! Yet her confidence in their youthful innocence was not quite what it had been twenty-four hours before during that boat ride – unique, unbearable to think about now.

Padric was aware of Bega's gaze and even in some degree of her need, but he did not turn to meet it. He did not want to run the danger of explanation. His desire to return to his home had been confirmed in him the instant after he had guessed that she was to be married. In his youth, it did not strike him as having a vital connection. His open admiration of Maeve, whose obstinate character and desire not to appear a slave genuinely attracted him, did not strike him as any attempt to antagonise Bega. He saw that he had come to Ireland – at the command of his father – to learn, and he *had* learned. He had come to make contact with those who had been forced to flee from Rheged and he had built up his contacts, his alliances. He had seen the Irish ways of fighting and living and that would be useful. But he had dawdled too long and this close friendship with young Bega now seemed childish.

His sole duty was to be back in Britain to regain the independence of his tethered kingdom. This simple conclusion both calmed and buoyed him and he used the journey through the bleak boglands to plan strategies, devise escapes should the column be attacked and imagine how he would defend those put in his charge. He smiled, despite his determination to put aside all such thoughts, at the notion of Bega needing anyone to defend her.

The closer she drew to her home, the greater grew Bega's fear. A fear she had never in her life experienced. A fear that was like a sudden night fastening on her. Inside her was all darkness as if Christ had fled. The cold of her flesh made the fear worse. Perhaps she was dying. She wanted to cry but would not give in to that weakness. Then she wanted to shout aloud but to whom? For what?

At dusk they topped the last hill and looked down at the flares of light which marked out the extent of her father's household – the great hall, the high wall, all the other buildings hugged together like a small fortified town. Indeed such rare settlements were the nearest Ireland came to boasting a town. Outside the walls were buildings propped against it as if queuing to get in to the power place of King Cathal of Connachta. Usually the sight made Bega feel proud, even arrogant – that all this had been made by her father whom she could talk to as freely as his sons. But now. The place frightened her.

Padric looked around to check his troops before the final descent. She caught his eye, her pleading look: he turned away. She wanted to escape, to go back to that exultant feeling of freedom on the sea. With careful steps her horse went down the hill. Murcha and the other dogs began to bay and the dogs inside the compound howled back at the approaching band. Padric finally took his right hand off the hilt of his sword where it had stayed throughout the journey.

Her father came to the gate, legs apart, powerful, short, a man many times wounded and scarred for life, a man who had changed gods and women and friends and allies. A man never beaten in battle.

CHAPTER THREE

K ing Cathal, son of Rogallach mac Uatach, whose great ancestor was Brion, son of Echu Mugmedon, could stand there for only a few moments because of the imperative call of the diarrhoea, so Bega and her party entered his tuath, his household, unwelcomed.

Even in her cringe of fear, Bega was impressed anew by the sight of what her father had built. As he had made more conquests and fought his way from a hovel in the boglands to become one of the four kings of Connachta, she had heard many epic poems describing his battles, the cattle raids, the individual challenges and bloody ventures. But nothing for her matched the kingly settlement which had been planned and completed in her twelfth year.

At its centre stood the great hall, more than seventy feet long and twenty feet wide, with stone making up the first few feet and then the rarer and more valuable, more royal split logs flat side in, semi-circular side rippling up outside to the high thatched roof. A cowl protected the hole which ventilated the smoke. There were no windows. It was the largest building for miles, for a day, for a week's ride, Muiredach their poet would boast. Bega had always felt secure in the place. Even burdened by her new fear of the future, the solid mass of the settlement made her proud.

Inside the hall were the wall hangings she had helped to weave; the peat smoke drifting to the open timbered ceiling, gently kippering everything it touched; the great oak table for feasts, the chairs, the ordering of the wooden plates and cups. Large thick cloaks draped the floor, which were used as beds by the close male members of the family. Cathal had the only private room.

On the walls were displayed shields of beaten enemies and the severed heads of those who had been slaughtered. Bega's father still held in part to the old pagan faith and, when a ferocious enemy had been vanquished, he followed the example of his hero King David and of so many warriors in so many sagas: he hacked off the head. For some weeks they would be skewered on the sharpened poles just inside the gate and when wind and weather had honed them, they were brought in to ornament the great hall.

As the horse walked the last few paces towards the stables, Bega caught the face of a friendly slave here, a child of a slave there, heard the loud voices of her brothers and cousins and warmed to the close weave of the self-sufficient place. It gave her a sense of being as safe as a root in the half-comprehended dark. Much as she had enjoyed being at the nunnery, she had still lulled herself to sleep by switching her mind to this place, usually at this time in the dwindling light of first nightfall.

The three slaves from the small island closest to Rheged were laying branches and bracken in paths to control the slithering mud. Though the hail had stopped, a steady drizzle persisted. Around and about the hall a higgledy-piggledy arrangement housed two hundred or so people. These buildings, propped against the hall like buttresses, included the women's quarters, the special room for Cathal and his queen, his concubine or one of his mistresses, the brewery, the blacksmith's, the washhouse, the stable for the war horses. Further stables were quartered against the outer wall, which Cathal had built particularly high with a large quantity of stone under the thick, covering sods of turf. There were hovels for the slaves, rather better quarters for the free men and patches quartered off for the two-wheeled, long-shafted war chariots.

Much of the arable land farmed was outside the walls, but inside grew a fair spread of vegetables. All of the many long-horned cattle, the pride of Cathal, were there, all safely in their pens, some of the goats, and a few sheep, although the majority of those were outside with the shepherds. Pigs truckled about at will, as did the hens, the ducks, geese and the innumerable lean and hairy dogs. Strong smells, stenches which carried the best reminders of childhood, the full steam stink of excrement from a variety of intestines, the tang of peat smoke, the odours of the meat roasting, the cauldron of broth all but permanently brewing, the sweat of men, women and animals, all this was inhaled affectionately by Bega.

A slave led their horses away. Padric sought to avoid her, Bega thought (although he was merely absorbed in seeing that the gifts to Cathal were carefully handled) and so with Murcha as ever sniffing about her footsteps, she took the hard course and went to wait for her father in the hall. Her one pocket of hope was that throughout her life he had prided himself on denying her nothing.

Inside the hall she shivered from the warmth. Its brown and yellow-beige colours lit by a few rushes and the tall fat candles promised some sort of reassurance. Women were preparing the meal. Others were weaving. None was idle. Most of the men were outside seeing to the animals, cleaning their weapons, butchering the fresh game or leisurely tasting the last of the day beside one of the open fires which smouldered even against the drizzle.

Cathal's diarrhoea was the complaint he most detested. He could endure the bleeding gums, the teeth could be anaesthetized by strong beer or mead on occasion, the rashes on his skin could be scratched or soothed depending on his mood, wounds and scars were to be borne as a matter of course, but this diarrhoea which sent him scuttling away like a child with the least warning, was intolerable. Cathal blamed it on the famine he had just managed to live through when a boy. Conditions had been so extreme that men ate horses, dogs, cats, rats, roots and, it was rumoured, in some less controlled places there was cannibalism. Surviving that experience had helped sustain the anger which had taken him from being princeling of a small chieftain's dun to a king in his great tuath, fit to challenge even the mightiest kings in Ireland. But it had left him looking older than his forty-nine years – visaged like a gargoyle of bitter fury, scabbed, pock-cheeked, scalded with a sense of urgency, cruel and vicious in warfare to a degree already legendary. He cared about three living beings only: his favourite horse, his favourite and now old and near blind dog, and Bega.

The exercise of sentimentality on these particular beings excused him all other acts of kindness.

He had prepared a speech for Bega and when he had sluiced himself down and taken a hunk of crust said, by his poet, to be the best long-term medicine for diarrhoea, he sought her out and brought her to the seclusion of one end of the great hall.

His slaves brought down the fine carved armed chair which he had looted only the year before and Bega sat at his feet, deeply comfortable on many layers of animal skins. She made herself a study in deference.

Even the crust, to his dismay, was often too much for the few teeth that could champ effectively. But his gums were hardened. He would be fifty years old soon – a good age – and he felt it except, he boasted and with truth, when he went to war. Then the years evaporated as the heat of anger and the lust to kill lifted him into a state of youthful ecstasy.

Just as he was about to begin, Bega said:

'Cathleen has sent you a cure.' They both knew the ailment but Cathal would never allude to his disability nor allow anyone else to do so. 'I will make it up tonight.'

'How is the woman?'

'Near the end. Pray for her.'

'She had a long life,' said Cathal, envy undisguised. 'She always fed herself well.'

'She gave me a rhyme and said if I followed it I would live as long as she.'

'Yes?' Cathal's lack of interest was such obvious pretence that Bega had to put her hand to her mouth to stop the giggle. He was obsessed with living to a mythical age yet liable to flare up at the affront to his dignity that such an admission would bring.

'I have it by heart.'

'Is it long?'

'No.' He was relieved. Poetry tended to be long. His genea-logical tree he could have wished longer, but nothing else. Riddles pleased him best. She began:

> 'Watercress, apples, berries, beautiful hazel trees,
> Blackberries, acorns from the oak tree;
> Haws of the sharp prickly hawthorn,
> Wood sorrels, good wild garlic,
> Clean topped cress, mountain acorns,
> Together they drive hunger from me.'

'Nothing about pork?' he asked.

'No.'

'There never is. Nor cattle, nor deer, nor duck, nor goose, nor any living animal. How can we feed the meat we are if not with meat from others? How can you make *blood* without the meat that *breeds* it? Could she answer that?'

Bega was silent. She had gained a slight initiative and that was enough. Immediately, she had felt the need to unsettle him, to prepare him for a conversation not to his liking. As he reset himself for the speech which in parts she had heard several times before and which had always affected her, Bega searched furiously for an escape.

'Your mother,' he began, in a rather cooing tone of voice exclusive to this specific subject, 'was the most beautiful woman in all Ireland. Indeed she was so very beautiful and so rare a beauty that only a very few of us could see the truth of it. The poets saw it and the abbot, one or two of the scholars and O'Neill himself and so did I. She was unlike all that they say an Irish beauty has to be. Where it says fair, she was dark, where eyes were blue, hers were speckled green, and there was a light yellow grain on her face like an ash leaf with the sun coming through it. She was sharp in the face where full in the face is the style and her hair, though it was long and black enough, had red in it and was glossy like a horse's coat, not silky.

'I had a wife already but your mother became my concubine as is prescribed by the kings and prophets in the Old Testament and while she was with me I took no other mistresses.' He paused, sincerely affected by his fidelity. 'No one knows . . . poets cannot sing the life . . . and then you came with such pain for her that in less than two years, she died.

'There were days when I hated you for it. There were days when I got up and rode away and did not care where I arrived or what danger I ran into. I hunted for danger. I wanted only to kill as many as I could to avenge her death. And I did. By God and this right arm, I did. Still I could not bear to see the whelp you were and Cathleen moved you away from me. Then one day I came back with my sword stained to the hilt in blood and a wound on my arm that bled like a cut pig. They bathed it and were bandaging me and I was dizzy by then; it had been a long ride and a hard struggle for the three heads I brought back.

'I remember a mist in my eyes – like the tears I shed the one and only time before, at the death of your mother. Through this mist I saw her again, smaller, not as beautiful – no one could be as beautiful – but *her*, a dot of a thing, pulling out my sword quite unafraid of the blood, looking at me without any fear. It was you. You came up to me, trailing the sword behind you and tried to heave it up into my hand. I reached out and took it and lifted it high and your little wide open eyes followed it into the air as if you had seen an angel or a saint and then – you clapped your hands.' He nodded somewhat grimly but she knew how moved he was. 'And she was born again in you – imperfect of course, only the Mother of Christ Herself could beat her, but it was then that I softened to you and since then I have denied you nothing, have I? Have I? You became my luck.'

She stroked the leg she leaned against and let him have his silence. She was shrewd enough to know that if her mother had been at all like her then the great beauty was in the eye of Cathal alone, or Cathal and those unwilling to contradict him. But this praise, this wildly uncharacteristic but consistent outburst of affection, moved her. She knew now, though, that the debt, as he would see it, would have to be repaid and in what voice, by what means could she refuse? For the first time in her life, she felt a chill of fear before him. What would he do if she did refuse? Would his love then be stronger than his will?

He then recounted the stories his poet had worked into an epic: the heroic advance of King Cathal whose every victory was dedicated to his dead concubine who had been his Luck. As he spoke she felt pride in his pride, remembering how fiercely pleased he had been when she had asked him to teach her to use a sword and spear and then to drive his chariot; when the abbot and then Padric had found her so easy to teach and, unlike her brothers, able to remember what she had been taught. How unique she was in that household for never once feeling the force of his fist, the flat of his sword, the venom of the man. Yet now that counted for nothing. For all she was doing while he spoke was to devise a way to refuse what was, in effect, his first request.

'But now we are moving to even greater things,' he said, and the excitement in the words was palpable and new: he had lived very largely without care for the living. 'Niall O'Neill is your man. He has been given his name for Niall Noigiallach, Niall of the Nine Hostages, High King of Ireland even before there was an Arthur in Britain. And beyond him,' Cathal's voice lowered, 'is Echu Mugmedon' – to whom Cathal feigned to be related – 'and so back and back to Adam and Eve.' His tone became sonorous, almost mesmeric. 'A son of O'Neill wants you as his wife. He has heard about you – from me, from others, and he will come with his men to this household in fifteen days. After the biggest feast that has ever been witnessed, Solomon himself would not better it, you will go and bring forth sons who will be kings of all Ireland.'

Though not strictly true, there was nevertheless sufficient reason for Cathal's natural and commonly obtaining exaggeration to be a possibility. For both knew that under Irish-Celtic law, the king's successor could be his brother, his uncle, his son, his grandson, his nephew or his grand-nephew. Given the high incidence of death in battle among the fit men of the time and the wildly erratic life spans, it was as much a fair bet as a boast. At that moment, Cathal was blazingly certain of it.

'Kings of all Ireland,' he repeated. 'You yourself could be the wife of the king himself with all the rest of them forced to pay tribute, forced to bow the head or by God and your king's right arm he would cut off that head and show what a king was made of.'

She looked up and saw that he was looking along the great hall as if he could already see, in the pictures of the flames, in the moving shadows on the wall, from the womb of that place built on so much blood, the issue of greatness in a procession before him for ever ruling the land. Perhaps in all his life, Cathal had never been so transfixed, so near to touch the glory he had only dreamed to meet.

Bega had this one chance and St Brigid was at her shoulder as she said 'Father, while I was with Cathleen, I had a—' a vision? That would be a lie. A call from God? Not true. '—a powerful sense that God wants me for His own. Abraham was told by God to leave his own land and Jesus Christ commands us to leave our father and mother for His sake.'

Her smooth use of Abraham and Christ alerted him. She had long ago passed him in learning. He could neither read nor write and he took the greatest pleasure in the fact that she had so decisively outsoared her brothers whose presence on earth constantly and bitterly reminded him that someone else one day would take what he had made. But he could tell a false note in a forest of sounds and her coupling of Abraham – one of his heroes, especially in his willingness to sacrifice Isaac – and Christ, her own ideal, was suspicious. Cathal had great trouble with Christ, not the birth but much of the teaching and everything about that compliant death. He sensed a concealed motive for all this piety and he concentrated.

'You have always said how the greatness of Ireland rests on its kings who are without fear and its missionaries who take the word of God to the distant places on earth,' Bega went on. There was no turning back now. 'I cannot be a king, Father, although I would like to be and I *could* be . . .' She paused, but he was not playing his usual game, she could not tug him along that easily. 'But to be the one who takes the Gospel to the barbarians over the sea, to go where you cannot know the language or the people . . .' Bega's words began to sweep her along, and she saw herself as the lone voice of Christ entering a wilderness of pagan souls, risking torture and death, but with God at her side triumphing over evil and dark forces. 'I would like to go to study and prepare for such work. You would be proud of me, Father. The stronger I became the stronger my prayers would be for you.'

Cathal had always been able to bide his time. One of his many strengths in battle and particularly in the individual combat which he always sought out, was that he could withstand taunts and even blows which would incite others to a quick and unsuccessful response. Now he said nothing for a while, but bent his efforts to muscling down the gripes in his stomach and eventually, in a neutral voice, asked, 'Cathleen was to you as your mother would have been – she tried to be that to you, did she not?'

'Yes.'

'A good woman, Cathleen.' Cathal was aware that Cathleen would soon be in Heaven and he had no wish to lessen the value of such a rare supporter. He sought his words carefully. 'You must be very upset seeing her so ill.'

'She is about to receive her heavenly reward,' said Bega. 'We ought to rejoice. Death is life for her.'

'We ought to.' Cathal nodded firmly. Nothing was more fearful or hateful to him than death. 'Yes, now, indeed we ought to,' he repeated, aware that his tone was not convincing. 'What I mean is that when these things happen, minds can be turned. There you were, well set on this mission, so when the news came – of the wedding – it was a fight.' The single word 'fight' put him back on track. 'But it is not a real fight, Bega. You were ambushed by

Cathleen but now you are back on home ground you can see the real battle plan. It is that you marry Niall O'Neill. In the next days, with the women, you will prepare your dress for the wedding; I will give you the finest jewellery seen in all Connachta. This hall will see a feast for three days and nights and no-one will leave until everything is eaten and everyone is drunk. We will drink more than Finian himself. We will feast as if we had won the final battle with the Old Deceiver himself.'

Bega knew better than to press further.

When she had gone, Cathal had a slave bring him a large wooden sconce of beer and more bread. The smell of the pork being cooked for the meal incited his appetite but he knew enough to be cautious. He would wait and ponder until his wife told him that the crackling was burnt gold.

His instinct told him that this was the fault of Padric. He had been foolish to allow them to spend so much time together. But Padric was not to be treated in a summary fashion. His family was a great family; it had followers all over Ireland. Padric was to be watched – he could trust no one but himself – and encouraged to leave soon. From his understanding of Bega he guessed that she was unaware that Padric meant so much to her. She saw him more as one young man sees another, like Jonathan, he thought, saw David. But that was dangerous enough.

He sent for Donal.

Those few minutes in Donal's life were as worrying as any he had ever experienced. The venom was arrow-tipped and hit home without fail; jabbed, rammed down with a blunt forefinger, which had long lost its topmost section.

'Why are you encouraging Bega to become a nun?'

'Why did you not keep her away from the ravings of Cathleen when you saw that the old crone was in her death rattle and making no sense?'

'What have you been telling Bega about those mad missionaries?'

'You are entirely to blame if she does not give up this foolish, stupid idea and I will punish you, monk or no monk, until you scream.'

'Seek her out, stop this stupidity, I will hear not another word of it.'

'I'm looking out for you, Donal.'

Though physically fragile, Donal was not a weak man. Someone who counted himself the merest speck on the landscape of
religion – yes; but his faith had given him resources over many
years, in situations often more obviously dangerous than this. Yet
Cathal shook him as no one had ever done before and, as he left
to seek out Bega, he had to combat a sudden weakness in his legs,
a palpitation of alarm which made him shiver, a chime of dread
somewhere out of reach of prayer. He all but ran away.

Cathal sighed and called for more beer. He would get good
and drunk and take his sons with him. Bega had disappointed
him but she would see sense. She was his girl and would do what
he wanted. The strong beer was sunk greedily. The sons, Dermot
and Faelan, came into the hall and sat at the table with the rest of
the household – relatives, warriors, young men the sons of lesser
kings there to learn about war, and partly as hostages against the
loyalty and obedience of their fathers.

As more lights were brought in and more men came in to sit
at the table and the slaves and women began to serve out the
food and beer, Cathal softened a little. Bega was clearly upset by
the impending death of Cathleen. This, Cathal thought, could
unbalance a woman. But she was strong – if only Dermot, sullen
but reliable, and Faelan, quick but needing to be watched – had
a mite of her treasury of qualities, then Cathal could look forward
to death in the certain knowledge that all he had built would be
passed down and his name in the genealogies would be as secure as
those in the great roll calls of the Old Testament. He muttered to
himself 'Adam, Sheth, Enoch, Kenan, Mahalalech, Jeral, Hanoch,
Methusaleh, Lamech, Noah, Shem, Ham and Japheth.' That was
all he could ever remember, but it was enough. That a lineage
could be traced to the beginning of time! Would his own poet
ever get him there? That was glory.

Bega would wed O'Neill and with her powers she would take
his name all over Ireland, sons and sons after them would sing
out about the deeds of Cathal at Feast times until the Last
Judgment.

After more beer, he set off for the table. But the unmistakable
wince in his rectum sent him scurrying out in a way insulting to
his dignity and he thought he heard a mocking laugh come from
the table from the region of his sons. At such times he could
willingly have slit both their gullets and watched them squeal.

CHAPTER FOUR

G od would not tell her what she should do and there was no one else.

Although she trusted Donal, she felt that he could not be leaned on for such a decision. Maeve would simply reinforce the directive of Cathal and perhaps tell tales of their conversation. Cathleen was far away and Padric, to whom her thoughts turned time and again, had been sent by her father on a mission of which he had not bothered to inform her.

Bega's accumulating unhappiness had been increased by the unfathomable behaviour of Padric since their return. When he saw her he would duck away or, if he could not avoid her, give the curtest nod, the barest words and, she could have sworn, the occasional blush. In the two days before he had set off with the cattle and six of her father's best men, it seemed they constantly stumbled across each other. Nothing came of it save transparent unease for Padric and growing irritation for Bega. By the time she had resolved to force him to tell her what was wrong, he was gone.

He had been away for nine days now and Bega was beginning to experience panic. She had never encountered it before and the breathless sense of terror doubly alarmed her: both in itself and in the confusion in which it left her – for what *was* it? Was a devil possessing her for being so wicked as to think of defying her father? Or had the devil worked out that she was not truly devoted to the idea of being a nun and this was punishment for pretence? Perhaps it was not the devil but, much more frightening, God Himself who was shaking her for taking the vocation of His servants in vain.

She began to long for Padric. She would wake from her sleep in the black of night convinced, from a dream, that he was standing over her holding out his hand, tall, challenging, as he had been on the boat. Despite the cold she would be sweating.

Maeve, who was a little older and much more aware of female aspects of life which Bega was late coming to, watched her distress with some satisfaction. Maeve had no illusions. Some day soon she would be forced at best to become the mistress of one of the men, one of Cathal's sons, Faelan most likely, who touched her brutally whenever he could find her alone. It would be rape. The world would not be surprised. She would be paid some compensation and if the child were a strong boy then she could devote her energies to ensuring he received the full rights which would be due to him under Irish law. If it were a girl then only her looks would stake her future. By sticking close to Bega and her official guards, Maeve had escaped that fate so far. She knew that to be a full wife to a nobleman was beyond her. She would far prefer to be the concubine of a rich and powerful prince – even Faelan – than the wife of a herdsman. What she saw in Bega was the beginning of the great transformation. Maeve saw Bega struggling with feelings which were too much for her, and she offered no help.

After another broken night, Bega stole out of the women's quarters an hour or so before dawn. She cooed to calm the dogs at the door and stood, barefoot in the sharp frozen mud, looking at the sky, wanting a miracle. There were so many, Donal said, and she wanted no great favour, just . . . help.

She let herself get very cold. She had not brought out her heavy cloak and, when the icy air began to penetrate the loose woollen shift, she forced herself to endure it. The sky was hazing towards early light, stars pale, a moon only intermittently seen as thin streams of dark grey stroked across its face. As Bega grew colder, she thought she heard the howl of a wolf setting off some of the dogs, making the cattle anxious, a few tremulous bleats from the goats, high pitched calls from the sheep.

She thought of the sea and remembered that sense of freedom. It was like a candle. Her mind warmed around it as her limbs began to shake. The shivering grew more desperate and she tried to think of Cathleen and wondered if she would know of the moment of her death so that she could pray for her ascent into heaven. She had been cold before many times but had never trembled so fiercely. She remembered a slave who had been possessed of the devil and rolled over spasm-seized, frothing at the mouth, so much so that some thought he was Beelzebub himself, until her father had pinned him down and forced the fit to subside. He had been thrown out of the settlement as soon as he had regained his senses.

Now her arms were shaking out of control, the muscles in her legs and body shivered and fought the cold as she heard the sound of her teeth trembling and chattering. But in all this she took an obstinate pleasure. She was testing herself, and she would not give in. The shaking almost became a dance.

She felt sleepy and heard the first few birds of dawn as if they were voices of angels. Perhaps they were. As a stream of cloud parted, she saw the moon full and was sure that Cathleen had joined her mother and that they were smiling down on her benignly. Her two mothers united in peace. It was such a sweet blessing, such a sleepy sweetness, that she thought she would lie down . . .

Padric would go back to his own land and marry. He liked Maeve. All men liked Maeve. No use her father telling her about beauty. Too dark, like her mother, they said. Maybe she came from another island far beyond the journeys of St Brendan where the cattle were white and it was always warm and the sea was hot all day and all night.

When they carried her in, her face, even that dark face, her lips, her fingers and toes, were blue. As warmth came back into the fingers and toes they pinched and ached as if a hundred tiny imps were jabbing at her, lancing her, warning her of the terrors to come were she to oppose the will of her father.

At last they had the torque and the four rings. They had been obliged to wait three further days until all the rings were set with the requested precious stones which had arrived late. When all was all done and presented, Padric was awed.

These gifts from Cathal to O'Neill were indeed kingly. The

magnificent torque, of heavy twisted gold with a clasp in silver, was fit for the neck of any warrior king on earth, he thought a little enviously. Made by the best craftsman in Ireland, the rings, two for Niall and one each for his brothers, were as big and fine as any Padric had seen. Truly, Cathal would gain great honour from giving such rare presents. The cattle they had brought to complete the bargain had been just enough. Their loss seriously diminished his wealth, but the gifts, like the marriage and the feast, were to be spoken of for ever in poetry and song and Cathal was seeking comparison with men of legend.

It was a great honour, as had been made clear to Padric, to be chosen and trusted with such a mission. It was also an effective way of removing him. Padric had been aware of this. But the king had been good to him and Padric wanted nothing to impair his gratitude and any future alliance. He had taken his command willingly and used the moment to ask if he could leave for home as soon as he returned with the gifts. After the feast, said Cathal, who wanted word of that great event to travel with Padric across to the kingdoms of Britain and even into the country of the Northumbrians, who might in turn send back to their old territories in the Teutonic lands stories of Bega's unstinted marriage to the O'Neill and the glory of Cathal.

As they hacked back across country, muffled against the rain, Padric turned again to that last meeting with Cathal. Although she had not been mentioned, Bega had been present and her presence had grown in Padric's mind ever since. Clearly Cathal had thought Padric responsible for Bega's stubbornness – or her sudden sense of vocation. Padric knew his man. There would be no argument. Although it made his immediate future plans simple – he could go home – he was nagged by unease. It drizzled through his mind as bleakly as the cold rain settled on his face.

Padric was someone who found no great difficulty in enjoying his life. He had always been at ease with himself. He was well connected, educated far beyond all others in his own country, athletic, inclined to generosity, strong in friendships and clear about his future course.

Uncertainty unnerved him. His emotions prowled around Bega without closing in on the obvious. It was not right that he should be trapped in such a small personal matter, he thought, when the world was full of great deeds waiting to be done. It was inconceivable that the waspish, ever-teasing, restless girl he had met three years before could have grown into a young woman who could unsettle plans and ambitions carved on his mind by ancestral imperatives.

Yet the fidget of unhappiness would not go away. The long track over sodden boglands encouraged him to endure an increasingly melancholic mood which was strange to him.

He insisted on going to the monastery at Durrow to keep a promise he had made to Donal. He was shown an illuminated gospel being worked on by the monks. As he looked at that glow of characters and colours, he thought – Bega would want to see this, she would understand it as I do, but she never will see it and never again will we talk as openly as we used to. With no one else could he share the sense of solemnity and the allied sense of high adventure. This was knowledge. This was learning. This was unknown to all but the merest fraction in a time of triumphant illiteracy and barbaric vengeance on words. With Bega present he would have imagined the future. He would have foretold the day when books such as these would be carried all over the world and smite all pagan peoples. She would have steered him to that mysterious, ineffable feeling of significance that learning and the words of the Bible gave both of them.

He went over the ground yet again. Cathal had banished him because he wanted Bega to have nothing to distract her from the historic conjunction with the O'Neills. He must have thought that he, Padric, would be an obstacle. How could Cathal think that? It was a marriage of which any princess in Ireland would be proud. He was pleased for Bega. He was. He wished her well. He did. Truly.

The abbot of Durrow knew of Padric's family and gave him gifts and messages to take back to Rheged. He himself had come from there 'more than two score years ago. You are lucky to be going back home,' he said. 'I shall never see it again, God's will.'

'Yes,' Padric replied rather bleakly. He was lucky to be going home.

Padric had sought solace in Durrow but left more disturbed. It was as if he were hunting in the forest and he could hear and sense the prey, but never set eyes on it. His frustration grew and by the time he returned, he had determined not to see Bega at all.

⊗⊗⊗⊗

The O'Neills drove down country like a pack of wolves. They gave the impression that life either cowered or scattered before them and only the brave stood to gaze and then they admired.

Three brothers, tall, with the O'Neill black crinkled hair, red, high-boned cheeks, blue-eyed, ready for any game, any quarrel, any fight. They rode with their best men, like themselves fine-tuned to any action called for, the more perilous the better. Niall planned to get there earlier than his messengers had announced, just for the hell of catching Cathal at a disadvantage. But Cathal had prepared his reception well. For three days before the promised date, he was ready. Padric and his men had returned with the gifts. In the household everything had been organised. His sons and the young men who fought for him were drilled in their roles. Cathal had prepared as if for battle. You never trusted the O'Neills. It was the first rule of Irish warfare.

Once Bega was married, once the feasting had been done, once he had sent one of his sons hostage to the court of O'Neill and kept one of the bridegroom's brothers under his own roof for a while, then a different strategy might be entertained. But for now, when the O'Neills rode down on you, you prepared as if for battle.

Cathal would admit that he enjoyed the prospect of a battle more than anything save the battle itself: more than gloating over the gifts and admiring his own unparalleled generosity – the poet had changed his lines and begun working on new ones when he had seen the torque and the rings; more than the laying in of unmatchable quantities of beer and mead and food; more even than the deeply satisfying sense that everyone in his household was frightened of him and worked solely for what he commanded.

He had taken precautions against anything that might diminish his dignity and greatness. All the bejewelled clasps which fastened the cloaks had been burnished. Fresh straw had been brought in to put under the skins which served as beds. The six silver goblets he had looted from the raid into Munster now shone 'like the sun' as he had demanded. The trophies on the walls, the enemy spears and swords and shields, had also been highly polished and beeswax had been rubbed into the table to make it shine and glitter under the rush and candle lights.

Cathal had also entered into combat with his diarrhoea. The prayers of Donal had been useless. Christ was not interested, nor was St Columbanus, and Cathal did not blame them. The medicines of his wife – whose only claim to his attention now that she was old was her boasted skill in cures – had failed. Bread was not enough.

Cathal could not be humiliated in front of the O'Neills. With his two closest men – men who would not babble – he went, as he had done so often, to the cell of Cassayr the soothsayer, whom he allowed to live in a dry cave on his land. The slaves would take her food in the hard times. She had been one of his mistresses but her age, her strangeness and weird ways had lost his interest. When she asked to go he had effortlessly agreed that she could leave the settlement. Once gone, he had begun to miss her wisdom and her sexual curiosity, and several times he had gone to seek satisfaction or advice. The visit was always represented as an accidental and casual stop for water or some berries in a hunting trip.

Inside the cave, behind the fire at its mouth, he sat and took the strong herb drink she offered him. He had left his two henchmen on guard outside. Their presence would have embarrassed him.

Cassayr advised him on what to eat. Then she explained that at feast times he should put a thick wad across the hole, pressing it into the hole itself, and truss that around with seven layers of clean rags all soaked in the herbs she would give him. The diet and the material precautions would see him through. Finally she cast a spell on the herbs and the salts. She spoke this in Hisperic Latin which always convinced Cathal that matters were being conducted seriously.

He rose to go but paused when she asked about Bega, whom she had known well.

'What have you heard?' he demanded.

'She is unhappy with what you want her to do.'

'She is a child.'

The woman paused, wondering whether or not to risk his temper. 'She may be obstinate.'

'She will do as I want.'

One last warning? 'The answer lies with the man from across the sea.'

'The answer lies with me.'

She sensed the blood-throb of his sudden steep acceleration of temper which could flash to loss of control in a moment. She said no more and sat rigid.

He had brought her the two mature geese he had previously promised her – as guards, now that her dog was so old. As he went out he picked up one of them, ignored its beating wide-winged hysterics and vicious pecking, and swiftly wrung its neck. The suddenly slack white bundle dropped softly quivering on to the earth in front of her.

If the medicine did not work he would punish her for that impertinence. Bega was now in the hands of the women. Donal reported that she was becoming more devout but that was not unusual at such a time. Come the moment, she, like her mother, would only do him honour . . .

So on the next day when the guards called him and he saw the line of O'Neill and his men on a low rise near the horizon, he was a man who had left nothing undone.

Niall O'Neill, prince of a great dynasty, in his twentieth year, pulled up immediately he saw the settlement. He was aware of the smoking beacon some hundreds of yards behind him on a strategic hillock and was well pleased that the old warrior was not to be outwitted. Like all the men in Ireland he had heard tales of the unmatched bravery of this upstart, King Cathal. His father had fought beside him; his cousins had been spared by him in one of the few politic and magnanimous gestures of his warlife. Niall looked at the settlement with respect. It was the place of a true king.

He saw the smoke wisping into the clear winter afternoon; he saw the long, stone-based, evenly thatched roof of the great hall; he appreciated the circumference of the earthworks and the stone which supported the thick carpets of sod. On nearby hills he could spy many sheep and goats and noted with approval the way the settlement had been located for maximum defensive advantage. He had heard of this woman Bega only from the poet sent by Cathal and, even after discounting much of it as you had to do with poets, she sounded acceptable. He had a fine mistress already among the slaves and a sturdy young son. What the O'Neills wanted was the fighting power of Cathal and access to the wealth he had reaped over the years.

Niall had brought eleven men besides his two brothers and they formed up in a line across. Behind them were the slaves on the packhorses with gifts and all the chattels necessary for the long journey down country. He scanned the landscape yet again to see if he could spot Cathal's men but they were too well hidden. Still he waited. The horses, best of their rather short and stocky breed, pawed restlessly; they could sense other horses, could hear the distant chorus of beasts and fowls, could scent food and rest after days of hard riding and hunting. All the men had only one hand on the reins, some of which jangled as the wind lifted and ruffled the small discs of ornamental metal sewn on to them. There was no saddle, just a blanket, no stirrups; the control came through forearms and thighs, all but bred on horseback.

Cathal had also waited and now he came to the gates in his war chariot, drawn by two horses, his spear-carrier leading them. Dermot and Faelan each led out about a dozen men, among them Padric, all armed and on horseback, and they lined up across on either side of Cathal's chariot.

Niall rode forward steadily, his men well alongside him, one hand on the hilt of the sword, the other almost casually holding the reins. Cathal and his men did not move.

Niall glanced left and right to his brothers and grinned as if to say 'What hell we could raise if we pretended to ride in to take them on!' For a moment it crossed the minds of all three that such a battle as they might have was too good an opportunity to miss and this tension went into the horses and rippled across the line; tension instantly noted by Cathal who barked an alert to his men. Then Niall relaxed and Cathal nodded to himself and thought – for that moment they *were* going to come for us! The treacherous murdering bastards! He loved them for it.

Still they came steadily until they were on the open and level ground which stretched for a few hundred yards. Niall took his hand off his sword's hilt and raised it, both as a greeting and to show he would not draw his weapon. The others followed his example. Cathal did not respond.

Niall had behaved himself for long enough. With a hundred or so yards to go, he kicked his horse into a gallop and with both hands now upraised and free, yelling loud enough to frighten all but the strongest, he led a full galloping charge straight towards Cathal's chariot.

Cathal did not flinch.

The O'Neills, suddenly a horde on the rampage, a force of horse flesh, speed and baying warriors, split into two lines at the very last moment and then galloped on around the whole settlement, crossing at the back of it, yelling to put the fear of death into all within. They arrived back in a thunder of hooves, suddenly arrested as Niall slung himself off the horse, walked towards Cathal and stood before him.

Cathal came out of his chariot doing all he could to restrain himself. Oh, these were the warriors after his own heart. These were the reckless fighters you could ride with into the jaws of the most flame-tongued dragon at the furthest ends of the earth. These were the arrogant, unconquerable, lords of the earth, the O'Neills. And they had come to *him*. Soon he would be of their family and they of his and when the poets sang of the O'Neills, he, Cathal, would be in that song.

He took off his sword. Niall followed suit. The two men took each other firmly by the arms and in that small gesture made a physical show of friendship and, in those few seconds, made a first quick assessment of the other's strength.

'You are welcome to my house and all I possess,' said Cathal and led him in.

Cathal had placed Padric on the extreme right of his flank which helped give him a measure of detachment. Padric was irritated that he could not seem to concentrate and give the occasion the focus it deserved. His thoughts were on Bega or on his return home. He wished he had left before the feast – Cathal, he now realised, would not have been offended. Yet the thought of departure made him feel obscurely resentful. He had not talked to Bega in the three days since his return and he now suspected that there were orders to prevent them meeting.

It was stupid, he thought. More than that, it was outrageous. He, Padric, not to be trusted. He, thought to be a danger to the girl he had tutored with such responsibility. Why did Cathal suspect there was anything but companionship or convenience in their association? He was not a hostage or a servant, to be ushered away when circumstances called. As for Bega, the most that could be said of his feelings for her was that they resembled those he experienced for his younger sister. And she regarded him as a tutor, no more no less. He struggled to pretend to himself that any carnal feelings he might have were directed to Maeve.

He had been away from home for too long. Once back, with his goal clear and his tasks set out before him, the unease would simply evaporate.

O'Neill was the chief reason for his decision to remain, he told himself. A future alliance with that large clan could be of critical value. Had this opportunity not come his way, he would have attempted to secure a meeting through some of the more powerful among those of his own scattered and exiled Rheged tribe. Now he could not be better placed: tutor to the young bride whose qualities he would cite at the feast, friend of Cathal and, perhaps, in the games that would be played, he could make a mark. So in the longer term he looked at the O'Neills as partners, but in the short term, bold competitiveness might suit his purpose better.

When the O'Neills charged at Cathal's line, Padric chose to think of it as rather childish. It was impressive – could they ride! – but it was such obvious swagger. His interest sharpened, however, as he sought out the face of the man who would take Bega.

Niall's flamboyant gesture of command to split his men, marked him out. Padric waited impatiently for the over-boisterous troop to finish howling around the wall. As soon as they came back in view he fixed on Niall. The man was fine-looking. He rode magnificently, hands free, thighs guiding and urging on the sleek horse to its fullest gallop, well ahead of the rest. Niall felt Padric's gaze on him and grinned back, white teeth suddenly relieving the raw face. As he came close to Padric, he lunged across, feinting a blow. Padric's hand fled to his sword and his horse pulled back. Niall laughed aloud, and slapped his horse for one last burst of speed.

Padric felt foolish and a flush came to his face.

CHAPTER FIVE

Bega heard the war cries of the O'Neills and a thrill of dread raced through her blood almost causing her to keel over. She was on her knees in the tiny hut allotted to her sole use for this great occasion. She was praying to St Brigid as she had been doing steadfastly for days.

Dread of a different kind inhabited Donal, who prayed alongside her. Dread of what she might do. She had fasted severely for two weeks now, and would not take his advice of moderation. She looked wasted and was bound to be weak. She spent too much time in prayer but again, when challenged, she either said nothing or quoted impeccable scripture.

Her prayers were buoyed up by her belief that she had been accorded something approaching a miracle. Word had come that Cathleen had finally gone to her heavenly reward and sat with the apostles and saints and martyrs in the kingdom of God. Bega was convinced that she had been given a sign on the morning she had allowed herself to endure great cold. The report fixed Cathleen's death at approximately the time she had seen the clouds part to reveal the moon, certainly early the same morning.

Bega took great strength from this and offered it to Donal as proof that her calling was not a matter of whim but a true vocation come to her perhaps, though she was most unworthy, from the very Highest. 'You see,' she said, 'it is a sign. How few have been given such a sign? How can it be disregarded?' He could see her disappearing into a bottomless well of holiness.

Donal was in despair. He had assured Cathal that her notion of giving her life to God had been abandoned. This was not true. Every day he saw her convincing herself that her life was destined not for marriage but for God. Donal had pointed out

that the two need not be irreconcilable. He knew several monks
– there were even abbots – who did not choose to achieve the
higher state of chastity and lived good lives, useful to God, while
being husbands and fathers. He had heard the same of nuns and
at least one abbess. Not St Brigid, was Bega's reply.

Over the seas, said Donal, where the Celtic missionaries had
moved into the darkest areas, risking and frequently meeting
torture and martyrdom, it was often the case that a queen or a
woman of the royal household, married, a mother, had been the
first to welcome the missionary. She had then become as devout
and holy, as loved by God as any nun on earth. Chastity, replied
Bega, was the highest gift a woman could bring to Christ and
she was determined that she should offer Him that as well as
obedience, love and unquestioning toil. She would be His soldier,
she said, and chastity would be her shield.

Donal pointed out that Mary had been a mother, of Christ
and others.

Bega said that she was not worthy to compare herself with
Mary.

Donal said that her father had given her everything and asked
only for this one gift in return.

Bega said that her constant prayers for her father would be a
far greater gift than any earthly addition.

Donal was forced to draw attention to her father's temper: to
thwart his will was to invite a terrible retribution.

I accept that, said Bega. It is in the hands of God.

Donal had gone to see her stepmother.

Una, bitterly abused wife of Cathal, came from a family which
had once seemed great to him but now seemed puny. She loathed
Bega, who could do no wrong in her husband's eyes, who had been
indulged beyond endurance, who would ridicule her own sons and
never attempted a response to her offers of guidance. Admittedly,
these had been hypocritical, but they had not deserved the rebuff
of a child.

She went to see Bega and spoke to her for some time. It gave
her some pleasure to tell the equally detested Donal later that
the girl was fully bound on her course to dedicate herself solely
to God. It gave her even greater pleasure to discern that Bega was
in love with Padric – though probably unaware of it – and now
stood to lose both men: Niall through her stubbornness and Padric

through misfortune. Una also relished the prospect of the torture to which Cathal would undoubtedly resort, even of Bega, if his honour were to be so publicly stained. Bega had never understood that this was more important to him than anything, certainly than any woman.

The sound of the O'Neills' arrival finally prompted Donal to urgent action.

Donal left Bega in her trance of prayer and went out to seek Padric.

⟨೫⟩⟨೫⟩⟨೫⟩

Niall's compliments were courteous and generous: Cathal had no need either to play at modesty or to boast. The stone-based wall was kicked and lauded. The seething winter cattlepens were lingered over as the two men prodded the buttocks of the long-horned, hairy beasts. All the buildings were admired and once or twice there was a ready admission that matters were better ordered here even than in the kingdom of the O'Neills. The long-shafted chariots, the horses, the armoury, the weapons . . . Niall knew that he was being shown power – and also that some judicious deaths could make all this his. Nothing was too trivial to pass by.

Women were milling with hard querns or walking, distaff in hand, the children keeping the pigs and fowl in some order. At the bleaching house, Cathal joked that he had ordered his men no longer to contribute their urine as the bleaching went so much better with the non-alcoholic urine of women. And women's was far better for the teeth. Niall had heard these remarks before, but he smiled, taking in the wealth of activity around him. Some of this was Bega's, Cathal confirmed, inherited from her mother, legally belonging to her – and there would be more.

It was a royal route.

Last of all the great hall was given its full due; paced out, praised in every particular – the beams, the tapestries, the huge iron pots, the leather and wooden bowls, the spoons, some of wood, some of horn. The deer and calf and wolf skins on the floor, the well-protected peat fire sending up its constant smoke and tanning the wall hangings a rich dark yellow.

The severed heads and shields were counted and Cathal offered that at some time during the feast his poet might tell of the battles in which they had been won.

'The feasting begins tonight,' said Cathal, 'and it will last for three days. After that – the marriage.'

'Do I see Bega?' Niall pronounced it with a short stubbed 'e'. Cathal frowned.

'B*ee*ga,' he corrected. Niall should have listened more closely to his poet-messenger.

'Do I see her now?' Niall smiled. 'B*eee*ga!'

'I will see if she is fit to see you,' said Cathal, evenly. 'She is a little nervous of so magnificent an event. I would be ashamed for her were she not.'

'Everything I hear about her does you the highest honour.'

'And now,' said Cathal, with a terrible smile, 'the weapons. At a feast, no one but myself and the guard man carries a sword or a spear or a dagger in this hall.'

The pause was just perceptible.

'I have a hut where they can be stored,' said Cathal. 'Two men can guard them – one of mine and, if you wish, one of yours.'

'That will not be necessary,' said Niall, handing his previously unbuckled sword to Cathal.

His dagger he kept hidden in its usual place. He knew that Cathal suspected as much. He hesitated. 'All my men will surrender not only their swords and their spears but also their hidden daggers,' said Niall. 'I will order them to do this.'

It was victory enough, Cathal decided.

'The O'Neills are everything I expected,' said Cathal, and nodded happily, unconsciously fingering the silver handle of his own concealed dagger.

⊗⊗⊗⊗

'It is simple. If she is not persuaded otherwise she will not go through with the marriage. If she does not, I fear that her father

will put her to death and in the most protracted way possible,'
said Donal. 'He could not be seen to give her any mercy in front
of the O'Neills. Only the greatest sacrifice would satisfy them.'

'Has she met O'Neill yet?'

'No. But soon she must.'

'She will change her mind when she meets him,' said Padric,
with a bitterness which surprised both of them.

'She may not,' replied Donal. 'I think she will not. She is not
used to changing her mind.'

'Then her father will come and force her to do it.'

'I very much fear she would welcome a chance to show him the
strength of her faith.'

'Then what influence could I have?'

'Talk to her.' It was a plea.

Padric saw that the old man was tearful and afraid. However
much he and Bega had teased Donal, they respected his age and
his dedication which such a display of emotion reinforced. He
followed him to Bega's hut.

Donal left Padric with Bega.

The hut was small and, even though they sat as far apart as they
could, the intimacy was oppressive. For days they had thought of
each other without seeing each other, dwelled on an increasingly
seductive past and suppressed impulses which contradicted the
paths chosen for them. Now they sat in silent embarrassment.

In the silence hung the memories of golden years of teaching,
of talk, of learning, days of innocence and of illumination. In
the embarrassment lay the realisation that Bega was no longer
the boy-girl of a father's indulgence thrown on to the winds of
good fortune: nor was Padric, any longer, the neutral tutor from
across the sea, as harmless as the ideal brother.

'When are you going back?'

Her words invaded the silence, disrupting the melancholy
reverie into which both had sunk.

'After . . . After . . . the, after the . . . feast.' The word 'marriage'
would not come.

Bega nodded most solemnly as if he had announced the precise
date of Armageddon. This fractional movement alerted Padric
to the change in her appearance. Until then he had seen her
through veils of memory. She had become so thin. Her thick
hair, bound up as usual but unbound, he knew, long enough to

sweep down to her legs, was lustreless. The sharp, intelligent face looked hungry. There was a weakness about her and at the same time a concentrated attention which excited both his sympathy and his desire.

He wanted to reach out, lean forward across that narrow space, and take her hand. But Bega was about to be married and Padric lived in her father's household as a trusted guest.

'Why do you want to stay for the feast?'

'Your father invited me. I could not refuse.'

'You could,' she said and he smiled, recognising the blunt truth of her.

'I'll leave right after that.'

'So will I.' She turned to the wall and the gesture had so much sorrow in it that Padric did lean over and reach out to her. But she drew herself away from his touch like a snail pulling into its shell.

'Donal is frightened,' said Padric.

'I know.' She was still turned away from him.

'Why is that?'

Bega paused. It was hopeless. Her mind was a dark place now. She felt weak. Why not do as most women did and obey the word of her father? How sure could she be that a greater Father had a greater call on her? Why on one so unworthy as her?

'I want,' she said, turning to him as she spoke and looking him directly in the face so that he flushed with the intensity of it, 'to serve no man but God. I want to go where other missionaries have gone and tell the pagans of the truth of our God.'

Padric experienced an anarchic swoop of elation at hearing Bega so roundly deny her interest in the marriage. It made little sense. He did not care to examine it. But his smile ignited a responding smile in Bega and he saw her as the wild young girl he had first met.

'What does your father say?'

'He says that I must marry. He ignores what I say. You know him.'

'And?'

'I say I will be a bride,' her steady gaze shamed his triumphant look and he glanced down, 'but a bride of Jesus Christ.'

'But O'Neill is here.'

'I heard him.' It was uncomfortable for her to acknowledge that the sound of the O'Neill clan had thrilled rather than dismayed her. She had been brought up to love war and the sounds of warriors.

'Your father could never bear the dishonour and the humiliation,' said Padric, impulsively. Having uttered this, he realised the truth of it.

'Do you say I must marry him?'

'Why do you ask me?'

'You are my teacher,' said Bega, promptly.

'I was not asked to teach you about this.'

'You taught me the gospels. You taught me about the saints and our missionaries. You taught me about St Brigid and her principality. You told me how the kings of Ireland obeyed her will. How she issued laws and became as royal as any monarch.' Her voice rose. 'You taught me that your own ancestors put God before everything and everyone. So why are you surprised when I decide to dedicate my life to Him? Why do you want me to marry?'

Padric had often experienced Bega's temper. Her outburst now was altogether different: desperation had alchemised it.

'I don't want you to marry,' he said, avoiding her eyes, the words stumbling out.

Bega felt a surge of jubilation but she took care not to show it. It was weak to reveal your feelings too openly and too soon. Her father had drummed that into her.

'What do you want me to do?' She spoke in a neutral tone which put all the responsibility on him and trapped him.

'I am not the one to advise you.'

'You are.' She nodded, vigorously, and repeated, 'yes, you are.'

Padric longed for an interruption. It seemed to him that the whole of a life was being offered and he had to act like Solomon – instantly. There was no time for manoeuvre. The axe would fall wherever he swung it.

'You can't put yourself at my mercy,' he said.

'That is what I am doing.' Her responses were hot on the heels of his phrases, yapping at them, biting them.

It was like war. No time to think: strike.

'You must do what your father tells you.'

'I must marry O'Neill?'

'You must do what your father orders you to do.'

'You are telling me to marry this man.'

'Bega! We both know your father. If you go against him, he will torture you. We both know that.'

'Sometimes it is better to be tortured and killed than to go against the voice of the Lord. Didn't you tell me that? Didn't you tell me about St Alban? About—?'

'Bega, you have a choice which they did not have. You can marry a man worthy of you—'

'How do you know that?'

'The O'Neills are the—'

'How do you know that *this* one man is worthy of me? Or I of him? Have you talked to him? Have you listened to what his friends or his enemies have said about him? How am I worthy of him? What if I am not worthy of him? Why do you say such a stupid, stupid thing? "Worthy of you"!'

Bega began to cry and Padric felt helpless. He tried to keep steady.

'One man I do know is your father,' said Padric. 'I have seen and you have heard what he has done to those who oppose him: to men, women and children. Much as he loves you, nothing matters more to him than his honour. These are the O'Neills. It is too late for you to say no. It would be seen as a terrible violation of his word. Perhaps it was always too late for you to say no. But it is so now. Once he had decided that he would use you to give himself the greater glory, then your history was foretold. There is nothing you can do but obey. Nothing *I* can do but see you hurt as little as possible. To refuse is to meet certain death and to be the cause of many other deaths.'

'Yours?'

'That is not important.'

'Because he would see you – and Donal – as bad advisors, wouldn't he?' she said, calculating rapidly. 'His mind works like that, doesn't it? You would be tortured and killed alongside me.'

'Not just individual deaths. There would be war, Bega. And you – you are the one at the centre of it – you would die in a most horrible way.'

Cathal had buried enemies alive. He had cut off their hands and feet and dragged them out into the forest leaving them for the wolves. He had slit off the lips and nose of many a miscreant and mutilated his inventive way through scores of captured slaves merely, some thought, for the pleasure of it.

Both of them knew this. Both of them had heard the screams, seen the savagery, smelled the blood, known the terror.

'I would not mind that,' said Bega. 'I would welcome that if I thought that I was dying for the love of my God.'

She looked at him steadily as she said that last word. A few seconds seemed a great age, a life of time, but finally he could not hold her gaze.

Silence returned and the weakened young woman found that she was humming to herself.

'So, so,' she paused once more, 'so I must marry him. Is that what you tell me, Padric?'

Padric knew that an opportunity was passing him which would never return. He knew that this opportunity unlived would haunt him more than the ghosts of his ancestors. But he could not give her the answer she implored him to give: to agree would ensure the murder of both of them.

'Is that what you say?' Her tone was harsher.

'Yes,' he said, eventually, 'you must marry him.'

Bega smiled, a beatific and serene smile and reached out to take his hand.

'Then I will,' she said. 'Poor Padric. Poor Padric.' And for a moment she put her cold cheek against his cold hand.

ChaPTER SIX

After Padric had left, the message came for Bega to meet Niall O'Neill. She moved in an obedient daze, her stomach no longer nipped in hunger; her head no longer ached with tiredness; her eyes no longer strained with the effort of tight shutting in prayer. She would do as she had been bid.

Maeve brought her the new cloak, furnished with a golden spiralling clasp worked with pearls, amethysts and topaz. The two golden armlets were now loose about Bega's wasted upper arms and Maeve had to pad in some cloth to hold them so that they would show when the arm left the open sleeve. The large-toothed bone comb could do no more than neaten the hair which Bega refused to let fall. A touch of ochre was put on unresisting lips, and on her tired cheeks. Maeve was aware that Bega had surrendered and she was sorry for it. The thought of this unbridled young woman being at last at the mercy of a father she had so stupidly thought she could outwit had comforted Maeve during the jealous days of preparation for the marriage.

'You must not leave me, Maeve,' said Bega, in a pleading tone Maeve had not heard before. 'Promise me that you will come north with me after I am married.'

'Your father will decide that,' said Maeve, coldly, but not entirely untouched by the sorrowful timbre in Bega's voice.

'If I marry this man, he will let me have whatever I want.'

'*If* you marry . . .' Maeve loosened and brushed out her own hair and – to great effect – used the last dab of ochre on her own lips and cheeks. She continued 'Have you not yet decided, even now?'

'Why can't we be friends, Maeve?' said Bega, forcefully. 'I would like a friend at this time.'

'What about Padric?' Maeve knew that the question was cruel but she could not prevent herself. Once she saw the hurt it gave Bega, she felt glad.

Bega licked her lips, the throat suddenly very dry. What about Padric? She swayed a little and then half-stepped, half-stumbled forward and slapped Maeve very hard full in the face, leaving a livid red imprint – far outcolouring the ochre – on her poetic white skin.

'You can be thankful,' said Bega 'that I have not my dagger with me. Now – get behind me and do only as I tell you.'

Maeve wanted to claw back the offer of friendship but Bega walked past her and out into the cold air, the light just beginning to thicken.

Donal was waiting for her and he led the women across the branch and bracken path towards the great hall. The doors were open.

Donal pulled away and the women went in almost side-by-side, some guards before them. The half light squeezed their eyes. Bega saw her father with a tall man whose back was towards her. Seeing her, Cathal shook his head very slightly and instantly the two women stopped.

The voices, the heat and smells of food and sweat, of cooking and smouldering peat swept into Bega's starved senses and she breathed in deeply, reinvigorated. This was the life she had to live. Padric had given her the only advice possible. She must put away the child who yearned for nothing to change and the wilful woman who now clutched at God. She could never be St Brigid but she could be at the side of a great king and she would share his power – let him try to stop her! She would fill the court with priests and poets; she would have the gospels illuminated and decorated in silver and gold. Her children would inherit an earth of heavenly majesty.

What happened next can have occupied no more than the merest seconds but Bega always remembered it in such detail that it could have lasted ten, twenty, a hundred times as long.

At a tap on the shoulder from Cathal, Niall turned around and in that instant Bega found that she did a complete comparison between this man who was to be her husband and Padric who was to leave her for all time. Niall had a dark mass of crinkly black hair, sweat and oil shiny, scraping back from a square forehead;

Padric's hair was red, yellowing sometimes, she had noticed, in the summer sun, touched with gold, and it fell about his high forehead or flowed down on to his shoulders in an infinitely preferable way. The complexion of O'Neill was high, scarlet as raw meat, offset by blue eyes as compelling as the marble glints in the limestone rocks of Connachta. But how much more attractive the paler, lightly freckled skin of Padric, the brown eyes which did not need to stare in order to command attention. Niall's frame was strong, he was tall, almost, Bega conceded, as tall as Padric, yes, equally tall, but Padric's slimmer body – which would be just as strong, she guessed – would not grossen into the inevitable heaviness you could see foreshadowed in the puppy jowl of O'Neill.

She had not realised how handsome a man Padric was until now faced by one from the family sung abroad as breeding the finest looking men in the world.

Niall smiled and for the slenderest moment Bega was affected as the deep warmth that can come from a smile sped towards her: and passed her by. For it was towards Maeve that the smile was directed. A lustful smile, she now saw, a lecherous, coarse, salacious, unparticular smile. Bega did not move a hair's breadth but she could feel Maeve grow beside her, absorbing the promise of that smile which Bega now saw as no more than a groin-fed grin made outwardly more respectable by the undoubted style and poise of the young O'Neill prince. But it was Maeve he wanted and as the two women walked towards him Bega noticed from the corner of her eye that Maeve was not slightly behind her as she ought to be but walked by her side. Bega knew that Niall thought that Maeve was his bride.

The sense of fury at this gave Bega all the control she needed.

They stopped a pace or so before the two men and Bega glanced swiftly at Maeve, whose hair shone, whose eyes glistened, whose breasts swelled forwards like the puffy chest of a gull. In that same glance, Bega saw, in the dimness beyond, the pale and tormented face of Padric and needed all her will not to call out his name in encouragement.

'My daughter,' said Cathal, 'your bride.'

Bega smiled and stepped forward. Niall fought hard to keep the smile on his face. Bega bowed her head and vowed to herself and to God that nothing on earth would take her to this man's bed.

'The Feast will begin tomorrow!' said Cathal.

Cathal looked at Maeve. It would be good to have her, he thought, after Bega had gone north. He had waited long enough. She would squeal nicely. His smile was unambiguous and Maeve closed her eyes in terror.

CHAPTER SEVEN

'I will marry him but I will never share his bed,' said Bega. Donal, who had thought the matter resolved, bent his head in disbelief. Maeve, still excited by the visual caresses of Niall and alarmed by the lust of Cathal, was further inflamed.

'Why not?' said Donal. 'Why not? Why will you not share his bed?'

'Because,' Bega replied, with skittish solemnity, 'that way I can keep both my promises: to God and to my earthly father.'

And, Maeve murmured to herself, you can keep yourself for Padric.

'It has happened,' said Bega. 'In the *Annals* of Kildare, it was written . . .'

'No history please!' said Donal. 'Bega – please – I am an old man. Soon, I pray, every morning and night I pray, I will be called to my heavenly reward. I want to be ready for that. I need to suffer alone, to dwell on my Heavenly Father and all His works. My mouth is full of aching teeth. My stomach swells when I eat meat. I cannot spend all my nights and days agonising not about my Lord on the Cross but about what you are going to do next.'

'It is all resolved,' said Bega, biting heartily into a hunk of bread and honey. 'It is decided.'

'We need not tell anyone, I suppose,' Donal suggested, thoughtfully. 'Not until the marriage is done. You could say – you could find something to say – which would mean that you need not be bedded here that night – he will probably be too drunk in any case, after three days. You could go back with him and tell him when you arrive in the kingdom of the O'Neills and are his legal wife.'

'Not here?'

'Not here,' said Donal earnestly. 'To tell him here would be to risk losing him. To risk losing him would be to risk inciting your father. To risk inciting your father is to risk the lives of you, me, Padric, Maeve and anyone within reach of his vengeance. Not here. No.'

'Why would Padric be involved?'

'Because,' said Donal impatiently, missing, which Maeve did not, the sudden anxiety in Bega's voice, 'because he was involved with you. He taught you. Your father will conclude that he mistaught you. He will say I guided you wrongly. He will say that Maeve did not, as she should have done, strengthen you in the right way. He will take revenge and that will be the most terrible thing you have ever known. And the last thing you will know.'

'But I must tell him,' said Bega piously. 'I must.'

You must, thought Maeve, because you want to send a message to Padric. And for the sake of doing that you are quite happy to put all our lives at risk. If ever I had a softening of feeling for the spoilt child before me, then God and Mary and all the host of angels forgive me, for I will never suffer it again.

'He can have children by a concubine or by a mistress, can't he, Maeve?' Bega turned on Maeve sweetly but unmistakably.

Maeve was too sunk in her anger to respond.

'And the children of the concubine would have all the rights the children of a wife would have. Maeve would like to be his concubine, wouldn't you, Maeve?' Then, cruelly, 'but he will only take you as a mistress.'

'So why do you want to be his wife?' Maeve asked, sullenly.

'I don't,' said Bega. 'But,' piously once more, 'I must obey my father.'

'You need not tell the man,' said Maeve, reluctantly. 'I agree with Donal.'

'But if I don't tell him,' said Bega, losing all her playfulness instantly in that volatile way Maeve and Donal found so confusing, 'then he will have every reason to be angry. Who knows? When I tell him, he might accept it willingly and immediately seek out the woman he can rut with, the woman he can ream with in bed, Maeve, and all will be well. Why should I deny him that?'

Maeve flinched, even though Bega had not threatened a blow.

'If I fail to tell him and trick him, then who knows where his anger will end? You talk about my father's vengeance and I fear that. But what of the revenge of the O'Neills which we hear goes on throughout the world and for all time? Which never abates from generation to generation? Which is more foul than the crime of Cain and harder than the army of Gideon? What will my father do then if he sends me away as one woman and then learns soon after when a raiding army comes that I am another woman and have tricked both himself and my husband and begun a war which will never end? No. At least if I talk now, you, Donal, you, Maeve, and Padric I am sure, can take consideration of it and have some influence on the course of events.'

She paused, but only because she was thrilled by the events she could see herself shaping and wanted to enjoy fully this moment of control. Lives would change, wars might happen, mayhem and murder could sweep the land, and all because of her.

'May God forgive you,' said Donal, softly.

'My father and my future husband must be told.'

The declaration had not quite the climactic ring to which she had aspired. Donal's quiet intervention had made her slightly lose her poise.

'Who will do it?' said Maeve. 'And when? *And*,' she added, 'if we are to know this – why not Padric? He is part of it, is he not, Bega? Do you want Padric to be part of it? Do you want to see Padric, alone, to tell him what you have just told us? He is in danger now like the rest of us – maybe he can find a way out. He's a clever man, so? The "cleverest man in Ireland", I heard you say many times. He can read Latin and talk it too; he can play the harp and solve a riddle. That sword of his leaps in his hand like a living thing. He is the wizard from over the sea and he must have his chance. Is that not right, Donal? Or were you going to leave Padric to whatever fate is flung in his face?'

Bega turned away. Then she spoke. 'Come near me again, Maeve, when you and I are alone and although my soul will burn in hell for it I will slash your throat until you bleed like a sow. Now get out and bring Padric to me. Donal, you go too.'

Cathal took all the care at his command to do everything that would be proper to the daughter of a great king.

At his court he had a poet, Muiredach, who turned his epic exploits into epic verse which he learned and retained by rote as he did the epics and legends of a history and poetry stretching back several hundred years. He had been trained in his art for almost twenty-five years since his boyhood, when he sat confined in a dark room while he chanted and revised the verses and the histories of his race. Caesar had marvelled at the accuracy and stamina of such Celtic poet-historians who considered it a sign of weakness to write things down. Muiredach had prepared a great poem for the feast, one that would extend the genealogy of Cathal as it had never been extended before. Moreover it was full of particularly exquisite inflections and rhythms known only to himself and other poets.

Cathal also kept a priest at his court who could usually play the harp, but Donal, who had lived too long for Cathal's liking, could no longer stroke the strings with his arthritic fingers. Padric's arrival and his skills, including the harp, had been welcomed. He was always willing 'to pray or to play' as Cathal said, although he did not enjoy the taunts of Cathal's sons when he did either. To them a priest was a man who had failed to become a warrior. Despite this, neither quite dared face him in single combat. All of them knew that the more successful priests came generally from the same families as the more successful warriors and were as well able and well trained in all the arts of war, but the taunts persisted. Of Padric's scholarship they had hardly concealed contempt; of his musicianship they had nothing but deep and envious respect. But he played with their darkling little sister and that would always drag him down.

Cathal's lawgiver, who made up the fourth of the heads of the household, was Eogon, inherited from the last king conquered on Cathal's road to power. Eogon was known as one of the sagest of his kind. Other kings would send for him and Cathal proudly let him go with full escort. When he fixed a ransom for capture, a punishment for rape, a sentence for theft or wounding, it was done with such long-worded attention to all the circumstances that it had never been known to cause the spilling of yet more blood, as so often happened after a judgment.

Eogon in turn was entranced by Cathal. He knew that the man would respect the law and the gospels with all his might until the day or the minute came when he saw what he wanted and could not get it without slashing away the roots of all they stood for. Eogon, who ought to have deplored that and who did indeed deplore it in the case of others, forgave it in Cathal.

Two years before, Eogon had watched from a nearby wood in which he had been, luckily, looking for berries, when Cathal and a few men had fallen on his previous master's household. Well outnumbered, soon surrounded, he had watched in awe as the man he now served had roared and laughed for joy as he murdered his way through men, until those who had the power to flee turned and ran. Cathal – steeped in blood, his sword running with it, his tongue licking it as with heathen glee – sang as he counted the severed heads. He had found Eogon, stayed the moment to ask him who he was, recognised the name, and spared him. Recognised his name! Eogon by that one recognition felt a touch of immortality.

For this feast, everything was done in an order according to Eogon's advice. Other feasts, the feasts to celebrate the Church calendar, the feasts to celebrate the calvings and lambings, the feasts when guests came, the feasts on relevant saints' days, these followed an old form and had been no great burden. Cathal liked feasts. They fed his men and made them stronger than the rest. They showed how important it was to be in the household of such a man. And for Cathal, marked by memories of scarring hunger, every feast was another stride away from a past he would kill and kill never to repeat. This feast, though, had to be one which not only Muiredach, but poets elsewhere, poets eventually everywhere, would include in their songs.

The land that he ruled knew that it had one purpose – which was to serve this event. For days before, processions of men and women, sometimes with horses, sometimes with mules, sometimes on foot, brought food and drink from every quarter of Cathal's domain. From the nunnery he secured more dolphin, but also whale meat, salmon and trout. His own fishermen at the last moment brought oysters, mussels, crabs, winkles and limpets which the women cleaned and stored in an ice-bound pond inside the settlement. The bitter weather favoured the preservation of fish.

Throughout the three days, specially fattened pigs and cattle would be roasted together with poultry and the game hunted in quantities so unprecedented that scarcely a wing stirred for miles around. The butchers were instructed to be ready at any hour to replenish the stock: the appropriate beasts were already picked out, the knives sharpened to edges of such fineness that the least pressure from a thumbing test would slice the skin.

The pigs had been butchered and bled with especial care. Pork was the staple and Cathal's own favourite food. He ordered that it be served first. Whole mature pigs and three massive boars, one of which had killed Cathal's best hunter, would be turned on the spits both in the old kitchens and in the new ones erected especially for the event. The crackling succulent roast carcasses would be brought in by servants who had been ordered to kneel in front of every man and wait until he had sliced and hacked off as much as he wanted. Cathal had appropriated the lame cook from his wife's cousin's monastery who was praised by all for the ingenuity with which he would stuff one fish or one bird into another and then into another, pleats of tastes. His seasonings and herbs made sauces the secret of which no one was allowed to learn.

The women had baked enough bread for three feasts and Una had brought in the women from the southern lands where there were only sheep and goats. But the cheeses from these were so exquisite, their preparation so skilful, that these women – some of them dark like Bega, some even darker, with large oval black eyes and flat black hair and fleshy, ruby, puckered lips – these women alone could serve the resulting delicacies. Cathal had sent an escort for them, given silver and promised a few cattle: a promise he would break, as both parties knew.

As for the drink, that had been his personal responsibility and there was enough ale, beer and mead to service the forces of an unequalled length of days. They would all be drunk, he thought, all the time, and the thought gave him the deepest pleasure.

The horn summoned the guests for the first day. It was noon. Cathal had worried about the horn. They had managed without one until now but Eogon had mentioned a legendary feast at which this was used and he supposed that at the court of the O'Neills the tradition was continued. So a horn was found.

In the great hall, extra tables had been added. At the door, the armed doorkeepers looked for weapons – apart from the knives used for eating – and brusquely turned away any who had not been invited.

Some of the hangings had been bleached as new in a mixture made perfect by the women's urine and the peat smoke had not yet darkened them. The interweaving of fine gold thread tantalised the guests with a perspective of riches.

The cold outside was excluded by the heat from the fire, heaped up high for the feast. Two small boys, shorn-headed against lice, stick-limbed and ragged, stood by it, wearily feeding it with squares of peat which took them all their strength to lift. There were tall fat candles everywhere, some arm thick, yellow flames spluttering, flickering, dancing, swaying, catching the gold in the wall hangings, the burnish on the hung shields, the glint of skull bone, the mirror of metal and glossy wood on the table and the flash of the jewellery so proudly worn by so many.

All the men wore their finest jewellery. The clasps were of Irish gold or silver; the rings were enamelled or set with semi-precious stones which caught the rushlight or the candlelight and shivered a responsive pattern of broken coloured gleams in the darkest parts of the hall. Big belt buckles glowed like beacons; the necks of the wealthiest men were adorned with torques, though nothing that Cathal could see in any way equalled the gift he had purchased for Niall. Cathal's own jewellery was uncompromising – every finger bore a ring, armlets rode up each arm and three torques haltered his bull neck.

Among the men, the women and slaves came and went, serving. Una with Bega served the mead from a double-handled silver cup which Cathal had stolen in his unrepented past – a pagan interlude – from a monastery, but one in the land of an enemy. Maeve and other slaves served from the flagons of ale and beer.

Maeve's glance kept darting over to Niall as if answering the call of her name. How could Bega have thought that pale gaunt Briton of any account compared with the luxuriant features and qualities of Niall O'Neill? Her fingers itched to grip that thick black hair. When he had looked at her that first time the glance had sliced into her heart. She could never be his wife – though in other circumstances, uncaptured, unenslaved, he would have been proud to own her – but being his concubine she could somehow effect. This meant that she would have to travel with Bega. Once again, compulsively, her eyes flicked over to the O'Neill and she knew she had to have him. While he, noting her glances and encouraging them, felt that deep certainty in the base of himself that he would have her and hard and soon. The certainty gave the feast – already one to boast about – a sexual piquancy he relished deeply.

More than sixty men were present, served by as many slaves and the women. The slaves were controlled by those about to be freed, and Cathal looked on with approval as the food was brought in hissing and crackling from the spits, glistening with juices. The low growls of the many prowling dogs and the deep roar of the men in their finery created the murmur of masculine companionship which Cathal loved and which would rear up as they stoked up the night. Outside there had been a fall of snow and even that was seen by Cathal as a good omen. For all the better it made them feel to be in here, secure, warm, fat with food.

Behind him stood his sword-bearer, a short strong blond-haired, broken-nosed and toothless Jute, captured from a minor lord on a recent unfortunate coastal raid, the best wrestler Cathal had ever known. His freedom had been promised after one more year and he had been given a slave woman. Grotesquely squat and famously ugly, he added yet more splendour, Cathal thought. To have a sword-bearer, a guard man, was magnificent. It also emphasised that he, even Cathal, did not carry a weapon – save for the dagger which, like Niall and, he suspected, a few others, he kept hidden.

For some moments he looked at the play of light, the waves of movement, the soft low flames at the fire, the wandering strokes of the candles, the faces of those who had come to pay him respect, his guests, he the provider and giver, and then he caught sight of Bega, like her mother but like no other woman in the place, and he knew he was a king.

He had secured a family of tumblers and jugglers but he saved them for the second day. There were also three musicians, a piper, a fiddler and one who played a double row of bells. The harp stood ready for Padric should he volunteer to play it. Padric, a prince of Rheged, could not be asked to play as if he were there only for the purpose of entertaining. Were he not to play, however, it would be

thought highly impolite, indeed an affront, and retribution would
be sought.

Because of his rank, Padric was well placed in the order which
Cathal had imposed. Cathal sat at the head of one long table;
his sons, Dermot and Faelan, were at the heads of the other
two. At Cathal's right hand was Niall and on his left the poet
Muiredach. Next to Muiredach was Niall's older brother and next
to Niall himself was Padric, dressed, Cathal thought, like a true
royal man.

When Bega poured Padric the mead she avoided his eyes.
Although Donal had sought him out everywhere he could think
of, he had not been able to secure him and bring him to Bega as
she had commanded him to.

Bega was convinced that he had avoided her deliberately. Instead
of understanding that, if true, this may have had something to do
with her now openly declared intention of marrying Niall, she
chose to interpret it as an unforgivable snub, or worse, an act of
cowardice. When she poured his mead she overfilled his cup so
that it slopped over his hand.

After Bega had moved on, Niall, well into the rarer slices of pork
reserved for the higher ranks at the very top of the tables, turned to
Padric. He knew that this man was a prince of Rheged and had
been at this court for some time, and he saw a friend. Rheged was
also a name in war. Some of the wilder sons of Rheged who had
fought and then fled the Teutonic invaders, now paid allegiance
to Niall's father and rode with the O'Neills in their war parties. He
felt towards him as he would to a young friend he had known since
boyhood: swift and superficial friendliness was characteristic of the
O'Neills. It unlocked many doors, undid many hearts and caused
many sudden and unexpected deaths.

'Tell me about Bega,' said Niall, already in the first stages of
drunkenness. 'What sort of wife will she be?' He saw Padric
hesitate. 'Come on. Trust me. The woman won't hear of our talk.
What have I to look out for?'

Padric too was a little drunk. He had taken too much strong
mead too quickly in his nervousness, and the rich food, the
unbearable proximity of Bega, the uncomfortably obvious flirtation
between Niall and Maeve, and his own confusion still at telling
Bega to marry this man, made him unusually tense. Besides, he did
not like O'Neill. It was nothing to do with Bega, he told himself.

It was just that there was a profound unreliability about the man. Here was someone who would change sides in mid-battle, Padric thought, if he saw an advantage. Not that he did not need to court the O'Neill but he was easily courted, Padric concluded, dismissively.

'Talk, man,' said Niall with a big, companionable belch of encouragement. 'What have I bought?'

In as level a voice as he could manage and at too rapid a pace, Padric gave a neutral and tedious litany of Bega's virtues. Her abilities were itemised: her several accomplishments were dutifully described; her lineage was recited; her unexpected talents – the swordsmanship, the daring – were merely touched on, and dully.

'I thought as much,' said Niall and swept the leather cup to his lips, clearing a brainfilling scoop of strong mead in one swallow. 'I think I'll turn to ale for a while,' he said, and banged the beaker on the table. A slave appeared within moments and the thick frothy ale slid gently into the drained cup.

'What about the other one?' he asked. 'That's the one I really want to know about.' He laughed with all his brilliant teeth on show and raised himself slightly to fart, a salute to his own charisma.

Padric felt himself freeze. Was this an ambush? He said nothing.

'To tell the truth – but don't for God's sake tell her father – I thought that the slave was the real one when I first set eyes on them. The other one *looks* like the one, doesn't she? The real one's too much of a darkie for me. I like the white skin, the black hair. Maeve! That's the name. A great name in O'Neill country is Maeve. They can ride can the Maeves.' And he rode up and down on the bench, grunting. 'What I want to do – and I need your help here – I need everybody's help but no word to old Cathal or he'll slice my balls off – I want to take that Maeve along with me as well. I mean, I want Bega to take her first and me to take her later!' He laughed very loudly at this pun and Cathal nodded happily to see the young men getting along so well. His smile hid the growing pain in his anus which signalled the most unfortunate return of the squits.

It was a mercy, Padric thought, that they had been obliged to leave their weapons out of the hall. He made an excuse to leave but Niall grabbed his arm. 'You're a clever man, they say,' he began, and belched again very loudly into Padric's face. 'What I want to do to that Maeve is to creep up to her while she's churning, while she's working away bent over the tub with the big stick going! Have you heard this riddle, scholar?'

He chanted the riddle into Padric's ear with the richest tone of innuendo:

'There came a young man to where he knew her to be.
Standing in a corner. (Do you think that's Maeve?)
The lusty bachelor approached her, lifted up his clothes and thrust something stiff under her girdle where she stood,
Had his way,
So both of them were shaking. (Can you see her white cheeks all red now? She knows I'm talking about her!)
The thane worked hard: his good servant was sometimes useful
But, though strong, he always became tired
And weary of that work before she did. (She looks as if she could last a long course, our Maeve, doesn't she?)
Beneath her girdle there began to grow
What good men love in their hearts and buy with money!

So,' said Niall, 'what is the answer to that?'

Padric, who had endured enough, had time for no more games. 'Dough,' he said, dourly.

'You've heard it before,' said Niall, disappointed and a little angry. The Rheged man could have played along a bit. 'Nobody gets it the first time around.'

'I have something to tell you,' said Cathal as he left the table on the excuse of talking to Padric. He had to relieve the pain of excrement before its release brought about a calamity that would disgrace him, especially on this, the first day of the feast. Later there would be so much stink no one would know who a particular offender was.

Seeing them go off together, Bega thought that Padric had gone over to her father and abandoned her for ever. In her spasm of panic she spilled the silver cup of mead. The dogs licked it up gratefully and Maeve caught Niall's disdainful glance at his future bride.

chapter eight

Cathal squatted just a few yards from the doors and a huge pain recoiled through his bowels as the impatient excrement squirted and farted and splattered its way onto the spiky cold earth. The stiffened grass prickled his bulged out bottom.

He invited Padric to squat beside him on the white earth and, rather boozily in the cold air, Padric obliged and was also relieved.

'She is too much like me,' Cathal began, taking it for granted that the object of his thoughts was also the preoccupation of Padric. 'Aahh,' he said, 'that should clean me out. The spell was good but it hasn't worked fast enough. But we're near the end of it, I think . . .' He paused, considered wiping himself and then decided to wait a while.

Padric, though finished, still squatted alongside, for company. Nearby a small herd of swine grouted the hard earth. The waif who was the swineherd that night stood shivering in his thin cloak. There was a wooden bucket half full of pig swill, and the boy, guarding it to the last, occasionally took a fingerful for himself. Beyond the swine, dogs roved around, forever picking up the smells from the great hall, mad to be in there and driven madder by the happy yelps of the privileged ones allowed in. Cathal could identify every sound of the animals and the humans that made up his pocket empire and every sound rang a peal of achievement in his ears.

A dry, trumpeting eruption signalled the all clear in his anus but still he squatted, superstitiously convinced that the exposure to freezing air might act as a natural stopper, in some way ice it over, bung it up with cold rigidity.

'When she goes for something there's no holding her,' he said.

'I could see that from the start. You never saw her as a girl-child. Put her on any horse – you had to throw her on it she was such a mite – the most dangerous of them all and she would put her little hands in that mane and to get her to let go, you would have had to cut off those hands!' Even in the low light of the cloud-veiled moon, Padric could see the pride on the scarred face that matched the boast of the words. 'And she would start whispering in its ear, just child talk – I went close up to listen – and where I would have slapped its nose and pulled it down, that little girl put a spell on it. She put a spell on it. And when we got her off a bad bugger she would be shaking and nearly weeping, but she would want on again. Right away. Same when I let her use a sword. We had a little one made for her and she would go at it – her brothers were frightened off half the time – they pretended they didn't want to hurt her but I could *see*. She was a real one. She would die rather than be defeated. *They* could see that and when the enemy can see that there is no doubt who will win. Fear feeds on fear. Never show it.'

His tone deepened here, the words were very thick; Cathal was talking about himself. Padric knew that to win the battles he himself must win, he too had to find that irresistible courage and inspire it in others.

'But that, you see, is the trouble now,' said Cathal, at last rising and taking some of Cassayr's least damaged herb-rinsed cloths to wipe himself down. 'You have put this idea – you and Donal and that idiot madwoman Cathleen, God rest her soul – you have given her too much God and saints and well and good. I'm your man for your God. Whenever I've asked His help in a difficult spot, He's beaten all the others. And there's Saul and David and Gideon – men I can respect like the O'Neills. But she has to be made to let go of it now, Padric. That was for learning years only.'

He flung away the cloths and two of the livelier pigs snouted across to examine the product.

'Now then, Padric,' said Cathal. 'I've seen you fight and you can fight and I like that. The sword you have is a help but still it takes a man to use a sword and you can use it. You need a bit more—' here he hit Padric, hard, on the shoulder to indicate weight, thickness, strength. Padric staggered but did not fall. 'But you're fit to do what you tell me you want to do with your own people. And by your own God, Padric, I am on your side. Drive them out that came to take your lands! Slaughter the lot of them. They came from another country to claim your country. That's no good. We knew the British were made soft by all the other conquerors and, save for King Arthur, they made useless treaties and ran away on the battlefield, but not when Arthur turned up, eh? And not under your grandfather Urien.

'You are cornered over there all right, but I have told you: when you are cornered you can be at your strongest. When all the world except those you truly trust are at your throat – then the battle is the sweetest and victory is just a snatch away. They think they have you: that helps *you*. When you are cornered, Padric, as I was in all my beginnings and as I have been since, then the gods send you all their strength and your God above all sends you His strong right arm. When you are cornered you have no alternative but winning, Padric, remember that.

'Now that you have been with me, now that you have made your alliances over here, now that you have got your learning, you are ready. But before that you will do one favour for me. With this favour you quit all your obligations. I will give you treasure when you leave but want no treasure from you save this. I will give you alliance whenever, *whenever* you want it but call nothing from you at any time. But you must do this. Listen.

'You must break Bega of this will to give herself to God. You must make her certain to marry. No more doubts. If she shames me, Padric, I will have to kill her and,' he looked away, a sob threatening, and it seemed to Padric, the better to ensure the words carried all the impact intended, 'I will kill her by degrees. I will have to, you see. To kill all my shame I will have to torture her slowly and everyone must witness these tortures. Even that might not be enough. Even that might not prevent an eternal war with the O'Neills. But, hear me, Padric, that I will do. She will listen to you. I want that from you. You will do this for me.'

Abruptly he set out for the hall – the broad back, the short legs, the supremely cocky strut, the hair dangling down. As the doors opened on a waft, a drift of warmth, a wave of noise, the roar of drink and rare gluttony, the deep growl of contented male dominion came out to warm Padric. He was part of that and so was Bega. His was to dominate; hers to serve. Cathal was right: it was his world, it was O'Neill's world and Bega must obey.

He shivered and wrapped the long woollen Irish cloak around

him and then decided not to go in. For some time he wandered
under the scudding clouds, under the intermittent moon.

Niall was not much disturbed when Padric failed to return. He
had been a little too quiet for his taste. And although Padric had
drunk, he had not really sunk the mead and the beer as if he
meant it. You could never trust a man who did not drink with
you drink for drink. Mind you, the O'Neills never fully trusted
anyone, not even other O'Neills.

Niall was pleased. The poet had delivered an interminable
saga on the lineage of Cathal. No one had dared interrupt,
scarcely whisper, as Cathal sat so still ready to take gravest
offence at any slight. He was a fierce man, this Cathal, Niall
thought, and smiled to himself that some day they might meet
in combat. Then the poet had commenced another dirge about
Cathal's exploits. This was something Niall wanted to learn more
about but Cathal insisted on engaging his poet in self-puncturing
ribaldry, dismissing the deeds so dangerously accomplished and
so painstakingly and elegantly rhymed. Occasionally a couple of
lines came through, or Niall recognised the name of a dun or
tuath or tribe which had met the full assault of Cathal and
his men. And when he heard mention of a raid which had
reverberated through the ranks of fighting men, he strained to
catch the sonorous details but Cathal would almost always cut
across the poet. Niall suspected it was a form of teasing or an
even greater show of power: let the world know of these deeds
but show the world how little they mattered to the man who had
done them. Niall appreciated that. He would have the poet tell
him the details another time.

It was a mighty feast, one made for poetry and song. Now,
deep into the night with the snow and the dark outside and the
fire still fed fat with rich lumps of peat, every man was drunk.
There had been no quarrels. Many of his own men were dozing
or down on the floor asleep – a sign of confidence in the place.
The slaves were still in attendance, those who could keep their

eyes open and, although Una and Bega had gone, Maeve, he saw, was still in the hall and he lifted his cup, beckoning her to bring him more mead.

The poet had finished and Cathal was walking among the tables, openly checking that all was well and would remain well. His guard followed him, bearing Cathal's broad sword like a banner.

Maeve came close to him with the two-handled silver sconce. Niall first held out his cup and then pulled it back a little further, a little further yet, so that she had to bend down close to him as she poured. His free hand found her breasts and then her thighs which parted as she moved her legs slightly to let him reach into her. She stayed close to him, not impeding his hard, knowing fingers which foraged and plunged deep into her and twisted and turned so fast and coaxingly that she felt faint. When she had to stand up straight, she breathed out, heavily, and looked down on him without any humility or disguise.

'I will find you,' he said. 'Soon I will be there.' He put the cup to his mouth and smiled.

She nodded and moved away. Her body ached and tingled as uncomfortably as if she were wearing a hair shirt. She wanted to be on her own. She wanted to be near him again. She wanted something to resolve this fiery agitation.

As a girl, Maeve had often been fondled and excited by men pretending or only half-pretending to play with the pretty little thing. Becoming the servant of Bega, however, had put a stop to that. People were too afraid of the wrath of Cathal. They knew how much he cared for his daughter and therefore anyone belonging to her enjoyed security. Faelan would attempt to waylay and grope her but she found him easy enough to evade; her distaste for his heavy eyes, lank hair and brutal ways made avoidance almost a necessity, although she realised that he could be her best bet for concubinage. Maeve was aware of her sexuality and of its power. Niall had touched it into possibilities of which she had only dreamt. She wanted to be with him alone as soon as she could: to find out what more there was, to give in to this deep itch, this uneasy pleasure, this prickling desire.

Niall sank the large measure of mead without taking the lip of the cup from his mouth and as the strong sweet liquid ran down his cheeks and on to his neck, his head swirled and swung in a

dark heaving dance and he felt that no one under the sky could
be as stuffed full of favour as he was. Then he went out like a
snuffed candle. Soon the hall was a low chorus of snores and deep
sighs as the slaves wearily cleared the wreckage and the boys took
turns to sleep while keeping vigil beside the ever-smoking fire.

CHAPTER NINE

Padric slept badly. He had, in effect, given his word to Cathal. He had not formally done so, but he had not objected to the request (more like a command) given him. Now, as the white dawn brought alive the shivering noises of the hens and the cattle, as the pigs began their all-day pigging and the dogs came out to scavenge their first snacks, the women and children rose to build up the fires and the men slaves left the stockade to gather more supplies of cut peat. The women slaves took out the frozen game and fish and meat for the second day of the feast, and Padric forced himself to walk towards the small hut leaning against the north wall of the hall which had been given to Maeve and Bega for these few feast days.

Maeve was asleep on her side, her body sprawled half out of the narrow cot, her hair sweeping down to the skins on the floor, her limbs, as he watched, moving slightly as if in yearning. It took a further moment or two before he identified Bega. She was in the far corner wrapped around by her old shag haired wolfhound, Murcha. All he could see of Bega was her face. Small, defiant, it seemed to Padric an isolated patch of human skin in the middle of sheepskin rugs, dog and grey woollen blankets.

Maeve opened her eyes but did not admit to being awake. Padric came over to her and took her lightly by the shoulder. She resisted for a while and then rolled over provocatively, knowing that her breasts would ride up through her shift. Abruptly she lifted up her eyes and looked at him intensely.

'I want to speak to Bega,' he said.

'She's over there.'

'Alone.' Maeve dug deeper into her bed. Padric's hand came

down on her shoulder a little more heavily. 'You will have to go,' he said. 'Now.'

Padric had always been soft-mannered with her, as indeed he was to most people. It was this even more than his scholarship which marked him off from Cathal's sons and henchmen. But nobody had ever taken Padric for a fool and Maeve was shrewd enough to realise that it was no time to pick an argument. Besides – she flung aside the coverings and stretched, a full deep stretch to show him what he was missing compared with the skrimshanks skulking under her smelly pet dog and threw on her cloak – Niall might be up early. She had gone back to him after his head had hit the table but he was out cold. She knew, though, that men like Niall prided themselves on an early rise after such a bout – Cathal did – and a cup of cold beer and much talk of what an almighty night it had been.

Maeve's leaving disturbed Bega awake. She fixed her eyes on Padric and he gathered his arguments together.

'Don't come near me if you have come to do my father's business.'

'I have come to help you.'

'That's what traitors always say.'

Still she lay coiled and burrowed inside the cot.

'I am not a traitor, Bega, and you know that.'

'What are you, then?'

'Your tutor.'

'That finished when I was told to be a bride.'

'I do not want you to be hurt, Bega.'

'So you'll have me marry that O'Neill joint of meat who'd flay the skin off his sister to get his way. Do you know he has a woman already and a child by her?'

'How do you know that?'

'From the servants. But it isn't so bad, is it? You are about to say. And it isn't. I would be sickened to be the sole object of that vain monster's attentions.'

Padric sat down to be more on a level with her. He had never before thought of Bega as vulnerable. Now she was exposed. As she curled in on herself, Padric saw a wild animal, cornered, the pack all around, no means of defence.

'Bega, you have to marry him.'

'So you tell me.'

'I promised your father that I would bring you to it.'

'Is this the tutor?'

'Yes.'

'The tutor taught me about a God in heaven mightier than any father on earth, even my own father. Did he not?'

'He did.'

'This same tutor told me that to obey this God was the most important matter in our earthly lives. Did he not?'

'I did.'

'This same famous tutor from across the sea with all the ways and the talk has taught me that this earthly life was no more than the flight of a fly, the blink of a cat, the twitch of a rat's tail. The real life was the heavenly and eternal life. And this existence was a test for that real life. And to sacrifice anything, anything at all for that eternal bliss would be stupid as well as sinful. Am I still with the same man?'

'Yes.'

'So. The first bark from the old hound and all of the religion runs around like a topped goose.'

'No. You can do all these things, Bega, and still marry O'Neill.'

'You don't like the man, do you?'

'That is not the question.'

'*You* don't have to marry him. I know you don't like him. So why should I?'

'That is of no importance at all and you have always known it. A princess does not marry because she likes or dislikes the set of a man.'

'I want to serve God as a nun, Padric. I want to go on missions. Do you object to that?'

'Are you sure of this vocation?'

'I knew it when Cathleen was dying,' said Bega, overpromptly. 'And when she died and God let me know that she had died, then I was certain sure. Anyway, what do you care? You're off to your own land as soon as this is over. Aren't you?'

'I am.'

'So what am I to you? And indeed, what are you to me?'

At this, the small face withdrew even more, suffocating the last words, the arm was drawn in, and all he saw was a heap of skins with the slow heaving body of Murcha slung across them.

Padric felt uncomfortably new to himself. A perfectly straight-forward talk was making him short-breathed, almost nervous, but not in a way he recognised.

'What do you want, Bega?'

Padric was aware that the noise of the ceremony announcing the beginning of the sports was growing more insistent. He could not be prominently absent. Cathal wanted him for the spear-throwing, the running, the game of hurly. 'What do you *want*, Bega?'

She rose from the disarray and stepped out to face him. Her shift was down to her ankles, the material as thin as Maeve's had been, but while the soft full breasts of Maeve had not stirred Padric, the hard swing of Bega's smaller bosom did. Her hair fell all about her, down the side of her face, down the front of her shift, down her arms, doubtless tumbling down her back, dark in the dark hut but still taking reddish glints from the dawn light coming through the door.

'I want you to go away.' Her fists were closed tight, her arms jammed down by her sides. 'I want you to go away. I want to pray and I do not need a tutor to do that any more.'

'Bega.'

'Go *away!*' The voice veered high like the sudden soar of a hawk.

'Shall I tell your father that? I can try to persuade him that you are serious. That your vocation is too strong for you to give up.'

'He won't listen. You *know* he won't listen.'

'Bega.'

'Padric, leave me. You see war. I see Cathleen already in heaven. Your battles will be against your earthly enemies and I want you to win. Mine, if I have the strength and if I am allowed, will be against the enemies of God. I want to teach His word, Padric, I want to carry it into the dark places so that not just two or three can see it and understand it but whole peoples can know His glory and be converted into His service. I know that is what I have to do, Padric. I have prayed and I have been given a sign. You go now. Go now.'

She ended gently and Padric found he had no more to say. He was rooted. Neither of them moved.

Bega looked at him calmly, waiting. Padric held her gaze but only for some moments. A shiver went through her and she smiled and turned to put on her long woollen dress. When she turned back, Padric was gone. She clenched her teeth against the tears and began to pray as Padric, with Donal and Cathleen, had taught her.

CHAPTER TEN

The second day was accounted Padric's day and even the O'Neills were ungrudging. The spear-throwing was won by Cathal from Niall, who gave his followers to understand that this defeat was a necessary act of pre-filial respect. Padric did well enough, though not as well as three of the O'Neills and Dermot. In the leaping and such running as could be managed on the snow churned to slush and reluctant mud – the thaw was very slight – he won without seeming to try. In the hurly he was the most skilful and, though he was knocked down rather more often than the rest, his game brought applause from the athletically besotted warriors. The ground was considered too difficult for the horse races around the settlement.

It was inside the hall, however, that Padric excelled, at the very end of the evening.

The feast began a few hours after noon and once again the slaves groaned with the weight of food they bore in and the men, freshened by the cold air and the fast chaotic exercise, dug in to show off their paces as trenchermen. Meat was stabbed as if it were a live creature trying to escape and the knife point disappeared into the salivating crimson mouth to be juiced with drink and more and more drink. The cheeses from the south were brought in and eaten with great burps of appreciation and then pelted around the hall.

The slaves stood back and waited for this warrior excess to spend itself and then they moved in to feed, to offer drink, to clean, to be cuffed, shouted at, pinched, abused, ignored and occasionally addressed directly. But the warriors were too far above them to notice; too far above everyone in the land. The land existed to support them, the few, the warlords, the makers of legends.

Niall had brought what he called an apology for a poet who began the orations with an account of the O'Neills' rise to pre-eminence in Ireland. The kings and prophets of the Old Testament had passed on direct their cunning and warlike skills to the O'Neills; the Romans who had wasted the island of Britain for so long had not dared come across to Ireland because of the O'Neills; only here was God's word safe for those who could read and that too was thanks to the greatness of the O'Neills. More and more could be told, said the poet, but in the house of a man like Cathal, soon to be blood-joined to the O'Neills and none more worthy, enough had been uttered for the moment.

Muiredach felt he had scored only half a success on the previous evening – the genealogy had pleased Cathal but the epic, so much better worked and with wholly original rhymes, had been lost in Cathal's banter which had distracted and diminished him. Now he gathered himself together and stood on the poet's step beside the peat fire, where the light was most concentrated and a good oration could make everyone wonder at him.

He had changed his mind during the morning and instead of the histories of ancient Celtic kings, he decided to go for a guaranteed favourite: the Voyage of St Brendan. Brendan was their favourite saint, as touched by miracles as any of the apostles and a man who dared the sea – an element fearful to these landlocked horsemen warriors. All carried pagan charms and totems about them. In a crisis many would as soon go to a superstitious deity as to the Lord of Hosts they swore by in great battles. But Brendan was their man. The story of their own ancestral saint who with forty monks set off into uncharted and perilous seas, seeking the land of promise, the land of the saints.

Muiredach was not a tall man nor was he imposing. But when he threw his bardic cloak around his shoulders and took in his hand a candle to represent the ship in which St Brendan and his followers wandered through the wildest reaches of the sea, he became majestic.

He spoke of the magical island inhabited by saints, scented by fruit trees forever ripe with fruit; of the gorgeous hall which suddenly appeared, in which they were washed and reclothed and fed with extraordinary white bread and of the miraculous arrow which flew in at dusk to light the lamps. Muiredach played with three small stones when he told of the juggling of the Ethiopian boy who suddenly appeared in the tale and the juggling brought drumming to the tables.

The poet told the story in his own order and, because of the reception, he returned to the pure white birds in the tree of colossal girth which had caught the imagination of the company. He put on a special bird-voice – 'We are fallen angels, part of the host which was banished from heaven through the sin of man's ancient foe'. The men shouted out for him to do it again. This was Muiredach's finest moment. 'Our sin lay in approving the sin of Lucifer,' he minced out, feather-like in his utterance. 'When he and his band fell, we fell with them.' When the birds sang the vespers – 'Thou, Oh God, art praised in Sion: and unto Thee shall the vow be performed in Jerusalem', then Muiredach let his throat open full throttle and the words soared to the roofbeams, rang around the skulls and shields and drew in the men like a battle dirge.

When Muiredach reached the Easter vigil, which was spent on the back of a gigantic whale – prophesied by one of the birds – he rocked a little and pointed to the ground, saying that perhaps the earth beneath them would be changed into a whale to mark such an occasion as this marriage. Many men looked down uneasily.

When the gryphon flew towards Brendan and his monks on the boat, extending its claws, threatening to take up the monks and devour them, Muiredach flung open his arms, let his bony hands slide through the sleeves and swooped down on the children at his feet. Their screams hid the terrors felt by some of their drunken elders, now in fear for the fate of Brendan, for yet to come was the volcano. The entry of Judas Iscariot 'I am of all men the most wretched' brought the relief of loud boos and catcalls from the men, who at last had found someone to whom they could feel superior. 'My punishment is to burn like a lump of molten lead in a crucible, day and night,' said Judas, and those who had done as badly and even worse to their prisoners cheered this just desert. Just as when the hermit turned out to have dug a grave for the real St Patrick there was a deep nodding of the heads: the saints were as near as that for Brendan himself. And then, with all his powers, Muiredach described the attack of the killer whale, the defending whale of God, the turmoil and blood in the sea, the fury of it, the victory, his words and actions roaring and spuming through the great hall like a hurricane. The battle was roared on and goblets and fists hammered on the table. When Brendan returned safely home, the men stood and cheered Muiredach and Cathal took off one of his best rings and threw it to him.

It was then that Cathal decided to give the presents. Eogon had been pre-warned and he came with the gifts which he gave to Bega and her father. They had gone halfway down the hall to receive them and now they walked back up together, Cathal followed by Bega, who carried the brilliant jewels. Everyone stood to peer and some saw but none appreciated the splendour of the torque until Niall put it about his neck. Flushed with possessing such a magnificent object, he stood on the table, took two rushlights one in each hand to show the torque to the hall. The rings too, for his brothers and himself, were shown to all.

The O'Neill gifts would be handed over on the following day, the wedding day, but everyone already sensed that they would not match the splendour of Cathal's. No one, it was agreed, had seen their like.

Bega saw the greed in Niall's expression as he took off the torque and let his fingers linger over it. Another reason for hating him was bolted into place, although she did not let its expression cross her face.

Now the hall was blistering with excitement. This would be a night to boast about for ever more: the night of the great retelling of the tale of St Brendan; the night of the fabulous rings and the unmatchable torque made in the inner cave by the finest craftsmen under the canopy of heaven and benefiting, some already muttered, from the skills of black and unknowable arts. Such bright gold had surely never been seen; such tones of gold and twists and turns of design, such clusters of precious stones . . . it was a piece of jewellery which would outlast time itself and go of its own accord to the throne of heaven, fit to be worn by an apostle and even Our Lord Jesus Christ. Just *look* at the thing.

Cathal's sense of occasion was replete. No more was needed for that night except to eat to the point of gluttony and drink into stupor which was what all of them intended to do, when the sound of the harp, tentative and disconcertingly sweet, swept like a hush through the men and they saw that Padric had taken his place.

He had to play. He had to do something. The sight of the resigned Bega and the increasingly coarse and obvious O'Neill

was driving him beyond distraction. To play the harp he had
to concentrate with all his forces: to forget everything but the
playing. That was what he wanted.

As his hands strayed across the strings the men felt their hearts
plucked into attendance. Music like this was rare and Padric had
the composure of someone who knew what he was doing. Cathal
caught the eye of Niall, taking a moment from consuming his gift,
toying with it, trying to believe it was really his and admiring it, as
he thought, secretly so as not to betray the extent to which he was
impressed. The men smiled rather foolishly to one another. The
gift had made a bond and each now had the other's measure. But
the smile was also about Padric. It said: the sound of the harp is a
fine thing and the man who plays it is to be valued, but however
much we are moved – and we will be moved – the playing of such
a thing is not for us; and we are stronger than the Briton because
it is not for us.

Padric began to sing. His own language was near enough to
the Irish for them to understand without much difficulty. The
songs in any case were simple enough. But they were new to the
Irish. A few were about the love a man can have for a woman.
David and Bathsheba was one, Samson and Delilah, the treachery
of women, the danger of women, but then, something none of
those in the hall had heard, two short songs about the love of a
man for a woman, simply that.

Bega, who had been rooted from the moment Padric touched
the strings, knew that the lament was for her, but new. Padric
had taken old airs – she had heard him sing them before – but
the words were his words. They were her words. The story told
of a man and a woman, young, bold, royal, who loved each other
but were forced to part because he had to return to his native land
– far beyond the courts of Rome, Padric sang – and she, from birth,
had been promised to a man, an old man now, who had once saved
the life of her father. However hard the two fought to resist this,
fate was greater than either of them and the song ended with the
man leaving for far distant courts, the young woman saying that
her soul would meet him there, her body alone stayed behind.

The freshness of this song and its directness together with the
plaintive and melancholy air moved the men to a serious silence
and, when Padric finished the words and stayed for a few moments
just to sweep the strings and bring it all to an end, the sound,

the melody seemed to possess many of the drink-softened heads, discovering undeclared, despised and hidden vaults of femininity. They loved and yet mistrusted Padric for bringing them to this pass. Perceptive as he was, Padric understood that the music disturbed into pleasure sensitivities their warrior discipline had beaten down since childhood. And yet, Padric could see from their faces how much they longed to follow the notes and let themselves, in that moment, be taken on voyages unknown to their compulsive codes of war.

When the last sounds had faded, he stood up and began by swiftly enumerating the qualities of Cathal, their lord for these days, his lord for more than two years. In short and quick sentences he drew them a portrait of the man so many knew and feared. Yet again Cathal was lifted up on a night such as he had never known, for in the gloaming of the distance sat Bega now looking as enraptured as any bride-to-be should look, and around him was the flower of men all bowing to his strong arm.

Moving on from Cathal, Padric told them one of the tales of his ancestor, King Arthur, known to all of them and claimed by some as having an Irish mother. Of how he had come back to the great Roman city of Caerel near his boyhood home and found it suffering from the early signs of ruin. Of how he had declared that from this capital he would raise an army which would regain for the British what Rome had only borrowed, never taken, and of the testing of the men he gathered around him. As Padric spoke of those first men Arthur brought under his standard, he could see the backs stiffen, the heads lift, the warriors' pride of lineage ripple about the hall as the men regained the character they knew and trusted most and exiled that seductive interloper which music had set loose on their undefended feelings.

From Arthur, Padric seized the advantage for his house and leapt to one of his most famous descendants, Urien of Rheged, his own great-grandfather, and a man known to all men who had taken part in battle. For at the fortress of Bamburgh, as the seas which brought the Teutonic invaders to Britain beat against the wide white strands of shore against the rock, Urien had thrown back the pride of all the foreign races and for three days outside the fortress, he had threatened them with extermination. They were saved only by the arrival of a score more boats, hundreds more men bright in armour, fresh for battle, forcing a retreat west, but a retreat without being conquered. Urien would have regrouped and conquered them had he not been so treacherously betrayed.

Since Urien, there had been the ever bolder incursions of the invaders, the British sometimes suing for alliance, sometimes fighting, but now, Padric concluded, locked in in the west, in hills and rivers of country very like Connachta. The British were hoping to fight one last campaign, to take back the lands stolen from Rheged and all the other tribes.

In this campaign they would need men who loved war as Cathal did, as the O'Neills did, men who could do battle as the giants in the Golden Age did in legend and in song. He, Padric, would be back one day, in however many years it took, to ask the finest warriors if they would cross the sea to join in a battle that would shake the mountains of memory. Would they listen again when he came not in peace but in conflict? They roared out, delighted at the prospect of glory in battle. Would they fear that the odds against them were mighty? No – so much more glory for the few who fought. Would they come, then? Did he Padric of Rheged have the word of the men of Cathal and Niall? He did! He did!

Cathal was on his feet, glowering with the anticipation of such a journey and such a war. His cup was now full. From famine and mean roots he had come to be lord of all he saw: and he saw heroes before him. Niall raised his arm to his followers who stood and acclaimed the words of Padric. Padric looked around for Bega, whose close and profound concentration had so moved him when he played the harp, he believed, as never before. But in the middle of his oration, when he had spoken of going back to his own land, her heart which had been so full after his music, suddenly squeezed tight with a cramp of pain and, helped by Donal, she had left.

For Maeve, the night was not yet over. Although she had been given permission to leave, she had not been commanded to do so. She kept herself respectably busy on the periphery but every so often she would cross Niall's eyeline or go to offer him more mead. He knew that she was waiting for him and the thought velveted the last phase of the feast.

Stuffed, distended, seeping with alcohol, a regular trickle of men went to and from the door to meet the night with vomiting and other excretions. It had been a punishing session. Almost ten hours of eating and drinking with the competitiveness of these hard men fully engaged. You could not pull back from the offer of a fat crackling leg of goose or yet another deep cup of beer. Private toasts and wagers took the scoffing and swilling to absurd and crazy lengths, but you ate until the food could no longer provoke the act of swallowing, and you drank until you dropped. That was what a feast was for. This was one of the chief events which marked out the warriors' status and power to all who served them. When it was enlivened, as this had been, by stories and songs and the heady sight of that royal torque, then you ate and you drank even more to do it greater honour.

Now the time of unconsciousness was approaching and as one slumped or fell to the ground, another followed. It was as if sleep became a rapid and invisible affliction. But the noise was scarcely lessened. Loud, ripe and ricocheting farts, spasmed grunts, deep gut, repetitive, cracking belches and the disharmony of dozens of rattling, membrane-straining, mucous-lubricated snores turned the place into a zoo of animal sounds and smells. These were scavengers as much as hunters; looters and robbers and thieves used to exploiting sudden excess as well as warriors. All of them believed that the food and drink they had had would give them not only strength in days and weeks to come, but some of the qualities of the animals and fowls they had eaten. The aggression of the wild boar, the strength of the long-horned cattle, the speed of the birds, so ingeniously stuffed the one into the other; the elusive intelligence of the trout; the grace of the dolphin; the power of the whale; and the courage of the gods in the drink.

Cathal rose and left when all but a handful were asleep and, with his going, the feast was over. He was still followed by his blond Jute guard whose ugliness made Maeve shiver. She pressed out the guttering candles and put a few tall new ones in the more elaborate holders where they would be safest. There were boys to look out for the candles through the night but, like the boys at the fire, they could not be trusted. Two slaves were detailed to see to it that nothing went amiss, for the worry was always that fire might destroy the hall.

Eventually, when all but the last dogged crew, almost somnambulistic in this final drinking, were endlessly repeating incoherent lies, Niall rose to his feet, fingered the precious torque yet again, sought her out, and moved slowly, almost aimlessly, to the main door.

Maeve quickly went ahead of him, keeping quietly to the shadows by the walls, nimbly stepping over the splendid, foetal, palpitating bodies.

She had no clear plan. She was driven by desperation. There was only one more day. The next night would be the wedding night and Bega and Niall would be bound together not only by the marriage but by intense public scrutiny. They would never be out of sight. Everything would be discussed – the political course of their marriage, the number and gender of their children, the new balance of power. There would be no chance for Maeve. And on the day after the marriage, the O'Neills would ride back north with their bride and their treasure and a handful of the bride's servants. Bega had not asked Maeve to go. Cathal wanted her to stay. The thought of that terrorised her.

This night was her only chance.

But to do what?

She had let O'Neill touch her and inflame both himself and her because it was the fastest and clearest way she could tell him to take her. But she did not want to be taken as a mistress. Nor did she want him to think she was a whore – and how could he know otherwise? Gossip in the settlement would be unreliable except in its certain malice. She had to find a way to make him ask Bega to take her along with them and stoke up enough interest to make him want her as his concubine, equal in all things to Bega, only more loved.

Maeve knew about the appetites of men. She had seen slave girls raped; she had seen women beaten; she had seen bruises, torn skin and blood. She had heard the screams and the stories of assault. But there were also those who smiled at the telling of it and longed for it again and again, like the men. Whatever, she had no option. It was clear to her that, once Bega left her, she would be without that special protection and if Cathal were interested, then she would become just another mistress.

There was something about Niall, she told herself, desperately, something . . . Clearly he desired her and she had steeled herself, wanted to do that. Her body was still aroused by him. But it had to be done in such a way that he would want to do it again. And to take her back with him: he could insist on this to Bega. It was a gamble – but what else could she do?

Once through the door and outside into the still, white snowscape lit bright by the big moon, she stroked the lucky green stone in her pocket, the one she had found recently on the shore when going to meet Bega. And she prayed to all the gods.

She stood in the moon-shadow of the building. Niall saw her but ignored her. He walked a few yards in the opposite direction, unhitched his trousers and delivered a piss of equine proportions, long, hard and steaming. Then he stretched his arms wide – still with his back to her – and belched, as he had belched at Padric, a rude, rattling, practised belch which gave him great pleasure. The cold air soothed him but it also began to act as an added intoxicant. He breathed deeply, satisfied, indulged and spoilt to the core.

When he did turn to Maeve she could not see the full, vicious lust of his expression. He pointed to her, indicating she should lead, and she walked to a hut some distance from the hall. She had made sure it would be empty.

She stood at the entrance and he bent low, almost double, to get in. Shivering, from the cold she thought, she followed.

There was a low glow of ruddy light from the peat fire and slivers of silver moonlight came through the hole in the roof which let out the drift of smoke.

There were a few poor skins on the floor, a pathetic huddle of domestic utensils. Nothing more.

Niall lay down and waited for her to lie beside him.

Now, before she did, was her chance: her one chance.

'I, you,' her throat tightened, dry, the words stuck. He made no sound. Fear crept over her. 'Bega,' she said, eventually, licking her lips, 'wants to – to be a nun. She will marry you but not for – she will give herself only to the Lord. I, I—' Now the fear crept into her pores, running under her skin as the silence hardened and the man's breathing dropped low. A stroke of moonlight caught the torque and it glittered like a creature in paradise. 'I want to – to come with you and I will do that which Bega will not do if I can be another wife to you.'

O'Neill did not move. The news that Bega was going to refuse his bed made him feel almost insane with rage, even though he had not the slightest desire for her. But the offence to his manliness was unacceptable. If word of this refusal got out, he, Niall O'Neill, a prince with more than twelve deaths to his credit, would be laughed at and talked about and mocked. It could not be borne. It would not be borne. His temper drew itself back to spring and destroy.

And that this slave should purvey this news to him! To an O'Neill! Who else had she talked to? What reliance could there be on her word? How dare she talk of his virgin bride at all, never mind in such a treacherous way? Who was to know she was telling the truth? Her tongue was danger.

But battle had taught him how to wait for the right moment to act. When he held up his hand, Maeve, though now impregnated with fear, her eyes searching for escape, the sure dread of something terribly wrong all about her, the pressure of danger almost making her sick – when he held out his hand, for that small moment she was sufficiently soothed. She reached out her own and he pulled her down on to him. She felt the enormous strength of the man and let herself flow towards him, wanting to have what he desired.

It was a brutish violation which, in its initial deliberate slowness, could have been misinterpreted as tenderness. He splayed her with his hand and when she began to cry in protest, his other hand slapped over her mouth, his fingers digging into her soft cheeks, threatening to tear the white skin. When he entered her, he did so in the most violent ramming way he could and her body shuddered as his groin battered against her mound. Breathing through her nose only, she sounded as terrified and helpless as she felt. She tried, for a few early moments, to find pleasure in this, to discover the satisfactions some of the slaves had told her about, but the hurting was too severe. It took all of her mind to attempt to block at least some of the messages of pain, the screams for help and relief, flooding up her body into her drumming heart and into her agonised mind. There was blood on her thighs.

He pulled himself out and for a moment kneeled gasping above her and the sudden stopping of the pain all but made her swoon.

Almost compliantly she followed his will when he turned her over and hoisted her up on to her knees. Then she had never known such a sear of pain as he stabbed himself into her from behind, while leaning down to stopper her mouth. Now Maeve tried to fight him. She bit his hand hard, but he was far too strong – forcing her wherever he wanted, cruelly, suddenly exulting in his possession of her – and every twist and turn only seemed to serve him better and drive him more frequently into her: more blood, nails tearing down her back, hair yanked like reins of a runaway horse. Once more he pulled away; once more she had the blessing of a fleeting moment of ease and then he had her by the hair, forcing her head down on to his sex and trapping her.

He hit her face so hard the jaws felt broken; his hands on her breasts became fists; when she attempted to cry out he would muffle her or lash her with his callous, hardened hands. Over the next hour or so he raped and abused her in ways which hurt and horrified her. Three times he said, 'We'll see who has the lying tongue. We'll see about that', and this simple utterance drove him on. Finally, just before he left, his own chest heaving with the violence, he took out his dagger, pulled out her tongue and slashed off half of it. Her long, low, desolate howl was indescribable.

Outside the door of Bega's hut, stuffing her mouth with snow, Maeve was caught full in the moon's bright, snow light. Her clothes were ripped, her feet bare, her movements convulsive as she shook and keened with a low moan and pushed more hand-scoops of snow into her mouth.

Bega helped her in and lit a candle from the fire. Maeve's face was bloodied and bruised badly; she shivered uncontrollably. It was a terrible omen, something a pagan's god would do. She held Maeve around the shoulders and waited for her to grow calmer, waited for her to speak.

CHAPTER ELEVEN

'**b**e has to be punished immediately,' said Bega, excitedly. Eogon looked away, rather shiftily she thought.

'You are the lawgiver. You must execute the law.'

'I know the law,' he said brusquely. 'The law is the law and it will be employed. In full measure. But it is difficult.'

'Why?'

'She cannot speak.'

'She can point.'

'What if the man denies it? How will she press her accusation?'

'I will do it for her. I will ask questions for her. I have learned enough from her – even though she cannot speak.'

'Today is your wedding day, Bega.'

'This is more important.'

'Your father will not agree with you.'

'My father believes in the law.'

When it suits him, Eogon thought, but held his peace.

Bega had cleaned up Maeve's face a little and she had put on other clothes, but still, trembling even now in the cot, she was a pitiful sight. The healing woman had packed a staunch against the wound and Maeve held it there, but the blood seeped through continuously and the next stage would have to be cauterisation.

'It was Niall O'Neill,' said Bega, vehemently. She had known this from the moment she had seen Maeve. And in pitiful, fearful dumbshow, Maeve had admitted it.

'It is a grave charge.'

'What are the penalties?'

These were carefully and exactly graded. A guest attacking the

slave of the king's daughter would be heavily fined. It was the
dishonour, though, which weighed with Eogon.

'The penalties are sufficient,' said Eogon. 'Although I would
have to hear his side of the matter and you must not say it is the
Prince O'Neill unless you are certain sure, Bega.'

'I am sure,' she said harshly. 'And I expected no better from
the moment I was cursed to set eyes on the man.'

'Bega!'

'You have to tell my father of this and then you have to carry
out the law.'

'I know what I must do.'

'Good!'

'Bega,' Eogon paused, 'this is your wedding day. Whatever
course this accusation takes, it will stain the day in your memory
and in the eyes of your father who has stalked it for so long.'

'Stalked it?'

'You know what I am saying, Bega.' Eogon's voice was sharp.
Did she really understand the strength of Cathal's sense of honour?
It was what made him. If he were not careful this young woman
would set off a quarrel which could become a bloody battlefield.
Maeve's wound was superficial by comparison.

'I will not marry a man who rapes my servant.'

'I repeat that we have no proof.'

'*You* might not. I do. And I am the one who is not going to
marry him. I want him to face Maeve and I want you to give him
his due punishment. And then if he still wants to marry anyone,
he can marry her although she would die first. We have to go to
my father right away.'

'Your father, Bega, is asleep. Most of the men in the hall are
asleep. Let us use that time to consider most carefully what we
should do.'

'Call him out,' said Bega. 'Accuse him. What else?'

Eogon steeled himself to resist her urgency. But Bega would
not be checked. Soon they would come to bathe her. In an
hour after dawn, Una and her servants would dress her for the
wedding. The robe had been made in finest cloth, decorated and
lavishly trimmed. Her hair would be oiled and sculpted into a
shape which fitted the traditional head-dress. Her face would be
exquisitely highlighted with subtle ochres. Her arms and hands
and feet would be painted with colours and shapes to encourage

fertility and increase her husband's desire. Scents would be rubbed over her body and the armlets and rings and necklaces would be put on her. Finally she would be given the gift of obedience for her new lord and then she would be carried above the mud and dirt of the day, into the great hall for the ceremony.

Bega wanted no part of it. 'You cannot be thinking to let it pass,' she said.

Eogon was offended.

'You will not tell me my work, woman. You will respect who I am and what I do.'

For a moment Bega was subdued.

'Look at her,' she replied. 'Soon she will faint with the pain of it and need to sleep deeply. If we have to put the burning blade on her tongue, then we must make her sleep, if we can, by whatever herbs and drinks we can find so that the fire and the iron do not kill her with their heat and force. If something is to be done, it must be done quickly.'

'Why?'

Bega saw his game. 'Because tomorrow he will be gone.'

'If it is he.'

'And I want to know whether or not it is he before I marry him. Eogon! You have known me for two years. Do you want me to marry a man who will do that to my servant – to anybody's servant? Do you?' She paused, but the prospect that her marriage to such a man might indeed take place if Eogon did not act, galvanised her to fury. 'Is *this* what you want me to be?' She pointed at Maeve. 'Do you, Lawgiver, want me to bleed and weep and be beaten near to death? Will my father forgive you that? Will Our Father in heaven forgive you that? Christ was not afraid to face those who broke the law. Look at His actions in the temple. We must follow His example or we are doomed and we are doubly doomed if we know what we should do but do not do it because of earthly fears. For God will never, never forgive that.' She was rigid with conviction.

Eogon nodded. 'I will seek out your father.'

'Now?'

'Yes,' he sighed. 'Now. But Bega,' a last thought, 'are you sure that you want her to go through all this *now*?' He directed her glance to the wretchedly unhappy, shocked and mottled white, ill face with the blood-red mouth stain. 'Is it for her you are doing this or for yourself?'

It was a wild stab but it caught Bega. She paused. 'Maeve, can you, have you the strength to go through this, to accuse the man who did this to you? Can you do it now?'

The words came so feebly to Maeve through the thickets of pain that she scarcely registered them. She had followed the sense of the argument but the sapping and relentless demands of the outrage in every orifice of her battered body, and the ferocious searing of her tongue made her so faint that much of it passed her by. She made no response.

'It is not for her to decide,' said Bega, seeing no ally there. 'The law must decide. Not the person.'

'But do we want to subject her to yet more at this stage? Of course the law is the law and will be enforced. But a few hours, a day, time for her to heal, to think clearly. Does she not deserve at least that respite?'

'Maeve!' There was some desperation in Bega's voice. 'You cannot let him get away. If you wait, I will be married to him, I will not be able to tell your story and he will go away, leaving you, Maeve, and taking me. If the law gets to him first, then both of us might stay here and I swear, Maeve, I will help you.'

Maeve saw the strain on Bega's face and then she began to cry. Bega was likely the only person who would help her and yet she had wanted to steal her husband from her.

'Tell me, Maeve,' said Bega. 'What is it you want? Can you stand up to him – soon?'

Maeve nodded and that small action started a distorted, bestial gurgling of sobs. Bega went across and put an arm around her.

'That is your answer, Eogon.'

The old man left them, cold in his body and fearing its impact on the persistent, draining ache in his stomach. He was annoyed that the girl felt that she had directed him on the course he would surely have chosen for himself. Pity for the condition of Maeve did not find a place on the agenda of his thoughts. She had caused unnecessary fuss and could go on – under Bega's wilful influence – to provoke ructions beyond belief. Eogon went first to the kitchen to take some milk to soothe his burning stomach. It would also give him a little time to work out how the law could help ensure that the marriage went ahead.

⊱⊰⊱⊰

It was the night when Padric realised what Bega meant to him. After his triumph at the harp, when the music possessed him and he seemed to exist in an element not of the earth, his disappointment at her absence crashed down on him. Cathal's praise and the boisterous approval of the bonded hall of drunken fighters interfered with his thoughts. Bega had gone: to follow her was to risk too much for both of them. Yet he found himself drifting out of the hall on the usual pretext and after emptying a steaming bladder into the slush, he wavered before returning for the final lap of gluttony.

Three men were left from a contest begun in mid-afternoon, to see who could eat most platters of beef. The measures were watched so that no advantage was taken. Bets were on. Two of the men were from the O'Neills, the other a scarred comrade of Cathal's from the old days. Loyalty to those who had shared the early and the hardest times was part of Cathal's nature and his policy. This man had also challenged them to drink in parallel but he had won that long ago. Their drinking was now an occasional gulp to his uninterruptedly emptied cups.

Elsewhere some were playing bones, others were listening to individual stories. Muiredach had been commandeered by a sottish clique of northerners who wanted to hear again highlights from the story of the Voyage of St Brendan. Cathal was in earnest conversation with the youngest O'Neill brother but both men were nodding. Sleep and stupor were creeping in like a slow paralysis.

Padric tried to pinch himself into enjoyment. Here were men he would be glad to ride with, food and drink, in quantity and quality he had not encountered before and would be lucky to meet again. All power to those who gobbled and sluiced as if their lives depended on it: out in the cold it would be bare pickings for months or the monotony of a diet fit to wage war on the human body. He too had enjoyed the chanting story of Muiredach, been impressed by the ultimate genealogy of the O'Neills and felt the sweet sense of oblivion when he had played and sung. Everything had been done in the knowledge that he was either sharing it with Bega or doing it for her or certain to find a way to talk to her about it.

He was amazed at the desolation he felt when ostensibly he had everything to be thankful for. But he was no longer able to obscure or sidestep the root of it.

He wanted to stay with Bega or Bega to come away with him. She had simply left the hall and he felt bereft.

The force of his longing took him by surprise. He had not yet unravelled the history of this feeling but he sensed already that it had been building and growing in the hidden side of his mind for a long time. He had grown from strong adolescent to man as Bega had taken the journey from girl to woman, and they had done so together. The strategic presence of others and the watchfulness of rules had blocked any public display of affection and appeared to nullify any possible flow of erotic feeling. But it had not been blocked out, only diverted.

The past was now alight in Padric's mind and again he went out of the hall to cool his thoughts. Insignificant gestures, half-remembered glances, the fragrance of a lost conspiracy between the two of them as their maturity intertwined in scholarship and playful adventures engulfed him. He began to feel he was infested by Bega.

How could he let her marry someone else? Especially O'Neill, whom he had seen relieving himself and then tacking over towards the slave quarters in search no doubt of other relief. How could he return to Rheged without her?

Once more he went back into the hall, determined to say some of this to Cathal, but Cathal was no longer there. The eating competition was over. The pride of Ireland lay on the floor, ripe for extinction by a couple of nimble men with quick daggers. Only Muiredach wandered about, still inflated by his success, admiring his ring in the guttering candles. He offered to play chess with Padric but the younger man refused.

It was as if Bega had put herself inside his body like a demon. Wherever his thoughts turned they turned to her. He was encircled by her. He tried to sleep but the chance of discovering that great escape was nil. He twisted as if his body ached with fever. Indeed his limbs did feel strained and nervous with agitation. Now on his back, now sitting upright, now on one side, now on the other: amid that deafening mass of unconsciousness, he was fully alert. Unbearably alert.

She would be sleeping now. Peaceful now. Resigned to her marriage – a fate which he had urged her to embrace.

He could not stop his imagination from stepping out the path she would take on the next day. The emergence of the bride opulently dressed in splendour. The entrance into the hall. The exchange of gifts. The words of Eogon. The words of Muiredach. Donal and his prayers. The affirmation of Cathal. Then the final and grandest day of the feast, during which Bega and the O'Neill would be taken to the room, Cathal's own, prepared for them for the night.

Padric somehow hoped that by allowing himself to imagine it, then it would go away. But it intensified. Once more he got up and went outside.

It was the middle of the night and the dead coldness was whipped into bitterness by a cutting wind. It moaned through the ramparts and when he listened carefully he could hear those moans echoed in some of the distant huts.

Why had he not realised this before? How could he not have seen it?

There were only a few hours. He could see Cathal and confess this and . . . as a plan of action it crumbled away before it had been half-formulated. He could talk to O'Neill – he had seen the man just before he left the hall, whispering to one of his brothers. O'Neill was not taken with Bega – Padric could see that as well as Bega herself. Maeve was more his sort – and if he could keep the torque and the rings and promised more wealth and gifts from the kingdom of Rheged, then perhaps. Perhaps (Padric's thoughts gathered pace as his toes nipped, his ears stung, his nose chilled in the cold), he could persuade Bega to hold on to her vow of chastity; appeal to the highest authority with Cathal, see the marriage somehow unmade because of the insurmountable intervention of the Lord Himself, and then ask if he could take Bega with him across to Britain. Cathal would want to see the back of her if that happened.

It was not a plan. It was a wish but it was the best Padric could formulate as he felt almost choked with the fear of Bega's absence. He could not see beyond her: he could not see a life without her

near him or there to return to or to accompany his thoughts on a solitary journey.

Still unweary but wanting to have all the strength he could muster for the next day, Padric went back for the last time into the hall. Beyond reason, the ramshackle plan at which he had arrived gave him hope. He was sure he could encourage Bega to embrace her chastity as a direct instruction from God through the intervention of St Brigid. He was sure that Niall would not want to marry someone committed to virginity – although this was not entirely unknown – and if Cathal could be swayed then O'Neill could be bribed.

O'Neill could be further bribed by taking Maeve as his concubine, Padric thought: he had noticed Maeve's tender glances to O'Neill and seen them returned. To be concubine to such a prince would be the very best that Maeve could get. Coaxing Cathal, after all the welter of feasting and boasting and doing so without even scratching the skin of his honour, would be the hardest task of all. Think of it as a riddle, Padric told himself as he found a place near the fire and curled up in a pleasant shiver of anticipation. And pray to God that when you awake, as sometimes happens with a difficult riddle, the answer is there, like a gift of the dawn, waiting.

He slept deeply and long and the dawn was well past before one of the boys feeding the fire tripped over him. The slaves were already preparing for the wedding feast.

In that half-awake half-sleeping state before fully breaking the surface into full consciousness, Bega had seen Padric hold out his hand and pull her to safety. For a few fragile moments, she had luxuriated in the image. The sound and sight of Maeve and the encounter with Eogon had dispelled it but now, with some pause after the departure of the lawgiver, the thought of Padric overwhelmed her.

Why had he not come when she had thought about him so hard? Often, when for some reason she had felt that she must see him, she had been able to think about him and conjure him up in her imagination and he would appear. This was one of her powers. But when she needed it most, it had failed her.

She had brought in Bheartha who knew all the spells and cures. She had asked if she could take Maeve back to the hut where she kept her herbs and her secrets. When the two women had left and she was alone, she felt panic.

Eogon could not influence her father to go against his will: she knew that. Padric had told her to marry. Twice he had told her that. She closed her eyes as if in prayer and willed Padric to come into the hut so that one last time she could see him. That was what she wanted.

The simplicity of it calmed her a little. To see him.

It was Donal who came in. Her dismay was undisguised.

'You must find Padric for me,' she said. 'And you must tell the women to wait until – I have done with my prayers.'

Her agitation transferred itself immediately to Donal. He stood quite still and let the fear go from her and into him. She told him about Maeve. She told him it was Niall. She told him she had seen Eogon and demanded the force of the law and that she would never while she was alive marry O'Neill. She wanted him to find Padric.

'There is something begun you cannot stop,' said Donal finally, 'and you must not try, Bega.'

'I will not marry him. I will marry no one,' said Bega fiercely. 'If I am strong and if I am called then I will serve the Lord but I will marry no earthly man.' She paused. 'Where is Padric?'

Donal did not answer. The time was here, he realised. Bega would stick to her word, he knew that now. Whatever the outcome, she would be in danger. Most likely the danger would be mortal.

'Oh, Lady whom I saw in a sweet visitation,' he prayed, palms upturned outwards, eyes lifted upwards, 'tell me, is it now that I fulfil the heavenly task You gave me on the mountain those years ago? This is the girl I met as You foresaw. I have watched over her as best I could but now I am old and she is in great peril. Is it now, is it here, that I pass on to her Your glorious gift?'

Bega was accustomed to the impromptu prayers of Donal but the intensity of this outcry and her mysterious involvement stilled her impatience.

'I have something to give you,' said Donal. 'We must kneel.'

The old man sank clumsily to his knees. In moments such as these his increasing fragility was most poignantly revealed. Bega kneeled beside him. The hut became deeply silent, so silent that it was as if an angel had enfolded it with its wings, baffling all outside sound.

Donal told his story, the story of the call, of the climb, of the prayers he had recited and the psalms, of the calls to St Columbanus to strengthen his belief. He told of what Our Lady had said to him and mentioned that a gift had been given him to give to a girl, Bega. Then he told of how over the years he had watched and prayed. He had tried to steer her in the ways of the Lord of All and been comforted by the ease with which the Lord had allowed her to learn, to read and even to write. Several times when he thought his own life was coming to its end, he had wanted to pass on this gift but always a voice had said 'Wait, there will be a better time, there will be an inevitable time' and he had been spared for this purpose only. Padric had been sent by God to help him with his work in making her a chosen instrument for anything she might be called to do but now Padric could not help her. Nor could he, Donal, who knew that very soon he would be called to his heavenly reward.

He took out a tiny bundle. The original rag of garment had long been replaced by another and that in turn replaced and each time by the freshest square of cloth which Donal could tease from the women. He unfolded it and held it before him.

'This, Bega, is from the True Cross on which Jesus Christ Our Lord and Saviour suffered and was killed. This has come to me from His Mother to give to you when your life or your faith was threatened. You must have it now, Bega.' Holding the fragment of wood in both hands, he bowed his head as he passed it towards Bega.

Bega was in sudden awe of Donal: that he should have been chosen for such a visitation. She blushed to remember how often and how comprehensively she had dismissed him. But almost immediately she was compelled by what was held before her.

Bega was transfixed by it. This wood had borne the agony on the cross. This wood had known the breathing and the dying body of the Saviour. This wood had perhaps drunk His blood, taken His sweat, soaked up His tears. It lay in her hand with no

weight at all. She looked at its dark-stained, runnelled jaggedness
and could see it being clawed from the cross by a zealot, perhaps
even an apostle, and carried about as the surest protection through
all the persecutions and martyrdoms that the saints had so piously
endured.

Why her? Bega felt a wholly new presence in her mind, in her
soul. She had been chosen. She took the fragment and offered
up a prayer of thanks. Her way was clear. From Donal she took
the cloth and wrapped the wood. Her life was to serve. She felt as
right and as powerful as the fragment of wood, as the holy feather
lightness of the True Cross itself.

'Pray now to the Mother of Christ,' said Donal, firmly.

He felt strange, drained, faint.

'Close your eyes,' he said. 'Close them and think of the Mother
of God who gave to Her most unworthy servant this great gift
for you.'

Bega did as she was bid. The marvel of it, the extra-ordinariness
of what had happened began to percolate through the initial spasm
of astonishment and she felt dizzy. To have touched a portion of
the cross was an almost unimaginable blessing: to be singled out to
receive it . . . What work was there in store for her? What conquest
of souls had she to make to justify this?

'Close your eyes,' Donal repeated, just able to repress his
excitement. 'Close your eyes and pray.'

For he saw, beyond the smoke and glow of the fire, the outline
of a shape he was sure could be the Blessed Virgin. He could not
make out any features distinctly, but he was sure he could see the
smile. His mind, lightened by the execution of his duty, heaved.

'You have done well. And now you must do one more thing.'

'Yes,' said Donal. 'I will do anything. Ask.'

Bega sensed a presence which she could not distinguish. Donal's
words were clear and were in answer to someone. Her body was
suffused with the alarm of profound awe as she sensed that
something of the perfection of the Mother of Jesus Christ might
be near.

'You must help Bega to live for her faith,' the whisper was low
but Donal caught every word. 'There will be those, here, who want
her to die for her faith. She too will be tempted by that. You must
help her escape that death even at the cost of your own death. She
will go from here, but only if you help her. Promise me.'

'I promise,' said Donal, loudly. 'I swear on the vision before me now. What is my death? I swear to you.'

Bega now ached with a curiosity she knew to be base. She longed, longed to open her eyes. When the puttering of the fire was a sound only slightly overlain by the sigh of her breath, she let her eyelids open the merest slit and looked.

Only the wreath of smoke snaked up to the rooftop.

Her faith was not yet strong enough.

There was silence and a long pause broken by a groan from Donal.

'I am suddenly a very old man,' he said, struggling to his feet, yet helping Bega to hers. 'It is as if I had been borne up all these years just for this one purpose, and now that it is accomplished, I am near the end.'

Indeed, he looked as if he had aged greatly in the past few minutes. Always rather frail, but with a stringy, sinewy endurance, he now appeared almost waxen.

'Who were you talking to?'

'The same who gave me that gift for you.'

'Was She here?'

'Yes.'

'And you could see Her?'

'Not as distinctly as before. But enough. She was here.'

'What did She say?' Bega was crushed with the distinction bestowed on Donal.

'She said that I had to make one last act of protection to you. And so I will.'

'And me. Did She say what I must do?'

'She said you must live for the faith.'

'Live for the faith.'

'Just those words.'

'Live for the faith' – words spoken about her by the Mother of God Herself. So how could she ever do otherwise? Finally all the veils were thrown aside and her true life was revealed. It was to be the life she had begun to embrace in rather bad faith with Cathleen: the vocation she had used to challenge her father; the existence she had until now seen chiefly as a way of avoiding the one demanded of her.

But to 'live for the faith' was to avoid nothing. To live for the faith was to go out into the world and encounter all its sins and its monsters, the arrows of evil flying through the air, the venom of the devil in the minds of the ignorant. It was to be as much of a warrior as her father had been or as Padric wanted to be.

'It will be a great thing to do,' she said, 'if I have the strength.'

'You will need all your strength,' said Donal. 'Today is easy. A few days are easy. A lifetime is a lifetime of pain.'

But Bega felt only elation. The notion that this exhilaration, this knowledge of being so honoured and chosen could be at all associated with pain or any doubts or discomforts was ridiculous. But she held her tongue. Donal had seen what she had not been allowed to see and her new veneration for him prevented any slighting remark.

'I know you doubt that,' Donal said, 'but it is always the going on that matters. There will be days like cliffs, Bega: and there will be days when you feel buried alive. There will be days of peace also but they could be the worst of all for inside that peace the devil could well be lurking to find a gap in your defences as you forget your high calling. To live the faith is asked of few and few of those few can do it. So bless you for the happiness you now feel and guard you in the misery which will surely be your lot.'

'Except that I will have joy in the knowledge that I am being of service.'

'That may be true.'

'And joy in the companionship of others in the same service.'

'Perhaps so.'

'And in the hope of entering eternal life.'

'The devil is in the hope as well, Bega: he is everywhere waiting for us. Are you sure you are strong enough to resist?'

Once again Bega allowed herself to be silenced, momentarily.

'Now I can never marry the O'Neill,' she said, abruptly, and laughed aloud, clapping her hands.

Donal nodded and smiled thinly in response. That would be his sacrifice. It was clear now.

chapter twelve

Rumours of the rape and mutilation of Maeve flew through the settlement. There was anger among Cathal's people. Maeve was a favourite: not haughty and volatile like Bega; not imperious like Una or unreliable like the royal mistresses. She was a beauty who smiled. What lay behind her smile may have been thoughts of the utmost contempt for all around her but it was the perfect disguise. She had a warm, seductive, conspiratorial smile which led those who were the object of it to believe that they and they alone had earned and deserved to be given this rare glimpse of softness in a hard world. The speed of rumour and its compulsion to grow ever more vigorously meant that by the time Padric had woken up it was being said that the O'Neills as one man had tortured and raped her in turn and then cut out her tongue by the roots so that she would not tell the tale.

There was a consensus of outrage.

Padric heard from Muiredach that Cathal was with Eogon and Niall O'Neill who denied everything. The problem now threatened to move into an uglier phase. Hence the closeting of the three men.

Padric went to the hut where the swords had been lodged.

'No one can take a sword into the hall.'

'I am not going into the hall. I have to go away.'

The young man was only mildly suspicious. He was new on guard and had been an admirer of Padric's performance on the harp.

'Could I learn to play the harp like that?'

'Anyone could.'

'Not just anyone.' He sounded a little disappointed.

'Anyone who had the strength to believe he could,' said Padric,

flatteringly. 'You could. I can see it.' He wanted the sword before
the O'Neill guard came back – although should he come back in
the present atmosphere, he would be quite likely to return with
his friends and strip the place of all its weapons.

'Do you think I have the skill?'

Padric hesitated and looked solemn. 'I have no doubt,' he said.
'You can practise on the harp that is there. When I return I will
help teach you.'

'Aha!' The young man pulled out the sword that Padric pointed
to and held it up to the light. 'What a fine piece of work. Are all
the swords in Britain like this?'

'Almost all,' said Padric.

'It's too long for me,' he held it out, scabbard and all, and
executed a few slashing gestures, 'but you are taller than I and with
your long arms, nobody could get near you. I've seen you practise.'
He slashed the air once or twice more and then handed it over.

'So where are you going?' he asked.

'Going?' The question was not grasped by Padric and the
expression on the young guard's face began to hint at suspicion. 'To Durrow,' said Padric, emphatically. 'I am wanted at
Durrow.'

The youth nodded, convinced enough, and Padric walked away
as steadily as was expected.

He made his way to a fire at which Dermot was standing, tasting
a cup of warmed milk, and all too clearly spying out the land.

'She's nothing like as badly hurt as they are giving out,' he said,
aggressively.

Padric was offered a cup by the slave at the fire and took it
gratefully.

'She was always a bitch,' Dermot continued, blowing on the
milk, his eyes never still. 'A troublemaker,' he added. 'My brother
Faelan should have been let deal with her when she first got here.'
He slurped the cup empty and dropped it on the ground. 'O'Neill
never did it, you know. He swears he never. You believe that,
don't you? I believe that.' Dermot stared mulishly at him. He
was rattled. 'He never would, you know. Not Niall. I know the
man.' There was a boast in that last sentence.

Padric sipped his milk and said nothing. He remembered the
flirtations of the night before and had no doubt that Niall was
wholly or in part responsible. Besides, he would have expected

no better from the man. He slowed himself down. Too much
was teeming into his mind.

What he wanted to do was to go and seize Bega and take
her back with him to the kingdom of Rheged where she would
become his bride. That simple course would in some way have
to be pursued if he were to get what he wanted. But it needed
to be disguised.

How could this promised marriage be uncoupled? That was
the heart of it. And how could he take Bega away from men
as powerful as Cathal and O'Neill without provoking not only
their present wrath but their long-term revenge? He had come
to Ireland partly as an ambassador to make contacts which could
eventually turn into alliances. To alienate Ireland's most famous
warrior and its greatest family in one selfish action would not be
forgiven either in Ireland or back in Britain. Moreover, those
of his people in exile in Ireland would not forgive him were he
to be thought to have slighted the house of O'Neill. Their lives
were somewhat on sufferance already. They could easily become
victims. Their foreignness made them a convenient enemy. And
there was his own persistent sense of obligation to Cathal. No: a
way had to be found which threaded through all these obstacles.

If only he believed in the elves so beloved of some in the
boglands here and around the estuary that was at the centre of
the Rheged lands. They could have been called up to weave a
magic spell. Or Merlin. But the only spellworker here was the
soothsayer in the woods and she would be too scared of Cathal
to do anything that might diminish him.

For a wild moment he thought that if he fomented the struggle
between Cathal and the O'Neills, then the resulting fury and
bloodshed would give him every reason to take Bega out of
danger. But that, too, fell at the hurdle of Cathal: Cathal had
to want her to go and Cathal had to ask Padric to take her.

Padric nodded to Dermot and went towards Bega's hut. He
sensed Dermot's eyes focusing on his sword but he offered no
explanation. As he walked he felt that he could almost touch the
force of rumour which was looping and feeding its way around
the settlement. He entered her hut not knowing what to expect.

Bega was transformed. There was a high calm about her as
if she had not now nor had ever encountered any fears about
anything. She seemed to be totally under control and yet somehow

threatening to explode into wild songs and laughter. Donal was sitting on the edge of her cot, a tired and ill old man, Padric thought. But he too had a serenity about him.

'I have heard about Maeve,' said Padric. 'What do you know?'

Bega told him – about finding Maeve, the horror of it, and her conviction that it was Niall.

'And so I cannot marry him,' she said. 'Not even as a chaste wife. No one will expect me to do that now.'

'He will deny it,' said Padric.

'Maeve will point him out.'

'It will be his word against hers.'

'I know who I will believe.'

'But who will your father believe?'

This was too close to Bega's own quick suspicion. 'Whatever my father believes, I will not, I *will* not marry him.' She smiled with a maddening superiority. 'And there is another reason, but I cannot tell you of it.'

Padric looked at Donal. The old man was impassive. Bega said no more on that subject and for a moment she looked chastened and glanced fearfully at Donal.

'What do you say, Donal?'

'Cathal will believe O'Neill.'

'Will Eogon? Will all the others?'

Donal shook his head. His task now was to save his strength for the sacrifice.

'The only way,' said Padric, 'is to tell everyone that you have been called by God and to ask O'Neill to forgive you in the name of the only power greater than he himself is.' Padric was so struck by the simple solidness of his own plan that he did not notice the complacent expression on Bega's face. 'Cathal will have to let him keep the torque and so the question is – how do we convince Cathal?'

'I can convince him,' said Bega. 'I will convince him.'

Padric had not quite realised until now how splendid Bega looked. Her determination gave a character and command to her face which far outstripped conventional notions of mere prettiness. But why, he wondered, could she not understand that he too was changed? Why did she not respond to this new Padric in front of her?

He would challenge O'Neill to single combat! No sooner

thought than expressed. Bega smiled and reached out to touch
his hand.

'Padric,' she said. 'Oh Padric. What would that do?'

'It would clear the way for your father to let you go. You
want to go?'

He meant, to go with him.

'Oh yes,' said Bega, fervently. 'Oh yes.' She meant to go into
the world and become a missionary.

'But why,' she laughed, 'why should he fight you?'

'I will challenge him for you. You have been called on not to
marry this man, called by God. If he insists, he is challenging
God. Therefore I accept that challenge.'

Now he could see that she understood. Her eyes gleamed with
the boldness and the danger of it. He reached out to take her
hands and she did not resist.

Meanwhile, Padric thought, he would have a boy take his horse
and Bega's beyond the gate, say he was going to exercise them, put
on the blankets, ready.

⚬⚬⚬⚬

'Bring her here,' said Cathal. 'We will decide it in front of her.'

Beohtric, his guard, went to fetch Maeve. Niall looked down,
sulking at the cup of beer on the table in Cathal's quarters. Eogon's
beer was untouched. He knew that by even bringing the news he
had risked becoming one of Cathal's enemies but some deeply
trained and surprising obstinacy had made him stick to the law.

'You are not going to take the word of a slave against mine,'
said Niall. It was a statement, not a question; a challenge, not an
enquiry. Cathal ignored it.

'Will this satisfy you?' he demanded of Eogon.

'She must be here to speak to him face to face,' said Eogon,
doggedly, as he had done several times.

Cathal spat at the fire but there was no doubting what the
action intended to convey. Eogon was to be respected, although
in older, rougher, better times Cathal would have acted first and
come to the law later. But as one of the four kings of Connachta,

and of those the greatest, he could not act in so primitive a way. Friends would no longer trust him; alliances would be harder to bind; enemies would use it to stoke up hatreds against him.

Eogon should have found a way around it.

The two warriors brooded on why they took notice of this feeble-bodied man and his laws which threatened what they wanted.

Why don't we just kill the lawgiver? was a thought which passed through Niall's mind and a glance at Cathal indicated that he would have found a sympathetic listener had he turned the thought into words. But he too had to be seen to let the law run where it had authority.

The act was not such a terrible thing, Cathal thought. Not at all. It was the timing that made it terrible; that and the unpredictable consequences a harsh judgment might have on the tinder-honour of the O'Neills.

Maeve came in and the moment she set eyes on Niall, Cathal, Eogon and Beohtric knew beyond any doubt that he was the guilty man. First she turned away as if she feared being hit and then, her face horribly bruised, her mouth gobbing out a wad of bandage already blood-stained, she rushed to him and with honking, panting grunts and tears, flailed at him with her fists.

He knocked her to the ground, hitting her across the face. The blood began to spurt.

Cathal looked furiously at Eogon. He in turn looked beggingly at Cathal, who did not relent. Nevertheless, he performed his duty.

'Is this the man who beat you?'

Maeve, her hands over her mouth, nodded violently.

'You liar! How can you prove the thing? You bitch!' Niall was about to attack her again when Cathal stepped in front of him. He nodded to show he meant no censure. But Eogon had to be heard. It would not do if Cathal were to be talked of as the king who behaved like a peasant-bully. Cathal was new to such diplomacy and the fresh territory was unnerving, but his instinct told him that he had to walk this tightrope for as long as he could.

'I have been told that you were raped,' said Eogon, taking a little confidence from Cathal's intervention.

Maeve was now on her feet. Even bruised and bleeding as she was, Cathal thought, she was still an object worth his lust. It was

a pity Niall had wasted her. He himself was partly to blame for
not getting there first. He had respected too much her position
with Bega.

'Were you raped by this man?' he repeated.

'Was it in the dark?' Niall interjected, angrily. 'And where was
it? How could she tell who it was if the thing was done in the
darkness? And where was it done? I was in the hall all the night
through – my brothers will tell you that, they and many more will
tell you that.'

There was no hope. She had been a fool to expect anything from
this terrifying man. In the full knowledge that she was inviting
her own early death, Maeve looked round at Eogon and nodded
emphatically.

'And did he further,' continued Eogon, 'so mutilate you that
you cannot speak?'

Maeve hung her head as if in shame and pointed to Niall, who
turned away.

'Do you want to ask her anything?' said Cathal.

'Ask her why she was born a liar,' said Niall, his back still
turned.

'You have the right to question her in front of any witnesses,'
said Eogon.

'How can you question someone who knows nothing of the
truth? What answers can you expect?' He turned to face her. 'You
are jealous of your mistress, are you not? *Answer!* Are you not?'

'*Answer!*' Cathal repeated. The growl in his throat was like the
growl of a dog before the attack.

Maeve did not move.

'What does no answer mean?' asked Cathal.

'You must answer or the question will be held against you,' said
Eogon. 'Are you, were you jealous of your mistress?'

Still Maeve made no move.

'So we conclude that you were,' said Eogon.

'Were you not familiar with me at the feast? Did you not wait
on me closely and ask me to caress all your womanly parts?
Answer.'

Again, she would not answer. Now she was staring at Eogon
as if hypnotised.

'Therefore we conclude that what Niall O'Neill has accused you
of is true,' said Eogon, swiftly.

'Ask her when this rape occurred. Ask her was it the dead of night?'

'You heard the question, Maeve,' said Eogon. 'Was it the dead of night?'

Maeve nodded.

'And what sort of a moon was there last night?' Niall asked.

'Now that is important!' Cathal added. 'Answer! What sort of a moon? Were the clouds out? When were they out and what could be seen? What were you doing out of your quarters in the dead of night? What were you doing alone out there?'

Maeve now turned her frightened stare to Niall and her eyes offered one last plea. How could she answer, her tongue running with blood?

'That is the best question of all,' said Niall. 'Never mind the moon! What took you out there at dead of night if not by pre-arrangement?'

'That is so,' said Cathal – and he looked at his lawgiver – 'that must be so.'

'Is it the truth of it?' said Eogon.

Slowly, Maeve raised her hand and pointed at Niall O'Neill. Once again the other two were convinced, but the gesture, like the flailing fists, was no proof.

Niall laughed.

'You saw me at the end of the feast there, Cathal. What was I fit for? What was this fit for?' He pointed to his groin. 'Emptying out what had too much come in, that's what this was fit for. And then some talk with my brothers and men about the fine feast – the finest of all fine feasts we were having and after that, Cathal, I was snuffed out. This is all a madness. She has been attacked, this spiteful woman, this witch, and now she wants to destroy everything around her and most of all, Cathal, hear this, wreck the wedding day of your daughter. Envy of your daughter has driven her mad and now that her life is ruined she wants to ruin the life of Bega as well. That is what we have here. A demented and vengeful woman.'

'Do you have any other proofs that it was this man, Maeve, and no other man?' Eogon felt the ground firming beneath him.

Maeve darted across to Niall and grabbed the hand she had so deeply dug her teeth into as it had all but suffocated her. Niall snatched the hand away.

'She wants me to see that hand,' said Eogon, 'and I must see it too.'

Niall held it out, carelessly defiant. The imprint of teeth was clearly visible and some skin had been torn.

'One of your dogs,' said Niall, laughing. 'That will teach me to offer it a handful of pork.'

'Too good to waste on the dog,' Cathal agreed and nodded heavily. 'Is that all, Maeve?'

The young woman took a step backwards and looked around the three men desperately. There was no chink. Then she tried to talk and a gush of dark blood flowed over her chin and down on to the ripped cloak. Cathal looked to Eogon.

'You have falsely accused this man,' said Eogon. 'For this you will be punished most heavily. After talk with him and with Cathal I will tell you what that punishment is.'

Cathal called out for Beohtric who had left to stand guard at the door.

'Take her. Do what you want with her. Her punishment will be told after the wedding feast. Keep her away from us.'

Beohtric's face did not crack open until he got outside. He did not understand a great deal of this language save 'do as you want with her'. He turned and gave her a grin which did full justice to the black stumps rotting in his mouth. Bruises would go, he thought to himself, wounds would heal, bleeding would stop, and if she could not talk this infernal language, so much the better; the people here talked too much anyway. He led her over to the squalid wattle and stick hut which served himself and his woman. She would have to move over now. Perhaps, after her punishment, Cathal would give her to him outright. He would ask.

He lashed her hands together behind her back and with the same hemp he secured her feet. Then he nuzzled himself against her and groped everything he could within full sight of his woman. She was told to feed and guard Maeve and told in a way which promised a beating for the slightest disobedience. But Maeve would never slip those knots. He returned to Cathal.

Eogon was publicly addressing all who wanted to listen – and most of the warriors had gathered around. He described how Maeve had been assaulted. He then continued:

'She accused a man among us, a guest, of this wrong deed. I questioned her, without fear or favour, and found that her accusation was foul and malicious. For this she will be punished. But there is also one other who deserves a punishment and that is the man or the men who did in fact assault, wound and rape this woman. This man or these men are still being sought but the object of much rumour and the man accused by Maeve is wholly without blame. I, Eogon the Lawgiver, in the presence of Cathal King of Connachta, tell you what the law has decided.'

The muttering of scepticism was unmistakable.

'Now,' said Cathal, 'this has been a bad start to a good day. But it is still only the morning. Soon the feast will continue. Soon the men from the north and ourselves will be big-bellied with mead and food and beer and stories. The wedding will wipe away the bad start and the foul taste. We are to forget now all that has happened. The law is decided and punishment can wait. Today we rejoice.'

The last sentence was flung out, daring contradiction or any murmur of qualification. There was none.

Niall beckoned to him and the two men walked apart.

'I am told that Princess Bega will marry me but she wants to remain chaste and to serve God,' said Niall bluntly. 'Do you know if this is true?'

'She has been instructed very closely in the gospels,' said Cathal, his stomach clenching in rage against whoever had revealed this to O'Neill but not to him.

'I did not come for a wife who will stay a nun,' the younger man said. 'It would not be right for me to have her on those terms. Those were not the original terms.'

'I think it is nothing more than fearfulness of the state of marriage,' said Cathal, soothingly. 'I am told that it affects women in many different ways and, besides, when you have her back in your own land, then she will do as you want her to. She knows that is her duty. She knows that from me. She obeys me.'

Niall stopped. They were near the hut to which he had been led by Maeve. His hand went up to his torque, which at one stage she had almost torn off. Cathal noticed that there was a scratch in its smoothness and his suspicion of Niall's guilt returned. But he would not dare behave in such a manner with the Princess Bega, Cathal thought. And the wedding was politically imperative for them both.

'I take your word, Cathal. Our alliance will be stronger after these troubles.'

The younger man looked intently at him and then walked away.

As Cathal came across the snow now rapidly thawing, he saw Padric coming from Bega's hut and beckoned him over.

Bega saw that the two men would be talking together for a while and used the moment to manoeuvre herself out and, unseen, make her way rapidly to Beohtric's hovel where, she had seen, from the entrance to her hut after Cathal's speech, Maeve had been taken.

'Why did you not make her do what I asked?' said Cathal.

'She has her father's will.'

Cathal was momentarily flattered. 'Her mother had a fine temper, too,' he said. 'But this must be reversed.'

'I fear she is bound to it.'

'And I am bound to this marriage. O'Neill wants a bride not a nun. You have failed me.'

Padric would not be bullied.

'She is not behaving in a small way,' he said. 'She is asking to serve the greatest of all the Lords of Creation. Because of her duty to you she is willing to marry but her duty to God has come to seem the foremost thing and I doubt if you will sway her.'

Cathal was further inflamed: so Padric, too, knew about her decision. 'I do not have to sway. I command.'

'Why not let her go on the route she has chosen? Others have done this with great honour.'

'No.'

'What if she refuses?'

'I will not allow her to refuse. Even though she is my daughter, and the daughter of my beloved concubine, who would have respected me in this. Bega will not refuse.'

'I will take on her tortures,' said Padric. 'Because torture is what you mean. Isn't it?'

'Why do you say this?'

'It was I who encouraged her over the last months to develop a passion for chastity and the love of God, therefore if anyone is to be punished it must be me.'

'It is Bega who must know how much in earnest I am.'

'She will know through me. Believe me, my suffering will show

her what is in store for her. You would not want to blemish her
or humiliate her in front of O'Neill. Show her what your anger
can mean and use me.'

'You have been with the woman too long.'

'Or let me fight with O'Neill.'

'Why is that?'

'I will fight as her soldier, as her arm, to show that what she
wants is something she is prepared to die for.'

'I cannot allow this.' Cathal looked at him closely. 'Who has
poisoned your blood in this way? Did Maeve prepare a drink
for you when you were off guard yesterday? Did Maeve fill
your cup?'

'Yes. She did fill my cup. And the cups of others.'

'They have not gone mad. You have. Tell me. Did these
thoughts of fighting O'Neill and offering yourself for torture
occur to you before yesterday's feast?'

Padric rued the necessity to be truthful. 'No.'

'I thought so.' Cathal put an arm around his shoulder. 'Maeve
is a witch. She has tried to destroy the wedding feast. She has let
loose accusations and slanders which filled the air like uncorked
devils and you were also in her net. Come. There is an antidote
known to my wife. Quickly. Come with me and take it before the
poison moves from your heart to the soul of you and you begin
to shriek with the frenzy of a witless man. Come!'

Cathal's urging allowed no refusal and hoping that this would
give him more time to state Bega's case, Padric went with him.

'Leave us!'

Beohtric's woman swayed reluctantly. She was heavily pregnant,
the added weight merely accentuating her bulkiness. There was
something bestial about her, Bega thought, either there in the
blood or brought on through life with Beohtric. Bega was like a
terrier in front of an angry cow, but she snapped out her will.

'Leave us now!'

Still swaying, the woman went to the door and ducked through it, hovering as near as she dared. Bega lowered her voice to a whisper.

'Let me cut you free.'

This took moments only. When she had done it, Maeve reached out for the knife. Bega hesitated but Maeve's hand was insistent. The sharp-bladed dagger transferred from one hand to the other. Maeve slid it deep inside her clothes.

'You must try to escape,' Bega whispered. 'I will get a horse for you. When I have gone, pretend to be tied still – I will rearrange the rope – and then when you feel it is the time, go to the single gate where we let out the horses and someone will be there. Ride towards your own people. That is all I can do.'

Maeve nodded.

'I must go now.'

Maeve held out her hand. Bega took it. Maeve pressed it against her bruised cheek, pressed it hard and passionately. When Bega took her hand away, she felt the tears.

'God be with you.'

Quickly she reassembled the ropes, retying them though loosely here and there, making a convincing camouflage. Then she left. Maeve was in great pain. Everything he had ripped and cut and penetrated scalded her body and her mind.

Beohtric's woman came in immediately and sniffed around Maeve. Maeve turned her face to the wall. Her life was over.

chapter thirteen

Cathal left Padric in his own quarters, guarded by Beohtric the Jute. He posted more guards outside with the instruction that Padric must not pass. Cathal's latest mistress, a girl who had originally come from over the sea to the south and was dark, much darker even than Bega, was stirring a potation of herbs which, with the correct spell, would drain out of Padric the poison put there by Maeve.

Padric's objections were flattened by Cathal's insistence that he was saving his soul. This had to be done, Cathal insisted. Maeve had proved to be a woman of the devil. Even he, Cathal, was wary of her now and would have to seek some special unhallowed place to put her down. But what if she were innocent? Padric protested. Eogon had given her a trial and there was no better man of law in Ireland than Eogon, Cathal said, stonily; Eogon could reel off law faster than Muiredach could tell an epic and no one had ever questioned Eogon. Padric's gut certainty that Niall had been the assailant was, he could sense, undoubtedly shared by Cathal.

'Whatever we may think,' said Cathal, coarsely aping piety, 'Eogon's judgment is the law. We must accept it. The woman was lying: a devil has taken possession of her. I will have Donal see what he can do tomorrow to exorcise it but I fear the worst.' All this was spoken near expressionlessly and without a blink, daring contradiction. In the light of the lawgiver's decision, there could be none. What were Padric's suspicions weighed against the gravity and ancient certainty of Eogon?

Cathal walked over to Bega's quarters and, as he walked, he steeled himself. All who saw him stride across that space were glad they were not the objects of his visit.

As he approached, Una and two other women were leaving. They were carrying the wedding clothes. He went across to them.

'What is this?'

'She says—'

'Silence!' Cathal looked around. No one dared to be near him. In these moods he carried his own wasteland around with him. Cathal looked at the two other women. 'If either of you repeats a single word to a single person about what the Princess Bega has said, then you will be butchered, cut in pieces and fed to the dogs for treachery. You will stay here and then you will go with Queen Una and you will not leave her side nor utter a single word.'

The petrified young women stood like statues with just enough energy to nod.

Cathal took Una aside.

'She says she is not to marry,' Una reported, concealing her pleasure with difficulty.

'She says that.'

'She says that she has been called and that the Prince O'Neill is an evil man.'

'She says that.'

'She says that she is prepared for any punishment.' Una paused. 'Because she will be protected by her God.'

'*Her* God. She said that? *Her* God.'

'*Her* God.'

'Anything else?'

Una clearly wanted to stoke up the fire more fiercely but she was already faltering. The fury that was taking hold of Cathal beat off him. She wanted to be out of his way.

'Nothing else.'

'Is she alone?'

'Donal is with her.' She hesitated. 'I think he is sick. He lies on the cot and says nothing.'

'He'll be sicker soon.'

Cathal took several short breaths. It was not good to lose control. Not with Bega. He tried to conjure up the images of her mother but the storm of blood to his brain blotted them out.

'Keep those women quiet or they'll end up like Maeve.' He turned. 'Like Maeve!' he said, very loudly, and the women-statues almost shattered. 'Be ready to come back with the wedding garments, soon.'

Una walked away, the two young women one at each side of her, almost bumping into her in their frantic desire to feel the touch of security.

Cathal went in. Bega was kneeling beside the bed, rubbing Donal's surprisingly large and knobbly red hands.

'Donal, I want you out of here.'

'He's weak, Father. I think he may be . . .' She bit her lip, distressed at the thought of a world without the reliable and devoted monk, whom she now saw to have been her friend and guardian throughout her life.

The sentence was never to be finished. Cathal was across at the bed, Donal was lifted out, carried swiftly to the door and ungently dumped on the heap of slush outside.

Bega's protest died in her throat at Cathal's expression. She had never witnessed him behave like this. The anger that came off him was also new to her; she felt she could touch it but if she did, it would burn.

'Later today, you will marry Niall O'Neill,' said Cathal. 'After you have wedded him he will bed you and there will be those there to see it happen. Tomorrow you will go back to his household to take your rightful place. You will do this.'

Bega tried to speak but an involuntary intake of breath blocked the words. She calmed herself.

'I would have married him for your sake, Father. But I would not be childed by him because I am now given to the Lord.' She swallowed some helping saliva down the dry throat. 'But now I will not marry him for what he did to Maeve.'

'Eogon has judged him: the accusations of Maeve are the work of the Devil.'

'I believed her,' said Bega. 'And you would not want me to marry a man who used my servant like that, would you? On the night before he was to marry me? And with such brutality?'

'I have told you what I expect.' Cathal's voice was unusually low and calm. The desire to take this defiant young woman and break her bones, hurt, hurt and hurt her again for so obstinately refusing to obey him – and he such a father to her – was drawing on his deepest resources. Anger was Cathal's essential element. It solved his problems. It established his pre-eminence. It underpinned his rule. It purged his feelings. It made him know himself. Now, faced with all the provocation he needed, he had to push it down, down to where it would ferment and turn bad. Down into his aching stomach and uneasily repaired bowels. But he could not unleash himself or Bega would be too injured to move for weeks.

Did she not understand what a sacrifice he was making for her? 'You will do this.'

Bega dredged up her courage. 'Even for you, I cannot.'

Cathal turned his back on her and let the anger spend itself on his own body: he shivered with the force of it. Then he turned back. 'If you do not do this, let me tell you what will happen. And it will happen now. It will happen where the O'Neills can see that I will not have my honour challenged. Listen, Bega, listen.' He paused. 'This is what I will do to those who have turned you against me. I will see that Beohtric breaks every bone in Donal's body – breaks them, Bega, across his knee or with the flat sword.

Afterwards Donal will be put out on the mountain covered in honey, blood and meat which will bring all the beasts of the night to him. I will do this.' He nodded, and still he spoke in an unnatural, even monotone almost as frightening as the threats to those she loved.

'Padric will be slaughtered by my hand. If the tribe of Rheged rises up against that – so be it. They are far away and I am not afraid of them.' Her face widened. 'I will do that, Bega. He is my prisoner now in my lodgings. I have law. He has corrupted you. Eogon will decide for me.' He was breathing more steadily now. 'Then, outside the gates, we will dig through the snow and make a grave which we shall throw him into.' He held her gaze and she had never seen a look as cruel and blank before. '*You* will be put in that grave alive with his body and we will cover it with earth and stamp it down. I will do this, Bega. Your God understands. The law has to be obeyed and a father has to be obeyed. He is my God as well and I know this.'

Bega felt that she was nothing but bones and skin: there were no thoughts in her; even more strongly there seemed to be no feelings in her. Had she turned to stone? Where was a voice and what was it to say? Before her stood a father who was not the father she had known all her life.

Cathal had to go. This stunned, rigid figure was rapidly losing

the identity of his child. How could he ever have thought of her as
any successor to her mother? He had to do something. Every item
in his body and mind and spirit craved release in action. He turned
to go. A sound rather like the high cry of a gull stopped him.

'Padric?'

His stride did not falter.

'Not Padric.' The voice was lower, the desperation unmistakable.

Cathal felt a sick heave of feeling. His shoulder was seized by
her hand and he turned to her. All trace of the woman who had
borne her had vanished from her face, he thought, which was too
thin, too sharp, held no softness, no whiteness of skin, rose of
cheek, jet of hair nor anything of the utter opposite characteristics
which had belonged to her mother.

'And not Donal.'

Cathal had seen many people break. Now was the time to wait.

'Me. Yes.' Bega's hand went into the side pocket where the
wrapped fragment was kept and the touch of the cloth on her
cold fingers gave her sustenance. 'Do what you want with me,'
she said, but even as she said it, a voice inside her whispered 'Live
for the faith. Do not die for the faith'. Bega's face expressed the
rack she found herself on. Cathal assumed it was all caused by
her fear that Padric might be killed. He knew then, if he had ever
doubted it, that he would have no mercy.

'If you have to kill me,' said Bega, fighting down the words
inside her – words, in a sudden flash of alarm, she thought might
be the voice of the fragment of the True Cross – but fighting them
down, just, in a low voice she all but pleaded 'but not Padric – he
is innocent. And Donal,' she added, 'he has done no wrong.'

Cathal's eyes were so hard. How could she not have noticed
that his eyes were so hard? And the scars on his face which had
once made her so proud were now nothing but cruel livid streaks
of pink puckered flesh reminding her of the sword and its edge.
'Live for the faith,' the voice said, and she wanted to cry aloud
'No – don't you see? – I can't do that if it means that I must
marry this terrible evil man!'

'I will marry him then,' she said. But a last surge of independence or wilfulness or foolhardy courage swept her on to say 'But
I will never, never while I have any breath, never let him get a
child with me. Never!'

Cathal drew his mouth wider in what just might have been a smile or sorrow but could also have been the grim and anticipated realisation of his hopes.

He moved, but the instant he moved she flung herself on him, cleaving to him. 'Spare the others!'

He let her cling, yielding nothing. He would spare no one.

'Live for the faith,' whispered the voice inside her.

With one rough and untempered hand, he took the length of hair behind her back and pulled her away from him and then flung her apart.

'I will do it!' she said. He waited. 'I will do what you tell me to do.' 'Live for the faith'. 'I will do,' she repeated bitterly, 'all of it.'

Cathal felt more disappointment than satisfaction. Mayhem had risen up as seductive as ever was; and the perfume of blood had begun to tantalise his nostrils.

Without a word, without the slightest gesture which could be admitted as gratitude, relief or affection, but in a character as warlike as that in which he had arrived, he surrendered the ground to the vanquished. He walked away.

'Live for the faith,' Bega murmured to herself, still dazed by her father's implacability. But it was the face of Padric and not the glow of bloodlight signifying God or His Saints which came into her mind. Padric alive!

'Donal.'

The old man had been waiting humbly for the summons. He had heard everything. He came in, sodden with the thawing snow, shivering, frailer it seemed by the moment, but with pale eyes bright.

'You do right to live,' he said. '"Live for the faith". That was strong of you. The Mother of God was guiding you. She was helping you. Let us give thanks. Oh Mary, Mother of Our Lord . . .'

Oh Padric, she thought, will you ever know what I did to save your life?

Some days later, the woman who had attended to Maeve's wounds said that she had known of her evil powers. The tongue had refused all her treatment and the blood from it was brighter than a crimson berry. Cuts grew bigger when touched; bruises darkened. The black hair, clotted with dirt and dark tracks of blood and sweat, had moved with an independent force. Later she said she had realised that a nest of vipers lived there, coiled in docile patterns, moving sluggishly but always ready to be called to the will of the witch.

The woman of Beohtric said that a spell had been put on her and under that spell – for she had stayed awake – the ropes had of their own volition slithered off the limbs of Maeve and bound her in her place. There had been a long silver dagger held at her throat, the point scratching her neck (a small scar remained), and then Maeve had stood in the middle of the fire, become a coil of smoke and slowly twisted up to the roof and out into the open sky.

No one had seen her cross the compound. Unless one poor slave girl was to be believed. She said that a ghost, very like Maeve, had moved slowly over the melting snow, her garments not touching the ground, red flames coming from her mouth, and dogs had whimpered and turned tail, geese and hens had scurried and fluttered away and the gliding figure had finally gone through the solid windowless wall of the great hall.

Most believed that she had stayed as the coil of peat smoke and let herself drift imperceptibly upwards where she had joined with the imps and venomous ones who were always in the air, always waiting for a chance to pounce on the unwary. They had borne this transformed being to the very top of the roof and guided it to the belching hole of smoke which signified the fire beneath. The smoke from the hall – several reported this – then died away completely so that there would be no interference with the entrance of Maeve and slowly she had twisted down into the large peat fire where she changed again. This time into a shadow.

There were those who saw the shadow creep along the wall and remembered later that they had felt a chill of horror when they realised that the shadow was without a body. But others had seen the ghost come through the wall and, still gliding, move up towards the table where Niall in all his wedding finery, the torque glittering, waited for his bride.

For it was then that Bega had entered the hall. Donal was on one side of her, Una on the other. Bega looked severe but her face had been painted as tradition demanded and the dress was encrusted in seed pearls; high on her brow rode the head-dress and on her arms she wore gold armlets.

Her father stood and the musician banged the drums. As Bega walked slowly down the hall, Muiredach recited her virtues and the qualities of her ancestors. The poet of the O'Neills responded with a list of the qualities of his prince and the drink-sodden, belly-stretched warriors growled in recognition when a name or a deed was uttered which they knew.

It had been the shadow of Bega, some said much later, racing before her, running from the fearsome terror in her face. But how could you tell? asked others. The candles were all new and tall and the hall was full of shadows as the men moved and the slaves and the servants came to see the event and the procession entered from the one door, past the fire, towards Cathal and O'Neill.

Like a deer about to bound across a ravine which would defeat the hunting dogs, Cathal would soon have everything. There was no calm in him now, though, and the jubilation had been corroded by his bile. He had lost Bega. That bond between them, so strong since her childhood, had been snapped by her destructive stubbornness. He was insulted that he had been reduced to uttering such threats to make her do his bidding. She owed him more than that. Threats against her diminished him. She ought to have been proud to do as he wanted after what he had given her. The sooner she was taken away from this place the better. Only a few moments to go, only a few more steps, a few more words.

Bega felt like stone. Her body was its own being. The legs moved forward inside the stiff clean garments. Cold became numb. The hubbub surrounded her like sea-surge on a distant shore. Donal walked wraith-like beside her. Her thoughts were locked: fear for Padric; fear of Cathal; love of God, live for the Faith, rape of Maeve. Where was Maeve? Without any doubt, O'Neill had done that to Maeve and would do it to her unless she complied.

Padric watched helplessly. By now he had shaken off the drowsiness which the herbs had threatened to induce. His sword had been removed and placed with the weapons of all the others. At the back of the belt, though, was the long dagger from which he was never parted.

He saw Maeve plainly as she slid out of a shadow and headed slowly along the wall towards the table to which Bega was aimed. He saw that she carried two flagons of beer high like a serving woman so that when she dipped her head, the lower face was hidden.

She walked ahead of Bega and Padric's eyes swung between the two. They settled on Bega. Her expression mirrored his feelings. How could he watch her walk so steadily towards a man such as that? He glanced across, beyond Bega, but Maeve was no longer to be seen. Why did he not cry out her name, or shout out 'No!' or seize her and try to fight his way out? Like a sapling bending low in a high wind, he swayed with the power of his feelings, but still stood, among the others, rooted.

O'Neill saw the candlelight and rushlight playing on the jewels on her dress. The armlets glittered softly. The necklace was heavy with gold and silver and enamel. The clasp which held her new wedding cloak was a great Celtic spiral of silver encrusted with semi-precious stones. He had brought more jewels for her: a special brooch, rings and a necklace made for the occasion, which were on the table before him. He too was dressed in high style and the knowledge of his fine looks had put him in a good mood. She would be broken in. Once he had wrested her from this backward settlement and brought her to where real splendour and confidence resided, she would not be able to resist. And if she did, so much the worse for her. And who would care back in the north where the writ of the O'Neills ran over man, woman, child and beast.

In her wedding garments she looked much better. There was a virginal seriousness about her face that paid him his due respects. She could turn out to be a good ride and a good breeder.

Almost gathered in, thought Cathal.

The pressure against her made Bega feel as if she were walking against a force of air which grew in thickness and opposition until it became a wall. Padric's mouth was open as if a shout had been uttered, but no sound came. He had edged himself up the hall at her pace, keeping parallel to her, back behind a couple of rows of men now slowly, rhythmically banging the table in approval as the bride was about to be offered up to be taken and deflowered and made to submit.

Here they saw the woman doing the man's will and the event of

the morning, the gossip about Maeve's rape and Bega's unwilling-
ness, made it all the sweeter that this virgin princess would surely
kneel in front of the warrior O'Neill and become his.

Padric saw Maeve emerge from the deep shadows at the end
of the hall where there was no door: the flagons still before her.

Cathal felt a wave of unease and widened his nostrils. He
reached back to tap the arm of Beohtric and put him on even
greater alert.

Bega's vision was now filled entirely by the face of O'Neill,
staring at her as cruel-eyed as her father. She stumbled – only a
few yards away now – and Donal took her arm to steady her.

There were those who said they heard a cry like the high pitch
of the devil when he carries you off to your death. Others said
that the lights had gone out and then, when all the candles burst
into flame again, the deed had been done.

Padric was aware that he had begun to move forward: he had
to be beside Bega.

Maeve had with her a small piece of bone given to her by her
wet nurse long ago to bite and stop her screaming while the forces
of Cathal were encircling their settlement. It had saved her life,
she believed, when so many had been killed – her father, mother
and brothers among them. She turned her back to the backs of
the men, put down the flagons and pressed the bone between her
teeth and bit on it. Still with her back to O'Neill and his brothers,
to Dermot and Faelan now flanking Cathal, and Beohtric just
behind him, she dabbed away as much of the blood as she could
and took out the knife.

Almighty God who let His people slay their enemies would be
at her side. The Mother of God who had seen what had happened
to her would bless her. Bega whom she would save from this would
pray for her heavenly life.

She turned slowly, taking good care not to disturb the men
for, even though they were intent on the arrival of Bega, they
were warriors whose intuition of danger was as sensitive as that
of a deer. She took a deep breath. It would, she knew, be one
of her last.

They said she had slid down on a strike of lightning; that the
blade had appeared from nowhere at all and, guided by demons
and elves, it had been put into the hands of the woman who had
been the mistress of Lucifer.

Maeve stared at the bare neck and, taking Bega's knife in both hands, with all her force and last fury, she plunged it into the bare flesh again and again. Stabbed and stabbed and stabbed again, deeper each time and growling with satisfaction at the answering groan of blood in the throat of O'Neill. The golden glowing torque stained dark red.

Her hair was being torn with a hand. Her head twisted around. The face of Cathal was above hers, his dagger glinting above her and then – Oh praise Him! Praise the Mother of – the knife rammed into her throat, twisted, twisted, pulled out and then slit wide open the bloodied neck. Maeve was thrown aside and in her death throes quivered alone on the ground, her own knife still gripped in her hand. The hand opened. Cathal saw it was the dagger he had given Bega. He swooped on it.

The brothers of Niall held him up and then laid him on the table, flinging away all that encumbered it. The clan O'Neill threw themselves up the hall to be around their stricken chief.

Padric now forced his way to within a few feet of Bega.

The hall was ugly and in many hands the secret daggers were ready.

On the table, O'Neill writhed more and more weakly, clutching at his throat as if trying to loosen a strangulating rope.

Cathal indicated what Beohtric must do and then clambered on to the table, a dagger in each hand. For a moment he stood poised over Niall's dying body, about to jump down to where his daughter stood as if turned into a pillar of salt. In that moment the ardour of the O'Neills for battle cooled just enough to hold them back and then Cathal, showing Bega the dagger she had given Maeve, leapt down and struck – but it was Donal who stepped between them and took the blow. The force of the dagger went clean through his ribs and he fell against Cathal, clung to him, would not for a few precious moments be thrown off, and in that time Padric arrived to push Bega back and stand between her and her father.

The roar of throats, the babel of accusations and terrors filled the great hall as Cathal pulled out the dagger. Donal slid down the front of him and as he did so Cathal saw that he smiled. Donal heard the sound of those coming to take him to his heavenly reward. Before those looking at the dying monk, his hair turned as white as the snow outside. Some said they heard the songs of angels and one even said he had seen the very soul of the good old man float up towards heaven.

Cathal sought out Bega and saw her face locked solid in terror, a piece of cloth in her hands, her eyes closed and prayers unheard by him issuing from her mouth. The mouth, he could see it again, traces in the face, yes, it was true again, were those of the woman he had loved, the only one.

As he hesitated, Beohtric stood on the table swinging the head of Maeve, holding the long black tresses, swinging the head in front of him. 'This is the murderer,' Cathal roared in a voice that rose above all the others. 'Sent from hell to destroy the Prince O'Neill. This is the murderer. There is no other.'

Cathal saw a chance for advantage. He leapt up beside Beohtric and took the head from him. 'It is the devil's mistress that has done this foul slaughter,' he said. 'We will not do more of the devil's work by more killing. He is here now and that is what he wants us to do. Hold hard against this!'

The unexpectedness of Cathal's pacific words further confused the men but calmed them, too. Those who had tried to run through the doors for their weapons had been blocked by the few of Cathal's best warriors, fully armed with shield, sword and spear, forbidden to let anyone out until Cathal gave express word.

'Donal is dead!'

Muiredach, who had been attempting to staunch the wounds, announced this in a voice of real sorrow. The men were quietened. O'Neill's poet began a lament. Cathal threw the head of Maeve at Bega. It hit her breast and trailed its bloody path down the gold and yellow linen purity of the wedding dress, landing at her feet. She stepped back in horror. The dogs rushed to it just as they had grabbed and fought each other around the truncated corpse. Steeling herself, she began to move towards the dogs to rescue the severed head.

Padric caught Cathal's eye.

'Take her away,' said Cathal. 'Bring in the shields to bear the Prince O'Neill. I, Cathal, will go back to the household of the O'Neills with you men of O'Neill. With some of my men, we will form such a guard and escort for him as Ireland has never seen. And at his father's house we shall tell of the power of the devil's mistress and the madness of an evil day.'

⚜⚜⚜

'Take her away,' Cathal repeated the next morning.

'To Rheged?'

Cathal shrugged. 'I will never see her again. If you want her, take her. I will be in your debt. Take her as your wife.' It was delivered like a curse.

Padric nodded. 'We will go before the sun is at its height.'

'Good,' said Cathal: and went to prepare for his long journey into the jaws of the most powerful, who might now be his most bitter enemy.

He had hoped for glory. Now he could face dishonour and death. Anyone but Cathal would have stayed far away from the O'Neills when the butchered body of one of their golden sons was delivered out of the household trusted to provide him with a future. But Cathal would guard the death litter on its journey to the north. No one would ever say that he had backed down: whatever the poets finally decided, his utter fearlessness would never be questioned.

Bega would have to be ripped from his heart.

CHAPTER FOURTEEN

On the poorest of Cathal's horses, it took them four nights and five days to reach the coast which faced the kingdom of Rheged. The journey was further slowed down by Bega's deep lethargy which drained her energy and left her practically silent. Cathal had allotted them two of his least regarded men as bodyguards, but only for two days of the journey, and when they left – to Padric's relief – there was only a girl-slave and himself to help an increasingly enfeebled Bega. There was no Murcha to comfort her. In an act of spite, Cathal had ordered the dog's destruction.

To his questions as to the location of any pain or the possible source of the ailment, Bega usually shook her head or repeated 'It doesn't matter'. The phrase irritated Padric, as it so obviously did matter: she was in pain. But her stubbornness could not let him into her confidence.

What would he have found there? Her mind was still violently shocked at the memory of the bloodied scarlet head of Maeve swinging in the hand of Beohtric; her father's look of murder as he had leapt down at her with the dagger that had gone into Donal; the blood-spurting mouth of Niall, hands tearing at his throat; the dogs, tails quivering, snuffing so excitedly around the severed head. And then the banishment – for it was that – by an adored father who until recently had never given her an unkind look and now could not bear the sight of her.

Constantly she touched the well-wrapped fragment, but to the shame of her faith, she felt nothing but ever-increasing desolation.

They stopped twice at monasteries, twice at small settlements where Padric's obvious rank made them welcome. The slave's report that Bega was the daughter of Cathal added a great deal to their security. The slave was welcomed by everyone for she alone told of some of the murders which had occurred on the day of the death-wedding feast. Neither Padric nor Bega would utter a word about it.

At the coast they had to wait two days until the fishermen were sure the thunder had passed. The men had been caught in the open sea during one thunder storm and flames had appeared on the top of the mast, over-bright, elfin, scurrying across the waves. The water imps had danced all about them and only prayers to the old gods had brought them safely home.

Padric bartered the horses for some provisions. When he came back to their hut in the scrappy settlement near the shore, he found Bega tossing in a feverish sleep and the girl-slave gone. Either she had been abducted or decided not to risk the sea after hearing the stories from the fishermen.

Eventually, when the weather cleared, they set out at first light in their largest boat. Four men were ready at the oars. For most of the morning they rowed over a calm sea as the weather dipped colder and colder. Clouds began to come slowly and low behind them and the sail filled a little. When they approached the large island in the middle of the sea between Ireland and Rheged they quarrelled. Should they make for land and begin the next morning or go on? In normal circumstances a day was enough, but the cold was becoming bitter, the clouds lower. Many weighty looks at the sickly Bega and the clearly wealthy Padric prompted Padric to take out his sword and lay it across his knee. He suggested they move on and, knowing that at the end of the journey a payment of some value waited for them, they buckled to. The anguished cries from within the caves of the sea god Moni, who ruled the waters around the island, sped them on their way.

It began to snow. Very lightly at first, very fine. Snow brought a silence to the waters, interrupted only by the splash of strong-armed oars as the curragh sped towards its destination. By the time they pulled up on the shore, the snow was thick in the air, the land white as far as they could see.

The men would not stay with Padric and Bega. Something the slave-girl had said was remembered by one of them and they considered this couple bringers of bad luck. The provisions and their clutch of belongings were humped on to the melting snow on the stony shore. The reckoning was made. The four men drove back into the sea, seeking a refuge a mile or so down the coast where they would be safe from the ill fortune attacking the royal couple so strangely alone. And they had all noticed the silence of Bega, her occasional trembling, her low muttered words which they feared were spells.

Padric managed to place most of the more fragile bundles on his back or under his arms. The rest he stored behind a large rock. Bega held on to his arm and they went forward, gradually, walking in snow on snow, themselves covered in white settling flakes.

They came to a sheer wall, a height, as far as Padric could distinguish, a great cliff. He turned to go alongside it, to find the small fishing settlement which the Irish fishermen had sworn existed here. Padric recollected hearing of the settlement too from those who had taken him over to Ireland two years before.

But Bega would not follow him. He tugged at her arm, but she would not move. He came near to talk to her but saw that her eyes were closed, her lips moving, he assumed in prayer. The cold was beginning to bite his face and hands. The great cloak and the leather boots kept most of him warm but soon this quality of cold would test even the warmest garments.

Bega began to move forward towards the cliff. Padric followed her. The nearer they drew, the more sheer, the more gigantic the cliff face grew. Up and up it went, into the swirling snowflakes.

Bega found a narrow path hacked into the cliff face and set out on it. Still Padric followed as the path zig-zagged in shallow strokes and the snow blew against them, exposed as they were. They tacked slowly; soon the ground they had left was as invisible as the top of the cliff itself. The path narrowed as they climbed, heightening the sense of peril. Below them were rocks and their feet grappled wearily, sweat sliding down their necks. Bega, leading resolutely, did not look behind her. The baggages swung all over his back; his arms began to ache with the weight of the provisions he was carrying; his long sword more than once threatened to jam against the cliff and send him spinning down. The snow thickened.

Then Bega was no longer there. Padric stopped. They had just negotiated another tight-angled corner in the path's zig-zag route. He had heard no fall. His heart began to beat even faster and the first tremors of pain reached his mind. He called her name, loudly and then frantically.

He waited. Out of the silence came his own name in her voice. He turned to the source of it, looked up a little way and saw her, at the entrance to a cave.

Gasping with relief, Padric hauled himself up the few steps set in the rock and went in.

'Make a fire,' said Bega.

Padric took out his firestick which held the flint and iron and tinder to start the fire. He struggled a while, but the purse had been kept dry and eventually he succeeded. By the low light of the first struggling flame, Bega found a jumble of wood and turf further down the cave. Her movements were slow. The murders of Maeve and Donal were like a physical burden on her. All her limbs were heavy as if she were carrying them. Humpbacked because of the low cave, she gathered the wood slowly – noted there seemed an ample provision – and fed the fire. When it had grown, she put back the screen of thatched branches which formed a door to the cave. The world outside was completely shut out. The cave, silent but for the spluttering of burning wood, could have been the only habitation on the earth.

They cleared sufficient spaces around the fire to lie down and Padric took some mouthfuls, Bega a sip, from one of the bottles of strong mead.

Padric wondered aloud at the power which had guided Bega to this haven.

'St Brigid led me here,' said Bega.

Soon she was asleep. Padric watched over this woman given him as wife and allowed himself only to doze, keeping the blaze going, letting his eyes rove over the shadows on the wall, thinking through all that had happened to bring Bega and himself finally together.

He was back in his own kingdom. He had a high purpose and a bride. As he grew warmer, Padric relaxed into a sense of contentment, even of anticipated joy. He did not notice the chilling slowness of Bega's faint breath as she plummeted into a sleep near death, driven and ghosted by visions of the head of Maeve, the earth falling on her body in the double grave with Padric, the bloodied Donal, the terror of her father and the aweful weight of the fragment of wood wrapped in common cloth, clutched in her hand, bringing the death of Jesus Christ directly into her life: for what purpose? Why her? How could she bear it?

BOOK TWO

✪✪✪

PADRIC'S INHERITANCE
THE KINGDOM OF RHEGED

✪✪✪

A.D. 657

CHAPTER FIFTEEN

In the security of the dry cave, Padric finally slept. He was awakened by a sense of chill and by sounds of distress. The fire had gone low. He went across to Bega, who was shaking. Her brow was hot, while from deep in her throat a ripple of fractured sentences reached her lips only in indecipherable murmurs. Quickly, Padric built up the fire, blowing the embers gently and then more strenuously as the flames reached up to burn the slender steeple of twigs and kindled further to eat into the thicker branches which would throw out fast heat.

He moved Bega nearer the fire and covered her with his own heavy cloak. Yet still she shook. It began to resemble a spasm more than the trembling of a fever.

Padric took out a small pan, poured in a little mead and added a taste from the dried herbs given by Muiredach just before his departure. He carved a corner from the tough bread and when the mead was warm he doused the bread in it and offered it to Bega. Her lips parted at his encouragement but only a morsel was taken and even that was so difficult to swallow that she refused a second taste.

He took the cup of warmed mead and herbs and offered it to her and she sucked gratefully at the liquid: but again, after the first mouthful, she fell back.

Padric built up the fire once more and went out into the morning to look for water.

The snow had stopped falling. But it still weighed down the clouds which squatted on the sea, giving dark grey to dark grey. The water was calm but looked so cold that Padric felt chill. Without his cloak, the bite of air soon stung his flesh. He scrambled down on to the path and then decided to follow it upwards, hoping for a stream.

The cave was quite close to the top of the cliff and as he crested the edge he saw a white carpet which rolled steadily upwards, unblemished, still, reaching in the far distance to white mountains whose heads were smothered in the great grey underbelly of snow-heavy cloud.

After all the time away, he felt his heart ease and soar with pride and possession.

Padric breathed it in and for a moment all other thoughts, even those of Bega, disappeared. This was his land. From this place could grow a true resistance.

For even though the rampaging warrior tribes from over the sea thought that they had already won the battle, Padric knew, in every particle of his mind and soul and body, that from out of this place, he and his men could throw them back and breathe their own independent life once more as a British people. This snow would sooner or later be melted and its conquest of the landscape disappear, revealing all the quirks and particularities of the land beneath its even, white authoritarian surface. When the tribes who had settled in Northumbria were thrown back, all the character which he believed his country had would be revealed for what it was: unconquerable, its own master.

This is what Padric longed to do and in those minutes of dream, a lifetime of ambition, a history of hope, an ancestry of battle returned in full force after his self-sought exile.

When Bega was well enough, he would take her north from here, through Arthur's ancient capital city of Caerel and on to the household of Rheged.

As he scanned the territory, he noticed a boy and a man, some couple of hundred yards away. He waved and, after a period of hesitation, during which Padric realised that he was being carefully appraised, the man released the boy. Like a puppy unexpectedly let off its leash, he came over the snowfield, trying to run, Padric noticed with amusement, even though his short legs went into the snow up to his knees every few steps. When he did arrive, what Padric saw first was the smile. That was the most striking fact. The grin rayed from his grubby, red raw face under a thicket of tangled brown hair. The eyes were deep brown, almost black. He gave off an air of cheerful willingness. He turned and in his turn waved at the man, signalling 'I have made it' and 'I feel safe'. The man remained where he was.

'I'm looking for water,' said Padric. 'Do you think there is a stream roundabout which is not frozen?'

The boy thought carefully, screwing up his eyes to prove it.

'There's one that goes right down the cliff,' he said, in a broad accent. 'Most likely that won't be iced over.'

'Take me to it, then.'

The boy pointed no great distance and after one more backward glance he set out along a runnel in the snow which was a sheep's path on the head of the cliff.

The crystal air flooded into Padric's lungs and the walking and the deep satisfaction of being home made him almost lightheaded. He had never felt so buoyant, he thought, not in all his time in Ireland.

On the way to the stream – which did prove to be running free – he discovered that the boy was called Chad. His father was both fisherman and farmer, and Chad was responsible above all for making the wicker pots; he could count and had once met a monk who had taught him how to say the word DEUS – 'It means God,' he explained – and the cliff was especially favoured by God for sea birds which came every year and nested there so that while you looked down on it, it was like a beehive. The gulls' eggs were good.

All the time he was chatting on, his eyes kept flicking towards Padric's sword. After they had filled the leather bottles with water, Padric retraced the impressions in the snow. The man, who with Chad had been engaged in chopping wood from a frozen hedge, once more stood up and watched them.

When he came to the path back down the cliff, he took out his sword and let Chad swing it around a few times. Against the white of the snow, despite the dulling weight of cloud, the long blade glittered radiantly and Padric could see the boy imagining himself as the finest of princes, the prince of warriors.

'I've never seen a sword like this in all my life,' said the boy, who had seen very, very few and those stumpy and poor in his short, isolated life. He had never imagined being entrusted with such a precious thing. When Padric did not snatch it back immediately but let him swing and lunge and cut it through the air, his gratitude opened like a desert flower and in those moments he became Padric's disciple.

'Who are you?' Padric asked as the little boy gasped with

his own exertions and was caught up in the dizziness of his
fantasy.

'You,' he said, firmly.

Padric smiled and held out his hand. Immediately, not daring
to spoil the treat, the boy stopped his play and handed back the
sword, to which his eyes were riveted, until Padric had slid it back
into its scabbard.

'You in the cave?' Chad asked.

Padric looked at the boy intently. No: it was a wholly innocent
question.

'Whose cave is it?' he asked.

'Ours. Now and then I go in when a lamb gets stuck down the
cliff or we're looking for eggs.'

'Who made the door?'

'I did,' said Chad immediately, eager to show off his handiness.
'To keep it dry. And to keep out the goats and sheep.'

What he did not add was that until very recently it had been
the home of some of his father's slaves who had just been sold
on. Only females had been housed there and Chad's occasional
visits had been tinged with a disturbing excitement.

'I may need you again,' said Padric.

'I will come down there about this hour tomorrow, if my father
will let me.'

'I'll expect you. Tell him to come too if he wishes. He will not
regret it – tell him that. And bring some goat's milk.'

Chad nodded solemnly and then gave the innocent grin which
lit up the day. He watched the tall swordsman wind down the
path, watched until he could see him no more. Then he ran as
fast as he could back to the servant he had been helping. At every
step he slashed the air with an imaginary sword, slaying dragons,
wounding monsters, vanquishing all his enemies, and crying out
'Deus! Deus! Deus!'

When Padric came back into the cave he regretted the dalliance.
Bega's breathing was harsh and forced; she had flung off the
covering of his cloak and her skin felt burning hot, her brow
especially felt like fire to his cool hand. Again he warmed a
little mead, diluted it, added more herbs and attempted to get
her to take a few sips but again she could manage only the first
mouthful.

For the rest of the day her fever grew and Padric dabbed her forehead with water, tried, largely unsuccessfully, to persuade her to drink or eat even a little.

As the evening gathered outside, her fever did not diminish and the words which had been gurgling in her throat like a secret spring became fractured ravings. Maeve was much mentioned and her father; Cathleen and Donal; Niall O'Neill and himself and a grave. The broken sentences were all expressed in panic. Something terrible was happening and she was in danger. No words from Padric could soothe her.

There was no air-hole in the cave and the smoke from the wood and the sods, sweet-smelling though it was, began to fill up the space. Padric took out the skilfully plaited door and used it to chase out some of the fumes, but the wind fought them and brought in more cold. He stoppered them in again and endured the smoke.

The night began its crawl and Bega's fever now contorted her in spasms of pain. However much he bathed her forehead it would not cease to burn; however tightly he arranged the cloaks about her to warm her, she would throw them off.

Sometimes she was coherent, but only momentarily. Often she would say, 'O'Neill is the devil. The devil himself lives in him. He has to be killed or he will kill us all. Who will kill O'Neill?' Or she would call on her father not to hurt her – a pitiful lament of a cry. Her words about Cathleen and Donal were addressed to them as if they were no more than a step away. The name Maeve came out keeningly and sobbingly: the name alone, drawn out, long, 'Maaaeeeve', the sound full of hurt and loss.

Padric himself took only a little mead and the barest mouthfuls of food. He feared to fall asleep while her fever ran so savagely. Once or twice he went out for a few minutes, to clear his head of the numbing drowsiness. The cloud had lifted. The moon and stars were bright as polished silver. The sea beneath him was tranquil. On the backs of the waves the moonlight glanced whitely here and there, both near and far. In those moments he prayed for the life of Bega. By now he was beginning to fear for it.

Time decelerated and the fever seemed to be destroying her. She shuddered at the force of it and her mouth frothed at the corner of her lips as she cried out hoarsely against the rage of illness that was racking her. There seemed no way for her to settle, no way to get the rest she needed. As Padric watched, she grew more and

more wasted. Sometimes her hand went towards a pocket inside
her cloak but it would emerge trembling and when Padric tried
to discover what it was she sought, she moaned piteously and put
her weak hand on his wrist to stop him. 'Not yet,' she said, 'it is
not time.'

Finally, at dawn, with Padric sore with exhaustion, the fever
seemed to abate. Padric lay beside her to hold and calm her and
that seemed to help a little. The heat from her body transferred
itself to him and he held her more closely.

Sensing that Padric might be her hope, Bega pulled herself
against him and clung to him as if she were drowning. Shadows
leapt up from the fire; outside the gulls swooped and called as the
cold sea shooshed and sucked over the smoothed stones.

Perhaps this was the calm of healing, he thought, and she was
now recovered. He reached out for the cup of mead and held it
determinedly to her lips until she took in some sips. Then he
wrapped the cloaks around both of them and held her close,
rocking her.

As Bega sank deeper and deeper into herself, falling into
blackness, she envisioned the dead body of Padric in the grave
where her father had flung him and where now she would join
him. She had to save him and prayed for help. She wrapped herself
more closely around him to try to urge him back to life as the wet
gobs of earth landed on her. She looked up and there was Cathal,
a knife in each hand, beside him O'Neill, blood covering his
wedding cloak. Her father flung a clod of earth in her face and as
she flinched, she saw it was the head of Maeve. She screamed and
held to Padric ever more tightly as the earth now rained on them
and the darkness grew and the moisty suffocating burial forced her
to shield the body of Padric, to lie on him and keep from him this
fall of soil which pressed them down, embracing in death. The
image was so strong that she woke, fully, and she pulled Padric
to her unambiguously. She needed to be reassured by his flesh.
She had already felt him against her and knew he longed for her.
Padric responded and soon they coupled, awkwardly, painfully,
but whenever he eased she pulled him harder into her. She urged
him to give her the hope of his warmth. In the cave their gasps
and Bega's desperate cries sounded strange to their ears, as if an
animal were trapped there, crying for release.

After a short sleep, she woke as if for the first time since banished by Cathal. Odd unconnected images jarred her. She had no coherent memory of what had happened to her since the murders in her father's hall. She felt wounded with a weakness more frightening than the fever itself. She prayed as Cathleen had taught her and could not stop herself weeping as the words whispered within the cave.

CHAPTER SIXTEEN

C had brought goat's milk and food – licensed by a canny father who had put together his own conclusions from the reports of Chad and his servant. He was allowed in the cave and saw Bega who smiled at him and when she held out her ringed hand to take the milk, revealed two golden armlets. The splendour of these jewels was completely outside Chad's experience and he stared as if he would never stop. The Mother of God, he thought, must be something like this. It was some days before Bega in her mist of weakness realised that he longed to touch the golden spirals which encircled her arm.

Snow turned to sleet, sleet to rain, rain to drizzle. Bega almost obstinately refused to improve.

She gave no sign that she was aware of what had happened between them. After a few days, Padric came to lie beside her and the surprise and questioning on her face made him feel ashamed. She cowered away from him and he went and lay alone.

Was it possible that she had no recollection of what had passed between them? The act had made inevitable what both had wanted for so long but been too blind to admit. Once back in his father's household, he would marry her. Soothing the hurt of rejection, he thought of the wife she would be.

A wife who could read, write, fight with a sword and dagger, talk to poets and princes alike, understand war and yet seek to join the communion of saints. A wife like no other in Rheged. A wife, too, though he would not speak of this, whom God had blessed: the discovery of this cave was no less than a miracle. When he cast over the events which had led them there, he saw that their release from Cathal's household and Bega's escape from a marriage prospect she abhorred had been guided by a God who favoured her.

It was the shock, he told himself. The brutality of that day, the virtual flight to a new land, and then the near-death fever. What strength she now found, she devoted to prayer. Chad alone could bring a smile to her lips. In a mild way, Padric was jealous but in a stronger vein he encouraged Chad to return. Towards Padric she was rather formal. Perhaps, he tormented himself, she could indeed remember but wanted to give the appearance of one who had forgotten. Why would that be?

Several times he wanted to talk about it but his dignity and then his embarrassment forbade it. It could be that she would regain all memories when she was finally well. This was the surest of his consolations.

Padric was finding it difficult to restrain his impatience to return to his home. But Bega could not be left alone and was still too ill to travel, so he went to the nearby settlement and made himself known. A foot-messenger was found and sent north to his father. In the short winter days, for a good man, it was a three-day journey at the most.

During those days Chad became his little shadow and, seeing future advantage in it, his father did not object.

A week passed by and Padric's fretting became less and less endurable, but Bega appeared to have been beached on a low plateau of marginal recovery and improved no further. She refused to move out of the cave and into the nearby household.

It was as if she did not want to face this new world. The old one haunted her. Bega could not rid herself of images of blood, the loss and scalding of guilt. Had she not given Maeve her knife, then there would have been no assassination of O'Neill, no slaughtering of Donal, no murder of Maeve herself. Had she not been so selfish, then Donal would not have felt impelled to be at her side.

Sometimes she thought she had misread the signs and that tortured her more than anything. For Donal was a holy man and he had advised her to marry. Our Lady Herself had married Joseph. She could have taken the knowledge she had into the lands of the O'Neills and shored up their faith. She could have been a princess, perhaps even a queen in an Ireland which was giving to the world its instruction in the gospels. All her strength could have been allied to the influence of that great purpose. What might she not have accomplished? Had she failed God by being too weak to subdue her puny private feelings of revulsion? Such a marriage was no sacrifice compared to the martyrdoms and epic acts of the saints and the apostles. Why did she consider herself fit to be a chaste and effective servant of God? There was arrogance in that assumption. She was too honest with herself not to acknowledge that the idea had come to her at least partly as a way to resolve a dilemma. To use the noble idea of service to God as an excuse to get out of a marriage which in her lack of wisdom she found unacceptable, was surely a sin.

The sight of blood, the smell of it, the stain seemed still on her fingers from where she had clutched at Donal.

So she had brought about three deaths and, as Donal had prophesied, perhaps a war in which her father who only once had been harsh, might be killed together with his sons, his men.

What she wanted most of all was to return to the time before O'Neill when she and Padric were together, innocent and free and, now she knew, happy.

Chad became a welcome presence. He was a little like her dog in his undiscriminating affection and a little like a younger sibling she had never had. He quivered with attentiveness and every move she made seemed sacred to him.

Even closed into herself as she was, she sensed Padric's growing restlessness and when, after ten days, he asked if she was strong enough to talk, she agreed, even though she felt no better than on any of the previous days.

'We have to go soon,' Padric began.

At those simple words, Bega's eyes threatened to mist over. For they implied leaving this cave, this miraculous find which had been her world and seen her out of death.

It was well into the night. The fire was crackling comfortingly, only thick logs, no smoking turf. Beside her was the bowl of fresh goats' milk brought earlier in the afternoon by Chad. Padric had cooked some fish and although she had taken no more than a few bites, the smell of their grilled flesh hung appetisingly in the air. In the flickering light, Padric looked extraordinarily handsome, she thought, and her body sighed as she found that, despite herself, she had wanted to own his eyes, his shining hair, his fine clear skin, the ease and warmth of him. Why could it not stay like this?

The thought brought an intimation of danger and her hand sought out the fragment of the cross.

'The messenger brought me news which was better than I had hoped for. But they need me to be there.'

Bega warmed, as ever, to the boyishness in that earnest assertion.

'And we will marry as soon as we get there,' he said, firmly. 'My family will welcome you,' he continued, holding out a hand to take hers, which she declined.

'Marry?' Bega said, eventually.

'Soon.'

'I,' she paused and felt that dry rush of panic to the throat: and something else, something she could not distinguish, something that disturbed her but was dark, was hidden from her, tantalising. 'I don't have to.'

'You must!'

'But why?'

Her question was an innocent one, Padric could tell that. He was certain now that she had been unaware of the completeness of their coupling.

But what of the consequences? If it was outside her memory, then how could he remind her? If she had yielded to him in such a way but only in a state beyond remembering, then where did that leave his sense of commitment? Where did it leave the certainty he had since had that their love had finally been fully acknowledged and consummated.

'Do you not remember?' he asked.

'Remember?'

In his eyes she saw a message but she would not receive it.

'No,' she said, 'there is nothing I remember.'

Her hand tightened around the cloth-bound fragment and she was reassured. It did not burn her.

Padric nodded.

'Remember?' she probed.

Padric turned from her and made a small play of keeping up the fire. With his eyes averted from her, he said:

'But you will marry me, Bega.'

'I have sworn to dedicate my life to God and to offer Him the greatest gift a woman can bring.' It was an incantation spoken in a voice barely her own.

'That was in Ireland, Bega, and that was when you were frightened by O'Neill. I don't frighten you, do I?'

'No.'

'We have been friends.'

'We have.'

'As my wife,' he began and then stopped. His eyes were still averted and he had to force out of his tone the dismay he felt. But Bega was ill and she had seen too much death too recently. He pressed on. 'As my wife you would be part of a Christian household. It is a household which knows of the preaching of the apostles and the saints and wants to continue converting the heathen to the understanding of our God. You would be an ornament to our household, Bega.' And I, he did not add, would be a man to whom all happiness had been given.

'I thank you for this,' replied Bega carefully, growing tired now, 'but I must stay true to my vow – for as long as I feel I am called. If that calling is not strong enough, if I have been mistaken in it, then . . .' Bega smiled once more as if everything had been settled satisfactorily. 'I am tired now,' she finished.

That was the truth he had ignored. He had approached her too soon. He should have waited until they had reached his household. He wanted to lie with her again. By what seemed a law, the more she ignored his need, the greater it grew: the more unattainable she became, the more desirable she seemed. He was aware that he had loved her in the roles of wild youth, eager scholar and tease, but never as much as now, when she was a woman who seemed unaware of his feelings for her.

'We must set off to my household within the next two days,' he said, briskly once again, schooling himself to patience. 'I have talked to some of the men here. We will make a sledge and one of the horses will pull it along. You will be able to travel so.'

'No,' said Bega, faintly. 'I have been thinking – of the man you told me about, the man who lived on an island.'

'Yes. Erebert. What of him?'

'I want to go to him,' said Bega. 'I want you to take me to him and to leave me with him. There is so much I have to learn and you said he was a very holy man.'

'Let us see,' said Padric.

'No.' Bega was urgent. 'No. Promise. Promise, Padric. You will take me to this man. Promise.'

Her agitation gave her strength and she sat up, looking at him with an intent solemnity which he could not resist.

'I promise.'

'Thank you, Padric. Thank you.'

She relaxed at the promise and almost immediately fell into sleep. Padric waited until she was settled and then went outside and stood in the cold damp, looking out at the dark sea, hoping in that mysterious space to discover consolation: finding none.

❧❦❧❦

Padric bought what he needed. He had ample resources. He had spent very little in Ireland: the hospitality had exceeded even its renown, and only rarely had he had to make demands on his purse.

Chad's father sold them a horse and a sturdy old pony and provisions for the journey. The sledge was there should Bega need it – although her pride had put her on the pony's back, disdaining the public stigma of invalid. It was useful for transporting what they had brought. They loaded up outside the gate of the small settlement.

Chad stood at a distance, a pup in his arms. He was cradling it for comfort. The two dazzling people, the one with the magical sword, the other with jewels from paradise, had come into his world and talked to him. In those few days his life had been transformed. They had found him important. They had been kind. They had come with the scent of adventure and glamour. He was already feeling orphaned.

Bega caught his eye and her smile was too much. He felt a well of tears, common enough but until now provoked only by a beating.

See how his father grovelled, but once those other-worldly creatures were gone – see how he would hit out at his wife and servants and slaves and return to the rule of fear.

Padric went across to Bega who murmured something.

'Chad! Come over here,' said Padric. 'How would you like to serve the Princess Bega?'

Chad's glance fled to the fixed ingratiation of his father's face, who hid his surprise, thinking it would up the boy's price.

'He's very useful here,' he said.

'I'm sure of it,' Padric replied. 'We will value him. And of course . . .' He took out his purse.

'And the pup,' said Bega. 'It will warm me up.'

'Go to your mother,' the father said, 'and tell her that you have been given a great blessing by a great prince.'

Bega held out her arms for the pup and, after Chad had delivered it, Chad dashed through the gate and into the house which his mother so rarely left.

She was beside the fire, feeding the ever-hanging pot. As it was morning, she was alone save for a servant child of about seven. The skins on the floor testified to a certain level of wealth once enjoyed by Chad's father. But over the past few years his habitual poor judgment had caught up with him and, though not impoverished, he was, each year, selling off his possessions simply to live. His wife, who had borne him eleven children since her marriage at sixteen, was listless, wax-faced and weary often beyond endurance. Many of the births had been traumatic: only four of the children survived. The girl had left the household; the two older boys had brought their brides and now their own children into this flimsily partitioned hut. There were too many mouths to feed.

Chad did not know how to begin. He squatted beside her and watched, as he had done so often, waiting for instructions to help. Beyond a partition the roinking of the pigs seemed louder than usual, as did the clack of geese, the dog barks; the sounds distracted him. Yet he had been given an order by his father and he knew the price of disobedience.

'The man,' he began: his mother needed no other clue as to whom he was talking about, 'has asked me to go with him. Go away with him. And her.'

It seemed an age before this simple fact registered. When it did, the stirring stopped and she turned to look at him. It was a beseeching glance. Chad was not only her favourite, he gave her the help that enabled her to meet the ceaseless demands of the day.

'Go away?'

He nodded.

'When will you come back?'

His mouth opened a fraction as if to utter a reply but a

sudden clamp in his throat prevented the breath forming the words.

'Never?' she whispered, and his throat tightened further. 'Why do they have to take you away?'

Chad did not move a hair's breadth. He was in some terrible void.

His mother's face began to give way and her eyes, already large, grew even larger, magnified by the tears.

Chad had not thought of this parting. His excitement was quenched by her sorrow. He did not know what to do.

She turned from him, took a bowl, spooned some of the soup into it and held it out to him. He took it with both hands.

'Drink it,' she said. 'It is not too hot.'

To please her, he sucked at the worn wooden rim of the bowl and felt the thick soup slither comfortingly down his throat. She watched every sip, every swallow he made, and when he had finished she took the bowl from him and in doing so let her fingers, for a moment, stroke the back of his hand.

'Go now,' she said. 'Go now.'

His eyes prickled. He felt frozen beside her. She turned from him and held back her feelings until – triggered by his father's commanding shout from outside – he stood up and left.

And then she mourned deeply, quietly inside herself as if her tired heart would burst. The light of her life had been snuffed out.

Outside, Chad could look only briefly into the satisfied face of his father. He ran to the front of Bega's pony and took a handful of its mane to lead it along. Padric mounted his horse and the servant hired for the journey pulled the loaded sledge.

They set off on the silent snow and Chad did not look back, afraid that Bega would see his tears as he began to understand his mother's grief.

CHAPTER SEVENTEEN

It was the first Sunday after Easter, early in spring, and, as was his custom, Erebert fasted all day until sunset. He spent the time in prayer or reading. He liked to do this out of doors because in his weakness he knew that he was comforted by the robins and wrens that flitted about, by the occasional sight of a canoe or a coracle on the lake, even on this disappointing day when the damp of many weeks hung around the place and the very air was so saturated that a time without rain or drizzle or wetness seemed inconceivable. A vaporous mist lightly overlaid the lake.

He was speaking aloud, from memory, from his favourite gospel, St John, and the Latin words seemed to enchant the small birds which hopped so near to him. Perhaps they were listening to his words, Erebert thought.

'The same day, at evening,' he chanted, 'being the first day of the week, when the doors were shut, where the disciples were assembled for the feast of the Jews, came Jesus and stood in the midst, and saith unto them, "Peace be unto you".'

This passage always moved Erebert to a reverie. He would lean out his cheek hoping that he too might feel the breath of Christ on his face and receive the Holy Ghost. How could he ever deserve such a privilege? Yet although no one could compare with the apostles, he had heard the wisest of the monks speak of Aidan in terms of sainthood. He had known Aidan. He knew about Aidan's miracles and those of Columbanus, of Brendan and of Irish saints whose missions were fit to compare with those of St Paul himself. But, oh, to feel the breath of Christ on his face; to be granted a visitation from Him! Even more than the miracle which eluded him it was that which would make him feel that he was chosen.

In his dream state, he was unaware of the quiet plashing of oars until, out of the mist, he saw a tall, long-haired, gently posed figure standing at the prow of a large coracle. For a moment the others in the boat did not register with him. And in the breathless centre of the moment, Erebert's soul soared higher than the eagle: he had been granted a visitation from Jesus Christ Himself and on the anniversary of the very day on which He had visited His own disciples after the agony on the cross! Never before had Erebert felt the stretch of ecstasy which chimed in every part of him so that his body felt free of all weight, his mind purified, his soul purged, his eyes dazzled. His spirit soared.

The coracle crunched against the shore and the tall stranger leaped on to the shingle. Following him was Brin, the oarsman who was a free man in the main household on the bank of the lake. Still in the coracle sat a body so wrapped up that he could not distinguish who it was.

Erebert knew the man. It was Prince Padric of Rheged who had come to visit him before his expedition to Ireland. Now, doubtless, he came with messages and a request for a further blessing. Erebert rose to meet the nobleman whose father had given him the land he lived on; but even as he reached out his arms to welcome him on to the island, he was resolving what punishment he would administer to himself for the conceit of thinking that Our Lord would visit his poor and unworthy island on such a significant day.

'The Princess Bega seeks your guidance,' said Padric as Erebert steadied him on to the shore.

Brin tied up the coracle and held it steady as Padric helped her to her feet and supported the faltering steps on to dry land.

'Princess Bega,' said Padric, firmly, 'who will become my wife.'

Bega was too weak to deny this.

'Where is there shelter?'

'Follow me.'

Erebert led the way. Brin stayed with the coracle just as Chad, across the water, was guarding the horses, the pup and the sledge. Padric and Bega went into his small house, and told Erebert a little about their journey while they ate the bread and drank the water offered them. Erebert, long starved for company and a chance to indulge his old beloved habit of monologue, waited patiently for his opportunity. It arrived when Bega asked him to tell her about the life of a hermit.

❦❦❦❦

'In remote places such as this,' Erebert began, 'in what had been the vastness of the Roman Empire, a few isolated Christians, usually men, strove in solitude to lead the highest form of earthly life.

'Such was God's deep purpose,' Erebert went on, 'that it was not the missionaries who dared to go into heathen lands and convert the often antagonistic natives who were regarded by Him most highly. That distinction was reserved for hermits like myself.

'It was necessary to be outside of cities,' Erebert said. 'For had not the city in Roman times sent the early Christians into the Coliseum, where they were used as meat for lions and other exotic beasts, where they were crucified or made to copulate in public or butchered before the eyes of a pagan mob? And in the cities was there not temptation in all its multitudinous shapes?

'St Anthony whose life,' said Erebert, 'first inspired me, went into the desert, as did St Paul. St Jerome found his isolated cell and St Augustine went to North Africa to write *The City Of God* and Cassiodorus to Calabria to hoard what manuscripts he could. To save the world you must first leave the world.'

Bega, dazed and faint, thought that she had been led to an oracle.

'In their search for isolated spots, where nothing would come between their God and their life-struggle to be close to His will, few were as isolated,' Erebert almost boasted, 'as I am on this island.'

He had found this island on a lake in the most remote corner of the ancient Roman Empire. Large enough to support his life, it was still small enough to circumnavigate with a few hundred pulls on the oars. And he ended this part of his story by opening his arms as if the gesture could itself encompass his retreat.

❦❦❦❦

Here he had lived alone for five years, save for occasional visitors.

In that time he had begun, he said, though just begun, to perfect the Godly isolation he had keenly sought.

Exceptionally pious as a boy, he had been placed by his rich parents in the Celtic foundation at Lindisfarne. The monks there had come with Aidan from the island of Iona, before that from Ireland itself, and Lindisfarne, twice a day, also became an island when the high tide overran the causeway connecting it to the mainland. As the Mediterranean holy men sought the emptiness and protection against worldliness of the desert, Erebert pointed out, the Irish sought the same ends on islands.

From his youth he had requested permission to leave the community at Lindisfarne, but they had made him wait. First he had to serve, to help others, to preach in the lonely places along the coast, to help construct the modest monastery. During this time, Erebert longed for visions. He would try to fast longer than any of the others, although his health would often let him down and he would go into a faint so deep that food and water had to be given him to keep him alive. Then he would punish himself and pray until he was cramped with fatigue. Hearing of the wonderful exercises of the hermits in the desert, he would strive to compete. He became a man apart, not so much because of his holiness but because of the single-mindedness of his ambition. But no miracles were granted to him.

Finally the abbot decided it was more merciful to let him go than to let him continue in such anguish among them. He was given a route along which he had to preach and told to go to the king of Rheged, a Christian king, where he would be directed to a suitable spot on their lands. Here Erebert bowed to Padric whose father's house was a refuge for missionaries.

This island was his reward. During the five years he had built two houses, both on the beehive structure which obtained on Lindisfarne. He was very proud of them. The one they were in, his main dwelling, was built on a circular wall of large rocks found on or near the lakeshore. He had planted poles in the wall and thatched it with the reeds which were so plentiful at the southern, more marshy, end of the lake. The other was similar in shape but much simpler in construction: stakes driven into the ground, wickerwork woven between the stakes, wattle and daub plastering and thatch protecting the clay surface from the weather. Inside there were skins on the floor. Erebert's cloak was made from skins. He also wore a long woollen garment of Hodden grey, Irish fashion, beneath, and at all times leather shoes.

Erebert confessed that his exercises in the spiritual life were not matched by practical skills. He had been helped by Brin among others.

He had finally established a large and sprawling patch on a protected part of the south of his island in which he grew his vegetables: turnips, parsnips, carrots, kale and cabbage were planted, but seemed to resent growing. Nearby, enclosed by a wall of thatched stakes, was the herb garden, yielding, chiefly, sage, parsley and stonecrop in large quantities. Geese and chickens had been given him and their eggs were one of his basic foods; there were a goat and two sheep which gave him quite enough milk. In summer there was a little wild honey. He was lucky with the berries on the island – raspberries but more especially blackberries, which could be dried and kept, like acorns, the year round.

To cultivate all this, to plant and hoe and weed and pick and fish, gut, milk, boil, prepare, eat, took far more time than he had imagined and he resented it. But he endured. He had before him the example of the saints and of men of great memory such as Columba. Like them, he endured and blessed God that his incompetence made him strengthen his character to overcome his weakness. Yet what he yearned for was a miracle.

Sometimes, for hours on end, he would stand on the southern tip and look down the oval shape of the lake glittering, on a sunny day, wondering what he had to do to deserve God's supreme favour. Ahead of him were two or three other, smaller islands. Beyond them, in direct line, a huge crag on top of which, it was said, the British Celts had built a fort which had defied all the experience of Rome. On either side, flanking the lake along its whole length, were terrible mountains, to the east a steady high ridge, to the west one which swooped and rose like a bird on the wind. Behind him too, the most massive of all the mountains towered so high that on most days it pierced the clouds and sometimes threatened the ceiling of the sky itself.

Far from feeling penned in by this, Erebert said he felt secure on the island in the valley. The valley bottom, to those who did not know the paths, was one thicket of alder and willow not much higher than a man's head but a perfect stalking ground for predators. That was part of the reason why those around the

lake preferred to use the water for travel, as he himself did in a
canoe so clumsily hacked out that anything but the calmest surface
threatened him even on the short distance to the mainland. The
oak and ash, the hazel, the lime and elm on the fellsides, the birch
higher up before the bare tops all seemed, to the universe of Erebert,
especially designed to close him in and conspire in this concealment
and isolation he had sought and gained from the larger world of
men. It was the perfect place in which to concentrate all his forces
on his ambition for eternal life.

Bega was enraptured. Padric, too, was moved by the earnest piety
of the flawed hermit of the island on the lake.

❧❧❧❧

The journey had not been easy for Bega. They had come the most
direct route, taking a guide to lead them over the high pass. Chad
had never seen boulders and high crags, rocks poised for falling
and enormity of size like this before. The going was hard. Even
with the requisitioned aid of a guide and another man to help the
servant carry the sledge like a litter, Bega had not escaped a good
share of uneasiness. The narrow, slippery path and the wet stepping
stones had sometimes caused one of the men to lose his grip.

It was too early after the illness for her to be travelling. The
penetrating damp, the cold night on the wet fellside when the fire
could not be made to yield more than miserable comfort: these had
set her back and she wanted to be warm more than anything now
and to know that she would be warm for a good time to come.

As soon as she had gone into Erebert's house, Bega had shivered
with relief. The air was smoky, the place smelled over-ripely of a
strong broth but, by the time she had been arranged on the skins
and further covering given from Padric's cloak, she was almost
swooning into the heat.

If only the images of blood and the grave would cease to
exhaust her. If only she could make Padric understand that she
had promised her virginity to God and now, on the death of Donal
and Maeve, she had no alternative but to keep that promise. It
would all have to wait. She was with the holy man Padric had told

her about. When she was well she would ask him for guidance and instruction. He would show her the way.

After Erebert had finished his story, she slept. Usually her sleep was brief and mostly shallow. Now she slept as if she knew that she was able to float away in perfect safety.

The men went outside and Padric explained why he had come to the island.

'I must have spoken of you too often and too well and she has insisted that she must see you,' Padric said, attempting a smile, for the thought of leaving Bega and, more painfully, the knowledge that she wanted to be left alone, made him disconsolate. 'She has lived through terrible events which have disturbed her. In Ireland she studied the gospels and although she is young she was thought of, not only by myself, as a fine scholar. Equally she has prayed and devoted herself to the life of the Mother of Our Lord and to the Irish saints.' Padric spoke quickly to skate over the half-truths.

'In this new place which will be her home she felt she needed to begin with a man of God. Here I know she will find what she needs. There is a woman who lives beside the next lake whose herbs once cured my mother. I will send her here. I will also leave the boy Chad, her servant. He will do her chores. He will be of help to you. I am sorry to disturb your peace in this way. Please regard it as a trial from which you will emerge even stronger.'

Erebert nodded. Such an invasion of his island would have been unacceptable save for Padric's royal birth. Besides, as a future wife of Padric, Bega could have a powerful influence on the souls under his rule. If, like other Celtic missionaries before him, he could win the royal family over to become proselytisers for the faith, then that would be of great account in his heavenly reckoning. It could be the most important service he had so far rendered.

'I will see that she is warm and well,' Erebert said. 'And when she is ready, I will instruct her. And then I will bring her to your court.' Perhaps, Erebert thought, the elusive miracle would be given him in this royal obligation.

Padric looked in to take one last glance. Her body was turned away from him. He nodded. Then he went back to the boat, able no longer to conceal his impatience to be with his own people and about his business.

CHAPTER EIGHTEEN

As Padric came down from the mountains, his spirits lifted. He rode along a broad upland valley which led past the most northerly lake. Here he sought out the wise woman who knew the spells and the properties of herbs. Padric was struck by the woman's cleanliness and, more surprising, her youth and long flaxen hair. She explained that her mother had lately died but all the secrets had been passed on to her. Her name was Reggiani. He admired the sunken hut inside the small ramparted settlement which, she explained, her mother had fashioned on a rise just above the flood plain boldly looking across the lake. She agreed to go to Erebert's island to attend to Bega.

He came to the sunny brow of the last hill before the landscape swung down uninterruptedly on to the fertile, populous plain. He was arrested by the prospect before him. Surely Eden had been a place like this? The mist had cleared and the long view of a crystal morning in early spring, the lush slack downward roll on to the verdant flatlands ignited such a release of homecoming pleasure that he dismounted. For a while he simply stood and looked down on what could be, would be some day, the heartland of a once more independent Celtic Kingdom. He longed to be the one to regain all that had been lost. It was his sole duty. For though he was the second son, he had been picked out as the next king.

In the distance, answering hills from across the firth of water marked the beginning of the Pictish lands which had also fought against the greater numbers and forces of invaders. In the warming early sun the water itself was shaped like a broad tapering sword, coming in from the sea to settle any differences in the land.

At the sight of that sweep of firth, which Padric had ridden by and fished in and seen almost every day of his childhood, he realised how much he had missed it. The gaunt mountain lands of Connachta, the moonlit Irish rocks, the broad span of the waves and the empty ocean speaking of infinity, they and the tangled cluster of mountains and streams and lakes were beautiful and inspiring. But this coppiced, stream-snaked, humped, secretive wooded landscape, this easy domain of game-filled, fertile ground, this place of ancient warfare, was proof of God's beneficence. He almost vaulted on to the stolid little horse and clicked his tongue to speed its laborious passage down on to the plain.

Proven as a scholar, he had not allowed his skills as a fighter to wither. He had found the woman he would marry, whose body was so passionately sweet. Life was his! He whistled like a blackbird and the day seemed one set aside as a taste of eternity.

He urged on the rather clumsy horse, eager with every step to be there, to be engaged on his fate. He took the Roman road, quietly pleased in the knowledge that the latest invaders always avoided the Roman roads for fear of the ghosts of previous conquerors. Padric welcomed the ghosts as the exultant day wore on. He felt escorted by them. He paused only at an inn in the large ruined Roman fort which had once housed hundreds of Roman cavalry and now housed a few small settlements. Soon he was near the great and legendary city, Caerel, which was at the heart of Rheged.

Ecfrith, son of King Oswy, who had succeeded to a Northumbrian throne battered by son rising against father, cousin taking up arms against cousin, blood alliances giving way to blood battles, had come to Rheged with a small war band to collect the tribute. He and his six thegns had spent more time than they intended in the town of Caerel, impressed by the strength and fortifications of the Roman city and the opportunity such a large place gave for pleasure. Now the company ambled slowly and rather hungover northwards towards the settlement of Dunmael, who would still style himself king of Rheged.

Padric spied the war band a short way ahead in open ground

between two great clusters of forest. He began to close in on
them. It was twilight now, time of elves and mysteries in the
pagan world.

The war band halted and turned to face Padric as he drove his
horse hard towards them.

He did not slacken his pace.

Ecfrith and his men murmured appreciatively to each other.
There was nothing better than a little roughing up, especially
here in Rheged.

Padric knew that the odds were hopeless, but what were his
options? He could turn back – which was unthinkable. Besides,
nothing excites bullies so much as cowardice and their horses could
well outrun his own to catch him, ignominious and shamed. He
could slow down and not be quite so soldier-like in his advance –
but that would merely draw the business out. So he rode without
breaking his pace and stopped only when he had to.

The man nearest him looked at him with more than ordinary
curiosity.

Padric offered them a greeting which was returned. But they
did not shift to let him pass. There was a bank on either side of the
path. Not high, not steep, but to take it would be to back down, he
thought, and therefore to invite some sort of retaliation.

Stubbornly, Padric touched the flanks of his pony with light
heels and, holding the reins in one hand, the other free but not
too far from his sword, he pushed forward.

Still the intent and puzzled looks.

Unwillingly he pushed his way past three or four of them
until he was in their midst. A hardening of purpose made this
encirclement into a trap.

Padric waited.

'Is that you, cousin?'

From the front of the group, a horseman shoved his way
through. 'Is that – Padric, isn't it?'

Padric found himself face to face with a man whose looks were
disturbingly like his own. The same long reddish hair, a similar
cast of features though a little coarser. Tall on horseback like
Padric and most likely tall on foot. The freckled skin. Only the
eyes marked a difference: the eyes of Ecfrith were narrower, even
darker than the brown of Padric's, almost black. And the beard of
a few days straggled around his chin and throat.

'Padric!'

Now by Padric's side, he put out a heavily gloved hand and grasped his shoulder.

'Ecfrith.' Padric smiled out of courtesy but felt on his guard.

'Cousin.'

'I am pleased to see you,' said Padric, stiffly.

'I am pleased too, Padric.' He grimaced, stabbingly. 'Who lets you ride alone here?'

'In Rheged anyone can ride alone.'

'In Rheged maybe,' said Ecfrith, smiling. Oddly, the smile marked out a further difference between the two of them. 'But in the land ruled by us, we take more care of our princes. Ride with us. We are going to the same house. You can guide us the last lap of it. As I remember, it's very cleverly hidden away.'

Padric nodded and fell in alongside Ecfrith.

This was what he always hid from himself. Oswy, king of Northumbria, most powerful yet of the invading kings, had married the sister of Padric's father.

Rhun, Padric's grandfather, a prince, a holy man and one of the sons of Urien whose leadership had all but sent the Germanic tribes back across the sea before they were settled, had brought the famous King Edwin into the Christian church. Then he had made the marriage to seal it. This had linked the most obstinate of the British kingdoms to the fiercest of the invaders. It was a kinship which Padric found unbearable.

Rhun who, they said, had tried to mend where his father the warrior Urien had tried to break, was convinced that this marriage would guarantee the independence of the British kingdom of Rheged. So, for some time, it did. How many times had Padric heard the boast that in those parts of Britain – large territories in the north – under King Edwin's jurisdiction 'a woman could carry her newborn babe across the island from sea to sea without any fear of harm'. He had heard too, for this had been in the lifetime of Dunmael his father, that beside the springs on the highways, Edwin had placed brass bowls so that travellers could refresh themselves. So greatly was Edwin loved – not feared – Padric's father would stress, that no one stole those bowls or used them for any other purpose. Edwin, encouraged by Rhun, had even had a standard carried before him, as the Roman rulers had been preceded by the imperial eagle.

Unhappily, as Padric saw it, Rheged had prospered owing to this blood alliance. At his death, Rhun was exalted as a man of deep wisdom and farseeing strategy. Dunmael then inherited the throne and Padric was next in line.

While Padric sank into an obstinate silence, Ecfrith spent the rest of the journey rubbing salt in Padric's wounds by referring, unprompted, to the triumph of his immediate ancestors. Particularly he stressed their famous victory over the barbarous Celtic King Cadwalla, a victory brought about by God. Cadwalla had been a British hero from the Welsh mountains, fierce as a bear, apparently invincible, a brutal Arthur.

Padric refused to be impressed. Even when Ecfrith, who was only a few years his elder, described how he had been a hostage in the Mercian kingdom until another famous battle had rescued him, Padric would not let go of his resentment of Ecfrith's authority over what he saw as his own rightful land.

How much more warrior-like, Padric thought, irritatedly, to be a hostage with the Mercians than to spend three years in Ireland reading the gospels, meeting exiles and being teacher to a girl! That girl was to be his wife but, even so, the comparison rankled. Ecfrith had been initiated into man's estate. He led his war band over all the region; he brought in tributes. He patrolled the borders of his father's growing kingdom. He looked for trouble and provoked it. As now.

Ecfrith felt that he had been cursed at birth: to have a British noblewoman as his mother, of the race by whose hand so many of his fellows had been butchered and tortured. Why was it that he, of all the princes of the Germanic tribes, should have this yoke about his neck? His mother had died soon after his birth. But the thought that by parentage he was halfway one of the natural and lifelong enemy could drive him to acts of madness. When he came to rule – and he would: of his two older brothers Alchfrid was too much a talker, he thought bitterly, and Elfwin was lame and weak – he would eliminate the Celtic-Britons of Rheged. Like their own Cadwalla on his first invasion of Northumbria, he would raze the dwellings, pillage, burn, torture, destroy. The prospect gave him all the comfort he needed on cold nights looking for sleep. But he could wait. And tease this scholar-cousin along.

Ecfrith had learned to control his temper. With difficulty, he had learned it as a hostage, knowing then that to lose temper

would be to lose life. He had learned it again at his father's court
when he could not make him increase the weight of the tribute
due from the British. He was learning it yet again from his wife
Aetheldreda, daughter of the king of the East Angles, who had
brought him a great dowry and then told him that her life would
be devoted to perpetual virginity. He would hoard his temper. This
treasure would grow, the soothsayer had told him, until it would
become an armoury of fury, a furnace of fire waiting for its victims,
a force like a falling mountainside. Meanwhile he gambled with
any who dared meet his stakes, roving and terrorising the outer
reaches of his father's kingdom with a bunch of drunken friends.
He bided his time.

They finally struggled up the steep incline, through the four
small courtyards which led to the court of Dunmael, known to
his own people as king of Rheged.

The welcome for Padric was lost in the galvanised activity
necessary to accommodate the seven Northumbrians and their
four servants. The men were haughty as a matter of style,
disdainful at what they saw as the inferior establishment of this
so-called king (noting none of its subtleties and unaware that part
of the galvanised activity had been to rustle away as many of the
obvious riches as possible) and on the lookout for women.

Seeing them parade through his household in such a manner
made Padric want to unsheathe his sword and quarter each one
of them in turn there and then. Dunmael caught the look in his
eye and motioned him to calm. His two other sons, Riderch and
Urien (the latter named in honour of their famous ancestor), were
absent, trading cattle in the most westerly part of the Kingdom.

Padric's mother, a stoic, rather gaunt figure in this cold northern
household, wanted to ask her taller, thinner, more manly son,
to tell her all that had happened to him since he had left the
household. But that, like Dunmael's eagerness to know of friends
and kinsmen in Ireland, had to be postponed. It would not be
politic to talk intimately in front of Ecfrith. Although she had
missed Padric badly and longed to talk to him, she accepted that
her need was secondary. Her whole life had been spent moulded
about the imperatives of warriors: father, brothers, husband and
now sons.

Watching Ecfrith and his men eat made Padric lose his appetite.
How vulgarly they sprawled and spat and hawked and farted and

belched and mocked what they were given. How contemptuously they treated not only the slaves and the servants but his mother herself as she took around the large silver goblet of mead. Ecfrith sat insolently as if he were the lord of the hearth. The more he drank the more imperious he became and the servants could not believe that two men who looked as alike as Ecfrith and Padric should be so completely different in character. They noticed, too, how close Padric had come to quarrelling and how deviously Ecfrith and his men had sought to provoke him. Later, when the invaders had gone, there were long talks about the face and the features as a guide to character – the same face here leading in completely opposite directions. It was the work, most agreed, of the arch-deceiver.

Dunmael managed to conduct his way through the speedily prepared feast with a sort of nonchalance but also, Padric feared and flushed at the thought, a little cringing. The men were capable of wrecking all he had and, if the mood took them, they would. The privileges of Rheged were diminishing as the Northumbrian kingdom grew ever stronger; and when Ecfrith arrived Rheged trembled. Padric was all but bursting with resentment. He was blind to the skills of his father in shepherding and tempering this herd of potential murderers, this pampered elect of warriors.

When they had slid off into the guest house and into drunken sleep, Padric and his father went into his father's room.

'Why do we have to treat them like our masters?'

Padric scarcely waited for his father to come through the door. Some paces away, his mother looked with sorrow on what she feared could be a rift between them.

'We want to hear of your years away, Padric,' said Dunmael, aware of the fact that in his son's eyes he had failed, but too weary and too proud to explain the place of such complaisance in the scheme of defence.

'I know I must not, I know we cannot, but I feel that I could go to the guest house and kill them all in their sleep.'

'Has Ireland taught you no more than that?'

His mother came and sat near Dunmael; the three of them now around the low peat fire as the servants repaired the ravages of the roughly devoured feast in the great hall.

'I cannot bear those men to treat us like that!'

'We have to bear it,' uttered Dunmael, steadily. 'We have to bear it until we learn how to defeat it.'

'Why don't we fight them now?'

'Because we are weak and they are strong. And you never fight unless you must. If you did not learn that, you learned nothing.'

'We shall always be weak. They will always be strong. Our people are fewer. Theirs breed faster than we can count.' Padric knew that he was exaggerating but shame spurred him on. There was some truth in it, he knew that too. The polygamy of the invaders persisted like much else from their past, despite their public embrace of Christianity.

'If we wait to be stronger than they are,' Padric continued, 'we will never succeed.'

'There are ways and ways of being strong,' said Dunmael. 'Your brothers are out pursuing one of the ways now: to build up our wealth. We can talk of this when we know that we are safe alone. Now, before you sleep, you must tell us some few things about your own adventures in Ireland. But nothing about our men over there. That also is for when they are gone.'

Finally, Padric did as he was bid. He told them of the household and the power of Cathal; he spoke of the monastery by the sea where Cathleen had died and of Donal. He did not avoid telling them of the O'Neills and Maeve. He was open and bold about his love for Bega and described her and explained why he had left her with Erebert. He asked for understanding that he had moved to marriage without first seeking out their advice. There were circumstances, he said, which would take time to explain, which had made it essential that he bring her over to Rheged with him. She came with some jewellery, no gifts, no servants; but she came as the woman who would be his wife.

He was fierce about this and his mother smiled at his earnestness, the quickly impassioned sincerity he had displayed since a boy.

'Tell me about her,' she asked.

Padric began, and as he spoke he saw her in his mind, the young girl again, unruly, unkempt, teasing him, upbraiding him, always seeking him out, glancing over to him as if she needed his attention at all times to keep herself alive . . . Bega, Bega: if, in his mind, he called and repeated her name, would it flow to her on that remote hermit's island? And would she hear?

CHAPTER NINETEEN

In the morning when they met for the delivery of the tribute, Ecfrith's first question was: 'Where have you hidden all the young women?'

Dunmael smiled, rather weakly.

'Come on, uncle, own up.'

Ecfrith spooned in the thick oat gruel and paused only to swallow some beer. He ate ravenously and swiftly. Soon he pushed the emptied bowl away. 'Am I not to see my pretty cousin Penraddin? Is Padric the best you can put forward?'

Dunmael smiled once again as if conceding that Ecfrith was being merely amusing. Everyone knew that a dark undercurrent threatened to break the surface.

'Surely you don't believe the tales of Ecfrith and his monsters roving the earth like wild dragons breathing fire and feeding on the flesh of virgins? Do you?'

'Is that the story?' asked Padric. He had spent a restless night absorbing his father's pacific attitude to Ecfrith, attempting to understand and forgive it. Now his hatred of the further humiliation being inflicted on his household by this young, clever savage who looked so much like himself threw off the constraints of understanding. 'I always thought you were known as a sweet, polite, young prince,' Padric continued.

'I always thought you were a whelp of a scholar, cousin.'

'I always thought you were a man without a stain on his honour.'

'I always thought you had a big mouth and a wooden sword.' Ecfrith smiled: humorous insults were permitted and in his defence he thought he could claim to be humorous. All the weapons had been left outside.

Padric looked at Dunmael, wanting permission to return insult for insult.

Dunmael would not be drawn by his son's open, silent plea.

'Have you sent them up to the caves?'

Dunmael's honest face betrayed him.

'I thought so! All we have to do now is torture some poor slave into leading us to the caves and we can all bid good day to our cousin and her women. We would like that, wouldn't we?' He appealed to his men.

Those not too hungover gave their rather jaded agreement. They knew very well that the plan was to collect the tribute and then go further north hunting for animals on two legs and four wherever they could be found.

'I'll take you to the caves,' said Padric.

'To keep watch over us?'

'To see how this perfect prince addresses helpless young women.'

'Don't you know I am a monster?' asked Ecfrith, calmly.

'I have been away from home,' said Padric. 'We had our own monsters in Ireland.'

'And did you meet the cowards from Rheged who ran away to Ireland?'

Dunmael's face hardened and for the first time Padric felt a lift of hope.

'We have the tribute ready,' said Dunmael.

'Twelve wolfskins?'

'Yes.'

'Twelve sheep and goats?'

'Yes.'

'Twelve cattle, six pigs?'

'Yes.'

'Six full lengths of woven cloth?'

'Yes.'

'What jewellery?'

'This ring.'

Dunmael held out a large, beautiful ring, made by a craftsman who lived just past the lake which held Erebert's island. Ecfrith all but snatched it, tested it with his large teeth, and then threw it up and down as if it were a pebble.

'Do you think that this tribute reflects the glory of Rheged?' he asked.

'It is what your father and I agreed,' said Dunmael.

'The king has always been too easy on this matter.'

'Why should we have to pay tribute at all?' Padric asked, hotly. He could no longer bear the humiliation; he could not stand the patient acquiescence of his father. He was ashamed of him.

Ecfrith grinned. He liked to see a man lose his temper; especially when that man was outnumbered.

'Is this what your cowardly exiled friends in Ireland have taught you?' Ecfrith's taunt steadied Padric and he paused.

'It is a question I have wanted to ask for years. Now I am old enough to ask.'

'You pay tribute,' said Ecfrith, tossing the ring up and down in a steady rhythm, 'because we conquered or subdued *all* the British, Padric, and a conquered and a subdued people pays tribute to its rulers.'

'You did not conquer me.'

Ecfrith paused and then beamed with delight. 'We did not conquer *you*.'

'You did not.'

'Well then. Perhaps we had better take care of that immediately.'

'Man to man,' said Padric. 'Me and you.'

'No!' Dunmael stood up. 'Padric – Ecfrith – this is foolishness. We pay tribute willingly for the protection of our land.'

'We can protect our own land.'

'From others, perhaps,' said Ecfrith, still grinning, 'but not from us.'

'This is enough,' said Dunmael. 'The tribute is outside. We will go and see that it is all as I have said. Padric – you have spoken enough here. I forbid any more from you.'

To disobey his father would be to dishonour him in front of those Padric thought of as his enemies and so he checked his tongue. But his frustration hit him like a sudden stitch in his side.

'You are in my house, Ecfrith. No fighting, no threats. We are kin.'

'We are,' said Ecfrith. 'Though I cannot understand how the blood of my tribe came to mingle with this thin British water.'

He stood up to meet Dunmael face to face and the quick onrush of his perpetual and deep hatred shot to the surface of his skin, blooding it with an anger that made Dunmael flinch. Padric noted that.

'Your mother, my sister, had blood good enough to bear you, Ecfrith, and milk enough to succour you. I see her in you as I see Padric in you. There is no escape from that.'

'But there is no mercy for it neither. We want more for tribute next reckoning time. This small parcel is not what Rheged can give. We will have twice the amount.'

'That will be difficult,' said Dunmael. 'I will ride to King Oswy and appeal to him.'

'It is from my father that the order comes.' Ecfrith, they all knew, was lying.

'I will talk to him nevertheless,' replied Dunmael.

'My word is his word.'

'And my word is my own. He has not been here for some time. Perhaps he does not know of the blight of weather and the still flowing wounds from the last skirmish. I will go to him.' Dunmael looked steadily at Ecfrith who, seeing a possible confrontation which would take too much explaining, turned abruptly and went out to where the tribute had been gathered.

'Come!' he shouted to his men. 'Find your swords; find your horses. Make sure no thieves have stolen from you.'

Padric found it ever more difficult to bear these insults, but as he moved forward his father put out an arm to check him. The odds were far too heavily against them. All but two of the fighting men had gone on the expedition with Riderch and Urien. And it was easy to see that Ecfrith was looking for a fight.

Outside Ecfrith mounted roughly. His horse shied a little and he lashed it with the knotted rope. He detailed three of the men and two of the servants to shepherd and carry the tribute back to Northumbria and gather in two smaller tributes along the way. He would go north, hunting, with his three best men.

The small yard swirled with horses, cattle, pigs, goats, sheep and the two packs of dogs, one from Northumbria, the other from Rheged, snapping at each other, growling, threatening, as if in conscious imitation of their masters.

Ecfrith longed to smash someone or something. The calm face of Dunmael and the hard scowl of Padric each in their different way enraged him. His horse now stood obedient, welted, bleeding.

'I'll give you a riddle, boy,' he said to Padric. 'Listen. See if your bookface can read this—

"There is on earth a warrior wonderfully engendered:
Between two dumb creatures it is drawn into brightness
For the use of men. Meaning harm, a foe
Bears it against his foe. Fierce in its strength,
A woman may tame it. Well will he heed
And meekly serve both men and women
If they have the trick of tending him,
And feed him properly. He promotes their happiness,
Enhances their lives. Allowed to become
Proud, however, he proves ungrateful."

So what am I?'

'Between two dumb creatures,' Padric thought – that could be . . . and 'tending him' . . . 'feed him' . . . 'for the use of men' . . . 'What will you give me if I have the answer?'

'You could ride with us,' said Ecfrith, leering, 'and see how far that would take you.'

'I have the answer. I want a reward.'

'What is it?'

'The reward is that you let me ask you a riddle. And if you cannot answer my riddle, then my father goes to the court of your father without harm.'

'No one is harmed on land that we rule.'

'That is what I want.'

Ecfrith nodded. What did such a promise matter? And why should he have to give it when their court poet schooled him so well in riddles. They were the only learning outside genealogy which interested him at all.

'The answer to you is fire,' said Padric. 'Fire which is engendered between the flint and the steel, both dumb. Fire which can be used for harm yet tamed by a woman. Fire which needs to be fed and can bring happiness but let it grow too high and it will turn on its masters. It is fire.'

'It is,' said Ecfrith, truculently. 'I gave you an easy riddle because of your age and also because I want you to know that fire, harmful proud fire, is our ally in battle and in all disputes.' He looked around at the orderly run of buildings and small courtyards which ran up the hill. 'With the wind as its friend, fire, here, could consume the head and heart of Rheged.'

'But never the soul,' said Padric, obstinately, and the cousins locked eyes. The day of settlement between them would surely come.

Ecfrith waved to his men.

'My riddle!' said Padric.

'No more boys' games,' said Ecfrith. 'No more childish talk. I need no riddles.'

'Another time,' Padric said. 'I will hone it, just for you.'

But Ecfrith was on his way: the animals, already roped together where necessary, were herded out and the household of Rheged saw some of its hard-won substance diminish further.

Dunmael stood and watched until the party had cleared the last boundary wall and gone into the drifting, light mists of the morning.

'Now we can talk,' he said, pre-empting Padric's outburst.

First, Dunmael instructed his two soldiers to go to the caves by a circuitous route and, when they were sure that all was clear, bring back the women. Then he ordered his wife and her servants to quit the main hall. The gloom was alleviated by the lighting of some rushes. The boy who looked after the fire built it up then scampered away. Dunmael poured his son a cup of beer.

'It is no good speaking out against them like that,' he said. 'They will urge you on in order to have the excuse now or later to cut you down. You have marked yourself out as an enemy of the House of Oswy. That is not wise.'

'Why should we pay tribute?' Padric was a little sulky now; not ready to be repentant but aware that his father had much greater wisdom and experience than he had.

'You know why we pay tribute.'

'Why did Ecfrith want to double it? That was not the King – that was him.'

'I will talk to his father about that. We do,' Dunmael said, almost cursed with a sense of fairness, 'pay a modest tribute for a rich region.'

'Are we only a region now?'

Padric's reproach struck home. Dunmael had inherited much of the diplomatic Christianity of his father, who had seen Oswy as a husband for his daughter and his grandfather who had baptised the great King Edwin, first true overlord of all Northumbria. But Rheged was his home and his kingdom and Padric's sad question needed an answer.

'What should we do?' he asked.

'Fight,' said Padric. 'Fight.'

'We are outnumbered,' said Dunmael. 'The tribes from Germany can bring huge forces to the field of battle.'

'Cadwalla beat them. He was British.'

'He had hordes behind him and he could have held it for us,' said Dunmael, bitterly. 'If he had served our God and shown mercy he could have ruled over all the domain of Edwin and to this day we would have British kings in British lands. But the devil turned him into a murderous monster and God smote him down.'

'He still won.'

'He had armies, I tell you. From the Welsh, from us, from the Picts, allies from Ireland. He had many warriors, now buried or scattered. And he stained our name.'

'He beat the invader and that is what counts,' said Padric.

'Not if in doing that he ruined our name and we became the same as the butchers,' said Dunmael, firmly. 'We became part of men who pushed their spears through the bellies of children and held them high. We became part of men who severed the heads of raped women and threw those heads from one to the other like a pig's bladder. We became part of those on whom the invaders took a terrible revenge when the Lord let them arise and cast down the demon of Cadwalla.

'I knew Cadwalla. I rode with him. I tried to convert him to the faith in Jesus Christ. I told him how Christ had blessed Edwin, but he said he had a power more ancient than Christ. And for a time so it seemed. But he dragged us all down into a hell-pit, Padric: and that is why we pay tribute, and that is why we are few. God has punished us and we cannot say that He is being unjust.' Could he ever convince this stubborn son?

'Besides, Padric, the invaders have been here through the reigns of four kings now. They farm and fish; they build and settle. Is it not time to say – they are no longer invaders but just another tribe on this island, like the Mercians or the Angles? As long as they do not try to crush us and stamp out our kingdom and our ways, why should we continue in this endless bloody vengeance against them?'

Padric was silent for a while. His father's wisdom had to be respected. But he revolted against every breath of it.

'Yes,' he said, acknowledging his father, 'but unless we begin now, we will be too old. We will lose the need. We will – all your sons – take wives and even one day fight perhaps for King Oswy and pay tribute and bury for ever all that this kingdom was.'

Padric looked at Dunmael and saw that he was moved by the quiet forcefulness of what he had said. He went on. 'It was you, Father, who told us about this place in which we were born. It was you who taught us to be proud of being of the Celtic family of Rheged. You who told us about Bishop Ninian who became a saint and who went from our estuary over to Rome itself in the time of the Great Empire and despite all the dangers brought back the true Word to teach us here. And then St Patrick, suckled on the teachings of Ninian – he too was born here and even after he was taken into Ireland, it was still to here he returned to make sure that Rheged was true.

'Rheged always strove to be true to the British people, to itself and to God. That is why God allowed Arthur to be born here, to find Merlin in the lake where Erebert now lives, to rebuild the Roman city of Caerel and – with just a few men – to make the land ours again so that the centuries of domination seemed no more than an instant of interruption.' Padric was giving tongue to feelings and hopes pent up in Ireland for many frustrating months. He was a man bound to a dream and nothing would change him. He saw service to this cause as the only possible course and the pursuit of his dream as a destiny and a calling which he could never surrender. His father was moved as his son continued, 'Our poets tell us of these saints and heroes, more glorious than any others and we walk today on the ground they walked on then.' Padric paused and went on more quietly. 'It is our ground.

'Was all that for nothing? Why were we blessed with such men if not to keep what they held? Were they sent by God to this particular place and this people so that we should surrender their inheritance? Yes, the invaders steal some of our ways to ingratiate themselves but they are not like us.

'We have our own history. Is it all to end in paying tribute to a vile prince? Is this all there is for us? It is not for me, Father.

'I will soon have a wife. I have a sword and a horse and some things I can trade. I will not be one who continues to sit and barter over tributes! I want our freedom. I will go out and find men who will fight with me for it. I listen to those voices from our past. They are telling us to rise up and fight again, Father. They are telling us that this is our own soil, and that we are an ancient and free people. When my brothers return I will ask them to join me. I do not ask you. You are old. This is for us who are young and have a full life to give to it.'

Dunmael was silent for some time. The cub had grown, the chick now soared out of the nest. It was dangerous and it was most unlikely to succeed. But he knew now that he could not stop the course his son would take. Though he could think him naïve and even foolish, the old man envied the young man's faith and daring as he sought to vault from their ancient glory into a future worthy of it.

CHAPTER TWENTY

S louched on his horse, scowling around the misty countryside, Ecfrith sank into his habitual disconsolate state. Many
interpreted his melancholy silences as evidence of deep thought
and close-guarded powers.

His three men kept a little distance from him, recognising the
mood. They did not blame him. He was the fiercest of the sons
but always the one to be overlooked or disparaged. Meanwhile
Ecfrith watched the manoeuvres at court and kept his counsel.

His thegns thought his reluctance politic. To a degree they
were right. Ecfrith was the careful one in a tribe renowned for
its excesses; indeed its excesses could have been the seed of its
formidable achievement in crossing a wild northerly sea, wedging
into a foreign land and then so efficiently spreading over much of
it as conquerors within two generations. Although primogeniture
was not the rule, the eldest brother Alchfrid was by so much
the most powerful of the three sons that he had been seen as
the ultimate successor since his first battle honours at the age
of fourteen. Elfwin, the second brother, had inherited the full
impact of his mother's Christianity and with her he was devoted
to helping the Celtic missionaries to build what Ecfrith saw as
their peculiar little monasteries and continue their struggle against
heathenism and barbarism.

Ecfrith had always been seen as the willing hand. Ecfrith was
sent out for the dirty and tiresome business of collecting the
tributes, a task which brought him nothing but deep dislike and
even hatred. Meanwhile Alchfrid sank his fangs gloriously into
any strong war band he could isolate in the south and Elfwin,
on Lindisfarne, began to play with the idea of becoming an
abbot-monk.

When the Northumbrians had been defeated by their southern neighbours in Middle England, the Mercians, it was Ecfrith who had been left behind as a hostage. With the three men now in tow behind him, he had endured the humiliation and fear of that perilous, whimsical state at a time when a wrongly worded report could have sent a dagger to his throat or the antics of one of Alchfrid's more careless war bands could have ended his hostage state and seen him tortured as an example to others. For almost two years Ecfrith had endured imprisonment, tempered now and then by a little show of the hospitality due his rank. He had been cut off from all contact with his own tribe except for the crowing gossip of his captors, and cut off from women, and found only qualified pleasure in the enforced, rather brutal play with his three thegns. He felt abandoned.

Then he had been forced into a marriage with Aetheldreda, previously married to a prince who had died a few days after the ceremony without consummating the union. Aetheldreda, a woman of great wealth and bred to piety by a fiercely religious father whose lands were coveted by Ecfrith's father, had taken the sudden death of her husband as a confirmation of her desire to remain a virgin all her life. She had declared this openly. Yet Ecfrith had shrugged and, dutifully, gone through with the marriage. His father needed the alliance and the estates and Ecfrith was sure that he would encounter no sexual opposition once the marriage bed was reached. It never was.

How many people knew of this? Did they praise him for taking on such a holy woman – already there were those prepared to worship her? Did they laugh at him for not being able to break in a new wife? Which? How could he find out? He would break her. One way or the other.

His father would be laughing; he was sure of that. Alchfrid would see it as just another example of Ecfrith's bad luck. But he was stronger than Alchfrid, could bear what Alchfrid would never be able to endure. He could hide. Alchfrid had to be in the open. Ecfrith could wait for Alchfrid to show a weakness and then he would kill him. And he would inherit the kingdom.

The mist began to rise and soon it was clear. To his annoyance, Ecfrith discovered – when he went up a small rise to spy out the land – that he had drifted from the path. He had been steering north, but he could see now that he had strayed

around and had come a half-circle. He waited for the men to
join him.

They took some mouthfuls from the leather sacks of beer which
Dunmael had given them.

'What did you make of the boy?' Ecfrith asked, again making
much of his few years of advantage over Padric.

The men smiled, in a way which offended Ecfrith.

'We've been talking about him.'

'What were you saying?'

'He is very like a younger Ecfrith.' This was said quite tenderly.

'It's curious, isn't it?' Ecfrith was rather flattered. 'But he's
such a boy.'

'He'll be brave enough, I've no doubt.'

'He'll be foolish and filled with tales of antique heroism as they
all of them are in Rheged. You would think that no other country
had any history or any heroes but Rheged. Better saints, better
soldiers, better scholars!' The bombast was beginning to restore
him to a better humour.

'Could we recruit him?'

'A younger Ecfrith. Two of you! Think how we could baffle
the enemy!'

'He's not a perfect likeness,' said Ecfrith, seeking flattery.

No, they thought: the more you look at Padric the more you
are drawn to the fineness of the features: there is the difference.

'He has not your breadth of shoulder.'

'He has not your fuller height.'

'His hand is a splinter compared with the log of your great
fist.'

'His eyes are calm where yours are in flames.'

'But there *is* a good likeness,' said Ecfrith. He paused, and,
smiling at them in a way which made them understand that
he had picked up the undercurrent of their thoughts, he continued, 'He has a glow that I have not. He is now a passionate boy and who knows what sort of man will be born out
of that?'

Ecfrith dared them to contradict him. They stayed silent.

'I think I will have to love him or kill him,' said Ecfrith. His
mood changed suddenly. 'Ssshhh.'

He half-turned his head and all four listened hard.

Voices on the light wind. Light notes. Women's, girls' voices, and laughter.

Miming utmost caution, Ecfrith slid off his horse and led it until he found a big enough rock around which to loop the reins; the others followed.

Stooping and finally belly-crawling the last few yards, they came to the crest of the small rise and saw, in the little valley, five young women splashing their feet in the wriggling stream and two soldiers, recognised from the house of Dunmael. They sat by while their horses cropped the first growths of fresh spring grass.

For some moments, Ecfrith and his men simply watched. It was a tender scene. Snowdrops carpeted the thin woods running alongside the clear flowing river, the morning sun fell on the water, shining it, sparkling the wave-froth. The gaiety of the young women, released after a night of trepidation in the dark caves, was like the spring itself. Stepping into the icy water from deep in the hills to the east, their laughter and small screams as they splashed each other made a rare picture of light feminine careless play.

Ecfrith pointed out how they could creep down to within a few yards. The men crawled on elbows and knees through the long, wet grass and the concealing shoots of new saplings, suppressing their curses as the gorse pricked their hands and faces.

When they were all but there, Ecfrith gave a sign and mimed what they should do. When they stood up the women thought that four big men seemed to grow out of the grass. They were simply delivered from the ground which opened up to present them.

They walked forward casually, sword hand deliberately away from the dangling sword.

On the further bank, Dunmael's two guards leapt up, pulled out their swords and called out to the women to come back to them.

Ecfrith held up both hands and smiled.

'Padric?' The young woman's voice directed Ecfrith's steps.

The mistake over his identity gave him a sensuous tingle, fur rubbed the wrong way. He saw a bold, willowy girl, echoing the looks of Padric and therefore of himself. Her hair was nearer blond, the skin a little freckled. The close-fitting gown indicated enough of a young, voluptuous, growing figure to incite his easily roused lust. But he would play this one carefully. There would be pleasure in the waiting. Besides, he did not want to spoil what he looked on as a wholly successful and crushing visitation on the household of Rheged. And he loved the mistaken identity: it made him feel picked out. He walked towards her.

'Padric?'

The joy in her voice made him jealous. Nearer now, he saw the plump white cheeks, the delicious young lift of her body, the trembling delight in her smile as she held open her arms.

'You came to meet us!'

Ecfrith came to within two paces of her and then stopped.

The other women had rushed back to their protectors. His own three warriors stood aside from this encounter.

'Am I Padric?' he asked.

'Of course you are! I am Penraddin?'

'You are.'

Padric's thirteen-year-old sister came to him and held out her hands. He took them and gazed at her intensely. What would it be like, he wondered, to take such a fine young virgin, not for the brutality of forced lust but for a wife to train and use as you needed? Someone so trusting, so unchartered, so innocent, it seemed, of the bleak dark certainty of life. Would it ever be given to him? He felt himself beginning to rise for her. He knew he could take her now – his men would easily deal with Dunmael's clods. How savagely satisfying it would be. And how foolish. It could be done less damagingly, he was sure, and she appealed to a finer instinct.

But in the flash of a second the brutal thought occurred, Penraddin recoiled and pulled away from him.

'Why do you do that?' he asked.

His tone was plaintive. It was unlike any public utterance he had ever made.

'I don't know.' Penraddin looked at the other men some distance behind him. 'Are those men from Ireland?'

'Are you of the house of Rheged?'

Penraddin glanced behind her. The guards who had been sent for her were almost over the river. Their swords were out. Why should this be? She looked again and saw something about the eyes of this heavier, bigger Padric that disturbed her. She did not like it.

Suspicion and dislike came freely to her face and Ecfrith felt it as a slap to his cheek.

'I am Ecfrith,' he said. 'Your cousin. Son of Oswy, king of all these lands.'

Her head tossed at this last phrase. She had spirit.

'Padric is safe at home,' he said. And added, loudly, 'And you are safe abroad, now that I am here.' His voice grew louder as he spoke to the two guards now almost beside Penraddin, swords ready. Ecfrith ignored their show of force: Penraddin noted that.

'You have failed in your duty,' he said to the guards. 'Dunmael sent you to bring back the women safely. You let them play and shout here when you should have shepherded them discreetly and swiftly home. Are you to be trusted to return with them or shall I give over the task to my own men? Children led by children! Women led by babes!'

The soldiers of Dunmael could not dispute the truth of what had been said. Besides, they were outnumbered and Ecfrith and his men were widely known for their cruelty.

Ecfrith's thegns kept their expressions stern. Disappointed, though, that what they had hoped for seemed no longer possible.

'They will take us home,' said Penraddin, wanting at all costs to avoid the shame of being delivered to her father by his conquerors. 'It was I who asked to stay here a while.'

'And you let your judgment be swayed by one so young – however bold?' scorned Ecfrith. 'I still have half a mind to escort all of you back. That is why you British had to be conquered. You were always children.'

Penraddin blushed and checked her tongue. She knew that if she defended her tribe then either Ecfrith would just laugh at her, which would be unbearable, or her guards would feel impelled to intervene, which, she guessed, would be fatal for them. She could not, however, prevent herself from giving a look of such pin-point fury that Ecfrith felt a stab of pleasure. This was the force he wanted to harness.

He noted a black temper which, he thought, mated with his own. 'Or I could keep you here all day until Dunmael himself came to look for you.' The guards, who had listened most uneasily, now dropped their heads. Penraddin still stared viciously. Ecfrith smiled and waved his arm in a stiff and unnatural gesture of largesse. 'But go. Go now. We will watch from that hill and see you some distance on your way. And you—' to Penraddin

'—make no more requests which these men seem to interpret as orders.' He smiled. 'Although,' his voice softened and dropped, intended to reach her alone, 'I can understand why men would want to obey you.'

Penraddin blushed a little but turned immediately to be on her way.

Ecfrith watched as they crossed the stream and regrouped. He climbed the small hill slowly and tracked them with an intent gaze and thought about the girl. Without the dreadful marriage around his neck, he could have sued for Penraddin and won her. What pleasure it would have given to Oswy and to Dunmael! What confirmation to both peoples. And what pleasure he could have had with that newly formed body, that high spirit to be broken in, that young beauty which all would know was his and his alone. Still, if she could not be his wife, she could be his concubine. He would work on it.

He waited until he lost sight of them.

He turned his face to the north and soon the three men regained the track and moved quickly into the hills, the haunt, among others, of a small tribe who worked these parts with a few cattle and goats and sheep and little else. The women were open to all men for a price and boasted that they took only the noblest, but in the open. As the hooves drummed the drying earth, Ecfrith forced his thoughts into the imminent slaking of lust in all its forms.

After a day of welcome and stories, Padric wanted to ride out and look over those lands he had missed so much.

Penraddin had been particularly pleased to see him. When he heard her story, he understood why. He treated Ecfrith's seeming gallantry for what he saw it to be: an expedient. Penraddin's over-excited state told him a truer story: she had been truly frightened. But she had wanted to forget the meeting and hear him talk about Ireland: about the famous wild horses she had heard of; about the wizards and goblins said to live on in the boglands and the fairies that lit up the paths of souls travelling

by night. When it was revealed – by Dunmael – that Padric had
brought back a bride, Penraddin flung herself into questions: her
hair, her skin, her age, her words, her learning, her horsemanship,
her brothers: to have an Irish princess in the household!

His two older sisters were much less demanding, though they
too made no secret of their pleasure in seeing him. Dunmael
put on a small feast for the middle of the day and promised a
great feast when Padric's brothers returned and the household
was once again complete. All sorts of dammed up feelings and
sensations were released in this flood of homecoming, and yet,
by mid-afternoon, Padric wanted to be away to look around.

The mist of the spring morning had gone. Now the day was
clear and Padric was soon near his objective without sensing any
loss of light. This countryside was so dear to him: small infolded
valleys, twisting brooks, well-furnished woods. The smoke, like
a greeting, rose gently and straight in the windless air, from
hundreds of turf and wood fires in the well-settled area.

He came to the enormous rock – almost three times as tall
as he and proportionately wide. It rested on an eminence of
land which jutted out rather like a frozen wave. The object of
great speculation, this isolated boulder tilted on the edge of a
smooth steep of green turf. The commonly held explanation was
that God had put it there to test Arthur. First he had buried a
sword in the rock and only Arthur's skill at answering the riddles
posed by the three ghost-women who guarded the rock and then
his own physical cunning had enabled him to find the sword
within the rock and draw it out. Then Arthur's wizard, Merlin,
had made the rock invisible for some years. It had reappeared
many years ago when Rheged was in danger and it was known
as Arthur's Stone.

Here Padric came and sat cross-legged before it. He had
deliberately put aside the pacific garments of Ireland and put
on the clothes of a warrior. Wolfskins and squirrel and wildcat
skins made his top garment. Long boots of hard leather rode up
to his knees. A leather helmet with metal arches across it gave
him protection, as did the vast, heavy, curved shield which he
had left lashed across the rump of his horse. Besides his sword,
he had two daggers and a spear, and around his shoulders a bow –
the quiver of arrows was slung at the horse's side. Few warriors in
Rheged were as fully equipped as Dunmael's sons. It took many

tributes from within the old kingdom to purchase the weaponry and the horses and thus maintain the readiness of those mostly highborn young men. But it was found. The men and their arms were the guarantee of the people.

On his left, the sun, a clear and huge ball, was growing golden as it began its fall into the other world. It lit up the long streamers of clouds to streaming shades of crimson and a pink more delicate than any dyes Padric had seen.

He wanted to tell the Lord of Heaven that he would never abandon the faith which he knew was superior to all others. He wanted to vow that after victory in battle he would establish monasteries, he would see that the recently started work of copying out the saints' stories of Jesus Christ continued. But first he had to turn back those pagan pretenders to the faith: those heathens from across the sea who, he was convinced, had professed to adore the One True God only because the cross had won them battles. Padric detested the political nature of their faith. A Celtic Christian believed in good times and in bad. These others had taken up the cross merely for earthly glory, so they would let it fall were earthly glory to desert them.

'To do this work I need help,' he said aloud, self-conscious but determined. 'It is a lot to ask You to give these gifts to one person and to one as young and untested as I am. But I have studied the books of Your saints. I know the works You have done on earth and the words You have put in the mouths of Your prophets. I am young but I need to begin now.'

Padric prayed for a sign. In the west the beaten copper sun stood still, resting on the rim of the sea, irradiating the hills for one last spell before it went to its resting place. Padric shut his eyes and swayed a little as he had seen Donal and Cathleen do. And from the darkness within him he began to feel a spring of power.

He let his mind take what it would, as Donal had instructed him, while murmuring Latin lines from the psalms: '*In te, Domine, speravi* . . . In thee, Oh Lord, have I put my trust: let me never be put to confusion, deliver me in thy righteousness. Bow down thine ear to me: make haste to deliver me: and be thou my strong rock and house of defence: that thou mayest save me. For thou art my strong rock and my castle: be thou also my guide and lead me for thy name's sake.'

As he murmured and repeated the lines of the psalm, as he

swayed to the feeling of hopeful joy, he began to remember the time he had lain with Bega in the cave to which she had so miraculously led him. He remembered the touch of her flesh. She was his guide then. He saw the cave, their shadows on the wall, heard her cry for help, felt the wetness of her brow, her clinging to him and he surging in and out of her as the sea below them came and withdrew on the shore. In his earnest trance, as the sun went from full to half-wide – he saw again her eyes seeking him, the murmurings of her soul reaching out to his. That was the sign. Bega was the sign. It was she who would be his guide and guardian angel! All the instances of exceptional grace he had noted and stored over those two innocent years together, all the growth of unremarked love which had secretly spellbound them, was now revealed as the will and plan of God Himself.

In his young and intense hope, Padric believed that God had chosen Bega as His special messenger and she had been directed to himself as the man who could best help her take the message of the Lord to defeat the pagans and convert the heathen.

As the final tip of the glowing orb sank hissing into the sea, he stood up, deeply refreshed, bursting with the desire to go now and claim his wife and begin this mission in arms and in words which would make Rheged free and ascendant once more, and to bring the word of God to the heathen across many dark lands.

chapter twenty-one

Bitter though it was to accept, Erebert had grown fond of those evenings when he allowed himself to join Bega and Chad in her hut. Solitude ought to have been his unshakeably preferred element. But every night the three of them would talk before Chad moved off to his tiny hut. What they found to talk about for so long and so often Erebert would never quite understand.

Partly, with Chad, it was the language itself. Though Bega's Irish was close kin to Chad's Celtic-British, there were sufficient small differences to make it fun to try to confuse each other. Bega had honed her knowledge through speaking with Padric but he had been so easy with the Irish branch of the language by the time he reached the household of Cathal that she had not encountered knotty differences until Chad's local chatter checked her. They spent hours talking while they played with the pup, which both of them pampered far too much. Already Chad had taught it obedience to its name – Cal – and he was on the way to teaching it a few simple fetch-and-carry tasks.

The boy was a blessing to Bega. She still felt very weak and though Padric had sent two men to escort her to his home, she had been too ill to accept and they were waiting for her on the mainland. There was an ache of homesickness which sometimes seemed to permeate every moment. Even the hills did not soothe her, near though they were to the hills of Connachta, softer and gentler, though higher. They reminded her of what she had been ripped from so abruptly. To leave her father without his blessing. The blood of Donal, the blood of Maeve, on her hands and on her conscience, never to be purged in a lifetime of prayer. The pain she felt in her heart was the pain of their blood.

Chad too could feel devoured by homesickness, especially when he was alone at night, when he would sense a blackness in himself full of terrors just as the dark outside was infested with ghosts and demons. But when he was with Bega, he could all but forget his mother. His cheerfulness, his transparent belief that life now was such a glorious and royal matter, brought her much more comfort and relief than she could have hoped for. It was Chad, she divined shrewdly, who drew Erebert to their fireside. She saw the hermit's face dance in the firelight at the boy's talk. But Erebert himself had some awareness of this and would punish himself with questions. Was this a longing for a son? Was he so weak in his service of the Lord that the easy laugh of a common boy could draw him from prayer to be part of this fireside?

Chad had tidied his gardens so that for the first time they looked truly workmanlike. He had built for himself the neat and cosy little hut in which he slept. He collected wood from the other islands and rafted it back. The fish seemed to rise to him, Erebert thought, the goats stood stock-still while he milked them and did not fret or buck as they did so often at the nervous fingers of the hermit.

Erebert began to fear that Chad undermined the life that he was pursuing, and to long for these intruders to be on their way. But he could not disobey a prince of Rheged who owned the very land he lived on. Yet how was he to continue the life of solitude when he was not solitary? His spiritual exercises were still observed but he was not alone and that single fact diminished them. What – in panic he sometimes woke up at this thought – what if he were called by death when his life was in such disarray?

More importantly, though, Erebert feared that he was becoming too fond of a non-solitary life. Though Bega was ill, she had grace and spirit and knew her gospels well enough to dispute with him. Chad was a spring of felicity showing how the goodness of the Lord could shine through even such a common spirit as his. It was so wickedly comfortable to be with those two. Life was undoubtedly sweeter. But this was a deep sin. Solitude was the rule. Without that he could not be God's shield. He had heard that a remarkable new young holy man from Lindisfarne was preaching in the area and would stay a few days at Caerel. Erebert decided to go to see him and confess this unaccountable liking for company other than his own and the presence of God.

He needed to be reinforced in his calling. He needed to be told that he was still fit for it. Calculating that it would be a short time before they were gone for ever, Erebert cowardly took what advantage he could while it was available and time and again he would dawdle along to Bega's hut.

As always, the closed murmuring and easy laughter between Bega and Chad stopped when he bowed his head and came to sit beside a fireside brighter and less smoky than his own. Bega was mending some of Chad's rags. Chad was carving what he intended to be a figure of the Virgin Mary which he wanted to give Erebert as a present. The boy was already in heaven. No one had hit him or shouted at him or told him he could not eat that day or pitched him out in filthy weather. No one had done that since he had been chosen by Lord Padric and the Princess Bega. Life, for Chad, had not anything else to offer. Most astonishingly of all, he had not once been left hungry.

'Chad was telling me about the bears that still live in the mountains hereabouts,' said Bega, glad for Erebert's presence. Glad for any diversion which took her attention away from the pains which had begun to grow in her stomach. Cal snuggled against her and his soft pressure was a help.

'In the hills,' said Chad, nodding hard. 'In the hills where nobody dares to go.'

'How, then, does anyone know what happens there?' asked Erebert, amused as always at the boy's passion.

'People have been killed,' answered Chad.

'Then they would be even less likely to tell us anything.'

'I wouldn't go into those hills for anyone,' said Chad.

'But you came over a big hill, a mountain, with Padric and myself.'

'That was with Lord Padric and yourself,' said Chad. 'He has his magic sword and you can do miracles.'

Erebert heard the word and felt a slight chill of apprehension. It was the first time he had heard the word in connection with Bega. He noted it and would come back to it, by a shrewd route. For Bega, this much he knew, did not like to be questioned directly: not about Padric, nor her homeland, nor her family.

'There are the wild white cattle in the forests,' said Erebert, 'wild as wild boars. But no bears. Boars, you see,' he repeated, rather reproachful that no one had even smiled, 'not *bears*.'

'Someone saw footprints,' muttered Chad, doggedly.

'Wolves, now,' said Erebert. 'We have enough wolves to make up for the bears. Since the last battles they are said to have increased. And wild swine, as I mentioned, much more dangerous than wolves. I have been charged by swine in the forest but never, surprisingly, even in deepest winter, when they howled all about me, never challenged by wolves.'

'What did you do,' asked Chad, huddled over his knees, loving the warmth, wanting to be scared so that he could scud back to his little hut deliciously quaking, 'when they charged at you?'

'I climbed a tree as the Lord instructed,' said Erebert. 'It was a very splendid oak and I found a pair of branches so thickly branched themselves that they made a kind of cradle where I rested until morning by which time the swine had long since departed and so did I.' He paused. 'Even the cats are worse than the wolves – a polecat or a wildcat will turn on your dogs whereas a wolf will give them a wide berth, recognising a cousin perhaps. The cat is hard to beat off: he's so fast in his movements and those claws can rip open your skin in one rake.' He could not hesitate any longer. 'What is it that is miraculous about you, Bega?'

Bega felt herself in debt to Erebert. Not only had he given up much of his island and allowed his life's work to be jeopardised, he had nursed her through more than one night of horror. He had allowed Reggiani, the pagan healer from the neighbouring lake, into his presence – indeed he had, however reluctantly, assisted her when she came to give Bega medicines and put on hot and cold cloths which had helped Bega greatly. She could not refuse to answer.

'It is not I,' she answered, seeming to withdraw, as she spoke, into the shadows of the hut.

'Who is it, then?'

Bega paused. To say his name was to see him die yet once more. But the name appeared on her lips.

'Donal. I think I have talked about him.'

'The monk who is dead.'

'Yes. The monk who is dead. He was given a miracle.'

'Many say that,' said Erebert, trying to cut down the shoots of envy ever ready to leap up at this particular provocation.

'Oh,' said Bega, wanting to do full justice to Donal, 'this was a true miracle.'

'Let me hear about it,' said Erebert, humbly, 'that I may know ever more surely the power of the Lord.'

'First I must ask you not to tell anyone what I shall tell you.'

'Why? Is the light of our God to be hidden?'

'No. But I ask for my poor sake that you tell no one. The burden would be too great for me to bear if others know of it. I cannot believe that God wants me to bear that burden yet.'

'You have not the strength? Perhaps God's will is that others give you the strength. We have not talked enough of this, Bega, but I am still unclear as to your final intention – whether it is to be the bride of Padric or the bride of Christ.'

'Oh,' said Bega, 'there is no doubting my final intention now.'

Erebert waited, but she did not give him the answer he wanted.

'This miracle?'

'Only if you promise to tell no one without my permission.'

Erebert was doubtful. For him, all of God's interventions in earthly life were meant to be revealed. It was also extremely useful to be able to quote a new miracle when faced by the heathen. Nothing impressed them more. It could be very helpful just now. He was about to set off to Caerel to see this new young holy man so beloved by the king that already he had been granted large holdings of land, so beloved by the queen that she went to the monastery where he was guest master just for the heavenly joy of seeing perfection. On that journey he would encounter many heathen and a fresh miracle could be effective.

'I cannot promise until I hear it.'

'Very well,' said Bega. 'I will trust you to be silenced by what you hear . . . Chad – leave us.'

The boy's hesitation was barely noticeable. But as he fled across the cold turf, he wondered what miracles were being told. Perhaps one of those stars so clear this night had been plucked from an Irish mountain-top in honour of Bega. Perhaps she had cured the palsied, made the blind see, raised the dead. Nothing would be beyond the powers of Bega and Padric, the boy thought as he shivered himself to sleep under the cloak she had let him use, still dreaming of bears.

In quiet detail, Bega told Erebert of the visitation of the Mother of Jesus Christ, of the fragment of the True Cross and how it had saved her in a time of carnage and again on a snow-blanked sea, and then led her to a secret cave. She showed him the fragment. Erebert took it in trembling hands and raised it above his head, swearing to God that he would never speak of this unless granted permission by Bega herself. He swayed with the ecstasy of it. Never had he thought to be so blessed. He praised God with all his might.

When the cross left his hands to be wound up once more in the strip of cloth, Erebert experienced a sudden total loss of strength. He even lay down for a while, enfeebled by the responsibility and the awesome nature of what he had touched.

'It is such a gift,' he said, eventually, his voice choking with feeling. What had Donal done to merit such a gift? 'Was Donal a wonderfully wise man?'

'No.'

'He was learned, then, was he not? One of the scholars of Ireland?'

'Oh no, he was no great scholar,' said Bega.

'He had done some brave deed then, some marvellous act which deserved the reward of a miracle such as this . . . ?'

'No,' said Bega, 'none of that is Donal. He was a humble poor man. He would say himself he was the most humble creature called to the service of Jesus Christ since He took the donkey to ride into Jerusalem.'

'That could be it,' said Erebert, thoughtfully, restored now, wanting to nail this one before the envy of it overcame his due and sincere awe. 'But I think it was you the miracle was for. Donal was the messenger only. It is from you He expects the marvellous life, Bega.'

'I have no marvellous life to offer anyone,' said Bega firmly. 'I am sick and confused and thrown out of my home into a foreign land.'

'Then it is sent to try you,' said Erebert sternly. 'It is often the starting point for the most holy that they are ripped from their land and taken to a foreign place. It is there that their virtue can stand uncluttered. Look at St Anthony. I know this myself from Aidan whom I saw and met and talked to.'

Bega nodded. She had heard Aidan's story but knew little of his works. 'Go on,' she prompted. Somehow the telling of her story and the revealing of the fragment of the cross had left her feeling low and weepy. She stroked Cal to calm herself.

Erebert needed little encouragement. 'Aidan,' he said, springing into explanation with the fanatical enthusiasm of the unquestioning disciple, 'came from the island of Iona which is in the sea beside the most northerly land of the Picts. St Columbanus had brought Irish monks to this remote place to be free from all worldliness and devote their lives to God. King Oswald took refuge in the Pictish lands after defeat in battle and as soon as he became king he sent into the land of the Picts for a holy man to help him convert the heathen of his own Teutonic tribe and the other heathens and pagans he had encountered. Aidan was that man – a man of supreme holiness. He obeyed all the Celtic rules of Our Lord.' Erebert's eyes glistened a little. The slight, elegant figure of Aidan seemed to rise up before his eyes in the lonely hut on that isolated island.

'Aidan sought an island,' continued Erebert, pausing to allow Bega to appreciate how closely he had followed in the footsteps of the Celtic monk. 'King Oswald gave him Lindisfarne. It was there that Aidan built his first monastery and then, with the help of more monks, he moved into Oswald's kingdom and built churches and monasteries wherever he was given land. The king himself used to act as interpreter for Aidan in the early months until Aidan mastered their language. He was a man who lived as he taught.'

That sentence caught Bega and she asked Erebert to wait a while. She wanted to let it hang in the air so that she could almost see it, reach out and touch it. To live as you taught: that was what she wanted. She breathed it in as the silence between them grew and enriched their communion. She moved Cal a little to warm up another part of her stomach. The aching was not as acute now.

'He meditated and prayed whenever he could. He made his monks learn their psalms.' Erebert all but chanted these phrases. Bega smiled at the warmth of the man's affection. 'He ate sparingly. When he was given money by the wealthy he used it to construct a holy building, or gave it to the poor, or bought up the ransom of slaves, many of whom followed him and became monks. His life was like one who accompanied Him around the Sea of Galilee and indeed there are those who think those times have come again.'

Erebert's deepest longing was that somehow God had chosen *this* time and *this* place, as He had chosen Israel, to make evident again His power on earth. For in their remoteness and humility and tenacity of devotion, he thought, the infinitesimal number of monks and missionaries in this furthest corner of the known world could be compared with those called by Jesus Christ Himself.

'He died,' concluded Erebert solemnly, 'only six years ago. He sat against an oak pillar in a church as he died. Later the church burned down but that holy oak pillar was left untouched. I met him,' Erebert repeated proudly, 'and I spoke to him on five occasions. He is surely with the saints in Heaven. And now I am told comes another similar man – Cuthbert. He is still young, but already they say with the marks on him. I will seek him out in Caerel and I must begin my journey in two days' time, Bega. If you want to accompany me, I would welcome it. If you are weak, you and your men must stay here.'

Bega caught his anxiety. 'Would you like our company?'

'It would be safer,' said Erebert, honestly. 'Along the way, there are those who worship nothing but water gods, gods of the lake, gods of the streams and springs, gods of the rain. There are those who still sacrifice animals not for the feast of the birth of Christ but for the blood to be drunk by the earth gods and by themselves. They do not like the servants of the true God. Others drink themselves into a frenzy with beer and often leap down naked from the top of the highest crags to fight the devil whose red tongues they have seen in the depths of the rocks below. And there are those who are magical, like Reggiani, but their gifts are not the miracle of the Lord.' He grimaced. 'Many do not trust me; they do not know why I try to live alone: they think I am sent to spy on them or to criticise them.' He stopped, abruptly. Tales of bestiality and child torture, of incest and unpredictable violence would be too upsetting for Bega at this time, he judged.

'Do *you* think that what you are doing is strange?' Bega asked.

'I am doing the highest work of the Lord,' said Erebert, simply and unaffectedly. 'Every day I do battle with the devils which tear against me. I give witness that one of the Lord's weakest vessels can stand firm against the strongest forces which rise up against Him. And by my prayers – with those of many others – if I am worthy enough, the work of God is done as He wills it.'

'But does He not want you to be out there,' Bega pointed towards the mainland, 'in the world, converting the heathen and confirming the faithful as Aidan did?'

'Aidan himself longed to lead the life of a hermit. God had other designs on him. Christ Himself showed the way in the wilderness. It is agreed by all that it is the hardest and steepest and therefore the most desirable path to Heaven,' answered Erebert with utter conviction. 'See what men have done to themselves in order to be fit to be hermits. Origen took a knife to his organs of reproduction and castrated himself in order to be rid of the evil of lust. St Anthony, when he felt temptation raise its serpent heads, threw himself into thorn bushes. Many have whipped themselves to beat the devil out of their bodies. In the deserts of the east there was a man, raised by his mother to be a hermit, who sat high on a pillar of rock for more than twenty years, scratching his open sores to show to the crowds how little he cared for earthly flesh and pain compared with the glory to come. How can you ask this of one who follows the example of such a man as St Jerome?'

His tone reproached Bega and she fell silent. But how best to serve God? Was this hermit's way truly the summit of Godly earthly life?

Bega was reluctant to go to Caerel. Padric would be waiting for her at Caerel, she guessed, for he too would want to see this new holy man. She needed more time. What must she do about Padric?

'I will go with you in two days,' said Bega.

'Will you be fit to travel?'

'Yes,' said Bega, 'I will be ready.'

Erebert glowed with gratitude. He rose to leave, but then he faltered. Bega knew exactly what he wanted.

From deep in her pocket, she took up the well-wrapped fragment and revealed it to him once more.

Erebert bent over, overtaken with devotion, and pressed his lips to it.

'He died for us on that cross.'

'Yes,' said Bega.

'He must have picked you out for some miraculous task,' said Erebert generously.

'I am not worthy.'

'He will decide,' Erebert responded, as gently as he could. She ought to accept the gift more gracefully, he thought. 'He will judge.'

Erebert left the hut and walked surely in the darkness to a tree stump by the lake's edge. He kneeled on its jagged surface and decided that he would remain in prayer until dawn. This would be some small thanks for the great blessing he had received. A wafer moon occasionally shone through the clouds and the still lake shone back its yellowing-whiteness into many parts of the shore, making a map of shadows.

The lapping of the water calmed Erebert's agitation. To have kissed the True Cross! Would God forgive him for that? He was not worthy.

He shifted from knee to knee and noted with appreciation that the pain and the cold were both beginning to grip him. Still, though, his mind would not settle, despite using all the techniques he had been taught. He would miss Chad very much. The presence of the boy reminded him of the lives he could not lead, hard to relinquish. Bega did not understand that. She did not understand that the more you denied yourself the more you served God. The only purpose of life on earth was to serve God as perfectly as you could and see the earth as the transitory place it was. The more alone, the greater the sacrifice, the nearer you were to Him. But the devil also knew this. Therefore the devil sent his strongest demons to torment those who took up the solitary battle.

Erebert longed to visit this new holy man for guidance and for his blessing. Then he would come back to the island and insist that he must be in solitude. This empty and wild place. Wolves in the woods. Polecats which had scarred him. And bears? He smiled.

His body was deeply cold now, his legs beginning to cramp. The thought of Bega's snug hut, the fire, the dog for warmth, the smell of the soup simmering.

Drops of rain began to fall bringing, at first, relief. It warmed him. Spring rain. And then the shower grew in strength and left him soaked to the skin. But still he persisted at the edge of the island, kneeling in prayer, daring the ravening devils to come through the night and eat into his faith and try to feed off his belief and lessen it, destroy it.

He shivered and recited the psalms. He was ready for them. Let them all come. He had touched the cross on which His Lord had suffered and died for the sins of the whole world. Nothing on earth would ever be more precious to him. 'Thanks be to God,' he murmured, and then, aloud across the shadow-scudding lake, 'Thanks be to God!'

CHAPTER TWENTY-TWO

In late morning, Padric rode down to Caerel with Riderch and Urien, his brothers, and three of their men. It was a fine light grey morning, the views long and clear, the air refreshingly tangy about the face. The six men all armed and well horsed were a striking sight. There was a grandeur and confidence about them which caused heads to rise from dull and obstinate ploughs, children to run a few yards after them as the glint of spear tip and sword hilts flashed across the level fields and caught the eye. To the many enchained in work and most often prey to disease and misfortune, all these big well-fed, richly accoutred men were kings. Most of them felt proud of their warriors. For, however expensive to maintain, these men guarded them and promised them a better future.

A message had come from Erebert that he and Bega and the escorts would be in Caerel that day. Padric would have gone further to meet her but his brothers had only just returned and he had to talk to them at length before racing off to collect his bride.

The three of them rode well together. Padric, the middle brother, had emerged as the strongest. In single combat the much broader and stronger Riderch could well have clubbed him down, but he was neither as fast nor as cunning as Padric. Urien was more Padric's build and even faster with a sword, but he lacked the wiry stamina and the athletic agility of his older brother. In neither case had it been put to the test. What mattered more was that neither cared as much as Padric about his mission.

Riderch's easy good nature had eventually been enrolled by Padric's fierce vision. Urien's lazy, cynical, personal sense of the satisfaction of battle meant that he was quite prepared and amused to follow his dedicated brother – as long as the path led to action.

Padric could scarcely wait to see Bega. In his mind's eye she now seemed to be perfection. Her thinness of face was a distinguished slenderness. The wild tumult of her hair was evidence of the passion and vitality of the youthful Bega. The faded blue of the eyes was far more subtle and intriguing than the standard, pebble-hard blue of the Irish beauty.

He knew Bega's mettle and had no doubt that her martial qualities would bring them a family of great warriors and scholars. But the scholarly, even the religious part of his life was losing out to the military feeling which now governed most of his thoughts.

He would first settle the marriage business. Riderch was married. Urien preferred to find prostitutes or willing slaves. Padric wanted a family to continue the line. Caerel was the place to meet.

The town was well positioned. The broad and richly stocked river flowed between two hillocks which breasted the waters. The Romans had chosen well and put a fortress on each one of them and even now, three hundred years after they had left the northern garrison town, enough remained to reveal how doughty those legions had been. The town was the most splendid for many, many miles around. Nothing that the new invaders had built could begin to compare with it. The river took boats down to the sea, and trade came not only from Ireland and Cornwall but from warm countries in the south, from ports near Rome and markets in the east, near Jerusalem itself.

There were still shrines to local Celtic gods. Balatucadros, who had held his power since before the Romans arrived, continued to attract worshippers. Altars to the Roman gods – Jupiter, Juno and Mars – had survived too, ruined but potent. Again they had their worshippers. The whole town had been linked by roads south and east and these, unrepaired as they were, remained the best routes to follow.

It was here that the first Urien, Padric's great-grandfather, had been born, hence his name 'city-born'; and before him, it was here that Arthur had raised his court. Though fallen away somewhat, the city was a thriving marvel in the middle of an abundant plain. When Padric rode to Caerel he felt that he was, in truth, riding into the heart of his kingdom.

Bega thought she would not reach the town. She had stuck to her word but Erebert could see the strain. He had offered to go on alone but she had insisted on following the original plan. Besides, she wanted to see Padric.

Once again the sledge was employed, but after a mile or so she was so bumped by it that she asked to be put side-saddle on the quietest horse. The soldiers were smaller than Padric, rather squat, not armed to the most expensive degree but certainly more furnished with deadly weapons than any they were likely to encounter. One of them had already offered to escort Erebert back from Caerel to his island. He was much impressed by the holiness of the spindly hermit and saw virtue and otherworldly reward rubbing off on him for this deed.

The hermit felt nervous. Prayers seemed impotent to calm his fear, heightened now by the heavy, head-clogging cold which had possessed him after his night of prayer. His loud sneezes became a joke between the soldiers and they mimicked him, to Chad's embarrassed delight.

One of the soldiers led the horse to which Bega increasingly clung. Soon he was alongside her and employing one hand in holding her steady. Chad walked along on the other side with Cal, ready for any fall or fainting. Their pace was slow.

When they left the mountains, Bega felt even weaker. This lush spread before her was alien ground. She saw no rocks, no steep sides, no stony acres, no reassuring barrenness to remind her of her childhood in Connachta. Only the verdant carpets of field and budding woods in which there nestled hundreds of strangers distinguishable by the multitudinous waverings of smoke coming from constantly burning fires. Some had been alight in those same households for generations. But it was all too open and exposed, as she felt herself to be. Where were the hiding places?

They stayed over in a firmly built inn which had recently received Padric, and Bega was given the respect accorded to him. It seemed to Bega that the talk around the fire was desultory. These were people who found themselves in a bleak world of work and little else save for the ills that were so readily visited on them. She found their dialect too raw, little learning in the talk, too much cruel evidence of disease in wretched deformities – a leprous face, a crushed hand, deeply pocked skin; and dirt even thicker than on the slaves she had known in Ireland. Used to the comparative wealth and ease bought by Cathal's successful looting, and the rather fastidious society of the hermit on the island, Bega shrank from what she saw as the coldness of the people. Their attitude chilled her as much as the damp night air and she yoked them together in her apprehension of this place which would bring her no good. There is no grace here, she thought.

Her sleep was restless. Chad scarcely slept at all, hearing her moans. Erebert translated the sounds into the menace of wild beasts and he too was sleep-broken and shivering from his cold in the dour and crowded inn. They left at dawn.

By now, Bega's stomach was in constant pain and the blood-soaked images of her last night in Ireland began to mingle with the daze of her unhappy thoughts, which no prayers seemed able to clarify or dispel.

❧❧❧❧

The young man in the market place, his hair a striking gold worn in the Celtic style of tonsure like Donal and Erebert, shaved at the front from ear to ear giving him a high-domed aspect, appeared effortlessly to gather up the souls of all who were listening to him; and to point them straight towards heaven.

Cuthbert, not yet thirty years old, was on a mission from his monastery at Melrose and had come across country to Caerel, at the request of King Oswy's fervently Christian wife. She had promised him property in the area which had bred her. At the end of a strenuous mission in the hills beyond the Roman wall, Cuthbert had come to inspect his latest bequest. But as always, he took the opportunity to preach.

His custom was to find a suitable location and wait there until his fellow monks had collected a congregation from around the

district. The congregation would be encouraged to bring simple
gifts of unleavened bread, berries, roots, fish perhaps, some milk.
Cuthbert would make a point of eating nothing until he had
preached the word of God and attempted to bring to God all
the doubting and heathen souls before him. Only when his work
was done would he take some food and that would be as little as
he could manage.

Erebert had left Bega in a house nearby where two nuns from the
just established mixed house were taking care of her. He had been
unable to contain his patience any longer. Chad would come and
tell him if there was anything more he could do for her. Meanwhile
he had to go and join the throng around the golden-haired man.

He had been drawn here and to this holy man, he knew, by a
power which would shape his life and his death. As he listened, he
heard words that he had always wanted to say. He felt a conviction
in the voice that he had always longed to have. Glancing about him
he saw a devotion he had always longed to deserve. He surrendered
to the presence of the man who spoke with the tongue of an angel.
Others too were in his power. They swayed. They picked up and
repeated key words. 'Amen,' they said and 'Praise the Lord' and
'Thanks be to God.'

This was the biggest town Cuthbert had visited on his current
mission. Usually he sought out the most inaccessible settlements
deep in the hills where little traffic of men or news ever penetrated.
There he had converted family after family, sometimes whole
tribes in a day. Often, King Oswy and Queen Rhiainfellt had
made him a gift of lands in those remote places, knowing that one
day he would attach them to a monastery and see that they were
held secure. King Oswy saw political advantage in that security.
He was happy to reward such an ally. Thus as he spread the word
of the Lord, Cuthbert's own wealth grew.

Cuthbert was ashamed of his love of wealth and strove against
the lust it drew from him. As envy was the bane of Erebert, so was
the love of wealth the splinter in Cuthbert's soul. So far he had
reassured himself by adding the new lands to the lands held by
the monastery at Melrose, though they were still held in his name.
This was no sin but he recognised it as a weakness, which was why
already – though so young – he wanted, like the Prophet Jeremiah,
to 'sit in solitude and be silent, because he will raise himself above
himself.'

It was the hermit's life he addressed in the market place and, as the crowd thickened – some of them climbing on to the pillars of the old Roman forum, some on to the thatched roofs, children on the shoulders of fathers, other children wriggling through the crowd to be at the front – Cuthbert decided that he would preach all through the day until the sun set. This was a place of conquests and he too would have a victory here. He had heard that Prince Ecfrith, who had been more open-handed to him than all the other princes, was in the vicinity. Word of such a feat would soon reach him.

Erebert's radiant attentiveness and the respect paid to him by several in the crowd, who knew that he was the hermit on the island in the lake, soon drew one of Cuthbert's disciples to him. He quickly discovered all he needed to know from the enraptured hermit. Erebert's blessing, he decided, would greatly reinforce and help Cuthbert. Erebert was reluctant.

'I do not want to be known,' he said. 'Even though the Lord brought me here expressly to see this Cuthbert and as I now understand to learn from him.'

'Let me take you up to him,' urged the disciple. 'He will revere your sanctity and ask only for your blessing.'

'No,' said Erebert, strung out between some satisfaction at the flattery and a firm resistance inside himself which he respected.

'He will preach until the sun has set,' the disciple said. 'Let me take you aside, as I can see that you are a holy man of God, and tell you something about this man the Lord has sent you to serve.'

Grudgingly, Erebert allowed himself to be led to a vast pillar a few yards away from the crowd. The disciple was lame from a slashed tendon but looked strong. Straining, Erebert tried to hear the sweet clear voice of Cuthbert. Very soon, however, all his words were muffled by the bombastic recitation of Cuthbert's life which was poured scalding hot into his ear. Despite his initial resistance, Erebert was swept up into the story of the man who would soon outsoar even Aidan in his private pantheon.

The sound not only of Cuthbert but of the town itself seemed to fade away. Dogs no longer seemed to howl, the squawking of geese was muted, the cries of children, the hammer at the forge, the hooves of horses, the sighs and acclaim of the crowd became like the lapping at the lakeshore as Erebert's miracle-hungry soul received the full benefit of the life of Cuthbert.

'When he was still a boy Cuthbert's leg was seized with great pain,' the monk began. 'Much as mine is now,' he pointed out. 'No one could cure it and he had to limp everywhere. Mostly, though, he lay in the house of his father and one day his servant took him out – Cuthbert came from a noble family – because the day was so fine. A horseman dressed in white approached on a noble stallion. He asked for hospitality. Cuthbert said, "I would give you all the hospitality in my father's house, but I am crippled by this knee. My sins have pinned me down. No doctor can cure it." The horseman looked at it and said, "Boil some wheaten flour in milk and bathe the tumour with it hot and you will be healed." Then he rode away. Cuthbert did as he was told and soon his knee was healed. Then he knew that the horseman was an angel, just as God sent the archangel Raphael to cure Tobias's eyes. This was the first real miracle.'

'Thanks be to God,' Erebert murmured. 'Praise the Lord.'

The monk added a prayer for his own lameness. Then he went on. 'When in the last days of his youth, Cuthbert was with some shepherds watching his father's sheep in the hills, he suddenly saw light come down from the clouds like a celestial stairway. Heaven opened. He heard the singing of choirs. He saw a host of angels white as the moon come down to earth and gather in a soul and take it back into the heavens which closed over and shut out the light. Only Cuthbert had kept vigil and seen these things and it was this which told him he had to enter a monastery – which he did the next day. It was then that he learned the soul he had seen gathered in was the soul of Aidan.'

Aidan. Erebert was transfixed. He asked the young man to repeat that story and bring as much detail to it as he could. At what hour did Cuthbert begin the vigil? What prayers did he use? Were the shepherds men who believed? What sort of countryside was it – was it especially high, for instance, so that it would be nearer to God? To see the soul of Aidan gathered up by angels! Erebert could scarcely believe it. Yet another blessing had been granted to him: to see and hear a man to whom God had given such distinction.

There was more. 'It was Cuthbert, still a youth, who was chosen by Bishop Bois to read to him during the last week of his death. They read, with a commentary, the book of St John the Evangelist, and during that time Bois said that Cuthbert would be a bishop.

Cuthbert himself always wanted the hermit's life. He longed for a solitary rock in the middle of the wild ocean to be free from the cares of the world,' said the red-faced priest, as he thought, cunningly. And this was why he would want to meet Erebert.

First Erebert prayed. A man who had seen the soul of Aidan go into paradise! He was persuaded.

The two men went through the crowd. The disciple pushed and shoved and called out 'Make way for the hermit!' in far too loud a voice. But no one seemed to mind save Erebert himself. The disciple went forward and whispered to Cuthbert, who then came across to Erebert. Erebert held out his hands. The handsome preacher made him feel much older than his years. Cuthbert suddenly kneeled down in front of him.

'You, Erebert, are living the life I long to live. These worldly demands and gifts hold me from my goal. Prophecies tell of my being a bishop, but I want no more than has been granted to you. I ask for your blessing. With your help I may succeed.'

In that instant, Erebert became a disciple. He wanted to extend his hand and let it hover over the blond head of Cuthbert – the frontal Celtic tonsure was more than compensated for by the flow of hair at the back – but no words came. The crowd, impressed and surprised at the abasement of this imposing messianic preacher at the feet of the ragged, rather sickly looking hermit, fell silent and waited to see how the drama would develop.

Cuthbert had fallen to his knees on a particularly hard jut of old Roman paving stone which jabbed into his still rather vulnerable knee. He praised the Lord for the pain.

Erebert was unable to act. He wanted a sign. He was being asked by someone who would surely sit on the right hand of God and enjoy the communion of saints to give him his blessing. He had been asked to help a man of miracles.

He looked up into the solid grey sky above Cuthbert and thought he detected a ray of yellow light struggling to free itself through the obscuring mass. Could that be a messenger of God trying to reach him? The clouds seemed to loosen and Erebert's hand pointed upwards. The crowd followed his gesture. Cuthbert was patient. The pavement dug even more insistently into his knee.

The clouds closed over. The sun was wholly blocked out. Erebert swallowed his disappointment and in that movement of the throat found voice.

'I bless you in the name of God and of Jesus Christ and His saints,' he began, firmly now that he was about God's work, 'that you will cast your net wide and bring in many souls to the Lord. That your name will ride in glory long after your earthly death and be an inspiration to those who follow Christ. We ask you to help us, sinners as we are, to reach the Heavenly reward which surely will be yours.' Erebert turned to the crowd, some of whom were already kneeling. 'All kneel,' he ordered them, discovering an authority.

The crowd did as he told them.

Erebert put his hand on Cuthbert's head. 'I ask you to pray for the soul of this man Cuthbert. We pray for thy soul.'

'We pray for thy soul.' The murmur of responses in guttural thick dialect came fervently from the crowd, a low, single, rather bestial voice from the belly of the mass.

'We ask to be remembered in Heaven.'

'. . . Remembered in Heaven.'

'We will do His will according to the word brought by thee. Pray to do His will.'

'We pray to do His will.'

The power left Erebert as unexpectedly and swiftly as it had come. He felt faint and, as Cuthbert rose up, he all but fell to his knees. Their heads bumped together. Cuthbert held him. After a moment, Erebert recovered himself and stood free.

Cuthbert looked around at the bent backs of the crowd. Behind it some horsemen sat looking at him. A swell of power threatened him and, despite his internal prayers to beware vanity, the feeling flowed through him. All these bodies and souls would be won to God by him. To deflate this mood of unworthy triumphalism, he turned to Erebert.

'What can I give you in return?' asked Cuthbert.

'I want to die at the same moment as you,' Erebert answered: the reply was prompt and sure and it came from he did not know where. 'Then you might help me into our Father's House.'

'That would be a miracle which only He can give.'

'I know,' said Erebert, 'that is what I will pray for. Will you?'

'I will,' Cuthbert replied, after a due pause. Softly he repeated, 'I will,' and Erebert's hopes soared.

'Thank you.' Erebert took Cuthbert's hand and kissed it. It was a small hand, he noticed, and only very lightly calloused. 'We will pray together.'

'Now I must continue to preach,' said the young man.

'One other request,' said Erebert and, aware of a tremor of dispatch in Cuthbert, he hurried on, 'I have with me a princess from a holy place in Ireland. She is unwell and in great pain. She is on her way to marry a prince of Rheged and would, I know, be made whole in health again were you to see her.'

Cuthbert turned to the crowd and said 'I promised that I would stand on this spot and preach the word of God until the sun sets. I promised that I would explain the parables of the lost sheep, of the talents, of the prodigal son and many others. Now the hermit Erebert has asked me to see someone who is sick and who may be helped by Our Lord through me. Will you let me go and see this woman and then return to you? I ask your permission.'

No one talked to them like that. Almost everyone in the crowd had spent a lifetime receiving orders. This dashing young man's humble request struck them as further proof of his uniqueness. A ragged salute of assenting voices let him go.

Erebert led him to the building in which he had left Bega.

The crowd followed and would have invaded the dark stone space itself had not the several disciples – most of them brawny young men like the lame monk who had spoken to Erebert – held them back. They jostled, but kept voices low, straining to hear what was being said, longing to be present at what could be a miracle.

Cuthbert looked down at the girl, for such Bega now seemed. Her face had a dark tinge but the illness and the pain had paled it. Her hair, thick and long, spread out around her rather small pinched face, a bounty of red and dark waves and curls, itself a pillow. In the crook of her right arm she nursed a large pup which looked beseechingly at Cuthbert. Beyond her was a boy, nervously stoking the fire to distract himself. He too, after Erebert's quick description of Cuthbert and his powers, looked puppy-like at him. The two nuns had made Bega as comfortable as they could. Cuthbert heard their whispered opinion in silence.

'Will you allow me to touch the place where the pain has been sent?'

Bega nodded. The pain was sharp now and insistent. Her stomach felt vastly swollen yet when she touched it, it was no great size. Her mind felt fevered and yet on her brow was only the merest dapple of sweat. She was frightened at what she could not understand and wondered why Padric was so late.

This young monk appeared to be a good man. His cold hand pressed on her stomach. His fingers were slender, his hand did not seek out the pain but touched on it, lightly.

'Did it hurt on the sea crossing?'

'No.'

'Were you ill then?'

'I was.'

'But not with this pain?'

'Not with this pain.'

Cuthbert nodded sombrely. 'Erebert tells me that God led you and Prince Padric to a cave in the rock.'

'We were led there.'

'Do you remember what happened there?'

'Yes. I was in a great fever and Padric nursed me.'

'And then you came to Erebert's island?'

'We did.'

'Was that journey difficult for you?'

'It was.'

'And the journey to Caerel – that too?'

'It was.'

'God is there,' said Cuthbert, looking at her intently.

He raised his eyes and put his hands in a steeple of prayer. Then he kneeled beside her and took her hand in his. She felt a tide of warmth in her body. His face tightened in concentration. Erebert too dropped to his knees as did the nuns and Chad.

The room appeared to hum with an invisible energy which emanated from Cuthbert. There was no denying the monk's force. The enclosed space seemed to throb as his lips now and then moved, intimation of his silent, intense prayer. Later, Erebert was to remember a particular delicate presence brushing against his body and be ready, almost, to swear that angels had descended to help Cuthbert in his holy work. The atmosphere was such that Chad felt the hairs on the back of his neck lift as they had only before lifted in terror in the woods. Cal kept whimperingly unobtrusive.

Cuthbert himself felt hollow. Within him was an imperative. His concentration became a white light in his head; the darkness in front of his hard-closed eyes turned to blood red and he saw blood pouring from a wounded neck, blood covering the long garment of a saint, blood pouring over Bega. He prayed for her to be saved to dedicate herself to Christ.

When he had done, he said, 'You will be safe, Bega, but there is much blood about you. Is there not?'

'There is,' Bega sobbed. She held Cal even more tightly and he whimpered a little.

'The blood has to flow,' he said. 'The blood has to flow to cleanse the sins of the lamb. You must stay with these nuns until that is done. I do not know,' said Cuthbert, 'what blood it is; but I see it before me just as a raw sunset sometimes shows the agony of the failing light. But once it is gone we have perfect darkness; for you to reach a more perfect state, there has to be what I have prophesied.'

Bega licked dry lips. She was so helpless. Where was Padric? How could she defend herself if the O'Neills sent over men to find and kill her? She had no sword, her dagger would be useless, Chad could not fight. She was too weak. She tried to sit up, to disprove her weakness, but even that small effort was too much for her and she fell back.

'I will see you tomorrow,' said Cuthbert. 'Let us talk more then.'

He left and stopped at the door. While he had been inside, the crowd had reorganised itself so that the sick and lame were gathered at the front. There was a young gaunt man of shaven skull repellently disfigured by warts on his face, his hands and, for all Cuthbert knew, on every other inch of flesh. A large woman stood next to him, her misshapen head as it were balanced on a pumpkin of flesh, a goitre the size of a duck's egg. Beside her, a child – or was it a shrivelled young woman? – was raised from the ground on two twig arms, the equally thin and useless legs dragging behind her. There was a blind girl and an old lumpish straggle-bearded man held between two women, white as bleach and shaking from a recent attack of falling sickness. As Cuthbert stepped out into the light, they and others moved forward to touch him, to grip his hand, to be healed.

The young noble-monk steeled himself against the stench of the afflictions and the horror confronting him. He forced down a sickly heave of revulsion, his weakness, as he saw it, when unexpectedly faced by such brutal evidence of the misery of the earthly world.

He opened his arms wide and those nearest nuzzled up to him. He did not flinch and let his arms close around them.

'We must pray for all the sick. For Princess Bega, for those I see before me now, for those in torment elsewhere – let us pray for them and as the day brings more prayer perhaps it may be given us to help some of these so blemished and stricken.' He let his head fall forward and began to recite the Lord's Prayer. Soon the words murmured about the crowd, a communion of hope.

Cuthbert moved slowly through the crowd – touching, blessing, holding – finally back to the stone steps he had stood on in the market place. The crowd once more grouped around him. Immediately he launched into the story of Lazarus and explained why only Christ could command such a miracle. He had read the commentary on Lazarus written by a holy monk at Melrose and used this to amplify his talk. He also called on local instances which he had heard of on his way to Caerel. Two of his monks had come before him and gathered information and gossip, stories which wove their way into his words and gave veracity and deep local comfort to his evangelism. For at one moment they were in the Holy Land with the apostles and the next they were beside their own river or in the villages with names they recognised.

Although the day was fresh, Cuthbert wore only the flimsiest sandals on his feet which were blue with unacknowledged cold. His woollen gown was dirty from travel and overuse. His face was slim from the severe fast he had set himself. But out of this figure, almost singing his words – powered by quotations in Latin – as he swayed through the hours, came a message which penetrated the hearts and minds of all of them.

Erebert spent only a few minutes longer with Bega and then came out. He felt as if he were carrying a vessel of priceless wine, full to the brim. Were he to put a foot or a thought wrong, he would spill and waste some of this precious liquid. He was the vessel; the wine was the spirit poured into him by Cuthbert. This was the day he had met a miracle-worker and might indeed have witnessed a miraculous prophecy. He had been given the courage to make a plea for a future miracle of his own. He had to tread most carefully for he felt he was treading in the footprints of godliness.

chapter twenty-three

When Padric and his brothers saw Caerel they whipped on their horses. It was late into the afternoon. They had been diverted by one of the few wealthy noblemen in the area who had insisted on giving them bread and cheese and mead. It was a casual act of hospitality but even so it could not be rushed. Padric had hidden his impatience with difficulty. His brothers had noticed this and smiled at each other and softly chaffed him about Bega.

It was undeniable. The nearer he got to her, the more ardently he thought of her and the more unbearable her absence seemed. She was in his mind all the time. He was never more than a thought away from her. Had it been like this since he met her? Perhaps it had. But in Ireland he had been sure of seeing her and being with her. He remembered the way in which he had persuaded himself – and so easily – that Bega had been no more than a pupil, at the very most a friendly younger sister, but no one to cherish. He shuddered at his flirtation with Maeve, for mild though it had been it must have hurt Bega. It would not have escaped her.

As he galloped the last stretch to the twin heights of the town, he cast away all care. His face into the wind, his favourite horse, the men beside and behind him, so much to be done, what life could be better than his? The woman he loved waited for him in a city he would one day make the capital of his people once again.

They went through runnelled streets, twisted through the crowds and parted the strutting army of merchants, visitors, townsfolk, traders, children, beggars, craftsmen, all making a market of every turn and corner of the city. In the centre, they reined in at the edge of Cuthbert's congregation and twitched their country noses at the particular odour of the town. Ragged, dirty-faced boys appeared to look after the horses and they dismounted, in their usual style, cocking one leg in front of the other and sliding idly off the bare back as if the whole business were an absent-minded afterthought. Padric spotted Erebert slightly swaying, from fatigue, and went straight to him to find out where Bega was lodged. Erebert gave him that and other information and Padric left immediately, not hearing more than a few sentences from the preacher.

The others decided to listen a while. They had their own business to transact in Caerel but there was time and they would meet up later.

The house was not difficult to find.

Bega opened her eyes, immediately smelling his presence, and her smile, her sweet, open smile shot through him like a fire arrow lighting up the dark. He kneeled beside her and she levered herself up to be taken in his arms.

On the other side of the fire Chad grinned happily. Cal licked Padric's face. The nuns smiled to each other, recognising a positive potion when they saw one.

'Are you still unwell?'

'She is in great pain,' said one of the nuns.

'I am much better now,' said Bega, feeling light, even giddy.

'Why did you travel if you were in pain?'

'That's right. You tell her.'

'I had been too long – away—' 'from you' was unsaid, but so plainly implied that Padric preferred the privacy of its being unspoken.

'She is pining half to death.'

'I am much better now.' Bega eased herself back. She hoped that by doing it slowly she would be better able to bear it, but its signal could not be deflected from her face.

'You are not at all better,' said Padric.

Oh, but I am, Bega wanted to say. She tried to convey it in her eyes. I am whole since you entered the room and looked so keenly and directly at me and made me feel as I know you feel – with the force of that love the poets sometimes sing about, the love that made the heroes go and fight for their women against dragons and giants, the love that made the women themselves strong.

Padric leaned forward to help her settle. Had he understood what she had left unsaid? 'Live for the faith' – where was that?

The pain returned vividly and she groaned deeply.

'Is there nothing you can do?'

'We have applied all the herbs and compresses that we know,' replied the younger of the nuns anxiously.

'Erebert spoke to me of blood.'

'Yes. But Cuthbert is preaching in the market place. God has granted him many miracles and Erebert brought him here. He came – himself,' the nun still tingled from the contact with Cuthbert, 'and kneeled and prayed with the princess. It was he who spoke of blood.'

'And of safety,' said the other. 'She will be safe.'

'What is this blood?'

He looked at Bega. She shook her head. All her might was concentrated on getting herself through this pain. Whose blood was he talking about?

Padric too remembered vividly the slaughter in Cathal's household.

Her face was now glossy with sweat.

'I will give her some more of this,' said one of the women and went to the fire to take the pan of gruel.

'Let me feed her,' Padric said. He could not bear to do nothing and besides, 'I fed her once before.'

Bega nodded and knew that he was telling her that she had suffered and recovered then and would do so again. Because it was Padric, she swallowed two spoonfuls but that was all she could manage. To hide the struggle from him, she closed her eyes.

In her thoughts she saw Padric, or rather she sensed the form and presence of Padric enveloping everything she did. Padric was the warmth she had. Padric was safety. Padric was everything that was not this dagger-point now slaving to reach a peak of agony. Padric was the faith.

God must understand. God would understand. She would serve Him always but she had to live with Padric. She was a miserable sinner and too weak for the high purpose of which she had thought herself worthy. Padric was . . . Padric . . . the warm presence of Padric, the two mouthfuls of warm gruel worked on her . . . she took refuge in a short oblivious half-sleep, half-swoon.

Padric waited until he saw that she was in a deep sleep.

Then he went out to conduct some business. On his way back, he passed by the market place and stopped. The crowd was still as big as it had been, perhaps even bigger. Many were now seated on the ground. Some, like Erebert, were kneeling. Cuthbert stood on the few steps – once perhaps the steps into a well-proportioned town-house. Behind him the disciple who had importuned Erebert held a large wooden cross. The other four monks flanked Cuthbert, two on each side, holding pages from the gospels.

Across the crowd, Padric saw Riderch and the soldiers, as engaged as everyone else. Urien had gone off to see the woman he usually saw when he came to Caerel and not even a thunderbolt would bring him out until he had satiated his appetite.

The sun, pale yellow and bright, was setting. The heavy press of cloud had moved east; an open sky had followed with just a few long-sided, grey canoes of cloud sailing along.

'Just as our light goes out of this world to a darkness we may deserve, so God sends the sun over the edge of the world every day. By night it lights up the fires of hell and the damned are roasted time and again in its flames. You have sat in the sun on a hot day. You have felt it burn your face. How much more would it burn were you to be next to it. Remember what Judas said when he met St Brendan.' Cuthbert drove himself to bring in these souls before the sun set.

'Tomorrow I shall baptise those who believe. Tomorrow, at dawn, at the river, I shall use the power invested in me by bishops, holy men who themselves were baptised by bishops going back to the sacred apostles. I can guide you towards the true path. Through me you will be given a footing on the Christian way.' The murmurs grew as the twilight stole over the town and the crowd realised that hope was now being extended to them.

'Tomorrow I shall bring ointments for those poor sinful creatures who have offended God in some way and been stricken in body. First find the sin, I say, then repent and God will chase it out. Hound it away until it is frightened of you. Make your will so strong and your body so strong that no sin can enter in. "Let no sin enter here" is what you must say, daily, what all of us must say. For you must help me as I must help you. And then, by the power invested in me, I will try to heal what I can heal: I will heal what God will let me heal. Amen.'

'Amen!' 'Amen!' 'Amen!' The word tolled around the square, a joyous resolution, the sound of a promise. 'Amen!' 'Amen!'

Cuthbert extended his arms and stood motionless.

The sun slid, sudden, swift, below the horizon.

The crowd moved towards Cuthbert to touch his hand, his garments, his feet. After a few minutes his disciples formed a cordon around him and reassured the crowd he would be by the river at dawn. Eventually the people began to move away, praising God, and already recounting what they had seen in terms miraculous. Erebert, shaking from cramp, limped slowly back to the house where Bega lay.

The town began to settle. The fires stabbed into the dark, the dogs took over the streets, and the sounds of the night grew steadily, wolf-howl, ghost cry, until finally they encircled and sealed in the enduring fortress-town.

ChAPTER TWENTY-FOUR

'Cuthbert would like to talk to you,' said Erebert.
Padric was looking at a set of reins. The price was high
but the man had studded them with small circles of copper and
semi-precious stones which would glitter majestically in the sun.
He wanted to buy them for Bega. Erebert's intrusion decided him
and he settled for the price they had negotiated. They walked
slowly through the debris in the empty twisting lanes. Erebert
was carrying a rushlight.

'Did you hear him preach?'

'Some of it.'

'He spoke from midday to sunset and he had begun before
midday. The only time he stopped was to visit Bega. Have you
visited her?'

For some reason, Erebert's instant idolisation of the new man
exasperated Padric. Of course he had seen Bega!

'Yes,' he replied, brusquely.

'Cuthbert prayed with her. I could see that she was greatly
moved by it. So could the nuns. To have the prayers of a man
as holy as Cuthbert! What an honour he did her!'

'Is he far away?'

'Quite near where Bega rests. Are you resting here for the
night?'

Where would he go without Bega and how could he take her
until she recovered her health? He took time to calm himself.
Erebert was a good man.

'I shall stay until Bega is well enough to travel with me.'

'You know,' said Erebert, shyly, offering his own evidence, 'I
had a most terrible cold when I began listening to Cuthbert. When
he had finished speaking, it was almost gone.'

Padric nodded.

They reached the building in which Cuthbert and his men were housed. It was one of the biggest and strongest buildings in the town. The pillars were almost untouched since the Romans had departed. The face of the building was elaborately decorated and the pagan figures could still be distinguished clearly.

Cuthbert was in the hall, eating nothing, sipping a cup of wine. He sat a little apart from the others. The monks, unable to sustain his self-denying regime, were eating more amply. The owner of the house, who owed allegiance to Padric, offered him food but Padric had already eaten. He took a cup of wine. The owner moved to join the others, leaving Cuthbert and Padric together.

'I want to thank you for the help and relief you brought to Princess Bega today.'

'I was able to do very little. She is in great pain. God will decide.'

'She is safe, though, isn't she?' Immediately, Padric found that he needed this man's reassurance, though he was not so very much older than himself.

'Yes. I believe she is safe. But the worst is to come.'

Padric stood up. 'In that case I must go to her.'

'She is sleeping,' said Cuthbert. 'I asked for some seeds which I carry to be put in her gruel. They will help numb the pain.'

'Are you sure?'

'I am sure.'

Cuthbert took a delicate sip of wine and considered Padric carefully. The resemblance to Ecfrith was superficially remarkable. But – Cuthbert had to admit, although Ecfrith was one of his best patrons – Padric's features were finer in every point, his posture more athletic. He was easier in his skin. Despite his present anxiety, there was a charm, Cuthbert could see that, and it would serve him well.

Padric could not fathom why he did not like this man.

'I am much honoured by the patronage of Princess Aetheldreda who is married to Prince Ecfrith who is your cousin?'

'He is.'

Instantly Cuthbert knew how the land lay. He had his own personal reservations about Ecfrith, but Ecfrith was forever telling him of his alliance with the true God and Cuthbert rightly saw him as a valuable and enabling convert. There was faith and there was the business of faith. He pressed on. 'There is a real resemblance between yourself and your cousin.'

'In looks only, I hope.'

Cuthbert nodded. He was surprised that Padric was prepared to be blunt to a stranger. The dislike must be deep.

'He was recently in these parts?'

'Yes. That was our misfortune.'

Hotheaded, Cuthbert thought, but there was iron there and the impulsive boy could grow into a formidable man. He would have liked him for a friend.

'Was he here to collect tribute?'

'Why should we pay tribute?'

Padric could not even begin to admit that tribute was paid at all.

'I am not the man to ask.'

'You are a holy man, a friend of Ecfrith, you see his father Oswy and his wife, my aunt. Or is she just one of his wives now?'

Cuthbert shook his head slightly, indicating that he would not answer.

'Are they poor? Do they lack jewels? Do they need more cattle and wolfskins and sheep? Are their goats suddenly udderless that they have to send all the way to Rheged for goats?'

This conversation would be so welcome, Cuthbert knew, when Ecfrith asked him about his mission. Ecfrith always asked him about his missions. Nothing seemed too mean for his interest. Cuthbert and other monks under the patronage of the Northumbrian kings and princes sometimes went where the Court never trod. Their intelligence was greatly valued. But Cuthbert had always been most reluctant to play that game. He would give nothing away about Padric, he decided. Something in Padric's honourable openness of heart, his Christian openness, Cuthbert thought, made the monk ashamed of his few past favours to Ecfrith and he resolved to be no more considered a bearer of damaging tales.

Cuthbert wanted to cut through and speak some hard truths. He wanted to say to this blinkered young man, look: you have spent your life in a Christian household in Rheged or in Ireland where scholars and monks are more numerous and welcome and free than anywhere else on earth. I, Cuthbert, like Aidan before me, and all the others who move out of those precious protected corners, am engaged in battle. I am in the territory of the great enemy. The only way to survive is to make an alliance with the royal household. Only then can you begin to address whole populations who do not know God. Those royal families are fickle. Lose a battle, fail to produce a miracle and the avalanche of heathenism covers you up and buries the faith. God needs men like you, Cuthbert wanted to say, trained to fight in wars. He also needs men like me for his spiritual wars. I have to bow to earthly men although I do not want to bow; to smile when a smile freezes my mouth; to cosset and reassure because, without the backing of the Court, there is absolutely no hope for the handful of monks clinging to the sheer rock face of indifference. There is no need to hint to me of Ecfrith's failings. I know them. I try to help him to see the True Way. I try to guide him. But I cannot let him go because without Ecfrith there is no mission in this land and God has called me to bring His mission here. That is my duty and that is what I will do.

'He is a Christian,' was all he said, in fairness and rather wearily, although Padric did not recognise that.

'We in Rheged have been Christians since the days of Ninian and before,' said Padric, too haughtily. He was annoyed with himself for so publicly losing his temper.

'That is why it was so pleasing to do God's work here.'

We can do God's work on our own without messengers from Northumbria poking around, Padric thought. But this time he kept silent.

To Cuthbert he was transparent. The monk sighed. He would have preferred the young nobleman as a friend and patron. His example could move many of his subjects and their souls would add to the earthly power of God.

'Do you believe that there are none left to convert in your kingdom?' he asked, holding Padric's look, hard-eyed now.

Padric hesitated. That was not the point. 'Rheged has its people who have yet to come to God,' he conceded, testily.

'And how do you propose to help them?'

'We have just established a mixed house here. The monks and nuns will go on missions.'

'It is small and fragile,' said Cuthbert, almost dismissively. 'I will give it lands to make it stronger.'

'Rheged can give it all the land it needs.'

'We can work together.' Cuthbert was sincere and serious.

Padric was struggling. Abruptly he stood up. 'I must go now.'

Cuthbert stood up beside him. He was the same height as Padric but seemed a little taller because of his slighter frame.

'Will you come in the morning to the baptisms? I asked you here because I need you as an example to your people.' He reached out to touch Padric's arm, but Padric, by the merest tremor, betrayed his objection and Cuthbert did not persist. 'If they were to see a prince of the house of Rheged there and perhaps reaffirming your own baptism, they would clearly see God's work.'

It was a reasonable request, so why did he resent it? The man seemed to be able to hold you in an iron-fisted grip.

'I will be there if I can.'

'I pray that God puts nothing in your way.'

Bega may need me, Padric thought, but kept silent. He knew that Cuthbert, friend of Ecfrith, could be dangerous.

'I am pleased to have met you,' said Padric very stiffly.

You are trying to redeem what you fear was a costly loss of temper, thought Cuthbert. Let me try to reassure you. 'I am a guest in your land and I observe all the responsibilities of a guest. Gratitude is the first.' Loyalty is the second, he hoped he implied. Padric chose to ignore this. You do not believe that it is my land for a moment, was his silent reaction.

Padric went to the door and lit a rush to take him through the huddle-muddle of streets and spaces between buildings. Cuthbert watched him go with regret.

Padric found Bega's house again without difficulty. When he went in, the nun who was awake put her finger to her lips. Bega was still asleep. What she did not say was that Bega had woken up in severe pain and only the near force feeding of more of the seeds given by Cuthbert had sent her, just now, into this sweating, uneven slumber. Chad, still crouched by the fire, looked very frightened.

There was nowhere for Padric to sleep or lie down. He stayed a while. 'Call me,' he said eventually. He told Chad where he would be and left.

Outside, he tried in the cold air to cleanse his mind of the contact with Cuthbert. What sort of a commander would he be when he could be led to give away his feelings to a close ally of the enemy?

Padric's anger with himself was extreme. He would have to meet Cuthbert in the morning. He would think of some excuse to explain his surliness. He would find ways to be genial at least about his cousin Ecfrith and King Oswy. He would praise the chastity of Aetheldreda. He would start again with Cuthbert and before he met him he would talk deeply to Erebert: listen patiently; learn closely; accept that Cuthbert was a true man of God and powerful in the kingdom and needed to be regarded as such.

He could not sleep and so he stood at the door of the inn, looking into the blackness of the old town which had seen so much blood, held up against many a frenzied siege, been looted and restored and looted again. His gentle and profound love for Bega was overwhelmed by the agitations provoked by his mistakes. Like the moon, he thought, almost full, bright, calm, but scarcely able to shine through the congestion of clouds which hampered and hid it. He stood at the door until he could no longer bear his inactivity and, taking advantage of a break in the clouds, he set off through the streets.

Soon he came to the mounded rampart which faced north across the river to the other matching fortress and, beyond that, deep into the kingdom of Rheged and into the lands of the Picts. The moon was less hindered now and under the stars Padric could sense the ghosts of the town. All the warlords remained in their battle place.

Padric felt the force of them march through his mind as he stood and looked out on what had been the sovereign territory of famous ancestors. The cold wind on his cheeks seemed full of reproach.

CHAPTER TWENTY-FIVE

The bleeding began near dawn.

One of the nuns gave Bega a rag to bite on. The other took a pan of water off the fire and picked up strips of linen cloths. At first the older nun assumed it was a miscarriage. But there was too much blood. And the signs were not there.

Chad, who had finally surrendered to the weight of his fatigue, was cuffed awake and told to go for Cuthbert.

'Cuthbert?' He rubbed his eyes. 'No. Prince Padric.'

'Cuthbert,' said the more forceful woman. 'We need the man of God. Hurry!'

She is calling for Padric, Chad muttered to himself. Although the rag muted most of Bega's words, Chad could make out the low and desperate pulse of the name.

He went to where he knew Erebert slept. Erebert took him to Cuthbert who rose immediately and followed them on to the moon-shadowed streets. Chad still wanted to seek out Padric but he could not find him at the inn. He began a tentative search of the town on his way back, but the darkness confused him. He hurried back.

As he drew near the house his apprehension grew at the howl of Cal, which set off a yowling chorus of dogs right across the town. When he went in Chad looked at the dog as if to ask – is she so bad?

What if she were to die? The possibility almost felled the small boy.

'Muzzle that dog,' commanded Erebert.

Chad went over to Cal and took him in his arms. The pup was shivering. Chad whispered to him, and gently first, then firmly clamped his jaws tight. He strained to whimper, more like weeping, Chad thought. But the howl was gone and one by one those of the other dogs subsided.

Bega's gown was up to her waist. Her legs were apart. Blood seeped out of her. The thighs were streaked. The legs were newly washed but already more blood was streaming down them. One of the nuns knelt behind her and held her in a lock which was designed to stop her throwing herself around and bringing more injury on herself.

Her face poured sweat. The sounds from the ragged, gaped mouth were unearthly.

'It is the devil coming out of her,' said Cuthbert, decisively. 'He has taken possession and now she is attempting to throw him out.'

The nuns glanced briefly at each other and then lowered their heads in obedience.

'How did the devil find a way in?' He continued, ignoring them, 'That would be good to know. But she has great strength. See how she fights to cast him forth! See how her whole body shakes with the will of God! We must pray.' Cuthbert was on his knees, with Erebert, and both men pitched themselves into a fury of supplication.

'If she keeps bleeding like this,' said the older nun who was struggling to keep Bega in some sort of check, 'then she'll be dead, devil in or devil out. I've seen it before.'

Dead? The word came to Chad like a stone stunning his temple. He gave a small jump, a moan, and his hand left Cal's mouth. Once more Cal howled.

'Dog!' said Erebert. 'Dog – boy. Dog!'

Chad resumed his grip but now his mind was close to panic. What would he do without Bega? He could not go back. He saw that Cuthbert and Erebert were praying and he too began to pray, but all he could say was '*Deus, Deus, Deus*'.

'Padric,' she cried. 'Please tell Padric.'

'Padric will surely come when God has done His work,' said Cuthbert encouragingly. 'Boy – go and look for him once more and take the dog. Is the devil still in there?'

'Yes,' said Bega, gasping the words. 'I can feel him. He moves around. Now he stays quiet but just to catch me by surprise.'

Chad did as he was bid, almost suffocating Cal to keep him quiet.

'Have you any sin which you can tell God and weaken the evil? Any you have not told Him?'

Bega thought. She had confessed her harshness to Maeve, her disobedience to her father . . . all other sins were petty.

'I cannot—' The agony shot up into her and she yelled aloud. She wrestled with it and then again there was a snatch of calm. 'I cannot think of any other sins which would call up such a monster in me.'

'I can,' said Cuthbert, severely.

Bega looked at him. Then she glanced across at Erebert who looked away. Swayed by the power he felt in this young man, he had betrayed his word.

'You have been given the most sacred gift of all,' said Cuthbert. 'Is that not true?'

Bega paused for as long as she dared. This man was undoubtedly one of God's chosen, far above her, and she must obey.

'It is.' Bega whispered now. She sensed the outcome and she feared it. Perhaps if she spoke softly he would be kind to her. She was terrified of his sudden power: he seemed to speak directly to her soul.

'Where is it?'

Bega found it in the disarray of her clothing.

Reverently, Cuthbert unbound it. When the fragment was revealed, he pressed it to his forehead and kneeled over until his forehead touched the ground.

'Oh Lord, my God,' he said. 'I feel your suffering. Oh Lord, my God, the blood on this cross is more than all the blood spilt and shed since that cruel and evil day for with this blood You washed away our sins. My life is now complete. I praise and worship Your almighty continuing goodness to one such as me.'

Cuthbert stood up and held out the fragment in front of him. Bega looked up in fear. What she saw was such a strange expression. It was so savage. Almost like lust. Lust for this fragment of the cross.

'No one now,' said Cuthbert – and his glance practically sawed Erebert in half – 'will ever mention this – no one.'

He looked at the transfixed nuns whose heads dropped immediately. They would not talk. 'If you speak of this,' said Cuthbert, who had known right away that the fragment was a source of tremendous power, 'then God will use His strong right arm to smite you down in the fullness of your sins so that you will burn in hell for eternity.' The piece of the cross was too important to allow it to become – as it would – a focus of worship for the many who would then treat Bega as a figure of sanctity. She must retain it, of course. Cuthbert was clear about that: it was the will of God. But it must be kept secret until its true meaning was properly decided. That was imperative. It was miraculous. It had to be used at precisely the right time and in the right way for the furtherance of God's Kingdom on earth. Now – in a rage of sincere religious wrath – he turned on Bega and exercised on her all his untempered authority. The room, Erebert felt, seemed literally to quake.

'You have denied this,' said Cuthbert, angrily. 'You have been given this greatest of gifts and you have denied it in your desire for Padric.'

'I have denied nothing,' contradicted Bega, weak as she was. 'Surely God will understand.'

'You were selected from among all men and women to be given this which came from a visitation by the Virgin Mary Herself. This was a message to tell you to give yourself wholly and only to God.' In this Cuthbert found his bedrock. 'But you have disobeyed His clear command, this heavenly promise of eternal life, this most beautiful gift. You have rejected it for a son of man.'

'God gave Mary to Joseph,' said Bega.

'Are you to be compared with Mary?'

'No,' Bega sobbed. 'No, no. But it is possible to serve God and to have an earthly marriage.'

'Not for you,' said Cuthbert, solemnly. 'Not for you. Because the devil has got in you and he knows more than anyone when there is a—'

Bega's scream struck him dumb. The gag was clumsily rammed back in her mouth and a glob of blood and other matter heaved out of Bega. The more she writhed against the grip on her, the more this seemed to serve to spasm forth more of the dark pottage.

Erebert closed his eyes.

Cuthbert stared, unblinking, watching for the devil.

The attack was over, all over. Bega was greatly weakened but Cuthbert was relentless.

'You must dedicate your life to God,' said Cuthbert. 'That is what He expects. You must do it now.'

'Let me talk to Padric.' Bega pleaded feebly, tearfully. 'He will
help me.' There was water, it seemed, in her head, which seemed
to swim and float. The agony was gone but the part of her body
which had hurt so much now seemed so far away that it might
have belonged to someone else.

Cuthbert's face was beside her own. 'You must look at me.'

She turned and saw his handsome, gaunt face almost transfig-
ured with intense concern.

'I have a duty to win you from the devil,' said Cuthbert. 'God
has instructed me so. You must help me, Bega.'

'Yes . . . Padric?'

'Padric is not here.'

'Has he gone away?'

'He is not here.'

'He has gone away?'

'I do not know.' He weakened a little. 'Chad is looking
for him.'

Bega nodded and large weak tears came to her eyes and mixed
with the sweat on her cheeks.

'If the devil comes once more tonight, he will take you away
with him,' said Cuthbert.

'Padric not here?' Her voice had a baby's tone now, helpless in
her unhappiness.

Cuthbert came closer. He had to call her back to listen to
the will of God. The nuns, tense with prayer, began to murmur
encouragement to her out loud. Erebert was drained, grey with
the effort to make himself heard by God.

'Padric will be next,' he said. 'You must let God save you and
then He will save Padric. Otherwise you are both damned.'

'Padric?'

'The devil which kills you will move into him.'

'Will he have this pain?'

'More. Much more. *Much* more, Bega.'

'No. No.'

'You must tell God that you will be His and only His for
whatever life He gives you. You must tell Him this now. And,'
he passed the fragment to her, reluctantly but firmly, 'you must
swear it on this cross.'

Bega felt the small piece of wood in her fingers and suddenly
she conjured the image of Donal coming off the mountain that

day when she was a child. How could he have kept so silent about such a treasure! But she had. It was a sin. It was a deep and unforgivable sin.

'You must swear, Bega.' Cuthbert's clear voice was muzzy. Could he hear her?

'What does Padric say?'

'He wants you to belong to God.'

Bega understood. She was so tired now. The agony was gone, all gone, she was sure, but there was such an emptiness there. Yet something in the agony had been good. How could that be? It was as if her body had gone. Something of her own being had been taken away by the devil who had found her out. Live for the faith. She was different now.

The fragment was still in her hand. She was surprised to find it there. Cuthbert ought to have it. Who was crying? It was her.

'Put the fragment to your lips, Bega, and swear on it that you will be a bride only of God.'

It was so light, this wood. Was it light for Him? Of course not. When she kissed it, would she taste the blood? She could taste the smell of her own blood.

'Swear,' said Cuthbert, stone in his determination to claim this soul, 'and you will be saved. Swear.'

It tasted only of wood. Fusty, pocked and riddled, comforting on her soft tongue.

'I swear,' she whispered and, soon after, sobbing heavily, she went to sleep.

⚮⚮⚮

When Padric came to see her, Bega was sipping a little soup and, though pale, looked so much better that his spirits lifted.

The older nun who had been serving her the food withdrew, taking Chad with her. Chad had returned the greeting given him by Padric but he wanted to say much more. He had not the nerve to speak of what had happened. But the nun simply took hold of his arm and hauled him out.

Cal barked a few times but settled beside Bega and was soon dozing again.

'There was a great deal of blood,' she said, frowning. 'Did they tell you?'

'No.'

Padric waited for more information but Bega seemed disinclined to continue. There was something rather abstract about her, he thought: it was as if she were floating away, out of reach, serene, not earthed.

'Where did the blood . . . was it? . . . the blood . . . ?'

'Oh . . . it came from there.' Unabashed, she pointed towards her vagina. 'It was God's punishment,' she added, and his heart suddenly ached at her submission.

'For what?'

'For doubting what He intended me to do.'

Should she tell Padric about the fragment? She had withheld it from him until now. It seemed unfair that Erebert should know and the nuns; and Cuthbert should have prayed for her with its power and still Padric be unaware of it.

Yet Cuthbert's command, his threat had truly terrified her. Cuthbert was to be obeyed.

'What is it that you have to do?' Padric smiled. The illness had made her rather childlike and he felt that he could cast off his own new armour of responsibility. Together they could start again. Great pain could cause the mind to wander. He knew that. She looked very vulnerable in the aftermath of the pain.

'I have to serve God,' said Bega.

'You do. You will.'

Bega's chest constricted. There was something she had to say but it was suddenly very, very difficult.

'Cuthbert made me swear,' she said.

Padric quelled his alarm.

'Because of what was given to me,' said Bega.

'What was that?'

'He said I must not tell anyone.'

Again Padric fought down the impulse to assault this interfering monk.

'What I have been given means that I have much to return.'

'You will return all that is expected of you,' said Padric, soothingly, thinking her dark hints were no more than the inevitable confusion after such a trial. 'In a day or two, I will take you to my house which will become your house. There will be enough to do.'

'Cuthbert wants me to go to Coldingham. He says there is a mixed house there and it would be a good start for my training.'

'Cuthbert is looking for converts.' Padric spoke evenly. 'But in your case, you are already spoken for.'

'I think I have to obey him.'

'Bega, you have been ill for many weeks now. This monk has caught you at a time of great weakness. The loss of blood alone . . . '

'Why was that?'

'The blood?'

Padric checked his first answer. In the name of God, her question revealed the genuine puzzlement of the over-protected and much cosseted royal favourite. He took her hand. It was warm. 'You are very weak, Bega. Sleep some more and we'll talk later.'

Her hand twisted inside his and she gripped it tightly. Staring into his eyes, she said, 'I have to remain a virgin for the sake of God. I have to give myself to Him and none other.'

'This is not the time, Bega, to talk . . . '

'You must understand, Padric. I cannot marry you. Cuthbert told me that it was wicked even to think of it.'

'While you sleep, I must talk to Cuthbert.'

'After the baptism at the river he will be out of the town on a mission. He will be three days. He told me to be ready to go to Coldingham when he returns.'

Padric considered very carefully what to say next. She was far too fragile for him to take any risks. Before he collected himself, Bega interjected, 'After all that He has given me. He let Donal die defending me. He let me defy my father and not be killed for it. He saved me from the marriage. He brought me across a sea covered in snow and led me to a warm cave. All this He did for me and more. He gave me a marvellous gift. Now I must pay Him back.'

'I thought you were promised to me.' Padric managed to convey this without any pressure.

Bega looked at him and then looked away. In his simple sentence were worlds of memories and bonds between them. She would have married O'Neill rather than see Padric harmed.

But to disobey what Cuthbert had convinced her was the true and implacable will of God . . . that could not be done. Not even for Padric.

'I have promised myself to Him.'

But you are not a virgin, Padric wanted to say. He checked himself.

'Virginity,' said Bega, with a piety which unreasonably redoubled Padric's dislike of Cuthbert – for he could see the zealot's hand in this adamant dedication – 'is the greatest gift any woman can give to Him. He rejoices in our virginity. For Him it is the first evidence of a pure soul.'

When she was stronger . . . Padric thought, then he would try to get her to remember the truth. But for now there was no dealing with this fixed and maddeningly serene faith.

'God needs nuns and virgins and monks and holy men,' said Padric, alive to the fact that a good proportion of those who took holy vows did not keep them and took them in the first place for reasons as material as spiritual. 'He also needs holy and Christian men and woman to "go forth and multiply". It was a command He gave to Adam himself. Why does Cuthbert want you so badly to become a nun?'

'Because of my gift,' said Bega promptly. 'Not because of myself.'

'What is this gift?'

She shook her head.

'More than your virginity?'

'I must not say.'

'Not even to *me*, Bega?'

Bega felt a wave of tiredness move heavily through her mind. No, not even to Padric. Her hand wanted to move to the pocket which contained the fragment. But no, not even for Padric. Oh, what a loss to both of them, she thought, what a loss.

'Cuthbert forbade me,' she whispered.

'And if Cuthbert says that I can know of this gift – will you object?'

'Oh no. Oh no!'

'Very well then.'

'Are you going to see him?'

'I am,' said Padric.

'Please. Please don't . . .'

'Why are you so afraid of him, Bega?'

Bega paused and her eyes filled with tears once forbidden an approach under any circumstances.

'I have been afraid,' she said softly, 'since my father said he would bury me alive if I did not marry O'Neill.'

She did not mention the other part of her father's threat: that she would be buried on top of the dead body of Padric.

Padric put his arm around her and the pair – so careless of their past times together that they had utterly discounted them until now – felt the unique reassurance of clinging bodily comfort. Padric could feel her thinned body and sense the great enfeeblement within. Cuthbert must not be allowed to take her simply because she was ailing and confused. 'Would you like him to let you off your promise?'

Bega pressed her head more firmly into Padric's shoulder. She had been so secure when she had said yes to Cuthbert. The bleeding had finished. Her life was staked out before her – a life of service and struggle for the Lord Himself.

Why could a few exchanges with this young man who was far less insistent, far less emphatic than Cuthbert, provoke such disorder and uncertainty? What was the measure of her faith if it failed at such an unthreatening obstacle?

'I did promise Cuthbert,' she said. 'I vowed to God.'

'But you are weak. I will not stand in your way. Serve God, but be with me. Do His will, but help me too. Help me build up His Kingdom. Help me to rebuild this kingdom. There are souls to whom you can give an example. There will be the work of teaching – no other woman in Rheged is as learned as you. And with me you could provide heirs to two kingdoms.'

'I have to keep my promise.'

'I will talk to Cuthbert,' said Padric. 'And remember – you have not yet taken any holy vows.'

He kissed her forehead and left. Bega, with just enough energy to do so, berated her weakness.

chapter twenty-six

Padric was simply not prepared for the size of the crowd. As he stood on the mound to the east of where the Romans had built one of their forts, he looked down at the river and saw what he would have described as multitudes. As his eyes scanned the countryside, he could see them coming in all directions. It was a memorable scene. This was how people could be called for war, he thought. But through Cuthbert, they came for God.

His brothers, whom he had sent for, now joined him and they too stood for a little while simply to watch the gathering horde. Urien was very rosy-faced after good beer and a night with one of his favourite women. Riderch had slept well and alone but not found enough to eat in the morning. He was a man whose simple appetites needed to be attended to regularly if he were to be sanguine. Riderch, once fed and watered, was capable of considerable amiability: Riderch denied was incapable of directing serious attention to anything but the deficit in his stomach.

Padric had picked out Cuthbert and his followers immediately. They sat in a circle on a little mound of turf some few paces from the river. Beyond the small circle was an unpopulated space: no one wanted to be seen to claim a position beside them. But food was deposited in that space: eggs, chickens, milk, honey, wine, a goose, smaller packages which could have been bread or cheese or berries. On one occasion, one of the monks collected some of the food and took it around the circle. Padric saw Cuthbert raise his hands shoulder high, palms outwards, disclaiming all nourishment.

'I'm going back into the town,' said Riderch.

'He said he would appreciate us down there,' said Padric.

'We're all baptised,' said Urien, grinning at the fact of it, 'once is enough.'

'He said it would be a useful example for the others.'

'He's enough of an example himself by the look of it,' said Urien.

'I can't look at the monks neglecting all that good food any longer,' said Riderch. 'Later.'

He left them.

'See how many are coming,' said Padric.

'They say he held off all the baptisms all along this mission and told them to come to Caerel if they wanted to enter the Kingdom of God.' Urien gave a sly smile: he was always the one with any gossip, and always rather ambiguous. When he said 'the Kingdom of God', it had none of the plainhearted certainty which came from the mouth of Padric. Despite himself, Padric relished his brother's mockery.

'He must be a powerful man,' said Padric and looked on intently.

Until now, he had thought of Cuthbert principally as someone he did not like and as someone who had taken unfair advantage of Bega's illness. He knew enough about the ways in which monks would wheedle and torment. He was aware of their success with women in the royal household and their grasp of court politics in female conversions. Padric had also observed that entry into the church was slowly becoming a way to self-aggrandisement and riches. It was just beginning to boast one or two fortunes which could compare with secular wealth, not that he ascribed this motive to most of the monks. From his own experience, Padric could vouch for the humble aspirations and often the humble origins of most of these men. But there were a few who saw the powerful influence that the Christian religion could have on their fortunes. It was a way to enjoying status and power and grandeur by other means. Cuthbert, he had thought, was one of those.

Now he was not at all sure. There was something more, much more, to a man who could both inspire and organise such a gathering. For that was what struck Padric, the more he watched. Cuthbert had taken great pains with this. He had put together what would be, for all who took part, an unforgettable spectacle.

It was well past dawn. Many had arrived the previous day and slept out in the fields. Some had walked miles since the first crack of light. Others had calculated the distance and taken two or three days, leaving the last push until this morning.

What characterised this crowd was its reserve. Padric, as he stood and stared, unravelled that as well. There was a purpose which united them. He knew something of these people. Most lived lives of comparative isolation. Cross-valley, cross-mountain, cross-tribal connections were sparse, most usually, limited to war. To their chief they were loyal: to the Northumbrians they submitted in a surly manner. To each other they were as often suspicious as welcoming.

But Cuthbert had given them a common purpose.

'The man could be a commander in war,' said Padric, abruptly. Urien, who was lying down, chewing an end of grass and looking at a sky struggle to shake off the occupation of large grey slow-sailing clouds, turned his head and looked again.

'These religions,' he said, and shook his head. '*This* one especially. No stopping people. Life everlasting. Somewhere else. I can see that. We all can. Got to be somewhere better, they think, the poor. And the rest follow.'

'Not only the poor, Urien. We are a Christian family.'

'That's different. It's in our history. We don't need all this.'

'I still think we should go down and offer to be baptised.'

Urien rolled over on to his stomach and looked at this restless brother with amusement. Only back a few weeks and already in so much of a hurry!

'We could give a lead,' said Padric.

'Seems to me the man down there's the one doing that.'

'He asked if we would come and give a lead. He said it would have a great influence.'

'It would prove that he had a great influence over you,' said Urien, shrewdly. 'That's certain sure.'

'But what if I wanted it to be seen that a son of Rheged could be at the head of his people?'

'Why would you need to do that?'

'Because there are so many of them.'

'I still think that he gains more than you do.'

'Sometimes you take a loss to make a point. Come with me.'

'That water looks too cold for me. I'll come with you as a brother and with my hand near my sword but if you're fool enough to want a ducking, you'll do it on your own.' Urien had none of Padric's trusting nature. Though the baptism was a most Christian occasion, there could always be enemies of Rheged there. Padric would need someone to look out for him. Urien had always felt protective towards this older brother. Besides, he thought, there could be some fun down there.

Padric waited a little longer until the movement around the edges of the crowd was reduced to a few stragglers. Still, at the heart of it, the sacred circle of monks remained ever more dramatically untouched by the pulse and the gathering of men, women and children who waited as if ordered. Yet not a word had come from Cuthbert.

Purpose was central to power, Padric concluded. And the more it could be held as a mystery, the greater the chance it had of fulfilment.

He began his walk down, following the sheep's track. He came to the river and, with Urien by his side, walked towards Cuthbert. The crowd shuffled aside for him and the respect was visible. Padric grew with it. The brothers were taller than most of the men and women: their fine war-clothes were unmatched as were their great swords and shields and torques. Before them, the ripple effect warned of their advance.

When Padric reached the empty space which moated Cuthbert, his step did not falter.

'We have been waiting for you,' said Cuthbert and he rose and bowed. As he got to his feet he felt a slight pull of pain in his knee. So, despite his courtly welcome, he grimaced as if the show of good manners caused him too great an effort.

Padric steeled himself against the dislike which again threatened. He had to use this man and he had to prise away Bega from him. Waiting for him? He did not believe it! Never mind.

'I will be baptised by you to set an example for the people.'

'Your people.'

'Your friend, Ecfrith,' he said, lightly, smiling, 'might not agree with that.'

'I do not always agree with Prince Ecfrith,' said Cuthbert curtly. 'Have you seen Princess Bega?'

'I have. She seems a little better.'

'She lost a good deal of blood,' Cuthbert said, fixing that

abruptly strong, clear look on Padric, who could feel his own
eyes threaten to shift nervously. He held his gaze, but was relieved
when Cuthbert looked away.

'She had seen great losses of blood,' said Padric. 'I think she
feels that to lose her own somehow absolves her.'

'From what?'

The smile caught Padric unawares. He blushed.

'Let me take you once again into the Church of God,' said
Cuthbert, turning to what was most important to him.

He walked into the cold late spring river. He had chosen a fairly
shallow stretch but he waded into the middle and the water was
well up to his thighs.

Padric took off his sword and his belt and his leather boots,
lay down his leather breast tunic and shield and followed.

The crowd moved as a swarm and pressed to the bank.

Cuthbert held out his hands.

'Do you come to be rebaptised into the Church of the One
God?'

This was said very loudly. It could be heard clearly by a good
portion of the crowd.

'Yes.' Padric was determined not to be wholly used. 'I, Padric of
Rheged, from the family which has given saints to the world and
welcomed God's men into the royal household, which has bred
Christian commanders who fought for Rheged and for God, I
am happy to lead the people of Rheged once more into the arms
of the God who has done so much for their kingdom. And will
do so again.'

A murmur of approval went up at what was plainly a speech
designed to give notice of Padric's intention to the crowd.

'*In Nomine Patris et Filii et Spiritus Sancti,*' said Cuthbert as he
put one hand on Padric's back, another on his chest, and lowered
him into the water.

When Padric emerged he said quietly to Cuthbert: 'After this,
we must talk.'

'Go forth in peace,' said Cuthbert, and nodded.

The other monks then came into the river, followed by the
crowd.

Padric put on his long, warming, Irish woollen cloak and sat
on the bank near the mound now abandoned by the monks.

Almost all the men came up to him after they had been

baptised and grasped his forearm. The women would stop for a moment and then move on. Urien sat at some distance, satisfyingly distracted by what was happening.

Some of the crowd went up into Caerel. More turned in their tracks and headed straight back for an existence where survival demanded constant vigilance.

When, eventually, it was all over, and the field was left to a few who wanted to stay on the newly holy spot as long as they could, Cuthbert came from the river, walked apart and kneeled in prayer. Then two of his monks had to insist that he put on warm clothes.

Why was it, Padric thought, that whatever Cuthbert did he seemed to enact publicly? It was an unfair reflection. Why should he hide? And perhaps he wanted the cold of his clothes and the cool evening air to test him further.

He stifled his critical feelings and, when Cuthbert got up and began to walk away, he followed him.

Padric was impressed by the man's endurance. He seemed to have fasted for some days. He had baptised hundreds of people. He had disregarded the cold of the water. He had in his own way controlled the entire event. Yet his first free move had been to pray. Padric joined him. Cuthbert seemed unsurprised. The men walked step in step along the bank of the broad, clear-flowing river. Cuthbert limped a little.

'What an earth He has given us,' said Cuthbert. 'Look at that river. Water for our thirst. Water for the fish. Fish for our hunger. Food for the fish themselves. Stones which we can take out and use. And the water keeps the land moist for growing the crops we need. They feed the birds. The birds themselves . . .' He smiled. 'Sometimes I think that God moves in perpetual circles. Everything begins and then ends at its beginning. He gives us all we need and as He does that so His abundance breeds and nourishes thousands of others of His creatures. Praise Him.'

Padric was again unsettled by Cuthbert. It was difficult to predict his tone, his direction, his commitment.

'Sometimes I think that He gives us a taste of His heavenly rewards here on earth,' said Cuthbert. 'And then I remember the words of the saints and I see how wrong I am.'

He fell silent. It was like a declaration, his silence.

Padric had decided to take all the time there was.

Cuthbert resumed – not looking at Padric but with his eyes fixed ahead, as if indeed, Padric thought, he were happily speaking aloud to God and himself alone – 'How long do you think most of those people will remain interested in our faith? How many of them will seek out more knowledge? Will they come to the churches or make a journey to the monasteries to discover further truths? There are so many souls to save, Padric, and we are given so little time. Even here in Christian Rheged, there are many who worship the old gods as much as they worship Him. Even here there is more darkness than light. And beyond this favoured place, whenever report comes, it is of heathen black darkness, it is of bestial ignorance and sometimes, like your Welsh Cadwalla, brute antagonism to the Christian God.'

He paused, but did not turn to look at his companion. 'These are the hard times, Padric. The few who have been chosen for the gift of learning and faith *are* so very few. They are all needed. And if, like Princess Bega, they have been given even more than that – then we all have a duty to see that they are enrolled in this small army of Christ. For make no mistake, Padric, it is small. It can easily be wiped away. The few scraps of learning could die in the throats of a few hundred murdered monks and nuns. That is possible.'

Again he paused and Padric, drawn in by his musing passion, feared for a moment that he would not go on. But he continued.

'And then, where would those remaining find the Word? Where would they look for the voice of God Himself and the words of the saints and the prophets? It is crucial, Padric, as you must know, a prince, a son of Rheged, crucial that what has been so painfully wrested from the ruins and depredations of a once glorious past be preserved from the barbarians who are still all around us.'

Padric was taken by surprise. Was Cuthbert signalling that he was on Padric's side against Ecfrith?

'And that is why Bega is even more important to us. She is already a learned woman, taught by you, God praise you. She has been encouraged to take her vows by a holy woman and an even more holy man, Donal.' Now he stopped and turned to look at Padric. Mention of Bega had driven out all other thoughts. Cuthbert smiled and said: 'And then there was the miracle. She has told you of that gift, of course.'

Padric was utterly at a loss. To deny that he knew would naturally prove that he was not as close to Bega as he wanted to claim. To lie was unthinkable. He said nothing.

'And so you will know why any means must be used to help her fulfil her vocation.'

What was this miracle? What was this gift? Cuthbert must know that he did not know. Did he? Or not? This was clearly meant to torment him. But how could he find out?

'This gift . . . ?'

'It is better if we say as little about it as possible,' said Cuthbert, who knew for certain now that Bega had said nothing to Padric. 'Until Bega is strong enough to be able to withstand the consequences, we must tell no one.'

Cuthbert turned and began to walk back to where his followers had regrouped themselves. Their wet shifts were spread over tree branches, looking, at a distance, like many small tents. They had laid out some of the food given to them and were waiting for Cuthbert's blessing before beginning to eat.

As they drew nearer to the circle, Padric felt he was losing his chance of fighting for Bega. Cuthbert had somehow sidestepped the question he most needed to ask, even though he had not asked it.

'I wish to marry Bega,' he said, clumsily, and was furious with himself. It was as if he were asking permission. Why should he? Of Cuthbert? What had this man imposed on him?

'She has promised herself to God,' said Cuthbert.

'She can be useful to God at the court of Rheged,' said Padric. 'You know how fruitful the presence of a Christian queen can be at a court.'

'She has promised her maidenhood to God,' said Cuthbert and he stopped and looked directly at Padric. As Padric drew a breath to reveal once and for all that her virginity was no longer a gift she could offer, Cuthbert drove on, 'She believes with all her strength that this virginity – which she knows she retains – has to be returned in exchange for the gift she has received. If,' his hand went up to prevent Padric from speaking 'she were to be told that her virginity was not available to her – for whatever reason – then she would want to perish in hell because her life's work would be denied her. And all the good she could bring, the example she could be, would be lost. God would not forgive the man or woman who stood in His path by blocking her path.'

'What?' said Padric, 'What is this gift?'

Cuthbert nodded to himself and then came to his decision.

'By Donal, the monk, and after a visitation from the Mother of Jesus Christ, Princess Bega was given a fragment of the True Cross. This has already worked to preserve her. When she is stronger in Christ and when I give her permission, then we will see it bring more to the faith, multitudes more than seven times the number you saw here today.' Cuthbert was now unchallengeable. 'Nothing must be allowed to prevent Bega from her vocation. She has been picked out by the Highest, by the Mother of the Son of God. Let no man think his claim, however prior and seeming strong, can prevail against such a force. Today Bega is weak. When she is stronger I shall take her to Coldingham where she will be taught the ways of a monastery in the manner of Aidan of Lindisfarne. That will strengthen her. After that, we will all pray for guidance to advise on her future. Now that you know this, you must never speak of it. You are the last to know and you will be the last to be told. But I see that it had to be so. Thanks be to God.'

Cuthbert bowed a little, and walked on, still limping slightly. Padric let him go. How could he think of himself and Bega when so tremendous a gift and so significant a future were in opposition to him? But how could he stop thinking of himself and her? She *was* his thought. Life without her was emptiness.

CHAPTER TWENTY-SEVEN

Padric was finally impressed by Cuthbert. He did not like him. There was so much about Cuthbert he could criticise: the love of public spectacle which went badly, he thought, with the idea of Christian humility; the undoubted vanity and, Padric sensed, a barely suppressed avarice. But when Cuthbert believed himself to be speaking for God, he was inspired. God was speaking through his mouth – so Cuthbert believed and so did those who were convinced by him. Padric too was now convinced.

He took time alone before returning to Bega. If Cuthbert's story of the cross were right, then how could he, or any man, stand against such a decision? But how could Cuthbert be certain that the gift was intended for Bega? It had been given to Donal. Donal had passed it on. Was there a divine reason for this? The answer would help him decide on his course.

He realised that all he could think about was Bega. It had to be resolved, he thought. There were matters of far greater importance which had to be attended to, he told himself. This private matter should not take so much time.

Yet when he had climbed back from the river and into the town, he lingered. He needed to let his contradictory feelings settle.

Twilight came and the visit to Bega could no longer be postponed. The weavers he had seen, the forge he had loitered by, where he had discussed the cost of new swords and spearheads, the men who could carve fine stiff leather into a dozen shapes for as many purposes, the dark-skinned jewellers from the far south and the famous Caerel horse-dealers, the rather suspicious-looking men from the north with sheep and long-haired, long-horned, small, feisty cattle to sell, the milkmaid-faced old women with herbs and charms – all this had been sampled by Padric with the excuse that he was taking an inventory of a city which would at some time be his. But it was no more than an excuse.

His feet went slowly towards the house. It was as if some physical resistance met them. Was he going to pronounce his separation from Bega? The evening was calm. His mind was in turmoil. The nearer he came the less clear his arguments grew. The crisp question and answer rehearsals which had punctuated his afternoon were misted over.

Bega was combing her hair.

He doubted if he had ever seen her do that. She was averse to the pursuit of any beautifying activity. Most of all she hated to be seen to be paying attention to the thick and intertwined tresses of hair. Now, with a long wide-toothed comb of horn, she was stroking it carefully. Nor did she stop in embarrassment when Padric came in.

This was one sign that she was somehow – slightly but, it seemed, decisively – changed.

Another was the look in her eyes. If her detachment earlier in the day had rather amused him, this look unnerved him. It was as if she were under a spell. She hummed a little as the long comb first tugged and then drew sweetly through the hair which nestled over her shoulders like a shawl. She was alone.

'Where is Chad?'

'He went with Erebert.' She smiled. 'They took Cal.'

'But he will be back?'

'Of course.' The smile remained. It was sweet but it made him uneasy. It was as if someone else's smile had been put on to her face.

'Did you rest?'

'Oh yes.'

'Have you eaten?'

'They made me eat. They are very good.' She nodded. 'And then I prayed . . . I prayed for guidance, Padric. When I saw you this morning, I was so tired I do not remember what I said. Or,' she corrected herself, 'I do not remember it properly.' She paused. 'Tell me about Cuthbert.'

'At the river?'

'Yes.'

Padric began with a determination to be fair. But, as he spoke, the memory of those streams of people, their unforced orderliness, the controlling power of Cuthbert and the sense of God's work being done, moved him to an unrestrained enthusiasm which swept up Bega in its wake.

'He is a man chosen by God, truly,' she said. Padric was too full of his image of the hundreds of people lining the river bank obediently waiting for baptism, to catch the sad undertow in her words.

'Yes,' said Padric.

'He told you?'

'Yes.' Padric paused. 'But . . . how could you be certain it was for *you*? It was given to Donal.'

'It was given to Donal to give to the woman-child he would meet at the foot of the mountain and God had placed me there.' The sentence bore the brand of an instruction. This time, Padric did catch the tone. Who had schooled her to say that?

'How . . . ?' he said. 'How can you be sure? Donal can be sure. He had the visitation. But, Bega, can you be sure?'

'You are not doubting the word of Donal?'

'No.'

'You cannot doubt that the Lord put me in the place where Donal would meet me?'

'It . . .' He had nothing to say.

'My life is decided for me,' said Bega, and again the displaced smile settled on her face still strained and paled by the stress and illness. 'I must be glad. Are you not glad for me, Padric?'

'I am . . . I am, yes, glad that you were picked out for such a gift. But, truthfully, Bega, I think that we have been together in such a way that God might see you as my bride.'

Would that hint gently prise open a night which appeared as forgotten to her as it was inflamed in his memory?

'We have been friends. You have been my teacher. Through God's grace, I found a refuge for us on a night when we might have perished. Your strength helped me to rediscover my own. God cannot see that as sufficient for a bride: can He?' Was there a plea in those last two words?

'In any case, come with me,' said Padric.

'Cuthbert says that I need the discipline of a community.'

'Cuthbert spoke of founding new churches. I would give him land and help to found a mixed order near our household.'

'That would be to put too much temptation in my way,' said

Bega, simply. 'Because of you.' The smile left her face to be replaced by a tremulous expression which craved comfort. 'I think I am too fond of you for the good of my soul. If I go many miles away from you, then,' she spoke with difficulty, 'the distance will help me forget that. Distance makes earthly fidelities lessen.'

'Did Cuthbert tell you that?'

'Yes.' Her head was bowed. The comb was now in a listless hand. 'He told me that.'

'What else did he say?'

'Earthly love is less than dust compared with the force of divine love.'

'And?'

'To obey the will of God is to be full of joy.'

She stated this with such simplicity and sorrow that Padric knew her to be caught in the net of the monk. To try to take her away by argument would only hurt her in her weak state. But to let her go was impossible.

'Why does he want to rush you out of Rheged and into Northumbria?'

'I think that he knows that I am weak,' said Bega, looking directly into his eyes. 'He knows that I would listen to you and he is afraid that I will do as you suggest.'

So Cuthbert had prepared for that. Padric, like all young men of his background, had been taught to play chess by his father partly to develop the skills of future planning in politics and war. He felt now that Cuthbert had given Bega every necessary note to check any move he made.

He could, of course, try to force Bega to remember the event which would destroy Cuthbert's plans. But what if she refused to dredge up the memory and thought that he was pressing her merely for selfish ends? Or what if she did remember and never forgave him?

Padric wanted to fight on but she was in some ways too weak an opponent. To attack her argument would cause her nothing but distress. Yet in another way she was too strong. She had been given a sacred relic. Perhaps he was now standing before someone who would one day inspire hundreds as Cuthbert had done that morning.

'So I should leave you?'

Bega did not reply. The harshness of Padric's tone threatened her.

'If I leave you, there is no reason why I should ever see you again.'

Bega could not find an answer.

'Is that what you want?'

His aggression was not fair but he was no longer the master of his feelings.

'Do you give me no answer?'

Bega felt as if she had been struck dumb.

'Why don't you come with me, Bega? You can serve God and be with me. That is what you want. Isn't it? Isn't it?'

He was sitting near her. Now he leaned out and took her face to tilt it up. She saw the pain that was goading his anger and yet she could say nothing.

'Cuthbert has taken control of you. You are a great catch for him and when the time comes he'll put you and your gift on show like the bones of a martyr. He'll suck your soul from you, Bega. He is ruthless. Come with me. Be chaste if you wish; be bound in prayer and the works of God – but Bega: come with me.'

She saw a future in his eyes, behind his fierce plea. She saw days with him, days which they had passed before. Absorption, laughter, learning; the two of them wholly sufficient. All her lifetime he would be her friend, and husband, a father, she a mother . . . He wanted it so badly. And so did she.

But she had lost too much in Ireland and brought about deaths and disruption which could only be redeemed by service to God. Padric was her sole friend on earth, yet the weight of her heavenly obligation crushed her. She could no longer decide on the matters of her own life as she had done. God would determine everything.

The silence became a denial.

'Shall I beg you?' He was ashamed of the words.

Bega shook her head. He must not do that.

'I beg you.'

The feeling which charged those simple and humiliating words – words which should never be uttered by any warrior – proved too much for Bega.

She put up her hand and let it rest on the hand that still held her face. She longed for him. Her body moved slightly but surely, wanting to be completed by him. Would God forgive her weakness? Surely Padric's virtue would compensate for that?

'I must,' she whispered, almost breathless with the effort of the words, 'I must do as God and Cuthbert bid me. My life is different now. I have been changed.'

Padric felt drained of life. His hand tightened on her face, tightened hard and then dropped away. He stood up and she looked up at a man she might never see again.

'Please,' she said, but did not know what she wanted.

'I will go now,' said Padric.

'Give me your blessing.' Stay, even if only for the smallest moment longer.

'Oh Bega. How can you torment me like this? How can you?'

She gazed up at him and saw the tensed face, the hard sprung body, and almost tasted the passion which would never be hers.

'I will always remember you in my prayers, Padric . . . Will you pray for me?'

Again her hand reached out to seek contact but he stepped back.

'God be with you,' he said, hoarsely.

She saw him turn away. Again and again she saw him turn away. At any point even in that swift motion of turning, she could have said 'No, don't go'. But he turned and, without a word from her to hold him there, he was gone.

chapter twenty-eight

E rebert was impatient to leave the town. He had encountered so much more than he had anticipated and he longed for solitude to digest it. Most of all there was the promise, as he interpreted it, that he would die in the same instant as Cuthbert. Were this miracle to be granted, then he would indeed have lived a life of holiness. But he knew that it would only be granted were he worthy of it. The noise, smells and temptations of the town, the goods, the fellowship, the women, the alcohol, the rude boisterous excitement were too distracting.

He had searched most of the day but failed to find the man who had promised to escort him. It was a weakness and he had already laid out a severe course of fasting and punishment to redeem this sin. For the dependence on an escort surely showed a lack of trust in God to take care of one whose life was dedicated to putting trust in Him. But he dared not travel alone. He was scared and ashamed of it.

The day after the baptism, Erebert was with Bega and Chad, fretting that he was not already on his way. Bega and Chad were both preoccupied and unusually silent. Erebert looked around, seeking an object on which to vent his dissatisfaction. Something about Chad incited his rage.

'Who baptised you yesterday?' he asked. 'Was it Cuthbert himself?'

Chad looked frightened and his eyes fled to Bega.

'You vile and stupid boy!' Chad cringed from the blow but Erebert was too quick for him and the hard palm slap rang out. 'You did not go!'

'Don't hit the boy,' said Bega, sharply.

'He was told to go into the river,' said Erebert, ignoring Bega's interjection, 'He was told that this was the moment for his baptism. Why did you disobey?' Once again the hermit's hand lashed out and this time it caught the twisting boy slap across the face. He cried out and scampered behind Bega. Cal growled low but stood off the enraged man.

'Why did you disobey? Answer me!'

Chad sobbed.

'Why *did* you not go?' Bega asked, gently.

'Because the boy is a fool! He will always be a fool!'

Erebert's sudden eruption of anger at Chad was not unexpected. He had been finding fault with the boy ever since their arrival in Caerel when he realised that, inevitably, he would lose him. The boy had shown so much more affection for Padric than for him, so that it had been a problem to capture the boy's attention. Yet on the island he had been so helpful, so pliant, so devoted. Erebert's anger was one of the rougher disguises of jealousy.

Chad curled up to avoid the worst of the blows. He had learned that early on.

'Why did you not go?' Bega repeated, more sternly.

Chad shook his head and sobbed. He could not bear the reproach in Bega's voice. He had been utterly overwhelmed. He had never dreamed that so many people lived on the earth, never seen the drama of the full baptism. He had stood on the slope of the hill transfixed, fully expecting the heavens to open and a choir of angels come to earth and accompany this unbelievable sight. The thought that he could be a part of it was beyond him.

Bega sensed this. 'You must take him to the river and baptise him now,' she said to Erebert.

'Why?'

'You ask why? This is a soul which needs the purification of baptism.' Bega's words, echoing those of Cuthbert, made Erebert calm down. 'It is your duty,' continued Bega. 'Surely that must be so?'

'He should have kept his word.'

'But he did not and if God wishes to punish him for that He will do so. Now, before it gets too dark, you must take him. And Erebert, you must purify your heart to this boy. "Suffer little children to come unto me and forbid them not; for theirs is the Kingdom of Heaven". The words of Jesus Christ are clear.'

Erebert was vexed to be put down so comprehensively by this

girl. But he was sensible enough to recognise that she had won the argument. And she was a royal princess. Aristocratic birth excused much. Hierarchy was as essential in Erebert's earthly life as in his spiritual existence. Without an ordering of people there could be no sainthood. A prince in this world was no more than a feeble reminder of the brilliance of those who sat in heaven; nevertheless it was a reminder which had to be observed as another aspect of the ceaseless instruction for life eternal.

On that self-justifying note, he agreed to take Chad to the river. Chad looked fearfully at Bega, who allowed him to take Cal. The exchange had given her some vigour.

Late afternoon was a time of hurried bustle in the town. Newcomers arriving to stay overnight, looking for places to sleep; people searching for food for the evening meal; farmers coming in from the fields with their animals and dogs. Chad was sure he saw Padric down a side street where the biggest forge threw out a wall face of heat. But Erebert tugged him on, taking the boy's hand. Chad did not attempt to wriggle it away, even when the crowd thinned out. He was in a panic about the baptism. Though he fished and had pulled a boat across the sea and fresh water as skilfully as many twice his age, he was scared of being immersed in it. Perhaps that was the deeper reason for his refusal to be baptised that morning.

Erebert took the trusting hand as a gesture of apology. He found great pleasure in it. By the time they had walked down to the river, his benevolent feelings for Chad were almost restored. The deep loneliness of his life had left him with little resistance to open affection: one warm exchange could kindle immense reciprocal warmth; a single cold look could trigger deep dislike.

The nearer they came to the water, the tighter the boy's grip became.

There were only a few last loiterers by the river. The sun was beginning to set, scarcely disturbing the dour grey of the skies. There was a wind from out of the north, chilly. But Erebert felt expansive.

'As I baptise you in the name of the Father and of the Son and of the Holy Ghost,' he said, 'the Holy Ghost Himself, invisible to all but those given miraculous powers, will descend from the Heavens and take you into the Church of God.'

Chad practically seized up. He stopped and planted mule heels into the ground.

'What ghost?'

'The Holy Ghost, Chad. You say your prayers to Him.'

'I don't want him to come and take me.'

'He won't harm you, Chad.' Erebert smiled. The boy's fright was so genuine and dramatic that the hermit could enjoy a hugely comfortable sense of superiority.

'Nobody said anything about the ghost coming down for me.'

'You saw what happened yesterday. Come on, silly boy. No one was hurt. Children smaller than you. Many of them came out of the water shouting the praises of God.'

'I still don't want a ghost.' He clutched at Erebert's arm. 'Just you. You do it. I'll do it with you but no ghost. Please.'

Erebert was delighted at the confusion and superstition this revealed. He knew that he was surrounded by a dark and pagan world some of which pretended to Christianity when convenient. Few of their protestations convinced him. Even the display of the previous day was remarkable to Erebert not for the crowds but for Cuthbert and his few disciples. Chad was a true child of his time. He could and did appear to be happy to join in many of the outward signs of the faith. But it took only a single confrontation with one of its minor truths for him to collapse into babbling superstition. Those who kept the faith and told the word and, above all, those who strove to come face to face with God Himself, were few. Erebert saw strength in that. For a few could keep firm. The many, he thought, would always scatter to whatever force threatened most or promised most.

'Let me tell you a story,' said Erebert and he drew on an unwilling Chad. They sat on a small hillock just above the peacefully, glassily flowing water. Man and boy wrapped their cloaks around themselves and grew warm. At a safe distance, Cal sniffed out a multitude of new smells and was soon drunk and oblivious of everything but the complicated scent paths of the wild fields.

'There was once a man called Alban,' Erebert began. 'He lived in our country many years ago, when the Romans were here and ruled over all the tribes of Britain. They were a race of giants: taller, stronger, cleverer than anyone of us today, they had conquered the whole world. They were pagans but God allowed them to vanquish all their enemies for He wanted the world to be under one sole rule when He brought His Son to our earth. The stronger the Romans became, the more God rejoiced because He knew that to conquer the Romans, to conquer the conquerors would be seen throughout the world as a mighty victory. What men they were, Chad! You must imagine that the ruins on that hill were once a fortress with walls higher than ten men; and over the river, another such fortress. I have heard of camps and walls and roads that reached across every land and once existed only for the tread of Roman boot or horse or the run of a Roman chariot.'

Chad began to see the ghosts of the giant soldiers. He saw the stones, weed-choked, tumbled down, scattered, gathered up again into battlements which no one could ever penetrate. The ghosts of Roman soldiers trampled about him. He crept in closer to Erebert and the hermit put an arm around him.

'Before God converted the Romans, He tested us Christians fully in our faith. This man Alban – British like you and Prince Padric – was a pagan. One evening, about this time, a man – as that man walking alongside the river over there might be – begged to be taken into Alban's home and hidden. Alban took pity on him and let him hide there. When the Romans came for him, to take and kill him, Alban denied that he was there. The Romans went away.

'The man was a priest and his prayers and faith so impressed Alban that he asked to be taught the faith. The priest instructed him and Alban was a quick and a good pupil, even though he had passed the usual age of learning and become a man. One day, Chad, you may be thought good enough to learn. It may be decided that even one such as you can be taught to understand the Word of God.'

Chad was not at all put down by the crushing patronage of Erebert. To the contrary, he was thrilled that he might indeed be allowed to be set before a page of letters and taught how to decipher them. It was a dream, though, as Erebert's sentence implied, and as unlikely as his ever possessing a sword like Padric's.

'Then the ruler discovered that Alban, whom he thought to be his friend, had hidden the priest from the Roman soldiers. He flew into a terrible rage and ordered the soldiers to seize the priest. Alban heard them coming down the street – it was a great town he lived in, a town just like Caerel used to be, with wide streets paved in stone – and, quickly, he changed clothes with the priest so that it was he who was arrested. Of course when he came face to face with the ruler, he was instantly recognised but by that time the priest had taken the horse Alban had given him and ridden away to safety.

'The ruler said to Alban, "If you do not renounce Christianity and all the works of Christ then you will suffer all the tortures which we had prepared for the priest". He pointed to the blazing fire with the spear-points turning scarlet with heat; he indicated the whips and instruments of torture which I cannot describe to you without disturbing your nights for years to come. But Alban was strong in God and he refused to submit and instead he called on the ruler to become a Christian. The ruler was so incensed that he had Alban whipped on his back until the flesh hung off him in strips. He threatened to peg him to the ground and let the birds of prey feed on him, but Alban would not yield. Then he took the burning spear points and laid them on Alban's chest until his flesh burnt but still Alban would not give up the faith. The ruler was now at his wits' end and so he ordered Alban to be executed outside the city wall.

'The soldiers led him outside the city, sometimes he had to be supported because he was so weak, but all the way he praised God. A crowd gathered about him. When he came out of the city, just as we have come out of the city, there was a river, like this one here, Chad, and it was high in flood. Alban longed for martyrdom now and prayed to God to let him pass. God sent him a miracle. The river sank low and dried to its bed so that not only Alban and the soldiers but all the crowd could walk over in safety.

'They went up a lovely green hill, a place of beauty, we are told. When he had arrived at the top, Alban asked God to give him some water. At his feet, at that very moment, a spring came through the earth, a spring which is there to this day. When he had drunk and blessed the water, he was executed and went to Heaven where he became a saint.

'It is also recorded that the executioner was not allowed to see the fruits of his work for as soon as he struck the blow to the neck of Alban, his eyes fell out. It is also recorded that the evil ruler was so impressed by the death of Alban and the miracles which took place at the spring that he himself became a Christian

in due course as the Romans began to fall to the will of God.'
Erebert paused, moved by the story of martyrdom and miracles.
Such men and such histories sustained him. 'So to be afraid when
there are so many examples of Christian courage, like Alban, is
not worthy of you,' said Erebert to the boy. 'Now, before the sun
goes, I must baptise you for Christ.'

Chad was indeed fortified by the example of Alban's faith and
fortitude and he took off his outer clothes and, bracing himself
against the cold water, followed Erebert who went just a few feet
into the river and called down the Holy Ghost.

Although he never told anyone, although he sometimes persuaded himself that it was not true, nevertheless Chad was utterly
convinced that he saw the Holy Ghost, like a cloud, white and
dazzling and, as Chad's head came out of the water, it wrapped
itself around him for a moment and he knew that he had been
taken into the Church.

After drying themselves, they wandered back into the town,
Erebert thoughtful about the journey and the life ahead, Chad
working out which parts of him were new and reborn, wondering
how the reborn Chad would differ from the one he had been
before. For to see a ghost, and the Holy Ghost, must change you
for ever.

When Cuthbert and Erebert came out of the house in which
Bega lay, Padric was waiting for them. It was just before dawn. A
wind swirled around the buildings, sighing in the enclosed spaces.
Padric knew that Cuthbert was about to set off on a mission and he
wanted a final meeting. The two monks came straight to him.

'I will not see you for some time,' said Cuthbert, 'and, when I
do, you will have become a man of blood.'

Padric, who had intended to take the initiative, was non-
plussed.

'I ask for your blessing,' said Erebert, 'and for the man you
promised would escort me back to my island. I have been away
from it far too long now and feel that my work will be ruined

unless I return at once.' This had been his sole journey out of his island. It had been blessed. But now there would be no more. Not until his soul left his body.

He kneeled before Padric who blessed him and directed him to where his men were sleeping. After one more blessing from Cuthbert and the exchange of mutual praises to God, Erebert hurried away through the just-wakening town. He would not sleep, he vowed, until he reached his island.

'I have not taken her from you,' said Cuthbert, reading Padric's thoughts. 'She has been called to God. That call is stronger than the claim of any man.'

'A woman can serve two masters,' said Padric. 'Just as a man can serve a wife and the Mother of Christ.'

'That is so,' said Cuthbert. 'But Bega has now made her choice.'

'She has been very ill,' said Padric, stubbornly. 'I fear that when she recovers . . .'

'She will regret leaving you? I am sure she will. It will bring her great anguish. I have told her that.'

'Why should you wish that on her?'

'It is she who will wish it on herself. It will remind her of her love for you.'

Again, Padric felt winded by Cuthbert's unexpected line. 'What do you know of the love she has for me?'

'I can imagine it,' said Cuthbert, with a faint smile. 'I have felt its first advances. I have felt desire for a woman and I will do so again. It is my vocation to conquer the lust of the flesh, but I know of it. Even in my chaste, unspoken state it has, once at least, threatened me as much as any other temptation. I have never given full rein to it as you have. So has Bega, although she does not yet recognise it. If ever she does, she will need all our prayers.'

'I do not believe you can know what I feel,' said Padric.

'Temptation is a quick teacher,' said Cuthbert.

'Experience is harsher.'

'I am not so sure. Strength comes from denial . . . You experience some wealth. Your family has lands, farms, servants, soldiers, horses, cattle, slaves . . . I too was brought up in expectation of those blessings. Now that I have decided that my life will be without them I discover that I am sometimes tempted to dwell

on them more and more covetously. See me now. I am going on a
mission to the southern parts of your father's kingdom in the barest
mountains where pagan rites have never really been abandoned. I
will try, with God's help, to root them out and bring these people
to our way.

'But I am also going to look at lands given me by King Oswy
through his wife. Those lands will be used to endow a small
monastery or a church, but still, Padric, they are my lands and I
want to see them. I think of them as my lands and this torments
me. Just as lust torments me and vanity and the belief sometimes
that I am very powerful in my work – these are the devils I fight.
To win these battles I will have to leave the world, some day, like
Erebert, and struggle alone to rid myself of sins which will forbid
me the Kingdom of Heaven. But I cannot do it yet – because there
is work to be done in netting souls. I am one of His fishermen.
That is what I do. You saw it. But is even that vanity too?

'Temptation can teach you what your weaknesses are and that
is great knowledge. Bega . . . Yes . . . I understand.'

'You are a clever man,' said Padric, bitterly.

'I listen to those who tell me the follies of their lives. Out
of their mountains sometimes I sift some grains of wisdom.
But it is merely earthly wisdom. Only the soul can teach real
wisdom and that comes from the communion of love with
God alone.'

'You have turned her against me.'

'You must go in and see for yourself.'

'Why will I become a man of blood?'

'You will take up arms against Ecfrith and his father.'

'Is this what you will tell Ecfrith when next you see him?'

'No,' said Cuthbert. 'But if God needs me to bind in Ecfrith
so that His will be done, then I will obey.'

'Do you bless the wars of King Oswy?'

'I do. He fights behind the cross of Christ. The people
see that.'

'He ravages a kingdom which was Christian when he and his
ancestors worshipped stones.'

'It is our great work to convert the heathen. Praise God.'

By now a reluctant whitish light silhouetted the buildings and
the smoke from the fires grew in thickness. The cocks had crowed
and the dogs were out sniffing for scraps. Noise of horses and men,

noise of children and mothers' calling disturbed the silence which had enclosed the two men.

'I will go now,' said Cuthbert. 'God bless you.'

Padric could not return the blessing. He merely nodded and watched Cuthbert walk to where his disciples stood with bread and water waiting to breakfast before their journey continued.

He turned back to the house where Bega slept. He longed to go in and yet he knew that he had said and tried all he could. He stared at the place as if the strength of his longing could materialise the change in Bega that he wanted.

Chad came out, rubbing his eyes, carrying a bucket to fetch the water. Padric beckoned him across. He slipped an ornamental silver armlet over his wrist. It had been given him by Urien to protect him in Ireland. Urien, though he never told this to Padric, had bartered it from the richest prostitute in Caerel.

'Take this to Bega,' he said. He took a step forward, bent down and slipped it over Chad's hand. 'Tell her that this is my protection for her. Tell her that when she needs me, I will be there.'

The boy nodded, heavy with the responsibility.

'Go back in now,' said Padric.

The boy did as he was bid. The man turned. Cuthbert and his monks were gone. The traders were setting out their stalls. A man was leading three donkeys down the narrow street. Padric forced himself to leave, to go, to start a life without Bega.

BOOK THREE

✦✦✦✦

CROSSING BORDERS

✦✦✦✦

A.D. 657–662

CHAPTER TWENTY-NINE

'Stay until Ecfrith comes here once more,' said Dunmael. 'At least until then.'

Padric found it hard to return his father's beseeching look. 'I don't trust myself to be near him.'

'You can never know enough about your enemy.'

'He is our joint enemy, Father. And the enemy of everyone here.'

'You can talk to him.'

'What can you say to someone who has plans to stamp you out like an insect on the ground?'

'You can find out why he wants to do this.'

'He is a vicious man. What else do I need to know, father? What I need to do is to fight before he uses his advantage.'

'With the few you can raise – how can you hope for any real victory?'

'Better to try than to be content to be slaves.'

'You mean me, don't you, Padric?'

'No! You had no choice. You had to organise a retreat after our defeat. You had to provide a refuge for us here and help our warriors and their women go into exile. But that time is over, Father. And Urien, Riderch and myself must go away from here so that you and our mother and our sisters and our friends are not tainted by us. We will go far away for the first months; probably for the first years. We want you to rail against us, Father.' Padric smiled, finding it difficult to imagine great anger in his father. 'We want you to tell Ecfrith and his kind that you have ungrateful sons who have disobeyed your will. We want you to say that you have cast us off for ever more. You must deny us, Father. That is all we ask.' It was a serious request but, Padric hoped, by offering it lightly, he might get what he wanted.

'Even if I could do that,' said Dunmael, 'could your mother? Could your sisters?'

Padric wanted so urgently to be gone. More than anything he wanted to rip up the past and go, go far away, go deep into the north with his brothers and a few men and fight alongside the Pictish tribes. There he would gather the strength and the forces to come back and bring Ecfrith to a reckoning. He could no longer bear to be in his own house to which he should have returned with a bride. His parents had said nothing after he had told them that Bega was committed to the church. But even that silence unfairly irked him. This place had no future for him.

'I ask you once more,' said Dunmael. 'Stay until Ecfrith comes. His messenger says that he will be here in less than twenty days. He is going back to Bamburgh and returning almost immediately. It must be a matter of importance. The tribute is fully paid. He has another purpose. At least stay and find that out. Who knows, it may work to your advantage. Stay.'

In that final word lay just enough of a command and Padric was still sufficiently obedient to his father for him to bow his head.

He went out and found his horse and rode until he found the highest point that looked east. Only the thought of war could keep her at bay. Perhaps in war itself he would finally be able to destroy her hold over him. He looked out and felt her presence fill the immensity of the countryside. She was everywhere, as air and light. He let himself think about her, exercising this rite as a special privilege, like the compulsion of a miser counting his private gold.

***

'Who shaves the man who shaves every person who does not shave himself?' Padric asked, like a challenge.

Ecfrith shook his head. He had been humbled by Padric in this matter of riddles and questions. Each time he asked one, Padric had the answer. When Padric put one to him, it was either insultingly easy or as difficult as this.

'Let me give you an easy one,' said Ecfrith, ducking his obligation to answer that of Padric. This one was hard. He had learned it only some weeks before and his poet had sworn it was new.

> '"Many were met, men of discretion
> Wisdom and wit, when in there walked . . .
> Two ears it had, and one eye solo,
> Two feet and twelve hundred heads,
> Back, belly, a brace of hands,
> A pair of sides and shoulders and arms
> And one neck." Name, please.'

Padric was surprised. Until now, Ecfrith had trotted out rather obvious riddles and been unable to grapple with any he had not previously learned. Yet he was not a stupid man. Had he been tricking Padric by pretending not to know? Certainly this one was suddenly much harder than any of the others.

Two feet, two ears, twelve hundred heads . . . He concentrated and forgot that Ecfrith had made no attempt to answer his riddle about 'Who shaves the man . . .'

Two ears, one eye solo.

Ecfrith had brought a dozen thegns with him. Dunmael's household was not outnumbered at the feast but there was no doubting that Ecfrith was making a show. His men had come in full fig. Weapons had been slung about them in an abundance envied by the men of Rheged who revealed none of their envy, reserving it for when the Northumbrians left. Only the swords of Dunmael and Padric and his brothers could compare with the swords, axes, daggers, bows, helmets, fine shields and ornamental leather breastplates of these big warriors. They rubbed in their superiority by word and gesture and their hosts were increasingly strained. Many of them were blond or light-coloured, contrasting strongly with the dark or reddish hair of the men of Rheged. Some were bigger: only Padric or Riderch stood as tall as several of them and all of them were heavier than Padric. They ate massively, appearing to think it a duty to bloat themselves to bursting.

A pair of sides, and shoulders and arms. Padric brooded on. This was clearly a man or a woman.

One eye solo. One eyed.

Twelve hundred heads . . .

'A one-eyed garlic seller,' said Ecfrith, abruptly, fearing that
Padric might strike on it. His entourage laughed and raised their
cups of beer. 'As for your man who shaves everyone – I say he
should have his throat slit.'

'I am a man of Rheged,' said Padric, speaking with that mockery
he seemed to reserve for Ecfrith and which drove Ecfrith half-mad.
'Tell me. What do you say if I tell you that all men of Rheged
are liars?'

'Ha! You tell the truth. All men of Rheged *are* liars!'

'But I am a man of Rheged. Therefore I did not tell the truth.'

'So you lied.'

'Does that mean I told the truth? When I said that all men of
Rheged lied?'

'I have a question for the chief man of Rheged which will need all
his truth,' said Ecfrith, and the tone made it clear that he assumed
that, in this gathering, he was in command. It also indicated, for
the first time openly, that there was a purpose to this visit. 'Or have
you any more unanswerable questions, cousin?'

'Not yet,' said Padric.

'Then will you play for us? All men know that the house of
Dunmael is famous for its music.'

'Penraddin will play,' said Dunmael smoothly. He saw that
nothing would persuade Padric to play and the obstinacy would
have been seen as a slight. His guests seemed to be looking for
trouble. Dunmael glanced over at his wife who saw what she must
do. Her own manners had been tried. She and her daughters had
been chafed by the drunken guests as they had passed among them
with the wine and beer.

'Penraddin?' Ecfrith beamed, rather stupidly Padric thought. He
watched him as his young sister, younger than Bega but about as
tall as she was and more plumply built, came obediently to the
harp. Ecfrith could not take his eyes off her.

Dunmael took it all in. It was essential that the night did not
turn into a brawl. Whoever gained that battle, he and his family
would only lose. Ecfrith was pushing it hard.

The hall was hot and men and women had taken off their
long woollen cloaks. Penraddin was revealed wearing a shift
embroidered by the Celtic women in many-spiralled patterns.
Her young body was clearly and succulently displayed. Her hair

had been loosened for the feast and it fell straight, thick and long, so that when she sat to play the harp she had to spread it wide so as not to sit on it. Her face had the fine, unafraid, serene quality of someone very young who had never doubted her right to be regarded as handsome and noble.

She played and sang and Ecfrith motioned his sprawling warriors to be silent. As she drew in the attention of the guests, Padric took the opportunity to glance casually and carefully around the hall.

The weapons had been left outside under the guard of two servants, one from each camp. Padric, his brothers and their men had assumed strategic positions. Riderch, broad as any of them, was next to the fire where heated irons, still being used to grill last delicacies, could be snatched and used to damaging effect. Urien lolled furthest away, very near the door, beside the armed guard, a Rheged man who stood to ward off danger from outside but could easily be summoned into the hall. The most long-serving of the male servants carried long knives in their garments: at least two had swords strapped down their sides. They were never far away from the men they served every day. The women had been told what they must do if a fight were to break out and, although a number of dogs were inside the feast, a number, the fiercest, unfed, were ready, hidden outside, to be unleashed if necessary.

With such arrangements in place, Padric listened to the music calmly: but with little concentration. For his eye was caught by the sadness in his father's face. Dunmael, Padric guessed, was afraid of how he might respond to the demand which Ecfrith was to make. He had spent a lifetime yielding. It had seemed the only way. Now, the strongest of his sons was telling him that this was no longer any good. Padric had to think of a way to safeguard Dunmael and his mother and sisters and yet do what he planned to do.

He followed his father's apparently nonchalant gaze and saw that it played between Ecfrith and Penraddin. Now Padric understood the purpose of Ecfrith's visit.

He sat tight and made himself absorb it. He glanced at the gloating, beer-bloated face of Ecfrith and there was no mistaking the expression. Nor, when his eyes flickered across the faces of those unbearable thegns, could he see anything but coarse confirmation of the suspicion to which his father's look had alerted him.

Penraddin sensed the interest she was arousing and her bold
spirit rose to meet it. Her voice seemed to challenge the sparkling
sound of the strings and as she drew on the melancholy springs of
the lament, the sentimentality of all the men was tapped and they
listened in reverence.

When she finished, Ecfrith levered himself up, with only a
little difficulty, and went across to her. He took off an armlet of
glistening gold, which was twisted in several coils, the head of a
serpent at either end.

'This is a small gift,' he said, bowing a little and holding on to
his dignity, just.

Penraddin had disliked Ecfrith. She would have said that she
hated him. But her father had received him with all honours and he
had been *quite* clever at getting out of Padric's remorseless riddles
and questions. Most of all she had felt the power of his position
as she had played. She had seen how a single gesture had settled
the scattered anarchy of his men. And the armlet was so heavy, so
much gold, the serpent heads so beautifully worked.

'Hold out your arm.'

Penraddin was obedient. As he slipped it over her hand, Padric,
witnessing, remembered with terrible acuteness the armlet he
had given Chad to give Bega. Did she wear it? Where was
she now? Was she thinking of him as he, whatever strategy
he followed, could not stop thinking about her? Was his armlet
protecting her?

'This will protect you,' said Ecfrith, loudly. 'Let all men here
know that the Princess Penraddin will be protected by this sacred
gift and by Prince Ecfrith of Bernicia and Deira which makes up
Northumbria which will, one day, under my leadership, conquer
the whole of the island once called Britain.'

Padric looked at Dunmael, who looked away.

<hr/>

Just before dawn and before anyone was awake, Padric left the great
hall and went to the women's quarters.

He found Penraddin, woke her quietly – she made no fuss – and they went out into the last chapter of the night. It was cold but not uncomfortably so. In their big cloaks and leather boots they were soon warm enough, walking through the small courtyards, down the fortified hill. His plan was wrapped in a story.

'Let me tell you about King Edwin and his chief priest, Coifi,' Padric said. 'Edwin, you remember, was the first king of those who conquered our land. Our great ancestor baptised him, when our father was a child, and so Rheged was not put to the sword then. Edwin wanted an alliance with us and we welcomed it. I am telling you this because I want you to know that I do not hate all those who now rule over us. Yet there is one thing you must know. That is why I mentioned Coifi, Edwin's high priest.'

Penraddin held on to her brother's arm. They were still inside the mounds and stockade which protected the settlement, but was that the low call of a wolf she had heard? She was glad for his sword.

'At that time – and remember, our father was alive – there was no man at the court of Edwin, including the King himself, who could read or write. The Court is still illiterate today. None, of course, was of our faith. But Edwin was converted and he called his council and asked them to follow him in this new faith. All of them found it very strange. Then Coifi, the pagan high priest, spoke. "I have been the most devoted of all your subjects to our religion," he said to King Edwin. "I have worshipped at our altars and asked you to worship with me. No one has served our gods more than I have. Yet what have I gained compared with others? You have not shown me any particular favour. My life has not had any advantages. I gave our gods the greatest service and had very little in return. And so I think we should try this new powerful God who promises new truths. If His teachings are more helpful and if His protection is more effective, then let's worship Him."'

Padric had imitated the voice of an old monk who used to live with them when they were children and Penraddin laughed as he told the story. He continued. 'To show that he was sincere, this Coifi asked Edwin for a spear which hitherto he had been forbidden to carry – because he was a priest (unlike ours) – and a horse which also had been forbidden him. Edwin gave them to him. Coifi rode into the temple he had built and threw the spear at the pagan idols, desecrating the altars. Then, in front of all the people, who thought he had gone mad, he set fire to the temple.

From that temple he rode to others and everywhere he desecrated altars and burned buildings.

'After that he sought out a holy man and Coifi became a convert.' Padric laughed.

'Did he die in the faith?' Penraddin asked; she felt quite fond of Coifi.

'I don't know.'

'Did the people stop thinking that he was mad?'

'I think so.'

'I like to think of him riding on that horse and throwing his spear at the pagan altars!'

'But why did he do it, do you think?'

'Because he saw that our faith was best.' Penraddin's thirteen-year-old certainty was pat on cue.

'Best for what?'

'Just best.'

'Best for him. Just for him.'

'He said so. I liked that bit as well.'

'Why best for him?'

'Because the pagan gods had not given him enough.'

'Exactly. So he changed gods to receive more favours.'

'He hoped so.'

'I agree. So he hoped.' Padric squeezed her arm and they turned to walk back up the hill, and east, into the dawn now milking over the night. 'But do you not see? There was nothing there about faith. There was nothing there about the life and miracles of Jesus Christ. Nothing about revelation. Nothing about the word of God.' Penraddin was not as impressed as he wanted her to be. Indeed she seemed to smile on the cynicism of Coifi. Padric went further. 'He did it for personal advantage and nothing else. Ecfrith is the same. They remain pagans. Christianity to them is just a convenient battle-cry. Ecfrith has a Christian wife: she comes from a Christian family in the south. But not only does she not influence him, he wants to follow his old customs and take other wives. No Christian would do that.'

'There are Christians with more than one woman.'

'And I have seen them in Ireland, yes. A wife, a concubine, a mistress, perhaps more than one mistress. And Solomon had many wives. But Christ came to teach us different ways.'

Penraddin had not expected this. She had gone to sleep still glowing from the attention she had received. She had never been such a centre of interest. The experience made her proud. The armlet made her feel important. She had rubbed it until the moment she fell asleep and even during the walk with Padric, she had been conscious of it, waiting for the light to catch it and show off its lustre. She had been prized and now, she sensed, she was being pulled down.

'Does Ecfrith want me for his other wife?'

'I fear that is why he has come here.'

'Why do you fear it?'

'For you.'

'Why,' said Penraddin, who had courage even in front of her travelled and hero-worshipped brother, 'should you fear for me what I don't fear for myself?'

'He is not of our faith.'

'I could help him.'

'He is someone you hated, Penraddin.'

'I've changed.' She fingered the golden gift, lovingly.

'I do not trust him.'

'You do not have to.'

Their mother had been a good teacher to both of them. But Penraddin had to know the seriousness of it.

'If you let him take you, then you will be living with my enemy.'

The girl stopped and looked at her brother closely. She saw and knew that he said what he meant.

'Why is that?'

'You can't expect me to tell you my plans, Penraddin. It would be dangerous for you to know. But Ecfrith is my enemy now and he will remain my enemy until one of us is dead.'

'Tell me.'

Padric shook his head.

'It's not fair.'

Padric was expressionless.

'It's just that you don't want me to marry him. His wife is a virgin and she will soon leave him. All the world knows that she is a virgin. There is no shame in being the real wife. Our father's sister married his father. Why do you not accept this as it is?'

'And what is it?'

'We are part of them. And they are part of us.'

'We are the part that pays tribute,' said Padric, softly. 'We are the part that Ecfrith's father hammered into submission and exile when we exercised our independence and fought against him.'

'So if I do marry him?'

'Then, Penraddin, it is my duty to tell you that you go to a cruel man and someone who will some day make you weep and wish that you had never been born.'

'So stay here? Who is around here? Or go into Ireland and live like the others? What are you going to do?'

'"Follow the deer". That, at first, is what I shall do.'

'If Ecfrith asks me to go to his court – imagine the court, Padric! – then I shall go. You follow the deer!'

Padric let go her arm.

'We marry whom God sends,' said Penraddin, spiritedly, and went swiftly ahead of him. Perhaps, Padric thought, by opposing her I have egged her on. He watched her go.

The gestures of independence – the jaunt in the walk, the flicking of the head from side to side, hopelessly reminded Padric of Bega's gestures.

He would talk to his mother about Penraddin. Perhaps she could find a way to dislodge her impulsive certainty.

'There is nothing I can say to change your mind?'

'Nothing.'

Dunmael, Padric, Urien, Riderch and three soldiers stood in the highest courtyard of Dunmael's house, their horses ready. Two servants had packed the four ponies with supplies.

'If I had denied Penraddin to Ecfrith?'

'Even so I would have gone.'

'But you would have . . .' Dunmael wanted his son's good opinion but was too proud to reveal the need.

'Perhaps it is for the better,' said Padric. 'When we begin to attack him he will be less likely to come here for his revenge.'

'Must you attack him?'

'You know the answer to that.' He smiled. 'It is time to give up riddles and take up this.' He unsheathed his long sword and held it up to the sun.

'No. Not the sword. Look at what we have, Padric.' Dunmael swept out his arm as if drawing a curtain.

Padric followed his father's hand. There, in late morning, was the country of his youth and of his heart. The sense of being on the roof of the world filled him with deep happiness: the flash of the sea; the prospect of distant bounding mountains; the knowledge of the fortress of hills to the south, places where he had hunted and through which he had travelled with his father so often. This, his father was saying, this which meant so much to him, could be his.

'But what is the point of it,' he heard himself asking, sheathing his sword, quite bitterly, 'if it is not truly ours?'

'We live here. We rule over it.'

'But it is not ours. We will have to oppose them some time, Father, and I think we must start now.'

'We can live together,' said Dunmael, firmly.

'Perhaps you can,' Padric replied and added, 'Yes, I love this place. But if I am to have it for the future, I must leave it now. Give us your blessing, Father.'

Dunmael knew that his sons would have wished him to ride with them. He also knew that his alliance with Oswy had restricted what could have been a terrible carnage. So often in the past, a burning vengeance had been visited on the north. This time, by his wise compromise and by his use of the family connection, he had, he thought, prevented the worst. But for Padric and his brothers, that was not enough.

'I give you my blessing,' he said. 'Go safely. Return unharmed. God be with you.'

'God be with you.'

The response from several throats came like a ragged, rather lame, salute. They were leaving him because he would not fight. That was how they saw it and Dunmael endured the unspoken reproach.

He walked some way with them and looked on as they wended down the hillside and turned into the valley which would take them north. Even after they had gone he stood there, the dogs snuffling in the ground about him, his hand growing cold on the handle of his well-sheathed sword.

CHAPTER THIRTY

The journey to Coldingham exhausted Bega. She was impatient with the debilitating fatigue but the more she struggled
the worse it became. Brought up with good food and exercise, she
had not known illness until her banishment from Cathal's house.
Since then, she seemed to have been permanently tired or sick,
or both.

She had wanted to enter into her new life with all her might.
Instead, she was carried into the hospital on a litter. She stayed
there for several weeks. A kindly old nun who herself looked at
death's door came regularly to give her some food. Chad was not
allowed to visit. The nun explained that although it was a mixed
house, the men and women were permitted little contact.

As spring ripened to summer and Bega began to gain strength
enough to leave the hospital for short walks and attend the
church, she discovered that this was not true. The house was
in disorder. A number of the younger, often illegitimate, sons of
the Northumbrian noble families had joined the order for the easy
pickings they could foresee, determined to pass their daily lives as
comfortably and hedonistically as their more favoured brothers
and cousins who had been afforded the status and prospects of
warriors. The nuns were largely from peasant families – mostly
young in this new house – and those few from the better families
became caught up in the excitement.

She saw Chad on her walks and quickly obtained the facts
from him.

Bega was not shocked. The behaviour was no worse than she
had seen among her brothers and her friends and there were houses
in Ireland given over to sensual riot. Her upbringing in her father's
household made her well able to size it up and keep herself safe.

Besides, she had a double protection: the flimsy one that she was an invalid; the stronger one that she had been brought by Cuthbert whose early eminence held back even the most loutish.

As a formality, Bega asked to see the abbot who had not visited her in the hospital. This unusual lack of courtesy was explained as soon as they met. The man reeked of drink. He spent the whole interview praising Cuthbert which, Bega knew insultingly plainly, was meant to get back to him and be a form of insurance. This was the church outside Ireland!

She adopted the older nun, kept to the hospital as if it were her cell, and followed a routine as fully matched to her strength as she could tolerate. She cautioned Chad against the excesses of the place and told him to keep Cal within calling distance at all times. Chad was working in the gardens. Bega was relieved. It was probably the safest place for him.

Thus she spent her first few months in training to be a bride of Christ. The solitude had become a preferred state – for only when alone could she give full thought to Padric. She hunted out solitary time to be with him. It seemed useless trying to stop it. Soon, she thought, she would be stronger and then with God's help she could throw away thoughts which, though not impure, undoubtedly diverted her full energy from worship.

It was an uneasy interval. It seemed to Bega that everyone knew that there would be retribution but the grip of wickedness and the vice of illicit ungodly pleasure had taken fast hold. It was like a fever, she thought. As if they ought to be in the hospital and she, sick as she was, ought to be governing a place which was beginning to resemble an inn and a brothel more than any place of God.

Then Cuthbert descended on Coldingham from its founding house like an avenging sword. He came accompanied by monks and soldiers from the court of Oswy and bringing a new head of the house, an abbess of the royal blood. Bega saw him only briefly, for he ordered her to stay in the hospital until he had done his duty. There were expulsions, fines and, for those who pleaded to stay, floggings of the severest nature. When he had finished, the numbers were more than halved. Those remaining were crushed, those ejected disgraced.

'I ask your forgiveness that I brought you to such a place,' said Cuthbert, who had come into the small hospital.

'You could not have known,' said Bega.

'I will punish myself,' said Cuthbert calmly. 'If these heathens had dragged you into their licentious furies, what might have happened?' He shook his head. 'No, I deserve punishment much greater than that which I have given to these stupid, wayward children and I will bring it on myself.'

'No.' Bega felt sorry that the thin frame and the worn look on such a young man should have to endure what she thought of as wholly unnecessary torment. 'I have come to no harm,' she said. 'Perhaps—' timidly she said this '—God was protecting me because of what I bear.'

'What you bear,' said Cuthbert most solemnly, and his serious-ness cut through to her heart as it did to all who were swayed and converted by him, 'is the lightest grace and the greatest weight a Christian can carry. It has been given for some great purpose, Bega. That is why we must not tell a single soul. And that is why I must suffer for putting you where your gift could have been in danger, or could have been used for a trivial purpose.

'I will take you to Streanaeshalch, also called Whitby, where the Abbess Hilda will properly begin your novitiate training and show you the path that you will follow.'

The Abbess Hilda was a stern woman but also one whose eyes twinkled with fun. Behind her back they called her 'Mother'. She did not entirely disapprove. She might even, she considered, encourage it.

Hilda was tall, flaxen-haired, handsome in a rather horse-faced way, thin, supple and almost crushingly enthusiastic. As a girl – and a member of the pious East Anglian royal family – she had wanted to go to France to join her sister Hereswith in the community at Chelles. She would have followed other famous English women converts to France: Bathild, sold as a slave, who became the wife of Clovis II and the benefactress of Faremoutiers-en-Brie, as well as the founder of Chelles; Erecengota, Saethryth and Aethelberg, all of whom went to

Faremoutiers, the latter two becoming abbesses of the community despite their foreign origin.

Aidan had persuaded Hilda to stay and help him in his task. Heiu, another protégée of Aidan and the first woman in Northumbria to become a nun, founded the monastery at Hartlepool and Hilda took over as abbess after her death. Now she had been sent to the high cliff edge of the land, to Whitby. Her community looked directly across the sea, east, to the dark places which needed to be lit up by the illumination of the Holy Spirit. It was from the east that Christ had come and would come again.

Whitby was established as a double community – five bishops were to graduate under Hilda's teaching. As abbess she ruled over men and women.

When Bega arrived, the settlement of Whitby was less than half-finished. King Oswy had given Hilda several farms in the district, the rents of which would support the large community Hilda intended to install there. The community itself was designed not only to be self-sufficient but, through its general produce and the specialised working of jet into crosses and pendants, to increase the wealth of the abbey. Hilda made her own inheritance available. As the place grew on its spectacular setting high above the tiny fishing settlement in the natural harbour beneath, many were attracted to work and then stay there. Hilda could have been tempted to give thanks for the polygamy of the invading tribes which produced such a ready surplus of young men and women. The growing strength of the church made it an increasingly attractive alternative for those balked at worldly ambitions. Their pagan history made their submission to Jesus Christ all the more satisfying for Hilda.

'I would have preferred a community of women, far easier, without any men at all. But we are determined to prove that a mixed house can work,' she said as she took Bega round, a few days after she had arrived. Bega had never seen such intense activity. Scores of men and women were digging the wooden circular foundations, stacking thatch for the roofs, constructing pens for the sheep and goats, building the walls and laying out the gardens, creating, on a glorious summer day, a place bigger than anything Bega had seen, save Caerel. 'And men have their uses,' she smiled at an almost grotesquely muscular man who was carrying several heavy logs across his shoulders, 'they can speed things up in certain areas.' She walked with glorious confidence, as if her presence alone, failing all else, would raise up the walls and build this city of God on a barren cliff.

'This is the wall which will divide the two halves of the community.' It was the most complete of all the constructions. 'The only contact between the two will be myself.' She went over to where a narrow door was being put in place. 'This is my exit and my entrance,' she said. 'Coldingham went over to the devil. You are well out of it. My cousin is a strong woman. *Very* direct.' Hilda smiled approvingly at the Boudiccan qualities of another member of a royal household. 'She will control them – or get rid of them. There can be no half way in discipline in the spiritual army of God any more than in His temporal army. Do you agree?' Bega scarcely had time to nod, so fast had she to move to keep up with Hilda's lanky, urgent stride.

'Cuthbert is a remarkable man, don't you think? Undoubtedly he will be one of God's saints.'

A saint! The word shocked her. Were there, on earth now, among those she knew and had spoken to and touched, saints to compare with the saints in the gospels? Bega's look of astonishment communicated itself to Hilda.

'Don't look so surprised. We could have many saints. God decides when He will choose a people. He chose the people of Israel for the greatest possible honour, His Son, who chose the apostles. He has chosen us for a great work.' She smiled. 'I shall tell you what that is tomorrow, after matins. You are sleeping over there – Isidore will take you.' Isidore was small, blonde, young, sweet-faced, smiling, a little hunchbacked and utterly enthralled by Hilda.

'The boy can work in the gardens. On the other side of the wall. Or he can go and be a fisherman. I recommend that. He needs the experience. Look at the way they are thatching the monks' dormitory!' She strode over to the men who were too caught up in the lazy summer day to be careful enough for Hilda's standards. Her criticism clarioned around the site.

Chad had never been more than a couple of yards behind Bega. He had heard everything. Hilda's voice was unembarrassedly clear, loud and incisive. Cal had been rather subdued and Chad was convinced that the dog too was chastened by the tone in the voice of this terrifying abbess.

Bega watched her stride off and turned to Chad.

She smiled. The boy's worries glided away. Cal wagged his tail. Isidore went over to ruffle Cal's coat. The three of them clicked in Bega's mind. They were all, even Isidore, part of her little family. Already in this new place she felt on firmer ground than at any time since she had left Ireland. An almost forgotten gaiety returned to her.

'Let us walk to the edge of the cliff and give thanks,' said Bega.

It was such a day! Her spirits were lifted up into the bright summer sky just as the gulls were uplifted by the invisible wind, their wings outstretched, unmoving.

As she walked with Chad and Cal through the busy groups of people, men, women and children melding into a common purpose, the sounds of voices contrasting with the thud of implements, a snatch of bird song and child plaint, the thrilling calls of the circling swooping gulls, Bega felt a spring of release. She did not examine it. She dared not rely on it. She tried not to acknowledge it. All that she would allow herself was to note the bounce of her step on the turf, the salty sea-freshness on her face. When she came to the edge of the high cliff and looked out over the wave-crinkled, sun-glinted sea speckled with a few small fishing coracles, she seemed to open herself as wide as the sea itself and for the first time for months, call in all that life promised.

She breathed deeply and closed her eyes. It was as if she were breathing for the first time. The tangy, rough sea air sank into her body and seemed to drive out all the weakness. The light wind lifted her hair. She turned her face full into the sun and let its heat beat some colour back into the dark skin so drained it had become pallid. She stood there for a while, aware that she was neither working nor praying nor meditating nor learning but content just to be. Her body itself was worship. To be alive was prayer. To let the world swirl through her and take her was praise and thanks to God.

The glittering surface of the sea which made her eyes narrow, the sun which made her face hot, the wind that cooled her body, the thick turf under her feet, these alone made her feel good; just to be. She had no thoughts, no plans, no memories even: just this acute feeling of herself. No more than a leaf growing, staying and then falling from a tree.

Bega wanted these moments to go on, until they became her death. This might be the shape of death to one about to enter the heavenly kingdom. What she felt was not earthly although it was the forces of the earth which seemed to infuse her. 'Make me,' she murmured, 'the vessel for Thy will.' She floated. She journeyed beyond thought.

When she opened her eyes she saw Chad, staring at her, his brown eyes anxious. Bega felt rather faint and put out her arms. He ran to take one, Isidore the other. They helped her sit down.

If only she could have stayed where the moment had taken her. She squeezed her eyes tight to try to regain that notion of still movement, suffused lightness, controlled freedom, empty fulfilment. Had it been a vision? Had she in fact begun to drift towards God?

Taking a deep breath, Bega stood up, shook her head and went back down into the noise and reassuring solid things being hammered and carved and marshalled into solid earthly shapes.

The next day was warm but duller. Hilda was relieved. 'I wanted to talk to you about several matters, Bega. But I hate being indoors on a sunny day. God must have given me this cloud for your sake!' She smiled and showed her rather uneven and, in three or four cases, bad teeth. 'Indoors is so much better for serious talk, don't you feel?'

Bega nodded. She loved the way that Abbess Hilda ended many of her statements with a question but she knew better than to waste time replying. It was often little more than a conversational embrace. Hilda wanted to include everyone in her field of energetic optimism and this was just another way.

They were in what was to be the parlour of the abbess. The wooden walls were completed. The roof was to go on soon. The earth floor had been beaten down. There was a bare and crudely made table and two chairs. The women sat opposite each other – as Hilda preferred. The thatchers had been sent away.

Hilda wasted no more time on small talk.

'I told you yesterday that I would reveal to you what our great work was here at Whitby. Cuthbert,' she spoke his name with distinguishing respect, 'told me of your struggles and I was most impressed. But of course you are of good Irish stock. We owe so much to the Irish.' Hilda's smile of gratitude was hopelessly infectious and Bega found herself grinning back, accepting this compliment on behalf of all her race. 'My parents in East Anglia were converted by the Irish, you know. They're everywhere you look. While the rest of us were painting ourselves blue and running around worshipping waterfalls, there were enough of the Irish, thanks be to God, to keep the word alive. Are we still enough?'

She barely paused. 'You have been lucky. Erebert is not an easy man but he was quite brilliant in all his monastic exercises, and quite adamant about being a hermit, although he has never been well and he is fussy, but underneath that fussiness is a soul which is seeking to be perfect. To meet him was a privilege. And then of course you met Cuthbert. What more can one say about him? God has blessed us. And from what you have told me, Cathleen, Donal and Padric were fine Christians.' She smiled approvingly. 'You have lived in a small, privileged world, Bega. As I did.' Hilda paused and her expression which had been playful took on the severity which had already given her a wide reputation.

'But in the big world beyond the small fires of our faith there is a terrible darkness. Imagine us as a small house on a great moor. And beyond the moor are mountains and rivers. Beyond that there are plains and lakes. Beyond that there are more and yet more lands and seas and waters stretching so far that the mind grows weary at the thought of counting how much there is. We Christians are that small house. Out there is darkness, Bega. Even those who joyfully help us build the abbey today are mostly pagan and will go back from here to revert to their pagan ways. I was christened by a man who was the only man in the whole of three kingdoms of this country who could read and write. Imagine that, Bega! Let your mind grasp it.' She paused to let the effect set in.

'You come from Ireland. You have had the cross and the word before your eyes every day of your life. This is not what faces so many here and elsewhere on God's earth. They see no heaven. They know no gospels. They have no true faith. They are souls condemned to eternal torment, Bega, unless we save them. Each saved soul is our great gift to God. Yet we could so easily be made extinct. Some years ago a plague took away almost all the men in our first two monasteries. The victory of a pagan king in my lifetime included the murder of one hundred monks who had gathered unarmed on the battlefield to pray for the victory of the Christian cause. Their faith was not strong enough. God did not hear. God will only hear if we are many. Do you see?'

Now that Hilda was launched, Bega felt herself almost mesmerised. At first she had felt herself back at the knee of Cathleen or being a young girl tutored by Padric. Now she felt that she was an equal, being called to arms. She could see the darkness outside. Her memory reinforced it with close details from the first journeys she had undertaken across Ireland and then across the spine of North Britain. She filled in with her imagination and saw, as Hilda was bidding her, those few men and women as faint lights on endless sombre marshes of ignorance and resentment.

'This is why we women are so important,' said Hilda. 'Some say it is very cunning of the Celtic monks to go first to the wives and daughters and nieces of the kings and the nobles. I see it as God's guidance. For we have the time and the will to devote our whole lives – we need not be consumed with war – we can be wholly, body and soul, in the army of Christ.

'We must get out to the people,' said Hilda. 'We have to share our joy and we have to ensure that the word of God takes root as the acorn roots the oak. We have been given this time, Bega, through God's grace. It is not for us to understand why. But one thing I do know: this time will not come again. The people of Israel were given their time. You in Ireland had your time. Some say that elsewhere there have been groups almost as devoted as yours. But now it is our turn. And we must not let God down!'

Her eyes glittered. Bega was excited. She wanted to leap out of her chair immediately and race into battle.

Abruptly Hilda stood up, full of her hope and godly zeal for the future. 'What we can do above all is to teach,' she continued.

Bega was badly disappointed. She wanted to go into the forests where there were wolves and wild boars and find pagan tribes and preach, cleanse their fouled souls, bring them to Christ.

'We are an army which must march on its words,' said Hilda. 'Words, the words of the saints, the words of the psalmists, the words of Christ Himself, the words of God – these are what we need. It is hard to learn. You say your brothers were taught – did they learn? Of course they didn't – they will be ignorant oafs until they die spitting out a few half-remembered phrases like crazy old soothsayers.

'It is my mission to change that. My life will be dedicated to making men and women learn. They will know their gospels and their commentaries! They will know their grammars and their psalms: they will read books which will be brought from Rome. They will know those books and be able to teach others so that never again will the words of our faith be lost.

'Not only the words of God and Jesus Christ and His apostles, but the commentaries, Sidonius Apollinarius, St Augustine, the Institutes and Conferences of John Cassian Cassiodorus. On and on they flow!

'Imagine a world without the richness given to those of us who can read. The void. The terrors. The shameful ignorance. We must change that. And I see you, Bega,' she had begun to pace the small room and was now on Bega's side of the table, standing behind her, both hands firmly pressed on the young woman's slight shoulders. 'If all that Cuthbert has told me about you is true, I see you . . .' if Bega could have seen Hilda's eyes she would have seen a visionary, '. . . as one day, one of my chief aides. You have a power in you given by God. You have suffered. I know that. You know pain. I can see that. You will always be restless. I understand that. But you are the clay that I need. You are like me, Bega. All I need is a few more women like you, and we can do God's work so well that it will never be undone, not for a thousand years.'

Bega looked up. Staring over the wooden wall were faces, men and women drawn by the sound of that clear calling voice. Hilda looked around at them with an air that might even have been called triumphant.

'We will all do God's will,' she said 'and in His Name, we will light up the whole world.' She pressed Bega's shoulders one final time and made a shooing gesture with her right arm. 'Be off with you,' she said to the spontaneous congregation. 'Back to your work.' She smiled. The expression was oddly affecting and sweet despite the teeth. Hilda breathed very deeply and sighed with satisfaction. Then, in a completely different tone, brisk, quite hard, she said:

'I saw you go over to the edge of the cliff.'

'Yes,' said Bega. 'It feels like the end of the world.'

'Or the leaping off place for a new world?' Hilda suggested.

'I suppose so.'

'I didn't object to your going over there,' said Hilda, with a set face of fair play, 'but in future when you stray away from the site you must ask my permission.'

'I'm sorry.' Bega blushed, resentfully.

'Perfectly understandable this once,' said Hilda.

'Thank you.'

'We shall be good friends,' said Hilda. 'Off you go.'

Perhaps as a riposte to this peremptory dismissal, Bega continued to seek out that spot – sometimes with permission – sometimes it happened that she was there as if by accident. It became known as 'Bega's Place'.

CHAPTER THIRTY-ONE

It was only after three years that Bega was given permission to do what she had longed to do since Cathleen had filled her mind with lurid tales of the great Irish missionaries.

'You have been as attentive and disciplined as anyone could possibly have wished,' said Hilda, in a parlour now well completed and beginning to show one or two signs of luxury: a painting of Christ brought back from Rome, a rug in reds and yellows woven by men who had come first to Canterbury to work on the tapestries and then moved up-country, books, of course, more than a dozen now, glittering in the candlelight, some of them embossed with golden and silver clasps and semi-precious stones. She regarded her pupil with pride but there was, and Bega knew this, a little puzzlement. Bega had not quite come through in the fullness Hilda had hoped. There was nothing, nothing in the slightest, she would tell herself, which could be criticised, and yet there was a distance – aloofness? Haughtiness? Whatever it was it meant that she did not fully yield to Hilda as so many of the others did; and so was she fully yielding to God? Yet, the intelligence, the understanding of the commentaries, the dexterity in writing, the punctilious observance of the great currents of discipline which fed into this landlocked sea of faith – all these were exemplary.

'You have often expressed the wish to go on a mission.' Bega's body and her look became, immediately, much more alert. Hilda was pleased that she had identified the locus of interest so clearly but just a little disappointed that this should be something which would take the girl away from Whitby. Why did she concern herself so much with one out of so many? So, she continued, a little crossly, but fair, always fair, 'I believe that you have earned that right,' she said and could not but be warmed by the rush of

Bega's gratitude: for a moment she thought the young woman
might even launch herself across the room into an embrace.

'Thank you, Mother,' Bega said, fighting hard to moderate the
whoosh of delight the news brought her.

'It will last at least two weeks, but certainly not more than
three,' said Hilda. 'Tuda, one of the most devout and zealous
of the younger men, will lead it. He is already showing promise
of a glorious future. God may well have marked him down for a
bishop and I could not disagree. Ingaberga will be with you: as
you well know, she is one of the most steady and one of the few
to come unscathed through that terrible business at Coldingham,
which was much worse than I understood when first you arrived
here. It still strikes me as something of a miracle that someone
of your inexperience and youth was so protected. It leads me to
wonder whether you have a guardian angel?'

Did Hilda know about the cross? Bega could feel it deep in
her pocket, lightly padded against her thigh. It had been hard
not to share the secret with Hilda who had indeed been like
a mother to her and demanded as part of the process that no
secrets be hidden from her just as none were hidden from God.
Yet the unique responsibility and the promises she had made to
Cuthbert had kept her silent. It was uneasy. Like her dreams
of Padric, it undermined, she thought, her otherwise strenuous
attempt to purify herself and her soul for the duty of total service
to Jesus Christ.

'You do right to blush,' said Hilda. 'It would be presumptuous
of you to think that you do have a guardian angel. But,' and she
smiled, 'I can say it to you. Ingaberga is a little old now and
the pains in her arms are sometimes most severe but she is an
experienced missionary and ever eager to harvest souls. Isidore
will go to help you both.' Hilda paused. She had been aware
of being too demanding of Bega and had decided to show a
rare favour. 'I have also decided that Chad can accompany you.
He has developed well. He is a steady and serious young man
and his interest in the work of the illuminators and scribes is
very touching. One day perhaps we may be able to make direct
use of him there but meanwhile he is invaluable in the gardens.
Apart from anything else, do you know that he is already our best
apiarist?'

Bega felt proud of him. Chad was now becoming a young

man, a little taller than Bega, though nowhere near the height of Padric and Urien, Riderch or Cuthbert, Tuda and others of noble families. He had begun to make himself useful by helping grind the colours for the brilliantly illuminated gospels. Bega had watched him grow not only in height but in contentment and with a sense of purpose. She guessed, rightly, that he would have loved the life of a monk but would need courage to take the first steps.

'He will be very helpful,' said Bega, again making an effort to conceal her pleasure. 'He is most capable.'

'So there it is!' Hilda clapped her hands as she stood up; a characteristic double action much commented on and even once or twice slyly imitated by that ever-increasing body of nuns and monks who had followed her to this cliff-top city of God.

⁂

A few days later and they were on their way.

Bega waited until they were out of sight of the abbey before she let her spirits lift. Her conscience was troubled but there was no denying it: she felt released, at large, unconfined. Even more, she felt that this was work which she could do and work which the Lord needed. She could pray, but perhaps not as well as others. She could try to purge her soul, others seemed more successful. She could follow a discipline, but when so many did, what was the especial merit in that? she thought, in her still sadly unhumble heart. But this – out into the world, deliberately seeking the desolate places, putting yourself at real risk, daring to take the word of God where it had never been before and challenge lesser but older gods and those whose lives had depended on them – this was true work!

They quietly settled into a line. Tuda led, followed by Ingaberga; Bega followed with Isidore never more than a fearful half-step behind; Chad brought up the rear with Cal, who bounded around them on permanent alert. Tuda had been supplied with a sword; the others had been given stout staffs.

They went up-country, angling themselves inland, twice stopping at well-established settlements to make sure of their direction. On each occasion they were left under no illusion that the
tribes they were seeking out were dangerous and best left alone.
The news fed Bega with a thrill of recklessness, a feeling so
long unknown to her that it came as a jolt of pleasure. Isidore's
ill-concealed terror only confirmed her own sense of boldness.

By mid-afternoon, a dry, cold, late-summer afternoon with
unthreatening clouds briskly steering their way out to a sea left
far behind, they found themselves deep in the singular sphere of
ages-old forest with its own peculiar hidden sounds and underfoot
softness, the shadowed trunks of high-rearing trees and the
ominous entanglements of wild shrubs and briars. Whenever
anyone spoke, which was rare, the human sounds appeared alien.
It was as if it were better that nothing at all was said; that they
did not give away their human identity; far safer to hurry along
the bedded forest tracks like creatures of the place, claiming no
more than a safe passage as harm-free as harmless.

Bega had passed through such woods on her journeys from
the coast to Erebert's island and then to Caerel and across the
country, but then she had felt protected and, rightly or wrongly,
on friendly ground. This was not. She felt she was whispered
along the twisting paths between mighty oaks and elms and
alder, lime and hazel trees. The sight of a few huts in a clearing
would be as much a cause for anxiety as relief and the small,
skin-clad woodland people would stop whatever they were doing
and stare in an unmistakably unwelcoming way. But still Tuda
led them further inland, deeper into the dense and tangled miles
of forest.

Tuda had something of the look and attitude of Cuthbert,
Bega had concluded, which was not altogether surprising: many
of the younger monks modelled themselves on Cuthbert. He
practised the same punishing of his body by fasting and enforced
sleeplessness and even self-flagellation. There was a similar zeal,
but what in Cuthbert was driven by a troubled soul was here
reproduced in his follower by a more certain, even blinkered,
unquestioning spirit. There was no doubting the commitment
to Christ. He was, though, Bega thought, in every way a frailer
figure.

They spent the first night in a settlement recommended by

Hilda. It had been the furthest point of the previous mission and its thirty or so inhabitants had been reported as captured for Christ.

Bega could not remember such a collection of mean hovels nor such a group of sullen people. They made minimal efforts at hospitality. A small and rotting hut on the edge of the settlement – little more than a few large branches propped against the wall roofed with a few sods – comprised their accommodation. Food – a greasy, tasteless soup – was given sparingly. When they had eaten, Tuda went to talk to the chief and returned much later than expected.

He had eaten nothing throughout the day and, Bega had noticed, taken only three sips of his soup. A space was made. He shivered quite violently and clasped his hands around his knees to steady himself. In the firelight augmented by one crude candle, all five of them were pocked by shadows. The unaccustomed soughing of wind in the trees just outside the clearing added to their restiveness.

'They believe that they have been let down by God,' announced Tuda, abruptly. 'Rain has ruined the harvest. A boy guarding the goats was killed by a neighbouring tribe and the goats were taken. The chief's favourite wife has died. They go on to list a score of other mishaps – all perfectly normal,' said Tuda in exasperation, 'but all of them, so they now think, attributable to the new God. While without Him, their neighbours have flourished.' Tuda's impatience spoke directly to Bega. She understood. He did not want to waste the mission reconverting a small group who had already been converted. He wanted to follow in the paths and ways of the great saints and martyrs and go where no Christian foot had trod.

'We must pray,' said Tuda, resolutely. He unfolded himself and kneeled, as did the others. 'We must pray that tomorrow we merit the strength of purpose to convince these people not to abandon the God who will save their souls and offer them the chance of eternal life. Let us pray.'

The next three days were difficult, and unnerving. The Christian party prayed together in the middle of the settlement. Tuda preached to the people. Ingaberga, Bega and Isidore nursed the sick. Chad tried to assemble the younger children and teach them, but their elders kept stealing them back for work. The

weather became heavier, uncomfortably threatening rain without delivering it. The stubbornness of those in the settlement
appeared absolute. Again and again they complained of instances
of misfortune which this new God had done nothing to avert, let
alone bring them better fortune. The harvest was ruined; the goats
were gone; someone's wife was dead when the day before she had
been cooking happily; and so it continued.

'Show us a sign,' said the chief, a muscular squat man who
seemed to be bursting out of his layers of skins just as his upper
teeth pointed forward as if bursting out of his mouth. 'You tell
us about these miracles. Let us see one.'

It was useless for Tuda to speak of apostolic grace and the
saints and divine intervention and the power of prayer and God's
mysterious will: nothing but a sign would do.

On the third day, the chief, who had gained stature, it seemed
to Bega, in the eyes of his tribe by being so firm against these
Christians, made his move. He called the village together at
noon. He asked two women to bring the lame child. This was a
desperately spindle-limbed girl of about six who had no strength
at all in her legs and seemed condemned to crawl her way through
life. The child was put between the squatting tribe and the much
smaller group of Christians.

'Now,' said the chief, 'she must walk. Then we will do all these
things that you say. We will not revert to our old gods. We will
pray. We will listen to you. We will aim our souls to the sky for
Christ and find Heaven. But first, she must walk.'

Bega took him in carefully. He was a bully, a small-time chief
who was relishing what he saw as the humiliation of these foreign
and overweening figures. The sort of man her father would have
cut down with his left hand without a thought. Bega's dislike of
the man stiffened as she remembered her father. She also observed
the way he had ogled her and then, finding no satisfaction, settled
the focus of his lust on Isidore. The pretty girl was now most
uncomfortably aware of the much older man's leering attention
and Bega's anger was roused even further when he grinned
gap-mouthed and foolishly at the girl and rubbed his crotch. A
blush shot across Isidore's face.

'We will kneel and pray,' Tuda announced. He looked fragile,
Bega thought. He had not been well when they had set out and
now he was clearly getting worse. 'We owe it to ourselves to pray.'

They kneeled down. Bega's knees pressed down her gown into a gurgle of mud. It was trivial, she knew, but the filth of the place was depressing. At Whitby, the laundry – which was as well organised as everything else in that model godly city – kept the heavy, cumbersome clothes in a steady state of sufficient cleanliness. Hilda's rather advanced notions of personal hygiene had been adopted by all but the oldest or most superstitious of the nuns. Here dirt was like a common affliction. Even the girl in the middle who, as Bega had found when she had visited her and spent some hours with her, had scarcely moved from the corner of her hovel, seemed to have attracted all the muck of the fields in her hair, on her face and bare arms and feet, and the rags which covered her were pasted with dirt. Out of all this peeped a white, drawn face, large eyed, big boned, peering around, unaccustomed to the light; looking, Bega thought, for salvation.

She prayed for the girl and tried, through the exercises she had learned at Whitby, to put everything else out of her mind. She called on Cathleen to come down from heaven and bring a mother's kindness to this poor stricken child-woman. Tuda rocked himself backwards and forwards and murmured his prayers. The sound came out like a guttural chanting and the rhythm and steadiness of it reinforced Bega's efforts. This was what she wanted to be! A handmaiden of God, doing His best service here, face-to-face with the unconverted, attempting to wrestle with ignorant superstition, the lure of old gods and the devil himself and to win the day.

The praying continued until Bega's thighs began to threaten cramp, even though by now she was well used to lengthy supplication. The mid-afternoon had passed, there was the hint of twilight coolness.

The girl had fallen into a doze. The chief looked increasingly complacent.

Tuda, Bega saw, was trembling once more. His face was flushed and looked hot. She was not sure whether this was the power of prayer or the progression of his illness. At last he rose to his feet. He swayed a little as they all did and looked off-balance as the blood coursed through the tautened muscles. Bega felt the swoony but rather entertaining dance of pins and needles and she stretched her legs, unobtrusively, to bring her body back to normal.

Tuda stepped forward and approached the girl. He was a weak

but not a feeble figure and the sword which trailed at his side
gave him authority. He bent down and touched her head and
she looked up at him. Tuda put his hand on her head. Then he
clasped both hands together in prayer.

'I beseech You,' he said, looking up into the sky, 'that if in Your
mercy You have heard our prayers, You will give back to this girl
the gift of walking. Drive out the devil which has possessed her
body. Cleanse her from the sin which has allowed the corruption
of men to take away the use of her legs! We call . . .'

As his words continued, Bega's glance caught that of the
troubled and bemused girl. Both of them smiled. Bega had
nursed her and spoken to her perhaps as kindly as anyone had
ever done and the girl began to move towards her. Tuda, now
fully in a double fever, scarcely seemed to notice that she had
moved away. His prayers rolled on.

The chief fixed his look on the crawling girl and Bega saw
that all the villagers leaned forward to watch what would happen next.

The girl came to her, looked up and tugged at Bega's cloak. She
wanted her to bend down and talk to her as Bega had done before.
But Bega stood firm, her mind now intensified in prayer. The girl
tugged at first playfully and then a little desperately. When she
sensed that, Bega looked down and smiled and prayed to God that
the girl would at least stand. Bega nodded and looked directly into
the large brown eyes. 'Stand,' she murmured. 'Stand . . . for the
glory of God . . .' Ingaberga, hearing this, and Chad and Isidore,
prayed even more fiercely, praying aloud, encouraging the girl with
the noise. She began to haul herself up Bega, clutching her cloak,
taking one handful and then another of the thickly woven wool.

Bega saw that the chief and all his people began to rise up and
their voices grow in a unison of excited murmuring. Tuda turned
to follow the small crowd and his feverish face looked startled.
Bega lifted her eyes and her hands towards heaven and heard
clearly the thin voice of Isidore reciting the oldest and first of
Christ's prayers with an urgency near panic. Chad and Ingaberga
too, she could hear, intensified their pleas to God.

The girl moved so slowly. Bega was aware that perhaps she
was the first person ever to be kind to the girl and to touch and
bathe and comfort her with care. But never, Bega thought, could
she have anticipated this.

As the girl swayed in front of her and keened as if in grief, Bega used her strength to stand firm. She felt that her body was being assisted by a surge of energy, as if the blood were storming through her limbs in a sudden roar. She felt possessed of unusual powers, and of a savage joy. Oh let this girl walk! She felt the girl's hand clamp on the thickly wrapped up fragment of the cross which was always in her pocket and the poor afflicted creature seemed to move into a state of ease and Bega saw the wild eyes all but mad with effort and hope, thrilled with terror.

'Hallelujah!' cried Ingaberga. 'Hallelujah!'

Bega put her arms around the girl and felt the flow of power – whatever it was – rushing out from her satiated flesh into the rickety, spindly limbs and pinched body of the girl whose head jerked from side-to-side wanting to see everything and everyone around her.

'Let her stand alone!'

Bega saw that Tuda was still trembling. She took it to be part of the whole movement which seemed to be sweeping through her; from the cautiously advancing chief and his people, from the earth so that it seemed that her body drew on deep springs of force, from heaven itself to which Chad now looked, waiting for a sign, a pure shaft of light, an opening in the sky, an angel.

'She must stand alone!' said Tuda, loudly, unlike himself.

Tuda's demand was taken up by the chief, who called in his people and a ragged little chant began to assemble itself in this bleak hilltop settlement hidden above an ocean of forest.

But she can't, Bega wanted to say. I can feel her weight all on me. She must be allowed time to get used to the wonderful thing she had already done. She felt fear start to penetrate the body of the girl as demands were more strongly made on her.

'Stand back!' shouted Tuda at Bega. 'Stand back! Let God give her His support if it is His holy wish.' Still Bega did not let go and Tuda's fever winged him into a rage.

No, Bega thought. No, she will fall. Still she felt strong but that translucent soar of inexplicable power had already gone and she could feel now bone against bone, body weight against body weight, herself not the pillar to a miracle but a mere prop. Yet how could she let her fall? It is my own unworthiness, Bega thought, that having been given such a chance to prove God, I should not be able to carry it out.

She stood back. The girl looked at her with anguished reproach, made a faint attempt to stagger and simply crumpled to the ground, beginning to wail almost unbearably. Bega knelt down and cradled her.

Immediately the chief turned to his people and addressed them rapidly in a dialect out of reach of all save Isidore whose interpretative talent was ignored. It was clear that he was using this as proof that his own gods were superior. More – it seemed to Tuda – he was urging them on, perhaps to rush the Christian mission. He drew out his sword and waved it at them. They were nothing like as effectively armed, though the axes, clubs and a few knives which were their weapons could, in numbers, soon have battered through the sword. Nevertheless, he spoke out fiercely.

'You are not being given a miracle because you are not worthy of one,' he said. 'Your disbelief has found you out. Only when you are all baptised into the true church will your souls be pure. Then you will be granted miracles.'

'No!' The chief saw that Tuda was weak and set himself against him. Bega saw tension tighten the crowd and her eyes sought out Chad and Ingaberga, readying them. Isidore was scared and Bega beckoned her over, giving her the girl's head to hold while she stood up.

Tuda was in some trouble. His fever unbalanced a mind never clear about violent action although like all other monks, he had no illusions about its occasional necessity. He knew that on missions such as these there would be physical danger. Some elementary exercise with the sword had been allowed for, but Tuda was a man of persuasion and, as Bega had seen, he had struggled even to draw the sword out of the scabbard.

Bega could still see that the chief was looking over to Isidore who was shaking, though bravely murmuring comforting prayers over the bemused girl. There was no doubt in Bega's mind that the man was now in the palm of lust and saw Tuda as no more than a brittle obstacle in his way.

'We come from a mighty church,' said Tuda, beginning to step back. 'We have a God who will strike you dead if you dare to attack those who do His work.' But still he retreated and still they edged forward. Bega moved towards him and signalled to Ingaberga and Chad. They grasped their staffs and Chad, she saw, was ready to go for his dagger. Someone hurled a small rock which hit Tuda in the face. He stumbled back, tripped, fell, and released the sword, which Bega pounced on, stepping in front of his flailing body. The growl from the chief and his men clustering around him was unmistakable. Without consciously considering, Bega swirled the sword around her head, clearing a space as her father had taught her and, from that multitude of lessons and games in adolescence, she drew on an expertise and confidence far beyond Tuda's.

It was Chad who liked to describe what happened. He and Ingaberga stood on either side of Bega, fending off those who rushed her at the beginning, but once she began to advance, all they did was walk forward alongside her, exulting in her power.

Chad reported that a sound came from the trees near the settlement which could only have been angels' wings as there was no breath of wind that day. The spot became infused with a ring of light as God gave His aid to Bega, he said.

The chief was the first to feel the strength of Bega's sword. He was lucky that her eye was not yet true and he was hit more by the flat blade, although a bad wound was slashed across his shoulder and chest. Seeing this, his followers at first advanced but Bega's skill with the sword, the distance it kept her from them and the deadliness of its blade scythed them down like grass. 'They fell and groaned like souls in torment,' said Chad.

Bega was relentless, he would repeat, in some awe of her, and, even when they began to back away and their cries went up for mercy, she kept moving forward, the sun glittering about her, the sword seemingly dipped in fiercest light as it swung and slashed and stabbed, the blood itself glistening in the sun's light and Bega 'like someone who was not doing her own will but was the instrument of God. And there was such joy on her face,' Chad explained.

'Only,' said Chad, 'only when the chief crawled on his knees crying for mercy, and the women with children at their breasts and those men who had not fled but had fallen, wounded or dying, sent up a great plea for mercy; only then did Bega cease and look around as if amazed at what she had done. As if she knew that it was not she herself who had done it. And at that very moment, the sunlight was withdrawn and the grey covering of heaven was restored.'

The chief begged for his life and swore to Bega that never again would he doubt the power of the true God. Bega tried to persuade him to rise but he would not. He was joined by all who remained: women, children and those men who could join him, all on their knees, praising her and talking about the miracle that had possessed her. This one had seen fire lighting up her hair, flames curling out as high as the walls of the settlement. Another had seen angels also with swords, leaping from her breast fully armed and cutting down any who stood in their way. Everyone agreed that the sword had been wielded by a God who could never be conquered and who must be worshipped.

Bega gave the sword back to Tuda who used his remaining strength to order them to look after their wounded, pray for the dead and be ready to receive instruction in Christ in the morning when he would be healed.

Bega returned to Isidore who looked at her with such adoration that Bega felt uncomfortable. The sick girl too looked reverently and made a touching effort once again to stand, but Bega bade her remain seated.

Tuda was cared for and three days later Bega felt confident to leave the newly reconverted settlement and Tuda to the care of Ingaberga. The sword was given her. The new converts were subdued and subservient.

Bega, Chad and Isidore went on to further villages. There were no miracles but somehow the word of Bega's fury seemed to have spread. It was said that God had sent the archangels down to inhabit her and that seven pairs of hands had held the sword which had avenged the honour of the Lord. Bega did everything to discourage any sign of submission to her. It was God, she told them, again and again, who was the all-conquering one.

Only when she was sure that everyone was asleep; when Isidore had finally absorbed the noises of the night; when the sense of isolation and the scent of danger lessened; then, in the darkest hours, Bega could admit to herself how much she had loved being the instrument of God and how savage her sense of purpose and righteousness had been.

This, she prayed, was what she had been chosen for: to bring God's word to a pagan world, if necessary with a sword.

CHAPTER THIRTY-TWO

The story of Bega's courage for Christ raced around Whitby and, from being that reclusive, scholarly, rather aloof Irish princess, Bega's reputation became altogether more public and more exciting. She was allowed out on other missions and although none matched the drama of that first with her slaughter of the enemy and the saving of Tuda and Ingaberga, there was enough to keep the pot of fervour boiling. Bega had been marked out. Where before they had seen an ascetic, withdrawn young woman, now they saw someone absorbed in the power of God, harbouring all her forces, confounding the devil by pretending to be merely meek.

Hilda was prepared to let Bega go again, although more than once she was worried by the wildness in the young woman's expression and demeanour when she came back from a particularly arduous mission. Her plan for Bega was not that she should leave Whitby as most of the clever men did, but that she should stay and help Hilda build on what was increasingly seen throughout the north as a great foundation house in which to cultivate the work and the word of God.

Hilda liked to compare herself to Noah. She saw the world in a similar danger from – 'The flood of ignorance, the flood of heathenism, the flood of barbarism'. She saw the Whitby community as an ark defiantly riding the waters. 'That is why I chose this place in particular,' she said. She had sought out this high and exposed point: no hiding place from God. 'It feels like an ark,' she would say, 'doesn't it? Especially when the wind blows wildly!' She became almost excessively enthusiastic when describing the violence of the weather; her limbs would lurch into motion as if she were about to execute one of the strange

and disgraceful dances which some of the heathen still employed.
'When the storms pelt us, when the devil does his worst with the
sleet and the seas roar and shout against the cliff, then we can feel
that we are out in the great sea of the world, chosen and protected
by God to bring enlightenment to the pagans. To bring light into
their lives. To bring them the word of God – a word which will
be heard above any storm that can lash us!'

It would have been terrible to have smiled let alone laughed
even a little at such thumping and boisterous explosions from the
abbess; but sometimes Bega did sense a grin developing which she
kept inside her lips; and sometimes she sensed she was not alone.
However much they adored and respected Mother, there was still
room, among the brighter ones, for the affectionate smile which
seemed just a touch wicked.

The missions exhilarated Bega and all but drove out her regrets
about Padric and her guilt at the impure nature of her calling. It
was harder in the abbey, but habit helped. Habit kept despair at
bay. The ebb and flow of the great ecclesiastical timetable was
wonderfully numbing.

Bega took particular satisfaction from the rule which stated that
everything should be held in common. There were those who had
arrived rich and those who were poor. All were treated in the same
way. This was the ambition in many houses: Hilda made it fact at
Whitby. Nothing was considered to be anyone's personal property.
Even the armlet given to Bega by Padric was first taken from her
and then, after a year, returned to mark her arrival at Whitby. It
was returned not as of right but as a gift from Hilda who was the
standard of all judgments. Hilda took easily to judgment and her
scrupulous mind was never more happily employed than when it
was exercised in fine discriminations.

This denial of personal property appealed positively to Bega.
She felt free in it. In Ireland her father had been so concerned
by the numbers of his cattle, sheep and goats, the size of his
household, the lands he had seized, the looting; even the severed
heads were all part of the same unending ambition to own, gain,
have and hold more and more of everything that could be regarded
as wealth.

Bega herself had been part of his wealth. In the many hours
of solitude now enjoined on her, when she would rake over the
cinders of her past, she saw, with pain, how much of an object she

had been for her father. Though she had held a place in his heart through her resemblance to her mother, the deeper plot in Cathal's story was her value as barter. She had been fed with learning, let loose with a sword, cultivated all along as a distinctive, rare creature to increase her value on the genealogical and dynastic market. Now that she realised this, she did not resent it. She thought herself rather foolish for not seeing it more clearly before.

To have all property in common meant that all responsibility was shared. Hilda was very strict on this. The food that was eaten, the clothes and shoes that were worn, the books that were made or copied, the dwellings that were built, demanded the efforts of everyone. Of course there were specialisations: some were better gardeners, others good at weaving, the monks traded shoes for cloaks, but the idea that all belonged to all pervaded all and Bega was uplifted by it. For this was truly a different life, unlike real life. Therefore to obey in this could lead her further to be a true servant of God.

'It is extraordinary, isn't it?' Hilda agreed when Bega brought up the idea of community yet again as the two women were working together in the herb garden. 'One wonders why everyone doesn't behave as we do but, there again, one understands why not.'

'Why not?' Bega felt zealous about its universal possibility.

'It's too difficult to organise outside a community devoted to God,' said Hilda, crisply. She was kneeling on a coarse mat, looking dignified even as she trowelled away in the rather heavy spring mud.

'You organise it here.'

'Inside a very limited community. And then – one has to be totally honest – we still have servants here who do *some* of the work; and there are the slaves which King Oswy has given us; *and* we have benefactors who are very rich indeed. I think it would be a mistake for you to get carried away with it as an idea, Bega. It is not an *idea*. It is a useful discipline.'

'Was it not an idea for the apostles?'

'Certainly not. It was merely a convenient means to an end. To put too great emphasis on it is just as bad as putting too great an emphasis on riches. Living in common as we do is a way to bind us together and distinguish us. We must not try to pretend that the world can live as we do. It can't. Nor do we want it to. For what, then, would be the point of us?'

Hilda turned and beamed at her. She enjoyed such sallies of logic enormously.

Bega restrained herself but her trowel went in much deeper than she had intended and the tiny root was almost snuffed out. 'I still think,' said Bega, when she had rescued the root, 'that it is an ennobling idea.'

'I dislike the use of ennobling.'

'It makes me feel above the world.'

'It ought not to do so.' Hilda patted down the earth rather too severely.

'Why not?'

'I passed most of my life in the secular world,' said Hilda. 'As a member of the nobility – like you – I know what that means. It means that you are "above the world" as you say. It means that you are one of very few who have authority. The nobles rule and the nobles go to war in arms and in style that everyone else pays for. The nobles have great halls and many slaves and jewels – they have possessions. That is what a noble is. Someone with many possessions. Above the world on a mountain of possessions.'

Hilda's tone became increasingly hard. She could not let such a prize pupil drift into sentimental ways. 'Sharing property in common ought to make you feel closer to this community and through that more disciplined in your search for God's grace. That is all. Remember that God is the supreme king. Christ is His prince. The apostles are the nobles as are the saints. Our community is not an imitation of heaven, it is a means to get there. You must not confuse the two. Don't dig so deeply. You'll ruin it.'

Bega used her trowel more carefully.

As always, she took Hilda seriously and though Bega's affection for the communal life did not falter, she saw that to be too fond of it could be a sin. The awareness of sin was everywhere in that earnest striving house at Whitby. Although it was defended and almost self-sufficient and greatly respected, Whitby felt sometimes to Bega like the devil's favourite battleground. For when her prayers were at their most devoted, when she had fasted, sometimes for a week, with only sips of water to sustain her, then her mind did not flood with images of heaven as it should but with images from her youth. Times remembered with Padric, the hills and the sea smells brought in on a warm wind to Connachta. Not only her mind, but her body seemed to float and swim in those images and the glorious sight of the assembly of saints would not emerge. But much more damning than that was the terror she felt that when most she wanted to worship Jesus Christ it was the face and figure of Padric who appeared and then her body grew hot until it shivered with remorse. How could she see this mortal man when it was the Son of God whose face she sought? Did this not make her unfit to be a nun, unfit even to be a Christian?

At times she was afraid to pray. What was a life in Christ without prayer?

It was this which ate at the faith which otherwise she felt had been sent to sustain her. When she worked physically, when she went out into the world for however lonely a mission and met others and did something to help them, then the pressure on her soul would lift and she prayed with an outpouring of thanks to the God who had rescued her and brought her to a place where she could do good work. But at night, Bega could face the most implacable devil she had known. For surely it was a most terrible sin, a worship of something even more to be avoided than a graven image: to see a man where she ought to see her God?

CHAPTER THIRTY-THREE

The wind came in from the sea bitter and wild and relentless. Those who could cowered inside and stoked the fires which coughed and stuttered as it swooped into the chimney hole and blew the smoke back to its source. There was the ancient comfort of being safely and warmly inside while the elements did their worst out of doors, but few in Hilda's Whitby led a fully enclosed and sedentary life. Even the small and privileged company of scribes had to work the land.

Those of a rougher temperament could see it as a playful, boisterous wind. As you walked from dormitory to refectory to church, dodging your way behind the buildings which creaked complainingly against the wind, it would wait for you and then pounce, billowing your long dress or cloak, ballooning your clothes until you nearly threatened elevation. Bega was one of the few who positively enjoyed leaning into it. The feeling of being supported by this invisible force was exhilarating. Though it was only air, it could push against you like a material being. Or were these the good souls out loose teasing the stolid earthly bodies? She longed to race up to her place on the cliff edge, to stand there and dare the wind to do its worst, but the frantic business of the day prevented it.

'Wilfrid is coming,' Hilda had announced that morning, her face full of expectation. Wilfrid, like Cuthbert, had been brought into the church through the inspiration of Bishop Aidan. 'He will be here this afternoon.'

Wilfrid, Wilfrid, Wilfrid. The wind seemed to boom out his name. All tasks were to be done before Wilfrid arrived. It was late summer and praise God stocks of food were quite high. Hilda declared that there would be a feast. Enough of the royal remained in her, and she had not yet had a feast at Whitby.

Wilfrid, Wilfrid, Wilfrid. The name rattled among the nuns, gaining more and more in power and lustre as it was shaped and added to, as it was fantasised and mythologised. He was coming like a young lord.

Chad, who was on the outer edge of the home farmland digging an irrigation trench, could claim to have seen him first. It was a sight he never forgot. In the distance he saw the company of colours, that was how he first described it: colours swirling in the wind as, below him, on the broad path up the cliff, a pageant force drew nearer. It was led, he saw, by a man of tremendous power. Even at a distance, Chad felt that power and the excitement rising from the cavalcade impressed him deeply. In the steady days and deep silent nights of Whitby, in the earnest inner concentration which the place cultivated, this came as a rare dazzle of radiance.

Wilfrid was riding the biggest horse Chad had ever seen. Five strong dogs of a breed unknown to him bounded and galloped around the man, never straying too far. The six men behind him were dressed almost as splendidly and even the dozen slaves, on foot, leading the packhorses, looked like freemen. Wilfrid's appearance, his flamboyance, his arrogance, made him someone all young men would dream to be, Chad thought. Just such a warrior as that! Full of the sense of victory. Clothed, it could be interpreted, in plunder, glistening silver and gold.

Hilda had arranged a reception. By the time Wilfrid reached the gates of the abbey grounds, she had marshalled her forces. The monks were two columns deep to the west; the nuns similarly ranked to the east. Hilda herself stood at the end of what was, in effect, a path, a tunnel of faith.

For Wilfrid had been to Rome itself.

When Wilfrid came through the gate, they broke into prayer and, as the wind swirled and pressed and tossed their robes, the words were whisked and buffeted as if busy devils were determined they never reach heaven.

He dismounted and walked between the columns with never a sideways look. He was taller than any man there. His young face, eagle-beaked, handsome hatched; his hair long and thick, dark brown, almost black in parts, lifted in the wind. His cloak was in purple and black with five large clasps worked in silver. When he kneeled before Hilda and asked for her blessing, Bega noticed the small bare patch on the back of his head.

His obeisance to Hilda was not brief. After she had given her blessing, he remained on his knees for some time. Hilda stood above him and, Bega observed, for the first time, looked just a little irresolute. Finally, after what had seemed a long time even to those so accustomed to prayer, Wilfrid stood and looked around. His eyes seemed to meet those of every individual and most of them dropped their gaze as his near-black glance swept over them. Bega refused to look down. Did she detect a slight smile from Wilfrid?

How, she thought, could someone who looked and acted so like a warrior be acclaimed by the holy Abbess Hilda to be such a holy man? Bega enjoyed the puzzle.

Yet when they assembled in the church to listen to him, her view changed. Unrobed, head bowed, attendant on Hilda, his was still a noble warrior presence which overwhelmed the rest, a brilliant light which paled all others, yet there was about him an aura of holiness. He was not, or not simply, one of those noblemen who were turning to the new official religion because it gave them more scope for material advancement. He may have been a forerunner of the type but, in that small crude church, the wind whacking against it like the waves against an ark at the mercy of the unleashed ocean, he was a convincing holy man.

'It is very rare that I allow us to be together as a congregation,' Hilda began, indicating that both monks and nuns were present. The small church was fast packed. There were almost as many outside, including Chad. The door was left partly open so that a monk could pass on the gist of the event to those who were excluded. 'It is, in truth,' Hilda continued, 'only the second time I have allowed this to happen. The first time, as most of you will vividly recall, was when Prince Alchfrid, son of King Oswy, helped us dedicate this church some three years ago. You will understand, therefore, that I consider this to be a very important moment in our lives.' She stood on the chancel step and spoke loudly. The monk on the door had little to do.

Wilfrid sat to one side of Hilda on a roughly made chair, head bent forward into his long-fingered hands. He appeared not to move, a sculptured figure impassively impressive, young in body yet old in command. The high wind seemed to sound his presence there.

'You will remember Moses when he witnessed the burning bush full of a fire which consumed nothing. So it was with the birth of Wilfrid. His mother, a fine noblewoman whose friend I was at court in my secular days, was near her time with her women all about her. Suddenly those who were outside the house saw that flames leaped from the roof. The men rushed to the door to rescue the women, but it was not necessary. "A child has been born," someone said. And the flames went out damaging only a small part of the building. Wilfrid's mother was a most pious woman who died soon after his birth but, before that birth, she was told, as the voice told Jeremiah, "before I formed thee in the belly I knew thee: and before thou camest out of the womb I sanctified thee and I ordained thee a prophet to the nation". She knew that this would be her son and, young as he still is, he has already begun to fulfil what was foretold.'

Hilda's clear words, cutting through the blow of wind, inspired Bega. She glanced at a few others and saw that they too were caught. Hilda was a fine speaker. But rarely before had she begun a story in such a dramatic way, with the subject of the story there before her. It was as if she were talking of St Paul and the saint and teacher himself were there among them. The more Wilfrid's story developed, the more the wind howled; the more fixed her gaze became on the grave face of this young magnificent man, the more secure in her own faith Bega felt.

'Let me say a little more and then I will ask Wilfrid to speak. You will remember that Cuthbert, who comes from a family similar to that of Wilfrid, took himself into the hills when he was thirteen in order to live with the shepherds and be available for the words of God's angels. When Wilfrid was fourteen, he found himself forever taunted by his father's new wife, a pagan, and took himself and some servants to the court of King Oswy.

'All of you know that Oswy is a Christian king.' Hilda did not pause to fill in any qualifications. Oswy's illiterate Christianity was passionate when it saw territorial advantage. He was also convinced that a passage to heaven might well come from cultivating this strange sect and he did so with a flourish.

'You can imagine how warm a welcome he extended to Wilfrid when he arrived there! At first they thought he had come as a warrior, for, although only fourteen, he showed how he could outwit grown men with the sword and the spear, outrun them and even, for I saw all this, outwrestle some of the king's leading warriors. But King Oswy's queen – my great friend, God be praised – saw Wilfrid and knew that he was bound for the kingdom of heaven. She demanded that he be allowed time to consider his full will.

'After many prayers, he decided to give himself to God. His first task was to escort a nobleman called Cudda to the island of Lindisfarne. It was there he came under the influence of the blessed Aidan. All the Celtic monks on Lindisfarne, whose devotion we honour, saw that this was a true son of God, deserving, as they said, a share in the blessing which Saul received as Eli's servant.' Hilda stopped. For a fraction of a moment she appeared undecided. Then she took her seat.

Wilfrid did not move. He let the silence build.

Bega began to pick out patterns in the wind, the lulls, the blows, the different levels of sound.

Outside, the crowd was quiet, waiting for the man to speak. It was a day they would talk over for months and years. Already they were wide alert to all that was happening about them.

Wilfrid sank to his knees and prayed.

All heads bowed in prayer, all legs bent in prayer as the congregation followed him.

Eventually, after another silence, he stood up. First he bowed to Hilda, then he turned and bowed to the cross. Then he held out his arms.

'I stand before you a sinner before God. I stand before you as a man who tries with all his strength, but so often fails, to resist the many temptations of the devils who swarm over the world tearing us away from our one true work which is the worship of God.'

His voice was gentler than Bega had anticipated. There was a honeyed quality to it. He spoke without haste. The words seemed unpremeditated, as if he were simply opening his heart to the congregation and sharing his thoughts as he would have done privately with Hilda.

'Your revered abbess, whom the whole world honours – as I who have travelled the world know well – mentioned my fellow worker in Christ, Cuthbert. It is his example I urge you to look to, not mine. It has been given to me to travel and move away from here. In such work it is impossible to reach a sanctity which the more constrained life of Cuthbert can reach. I may go wide. He plunges deep. Let us pray for the mission of Cuthbert.'

Wilfrid closed his eyes and lifted back his head.

It was a very becoming pose, Bega noted. She had also been made uneasy about the reference to Cuthbert. It was as if Wilfrid saw him as a rival and wanted to neutralise him by this praise and prayer. Bega dismissed her suspicions moments after they had formulated themselves. Surely it was generous of Wilfrid to mention Cuthbert. She must not doubt. She was dealing here with a man approved of and celebrated by Hilda herself.

'I will tell you of some of the trials which God led me through in order that you might see how far His care extends even to His humblest servant and praise Him yet more. After the death of Cudda on Lindisfarne, I became restless. I was still a boy and though I revered the work and dedication and austerity of the monks, I wanted to go to Rome. This seemed to the people on Lindisfarne a wild and an overweening dream. You know how simple our life is there. In our small beehive huts we pray and read, we cultivate the ground and copy out the gospels in winter and spring. When the weather turns we go on long, independent missions, fearlessly seeking out the most barbarous regions to spread the word of God. I have met no men whom I could honour more. I see it as a weakness of spirit that I wanted to leave them and attempt what none of our people had yet attempted: to go to Rome.' The word 'Rome' sent a thrill through the congregation. Bega, like all the others, longed to go there.

'I returned to the court in Kent. There, after a year of waiting and planning, I found three companions bold enough to join me and one, Bishop Baducing, who had determined to go to Rome to die there. I agreed to be his servant and he provided the means for us to travel.

'Eventually we came to the city of Lyon, once a famous centre of Roman law and learning, now wolf-haunted and more debris-strewn than Caerel. But still it is a city and thanks be to God it had a bishop, Dalfinus. Dalfinus treated me as if I were his son. He had much to teach me and Bishop Baducing went on to Rome with his servants while I stayed behind. Bishop Dalfinus has a great and famous library, with books which I had never heard of and many which I had heard of but never seen. I had never felt so rich as when I was allowed to be alone in that library, reading and copying words which I would bring back – as I have brought back – for some he gave me and some I bought. They are for you.'

He pointed with a flourish to the back of the church and everyone turned to see two of his servants begin to walk towards him. Between them was a litter heavy with several large tomes and some bulky rolled manuscripts. The excitement rose to broken murmurs of thanksgiving as Hilda stepped forward to receive the princely gift. For a moment or two she simply stared at the literary treasure which had been laid at her feet. Then she turned to Wilfrid and, for an instant, many feared she might bow to him or kneel down before him. Perhaps Wilfrid sensed that too, because he held out his arms and she took his hands, whereupon it was he who kneeled.

'May God bless you,' said the abbess, in her clear tone. It was all the more crystal for having to overcome a slight hesitation which many construed later as a possible tear of gratitude. 'And may He bless all who can read these books so that they will learn from them how much mightier He is.'

The 'Amen' was fervently uttered.

Hilda indicated that Wilfrid should continue.

'I will be brief,' he said.

'Not on our account, I hope,' said Hilda.

'You lead me into vanity.'

'I want your story to be an example for all.'

'Let me avoid what makes me seem more than I am.'

'We want to hear everything,' said Hilda, firmly. 'Both more and less than you are. God has chosen you to be a witness. Like Abraham you left your own people. And as St Matthew said, "Everyone that hath forsaken father or mother shall receive a hundredfold and shall inherit everlasting life". Many of us here have done that. You, though, have done it on such a scale that it becomes a different matter. It is not usual for us to have a guest of your—' she sought the word carefully: not to flatter, not to underplay '—distinction.' She sat down.

'Bishop Dalfinus made a favourite of me,' said Wilfrid. 'He promised me his niece in marriage and said that I could govern a good part of Gaul. But of course I was bound for the service of God and so I took my leave, promised to return and went on to Rome. To *Rome*.' His pause was intentionally dramatic and

Bega registered that. Her distrust of this magnificent young man began to harden. 'My first visit was to the oratory of St Andrew to kneel before the altar above which the four gospels are placed. I ask you now to imagine yourself, like me, from this extremity of the world, transported across violent lands and dangerous heights to Rome itself.'

The gestures which accompanied the words reminded Bega of the poetic delivery of Muiredach. He went on.

'The fallen might of the Roman empire is all around in buildings of such size and strength! Difficult to believe that men could build so. But Christianity is no longer its proud empire. Indeed you could say there is truer Christianity and a keener spirit on Lindisfarne.' Bega nodded. She was both compelled by Rome and suspicious of it. Lindisfarne, home of the austere and plain Celtic monks, was a much better anchor, she thought. 'But still it is Rome,' he added. The word Rome was breathed like a blessing in the small church and each one thought to conjure up the magisterial nature of such a location. 'Where Peter founded the Church of Christ.'

He then seduced them with detailed talk of the relics: the bones of some of the saints, the dress worn by Mary when she delivered Jesus Christ, the staff of Peter – so many relics that even he had been allowed to purchase some and on his next visit to Whitby, he promised to bring some which would add to the holiness of the place. During all of this, Bega held on to her fragment of the Cross, feeling unaccountably guilty.

It was clear to Bega that the nuns and monks could have listened all day and more to the descriptions of Rome. Wilfrid hinted at a deep luxuriousness of sin and a breadth of wickedness there. Bega noted this and both resented the prickling of forbidden pleasure this caused and still responded to the teasing.

After a year he returned to Lyon, where he stayed for three years in the house of Bishop Dalfinus. Dalfinus still treated him as a son and, Wilfrid explained, he welcomed most of all the fact that, in Rome, Wilfrid had been converted to Roman ways. In Rome he had been convinced that the true method of calculating the date of Easter and all the other church festivals belonged not to the Celts but to the Romans. In many other ways he stated, briefly, without explaining in detail, he now took the Roman view.

'And then came the moment when I entered the church, weak

and unworthy though I was. Dalfinus asked me to take the Roman
tonsure, which, as some of you know, goes around the head –
unlike that of the Celts – and represents Christ's crown of thorns.
I did.' Here, for the first time, he smiled and dropped his head
forward so that all could see what Bega had thought a rather
disfiguring and unexpected bald patch. When he swept himself
upright again, still smiling, Bega forgave him the too-lingering
talk of relics and splendours and luxury and began to enjoy the
fun in what had become the fate of a dashing young man with
the world to conquer.

   'At the end of the three years an event occurred which may
be known to some of you. Queen Baldhild, who was in the pay
of the devil, just as Jezebel who killed the prophet, conquered
Lyon and all that part of Gaul. Her crimes included sentencing
to death nine bishops. They were asked to appear in the church
itself in Lyon, where she sat high on the altar above her dukes
who ate and drank and desecrated the holy place. Your abbess
has instructed me to tell you that I accompanied Dalfinus into
that church of terror and death.'

   He paused. Once more the wind provided a dramatic intermission. Yet again the congregation strained forward to hear. Outside
the silent crowd heard the report and they too were stretched in
concentration. Bega tried not to think of the tortures, yet she
wanted him to go on. She longed for him to tell a story which,
she knew, as they all did, would be told and retold down the years,
a story of true Christian martyrdom. And Wilfrid had been there!
Yet here was Wilfrid, miraculously alive. Almost, Bega thought
with sinful impatience, baiting the congregation which was so
humbly, unreservedly, in his grip.

   'We stood together side-by-side. Naked.' He paused. A delicious thrill of horror rippled through the congregation. Bega, to
her annoyance, was also taken with the image of the magnificent
young man stripped and vulnerable in front of the Jezebel. Then
he went on. 'Dalfinus replied in a proud and faithful voice to all
the questions hurled at him. But to no avail. He was dragged off
and murdered most cruelly.

   'It was cold but the fear made me colder than any ice I have
touched. I knew that God was present and prayed only that I
would be worthy to meet Him in His heavenly kingdom. Then
the queen asked "Who is this youth?" It was explained that I was

a foreigner, from over the sea. She smiled at me. I thought of the Mother of God and smiled back at her in forgiveness. "Then spare him," she said. "I will have him safe" . . . and so I was spared.' The murmur of relief around the church was like applause. He went no further, although Bega longed to know why it was he who had been spared and what this Jezebel had exacted in return. But these she deemed to be unworthy thoughts and she laid a punishment on herself for having them.

Soon afterwards, he explained, he was allowed to leave with all his books and relics from Rome and finally he returned to Kent and then to Northumbria at the court of Oswy, where he met up with Oswy's favourite son, Alchfrid, whom he had known as a boy.

'Because of the knowledge I had gained in Rome, Oswy asked me to stay at his court. Alchfrid welcomed me most warmly. They said that we were as David and Jonathan. Over the past year he has given me many gifts of land. His latest gift, though, was so generous that it will support an abbey and I intend to build one, at Ripon. This is partly why I am here with you now. For Alchfrid insists that I be abbot of this new foundation. I have come here to sit at the feet of the Abbess Hilda and learn, if I can, how to attempt such an awesome task. I ask you now, humbly, to accept myself and my men for what we are – poor followers of Christ come to seek from you the illumination to enable us to go forward into the darkness beyond and bring God to those who suffer in their heathen distress.'

His appeal for their help was consummate. Had there been the slightest chink in their adoration it was closed by this humble request. Over the next few days as he proceeded to do what he had promised and learn how a well-run abbey worked, he became an icon to the younger members of the community. Even the senior members would relax their severity when Wilfrid appeared. It was the combination of so much that was attractive which made him irresistible: he was very handsome, he was undoubtedly brave, he had endured hardships and trials, he had made a great journey, he was generous, he was a scholar, and he appeared modest, gentle and humble.

Bega feared, with some cause, that she was the only one who slightly demurred from this view. She would not deny his qualities, nor would she deceive herself by pretending not to be impressed

by him. The very size and powerful health and strength and poise
of the man among the largely introverted community made an
impression wherever it moved. But where others saw a humble
man, Bega saw a man who announced that he was humble and
then laid claim to virtues which never characterised a humble
man. Where others spoke of modesty, Bega prised open his
utterances and discovered again and again unspoken arrogance.
Where others saw a gentle man of God, Bega still perceived the
traces of a warrior's swagger. Even his generosity she saw as a
bribe to bring his fame to a wider world.

As the wild winds subsided to blusters which gave way to
tolerable late summer breezes, Bega kept these thoughts to herself
and was content to avoid Wilfrid as much as she could. She
considered her unease as something unhappily singular, marking
her off from her colleagues in a way which disturbed her. What
could they see that she failed to see? Did what she saw mean that
there was a failure in them? This latter thought was subversive but
Bega was never timid, least of all about her own mind. Perhaps,
though, they were right and she was mistaken. It was better to
think that. Better also to examine her motives. What sin of hers
blinded her to Wilfrid's goodness?

'You have been avoiding me,' said Wilfrid.

Bega looked round in alarm. She was in the scriptorium alone.
By elimination she had discovered that the best time to find it
empty was just before the final prayers of the day and this was
her preferred time. Hilda followed Wilfrid into the room.

'How could you possibly notice?' Bega replied, blushing.

'Our Mother has told me about you. I have tried to meet you
more than once.' He smiled and made a dodging gesture with his
hand. 'But you have always slipped away.'

'I'm sure there's been a good reason,' said Hilda. 'Hasn't there,
Bega?' She did not pause. 'After all, Wilfrid, you are rather an
intimidating young man. The younger women are terrified of
talking to you. They simply wouldn't know what to say.'

'But not you,' said Wilfrid, who had never taken his eyes off
Bega. She fought against a deeper blush. Why did he make her
feel that he understood everything she thought and could see her
as she really was?

'Well, here she is now,' said Hilda.

Wilfrid glanced at the older woman and Bega caught in

the glance a wish that she would go away. Hilda failed to see this.

'Aren't they the most *marvellous* books?' said Hilda. 'I can't tell you how much joy they will give to all of us. I've set my best people to copying them already. It is impossible to get enough books, don't you find? But where are we without them? Just words on the wind, Wilfrid. Not words on the mind. Holy books are the mind of God and the more we have the more we can make His mind manifest.'

'Many of the Irish have strange powers,' said Wilfrid, cutting through Hilda's enthusiasm and still, as it were, exercising his own power on Bega. 'Is that true of you?'

An involuntary gesture – not lost on Wilfrid – took Bega's right hand to the pocket in which she had secured the fragment of the cross. She shook her head. Wilfrid frowned a little.

'The Abbess told me that you were a bold, eloquent, questioning one. Why are you so silent now?'

'As I've said . . .' Hilda began, but Wilfrid lifted his arm a quelling fraction. Hilda obeyed the signal and fell silent.

'Is there nothing you want to say?'

Bega felt trapped. Common courtesy and the wish to prove Hilda right urged her on. Caution about her qualified opinion of Wilfrid held her back.

'I am told that you want to follow in the way of the Irish Celtic missionaries.'

Was this a trap? It was a very simple question.

'Yes,' she murmured, and that bare monosyllable brought a grin, youthful, to Wilfrid's face.

'Ah!' he said. 'We begin. Your missionaries have done famous work.'

'Yes,' Bega agreed. 'As you said of your time at Lindisfarne, they are such pure men.'

'What do you mean by the word pure?'

'Uncontaminated by worldly possessions and lusts.'

'Are not non-Celts capable of that?'

'Austere, plain, wanting no estates.'

Wilfrid bridled a little. Hilda looked on with some relief. Bega was her star pupil: this was more like it. The way in which Bega had avoided Wilfrid – who had tried to talk to several of her best nuns – had become conspicuous.

'Sometimes the possession of an estate can benefit others,'
he said.

'I agree,' said Bega, calmly, 'but it is still impure.'

'Would you have us all walk about in poverty?'

'Christ and His apostles did that.'

Wilfrid checked himself. He had fallen into that trap far too
easily. She was one of those not quite attractive enough young
women (on closer inspection) whose tongue had sharpened in
consequence. He had underestimated her.

'What if I said that the Celtic way was no longer useful for the
new world?'

'So much the worse for the new world,' said Bega. The surliness
in her tone began to alarm Hilda. Wilfrid was intrigued by it. He
had suffered enough adoring agreement.

'I am talking of a world in which the power of Rome is
restored.'

'That need not mean the eclipse of the Celtic church.'

'There can only be one centre of authority.'

'So there is. He is our Lord God.'

Again Wilfrid checked himself. The whelp! 'The problem with
the Celtic church is that each individual thinks that he can do as
he wishes.'

'That is not a problem I can see,' replied Bega. 'St Brigid did
as she wished. Our dear abbess is doing as she wishes.'

'Whitby, though inspired by Lindisfarne at the moment, will
soon be brought under the sway of Rome.'

'Why should Rome have sway?'

'There are forces of darkness, so vast, there are armies of the
heathen so ready to be at the service of the devil, that we have
to organise and arm ourselves for a mighty struggle. In the great
battle to come, a battle which will shake the foundations of the
earth, a battle between good and evil which we shall surely win, we
need a large and disciplined army. Rome alone can give us that.'

Hilda could not help being thrilled by these words, but not
if it harmed all her beloved Aidan had stood for. Wilfrid would
never betray that, she assured herself. He too, like herself and
Cuthbert, was a follower of Aidan and had known his saintliness.
Yet this new passion for Rome appeared to be serious. The Celts
and the Romans would live side-by-side. Wilfrid in himself was
a promise of this. At present this Roman fashion had swept him

away – but that was understandable in a young man. Underneath he, like herself, Cuthbert and Bega, was a child of the Celtic church with its own history and its own ways given it by those nearest Christ Himself and purer (a good word of Bega's) than one hundred Romes.

'The Celtic monks – and nuns,' Bega added defiantly, 'have also conquered the forces of darkness many times on their missions. Why do they need this Roman army? How can we trust a big army to be as true to God as one man or one woman who has been called?'

'It is difficult to give up the things we have loved in childhood. But now you are a woman, you must put away childish things.'

'What was childish about Aidan? What is childish about Cuthbert?'

'Cuthbert will see the strength of Rome,' said Wilfrid, very coolly.

'And if he does? Does that make him better? Surely Cuthbert is strong already because he is strong in the Lord?'

'You speak without knowing the gain that can come from the power of Rome. You speak without knowing authority.'

'Surely the only authority I need to know is the authority which comes from heaven?'

'Soldiers are needed on earth to fight the war for heaven. Soldiers must have a lead.'

'Rome seems a very unlikely place to look for a lead from what you say.'

'How is that?'

'Of course it has the holy relics,' Bega conceded, 'and the books, and the pope, but everything else you told us suggested to me a place which needed to be cleansed. I kept thinking – while you spoke—' (this was untrue, the thought had just occurred now, but Bega decided that she would pray for the lie later) 'what would Aidan have done there? What would St Columbanus or St Brigid have done there? What would Cuthbert do there now?'

'Would Cuthbert do so very differently from myself?'

'Oh yes.' The laconic certainty of her reply infuriated him.

'Cuthbert,' said Wilfrid, enunciating the name crushingly, 'has the wholly laudable ambition, thanks be to God, to retire as soon as possible to a place as inaccessible as he can find and pursue his own contest with the devil. This is given to few of us. But what if that were the ambition for most of our soldiers of Christ?'

'Then God's triumph on earth would arrive sooner,' said Bega, as pat as she could to annoy him further. It gave her a reprehensible pleasure to see this splendid and undoubtedly outstanding young man lose something of the poise she distrusted.

'You have trained her to have a short answer for everything,' said Wilfrid.

'Her tongue can be sharp.' Hilda was not altogether pleased, although she liked the way Bega had stood up for Aidan and Cuthbert.

'It is perhaps unfair of me to lean so heavily on such a novice, a young woman, when talking about the armies needed by God to win the battle we see before us.'

'Because I do not accept your arguments?' Bega began, her own temper suddenly rising up, 'there is no need—'

'Bega!'

Hilda's word was enough. Bega stopped.

After the two of them had left, Bega went through the arguments and concluded that Wilfrid had not been fully concentrating. It made her feel no better. She knew that she had presumed too much and was unsurprised when Hilda returned alone.

'Whatever possessed you?' Hilda began, rare for her, on the open offensive.

'I am sorry.'

'I am not – yet – asking you to be sorry. I want to know what you think you were doing.'

'When he began to disparage the Celts, I saw, in my mind's eye, Donal and Cathleen, even Cuthbert, who is not like them but was trained by the Celts, and I felt that I had to defend them.'

'Wilfrid was not attacking them.' Hilda was flustered because she recognised truth in what Bega was saying. Yet Wilfrid's reach and reputation were so much greater than that of anyone else in Whitby . . . how could he be wrong? Hilda was unnerved. She hit out.

'You have to be punished, Bega, to make sure that you understand fully how un-Christian it was for you to spurn the help offered you. From tomorrow you will speak to no one save myself. Wilfrid is to leave in the morning. I would not want him to learn of this. His generosity of spirit would surely blame the punishment on himself and I cannot give him that burden. He has enough. He carries the future world of God on earth on his shoulders, Bega, every bit as much as Cuthbert. Both are equally important. Nor will you go outside the walls, not to the farm, not on a mission, not on any of our walks by the cliffs. When I think the punishment has served its purpose – and it will certainly take a month at the least – then we shall discuss this again.'

'Thank you. I accept my punishment with joy that it will make me stronger in the Lord.'

'God bless you,' said Hilda, more icily than she had intended. 'Wilfrid brings us great good news,' she concluded, 'and we must welcome it and praise the Lord.'

Bega bowed her head and did not reply. In that moment Hilda lost a little of her special affection for this increasingly over-independent young woman.

chapter thirty-four

Not long after Wilfrid's departure – which provoked weeping in many a cell – four mud-caked, ragged warriors led tired horses up to the abbey and sought out the guest-house. The rule was that a guest who had travelled for more than seven days could stay two nights. The men expressed a wish to take full advantage of this.

One, the largest and most savage-looking, with black hair which seemed to sprout in every direction and grow even as you looked at it, was suffering badly from a toothache which had gripped him for more than a month. Big as he was, he feared to have the tooth pulled and wanted the herbalist to give him relief. The youngest, a man in body but a youth in aspect, handsome and charming under his dirt, wanted to sleep and scarcely paused to take the food offered him. One seemed of lesser rank than the others and made it his business to see to the horses. The leader, a tall, lean young man with a vicious scar running up the back of his left hand, said little and seemed always to be in a browsing study of matters known to himself alone. Three of them bathed and washed out their clothes which dried quickly in the light warm breeze. The youngest was happy to sleep and wake in a stink of dirt.

At that time of year, early autumn, the guest-house was not especially full and the four noblemen – for the quality of their weapons, glittering clean, attested to the nobility of their background – had most of the place to themselves. Despite cunning questioning by the guest-master, who was considered unbeatable in the art of extracting their story from all visitors, little was learned about them.

The guest-master thought this unfair. No charge was made for hospitality although an offering was gratefully accepted. The greater benefit, though, came from the news which the guests brought. It was surprising and refreshing to learn of the range of people who went through the guest-house. The guest-master's finest hour came when the abbess invited him to tell the community about the lives of those passing through their abbey, taking sustenance from the work they were doing.

He resented the reticence of the four warriors.

Not even the big one, who might have been expected to talk a little while his tooth was being nursed with a hot herbal poultice, could be prevailed on to loosen his tongue.

The guest-master failed somewhat in his attentions to them. It irritated him the more that they did not appear to notice.

Padric, Riderch, Urien and Owain, the soldier, an older man, had been through much fighting in the years since they had quit Rheged. Two of their soldiers and all their slaves had been killed. They had just recently escaped with their lives in a battle in Dumnonia. They had been captured and threatened with long and hopeless imprisonment and spared only by an unusual act of generous ransom from the king for whom they had been fighting.

Brief as it was, this respite was the first they had enjoyed for many months.

In the late afternoon on the second day – a mild, golden autumn evening – Padric took the men to the cliff top. They sat down on the still warm turf, very nearly on the exact spot known as Bega's Place.

For a while they looked out at the sea, part-hypnotised by it and refreshed by the light saline breeze which flickered on to their faces.

'I wanted to talk here because we cannot be overheard,' Padric began.

'The guest-master is going mad,' said Urien, smiling to himself as he dipped his dagger in and out of the earth. 'I thought of telling him some wonderful lies.'

'Keep him happy,' said Owain, solemn as always. 'Today's meat is better than tomorrow's feast and we eat well here.'

'Tell him nothing,' said Padric.

'The monk who soothed this tooth,' Riderch spoke through a wad which had been padded between the inside of his mouth and the rotting tooth, 'almost stopped when I did not reply to his question.'

'We have no need to fear them,' said Padric. 'They are isolated here, that is all. They are disappointed that we won't offer them stories of our worldly adventures.'

'I could entertain them, if you want,' said Urien. His youthful boasting failed to impress them, as he knew it would. But he liked to annoy. 'Provided they let me address the nuns.'

Urien's thoughts were never more than a few hours away from women he had bedded and those he dreamed of bedding. This was the principal distinction he made within the female population.

'I saw a few of them over the wall this morning when I went for my piss,' he said. 'Very choice. The pick of the crop here in Whitby. But we've always known about these Northumbrian girls; "the men go in for many wives the wives go in for many lives". I think I'll be a monk.'

'It's a prosperous place,' said Riderch, 'when you count up the cattle and sheep and goats, when you look at the farmland and see how many buildings they have. Many of them are small, but none of them is in poor repair. Somebody endowed it well.'

Owain nodded. 'A fine house does not fill itself,' he said.

'Oswy himself,' Padric said. 'And the abbess had wealth which she brought here.'

'The guest-master told you?'

'Yes.'

'What did you give him in return?'

'I told him we had ridden all up the land from the far southern kingdom of Dumnonia. I scared him a little by telling him how many of the tribes were heathen and how keen they were on war and I hoped the abbey could be properly defended.'

'He must have been glad he asked,' said Urien. 'No wonder I got no gruel for breakfast.'

'Your breakfast came and went while you slept,' said Riderch.

The brothers bantered and Padric enjoyed it. It was not often they felt so secure and so relaxed. The prospect before them, that wide, lapping sea, and the comfort of the abbey behind them added to his sense of spacious peace. Padric had found it harder and harder to relax. Too much pressed on him. This unexpected time was very sweet.

As they exchanged desultory talk, his eyes scanned the prospect. He noted with approval the neat outline of the farm fields. Various figures, tiny even at this distance, were diligently working the land.

Further down the cliff, in a well-protected place, there were pens for the beasts at present scattered all over the landscape, well shepherded as far as he could judge, by boys whose curled staffs for catching and turning and prodding the beasts were clearly in evidence. On the sea, near the shore, small boats tacked for fish, drawing their nets, seeming to enjoy good pickings. In the tiny settlement below, deep inside the harbour, turf smoke from the hovels seemed to send out a signal of contentment while the abbey itself appeared as a fastness of tranquillity.

His kingdom, he thought, would be like this. It would feel like this. It would above all have this sense of safety. Without that, he thought, no kingdom was worth its name. He was envious that the Northumbrians had been able to impose such a sense of security and knew from his travels that their laws ran and held as well as any.

'If we can take Rheged away from the Northumbrians,' he said, 'then we want to have a British kingdom which brings us security such as this.'

'There can never be the sort of security you like to talk about,' Urien said. 'Even if our plans work and in the next years we make it easier for the Northumbrians to leave us alone than to occupy us, they won't just go away. They will always want to fight again.'

'So will we,' said Riderch. 'We like it. Don't we, old man?'

Owain nodded. Fighting was his life. The dream of Padric which he had heard several times was to him as remote as the heavenly kingdom. 'Youth talks,' he said, 'age acts.'

'We have been away now for more than four years,' said Riderch. 'And we are heading back to Rheged. What can we say to our father that we have gained?'

'He won't recognise what we have done as any sort of gain,' Padric smiled. 'The biggest gain to him is that we have kept clear of Rheged for these years. But I am not sure that he would understand that.'

'Why do you think our father is so wrong?' Urien's questions, which were rare, had an idle appearance but a hard undercurrent.

'He has given up our cause and let our kingdom become a tribute-paying province.'

'What else could he have done?'

'Fought,' said Riderch.

'And would he have won?'

'Not then,' Padric said. 'No. Not then.'

'So what can we bring him that will change his mind? Because if we are going to raise the men of Rheged then we need the king's command.'

'Is that the way we should do it?'

Padric glanced around. He even stood up and walked the few paces to the cliff edge to make sure that no one was below on a ledge, listening. No. They were as isolated as they could be. Even the nearest boys in the fields were too far away for eavesdropping.

'You have seen what we have found. In the north among the Pictish people there is confusion. They are as happy to fight each other as to join forces against Oswy.'

'I liked the Picts,' said Riderch. 'What boys!' Riderch had been particularly struck by the lunatic bravery of the young men who would, in the ancient Celtic fashion, strip off bare before a battle and strut their naked painted bodies between the two drawn armies wearing only their golden torques and flourishing their swords challenging any or all to single combat. The wildness for war ran in the race and Riderch had been happier there than on any other part of their travels. 'What lads! Eh, Owain?'

Owain nodded. The fearlessness of those madmen in the far north had left him with great stories. Should God let him live and spare him to see his sons, then he would keep them spellbound for days on end.

'They will not be reliable allies,' said Padric, 'and even if we came to the field with them, their methods can scarcely resist these invaders,' he indicated across the sea, 'who have brought a better organisation to war. It is wonderful – I too enjoyed it – to see the Picts flaunt their fearless courage. But the Northumbrians would simply fell them with their great swords. Remember how they cut down the wild forces of Cadwalla.'

'No good, Cadwalla's people,' said Riderch. 'Don't trust them.'

'But,' said Urien, 'oh, their beautiful little black-haired, quick young women. No wonder Cadwalla had the strength of a hundred men. They make me groan to think of them, those Welsh girls just like our own but so much rougher. So *much* rougher!'

'They will come in with us if they think we will win. Even then—'

'Even then, watch them,' said Riderch. 'Don't trust the buggers. They smiled far too much for me. Too many teeth is a bad sign.'

'Is that why yours are coming out?'

Riderch grinned and then yelped. The melancholy certainty was finally percolating into his mind. He would have to pull out the bad tooth. Owain had offered to do it and told him that with a heated dagger point it took no time at all.

'In Dumnonia I had the most hope of a future alliance. Arthur's name thereabouts is so strong that you feel they would all ride slap into the ocean if they thought he was calling them.'

'I've never eaten as much in my life,' said Owain, and this time resisted a proverb.

'They honoured us because of him but we must have looked a rough lot.' Of them all, Urien was the most conscious of how they appeared.

'Yes,' said Padric. 'But I think that impressed them.'

By the time they had reached Dumnonia, they had lost their soldiers, their servants, the pack ponies and most of the small amount of possessions they had stocked up with them.

'They respected our quest,' said Padric.

Indeed, at the court in Tintagel, Padric had felt more at home than at any place in his life: more than in the early days at the court of Cathal, more than in Wales or among the Picts, more even than in his father's house. Down beside the crag-blackened coast in the warmer lands of Dumnonia, he knew that the dream and plan he had for the future was understood and supported.

'But they are so far away,' said Riderch.

'They will come when they know we are ready.'

'When will that be?'

Padric took his time. He had intended to wait until they reached Rheged before outlining his plans but here, somehow, on this bold promontory, as it were staring across the sea at the home and source of the enemy, he told them what until now he had only hinted.

'It will not be soon,' he said, carefully. 'We are few. They have many men they can put in the saddle. What we have done in these last years is to train ourselves in many kinds of battle. Each of us has killed and killed in numbers. We know about that. We have lost, almost fatally the last time, and that too is knowledge.

Each of us has been in danger many times and come through with our lives, thanks be to God. We know that. We have seen how a raiding party can harass and madden a big army. We have learned about ambush and night attacks. We have learned how to go to war not with great armies on open battlefields but with few men, moving swiftly, faster than the sun's rays, now here, now gone. We know war.'

'We should raise our men in Rheged or in Ireland, ask for alliances from Dumnonia and even Wales and march on Oswy in the spring,' said Riderch.

'No,' said Padric. 'God is on our side – all of us here know that. He has guided us and saved us whether it was when we were all but perishing of hunger on the long, icy route to Dumnonia or when you, Urien, were charged by the king of wild boars, or when you, Riderch, were surrounded by more than six men in the craglands of the Picts, or when all of us went into battle for the kings to whom we gave an oath to prove our worthiness. God is with us, therefore He will not fail us. When I pray to Him and seek the way forward, He tells me to be patient. He tells me to stalk and not to break cover. He tells me to wage war first in the hills before taking to the field. He tells me that there will be one great battle only between ourselves and these invaders and when that battle comes we must be harder than the rocks below us and more remorseless than the sea. That battle may be many years away, so we will continue to fight as a small company. We will continue to do service in return for future alliances. We will take our own time. But now we will begin to strike closer to Northumbria.'

'That will put our father's house in danger,' said Riderch. 'We can't do that.'

'You talk of us in ways I recognise,' said Urien, 'and a poet could make an epic of what we have done. They do it with much less. But we are still four men, Padric, whatever you say. Just four men who have lost two of their company and spent almost all their wealth.'

'Cast your bread upon the waters,' quoted Padric.

'A wise man knows both pain and joy,' quoted Owain.

'We are too few,' Padric said.

'When will we be stronger?'

'When they are weaker.'

'But,' said the big and obstinate Riderch, 'I will not fight in

Rheged unless our father is at our side and we ride as an army against the invaders.'

'He will never do that.'

'Perhaps he is wise,' said Urien. 'The old are supposed to be wise.'

'He is—' Padric struggled to balance his true assessment with the respect due '—he is of a different time of history.'

'So?'

'He trusted the invader.'

'And?'

'Look at what it brought us.'

'Was it so bad?' Urien's opposition was not unexpected. Although he followed Padric in battle and listened as attentively as Riderch, and although he admired Padric's learning and his skills in diplomacy, there were times when he could not stop himself wanting to tear down this certainty.

'We were slaves.'

'We were not.'

'We were worse than slaves. We agreed to be subordinate. We give the slave no choice.'

'We were conquered, Padric; some of our best men fled, most of them to Ireland.'

'Many a people has been conquered,' said Padric. 'The greatest are those who will not endure it.'

'Four of us!'

'Not in Rheged,' said Riderch.

Padric smiled and let the breeze and the air gather in silence for a while. He had noted more than once that the only times Urien and Riderch questioned the path he was taking was when they were safe, and felt at their ease. No call to action was ever resisted.

It was good to have these times, though, he thought. Too often over these years of almost incessant skirmishes and local battles, he had seen men urged to war who did not know the cause of it and did not believe in the justice of it. That was not what Padric wanted. His aim was still clear: he wanted to lead a crusade. The fact that outsiders might consider them to be pitifully few, their ambition over-vaulted, was of no account. Great matters unrolled at their own pace and no one but God could know which acorn would breed the greatest oak.

'We must find a way to have Father renounce us. Then he will not take the blame.'

'He will never renounce us,' said Riderch, whose physical resemblance to their father seemed to encourage an extra charge of loyalty.

'He will if he knows it is what we want.'

'Why should that stop Ecfrith retaliating?'

Urien appeared to be bored with the conversation and stood up to stretch himself. Despite the stink of him, he was a notably rakish, attractive young man and a man who knew his charms and was never shy about displaying his talents. Now he executed a backwards somersault he had learned from a tribe of dark-skinned nomads they had travelled with for some days before entering Dumnonia.

'If you think it will work . . .' said Riderch. 'But . . .'

'I know,' said Padric. 'Ecfrith must never have another excuse to destroy our country.'

'He wants nothing more,' said Urien, now a dozen or so paces away and preparing himself for a cartwheel, learned from the same teachers.

'Penraddin may have changed that.' None of them approved of her becoming Ecfrith's concubine.

'And I may grow breasts,' said Urien, who ran into the cart-wheel, executed it raggedly and then, with the impetus, raced the dozen or so paces to a shallow slot of a gulley where he dived down and emerged with Chad, his left arm twisted painfully up his back, Urien's free hand slapped across his mouth.

'How long has he been there?'

Urien shrugged. As soon as he had spotted a presence he had acted.

'No field is free from spies,' said Riderch as if rather pleased that an old adage had been proved.

Chad was thrown down roughly. He was winded.

Padric glanced around. He could not see that their disturbance had drawn attention. But then, he had thought himself safe up until now. How could he have failed to spot someone who could have harmed them? The abbey had lulled him with its 'peace' and 'security'.

'It is a deep little gulley,' said Urien, reading his thoughts and wanting to reassure him. 'And,' he added, a little worried that the exchanges between himself and his brother might have been partly responsible for Padric's lapse of concentration, 'if there had been any weapons carried, we would surely have heard it much earlier.'

Padric was not going to let himself off so easily but nevertheless he nodded.

The young man looked up at him and stared.

Padric frowned. There was something familiar about the youth. 'Chad.' He paused. 'I am Chad.'

'Chad.'

The saying of that name uncorked such a powerful eruption of memories that for a time Padric could say no more. The others waited for him. Chad looked up at them fearfully.

Padric gathered himself together. 'Why were you spying on us?'

'I was not spying.'

'What were you doing, then?' Urien accompanied his question with a dig from his toe which connected with Chad's side quite forcibly.

'I thought it was Prince Padric and I wanted to be sure.'

'How did you know this name?' Riderch asked. They had given no name to the guest-master.

'I was his servant on the island with Princess Bega and then we went to Caerel to be baptised.'

'It is Chad,' said Padric, forcing himself not to ask the one question he longed to ask. 'What he says is true.'

'But why were you spying?' said Urien.

'I've said.' Chad stood up and looked as if he would bolt at the first opportunity. 'I just wanted to see him.'

'What did you hear?' said Riderch.

'Be truthful,' Padric warned him.

'I didn't hear much. I had my head down. You were quarrelling, I think.'

'About what?'

Chad considered and the earnest concentration convinced Padric that he was harmless and knew nothing. 'Something about where you were headed next?'

'Something like that,' said Padric. He paused. 'You are much bigger now,' he said and wondered how long he could hold back the question now roaring in his ears. 'I will talk to him alone,' he said.

Urien's smile was not innocent. Although Padric talked about Bega very rarely, sometimes, when they had made him tell stories about his time in Ireland, her name had come into the story and Urien had understood his brother's feelings immediately.

The three men drew away from Padric.

'We first met near a cliff like this,' said Padric, 'on the other side of the country. You have travelled from sea to sea, Chad. Do you like it?'

'I would like to travel more.'

'You are here to be the servant of Princess Bega?'

'The abbess takes care of her now. She has her own servant – Isidore. But I am allowed on some missions with her.'

'Is she well?'

The question appeared to take Chad by surprise. Why on earth should she not be well?

'Yes,' he said, rather brusquely, but only because so clearly an answer was wanted.

How did she look? Was she the same? Did her eyes still make you want to laugh or feel prickled with teasing? Was she happy? Did she still race around the place like a wild thing? Was she over the shock and memories in which he had, wrongly, left her in Caerel?

'I'll see if I can talk to her,' said Padric, and recognised, from long back, the dry mouth of desire. 'Now you must go back before you are missed. Go. Tell no one.'

Chad hovered for a moment but he trusted Padric and saw the sense in what he had said. He made his way down the hill.

Padric looked down on the community now transformed. Somewhere in that small, hill-hugging huddle of buildings lived Bega.

chapter thirty-five

Would she want to see him? He was restless and could not sleep. The light from the fire caught his face and he felt Urien looking at him. Yet it would be too conspicuous to walk out and be alone again.

Her name, her pale eyes, the mocking smile, a thousand waves of memory were unloosened, crashing against his skull, salting him to sharp recollections. There was almost a noise about those taunting ghosts, a frenzy, as if a swarm of hornets had been locked in his brain and could not find escape.

And if they met, what had he to say?

It was not what should be consuming him.

Would she feel the same?

How could she, here in this place enclosed for God, surrounded by women dedicated to leading unspotted lives? But surely she must have realised or remembered by now the time and the act she seemed, in her shock, to have lost from memory? She would be changed.

Perhaps he had seen her, not knowing that he had seen her.

His body ached as if he had travelled too far and pushed himself beyond his limit.

The blubbery snores of Riderch and Owain, the humming of Urien, the coughing of the only other guest were all irritants. He needed silence. And they had to move on that morning.

He could find a camp for them nearby and return until she would see him. If she would see him. Finally he found a shallow sleep.

It was a long morning. The others were ready to leave but he told them that he had asked to see the abbess and she could not meet him until the middle of the day. The guest-master made

it clear that midday was a deadline they must abide by. Owain
mollified him a little by swapping some of his warrior proverbs
and sayings for some of the guest-master's plump store of Biblical
quotations.

It was an aimless morning but they prided themselves on
patience.

Padric was at the gate well before time. He was dismayed that
there were two others there before him. Another joined the line.
They stood, a meek male quartet, unspeaking, waiting for an
outdoor audience with the renowned abbess.

She gave short shrift to the first man. With the second it
seemed to Padric that she was interminable. Should he let
the man behind him have preference and then he could speak
without being overheard? He had registered every word of the
first conversation and this second — a detailed explanation of why
certain cattle had been moved from one pasture to another — was
delivered at the pitch of a public oration. The abbess appeared
to have no intimate tone. But if he waited longer then perhaps
her time for such audiences would run out. All he wanted was a
simple answer to a simple question.

'Could I see Princess Bega?'

'Why?'

'I was her tutor in Ireland.' Padric felt very young again in
front of this woman whose authority over his immediate life was
so great. 'I have not seen her for many years.'

'You must be the young Prince Padric of Rheged.'

Padric nodded.

'Cuthbert told me about you. Why did the guest-master not
tell me?' She scarcely paused. 'You did not tell him. I understand.
What do you want to say to Bega?'

'I — it isn't — we were — I suppose — it's many years — I
wanted to . . .'

Hilda smiled. 'Has anyone told you that you have a remarkable
resemblance to your cousin — that's right, isn't it? — Oswy's son,
Ecfrith? They must have done. Though, looking more closely,
you are . . .' she was about to say 'much more handsome', but
she desisted because she did not think that physical flattery was
helpful. 'Come through here,' she said, indicating a rough wooden
seat in the female half of her domain.

Padric followed her, not quite appreciating that this privilege was rarely extended and that Hilda had a weakness for clever or handsome men. She suspected that he might be both.

'Now,' she commanded, 'tell me all about Bega. I have to say that she impresses everyone here. If you taught her, you are to be congratulated. She is the best scholar among the younger ones. There is also a courage about her which I like – where did that come from? I suspect it is to do with the Irish – Connachta, wasn't it? A nest of saints and warriors. She has a will, sometimes you can see it. I'm sure you know what I am talking about. I remember now some reports of you and your brothers from a cousin in Anglia – I am told that you only fight behind a sign of the cross.'

'How is she?' Padric wrenched the conversation back to Bega. Hilda, who wanted to catch up on the life of this striking young Christian warrior, was rather put out. She took her time.

'Bega should be in the library,' she said, almost kindly. From the shape of the buildings, about half of which followed the beehive pattern, the others a square Teutonic shape, it was impossible to judge which was the library. Yet Hilda could feel the young man applying himself to what might prove an unfortunately successful essay in elimination. 'Or she might be elsewhere,' she said firmly, and added 'wherever she is, she is well.'

'Could I see her?'

'I think not.'

'I could,' said Padric, in a burst of temper, 'simply go and look in all the buildings.'

'Without my permission?'

Yes, Padric thought: but held his tongue.

'You see why I do not want you to see her?' said Hilda and this time she waited for an answer.

Padric refused to be drawn.

'She has, sometimes, a great sadness about her,' Hilda conceded, with reluctant honesty. Padric looked directly at her now, not pleading, but wanting the reassurance that certainty brings. Hilda was utterly open – the calm grey-blue eyes, the flaxen of her hair and paleness of skin emphasising her sense of control and measure, the few discoloured teeth somehow humanising the expression.

'Maybe this is to do with her exile – many of the young ones take some years fully to drag the past out of their hearts and souls. Maybe this is to do with you, Padric.' His name was caressed and Padric now trusted this woman completely. 'But I think it is because God has selected her for His highest purpose and, as is His way, He is testing her more harshly than the others. For there are other times – as when she is on a mission – when she is totally fulfilled and happy in God. In the library, too, she finds peace and even contentment in her heart. And this is growing. I see it month by month, year by year, as she is grafted into the body of Christ. You loved her, didn't you? You need not answer. It is for that reason that you will not ransack the buildings to look for her. She is well set but still just at the beginning of the long journey to perfection. You would not wish to disturb her.'

'I wish merely to see her.'

'That would be the same thing, wouldn't it? We know that. Already there are signs that Bega has been chosen. Some time just before Christmas, a great boulder fell down from heaven and buried itself fiercely into the earth not far away. God in His righteous anger has sent down many of them over the centuries. Our poets have told us that and it is written in the lives of some of our saints. Yet this great boulder which came down and buried a deep hole in the earth hurt no one. No one was harmed.' Hilda spoke with pride. The object from the sky had become the wonder of the area and she had rushed to associate it with the abbey.

'This we think was because of Bega's ministry. She had been visiting the sick in a remote area where the boulder fell. Many believe the plague still recurs in that district. Yet Bega insisted on going there. Only her young servant – and Chad of course – would go with her. Isidore told me that Bega devoted herself to the sick and did not spare herself. It is already being said in that district that angels came out of heaven itself to help her. It was because of this, they now say, that the boulder from heaven hurt no one. God wished to give us a warning but Bega's goodness softened His wrath and deflected the boulder. You see, already she is becoming one of those who are of us but not of this world entirely.' Hilda expected her words to settle the matter, to be law, as they so often were.

Padric's silence was obstinate.

Hilda reached out and touched his arm. 'I have to go now,' she said. 'But I will tell you one last thing. Bega has the true power of prayer. Some months ago, one of my oldest friends, a nun of unrivalled virtue, was dying of a most painful illness which consumed her stomach and ate into it day and night like a fire.

Bega visited her regularly and it was only Bega whose prayers could dull the pain of this good old woman. Soon she called for Bega constantly and whenever she could see a gap in her duties, Bega went and kneeled beside her bed and prayed. She would deny herself sleep in order to pray. And Bega's prayers eased the pain so much that in the last days the dying body was full of ecstasy, telling us all of the glory she would see, filling us with joy as she ended this wretched state and progressed to her heavenly reward.' Hilda smiled a little sadly at his intensity of attention. She had finally recognised the young man's passion and she sympathised. But she would not help him.

'This is a world of darkness and sin, Padric. Without those like Bega, who is both a scholar and a missionary, we shall all be conquered and overwhelmed by the devil. You have helped, through God's grace, to teach and prepare one who may serve with His saints in Heaven.' Hilda paused to allow the solemnity of this to enjoy its full effect.

Finally, Padric said 'I will come back.'

Hilda nodded.

'Will you tell her that? Will you tell her that I have been here and one day I will come back here? If she is not here I will find her.'

'Why, Padric?'

'There is something I can only know in her eyes,' he said, truthfully. He had no more to add.

He and his brothers left within the hour. Chad saw them leave. He watched them go until he was called back to his work.

It did not take the abbess long to plan her course of action. It rarely did.

Bega must not be told until she was out of her penalty of silence. Hilda had not mentioned this to Padric, since she feared, probably rightly, that he would have used it as an excuse to stay longer until her punishment was remitted. She would consider whether or not to pass on his promise that he would seek her out. She had not openly agreed to do so.

Padric, she was absolutely certain, would recover. She herself had been sentimentally engaged in her youth. It had not come to anything as the man's father had seen a better marriage elsewhere. She had recovered rapidly and was sure that everyone else could do the same.

Bega was to be treasured. Even though Hilda did not quite favour her as much as she had before the clash with Wilfrid, a new abbey needed such ornaments. The young woman was difficult and the next few years would be critical. She would need all Hilda's patience to become the example Hilda wanted her to be. The complication of a childhood attachment could not be allowed to spoil all this . . .

About two weeks later, Chad managed to waylay Bega. He told her that Padric and his brothers had stayed in the abbey. He saw Bega go very white and he faltered as he answered her question as to how he looked. Bega asked no more and he left her fearing that the news he had brought was not the good tidings he had hoped. His final word was that Padric had stayed especially to talk with the Abbess Hilda and left very quickly after their encounter.

Bega walked back to her lodging as if she were forcing herself to shove against a strong outgoing tide. Once there she lay down, practically inert, aching, unfathomably unhappy.

There had been so much in her new life and it had seemed strong, full of hope in doing God's work. Like the abbey itself she had built, she thought, a fortress on faith. The message from Chad destroyed it at one blow and she lay in a state of terrible loneliness, crushed by her unforgivable weakness.

CHAPTER THIRTY-SIX

All three – Urien, Riderch and Owain – saw that Padric changed. Each found a different explanation.

Owain saw it as the frustration of the warrior who could not find the action to meet his needs. 'All we know is fighting,' he said, when the three of them were discussing Padric during one of his solitary absences. 'Since we came back from Dumnonia we have hardly taken our swords from their sheaths. A warrior must fight or he has no life. The prince speaks wisely and when he speaks I am persuaded. I understand that we must make long preparations. I understand that the enemy is at present too many for us. But when a warrior does not fight, then he feels useless. The brighter the clearing, the darker the shadows. Look at the way he stays silent, sometimes all the day long. Or those days when he leaves us and goes to another part of the forest. As you know, I tracked him. My craft was unnecessary. He walked as if in a dream. When he came to a glade, he stopped and lay down with such weariness. There I saw a man who is lost because his purpose on earth is gone. We are all assigned a purpose.'

Owain, who rarely spoke at any length, would often wind up with a reference to God. He had heard learned men talk and what most impressed him was their command of references to stories in the gospels or in other parts of the Bible. Sometimes Owain would recognise that he too knew the stories but the knack of producing them at precisely the time appropriate to make the point was beyond him. His version was always to end on God in any speech lasting more than three or four sentences. He concluded, 'God gives to each creature its place. The bird cannot wield a sword. A man cannot fly. We who were made by Him to be His soldiers on earth must fight.'

Whether or not this was true or partly true of Padric, it was the whole truth as far as Owain was concerned. They had returned to Rheged after Whitby, spent a few unhappy days in the household of Dunmael and then back on horseback for month after month on what seemed to Owain to be the work that emissaries could have accomplished. Although he accepted Padric's strategy, he did not appreciate the value of the young leader meeting and talking with the head of even the smallest household, spending time with him, making his case plain. Only twice had they come near a Northumbrian war party and on both occasions Padric had pulled them away and gone deeper into the hills and lonely spaces where the scattered men of his race remained.

Now they were just north of the old Roman wall that ran from sea to sea. They had found a small clearing high on one of the rolling hills. There was a spring nearby: game, berries, fish further down in the river. They carried herbs and other stock. Within a day they had established a comfortable camp. Padric had decided to spend two nights there. It was Northumbrian territory but still within striking distance of Rheged. The time neared when he would have to summon a number of his countrymen and decide on the first strike against the enemy.

None of them knew that they had been spotted.

Ecfrith had decided to make use of the old Roman wall, once the furthest boundary of the Roman empire. The milecastles were tumbledown, the high-scaling barrier wall itself was breached in many places and here and there the stone had been plundered; but enough of the great camps remained, enough of the wall and the roads and the deep ditch and embankment. Ecfrith had seen a system he could use and it took little of his skill to persuade his father to let him draw up a plan of patrol. No one liked it. The warriors wanted to be at a court, in battle, in the saddle and always in a mass. The ones and twos of lonely duty out in the bleak uncertain landscape which bordered on the forest of their former enemies did not appeal to them at all.

Soon, Ecfrith was forced to use the youngest men there, no more than boys really, trained and armed in an elementary fashion but wild with ambition and, for that, willing to endure a lonely post. One, who patrolled about six miles of the wall, had seen the four heavily armed men with their laden packhorse. Tracking them carefully, at a safe distance, he had seen them set up camp.

He knew from all the signs he had lived with that they were not Northumbrians. He set out for the court, determined not to pass on this valuable news to the next warrior in the beacon succession Ecfrith had suggested. It was his exclusive news and he wanted to deliver it. The young man rode furiously, his head boiling with excitement.

After setting up the camp, Padric had gone off alone, ostensibly hunting game but clearly seeking solitude. After Owain's explanation, Riderch, who always felt protective towards his resolute young brother, spoke out, 'Maybe he longs for the battle as we all do,' he said roundly, his big hairy face both benign and puzzled. 'But I think he is still wounded. When a man is wounded on the body – as we all are – then we see the wound bleed but we know that if we take care the bleeding will stop and the wound will heal. Look at the hand of Padric himself. He took a terrible blow and we feared that all the blood would rush out of him. Once we had stopped the blood the wound began to heal. But there are other wounds.' Riderch was thinking hard. He knew that he was not as clever as Padric or as sly as Urien, but he was the oldest of the brothers and sometimes it seemed that behoved him to give an overview. 'He is still wounded after the quarrel with our father. It is a wound which will not heal.'

He referred to the disappointing days they had recently spent with their parents in Rheged. Riderch remembered it all, unhappily . . .

King Dunmael had proved unexpectedly stubborn.

'You must renounce us,' said Padric. 'You must tell the court of Northumbria that we have risen against you and disobeyed you.'

'I will never do that,' said Dunmael. 'You are my sons.'

'Then we are condemned to leave you all in danger.'

'Why not stay?'

'We have argued over this, Father. There is no room in my heart for any accommodation.'

'Take time. Invaders can become inhabitants. Who knows

which lands accommodate which people? They are trying to
embrace our God. They are good law-makers. Know them
better.'

Padric could not allow himself to consider this and responded
sharply. 'Like Penraddin?'

'She went freely.'

Padric did not exploit his father's embarrassment.

'I ask you to let me do this, Father.'

'What must I do to help you? Ecfrith will not be easily
convinced. So, shall I say I fought with you hand to hand?
Or that you have burned buildings which still stand or stolen
cattle which still graze? Or raided and harmed people who will
deny it? There is a peaceful kingdom here, Padric. Why should
anyone believe in a sudden outbreak of rage from a father to such
fine sons?'

'It is neither peaceful, nor is it a kingdom.' Padric did not flinch.
Nor did his father. 'You are king only in name. They rule. It is
peaceful for the same reason. They have conquered us. It is the
peace of the slave without weapons, without a voice and without
a future. When they choose to rip open that peace or put an end
to the pretence of kingdom, then they will do it.'

'You must say no more on that, Padric.'

'It is the truth.'

'This settlement will hold fast. It is good to live in concord
with powerful neighbours. That is what I have striven for. It is
what I have made.'

'You have . . .' Padric stopped.

'You must go on,' said Dunmael, 'or the unspoken words will
stay in the air and never find rest and be for ever between us.
What have I done?'

'In your time, what you did was all that could be done.' Padric
said no more and both of them knew that he had backed away.

'What I did will not live in the mouths of our poets,' replied
Dunmael sadly. 'I know that. It will not be sung at the feasts. It
has not brought me the regard of my sons.' He paused but not to
solicit a denial. On the contrary, his brief silence was a reproof.
However much he supported them, he thought they were badly
misguided and had misjudged him. 'A beaten people does not look
to the king to put them in more danger. They want hope. We are
still here, Padric, as a household and as a people. You say there

is no truth in my title as king but it is one which your brothers want you to inherit. The kingdom is shrunken and cowed but it is still here, unlike so many others. You say you have a plan. Why do you not allow that I, too, might have a plan?'

'What is that?'

'To trust in God.'

Riderch remembered yet again the quality of the silence that had fallen over the four of them – a father and his three sons.

'He will take us under His wing,' said Dunmael. 'For we are part of the new people He has chosen. Unless you tell me that you have been advised by God Himself, I will have nothing to do with your plans. Let our children grow in peace for a while, Padric. Let our families know each other and marry each other and form a stronger people in that union. Let our fields grow crops again and the cattle multiply. Let failures and defeats which are still so raw find time to steal away.'

'You have tied me more tightly than any rope,' answered Padric. 'I am bound in chains because you will not let me be free.'

'God may give us a sign.'

'I am not a man good enough for a sign.' He hesitated, and then, with unaccustomed weariness, he ventured, 'I will go on. I will do what I always meant to do. I will never forget my duty to you.' His tone became harsh. 'And I will never forget that when I came to you for help, you gave none.'

He walked to his horse, mounted it, took it a few steps forward and waited. Urien, the youngest boy, looked almost longingly at the father who had never loved him as much as Padric had been loved; and then he went to join his brother. And so, finally, did Riderch, leaving their father alone, old, spurned by his sons . . .

⬡⬡⬡⬡

'I waited for the king my father to say something,' said Riderch to Urien and Owain, who had heard him tell the story many times but knew that he needed to repeat it to lessen the pain of it, 'but he stood his ground and when I moved to embrace him there was a stone look in his gaze which felled my arms and I too joined

Padric. It is that wound which Padric gave to our father, the knife
is still in that wound and he turns it into his own flesh every day.
But he will not back down. That is what has changed him.'

Urien remembered that too: he also shared in the general
nervousness that they had not fought in a real battle for so
long. But important though these were, he had no doubt as to
the source of the anguish which so plainly afflicted his brother
and was changing him before their eyes. Although he was the
youngest, Urien knew, and said he knew, repeatedly. This irritated
the life out of Owain and Riderch, especially as he refused to
declare what he knew. Once he had put it as a riddle:

> 'The answer is one word
> It is not on our earth.
> Life will never be in the answer.'

Urien had noted it from the moment he had seen Padric return
from his meeting with the Abbess Hilda. It could not be admitted.
It was not part of any conversation. A warrior dealt with the
enemy, with monsters, with the devil. Women were for dynastic
breeding or irresponsible lust. The poetry of love was almost
always a story of loss. Women were admired because they were
like men or adored because they were like the Virgin Mary, yet
Urien, who had been in love many times, knew more than this. He
had always been involved with women. He was always open about
it. Women were necessary to him in a way which he admitted and
he was easy and natural with them in a way which they liked and
was not common. Had he not been son of a king and a noted
warrior, his proclivity would have brought him mockery and even
contempt. But very few, and none who knew him, would seek a
quarrel with Urien.

Padric was smitten. To Urien it was as clear as the plague.
Over the months Urien, saying nothing, had watched with the
interest of an expert as the disease had twisted into him, drawn
him down, lifted for a time only to regroup and attack once more.
Urien knew that the hours Padric now seemed to need alone were
times to breathe. The woman, especially the woman who could
not be attained, was demanding. He needed time alone with her.
When Padric went away, Urien knew that he went to be with the
woman he loved but could never live with.

He did not know whether his brother fully understood that. He suspected not. Padric's greatness – and he was the only man Urien had ever encountered whom he would follow – did not lie in such self-examination. He would neither see nor acknowledge that a woman could erode his will and deflect him from his set purpose. The story of Padric was written in capitals. It was not part of the scheme that love for a woman should subvert it. Yet Bega held him on an invisible rope and Urien saw it tugging and pulling at the man who became less himself, less open, less optimistic, less vivid, sometimes crueller as a consequence.

Padric returned late. It was still light enough. The days were long in midsummer and only for a couple of hours did any velvet come into the darkness. He ate little and soon slept. The others followed, Urien keeping awake until the stars were up. Lying there with the faint noises he knew so well, the scuffling of their dogs, the breathing and quiet chomping of the horses, he let his mind loose, as he often did on such clear nights and enjoyed a sensation of the vast spaces entering into him, a sense of all things whispering in a harmony he understood but could never describe.

CHAPTER THIRTY-SEVEN

Owain came into the clearing unhurriedly. He tapped each of them on the shoulder in turn. The gentle imperative woke them, instantly ready.

'There are about ten of them,' he said quietly. 'Near the great wall. I have looked around but could find no others.'

'How are they armed?' Padric asked.

'Heavily.'

'We must have been spotted,' said Urien. He worked it out. 'Yes. They had somebody along the wall. We should have moved further on.'

Padric nodded. He had felt so disturbingly tired that this appropriate little clearing had been too convenient to miss. But Urien was right.

'We will go north.'

'They know we are here,' said Owain. 'They look towards our camp. When we start to move, they will follow.'

'They will know this land as well as us,' said Riderch.

'They will have brought along someone who knows it better.' Urien looked thoughtful. 'Let me go and look them over.'

Padric nodded. Urien was scarcely gone when the camp was effectively struck, the packhorse loaded, everything ready for a quick move.

'Eleven,' Urien announced when he returned. He grinned at Owain. 'And a boy.'

'Good odds,' said Riderch.

The longing in his voice matched a glance towards Padric, which held a plea.

'Come,' said Padric.

He mounted his horse. With small degrees of hesitation, the

others followed. Riderch let loose a low whistle for the dogs. But however carefully they moved, there was no concealing their presence.

The Northumbrians followed.

They had only a few minutes start on their pursuers and the disadvantage of breaking the ground. When Padric saw a gap which took them clear of the forest, he went for it. On the open ground they drove the horses but the Northumbrians were not easily deflected.

Padric searched out hard ground: a steep gulley which they slithered down, the legs of the horses near breaking. At the bottom twisted a narrow path by the river, stone-strewn and wet, treacherous. The four of them who had ridden so much over the years, along cliff edge and mountain track, through swamp land and deep, entangled forests, picked their way with assurance, single file. It needed just one weak rider among their pursuers and they would fall far behind.

Padric kept to this path as long as he could. After some minutes the noise of their pursuers began to fade. Following more fast foot picking along this narrow course, he signalled a stop. They listened. There was no sound behind them. Padric pointed ahead to where a sheep path angled them out of the gulley and they made for it. At the top they paused to look around: no sign of the war party.

There was only one course to take. To go back along the gulley's top was out of the question. To follow the rise of the ridge towards the summit would be to isolate them on a barren hill top. Before them was a swathe of open countryside, rolling, dipping hills bowling north. Allowing the horses the benefit of a breather, they set off, centring themselves in this open vulnerable space, riding in a loose diamond formation.

It was in this formation that they rode into the ambush.

The Northumbrians had brought a boy who had been a shepherd in that patch of country. He had known where the gulley led and taken the Northumbrians back, on to the top. The leader had gambled on the boy's knowledge.

The ambush was well sprung. Padric led the four of them down a fairly steep slope into a bowl. When they were in the bottom, three Northumbrians appeared on the hill crest before them; two were on either side and when Padric turned his horse he saw that

five had ridden around behind them to cut off their retreat. Any
attempt to charge through the lines would be slowed down and
they would be at a disadvantage. The best course was to dismount
and fight.

It was a decision taken without a word spoken. When Padric
flung himself off his horse and looped the reins around a large
stone it was with relief. More than that. It was curiously light-
hearted. He saw the same gleam of joy in the eyes of his brothers
and Owain. Seeing what was happening, the Northumbrians also
dismounted.

It would now be a battle to the death in this wilderness.
Curiously, a certain sense of calm set in. All of them worked
swiftly. The horses were tethered. Padric directed them to the
place where they would make their stand. Spears were stabbed
in the ground to mark the spot and to be ready to hand if
necessary.

The ground was not altogether bad. The enemy had the slope
with them for the charge which would undoubtedly come from
all sides, but Padric had noticed a small hump of turf which
stood uplifted rather like a tiny island. A wide shallow stream
isolated it.

They stood in a square. Padric had heard stories of the soldiers
of Rome and the inviolable Roman squares. It was said that Arthur
had used this, especially when his forces were thin. Until now
Padric had never employed the square as an opening position. It
felt good.

He had always insisted that they carry exceptionally large thick
leather shields, often a clumsy burden but now, planted on the
ground in front of them, presenting four doors to be approached
with great caution. Though the spears were ready, the real fighting
would be executed with the sword. All four had swords as good as
could be found.

When quite young, Padric had asked for a sword longer than
normal. His unusual height had encouraged the smith and the
weapon which he could wield with such speed and finesse had the
extra advantage of giving him more distance from his combatant.
Riderch's sword was heavier: in the grip of anyone less strong it
would have required two hands. Where Padric used his sword
like a darting serpent, Riderch's blade came down like a cleaving
hammer. The handle was nothing like as ornate as Padric's, which

swirled with spirals and circles and yet appeared chaste compared with the elaboration of Urien's. His was the showiest sword with all that could be decorated finely embellished. The swagger of the tattooed blade could cause an opponent to think he was dealing with a man more of show than substance and Urien used that to his advantage. Of the three brothers, Padric was the most skilful and the fastest; Riderch the strongest and the most enduring; Urien the most cunning and the most vicious. Owain's weapons, sword, spear and daggers, were as finely sharpened and polished as they could be. All his adult life had been devoted to the spartan arts of warfare and his survival through so many battles was in itself proof of his valour.

All four had suffered wounds, the most noticeable being the livid scar on Padric's left hand where the sword of a heathen from Wessex had threatened to splice it. But, when they stripped off to bathe in a river, scars and discoloured lumps figured on all of them. All four were as strong and fit as was possible, thanks to constant riding, year in year out, battles and skirmishes, raids and single combat, and even in the months without combat, hunting, sport between each other and the martial exercises that Padric insisted on. All relished the imminent prospect of battle. They had been bred for this.

They loved the thought of it. The energy which the wild ride through forest and gulley and bare hills had pumped up now leaped high as a bird. You could see their nostrils twitch as the excitement drew in more breath. You could see the trance-like expressions on their faces as each in his way prepared swiftly for the assault. In Riderch, as in Owain, it was very near to joy. Riderch began a growling tuneless hum which was as near to happiness as he came. In Urien it was a flashing eye, the twist of his lips as they threatened a smile. Padric felt the deep refreshment of certainty. Now he was faced with the battle and with this real, earthly enemy, everything else was driven from his mind and the ease he felt seemed akin to jubilation.

He saw eleven men and a boy well enough armed but over confident in their numbers and two or three of them just a little unsteady, perhaps from too much drink. That was good. He did not think they would move in lines but he did not doubt they would fight to the death. They were big, too, some of them, some with long, yellow hair. Their shields were small but they wore the tough leather jerkins which could turn all but the strongest thrusts.

Riderch and Owain saw warriors worth the fight. They observed that the men took their time. They had no need of urgency now. They put on their armour in a measured way and called across to each other, boosting their courage. Riderch hummed thoughtfully and picked out this one's height, the left-handedness of that one, and thought he scented some nervousness or at least over-activity in a third. Owain looked down to see if how they were shod would be affected by the water they would have to cross as they came the final paces. He also wondered whether a spear might be useful early on: only if he could draw blood. He pulled a couple near to him and tipped them lightly in the turf, ready. Their shields would take all the spears that could be thrown. When he crouched he was fully covered but he knew the mobility those shorter shields could give.

Urien decided he would go for the legs. He muttered this to the others. He, like Owain, considered hurling a spear now but desisted. Better they just face the four shields and the men whose quality they did not know. Urien had taken a helmet from one of his victims – leather with a fine metal nose ridge. He slid it on. Riderch laughed at it and hummed louder.

Padric turned and rapidly lashed together two spears. He planted them as a cross. 'Pray,' he said.

All prayed with open, intent, eyes.

'Lord God of Battles, who routs all enemies, be with us this day. Give us a victory that will be Thy victory and show the world that the strength of the one true almighty Lord of Hosts can never be defeated. Amen.'

When he had finished, Padric lifted his shield and stepped forward.

'I challenge any one of you to single combat!' He shouted and the words rang around and around the steep sided bowl, a bony, empty landscape now lined with the vivid formation of battle. For in that fine midsummer morning, the glitter of the weapons, the anxious movement of the horses, the dogs crowded where Riderch had ordered them, the colours of the woven cloth on the Northumbrians – some blue, some green, some wine – all created a sense of occupancy where soon there would be death and slaughter, where soon men would use everything at their command to kill each other. The echo around the woodland bowl was a trumpet calling on the action to begin.

'If,' said Padric, 'you should win, then we will surrender and there will be no more bloodshed. If I win, then you will let us go free.'

Riderch and Owain had a sudden fear that this traditional offer might be accepted. Padric's tone of voice was so persuasive. Urien saw that the boy was looking a little scared and was sorry that he would have to be killed.

'We have not anyone weak enough to fight with you,' the reply was thrown back at them by one of the tallest, a flaxen-haired man, broad as Riderch, red-faced, thonged on legs and arms, his leather breastplate studded and shimmering. 'There is this boy but he is already such a warrior that we have had to force him not to rush at you now, alone, and scythe all of you down. Far better that you surrender to us now. To be slaves of people such as we are is no disgrace. We have no equal in war. Our ancestors came out of the darkest forests across the wildest of seas. Everywhere they trod they crushed the vermin who dared oppose them.

'One of us could settle you all. One here has killed fifty men in a day and the steam of blood from his sword was a cloud across the sun. Another here himself alone caused the Picts to swear that they would never more come into our lands. Our swords are forged in magical caves and woven with spirits which guide them to the hearts of all our enemies. Our armour is spell-cast bound fast impenetrable. We ourselves become dragons in battle. You will see the flames roar from our mouths and our skin turn to scales which no dagger can pierce and our hands will become claws, harder than the eagle's. Throw down your paltry weapons, you miserable Britons. You no longer own your land. You have come into ours like thieves. Like cowards. You have chosen the way of war but our gods tell us to give you this one final chance to renounce it and bow down to our greater might.'

'Your gods have no power,' said Padric. 'I know you. You are from the court of Oswy who claims our Christ is God but he has so little true faith that he cannot pass that faith to you who choose your old gods as soon as you are out of his sight. But King Oswy is wiser than you are. He knows that your gods have no more power. He knows that the God of Jesus Christ is the only one true God. But he does not know it as we know it. We have served the one

God for many reigns. The one God has tested us. He has seen us defeated. He has seen us slaughtered. He has done all that to harden us for the larger struggle which is against all the dark gods of the earth that you worship and glorify. Behind me is the cross of our God. This cross brings Him here on this battlefield. Our God is invisible but He is everywhere. Listen.' Padric paused and Urien smiled as he saw heads turn. His brother had a fine dramatic sense. 'Listen! Hark! Hark! . . .' Padric snapped out the words to create an echo. The echo was clear. 'That voice which rings around you is invisible but it comes from one source. So our invisible God will come down from this cross to help us in battle. Look up into the sky – see the crack – is that not the eye of our God?' They looked! Urien hugged himself. 'Feel the wind on your face – is that not the breath of our God? Accept my challenge or the great God we serve will fill this empty place with your dead bodies.'

Sensing perhaps that his men were being influenced by Padric's bold and seductive words, the Northumbrian leader returned his challenge immediately.

'Invisible God! Come and fight us with your invisible God! Why does your invisible God make you sit like four stones in that shallow river? Are you rooted in fear? Dare you not move? Are your legs too weak to bear you towards our terrible strength? Why does your invisible God want you to crouch like cowards behind those sheltering shields?'

At this, the Northumbrians beat on their own shields and, shouting in a babel of cries and threats, began to move forward. Padric stepped back and, throwing his shield out to the left, caught a powerfully hurled spear which could have thudded into the back of Owain. The Northumbrians advanced at an easy pace, now and then hurling a spear which was caught on one of the big shields. Riderch began to smile broadly as he felt the muscles tighten and flinch with anticipation. Owain put down his sword and plucked out the spear. The Northumbrians were now no more than ten yards away. One, two, three more of their spears thudded into the leather layered shields.

Quite suddenly, Owain stood up, put his shield half to one side and flung the spear venomously. It caught the target on his shoulder and as his howl distracted, for a split moment, the attention of the others, Urien launched his spear low and hard to pierce through the thigh of another. The Northumbrians in those seconds shed the carelessness of over-confidence, found even more energy in fear and vengeance and rushed towards the four men from Rheged, leaving behind the two wounded.

Padric told them to hold and wait until the instant he gave the order. The noise from the war party was now tremendous. Riderch's humming had turned to a strong chant which Owain punctuated. Urien braced himself and waited impatiently. He knew that this first manoeuvre was the best chance.

'In the name of God!' said Padric. 'Now!'

All four rammed their shields forward three or four paces, in almost every case throwing back and unbalancing the leading attacker. From then on it was each man for himself with always the ear open for the one further command – 'Back!' – which would throw them into the original, tight-sealed formation.

The force of Padric's thrust had caught his man flat-footed but before he could finish him, he was forced to cross swords with another who darted round and came in behind. As they were engaged, the first man, winded, got up and attacked Padric on the other side so that his shield was swung, now this way now that, and his long sword swayed before him, keeping both at bay.

Riderch had run forward the furthest and spreadeagled his man. As he passed him, he bent swiftly and stunned his brow with the hilt of his sword before rising to clash with the long, swinging strokes of the flaxen-haired leader.

Urien was unlucky. He had slipped on a skid of mud beside the water and a sword point had gashed the lower part of his shield arm. Only the speed with which he rolled over, wriggled away and regained a firm footing saved him. The wound made him angry and anger always made Urien feel cold and hard. He fought as if he would rip all of them to pieces with his nails.

Owain executed the manoeuvre perfectly and managed to wound his first attacker in the calf. He knew that this was not disabling enough but left him time to turn on his other enemy who was the biggest man on the field. Owain let him hurl great blows at his shield, waiting for the man to tire before he launched his own attack.

The boy hovered around the edges. Hopping literally from one foot to the other, now seeing an opening, hesitating, about to dash in, ready to pull back, excited by the clash of arms, excited by the spill of blood, admiring, wincing, waving his sword, now whooping, now whispering, slashing out at the thin air, still somewhat afraid of the invisible God, and that cross, flinching from the power of those men in death-struggle, feeling a hero, fearing a coward, a sprite on the fringe of the battle, a will o'the wisp darting across the field of blood.

What the Northumbrians could not have known was the strength of the men they had taken on. This realisation slammed home within seconds and the fight became grim. What they had not bargained for were the battle-trained dogs. These three large wolfhounds were expert at leaping at a face, savaging a calf, rarely pausing long enough to feel the cut of the sword. They were no more than harassment but they evened the odds a little.

'Back!'

The men from Rheged, inevitably drawn away from the base mound and from each other in the pull of battle, fought their way back into their tight, opening formation. When they had assumed it, the Northumbrians, at a similar command, also fell back.

The first assault had lasted long enough for all of them to be breathing heavily and in some cases with difficulty. The Northumbrian wounded were helped by their comrades, their gashes hastily staunched and bound.

The Northumbrians stood off at some distance.

Urien showed his arm to Owain who bound it firmly and tightly. The wound on the back of Padric's hand had been broken open and Owain lashed a wad of cloth on to it. Riderch had been slashed down the thigh but he bound it himself.

Two of the Northumbrians appeared to be out of combat. Two others were wounded, one of them lightly. There were still at least seven and the boy.

'The big one is strong,' said Owain, who felt that he had just escaped with his life.

'They will be harder now,' said Riderch.

'They will change their tactics.' Padric watched them carefully.

Urien looked around for more spears. The only two were the couple making the cross. Those bedded in the shields were too deeply sunk in to pull out without losing the protection offered by the shields.

'We need those two spears,' he said, looking at the cross. 'Owain and I could get out at least one between us.'

Padric did not hesitate.

Urien took one and handed the other to Owain.

'Front!' Padric shouted.

The Northumbrians were running at them full tilt, shields held mid-body to field any spear, swords held high, cries loud and blood-chilling.

The men from Rheged swung into a facing line and braced themselves.

'God be with us!' It was Owain's voice.

The phalanx of Northumbrians hit them hard and drove them back. It was almost impossible for the British force to do anything but hold to their shields as the dynamic strength of those insulted and vengeful warriors buried its force in them. The swords hammered against the shields. Back they were pushed until Padric felt a slacking in the frenzy.

'In the name of God,' he said. 'Hold!'

The four men steadied and braced themselves.

'Now!'

They pushed forward with every particle of strength. For some moments it was as if two mythic beasts were locked swaying against each other, steaming with will and sinew-straining power and then the desperate strength of the men who had to fight for everything began to prevail: a vicious stab in the leg from Urien; a breathtaking swirl and flash of sword from Padric opened the face of another; and the deep strength of Riderch and Owain plus the four shields rolled back the Northumbrians.

It was then that Riderch began to roar. His voice was monstrous. It was the roar of a creature, not a man, a roar of terrible warning and blood-lust. He bayed and the sound was taken up by Owain, then by Urien, then by Padric until it became a cry, a song of battle victory and slaughter, a sound which melted the guts of the boy who saw his heroes yield to this four-faced beast, howling like the monsters deep in the rock caves when the big seas beat against the land.

But the men they fought were not so easily frightened. Now, seeing death raw, they too pulled out all the skills and strengths which from boyhood had daily fed and gorged them on war and battle and death. In their heads were the songs of their own giants and men of unparalleled courage. Pain was banished as they fought back. But this howling, moving force was not to be defeated. Perhaps, the boy thought, it was not four men but one. Perhaps the four men had all disappeared and the invisible God had put the shields together and it was He who moved them across the floor of the bowl as they drove back the Northumbrians, now two fewer, two more in death spasms behind them.

The Northumbrians peeled away, forcing Padric and the others to split.

Then began the hand-to-hand struggles which seemed unending. The leader had sought out Padric and the two of them moved to ground a little higher, their swords ringing against each other, the sound of the blades on the shields echoing among the hills.

Riderch and Owain stayed shoulder to shoulder in order to take on three men and the boy, who was now discovering courage and energy to flit in and prick a wound as he did twice on Owain, once on the side of his thigh, quite deeply, the second a lesser one on the sword arm.

Urien had drawn the man whose sword was even heavier than that of Riderch. A man fit to be a Goliath and Urien, slight and agile, his David. For a while, Urien let his shield take the blows and dodged and ducked and twisted and darted out his sword like a serpent's tongue and finally saw it leap into the throat of the giant man where he pushed it in, twisted it further, brushed away the last wild spasmic furies of the clubbing sword arm and yelled aloud to see the blood gush from the deep, fatal wound.

He turned to help Owain and slid around to attack one of the men from the back. Without compunction Urien aimed his sword below the leather jacket of armour and then thrust it up into the body. The man jerked around and as he did so, an enormous swathe from Riderch hacked through his neck.

The wounded, now seeing that the battle was all but lost, still came towards the enemy, determined to inflict some harm before they crossed the line into death. Urien raced towards them and ended their days.

Padric had never fought against so fine a warrior and even as he struggled he admired the man. The fierceness of their struggle covered both of them in sweat. Limbs were aching, air sucked in desperately. Padric knew that he could kill if he could manoeuvre the man on to ground higher than his own. He had seen a way to reach out and slide his sword under the armour . . .

Behind them, Riderch and Owain finally overwhelmed their

men, who still fought but with less and less hope as the battering force steadily pushed them back.

The boy, seeing all would soon be lost, began to edge over towards the horses but Urien caught him, disarmed him, swiftly tied his hands and feet with thongs from his arm and left him for later.

He came back to help Padric but as he drew near he saw that his brother was in that controlled skill of battle which he had never seen anyone resist. Still he ran up towards him and, as he hurried, he saw the flaxen-haired leader turned on to higher ground, lunge down at Padric and then stop, as if in mid-air, let his sword fall, put his hands down on to the blade which skewered him and try to pull it out of his body and then suddenly collapse as Padric stood back and ripped out his sword.

Padric's action ended the battle. The four of them began to realise how weary they were although the exhilaration of the victory stemmed their exhaustion for a while.

'This victory is thanks to the mightiness of our God,' said Riderch, looking at the sky. 'You are the Lord of all You see. Your strength gave strength to us. See how we have slaughtered the unbelievers. In time to come we will talk of this and the heathen will go pale at another story of the power of the only God.' They sat down and regained their breath.

Slowly, Owain and Urien went over the battlefield and made sure that all the Northumbrians were dead. Only now looking at the faces of death did the real impact register. The thick blood still oozed, slashed flesh a tangle of veins and muscle, one man's guts hanging out, a feeding bag for flies and crows, an eye rolled out of its socket, an arm askew, amputated. They gathered all the weapons.

Padric sat and contemplated his strategy. He was satisfied that the tactic of the square had worked so well. Would it be able to work with much bigger groups not used to fighting together? He doubted it and so a sense of great tiredness began to overwhelm him. Not long ago the excitement following such a victory would have uplifted him for hours, whatever the cost in wounds and bruises. Now, as he wrapped up the opened wound on his left hand and felt where the stab of a dagger had entered his shoulder and the tip of a spear had scraped down his arm, he felt little of his former joy. In the demeanour of all three others he saw evidence of several varieties of pleasure. Would this force which pressed him down never leave him?

With an effort he forced himself to go over to the horses. He scarcely looked at the bodies for whom he would once have felt some admiration and sorrow.

The dogs were barking, maddened by the scent of blood. The horses jostled and stamped, high whinnying in anxiety. Urien, Owain, Riderch and Padric stood still, shoulders bent, suddenly numbed from the savage battle. The boy whimpered and asked for help from the invisible God.

∗∗∗∗∗

They took the boy with them into Rheged. There they found Reggiani beside the most northerly of the lakes. Padric remembered her skills from his time on the island with Erebert. Although she was a priestess of a pagan cult, he still trusted her. Because she was not a Christian she would be less suspect to their enemies. In the forests on the side of the hills she could hide the horses they had brought. Somewhere in the woods Urien and Owain buried the captured swords and daggers, spears and shields they would need some day for further men of their own.

Urien slept with Reggiani and knew that she would keep her counsel. If she did not he told her what she would suffer. Even if she did break her silence, it was only the loss of a few horses and weapons. There would be more. Their course had changed now. Padric knew that when Ecfrith discovered some of the best of his men slaughtered inside his own land, he would soon realise who was responsible.

For further safety they took the boy with them on to the island called Mann and then to Ireland where they would look for warriors to join them.

CHAPTER THIRTY-EIGHT

Abbess Hilda was beginning to regret that she had praised Bega so highly to Wilfrid. He had come back to see her following almost two years of yet more astounding travels and adventures but already he was preparing to be off again and Bega, it seemed, was part of his plans.

'I would very much like to see her,' said Wilfrid. 'Perhaps I can tempt her,' he smiled, 'if anyone is allowed to do that, Mother, on such holy ground.' Hilda nodded away the compliment briskly. 'Perhaps I can give her advice on the long mission you tell me she wants to undertake.'

'I am not sure she is ready for a long mission yet,' said Hilda, rather nervously, puzzled that she should feel ill at ease.

'None of us is ready,' he replied, steadily. 'Nor ever will be. But we must go, nevertheless.'

'There is no doubt that she has a remarkable spirituality. But before I can let her undertake a great journey, I have to be more sure of her character. There remains an element of self-will and even of secrecy which will not do. She understands this and helps me chastise her but there is more work to be completed.'

'You have described someone perfect for the work we do,' said Wilfrid, smiling charmingly. He loved using his power. He could not help it. He lived for contests and for victories. The stronger the opponent seemed, the more he relished the conquest. Hilda appeared to be easy, but there was iron under the clay. They were in her parlour-study, the turf fire high, beating off the cold which clamped down on the world outside as the bitter wind came off the sea, surrounded by her books, several of which he had given her, and a Greek painting of Christ which he had brought back from Rome – a languorous, dark, slim-faced, scholarly Christ. She was on her own ground but a little uneasy. Now he tried to twist her arguments as he twisted the lumpen gold ring given him by his great admirer, the chaste, Christian wife of Ecfrith.

'Let me see her.' The tone implied that she would be doing him, and possibly the church, a singular favour.

'In the morning,' said Hilda, finally.

'Do you think the night might change my mind?'

This was exactly what Hilda had thought.

'In the morning, then.' Wilfrid yawned, delicately covering his mouth with his multi-ringed hand. 'You make me feel so comfortable, Mother,' he said. 'Even in Rome there is not the ease that I find here. You have such an intelligence, you see, that I feel that nothing I say will be misunderstood or miss its mark. Worldly comfort' − his hand lifted from his fine fur coat − 'that is not important. It is comfort of the mind and of the spirit that we seek and you bring it to us, to me, more than anyone I have ever met.'

This was said with well-practised candour and his direct look into her eyes undoubtedly gave her pleasure, even as her gestures warded off the compliments.

'Read to me now,' he continued. 'From St John.'

Hilda moved the large gospel of St John − recently completed in her own scriptorium − nearer to the fat candle which gave such an intimate light. She was agitated by Wilfrid's emphatic presence. Wilfrid closed his eyes the better, she assumed, to concentrate on the words of the evangelist. It enabled her to glance across at him − so fine and well sculpted his face, so splendid a man fit to be the pope himself. She began to read . . .

Wilfrid was intrigued by Bega. He had carried away an unfavourable image of her. But over the two years he had found, to his surprise, that he had revisited her in his memory. The first occasion was at the time he was studying St Augustine. He was very taken with the saint's thoughts on memory. Undoubtedly that had prompted it.

Bega was unique in his experience of women. She was one prepared to stand up to him. He was far too wise not to appreciate the value which might accrue from that. To harness that force for himself would be to augment his own; she would reflect well on him. Hilda's confirmed his instinct. A subsequent account that Cuthbert had been very closely involved with her made her even more mysterious and more valuable.

Hilda saw no reason to be absent from the meeting between them on the following morning and Wilfrid concealed his annoyance at the intrusion with only partial success.

'You are changed,' said Wilfrid, the moment Bega came in. She said nothing, nodded, and sat on the chair indicated by Hilda. 'You look as if you have benefited from the guidance of our Mother here.'

What he also thought was that she had grown into a certain sort of beauty. Exposure to the sea air had brought a darkness to her skin which suited it. The hair was still luxuriant but not as wild; it was loosely knotted and fell in a thick strand down the oatmeal-coloured gown. The eyes – how could he have failed to notice? – were so palely beguiling, intelligent, capable of an intensity which interested him.

'Everyone here benefits from her teaching,' said Bega, calmly. She felt a small surge of distrust, knew that this man was clever enough to sense it, and fought it down. It was a fault in her, a sin for which she deserved to be punished. Wilfrid was already a man of greatness. He could speak to huge crowds – bigger even than those addressed by Cuthbert – and, at the close of his preaching, thousands would become converted to the one true faith. His work for God had brought him land, farms and money for the building of churches, so that he was, in that way, richer than most of the nobles. Yet it was all for Christ. She must be wrong! She had to drive the thought into her soul. She must look up at him now and in her eyes she must say 'forgive me'.

As her full unflinching gaze met his, a faint shiver went through Wilfrid.

'The abbess tells me that you are the most skilled in reading, the most conscientious about visiting the sick, and above all, as far as I am concerned, fearless in going wherever you are sent. You are a fighter: with the sword as well as the word. I like that.'

'I am no more and no less than what God has let the Abbess Hilda make me,' said Bega flatly.

'Praise Him,' said Wilfrid.

'Amen.'

'I am told that you were especially devoted to a study of the *Confessions of St Augustine* – one of the books I studied in Rome.'

'Oh yes!' Bega suddenly switched to delight. 'It is a wonderful book.'

'What especially moved you?'

'The struggle,' said Bega, simply, fearing she would be caught out. 'The struggle with the sins of the world.'

'With his sensuality?'

'That, yes.'

'Do you recognise that struggle?' Wilfrid asked, sharply.

'All of us who forsake the pleasures of the flesh know that it cannot be done without suffering. But the suffering is in the service of God which makes the pain a joy,' she replied.

He decided he would have to work harder. 'Do you remember the passage where he speaks of the man he is by day and the man he is by night?'

She did but she was not so foolish as to seem eager to remember. She merely nodded.

Wilfrid steadied himself for a moment and then, in Latin, he quoted: '"Thou commandest, indeed, that I should restrain myself from the lust of the flesh and from the lust of the eyes and from the ambition of the world . . ." That is how the chapter begins, if I am not mistaken. Augustine goes on. "But still there live in my memory (of which I have spoken so much) the images of such things, as my habits have fixed there; and these rise up before me, lacking indeed their old power, when I am awake. But in sleep they present themselves not only so far as to call forth pleasure, but also consent, and very like reality. Yes, so far has the illusion of the image power over my soul and my flesh that, when asleep, imaginations carry with them more force than realities when I am awake." And you remember his great cry? "Am I not at that time myself, O Lord my God? And yet how great difference is there between myself and myself, in the moment when I pass from waking to sleeping, or return from sleeping to waking? Where, then, is the reason which resists such suggestions when I am awake?"'

As Wilfrid continued his flawless quotation – which itself impressed both women – Bega almost cried out. How was it that he had chosen the passage which had most riveted and most tormented her? How did he know? How could he know that she went into that darkness of sleep in a despairing fury of anticipation because there, like St Augustine, she found images of sensual repletion which her horrified conscious mind banned? She looked at Wilfrid in some confusion. For a wild moment she thought he might be a wizard. Was it possible that the Devil could conquer the soul of such a strong holy man and use him for his own ends? Wizards were still at large. In Ireland her father had feared them. In Rheged, she had been told by one of Cuthbert's followers, wizards flourished and were constantly turning converts back to their pagan gods.

The atmosphere in the small parlour had become charged with the passion of St Augustine's words. Hilda was very uneasy. There was something shocking, even sinful, which she could not identify and therefore she blamed herself for the feeling. Perhaps, she thought, she had failed to live up to Wilfrid's high standards of scholarship. Why, otherwise, would he wish to put on such a wonderful display of learning not for her but for Bega? Bega, who sat transfixed.

'So,' Wilfrid concluded, well aware that he had struck his target, 'the question is that asked by the saint himself "Where, then, is the reason which resists such suggestions when I am awake?" Where is it, Bega? "Am I not at that time – in full spate of sensual sin – am I not myself, Oh Lord?" What do you say to that, Bega?'

Bega was silent. Her heart was too full, her head too dizzy with the impact of those taunting words. She shook her head. It was deeply intriguing, Wilfrid thought, how the most pious and unworldly of the young convent-bound nuns could shimmer with a sensuality that would shame the whores along the Tiber.

'It is a question which must be debated with the best scholars,' he said. 'And they, there can be no doubt, are only in Rome.'

There could indeed be a great debate, Bega thought. But what about the scholars from Lindisfarne, or from Iona, or from Connachta or Whitby itself? Her loyalty and her belief in the truth of what she thought pressed her to contradict him on the point but once again, with the discipline learned so painstakingly, she controlled herself. Besides, the great question remained. Was she truly the sensual person who loved in her dreams or the chaste person who was awake? Wilfrid had delivered a piercing insight into the heart of her fears.

'And that is one of the reasons I must go back to Rome,' he said. 'It is only there that certain books exist which may contain answers to questions such as these.'

Here he looked at Hilda and spoke the next few words entirely to her.

'I have long felt that a woman, a nun, from this kingdom should go to Rome. There is much to learn of the Roman ways, there is much to discover about the women who served the church in Rome when it first became Christian. Some of them, they say, conducted the Mass itself. There are stories, too, of our women saints and martyrs and they should be heard directly by a woman who could bring back news of this to her sisters. Of course, if such a thing were to happen, then the woman could only come from this house.' He paused.

'I . . .' said Hilda, 'I am overwhelmed, Wilfrid, but . . . there is so much to do here. I do not know what time I have been given and I must spend all of it here. Forgive me.'

Wilfrid's expression changed not a fraction though both he and, he knew, Bega, were aware that Hilda had excused herself from an invitation which was not being held out to her.

'God told me that you would say that.' He looked troubled. 'And I knew that if I sought to persuade you, then I would be guilty of stealing you from the work to which He had called you. Work which only you, of all women, can do. Already the fame of your abbey echoes around the kingdom. From here, we know, princes of the church and martyrs to virtue, teachers and golden scholars will emerge to glorify His name and forever perpetuate your own.'

Hilda, in her embarrassment, leaned forward and tapped him on the knee to check this flow of sinful flattery. 'And that is why I was so interested when you spoke of Bega. For in all you said I saw someone in your own image. Here, I thought, is a young Hilda! She, like you, has known a court; like you she has endured the dangers of the world outside the abbey walls; like you she is a scholar and, no doubt following your example and striving to imitate you, she is unafraid to visit the most afflicted of the sick. As you cannot, indeed you must not, go with me to Rome, let me take this disciple of yours to be your eyes and ears and mind in the city of Peter and come back to you with reports which will enrich this abbey beyond all others.'

In the silence, Bega felt her heart banging against her ribs. Surely the others heard it too? To go to Rome! To go through all those lands she had heard of, to meet pagan tribes and try to win their souls! To arrive in the most splendid city on earth and visit the shrines, see the relics, dispute with the scholars Wilfrid spoke of! Yet, with Wilfrid?

'We must think about it very carefully,' said Hilda, slowly.

'I leave just after Easter. The Roman Easter.' He smiled as did Hilda at the reference to the old Celtic–Roman disagreement which he had spoken of on his previous visit. Hilda was uneasy that the most holy date in Christ's life was celebrated at different times by the Roman and the Celtic community, but the difference was traditional and no harm seemed to have come of it.

'The six weeks of Lent will be good for us to seek the right way,' she said.

'And you?' he asked.

Wilfrid turned suddenly to Bega who discovered, to her mortification, that she was trembling.

'I will be led by the abbess.' The words were whispered.

'You could have no better guide,' said Wilfrid briskly. 'And you and I,' he said to Hilda, 'will talk of this further before I leave. There is more to be said.'

Bega was made to feel intrusive, so she left.

Hilda was relieved to have Wilfrid to herself.

'Perhaps,' said Wilfrid carelessly, 'she is not the one. Is there another you would choose?'

'No,' Hilda replied, scrupulously, 'if what you are suggesting is to come to pass, then Bega is a good choice.'

'It was only because of what you told me about her. But of course if you have any doubts now that you know the extent of the enterprise . . .'

'I have doubts, yes,' said Hilda. They were unclear but she knew they existed. 'I need to pray,' she said, nodding quickly. 'I need prayer.'

'I too will pray. And I need your prayers, Hilda. Your prayers go straight to heaven. Nothing *dare* stand in their way!'

Hilda smiled, rather anxiously, at yet another compliment and indicated that the meeting was over.

CHAPTER THIRTY-NINE

Wilfrid had business with some of the new land given him by Aetheldreda, wife of Ecfrith, and he left Whitby promising to be back to hear the decision in about twenty days. He did not see Bega again. Chad observed his departure. From his usual post in the vegetable garden near the main gate, he tried to note all the exits and entrances. Hilda was still rather dismayed that he had not followed her advice and become a fisherman. Perhaps because of her unease over Bega, she had become suspicious of his attraction to the scriptorium and his fascination with the illuminators. He was simply not fitted for anything but manual work, she had decided, which was, just as much as anything else, a way to worship the Lord.

Later that morning, Bega asked to see her.

Hilda was still perturbed and would rather have evaded an encounter with Bega, but she acceded. Bega sensed Hilda's resistance, almost her displeasure, and tiptoed in determined to progress with all her tact.

'I am in need of all your guidance and prayers, Mother.'

'I am aware of that,' said Hilda, noting, not for the first time, that Bega could be a little presumptuous.

'This is a decision I cannot reach alone.'

'You are not required to.'

'It would be far better were you to go to Rome. Wilfrid would much prefer that.'

Hilda was not mollified but she nodded her assent.

'I am worried about Rome itself,' said Bega.

'It is,' Hilda agreed, 'a fearful prospect.'

'Not the journey,' said Bega promptly and then regretted it. She longed to make the journey. Just to travel. To see so much.

To go. To let herself be cast on the waters. 'The city itself is what worries me,' she added hurriedly, 'because of the power it seems to exercise. If it can have such a strong influence on a mind as fortified as that of Wilfrid, how can my weak will survive?'

'What is it you fear you will have to survive?' said Hilda, much encouraged.

'This Rome,' said Bega, firmly. 'This place which seems to want us all to do as we are told, not by God but by men whose authority is directed at an earthly rule.'

Hilda felt she was being drawn into an argument she did not wish to have. But Bega's doubts had to be given air, she thought. Frankly, at this time Hilda was too consumed with the building of her own empire to be much worried by the designs anyone else might have. Rome seemed no threat, only an enrichment.

'Would Cuthbert wish to go to Rome?' Bega asked.

The introduction of a parallel revered figure spurred Hilda into a reply.

'Wilfrid and Cuthbert are as the sea and the rock,' she said, 'a comparison I have used many times. God needs both water and land. Cuthbert is the land. He will one day chain his faith to a small and simple plot of our earth and there fight all the devils sent to tempt him. Wilfrid is the water that runs from the mountains and carries us across the sea and comes down from heaven to grow our food and slake our thirst.'

They are also, Bega thought, equally ambitious and quite fearsomely determined to be first among the soldiers of Christ. One seeks glory in the life of the hermit, the other in the exercise of the church's authority. Neither, though she would not admit this, claimed her heart in the way that, say, Cathleen or even, in their moments, Donal and Erebert had done. This puzzled her, for they were undoubtedly the most remarkable men, profoundly devoted to the Lord of Hosts. 'I would like your permission to fast until Wilfrid returns,' she said as humbly as possible.

'When did you last undergo a fast?'

Bega told her. It had been severe, quite recently and she was not wholly restored. She still felt feverish. She knew that Hilda distrusted a display of virtuosity in this regard. But there were those whose excesses – in fasting especially – brought credit to the abbey.

'We will not tell anyone why you are undergoing this fast.'

'No.' Bega understood. 'No one.'

'It will be a fast which I have asked you to undertake for my own reasons.' She paused. 'I have good reasons and I bid you undertake this fast, until Wilfrid returns.'

'I will.'

Bega drew a deep silent breath in order to launch, as nonchalantly as possible, the question which was the real reason for her seeking out Hilda.

'I would also beg permission,' she began, with unfeigned timidity, 'to walk, at some suitably inconspicuous time of the day, and be allowed to pray and meditate overlooking the sea.'

'At what the younger ones call Bega's Place?' Hilda sniffed audibly. It was exactly the sort of notoriety she distrusted. But the dashing reputation of Bega had already begun to work in drawing young women of good family to the abbey. With their handsome earthly prospects and undoubted capacity for heavenly reward, they were becoming a force which, to Hilda's pride, competed well in so many areas with the men.

'What is it about that place?' Hilda asked.

Bega took her time. She knew that nothing but the truth would do. Though Hilda had weaknesses, her strengths far outweighed them and one was a scalpel ability to slice through an ill-prepared argument.

'I have no simple or clear answer for you because I have none for myself,' said Bega. 'I have thought about it often and although I can find explanations, none is sufficient. Sometimes I think it is because of the sight and smell of the sea. But why do I want that?' Here she saw Padric on the boat, one hand holding the mast, the other reaching out for her, the soft salty spray freshening her excited face, the lightness and soaring freedom of it, still now able to spin her soul into a unique happiness. But she said nothing about it.

'Perhaps,' said Hilda, 'you look at the sea and think of your home. We are all homesick. I notice that the girls who come from Ireland seem more susceptible than most. And from what Cuthbert said to me, yours was not a particularly easy journey.'

'It is true,' confirmed Bega, eagerly. 'I am sometimes very homesick and I ask God why? Is it because I am so weak that part of me still longs to be in the ease of childhood?'

'It could well be,' said Hilda, swiftly.

'Or,' Bega continued, feeling that if she could keep going then she might just get this favour so mysteriously but so very keenly ached for, 'is it that I see a mission to go back in the direction from which I came and try to convert the many pagan I saw along the way?'

'Have you had such a vision? Of preaching to the remaining pagans in your own land?'

'Voices,' said Bega, carefully, and added, 'not visions; and not often voices.'

'I still see nothing that could not be achieved in your cell. You can see the sea in all your daily movements around the abbey. Why you need a special spot of ground still puzzles me and I fear that there may be a sin in it somewhere. Pride?'

'Perhaps,' said Bega, struggling to put aside her disappointment and fight back.

'We must beware making ourselves too conspicuous.'

'I know that.'

'We are here to serve God, to live an unspotted life, to learn and preach His Gospel and to visit and cherish the sick. It is difficult to see where standing on a clifftop gazing out to sea fits in.'

'It is the sense of being alone with God,' said Bega firmly. 'I am a weak vessel, Mother. When I am surrounded by others then sometimes I feel comfort and support. At other times I feel that I am unable to focus my spirit. My poor prayers are lost in the flock of prayers which rise up to the sky. My feeble mind cannot fix itself on the object of adoration because it is so stupidly distracted by a coughing here or an overloud voice or the sudden sight of feet thick-caked in mud. It is my weakness which makes me beg you to let me go there – not often – but when I fear that within the community I cannot fully examine what God wants of me now.

'The community will help me. Everyone loves Wilfrid. We all know that he may number with the saints. He and Cuthbert walk here as the apostles walked in Galilee. We kiss the earth they tread. But does God want me to accept his offer? Magnificent as it is, might it be – for me – the offer of a devil? Not that Wilfrid is a devil – of course not. But we know how cunning, how very, very cunning, the devil is. Might he not have seen that Wilfrid wanted to take a nun and her attendants with him to Rome and directed him to me *because he knew that I was a weak vessel?*'

She paused: Hilda was very attentive. 'Wilfrid's high purpose will be brought low unless I can discover whether I am worthy. If I stay near all my sisters and near you I will feel strong. I will feel worthy. But is that the truth of it? I beg you, Mother, let me test my spirit alone, fasting in our own domestic wilderness where I can look out at nothing but sea and sky and praise God and wait for one of His saints to think me worthy of intermission.'

Hilda was moved by Bega's plea. She was also convinced by the sense of it. She agreed and she agreed in generous measure.

Bega kissed her ring and the two women prayed together.

She drank a little water with some thin gruel at dawn, a little at sunset, attended to an agreed minimum of her normal daily routine and spent the rest of the time in prayer.

For the first twelve days it was as she had anticipated. She knew the symptoms now. The raking claws across the stomach, the felling pain in the head, the aching eyes, the swelling of the throat, the languorous perilous drift of spirit, the lust for food which set off juices which opened to wounds unappeased. All this she knew.

About the twelfth day things changed. She felt a new pressure behind her forehead. There was a coldness which would not go away despite the mild spring and the warmth of her cloak. The simple walk up to the clifftop left her breathless.

This was nothing but a new test, she decided.

But there was something else that disturbed her. St Brigid, who had always been ready to be summoned by Bega's prayers, would not appear to her. However furiously the young woman prayed to her saintly exemplar, the image would not appear. And no other replaced her. In her fast Bega was locked in alone.

She found that although her faith did not diminish, her fear grew. She was nervous of everything. She flinched from the solidity of the earth or the wall of her cell when she awoke. When anyone came anywhere near her she feared they might touch or even attack her. The sudden howl of a dog made her start. Sounds, of wind or sea, which had become friends, could turn into the threats of the enemy.

There were forces gathering themselves to destroy her, she felt. Every pore in her body seemed open to this alert rash of fear. Something was being summoned up, she knew it. This feeling, these particular aches, had never happened before on a fast. Was she ill or was God testing her more severely for the great opportunity which had been offered to her?

Perhaps she was too weak. The abbess would let her off the fast. She would understand.

But she had promised before God. And she needed to know what to do about Rome. Was it glory or was it an invitation for a descent into hell? Was she worthy of it – honour that it might be? Or was she to become a sacrifice?

Wilfrid's eyes were so seductive. She shivered at the memory. Everybody loved and worshipped him. Why did her flesh seem to curl away?

'What are you praying for?'

That was the question put by the first of the devils who visited her. This figure was very like herself. She appeared late at night when Bega, chilled and full of pain, knelt on the clifftop facing the dark sea whose noise threatened to hypnotise her to sleep.

'What are you praying for?' the young woman asked.

Bega stared out into the darkness to find the form behind the voice.

'I am here,' said the voice. 'Don't pretend you can't see me. Just because you cannot answer the question. What are you praying for?'

'Guidance.'

'Of course. For what?'

'A decision.'

'Of course. Which decision?'

'Whether or not to go to Rome with Wilfrid.'

'Do you love him?'

'His is a fine Christian soul.'

'Not that! And look over *here*! This is where I am. Do you lust for him? Do you want him to couple with you?'

'That is not a question you can ask.'

'Don't be silly, Bega. You know that look in him. Remember St Augustine. Imagine a night such as this in a place

as lonely as this with your servants asleep and himself and
yourself praying together. Do you enjoy the thought of what
might happen next?'

'I have no such thoughts.'

'Hypocrite! Liar!' The voice became a cackle and a shriek and
a whip of wind stung Bega in the face. 'Ha! I know your dreams,
you hussy. You whore of Babylon. That's why you want to go, isn't
it? And that's why Hilda is so candlegrease-faced full of jealousy.
Ha! You all want him! Ha!'

Bega threw herself forward on to the wet turf and clasped her
hands to her ears. She pressed her face into the wet grass and
licked it gratefully. She stayed there until the shrieks finally
faded away.

That was on the fourteenth day.

On the sixteenth day she was walking a little way in the
afternoon along the clifftops. Some force drew her to the edge
itself. She tried to resist it but she could not.

She placed her feet on the very edge and looked down at the
swaying sea. She felt lightened, her body hollow as if ready to be
uplifted by any prayer and cast into the air itself.

As she gazed down she saw two black-winged tormentors. First
they skimmed across the waves, scissoring the surface and forcing
her to secure all her attention on them. Then, when they knew
they had her eyes and her will in their grip, they rose, two flights
of malign thought and tipped their wings and circled about her
head. She saw that though they had the wings of birds they
had the bodies of weasels and the faces of goblins, grinning and
screaming at her.

'You cannot serve God.'

'You love Padric.'

'Tell Hilda. Tell Hilda about Padric.'

'Too cowardly to tell. Padric so long ago.'

'Padric never came back to see you.'

'Padric walked away.'

'Why did he not stay?'

'Never saw you. Never tried. Not hard enough.'

'Didn't care.'

'Didn't want to.'

'Didn't come back.'

'Didn't come back.'

'Didn't come back.'

And they wheeled up into the slate grey smooth-stretched sky as Bega swayed forward and threatened to fall. She stood back. She kneeled. Again they swooped down.

'Where is he now?'

'Married.'

'Of course.'

'Married.'

'Why do you not hear?'

'Because he went to another country.'

'And married.'

'Of course.'

Up they went and performed great scimitar arcs in the sky as Bega sobbed for them to go away and sobbed for them to tell her how they knew.

She could not answer back. And down they came again. This time they were so close to her face she could see that their eyes were yellow and boiling with malice; their little teeth were green dagger points and raw flesh hung from them; the wings were black but their tips had been dipped in blood. On their bald goblin heads were sores and suppurating holes and from their foul, stinking mouths came the final jet hiss of hate, spitting on to her puckering, cowering skin.

'You used God, didn't you?'

'To avoid O'Neill.'

'To be free for Padric.'

'You used God. Didn't you?'

'And Maeve was killed.'

'And Donal was killed.'

'And O'Neill was killed.'

'And is your father alive?'

'Have you asked, is your father alive?'

'All this is false.'

'All this is a sham.'

'You wanted Padric.'

'Others died for that.'

'And you didn't get him.'

'Is Christ second to Padric?'

'Yes. He's second. Isn't He?'

'Can you go to Holy Rome such a sinner?'

'Yes. Because Padric is there.'

'You think you will meet Padric there.'

'On the way there.'

'He went across the sea.'

'He is never coming here again.'

'Never.'

'Never here.'

'Never.'

For some utterly terrifying moments, the two goblin devil birds wrapped their blood sticky wings around her face and sank their dagger teeth into her head and sucked at her eyes with their slavering, long, thin-lipped mouths.

On the seventeenth day she was too weak to leave her bed. She told a fretting Isidore that she would be fine, it was a passing phase, of no consequence. The truth was that she could not bear the presence even of so bright and innocent a girl. She needed to gather all her remaining strength in solitude as the devil prepared for further assaults.

She had not long to wait.

Down the inside of the wall, from the thatched roof, a large rat slid and slithered until it skidded on to the floor and crouched, glittering black eyes fixed on her. She dared not move. Indeed, the pain behind her eyes skewered her to the bed, giving the fear an ally. She had never known such a pain behind her eyes.

As she watched, the rat began to grow and soon it was as big as Cal her dog and still it grew, and then it stepped towards her as she closed her eyes in terror. For not only had it grown but, as it grew its fine shiny rat-sheen skin was sloughed off and a bloodied and yellow quivering fester of rotting flesh was exposed. The mouth hung open and emitted evil droppings which looked as if one touch would infect with death. Those glittering black eyes began to bulge forward and the small veins in them popped, making the surface blood flecked. But most of all the face, when she dared open her eyes once more, was what made her want to swoon. The rat face became a human face, but a face of bones with only the eyes alive, the rest a yellow-boned skull dripping dead flesh.

'I have been to Rome before you,' the thing said. 'Do you want to know what I saw?'

Bega tried to swallow and failed. But she nodded.

'I went with you and with Wilfrid and the others.'

The thing shook its head from side-to-side and the dead flesh swung towards her, threatening to brush her face. She could not move.

'Along the way we met a man who once loved you.'

The voice was so deep, it made Bega's ears burn just to listen. The words were spoken very deliberately.

'But he no longer loved you and when the pagans took him and opened up his belly and put in it a nest of wasps and sewed it up again, you were glad.'

Bega tried to pray to St Brigid.

'This Wilfrid took a sword and slew a forest. In the forest were hobgoblins. They came to you and sucked all the juice out of you until you were like my poor skull.'

What was it Cathleen had taught her? First say the name, then imagine the face and all the time repeat 'St Brigid, Holy Mother of all Irish women, please help me in my dark hour'. Could she begin to say that?

'In Rome he took you to a place of women where they fed you and filled you with wine and made you into someone else.'

'St Brigid,' she began . . .

'I see you still in Rome. Wilfrid is back here. You are lying on a cot and you cannot rise.'

'In the name of the Father, and of the Son . . .'

Still bigger, bigger still and then . . .

'That is where you died, Bega. In Rome. I travelled there before you.'

'St Brigid, Holy Mother . . .'

When next she opened her eyes, the thing was gone. Despite the pain, she forced herself to roll over on to her knees and then to crawl to the door and stand, heaving for breath in the blessedly clear, cold air.

How could she possibly think of going to Rome when that was in store for her?

But was that not the devil tempting her not to go?

Did that not mean she was right to go?

It must. There could be no other reason for such a dread visit. God was telling her that she had to go to Rome.

She experienced a sudden uplift of joy and liberation. It was decided. Rome!

The air felt so good. She took mouthfuls of it, she ate it, she felt it sweep through her body and shivered with pleasure as it sweetened the pain.

When Isidore came to see her in the evening she found her in a state of remarkable tranquillity and quickly reported this.

But when most secure, as she should have known, the most seductive devil of all appeared. Its arrival was forewarned by pain in her lower stomach which reminded her of the pain she had endured before the bleeding in Caerel.

She knew that if she could resist this pain then she would be able to resist the devil.

Bega thought she could force herself not to cry aloud. She did not know that her shouts were heard all over the Abbey.

The malevolent imps inside her tore under her skin with their thorn-pointed nails. She put her hands on her wasted belly to soothe it but the weak, trembling palms would do nothing to stop the rampage of the spiteful creatures trying to distract her. The image of St Brigid now swam easily into her mind and, as she stifled the groans against the red-hot poker pains lacerating her guts, she prayed to the saint for the strength to resist this attempt to weaken her.

She writhed on the bed as scalding prickle-backed serpents threshed furiously inside her poor belly. She shut her eyes tight to summon the concentration necessary to fix her prayers on St Brigid.

When she opened them after a long silent cry of 'Help me! Help me!' she saw or seemed to see the Abbess Hilda hovering over her. But was it Hilda? The attitude, the voice, the dress, all were hers, but the face was cloudy.

'You must break this fast now.'

'No!'

Bega heard her own voice. It sounded like the shriek of the first devil. That was what had happened. The first of the devils had returned when it had thought it had victory and it was now inside her squeezing its fang-flickering form inside the coils and twists of her body.

'I command you to break your fast. Here.'

Bega saw a cup coming towards her. A hand lifted the back of her neck and guided her mouth towards the warm herb soup. The luscious thick warm smell of it made her want to cry. Her nose seized on the aroma and flared with passion. The back of her throat longed for the soup and the juices, parched for so long, rushed out to slake their lust.

Bega closed her mouth tightly.

The cup was brought to her lips and tilted.

The soup ran across the brim, on to the tight thin hard cracked lips and then down over her chin.

'You must drink this, my child.'

The devil was pretending to be Abbess Hilda.

This was the final test.

The soup was withdrawn and Bega heard the whispering of several women.

The spasms in her stomach eased a little, which convinced her the women were in league.

'Wilfrid sent a messenger. He will be here tomorrow.'

So why should she not hold to her fast for another day?

'If you are to speak to him, you must at least take some soup.'

But to break a fast would be to break a promise to God.

'You have been ill, Bega. I should never have allowed you to fast for so long so soon after your last period of self-denial. But also you have been ill.'

That was the trick. To pretend that she was ill so that they could break her.

'Please. Take just a little.'

That was the clever way. 'Just a little'. But 'just a little' would still be too much.

Again the cup came up and her head was heaved up to meet it. Again she armoured her mouth against it.

'How will you talk to Wilfrid? You have no strength.'

I have enough strength, she thought, to say 'yes'. That is all I need to say.

'We will pray for you,' said the voice of Hilda. 'We will pray that you be delivered from your obstinacy. We will pray that you see the truth of your weakness.'

They have been defeated, Bega thought, in grim and silent triumph.

She refused to join in the prayer, knowing it was the mockery of the devil.

And finally they left her alone.

Then she laughed aloud. She shrieked. She beat her belly with frail fists to drive out the last of the devil's serpents which were retreating, sliding away, defeated.

When Wilfrid came to see her, she made herself get to her feet.

She held out her arms to him and then kneeled on the ground in front of him.

'God has blessed me,' she said and noticed, again, that the voice she used was not the voice of herself but that of the first temptress.

She saw Wilfrid backing away. 'No! No! No!' The words shrieked out as she crawled towards him.

'What have you done to her?'

'She would not listen. I told you.'

'I will come to Rome.'

'She has been ill.'

'Why did you not break the fast and nurse her?'

'The devil tried that and I beat him off.'

'She was very obstinate.'

'It is your duty – may I say that? – to command your flock not to fast when they are so ill.'

'I will not break a promise to God.'

She lay down before him, spreadeagled on the floor.

Had she seen his handsome, elegant, haughty face she would have been dismayed at his look of distaste. This pale, wretched, scraggy, suddenly unattractive, obstinate woman was revealed now as one of those wild Celtic self-flagellators who had no conception of the true business of the church.

'I cannot possibly take her with me.'

'No! You must! God has given me the strength.'

'This has been a wasted journey, Abbess, and I expected more from this abbey.'

'Let us feed and nurse her for a few days. You will see the difference almost immediately.'

'I see the difference now. And I do not like it.'

'Even the devil's rat could not destroy me.'

'I have wasted enough time here.'

'Please. We will help her and then – she could be so useful to you.'

But the wild, raving, pinch-faced, dirty hair-tangled zealot at his feet made him recoil.

'I will find someone else, along the way. Perhaps in Canterbury.'

'No.' Bega found her normal voice. Her composure returned as if an exorcism had been suddenly successful. 'No.' She hauled herself on to her knees and then, with difficulty, on to her feet. 'You must take me to Rome.'

'I have decided against it.'

'But I endured all this for you.' She pointed to her body and her face knowing that it must show marks of her struggle. 'I fought devils in order to test my strength before God. I fasted. I prayed. I did everything necessary to be thought worthy to go to Rome. I am ready now.'

How could he ever have thought of her as a possible companion – least of all attractive? In this calm mood the haggardness of her slender features seemed even more unappetising.

'I have changed my mind. You are not sufficiently strong.'

'You made a promise.'

'Bega,' said Hilda, firmly. 'We must get you something to eat.'

'You promised.'

Bega's hand reached for the small wrapped fragment of the True Cross. She took it out. It looked very insignificant and scruffy. She held it out to him.

'What is that?' said Wilfrid.

'She is not herself. She has been raving in her illness. And, I have to say this, she is possibly suffering because of what you have said to her.'

'Do you know what is wrapped in here?'

'I am leaving now, Abbess.'

'In here is something that could make the sun stand still in the sky at noon,' said Bega.

'I will collect my men and come back for your blessing.'

'Do you not believe me?'

'God bless you, Bega. When you are restored to health I suggest that you continue with your studies more assiduously and leave the tests of the flesh to those whose particular strength it is.'

'Like our dear Cuthbert,' said Hilda. Wilfrid nodded rather stiffly.

'Cuthbert told me not to talk about this.'

Bega had almost unwrapped the piece but the name Cuthbert stopped her.

'Whatever Cuthbert said must be obeyed,' said Hilda.

'It could be the first of your new lessons in obedience,' said Wilfrid, glancing dismissively at the unprepossessing wad of bandage in Bega's hand. 'I am shocked, Bega, to learn that you failed to break your fast when told to do so by the abbess to whom you owe all duty and obedience. If Cuthbert – who is one who can survive the rigours and torments of the flesh – forbade you to talk about that object you have gathered on your travels, then obey him.'

'You must obey Cuthbert,' said Hilda, 'and Wilfrid.'

There was a pause. Then, wearily, Bega began to rewrap the fragment.

Wilfrid left.

Hilda took Bega by the shoulders and led her back to the bed.

'I will send you soup which you must drink.'

'I will.'

'And a little bread to soak in the soup. That too must be eaten.'

'I will.'

'Then you will pray for the safety of Wilfrid, may God preserve him against all his enemies on this terrible journey he must take through tribes of dark pagans.'

'I will pray for him.'

'Good.'

Hilda looked down at Bega and felt at peace.

God had seen His own way to resolve a matter which had disturbed her a good deal.

'You are a strong young woman, Bega,' Hilda said. 'That is what I am looking for. Your fault is this dreadful obstinacy. You should have accepted it when we told you you were ill. We sent Cowla to you. She is old but she understands things and she feared you were getting the plague. But you would not listen to her either. But there is also something remarkable about you, Bega. God has prepared you for a special task. We will see that we make you ready for it.'

She too left.

Alone, Bega began to cry softly and helplessly. Her body ached so much. Her eyes, her head, her stomach, every bit of flesh tingled or smarted or pulled with pain.

As she waited for the food to come, she knew one thing only. She must leave Whitby now.

CHAPTER FORTY

Penraddin combed her hair with a comb of finely toothed bone. Like everything at this Northumbrian court, it was far richer than anything she had been used to at what now seemed the lowly and extremely humble court of Rheged. There was a great deal the young woman enjoyed here, even though she had quickly lost her infatuation with Ecfrith, and she believed that staying protected her family.

The court was on the rock of the fortress of Bamburgh where her own ancestor had famously threatened the invading Germanic tribes almost a century before. Now through the good offices of her aunt who had married King Oswy, she was welcomed there.

The household was, to her eyes, vast. Almost seven hundred people lived there or in the buildings set below the great rock. From the court you looked out across the sea towards the lands which the conquering tribes had quitted on their surge to this rich area. In the distance were the islands, nearest of all the half-island of Lindisfarne, the first home of the monks from Iona in this foreign land. No woman was allowed there, but Penraddin heard tales of the monks' miraculous powers and of the strength of their learning, the piety of their prayer. Twice she had heard men from Lindisfarne preach. On both occasions she had felt the true faith. Only Cuthbert had moved her more and he had been trained by those who came from Lindisfarne. It was consoling to have such sanctity so near at hand.

Much more exciting was the view to the west. Here, when she stood on the highest point of the rock and looked out, was the evidence of power, of conquest and of law. She could pick out scores and scores of settlements and homesteads, many substantial in size and structure. There was constant movement of cattle. Bands of horsemen rode through the land, war parties, tribute-seekers, messengers. The forests were being hacked down and the sounds of the axes on wood pealed across the plain. This was a people which would let no one stand in its way.

By comparison she almost blushed to remember the limitations of Rheged. In her father's domain the whole purpose seemed to be to underplay power, to display as little as possible, to act as a subdued, even a cowed people. Now she combed her hair for Ecfrith and waited with some impatience.

She had learned quite early – with help from the concubine of Alchfrid – how to satisfy his lusts. It was not too complicated. Spurred on by her early success, she had then sought advice from a soothsayer and procured not only aphrodisiacs but ways of driving him further and further into a madness of desire. In her extreme youth and from such a protected background, she found nothing in this but adventurous delight. And she too was drawn into the excitements. She loved the way that she had the wit to subject Ecfrith to her will. He called her his little Celtic witch and she loved that too. Witches had power.

The skill of the soothsayer had kept her free from children so far and that was a possible source of conflict. That, she suspected, was why he had asked her to come to his quarters in the mid-morning. Ecfrith wanted children. He had a virgin wife and now, it would seem, an infertile concubine.

As she walked, unaccompanied, past the large spread of buildings which dominated the rock and tumbled down to shelter behind it, she wondered, as she always had, what she would say to Aetheldreda his wife should they ever talk. This strange wife of Ecfrith who had taken a vow of chastity, fascinated the young girl who had supplanted her in her husband's bed. But Aetheldreda had never offered anything other than a sweet, annoyingly pitying smile and an occasional blessing.

Ecfrith had been given a large room off the main hall and made it magnificent. Rare skins hung on the walls and covered the floor so that it appeared like a royal hunter's cave. His father had returned to him some of the booty he had gathered in skirmishes and local battles, and these pieces, silver, enamelled objects, a studded shield, ornately worked daggers, were littered around with princely carelessness. Bishop Benedict, who had gone to Rome, like Wilfrid, but with a richer purse, had brought back manuscripts, rare silks, and painting on wood, which brought even more lustre to the place.

Penraddin had been impressed by the room from the very first. It was a cave of materials and ornaments almost lascivious in their gorgeousness. Her attraction strengthened as its association with pleasure and the enormous, dangerous task of bridling Ecfrith became the centre of her life.

He had been out with a war party and returned only that morning. He still stank of horse sweat and earth dirt, blood and too much mead, but when he opened his arms she fled into them and within minutes he was writhing in delight under her skills as she drew out his urgent desire into a longer and longer tension of deep sexual pleasure.

When he was satisfied and, with her help, had satisfied Penraddin, he let her pour him some beer before he began.

'It was your brothers,' he said. 'Your brothers and their men who killed our men. Now, it is said, they have fled abroad.'

Penraddin clenched herself against any compromising reply. She could not think of her family without regret. Her brothers were still her heroes. She poured herself a mouthful of the beer – he liked her to drink when they were alone together.

'You can sit down,' he said.

Ecfrith was sprawled on a heap of fine wolfskins. Penraddin sat at a rather formal distance. He liked to look at her half-dressed, at this reachable distance from him. The golden armlet glowed on her naked arm.

'So what do you have to say to that?' he asked, only partly bantering.

'Are you sure?' She fought against her nervousness: it would not do to let Ecfrith know of her continued allegiance.

'One of Cuthbert's monks saw them skulking towards the coast in Rheged. With the horses. And the swords.'

'Well then.'

'They should not have taken the swords. How can we bury our men without swords? Is this what Rheged has come to?'

'I don't know.'

Ecfrith's temper was quick to change and rapidly turned to fury. Penraddin found that she was letting herself become more and more submissive. Until now she had been prepared to pay

that price. But the mention of her brothers and the undoubted
heroism of their encounter (she had heard all about the battle)
unsettled her. She was entirely on their side and found it difficult
to support Ecfrith as he expected and as she had pretended to do
at other times.

'There must have been at least a score of them to defeat our
warriors,' he said. His humiliation at the defeat and slaughter of
his men had set him on a course of vengeance which only the
strongest ruling of his father had diverted.

'Is that what the monk said?'

'Your brother is too clever to travel across this kingdom with
such booty in one big war party.'

Ecfrith took a deep gulp of the cold strong beer. 'I have just
come back from Rheged.'

Penraddin felt her heart quicken.

Ecfrith looked closely at her.

'What would you do if I said that I met your brothers and we
slaughtered them?'

Penraddin lowered her gaze but gave no other sign.

'What would you say if I told you we burned down your
mother and father's household and murdered everyone who lived
there?'

Penraddin tightened her hands into fists but still she said
nothing.

'Come here,' he commanded.

She went across to him. He pulled her down to him by the hair
– not entirely ungently – and directed her head into his groin. She
did as she was bid.

When she was done, he waved her away. 'So you will always
be loyal to me?' he asked.

'I will.'

'And children?'

'Will they be the children of a princess or a woman with no
title?' she asked, roughly, glad to take the initiative.

'They will be my children.'

Penraddin rallied her forces. Were her brothers dead? Was the
household burned down, her mother and father murdered? Ecfrith
was quite capable of doing it.

'How can your children know themselves to be equal to any
other on earth?'

'They will be able to say that.'

'It would be better if others can tell them.'

Her father? Did he fight?

'I have one marriage,' said Ecfrith, rather sulkily. Penraddin saw a weakness.

'And yet it is not a marriage. But because of this not-marriage am I to have no title at all? And are our children to be untit-led?'

'She brought great lands to me. Her father is a most mighty king.'

And my father?

She knew that Ecfrith wanted to see if she would break down and ask about her brothers. She would not let him enjoy that. Instead, to take some of the strain from her body, she took his cup to the pitcher of beer and poured more for him, taking a long draught for herself.

'Make me your promise,' she said.

'Aetheldreda will not divorce.'

'Make her.' How often had she challenged him to do that?

Penraddin hated Aetheldreda at this moment. 'Make her,' she repeated.

'She has powerful allies, Penraddin. You are very young in these matters.'

'You thought I was young in other matters. But I learned.' She smiled. His mood changed.

'You did! Little witch. Where did you learn?'

'From you, Ecfrith! From what I know you wanted me to do. You were the one who taught me everything, Ecfrith. You are the most handsome of all the men, the most fearless of all the warriors, you are stronger by far than your brothers. It is you who should take the crown of King Oswy and I can help you. How can she?'

'She has all the church on her side. The monks on Lindisfarne love her for her piety and her charity. Wilfrid,' the name was ground out: he detested Wilfrid's very public friendship with his wife. 'She listens to Wilfrid who tells her that she is an ornament to the church.'

And her mother? Was she, too, slaughtered?

Why did she see Padric every time she glanced up at Ecfrith now? Although it had been strange in the beginning, his likeness to her beloved brother had been something she rejoiced in. Now she saw only the differences and at times like this she made comparisons which were not in Ecfrith's favour. But she had made her choice and must abide by it.

'Wilfrid has an influence which already outreaches any other monk in Northumbria,' she said, deliberately, knowing how much Wilfrid annoyed him.

'He can make some of them believe that he will be the pope himself,' said Ecfrith, bitterly.

He is very handsome, Penraddin thought. And his wealth exceeds that of everyone but the royal family itself.

'Aetheldreda gave him twelve more farms after his last visit to Rome,' said Ecfrith. 'Twelve!'

'They will be put to a good use,' said Penraddin in a pious tone which she knew was guaranteed to inflame Ecfrith further.

'Oh yes! He will build another monastery. But it is Wilfrid who will administer the land. It is Wilfrid who will decide where the tributes go every year. It will be Wilfrid's wealth *and* Wilfrid's monastery. Where will we be when all the wealth goes from the warriors to the church?'

Padric and her brothers would have fought. She would have heard already of the dead and the wounded. Ecfrith had no wounds. Just that lingering smell of blood. Her spirits rose.

'Aetheldreda must be stopped,' he said. 'The other royal women follow her example and with land given in good law they endow monasteries and churches, while many of the younger warriors cannot find courts or households rich enough to support them. And so they go into the monasteries and abbeys instead – like Wilfrid, who should have stayed a soldier, and he would have done had he not been given greater riches elsewhere. If it all rolls on, the church will bleed the court dry.'

It was a theme which Ecfrith had spoken of several times. It was one which made him popular with his men but regarded with suspicion in a court where women particularly, and their attendant monks, were devoted – sometimes almost frenzied – in their search for their heavenly reward. As more and more miracles turned their land into an imitation of Israel in the time of Jesus Christ, a madness seemed to possess some of those few who fully accepted the faith. On the vast lake of paganism and indifference were a few tiny zealous islands of Christianity. Here and there they had been wholly captured by those who would pay any price to ensure their eternal salvation.

'Wilfrid tells Aetheldreda that she cannot get a divorce.'

'Is Wilfrid more than you?' Penraddin asked.

Ecfrith did not like the question.

Penraddin knew that her thrust had hurt and she had no fear about twisting the blade.

'If he is more than you now, then as his power grows he will outsoar you, their friendship will mock you and who will have you for a king then? Make him tell her to get a divorce. Or take me openly as a second wife, her equal in all ways. And then you will have children. And you will still have me.'

The implied threat was ignored by Ecfrith, although he was well aware how addicted he was to her.

'Do you want to know about your father?'

'Yes.' Penraddin's tone was even but emphatic. 'Yes I do.'

Ecfrith let her dangle a little while longer.

'He is alive.' He sighed as if it cost him too much to admit this. 'And your brothers have fled, they say, to Ireland.' He looked at her for signs of relief and joy which would have been betrayal, but she was cleverer than that. He was disappointed. He needed to find weakness in her.

'But it was a bitter day for Rheged,' he added. 'We took many of them for slaves. Not enough. Next time, whatever my father says, I will sell them into the south. Padric will hear of it and that will help to flush him out. Your brother and I are now full enemies, Penraddin.'

'I know.'

The relief was suppressed with all her skill. He would never know of the tingle of elation which filtered through her body and made her thank God when he said, 'He is alive'.

On that day Penraddin confirmed two suspicions. Ecfrith would never have the strength to cast off or offend his rich and powerful wife; and she, older now, having had the excitement of outrage in agreeing to come with Ecfrith (although her parents had also seen it as a sacrifice for their sake), was still on the side of her family. And it was becoming more and more difficult to conceal it.

Ecfrith and his wife were in her room which was both rich and austere.

'The girl,' Aetheldreda always spoke of Penraddin with that deliberate vagueness which made Ecfrith furious but somehow gave him no way of answering back effectively, 'the girl . . . has been talking rather a lot with your captives from Rheged.'

'They are her own people. It would be surprising if she did not talk to them,' Ecfrith replied, although he was angry at the news.

'She is a traitor in our camp, you know,' said Aetheldreda, blithely.

'No one could be more loyal.'

'Those people never abandon their own kind.'

'When I told her that I had killed her father and her brothers she never flinched.'

'Very clever,' said Aetheldreda and immediately Ecfrith felt undermined. This cool, severe, chaste woman of title and vast wealth could always outflank him. He was hypnotised by her implacable self-assurance.

'They are good Christians, you know, these people from Rheged. Their tradition is much longer than ours,' she added.

'It makes them no less opposed to us.'

'Are you absolutely certain it was the Rheged people who caused all this new trouble and not yours? Did you have to take them as slaves?' Her southern clipped accent was another thing that provoked Ecfrith to a silent fury: another sign of this intolerable superiority. Even here in her room off the great hall of King Oswy, famed throughout the island for its magnificence, she seemed to look rather critically at everything as if she had seen and expected much better. 'And after all, they had very little chance, did they? Against a war party of the size you took out.'

'Our warriors had less chance against the war party that slaughtered them and took their weapons. Yes, those men were from Rheged and they outnumbered ours!'

'Yes.' Aetheldreda looked thoughtful. 'It *is* curious though that only four of them were spotted. *With* all the horses, *with* all the weapons. I suspect that on your expedition of retribution you took too many slaves which will not please your father and cause bad feeling.' She paused. 'They really are very good Christians. I went to talk to them myself. Very pious but also strong, like the men of my own father's household. That was when your – the girl – came down. I do wish you'd send her away with all the other slaves, Ecfrith. It would make life so much easier for you. She does torment you. You would be advised to take this as an omen.'

Her mission accomplished, Aetheldreda made it clear it was time for him to leave. As he moved away, she added, stingingly, 'I've decided to give more land to Wilfrid. His plans at Ripon are extremely ambitious and after taking council from Benedict, God guided me to understand that I had not been sufficiently charitable. It will be a further reward for the brave journey he took once again to Rome. He is what I call a soldier!'

Ecfrith nodded, added this insult to the list and, as he left, forced himself to remember that she was wealthier than the wives of all his brothers combined. She was a person of power in a church now growing in lands and estates to match some of the noble houses. Although no one was allowed to refer to this in her presence, she was quite unbearably beautiful. Beside her, every other woman, every other woman Ecfrith had known or dreamt of, was seen as an aspirant. Aetheldreda was the grail.

The force of this beauty was remarkable to witness. The cleanliness of her skin at a court where cleanliness was only a little better than that of the unhygienic generality, emphasised a pureness of line – nose, chin, high cheekbones, pale forehead, finely bowed mouth – all utterly unblemished. Her flaxen hair swung plaited below her waist and shone in the candlelight. Taller than many of the men, she moved with self-aware grace. Her teeth were the pride of the court. Her breath, they said, the sweetest in all Northumbria. Although she took care to wear the plainest looking gowns – the material nevertheless was as fine as it was possible to discover – it was clear to many an eye-lingering warrior that her shape could deliver a banquet of satisfactions. In all this, her often proclaimed chastity made her even more desirable. At least, Ecfrith thought, when others might be suspected of sneering at him, at least she was his wife.

After their meeting, Ecfrith went down from the castle on the pretext of asking a few questions of the captive slaves.

Penraddin was there and looked guilty when she caught sight of him. He barely nodded to her.

The captives were penned in far too small an area. There was a small shed with a space outside it and the men had come out there, leaving the building for the handful of women and children. Sounds of crying and a stench of excrement came from inside, spoiling the scent, Ecfrith thought, of a fine summer evening. Six men guarded the shed and the pen, a further six a few yards away. The captives were tied, their ankles roped together, their wrists similarly bound, a running collar lassoing their necks.

When Ecfrith came they stirred themselves and some stood to face him. There were fourteen men; inside the shed were four women and six children, three little more than babies. Some of the men carried evidence of wounds received in the struggle. All were dirty, hungry and stripped of all but the most basic clothing.

One, the leader, appeared unsubdued. He still managed a swagger; the cuts down his arms showed how hard he had fought. His hair was pitch black, the eyes hard blue, smile taunting. He had a look of Urien, Penraddin thought, remembering her rascally youngest brother with a quickening of affection.

'Where will you send us?' he asked, boldly.

'Where you can do no more harm,' said Ecfrith.

'Are you going to make slaves of all the people of Rheged? You would if you could, wouldn't you?'

'Only if you attack my men.'

'That was Padric and his brothers. Only four of them.'

'And the rest of you.'

'There weren't any others. You know that as well. We all know that.' The man looked over to Penraddin. 'Doesn't he?'

She nodded. She could not help herself.

Ecfrith felt a shock of rage. Would he always be demeaned by women?

'You have just lost yourself — and all the rest — any food tomorrow.'

'Maybe it was worth it,' the man said and smiled.

'This one has to be tortured,' said Ecfrith, as he turned to leave. He summoned Penraddin to follow him.

'We thought you were Padric at first,' the man said, as the heavily armed guard began to move in on him. 'We ought to have known that a man such as Padric was bound to have a devil opposite. That was why we let you into our settlements without fear. We thought you were made of the same stuff. But you'll never be a Padric.'

The guards had hold of him and he mocked them by not resisting.

'Padric will be remembered in our poetry and songs until the world ends.' The man's smile was now broad. 'You mind that too, Princess Change-Sides. Who will sing of you, Ecfrith? Will you, the treacherous sister of Padric?'

The guards pinned the man down and made him ready for their tortures. His friends began to yell and curse so that the sound swept up the rock and could be heard even in the small solid stone church where Aetheldreda said her prayers and dreamed of going to Rome with Wilfrid.

Ecfrith encouraged them to first whip him and then to heat up ploughshares which he would be forced to walk across. They would not torture him to death but he would bear the scars for ever. Penraddin stood beside him shivering although the evening was mild. She flinched as the guards began their work and winced at the sounds of anger and grief coming from her captured people. The man himself at first sang out and then was silent, only groaning as the blows landed relentlessly on his bloodied back.

Ecfrith suddenly turned to her and hit Penraddin with his fist. Hit her hard on the side of the head, all but stunning her. She swayed and shifted away but could not escape the second blow which felled her to the ground.

Penraddin knew that her place was gone. Those two public blows had turned her from a possible second wife to worse than mistress: a slave would be treated like that.

His anger with her multiplied by the second. Her shame gathered itself into loathing.

She stood up and touched her face. Blood from the corner of her mouth stained her fingers but she did not look at it.

'I would like to ask your guards to stop the torture of my countryman,' she said.

Ecfrith appeared not to comprehend what she had said.

'The people of Rheged should not be your slaves. That is bad enough. But to be beaten and tortured at the Christian court of King Oswy and in the holy court of Princess Aetheldreda is infamy.'

'If you say one word more,' said Ecfrith, 'I will never forgive you.'

Penraddin looked at him with all the loathing a young noblewoman who knew she had dominated this man could command.

'I shall return to my own land.'

'Who will have you? You are wasted. Who will want you now?'

'If I stay, what am I?'

'There will be a place for you here,' said Ecfrith. 'As a slave.' He felt tied up in one of her brother's riddles. He had to sever her from himself and yet if she went he would be deprived of her sex, which would be intolerable.

Penraddin knew better than he did that in this moment lay the burden of her life. He was right. She would be thought wasted. As a woman taken as a mistress and then returned or returning, she could only become a liability, a pitiable broken figure. But to stay as a slave in the open knowledge that he had thrown her to the ground, that was worse than shame.

In that moment she felt that God gave her grace. She knew what she would do.

'Stop beating that man,' she said, and the guards paused.

Ecfrith did not hesitate.

'Arrest her,' he said. 'Take her to the stone cell. And kill that man *now*.'

BOOK FOUR

❈❈❈❈

CELTIC SURVIVAL

❈❈❈❈

A.D. 662–664

CHAPTER FORTY-ONE

In the late spring of the following year, Hilda decided to send Bega across the land to visit Cuthbert who was building a monastery in the bay where Bega had first set foot in Rheged. She could take a woman with her, two guards and Chad.

※※※※

Bega left her woman and the guards in Caerel. She would have preferred to be altogether alone for this last lap, but she had been unable to resist Chad's pleading look.

As they drew nearer, Bega was seized by an agitated impatience. She felt that to reach this place would be to discover – what? Something which would clarify her life? Catching her mood, the dog, Cal, bounded ahead and then raced back again, as if herding them along.

The prospect from the clifftop was very fine. There was warmth in the late-spring morning and the meadows were luscious in bright new grass and speckled with wild crops of spring flowers. Glazed new leaves shone under the eye of a clear sky and the sea seemed to frisk under a playful wind. From sea to sea, she had walked with Chad and Cal. For some of the way they had been part of a company journeying from Whitby to Lindisfarne. They had peeled off at the old wall and followed the road alone for the first day. Oswy's warriors, occasionally seen, gave them a sufficient sense of safety and on the second day they had joined up with four monks making their way to Caerel. Bega had insisted on their making a diversion into the mountainous district to visit Erebert but they stayed with him only briefly. The visit quite long enough for a much more settled and confident Erebert.

Now the pull of the place where she and Padric had landed overwhelmed her. It was a force outside herself, almost a command.

Chad too was excited. This was his own country. Now, so much older and changed by the wonders he had seen and the people he had met, he scanned the fields eagerly for landmarks. He wanted to be seen by everyone he knew. How he could dazzle them with descriptions of the journeys he had made, the marvels he had seen, the magnificence of Wilfrid, the sanctity of Cuthbert, the awe-striking Hilda. Chad was boiling with an excitement he had never before experienced. And he longed to see his mother.

As hungrily as he burrowed into the land, so Bega's restless questing look raked the sea. Homesickness lurched up in her. There, there, at the other side of the sparkling sea was the land of her birth. She wanted to pray at the graves of Cathleen and Donal, to see again the gaunt and marbled hills of Connachta; to learn the truth about her father, about whom she had been fed no more than inconclusive scraps.

They walked more quickly as they drew nearer to where the cliff bowed down low into the small bay. The smack of sea-salted air freshened their lungs. They were fit and strong after their days of walking. Bega experienced a sudden rash wildness of joy. This was a journey's end which marked one beginning and somehow promised another.

There it was. Both of them stood still, thrilled to see that tiny harbour, the wet skin of sand shimmering, the tide well out, the pebbles and stones flung about the upper beach, the cliff and carved rock of sandstone finding its true dark blooded redness in the sun.

Neither spoke.

Chad looked at Bega and saw her as one transformed. He saw her as someone with special powers. No miracles had yet been credited to her, which he rather resented. His witness seemed to count for little. For example, on one mission he had seen a young girl possessed with devils since childhood and incapable of co-ordinated action. Bega held her close and spent a whole night shielding her from harm. The girl had fallen into a sleep from which she had woken healed and whole. Yet Hilda and the monks who decided on these matters were not convinced. On the other hand, Bega's fasting was held up, even by the abbess, as a standard by which all should be judged. Nor could her scholarship be challenged. Chad had heard that even with the most learned men she could dispute and discuss the gospels. And there was her sword-arm: Hilda had let him take a short sword for defence on this journey. But although he carried it, it was understood that it was Bega who would use it.

In all their time together, Chad had never seen her as elated, nor as beautiful and animated, as open to life.

The wind swept up the cliff face from the shore and lifted her hair until it flew out behind her like wings, he thought. Her eyes were closed, her face uptilted towards the southerly sun, her lips moved slightly, gently, in prayer and there was a radiance, Chad would swear, which could only have come from heaven. Yet suddenly, out of nowhere, he himself was seized by dread and fear. He fell to his knees and grasped his hands in prayer but he could not close his eyes. Bega compelled his gaze.

'Will you bless me?' he asked.

'Chad!'

'Bless me! I might be dead tonight and your blessing would save me. I beg you.' The devil was eating his soul.

She reached out and held his head between her hands, pressing hard: she gave him her blessing. He groaned and prayed with her. Finally he was calm.

'Now,' said Bega, 'let us see what they are building.'

They walked down the cliff path and Bega glanced at the other small route which led to the cave. She would visit that later. She would savour the waiting knowing that she could enter it whenever she wanted. The knowledge elated her.

It was Cuthbert himself who came to meet them. He had been fasting to help spur on the building of the monastery. His leg had begun to hurt badly again and he limped with fatigue.

Chad immediately dropped behind and called in Cal with a low urgent whistle. He sensed that Cuthbert wanted to meet Bega without attendants. He could use the time to see his mother.

After they had exchanged greetings in God, Cuthbert asked her why she had come to this lonely spot.

'Primarily to bring you a message from Abbess Hilda,' she said. After this had been delivered, Bega added, 'but I asked if perhaps one or two of your monks could come with me on a mission into these mountains. I remember when first I came to Erebert's island, he told me that there were many here who were ignorant of the words of Jesus Christ.'

'We shall see,' said Cuthbert. 'The men are all working from dawn to the end of the day. But it is a good ambition and I would like to help.' He smiled and Bega saw how fine and handsome the man could be. But she sensed also the strain he put on his body and his spirit by so violently subjugating himself to the full force of Christ's rule.

'And was there another reason?' he asked. 'Perhaps the one that makes you look so very happy to be here?'

His smile and openness prompted a similar return from Bega.

'Yes,' she admitted. 'Although it is very selfish, I wanted to retrace my footsteps and come back to the place from which I truly began my journey to Christ. For it was here that I was saved by Him: I know that now. It is in my memory like a stone which I can touch even if I cannot wholly understand or comprehend it. Now, here, I want to ask God to guide my footsteps. Sometimes I dream of seeing out my life in His service alone in that cave in which I was saved.'

'It is not good for a woman to be a hermit,' said Cuthbert.

'I am not so presumptuous,' Bega replied. 'So first I want to know why God has given me this lust for making journeys. Both in myself and to other lands. It was here, where I almost died and He spared me, that I hoped to find the answer.'

He nodded approvingly at her humility and they turned and walked towards what was a building site.

There were five large beehive huts already in place – for sleeping and shelter. What was now being built was a small church, using stones from the beach to create the outside walls already four or five feet high. The location had been easily chosen, tucked behind the cliff and well back from the beach, beside a good river as Cuthbert pointed out which could be dammed up and bypassed so that a fine fish pool could be created. The land attached was also sheltered and there were cattle, sheep and goats already grazing, shepherded by boys much younger than Chad, while poultry and dogs picked their feet among the buildings and the workers.

'It is as if the place has suddenly come alive,' said Bega. 'But why here?'

'Some land,' said Cuthbert, a little shamefacedly, 'some land and farms that I was given here and nearby this is a place where fishermen have always come for safety ... and there is no monastery nearby ...'

'It will welcome those of my country who come here.'

'True. It looks to Ireland.' Cuthbert smiled awkwardly.

He led Bega away from the site, down towards the sea. There, on a giant slab of rich sandstone which presided over a market of small rock pools, he sat and, for a few moments, simply stared out to the ocean. He shivered a good deal. Bega was sorry for him. She recognised the signs of an over-zealous fast.

She looked at him closely. The dirt of the work had stuck to much of his clothing; the leather shoes were caked. His hands were roughed with mud, as was his hair – the foam of yellow all but obscured. He looked not only tired but unsure of himself. How could that be, she wondered, when he had received such gifts from God?

'We have a countryman of yours with us,' he said, smiling gently at her. 'A bishop, Colman, who comes, I believe, from land not far from your own birthplace. He is away visiting the sick at present but he will be back for our evening meal. You will want to speak to him.' He paused. 'Is the abbess in good health?'

Bega talked a little about Hilda and then found herself talking more about the abbey. Cuthbert drew it out of her so simply and yet sometimes she felt she might be saying things which she might regret. Yet she could not quite identify them. Nor could she quell a suspicion that Cuthbert was not really interested in Whitby at all. He had another aim in mind. In a way she was relieved to be proved right.

'I would like, if I may,' he said, most humbly, 'to look upon the portion of the True Cross.'

Bega nodded.

She noticed that as he had made the request, his eyes had roved around nervously behind her – across the higher beach towards the monastery. But no one would disturb them. Suddenly the cries of the gulls which Bega always loved and in which she had found mysterious consolation on the clifftops of Whitby, seemed to grow louder and become a lament.

'Not here,' she said.

'Not here?' He looked at her with the coldness she remembered

so well, a coldness which sat so very sternly behind his outward
pliancy of manner. 'You are right. But where?'

Instantly Bega thought of the cave and instantly she rejected
it. She had an appointment there alone, with her past.

'It was here that you landed with that young prince of Rheged
several years ago, wasn't it?'

'Yes.'

'I see.'

Bega wished that she had been more prepared against the blush
which revealed too much feeling.

'He has gone into Ireland, you know.'

Bega did not know but the association of Padric and Ireland
set off a secret keening as sorrowful as the sad cries of the gulls.

'It is a pity that he cannot make peace with his cousin. I know
that King Oswy would like nothing better.' Cuthbert looked at
her carefully as if asking – What do you know? About him? About
yourself? About both of you?

'We hear nothing about him,' said Bega steadily. 'We hear much
of you! The Lord grants you miracles. The abbess praises God for
you every day.'

'I am unworthy,' said Cuthbert, testily. He rubbed out the little
knife of pain which kept returning to his over-fasted stomach. 'To
show His might, the Lord of Hosts will use the meanest among
us. That is all.'

He got up from the rock and began to limp towards the cliff,
quite swiftly, forcing away the pain in his leg, yet again using the
opportunity to test himself. Bega feared that he might climb the
path and lead her to what she thought of as 'her' cave. But at the
foot of the cliff, now completely out of sight of all those working
on the monastery, he stopped. He sat on a slab of sandstone and
invited her to sit near him.

'You are right to be reluctant about showing me the cross,' he
said, and again, as she remembered from before, Cuthbert seemed
to unlock her secrets with ease. What could she withhold from
him? She blocked out her longing for the cave. 'I was wrong to
ask you to let me see it. It disturbs me, you see. Ever since I
first saw it I have thought about it and it fills me with a terrible
unease.'

'Why? Is it not a gift and a proof for us all?'

'It is. And yet I asked you to hide it. Why did I do that?'

'You were afraid of my pride,' she said promptly, for she too had thought this over many times.

'It was not your pride. It was my envy,' said Cuthbert, heavily. 'Will you forgive me? Will you pray with me for my forgiveness?'

Bega was not so foolish to question his description of himself. From her own repressed intuition it rang true, she felt.

'I cannot believe that a man as holy as you are needs help in prayer from one such as me,' she said, smiling, 'but I will pray with you.'

'Will you ask God if He can make me strong enough to beat off the temptations which surround me and which I feel so sharply.' He shivered and indeed a fleet of clouds, conjured up in the south-west, took away the immediate warmth of the sun. Bega sank to her knees as did Cuthbert. Bega spoke and held out the fragment of the cross in front of her.

'I beg you, Mighty Lord, to strengthen this most faithful servant Cuthbert against the promises and cunning of the devil. Because he is Your glorious servant, he is more beset about than others whose work and worth can never match his. But in his strength is his weakness. I pray You to send him some of Your all powerful love which was given to Your son on this cross so that He would live again and lead us into the kingdom everlasting.'

She held out the cross to him and, eventually, he took it.

'Now I hold this,' he said, 'let me tell you what also torments me. I long to become a hermit like Erebert my friend, but God will not let me. He keeps finding other work for me to do.'

'It is important work,' Bega protested. 'He gives you the power to cure the sick. He gives you the power to build monasteries. You baptise whole tribes of people. Perhaps He does not want to spare you from this work. Who else can do it?'

'Perhaps I am more in love with it than I confess,' said Cuthbert, bitterly. 'For now I hold this piece of the True Cross I can say that I truly love wealth, and I seek it; even though I give it away; even though I give the land to the church and use the other wealth for His sake, I still want it.'

'So does Wilfrid, I think,' said Bega, to reassure him. 'Some of us discussed this with Abbess Hilda at Whitby. She said that God gives to a very few such mighty talents that they must also be more greatly tempted.'

'But how can I be a true servant when I know that the love of wealth is at the root of all evil and yet, in effect, I do love it?'

Bega was moved. Cuthbert's distress clearly hurt him.

'I know that to lead a life alone and be seen to resist all that the devil can offer you is to make the greatest declaration on earth of God's dominion. Monasteries are stones and stones will come to ruin. Buildings will decay, lands will be taken from you, but the immortal spirit is the one thing that endures for ever.' Cuthbert's agitation grew and he stood up, still holding the fragment of the cross. 'What else is there?' he declared as the sky darkened further and the abrupt arrival of a sagging flotilla of fat rain-bearing clouds signalled yet another switch of weather. 'All that we are sent on earth for is to show God that we are worthy of Him. We are sent to test our souls. We are sent to show that we can join the saints and be immortal but only if we are unstained by sin.' He shivered at the word 'sin'.

He looked at his filthy clothes. 'I am caked with it. Look at this mud on my clothes, on my hands, in my hair, on my boots – this mud is nothing compared with the sin which clings around my soul and will not be washed away. Help me, O Lord! I cry out to You – help Your servant so that he can leave the world and, alone, alone battle against all the devils that can be sent to try him! Do you not see?'

He turned to Bega and she saw the anguish in his wasted face, anguish as fixed as a scar. 'Can you not understand living with the deceit of doing what the world thinks is good and yet I know that it is no more than pandering to my basest feelings? For all I do is amass goods, land, wealth – even though I despise it when I get it. The devil has me in his paw and he makes me scratch and seek it out. I *have* to leave the world or I will be consumed by it. Do you not see? This, this world, these riches, this land – all this is what I want.' He looked upwards.

'But now, Jesus, I am holding that upon which You rested in the ecstasy of sacrifice. I beg You through the intervention of this cross to let me too enjoy the sacrifice of solitude. Let me know the dizziness of sheer faith. Let me know the vertigo of making Your will triumph against all the deadliest lures of the Enemy. But let me first go from this sin-sated world that I swim in so successfully.'

By now Cuthbert was swaying in his distraught and famished

trance of self-loathing. Bega heard a high sound which sounded like the whine of a trapped dog and then she realised that it was Cuthbert. The sound rose higher into the air lifting like the sudden upward soar of a gull. He dropped to his knees on the hard, pebbled ground and, still with both hands clutching the fragment of wood, curled himself into a foetal ball and began to shake with visible spasms of frenzy.

Bega was numbed. She had never before encountered such a savage passion. It was as if he had peeled all the skin off himself and felt every fleck of dust prick against his rawness and could not, simply could not bear it. The distress was not only in the voice, in that strange howl, in the shivering, twisted, wasted body, it was there in the agony of his hands, the fingers long stretched, bone-aching, even contorted, but somehow holding safely and tenderly like a communion wafer the fragment of the True Cross.

Cuthbert had been overtaken by physical desire. He ached for relief. Was the woman the Jezebel or was she the Virgin Mary? His parched senses had been agitated by Bega and now he was in danger of a terrible excess. Bega saw his turbulence and she felt her skin flush hot. Cuthbert's graphic torments, his spasms and writhing were, she thought, evidence of a passion rare and compelling. That such a stern and disciplined man of God, so powerful in the sight of heaven should be visited by this violence of feeling impressed her more than all his sermons ever could. She felt as if she were being pulled into his soul: for help. She saw that though it was God who gave Cuthbert this terrible passion, it was the devil who was using it. Satan wanted to lure her and Cuthbert into a sexual coupling. She herself began to tremble. The devil had enticed her too. Did she want to reach out and take Cuthbert? Did he so clearly want her?

It was then that she called on the power of the cross itself. Fearfully, she went over to the most ardent of monks and wrested the fragment from him. She broke it. With one of the now tiny portions she made the sign of the cross in the air.

'In the name of the Father and of the Son and of the Holy Ghost I beg You to give strength to Your most faithful servant Cuthbert.'

She placed the most holy sliver of wood in Cuthbert's mouth. He appeared not to know what was happening but his jaws, masticating wildly, chewed and swallowed the offering. She stood back as his arms flailed out towards her. He fell forward in a faint. Bega's heart was pounding. She stood back.

Eventually Cuthbert stood up warily and looked closely at Bega. His mud-caked face was streaked with sweat and tears. The froth was still gathered around the corners of his mouth. He stared without saying anything.

Bega felt a little frightened.

'Who directed you to make that sacrifice?' he asked.

Bega shook her head. She had acted in so unguided a way that she had no recollection even though the act was so recent. How he had changed! And now changed again!

Still he stared at her and she found herself wrapping the linen tightly around the remaining fragment of the cross as if it were proof of a guilt to be hidden as soon as possible.

Cuthbert let out a huge sigh, lifted up his hand towards the clouds now beginning to let loose their rain, and said, 'How can I carry this burden within me, O Lord? I called for strength but how could I have imagined such a burden of gift would be bestowed?'

'But it was,' said Bega, her throat dry. 'What you have will give you the resolve you so despairingly prayed for. Acting without knowing why I was acting must have been acting under His guidance. How else would I have known what to do?'

'You delivered it like the sacrament,' said Cuthbert, 'which is forbidden to women.'

'I delivered it as I was guided to deliver it,' Bega replied, firmly.

'This must never be spoken of,' said Cuthbert. 'How could I bear the knowledge that others knew that the cross on which He died had passed my lips?'

'It was a miracle,' said Bega, steady now that he had released her from that fixed stare. 'I saw you wrench yourself into a condition fit for nothing but harm to all that our faith commands. Once the wood had touched your tongue the devils went out of you. There must be a purpose in this gift,' said Bega, evenly. 'Some day we will know why it was that such an intimate gift has been given to you. It will not be spoken of. We will be told, in His time, why this has happened. Thanks be to God.'

'Thanks be to God.'

'We must give Him thanks and pray that this is the strength that you need.'

'Thanks be to God,' Cuthbert repeated, humbly. 'I can feel the strength it has given my body which will be exalted by this miraculous gift even in death. His will be done.'

They walked back towards the new monastery in silence. Plump raindrops plopped and burst on their heads. The sound of the gulls now seemed to Bega even lonelier than usual, as if they had drunk in the anguished howl of Cuthbert.

The monks and those conscripted to help worked on. The tide had turned and the thin scum of sea ran greedily over the soaking sand.

'I will call this place Bega's Haven,' said Cuthbert.

CHAPTER FORTY-TWO

Cuthbert decided that Bega should be separated from the monks and he had instructed a single hut of branches and turf sods to be constructed at a significant distance from the rest.

'In Whitby,' Cuthbert said, 'Hilda took strict precautions to separate men from women and with good reason. Here we have many monks who have not taken the vow of chastity – few of us are called to try that – and your own state is not known to them. I want to put you outside risk. You shall sleep there and I shall lie in the open space between your hut and the rest of the settlement.'

The hut was barely large enough even for her modest frame. The ground was damp, the turf still stinking of cold and damp and the fire at the door smouldered too low for any real comfort. But she understood Cuthbert's fears and obeyed. Besides, a sense of isolation was welcome. She had come to this place to go to the cave which she was increasingly sure would dispel an unfathomable uncertainty which sometimes quickened her to alarm. The encounter with Cuthbert had diverted her from that. It would be good to be alone.

Chad sent Cal across to join her and she was glad of his warmth. The early meal had been very light out of respect for the twelfth day of Cuthbert's fast and, following the exercise of the day, the long walk and the turmoil with Cuthbert, Bega had been ready to eat well. Her frugal portion, though accepted with gratitude, was more of a tease than a satisfying meal. Yet she slept soundly.

It was just after dawn that she met Bishop Colman.

He lolloped across to her, almost seeming to roll across the ground, so round and tubby. She was sitting beside her fire, eating the bowl of gruel and the generous portion of nuts and unleavened bread brought her by Chad. Even before he came up to her, he had about him, she thought, that immediate open warmth which made her feel that she had known him, and known him well, all her life.

He arrived and stood still and stared down at her in a puffing merriment. 'It's the Princess Bega at last,' he said. 'We've heard so much. We're all so proud.'

His smile was a boy's innocent smile and his old face was all-boyish, round as a daisy, milk-white, fresh as spring-water, despite his fifty-three years.

'Don't ask how we know about you because we do!' He squatted beside her, as intimate as an old acquaintance. 'Well, to tell you the truth Cuthbert has been telling us all what a fine woman of the church you were and how he trusted you with secrets dear only to himself and the Lord and the praise that the mighty Hilda has showered over you. And the two of us are from Connachta, where before you were born I was priest in the household your father . . . brought down, shall we say?' He seemed to bring the best of her past into her face as directly as the special smell of a peat fire.

'I'm on my way back to my brothers in the see of York which they made mine, thanks be to God, against all expectation,' he explained. 'But Cuthbert is so persuasive. I've heard so much about the man – he'll become a saint, never doubt it – but I never thought I'd meet him and talk to him. He had me working for him in no time. I was detailed to carry on with the mission work while the stronger hands built up the walls. So I did. But I'm off tomorrow. And now thanks be to God I meet you as well. What a blessed place this has been for me!'

'And how was your mission?' Bega asked, 'I was told that even here there is still a great need.'

'So there is. I've seen more paganism in these hills in a few days – I tell you, Bega, there's an unbelieving, lost world out there.' He waved towards the hill country. 'The sooner we forget about building all these buildings and arguing all these cloudy arguments and get up and out and among the pagans with the True Cross of Our Lord, the better.'

'The cross?'

Bega was searching him. Surely Cuthbert, having so strictly forced her to suppress all information about it would not have confided it to Colman?

'I speak of our faith, Bega.'

'Yes!' she cried, louder than she had intended.

'I love your ardour,' said Colman. 'I know that you've been on missions. Would you go on a mission that I proposed?'

'Oh yes!' Maybe this was the resolution. Not the cave but Colman's mission. 'Oh yes,' she repeated.

'But I'll need dear Hilda's permission.' Colman sighed. 'We're getting ourselves all tied in knots with those permissions and buildings and the rigmarole of the thing, don't you think? What we need is good stout hearts of God to blaze out there in the darkness and gather up those souls consigned to hell, poor creatures, unless they are saved by the word of God. That's our business. That's what God wants.'

Bega almost clapped her hands.

Sensing her sympathy, Colman enjoyed himself, prattling in a naïve voice which sometimes seemed to represent all of him and sometimes seemed merely the tone he slyly adopted to disarm the world. Bega listened closely as he spoke of the wonders of the church back in Ireland. No miracle went unvarnished from the hand of Colman. No feat was too strange or incredible for the Lord of Hosts. The bishop appeared at times to live in the next world already, for every day some event chimed with multiple voices praising God for His glories.

'Your father,' said Colman, shaking his head and assuming an instant mask of sorrow. 'That was an act of darkness.'

Bega felt her heart constrict. She had kept thoughts of her father to the merest trickle and over the years fewer and fewer had surfaced. But this sudden reintroduction, with the clear forewarning of fatality, released a shock of feeling which blenched her face.

'Did you not know?' Bishop Colman's face scurried from surprise to apology and back again. 'I suppose what happens to a king on the edge of Ireland is not what they teach you in Whitby. But although he fell away in his last years, Cathal was a king fit to be a hero and a hero's death he surely died.'

Bega breathed in deeply and rubbed at her heart with her right hand.

'I did not know he had died,' she said.

'I am sorry to be the bearer of such news. It was not long ago.'

'As you say . . . a king in Connachta . . . maybe the abbess knew and did not want me to know until she thought it was time.'

'Oh!' Colman looked crestfallen. 'Does that mean I have crossed her plan?'

'No. No. I was just speculating. The chances are that she knew nothing of it. So,' Bega paused, 'tell me and then I will pray for his soul.'

Colman looked around. The morning was fresh. Clouds were flitting under heaven, high and light, not threatening rain. The tide was in and the sea's sound sucked reassuringly on the shore at no distance. The men were steadily finishing the stone walls: soon they would be able to put up the timber and then thatch the roofs. Bishop Colman was a little guilty that he was not occupied in a way which would have pleased Cuthbert. But Cuthbert was nowhere to be seen and, besides, this young nun he had spoken of so highly needed to know the story of the death of her father.

'We have to begin with the murder of the young O'Neill. God rest his soul. And what a terrible thing for you to behold. That mad woman. Yet some of the peasant women and the slaves swear by her now, you know, and pray on a little comb she had. Maeve! It was a terrible thing. For your father that marriage would have been the crown of his life. He was a rare man.' Colman paused and took stock. It would be better to tell it all, he decided. This young woman was strong.

'They will sing of him here one day. I have heard him in songs and epics already. He was one of those whom God endowed with no fear and a right arm always raised for the Lord of Hosts.' Bega let that pass. Clearly Colman had enrolled Cathal for Christ. The Bishop closed his eyes now and then, delivering some of the story in trance-like fashion. 'When he went back with the dead body of the murdered Prince Niall O'Neill, Cathal thought that his own head would be claimed as a punishment for his failure to guard his guests. Some say that he sought a death at that time, although I do not see it in a man who has dedicated so many victories to the God of Gideon and David. But the story of the wedding and the murder was told and the king of all the kings of Ireland forgave Cathal. Yet he rode home a sad and despairing man. Through you, Bega, he was to have gained the prize above all worldly prizes for him and the Lord would have blessed him. The devil's possession of Maeve robbed him of this. And you were gone too.

'No use when he arrived back in Connachta that the poet sang
of future glories. No one could help him cast off this heavy cloak
of sorrow. And, as the years went by, it grew even heavier. Cathal
the warrior of a hundred battlefields lost all his appetite for war.
Cathal who had harvested the cattle of his enemies and would
ride over half of the land to seek out a worthy enemy would not
even polish the hilt of his sword. No one could bring him to his
former self. No wife, no woman, no poet, no son, not even the
priest.' Colman gave a little grimace here as if he personally had
failed her father.

'His kingdom began to weaken but he did not seem to care.
His sons went on expeditions their father would once have advised
them against, but now he let them run wild and the court of Cathal
became an unruly house. Cathal was never crossed but the officers
of his house, including the priest, were often shamed by the sons
and Cathal would not hear their complaints. He carried too big
a grief.'

The account of her father's decline moved Bega close to tears.
She had been unable to think about him without seeing also the
bloody head of Maeve, the dagger through the heart of Donal,
the spurting blood from the throat of the man she had been
set to marry. Now she could see her father sunken, solitary, an
untouchable force in his own household, and she knew that the
dishonour she had brought on him was the cause. She began to
pray silently for the salvation of his soul even though Colman
had not yet told her of his death. She could see her brothers
blundering into wasteful raids. She could see the once rigidly
controlled household and proud would-be court which he had
gathered together with such effort simply falling into sloth and
feebleness as the centre which had supported it fell away.

'When the King O'Neill who had forgiven your father died,
there were those who wanted to ride out against him. Many of
the O'Neills thought the king had been too merciful. Though
there were reports that Cathal had become quiet, he was still
feared and, at first, wiser councils restrained the O'Neills. Yet
a younger brother and two of the others who had been at the
murder longed for a revenge and now they saw their chance. But
their uncle who took the throne would not let an army loose into
Connachta. Ireland has won its peacefulness with the loss of much
blood and the help of Almighty God. The new King O'Neill did

not want to be the one to plunge a place known throughout the world for its hospitality and learning into the bloody wars which once were its curse.

'However he could not put out a fire already lit. The young brother took five men and rode out for the head of Cathal.' Colman's pace began to quicken.

'It was only Cathal they wanted, they made that plain all along their way. When they drew near his court, they sent a messenger demanding that he come out with equal number and fight them to the death.

'We are told that when the messenger arrived, your brothers were drunk beyond all hope of action, and the other warriors were so fuddled by strong beer and confusion that they did not know whom to follow. It was no matter. Cathal declared that he alone would ride out and take up the challenge.' Colman looked around as if worried that anyone else might share this event belonging to a different land, whose greatness he wanted for a while to retain.

'Cathal rode out in a boldness that shamed the sun. Alone he went without his spear carrier or his chariot. His horse was all he needed, and that only to take him to where the O'Neills waited. There he dismounted and, with shield and sword, with daggers in his belt and torques and armlets, rings and bracelets glittering, and with his glowing shield reflecting the image of themselves to the O'Neills, he walked towards them, challenging them to battle. One man against the six.

'They called him to bring out his sons with him but he ignored all their calls. They told him they would fight man-to-man in single combat but he ignored all such words. As he walked forward, some said he became broad as a bull, strong necked as an ox, his sword flowing like water about his head, they said, and the sun-glittering shield blinded their eyes. They knew he would kill them unless they attacked.'

Now he was into the battle, Colman was martial, his expression fighting, his eyes launching every attack.

'Those who saw, who came to the edge of the field and watched as the sun rose higher on the bloody scene, say that Cathal was like the very creator of war. His sword divided and became ten, some said more, each one twirling and slashing, stabbing at the O'Neills as they tried to rush him and hack him to death. Where they ran, he leaped like a young deer, over their heads, to attack them from behind, and when they slashed at him, his shield caught the blow and threw it off so strongly that even the mightiest of the O'Neills staggered back. They say at one time all six surrounded him and marched towards him and they saw his sword take fire from the sun and scatter them with flames redder than blood.'

Colman's voice rose in a triumph of excitement. 'All day it raged, this battle and, as the sun began to set, bloodied by wounds, Cathal was head to toe in gore. His shield arm was hacked at the shoulder, one pass had slid into his side, his face had been gashed with a far-flung spear and yet still he roared and triumphed over two dead and two more badly wounded than he. But now they played a trick on him and drew back and back into a wood which lay on the further side of the field. Those who were observing all this in wonder, followed and peered into the lowering light and saw that they drew him into an ambush.

'There in the last of his battles he slew one more of the O'Neills, but no howls of pain compared with the great roar of agony when a sword finally took his life blood and went through his body, through that most noble warrior body. And as he faltered, further blows about the head and neck drew more and more blood until he fell. As he fell the earth shuddered as if a giant had fallen from the sky, as if a voice of thunder had been released from the inner earth. Cathal was gone.' He paused as if he could see the death before him.

'There is more that can be said of this event. I have told it simply in my own way. But you have heard what I have been told and it is all true.'

Bega closed her eyes and her hands in prayer.

Even before she had finished her solemn pleas for the eternal life of the soul of Cathal, Bega felt a fuse of exhilaration maddening through her. To die such a death! Not even Cathal could have hoped for a better. She could see the pageantry of the burial, see the face of Muiredach as he incanted the epic list of deeds. See her brothers shifting for position after his death, her stepmother taking sides. All that court so craven before Cathal now released to the four winds.

No one would match her father, she thought and felt her body straighten in pride as the thought formulated itself. As Colman had told the story she had been by his side, her hand his sword hand, his sword her sword, seeking for the flesh through the armour behind the shield. She had seen that square, squat, fast-leaping man laughing at the odds and urging his enemies to do their best and their worst as the blood washed down their sweat-stained bodies. How she would have loved to have been there!

In her excitement she had stood up and then began pacing about. Colman took her agitation for an attempt to ease the shock of learning of her father's death and he, too, stood up in respect.

Bega's head felt fit to explode. Images of her father and her many times with him beset her: of the favours and his savagery so adored, of his courage which would stare down a wolf and the deeds which rang to the high calling of his valour. How she missed that! How she longed for the warrior side of her to be employed more often. If she went on missions all the time, could she always carry a sword? Wilfrid carried a sword and he was unafraid to use it. Cuthbert carried no weapons but some of his followers did. She wanted her father's sword – who would get that? She was the one who would have claimed it. Could she not race back to Connachta even now and claim the blood-spilling lance which had taken so many men of the O'Neills to death with him?

'I fear I should have told it more gently,' said Colman. 'The trouble with me is that I am from that part of the world myself and,' he nodded over his own fault, 'I get carried away. You see, I have heard of the great deeds of your father all my life. The children I taught used to want to be Cathal when they played their games.'

Bega felt a hot press of tears at this. The fame that her father had so badly wanted had been there in the mouths of the children and now on the tongue of a bishop it was sung after his death. The tears came freely and somehow happily down her cheeks. She wanted to see him striding into heaven, all his armour bright to meet the Lord of all victories, but sensed that he was moving into the woods and sacred places of Ireland, where for centuries such pagan heroes had gone in their glorious death search.

The tears made her feel uplifted. Despite what he had done, Bega now experienced her father in the heroic vein in which Colman had so ardently reported his death.

'I want to walk to the sea,' she said. 'Will you come with me?' To look across the water to her own place and pay a tribute.

Colman agreed.

As they made their way, he began to talk about Cuthbert. To the pure-spirited and humble Colman, the wonders of rare men were the lessons of life and he never tired of repeating them. Now it was Cuthbert he celebrated. But Bega did not hear him.

When they were near the sea Colman fell silent. He let Bega take a few paces ahead of him. The gusts of air from the sea's surface, air, Bega knew, which came from the Ireland of her father's grave, filled her brimful with a jubilation of mourning. Had Colman not been with her she would have kneeled down and worshipped – the sea? The invisible land beyond it? The spirit and the ghost of her father? She wanted her soul to soar out of her, soar like the gulls and fly and dip towards Ireland and find her father and join him for one last moment, even though his flesh was cold. The forests and dark places had claimed him at the last but so too, she prayed, had the heavens which surely needed the boldest of warriors, soldiers fit to challenge the blackest creatures of the enemy.

Eventually, Bega returned to Colman. It was as if she were gently hauling in the kite of herself which had soared and sailed to see her father one last time. Now, calmed, and through the first shock of mourning, she rejoined him on the blustery shore and shook herself back into his company.

⚬⚬⚬⚬

'There is a cave,' she said, 'which the Lord led me to when I landed here with Padric those years ago. Had He not showed me this place I would surely have died. I must go there now. Will you walk with me, to pray for my deliverance? For when I arrived here I failed to acknowledge what I had received.'

He climbed the path with her and marvelled that in the dark and the snow she had been led to this refuge. This he told her was a true blessing if not quite a miracle.

He insisted on looking inside the cave.

'He led you to a place of life,' he said, and continued, hands clasped in prayer: 'Oh God, I thank Thee for the charity shown to my humble countrywoman, Bega. To preserve her in such a way is to show that there are great plans for her which we must wait to see unravelled. Thanks be to God. Amen.'

Bega echoed 'Amen' and stood as still as she possibly could.

Colman looked at her and thought that he saw a figure in a state of deepest meditation. Perhaps here in the cave where she had been so jealously sheltered, God was calling her to a high purpose. The sweet and reluctant bishop tingled between a yearning to stay and share in whatever grace might come and a fear that his presence might deter such an occurrence from happening at all.

'I will go back down the path,' he said, his expression both meek and solemn, 'and wait for you.' He had hoped to be dissuaded.

It is doubtful that Bega heard him.

In her ears drummed the sound of the sea or a sound of sea-like surging with an amplified slow rhythm as if the cave itself were slowing sucking in the thrust of tide and then exhaling it with longing regret. Slowly she drew in a breath, hearing its sound, dreamily stroking it with her mouth: perhaps it would tell her what it was that seemed so tantalisingly beyond the last pulse of memory. She felt as sensitive as a foal first tasting the air as she searched to uncover the layers of forgetfulness and find its origins in that cave. What could she see or smell or touch or taste which would help her? What would trigger the memory and make a pattern from the sensations, make a meaning from the rush, from this overwhelming sense of . . .

Nothing. She recognised nothing.

This was the cave. She had led Padric here. Here she had stayed and been near death. She knew that. Padric had told her and a definite, almost bone, memory of coldness also told her; so cold, she shuddered the rare times she touched that memory. Yes. Death had been there.

She turned to the entrance and knelt there and looked out on to the sea. As the Abbess Hilda had taught her, she schooled her mind to meditation.

The hardness of the sandstone rock ledge under her knees became an anaesthetising numbness. This, as she had been taught, could be a help. The breeze cooled her body and that coolness was a steady, reliable state which enabled her to begin to forget the body. She murmured her favourite words from the Gospel of

St John. Again and again the words whispered through her mind.
The words like oil on choppy water held down and soothed and
quieted the surface disturbance and made way for the soul to
emerge and show itself to God.

Bega could, on rare occasion, go into deepest meditation beyond
consciousness. She moved towards it now, feeling herself falling,
slowly falling.

Concentrating on the figure of Christ.

Christ on the Cross.

She began to sway slightly and, on the closed blank of her eyes,
gold and red forms appeared. She let herself fall further and further
until the sensation of falling was all the sensation she had.

Could she disguise from herself any longer that she was
searching for Padric?

Let herself fall and fall further.

Padric was here with her: a tremor, a disturbance. The image
before her eyes should be of Christ. But again as before, the face
and body of Christ was overlaid with the face and body of Padric.
Was this a test sent by God or the mockery of the devil?

Behind her in the cave she felt a gathering of forces she dare
not turn to see. Were they benign? Was that the rustling of angels'
wings or the scurrying of the slaves of the devil?

Bega felt herself grow hot as the memory of so long ago so
fiercely repressed, so unremembered, groped for a life of fact.
The memory wanted to become a reality and Bega longed for
the deep itch of it, its teasing, out-of-reach message to come
back to her. She panted now with the effort. Falling, still falling,
she reached out. For Christ? For Padric? Her body glowed with
a quite swooning warmth and began to move to the rhythms of
her breathing.

Padric had been here with her.

He had saved her from death.

She remembered the stone coldness of her body.

Almost there.

She dared not look around although the sounds behind her
grew. There was a scuffling, a fall of earth, a presence in the
holy cave. But to turn would be to lose what was almost in
her grasp.

Padric had been here with her.

He had lain beside her.

She remembered that he had lain down beside her stone cold body.

Oh! It was so wrong to see the face of Padric on the body of Christ on the cross. It was, it must be, the author of all deceits leading her into the pit of temptation. No earthly man could be compared with the Son of God. Yet they were, weren't they? Matthew, Mark, Luke, John, Peter . . . Ninian, Patrick, Columbanus, Aidan, Cuthbert . . . but should they be?

Her breath came harder now. Her body was moving it seemed of its own accord. The pressure of the presence behind her grew all but intolerable. She murmured the words and felt that they were beginning to strike on the mausoleum of that memory, to ring on its stone secret and summon it to life. It was there. She could feel it.

'Bega?'

Bega turned sharply, almost convulsively.

It was Chad.

'I thought you might be here,' he said. 'There was always this way in from the top. You have to push aside a rock but I remembered it. Cuthbert wants to celebrate a Mass for the monastery. He wants you to be there.'

Bega swallowed the dryness in her own mouth. Too rapidly, too easily, her body filled up with the normal pressures of life. The empty vessel she had almost succeeded in making herself was flooded with the world which seemed emptier now than ever before. It had gone. Whatever it was, it had left her.

CHAPTER FORTY-THREE

'have you *seen* Cuthbert say a Mass?' Colman asked as the three of them walked to the monastery. Bega shook her head. She did not want to talk. Useless though it seemed, she wanted the embers of discovering the hidden memory to be given a silent last chance.

'Well,' he went on, 'it is a sight to behold. The man is so given over to the suffering of Christ that – well, I won't spoil it for you.'

They arrived at the half-completed church. The monks were lined up. Cuthbert was at the large slab of sandstone supported on two pillars which formed the altar. A cross, also hewn from sandstone, stood square in the centre. The yellow sunlight nourished the deep red-blood colour and the altar seemed to have its own aura in the open air.

Cuthbert waited until Colman, Chad and Bega had joined the congregation. Bega sought out his gaze and was relieved to find the hardness back, the resolute-beyond-earthly-persuasion look which accorded so well with the miracles and the feats of self-denial and the friendship with kings and courts, queens and all the nobles. She felt privileged to have seen him unguarded and privileged to have given him the wafer of the True Cross which would, lodged in his body, procure so many more converts through the miracles it would engender. With the cold-eyed Cuthbert she felt secure. There was not the slightest sign of what had passed so privately and intensely between them.

The service began calmly. Soon, however, the congregation of monks and labourers, slaves and children, were moulded into one body. Cuthbert did this with no effort, it seemed, no dazzle or tricks. But he made them as one.

Bega found that this Mass answered to a deep need. In the cave she had sought and failed to find the source of the disturbance which had led her back there. But Chad's interruption had clearly been a sign. She should no longer look there. It was here, she knew, as she offered up prayers for the soul of her father, that she was to be made whole.

Cuthbert conducted the service with simplicity. He himself was immersed in it. At times it seemed that the mass was for himself alone but such was the force of his concentration that the minds and spirits of all of them were drawn in more deeply than at any other mass.

As the climactic drama approached – the turning of the wine into the blood and the bread into the body of Christ – and the fateful words 'and on the same night as he was betrayed' were spoken, Cuthbert began to find it difficult to continue. His voice choked over the phrases. The agony of his Lord seemed to become his own agony. The congregation caught his mood as other congregations had so often done. They went every step of the way with Cuthbert and Jesus Christ to Golgotha.

At this point, Cuthbert's power was absolute. Without openly instructing them, he made them do whatever he chose to do. Bega felt that she and the others would have obeyed any command he gave them. They were in his hand. Bega was tense as he paused to gather strength for the next scene in this eternal drama of resurrection. This promised all of them life everlasting and all of them believed that through Cuthbert they might receive it. When Cuthbert began to weep at the pain suffered by Christ, several and then most wept with him. When he was so overcome with grief that he lay down before the altar and spread out his arms in imitation of the cross, many did likewise.

Bega experienced and loved this charge of common purpose which Cuthbert gave them in this bleak remote harbour. She saw her single prayers multiplied and amplified by this force so palpable that the angels could have come down to earth and carried it back like a honeycomb from a hive. She glanced at the sky to see if some parting in heaven indicated that the strength of their prayer was reaching directly into the celestial habitation. And yet she wanted to hold out against it.

With a cry which seemed wrenched from his soul, Cuthbert

held the bread above his head and broke it. Broke it. The congregation shifted forward – all hungry in spirit now, needing to be fed this divine body at the hands of this saint. Bega went with them. When the bread came into her hands she broke it and thought, 'this is how the disciples broke bread in Jerusalem on that night: from today I will go out into the world and save souls. I vow again that never will I be unfaithful to Jesus Christ'.

Once she had said that to herself and eaten the fragment of bread, she felt a deep and weary peace. Colman kissed her on the cheek and she kissed Chad. The congregation began to cry 'Alleluia! Alleluia!' and the word ran towards the cliffs. The wilder some of the monks became, the stiller, it seemed, grew Cuthbert who stood before the altar as if he were part of it. 'Amen!' they cried. 'Amen! Alleluia!'

Bega was swept along. 'Alleluia!' she cried. 'Alleluia! Praise be the Lord of Hosts! Praise Him! Praise Him in Zion! Praise Him! Alleluia!'

They danced to the words of the faith and the more extreme monks set up a wailing of the words which was curiously exciting, stamping their feet in rhythm, some of them clapping hands. Bega joined in, released.

Here, where she had begun one new journey was where she would begin once more. This time the journey would be directed towards her heavenly reward. Alleluia! Praise be to the Almighty, the Lord of Hosts! Now there was no confusion. Work would be found for her. Alleluia! Alleluia! Amen! The hills rang with the chants and Glorias.

Cuthbert, immobile, watched what he had let loose.

It was a noteworthy procession. Cuthbert led, his own disciples followed, one of them carrying a cross; then Colman on a stout horse and his three monks from Ireland; Bega next and two other women who had been included by Cuthbert; finally Chad and half-a-dozen builders, carrying their implements. Cuthbert was

leading them across the country to Melrose, his first ecclesiastical
house, where extensions were being built.

Colman was going north out of his way in order to pay his
respects to Erebert who had once sat at his feet in Ireland. As
they went along the lakeside, Colman told them stories of the
boy Erebert's astonishing piety. It was that which had allowed
him to be released so young for a hermit's life.

Cuthbert and Colman took Bega with them across to the island
of Erebert. The rest of the party pitched camp under threatening
skies on the promontory rock which jutted into the lake from
the north.

Erebert was overwhelmed with joy.

He fell to his knees in prayer. He kissed the hands of Colman
and Cuthbert. He acknowledged Bega with praise.

They sat in the open on the rocks beside the lake. A warming
breeze ruffled the water and began to pitch the few patient
shore-hugging fishermen in their tiny raft-like boats. Bega found
it refreshing to be back on the island. Here was another station
where she could slough off confused memories of the old and
assert the newness of her determination.

Erebert, who, Bega thought, looked steadier than before –
and a look over his small estate showed it to be in much
neater order – could not resist introducing his longing for a
miracle.

'Cuthbert has said that he may help me to *one*. That I die in
the same moment as he does so that together we may take the
road to heaven.'

'You must not expect too much of me,' said Cuthbert.

'You are given miracles,' replied Erebert firmly and just a little
sadly. And he went on: 'What better proof do we have? Who
but He can make a spring rise up in stony ground? Who but
He can make the blind see or cast out devils or raise the sick?
When the people see them they say – "Yes. He is the God they
say He is. He is a God greater than our god." Miracles are our
best evidence.'

'But are those what we should be basing our faith on?' asked
Colman quietly, and Bega noticed the leaven of his authority.
'I am Peter and upon my rock . . . What is the rock? It is the
rock of faith. Is a faith sustained by miracles a faith built on a
rock? Miracles are few. Sometimes the miracle-makers' claims are

proved false. Ridicule and disbelief come from that and make it harder.'

'There is only one thing,' said Cuthbert evenly, 'that I have seen which convinces people more than a miracle and that is an unexpected victory in battle under the protection of the Lord of Hosts. For most heathen people, and for many who would call themselves Christian, faith is difficult. We ask for so much. We ask that everything that they have must be given to one single God who is invisible and eternal and unconquerable. One God who controls, as in truth He does, every inch of earth, every beast that crawls or flies or swims in the seas and the rivers and every breath we breathe. How can this be? Who can do all this? Where can He be seen? That is why a victory or a miracle are the best weapons we have in our struggle to win the world for our God. Look at what is ranged against us!'

'Who am I?' said Colman, smiling, throwing up his small plump hands. 'Who am I?'

The words and the gesture were part of his talent for bringing a disturbing discussion to a close. He directed the conversation to mundane matters.

Eventually they went back to the boat. The wind had dropped and the lake was calming down; the small craft were still on the water, nets being thrown in an arc guided by stones tied to the end of them.

'Do you think this is what Christ saw on the Sea of Galilee?' Colman asked. When no one answered, he continued. 'I do. And these simple fishermen became his fishers of men. Simple folk. We must never forget that.' He nodded at all of them. 'Simple folk,' he repeated.

Erebert escorted them down to the boat where an oarsman was waiting. The two men got in first. Erebert, who had given and received blessings from all, turned to Bega for a last word.

'I hear Prince Padric comes to these parts now and then,' he said, 'though we're not supposed to say.'

Bega made no answer.

Colman took her hand and helped her into the small wobbling boat.

The man rowed them across to the others and Erebert watched until they had landed and then he turned to be about his day.

Across the hump of sodden ground, reed-clustered, rushes-and-flower-strewn, they went until they came to the next lake, the most northerly and magical of those of Rheged. It was said that into this lake the dying King Arthur had thrown his sword.

Cuthbert walked with Colman and the deliberate way in which he sought him out made Bega fall behind, which suited her. She wanted to be alone with her thoughts.

Erebert's casual words had tested her new sense of purpose. This was timely, she decided; Padric was undoubtedly dear to her. It was foolish and unwise to deny this. By admitting it, she knew that she had already shamed the devil. But still she wished Erebert had said nothing.

She squelched through the ground, her long robe collecting mud. She looked about her as if she had not seen the landscape before, and indeed in her previous state she had noticed very little. It was a place, she decided, in which she could do the work Colman had hinted at, a place where she could begin to pursue her true vocation. The prayer and the spiritual exercises at Whitby had been excellent training. But the visits to the sick and the occasional missions were not enough. Out here, behind the hills, in the deep woods, even along the lake shore would be many who did not know of the Glory of Christ. It was in such a place as this that she could begin, and afterwards, if she had won victories, she could ask to take His word into areas of darkness much further away. To stand alone for God in a land of heathen ignorance and rejection!

But this lake which stretched so shapely up towards a rolling open valley, these flanking containing hills, this would be a start.

As she walked she prayed and when, in her prayers, she remembered Padric, she did not fight him off. She prayed for the safety of his life and the purity of his soul. And she thanked God for the strength He had given her to rededicate herself with all her force. Now she did truly live for the faith.

They reached a spot beside the lake where there was a wide

clearing. Beyond it was a point of land which stretched out into
the lake. To their right were open fields and then the sudden
alarming soar of the land into a mountainous mass which seemed
to touch the heavens. Across the lake were more mountains, and
thick forest and sounds of occupation which travelled bell clear
across the watery boundary. The day had calmed and a thin yellow
sunlight struggled to make its mark.

About two hundred paces from the edge of the lake stood a
half-completed building in stone. They leaned against it or sat
down to rest.

Bega walked to the lake's edge. Her eyes scanned it and she
breathed in happily. The spaciousness given by the lake was
deeply comforting: it felt part of her own mind. The hills, too,
their swoop and fold seemed to correspond to a configuration in
her mind. It was as if the place reflected her and she was already
inhabited by it. She prayed once more to be able to stay here.

Cuthbert was at her left shoulder.

'You spoke of wanting to begin a mission,' he said.

Bega turned to him.

'Bishop Colman and I have been discussing this. You see the
walls there—' he indicated the half-built church 'that was where
I began to build a monastery about two years ago. Then the place
which we have just left seemed more pressing. But King Oswy
gave me three farms and lands around here. I want to use that
for some good purpose. Would you like to stay here and begin
a mission from here? The two women I brought with us were, I
confess, brought with this thought in mind and they would stay
with you and help you. They are ignorant country women but
kindly, recently converted, and able to do many of the things
which need work. I will ask four of the men to stay on and put a
roof on the building and build some quarters. Over there by the
edge of the woods there is a woman, Reggiani, from whom you
can get skins and herbs and many of the necessary provisions.' He
looked sternly at Bega. 'Be wary of her,' he went on, 'for she is
against God. But there are ways in which she can help you. I have
brought some essentials from the other place and you can always
send your servant' – he indicated Chad – 'back there for more.'

Cuthbert took Bega's silence for resistance to the suggestion.

'There is another matter,' he said, quietly but unflinchingly,
and she saw coldness in his eyes. 'When you gave me that most

precious gift. You will have seen that I was quite unlike myself. Since then I have prayed without ceasing. I still do not know whether I was possessed by the devil or guided by God. I still do not know whether the cross of Christ is feeding the deceits of the leader in all lies or whether it is lodged there in my heart to become a beacon for others in Christ. What I need,' said Cuthbert, pausing only fractionally, 'is for there to be no talk of it at all until I have resolved the matter. Perhaps there never shall be talk of it, just as there never shall be talk of that remaining fragment of the cross which you have. What you must do – as I must do – is to wait for a sign. There will come to each of us a sign which will say, unmistakably, that we ought to reveal the supreme grace that has been accorded to you, through your priest in Connachta, and to me through you. Only when such a sign tells us so, will there be a purpose to our revelation.'

Bega still remained silent, rather like someone standing on the very tip of the sheerest cliff, frightened that one slightest wrong movement would plunge her to grief.

'I have discussed this with Bishop Colman as I said,' Cuthbert repeated. 'He will explain all this to the Abbess Hilda and I too will explain it to her in some weeks' time. She gave you her blessing for your journey and this would merely be an extension of the journey. You can stay here until I come for you or send a messenger to bring you back to Whitby.'

'Our silence,' said Bega, eventually, 'will never be broken by me.'

Cuthbert nodded and she saw his relief.

'I would be afraid in any case,' she continued, truthfully, 'to know what to do with this gift. I am so unworthy of it. I need guidance and I accept what you say about the sign. I will wait for a sign.' She hesitated. The tone of this must be precisely right. 'And I will do as you ask. I will stay here and when everything is in order I will begin to visit the sick and preach, with God's help, to the heathen.'

'Thanks be to God.'

Bega turned back to the lake. *Jubilate! Jubilate!* Her prayers had been answered. Thanks, indeed, be to God!

CHAPTER FORTY-FOUR

Afew days earlier, Padric, Riderch, Urien and Owain with five servants had sailed from Ireland across to the land of the Picts, crossed the country to the other sea, turned south and set their course for Bamburgh, the fortress of Oswy and the prison of Penraddin.

The expedition was at Urien's insistence. As the youngest of the brothers, he had always been closest to Penraddin who had applauded his escapades since his childhood. When he had heard that Ecfrith had imprisoned his sister, he had decided that he would rescue her.

Padric was against it. They were still in hiding after their battle with the Northumbrians which had already provoked one raid on their father's country. From what they had heard it was not the massacre it might have been if it had been left to Ecfrith alone but, even so, there had been murders, slaves taken, humiliation inflicted. It was madness, Padric said, to provoke them so soon again.

Urien shrugged.

Riderch and Owain had pointed out that Bamburgh was the most fortified and impregnable spot in all of Britain. They had not the resources to take it. It was far beyond any reasonable risk.

Urien said he would go on his own.

The argument lasted for one full day and deep into the second and stopped only when Urien suddenly put on his armour, collected his horses, secured a servant, and made it plain that he was on his way.

Padric went over to him and made one last effort.

'I will go,' said the younger man, 'whatever you say, I will go.

And if they stop me before I get there – then let's see how many I can take with me.'

Padric smiled and put an arm around his brother's shoulder. There was no doubting Urien! It would never occur to him to flinch. The high odds made it more attractive.

'We are wanted men over there,' said Padric. 'If they see any of us they will have no mercy. We have to build up our allies – here in Ireland, and then in the north, in the south, across the sea. We cannot abandon that. Even for Penraddin. She is my sister too.'

'I understand you,' Urien said. 'I know what you are doing. I know that it will take many years. I know that to be patient is to be strong and you bring us to good battles where we can prove ourselves.' He looked directly at his brother, to emphasise his sincerity. Usually, he rather mocked him, although he was always by his side. 'But I hate Ecfrith. I hate that man.' The repetition was hammered home. 'I am not going to let him cage up Penraddin and laugh at all of us that he has the daughter of Rheged at his mercy and her brothers will do nothing. I will not let him do that.'

'We had planned to stay here for another half-year.'

'You stay,' said Urien, with no blame in his tone. 'I am set on this.'

'I can see that,' said Padric and then he knew that he too would go.

They rode hard down from the north where Oswy's law ran weakest and where they could seem to be going to the Holy Island of Lindisfarne, as many now did. Padric's main tactic was to ride as fast as they could, squeezing miles out of every moment of daylight. Even if they were thought suspicious, he calculated that no patrol could beat them to Bamburgh.

When they came alongside Lindisfarne they saw not an island but a strip of sand connecting it to the mainland.

'This happens with the ebb and flow of the tide,' said Padric, who had been told about it by Erebert. 'The sea comes in rapidly and cuts it off and then when the tide goes out the monks can walk across.'

They paused, needing the rest, and gazed out at the seaweed-strewn stretch of sand, across to the swerve of tall yellow marram grass which formed a low wall around the island. They could not see the settlement of the monks but further down country, on the mainland, the rock of Bamburgh and its fortress crown were clearly visible.

Originally, Padric had planned to go over to Lindisfarne. It would have allayed some of the suspicions aroused in those who had undoubtedly seen them and might have been following them. Padric also had thought that they could somehow encourage two or three monks to accompany them. This would solve a number of problems. But now, looking out at the afterthought of land, he let that plan go. It would not do to implicate those men in what would be seen as a severe blow to the pride of the court on which they utterly depended. Besides, they could well be untrustworthy accomplices: they owed a lot to King Oswy.

He had thought also that Urien, Riderch and himself should impersonate monks. They could be seen as coming from Lindisfarne. The traffic in religion between Bamburgh and the Holy Island was well established and so their entrance to the fortress would be unimpeded. They could ask to be taken to Penraddin's place of confinement without embarrassment.

The flaw was that they would have to go on foot. Aidan's famous relinquishing of the king's magnificent gift of his most splendid horse had been taken as a necessary rule by all his followers. Very rarely did the bishop himself take to horseback. To see three monks mounted . . . Even if they went on foot and Owain and the servants followed behind with the horses, they would arouse suspicion. What would Owain's story be when challenged, as he would surely be, nearer the castle? How would he account for the armour, the number of fine mounts, the servants? And how slow it would be.

They rested and ate and waited for Padric to take them further. Urien was quite content to leave it to his older brother. They had discussed plans of attack but none had been wholly satisfactory. Padric had kept to himself the boldest stroke of all. He waited for the spy he had sent in advance to bring him the vital information.

They had ridden down country safely. The confidence and status of their group had swept them through, confidence flaunted deliberately by Padric; the sweep of the huge cloak he had bought from his friend the prince of the Picts, the richness of the promise on the laden pack-ponies which were indeed carrying stores, for the immense journey Padric intended to make after Penraddin had been rescued.

Knowing the strength of the fortress and calculating, from the intelligence he had received and from his own instincts, that the forces against them could be unbeatable, he had sought the simplest, most daring plan. He had found it, on his drive down the coast route, in the recognition and salutes occasionally given him, in the sense he had gained of being someone else. Now his spy returned and completed the plan.

He took aside his brothers and Owain and told them what they would do.

'You know that I am said to resemble Ecfrith,' he said, 'well, that is our way in. I have just learned that he is not in Bamburgh. I will act as if I were him. You will cover your faces so that you will not be recognised. Riderch will fall behind and bring the spare horses and servants to the foot of the castle. Owain, Urien and I will go in and find Penraddin and bring her away.'

Urien grinned. He liked it. Riderch's objections and the cautions of Owain were taken on board and discussed. How could they swiftly discover where Penraddin was? Surely, taking a spare horse (even one laden with bogus booty) would arouse suspicion? And was Padric, to an experienced eye, *really* like that coarse and brutish bully? Padric gave them very little time: he was impatient to move on.

They set off at a fast pace. The size of the Bamburgh rock made it appear deceptively near. As they approached it, the population thickened. Occasionally Padric would practise a surly greeting and it was returned, which gave him confidence.

None of them was prepared for the massive sheerness of the rock on which the fortress was built. Urien nodded to his ancestor of the same name who, those years ago, had locked up the whole first-thrust force of the invaders there. What a fighter he must have been! Urien settled more comfortably into himself. There was no going back now.

Following orders with some reluctance, Riderch fell a little behind the three leaders and Padric, Urien and Owain distanced themselves and turned up the steep path which zig-zagged up the rock.

It was a cold spring day. The wind from the sea bit into their skin. Padric was glad of it. There was some excuse to muffle up their faces. Now that they were almost there, the odds against them rose as sheerly as the rock itself.

There were guards at the gate and it was here that Padric took a breath, tried to imagine how Ecfrith would return and showed his face sufficiently to let the naked disguise be tested. He expressed a terrible impatience.

The guards looked a little surprised, but a curse from Padric had them hurrying to open the gates.

Urien and Owain had adopted a great weariness, half-slumped on their horses – drink and hunting had worn them down. They went in.

The space which gathered them in was as busy as the market at Caerel. Padric had gone no more than a dozen paces when a slave came and took the rein of his horse. 'Take me to Penraddin,' he said, leaning down to the man.

The slave did as he was bid and the three of them went through the parting crowd towards the furthest height of the fortress where a small stone building stood independently of all the others. Someone shouted the name 'Ecfrith!' Padric ignored it.

All three men strove to maintain a show of casual weariness; each one of them was a hair's breadth from the hilt of his sword. Owain had dropped back, as agreed, and, looking round in a desultory manner, he calculated what mayhem could be raised to confuse the enemy in the event of discovery. That fire could be spread about, that cart overturned, those pigs whipped into squealing, scattering frenzy.

Padric dismounted briskly and went to the door of the small stone building. Beyond it was the wall and beyond that the white sanded shore and the sea.

The guard let him in and Padric found himself in a musty room. The guard followed him, stirred by a slight sense of unease. Padric, without turning to face him, ordered him out. All his concentration was on Penraddin, who was staring at him, amazed.

Reluctantly, as it seemed to Padric, the guard went out.

'We are here to take you with us,' said Padric. 'Come.'

'How . . . ? You . . .'

'Urien and Riderch are outside. We have a horse for you. Put on your cloak.'

'I do not deserve . . .' Penraddin was breathing with difficulty. The shock of seeing Padric and being told that her freedom was imminent had numbed her. Padric saw that she looked ill, much thinner than she had been, her hair lank and dull, her body wasted. Most striking of all was her expression – no longer that of the bold, attractive Penraddin but of a young woman cowed.

'I deserve my punishment,' she said, looking around the room as if she would fight to stay in it.

'Put on your cloak,' said Padric, firmly. 'We must go.'

'What will I do?'

'Penraddin.' Padric looked around, saw her cloak and brought it over to her. She was trembling. 'Come!'

'He will hunt us down,' she whispered. 'He will torture us all.'

'Come. You will be safe with us.'

He put an arm around her bony shoulder but she shivered and resisted. Padric was alarmed. They had to move quickly. He put pressure on her to move but she stood her ground.

'Shall I carry you?'

She looked at him piteously. He knew that she had no will. He scooped her up and made for the door.

The guard was immediately outside and Padric pushed into him. He looked at Padric and then at Penraddin and his expression registered fast-growing anxiety.

'Urien!' Padric looked at his brother and then glanced at the guard who was clearly about to shout out or pull his sword. In what appeared a single movement, Urien slid off his horse and pushed the guard into the prison. As Padric put a dazed Penraddin on her horse, they heard a gurgling cry from within. Urien had used his dagger and found the man's throat.

Now he had to be Ecfrith even more openly. To adopt any aspect of disguise would be to alert those who must already be beginning to sense that something was wrong, something was strange and out of character about the behaviour, the actions, the manner, the poise of the Ecfrith-like person leaving so soon after he had entered without the usual marks of his arrival, accompanied by a pale, downcast Penraddin. Padric threw back his head and glanced around, unafraid to catch an eye, imagining himself as Ecfrith.

Owain went first. Urien was the rear-guard. Certain voices hailed them, certain shouts were directed towards them, there was more than normal curiosity in the eyes of those who watched this procession. But they rode on, through the gate, down to where Riderch was waiting for them. Then they flew, until they came to the forest where, from wood to densest wood, led by other desperate men and greenwood rebels, they made their way under cover, going further and further south until they reached the shore to embark and sail across to the place they called Little Britain, where they would stay and fight and build their strength.

When he knew they had been lost, Ecfrith obtained permission from his father to turn some of his wrath on the kingdom which had bred the traitoress Penraddin and her brothers. He went too far but this time his father could forgive him, even though he lamented the death of Dunmael. Now Rheged was leaderless. Oswy – to mark his displeasure at Ecfrith's excess – allowed Dunmael's widow to rule.

chapter forty-five

When Cuthbert and Colman and their company had moved on, Bega went down to the lake's edge, looked across at the sweet roll of mountains and found that a voice inside her said, 'Here, this spot, at last is your place on earth'.

She could not have chosen it beforehand. It was remote, isolated, apparently calm, quite prosperous, yet fearsomely encircled by giddy, tipped and dangerous mountains. She would learn, as time went on, why this place had been chosen for her. When the time came, God would reveal it. For the present, she knew and felt a deep strength of peaceful joy. Here she could be what God wanted. She stood contentedly for some moments and then, with a huge lift of zeal, began the work.

Cuthbert had made it clear that Bega was the leader of the small community. Therefore she needed to make little effort in exercising her dominion. The men set to and after building two small stick-and-sod shelters, they went to find wooden branches and thatching material to complete the stone-founded building. The women were watchfully obedient. With the means left her by Cuthbert and the promise of payment in kind within the next few days for those whose farms he now owned, Bega planned her estate.

She had asked Colman to make a plea to Hilda that she be allowed to start up a small nunnery, dependent for all its authority on Whitby and the abbess herself, but designed to be a starting point for mission in the barbarous mountains.

On the sixth day, she went across the fields to the nearest settlement she had spotted. She was seeking milk. It would have been easier and possibly seemlier to have sent one of the women but Bega was curious. She wanted to beat the bounds of her domain.

Reggiani had been waiting for her.

Bega recognised the young woman who had come to help her on Erebert's island those years before, but a sudden embarrassment caused her to conceal it. Reggiani welcomed her without suspicion or hesitation. She went to the goats and squeezed a good-sized jug of milk from their well-bagged udders.

Reggiani's hut was no more than four score paces from the edge of the forest which swung steeply up the mountainside. Her mother had selected the place with a fine eye for the water channels, as did everyone in this area. It was easily possible to be ruined by water. A few yards the other way, usually on a thin-turf covered hump of rock, you could build as solidly and snugly against the rain and water as it was possible to be. Reggiani's settlement and huts had been selected with particular cunning. It was, in fact, when examined carefully, a little fortress in itself, moated by two small streams – which could rage after heavy rainfall but not flood – and screened from the worst wind, the north-east, by a straggle of elm and Scots pine. Nearby was a shrine and Bega could see what she considered to be an ugly little statuette. There were also half-a-dozen less imposing buildings, homes to the other inhabitants of this, one of many settlements bunched between the game-filled woods and the fish-filled lake on land fertile enough to cultivate grain and protected enough for herbs.

'You do not remember me?' Reggiani asked as she handed over the milk.

Bega stared at her, reluctant to be reminded of her weakness. She took in Reggiani properly for the first time.

She saw a woman she guessed to be a few years older than her, about the same height, though plumper. Everything about Reggiani appeared soft and yielding. Even under the coarse full-length dress the undulating softness of easy curves could be seen or suspected. Her thick fair hair was spread over her shoulders and, like Bega's, reached down to her waist but, unlike the attempt on Bega's part to regiment the hair, this seemed cultivated to a seductive, entangling wildness, seductiveness being the most marked characteristic about Reggiani; in the parted red lips, the fine-coloured cheeks, in the slow saunter, but above all in the eyes, hazel brown and always, Bega was to find, seeming half-closed. Depending on her mood, her eyes could indicate a mood of distrust, or a sense of mockery so strong that the eyelids simply had to be half-closed to hold back the laughter. Despite the mud which was the given condition of that damp landscape, Reggiani was almost magically clean in herself and in her well-woven cloak and dress.

'On the island, on Erebert's island,' Bega acknowledged, somehow rather angrily. 'When I was ill.'

'You were very badly,' replied Reggiani. Bega felt uncomfortable at what she thought was a rather mocking stare. 'You helped me.'

Reggiani waved a lazy hand towards a large and heavily-stocked herb garden. 'That was what helped you.'

'That and God,' said Bega.

'God.' Reggiani smiled and her eyes brimmed with fun. 'Ah yes. You are one of the God-ones, aren't you? The Christians.'

'You are not.'

'He is much too difficult for me,' Reggiani replied, shrugging to avoid any argument. 'I have much simpler gods. But mostly, when people are badly, I have herbs.'

'The herbs are the gifts of God.'

'Ah yes. Your God makes everything, doesn't he?'

'He does.'

'The good and the wicked?'

'The good to combat the wicked.'

'And that is why you starve?'

'That is why we fast. That is why we pray.'

'We too pray,' said Reggiani, briskly. 'And we make sacrifices—' she indicated the shrine. Reggiani was the priestess of a cult well favoured in the valley. 'Every day. To the waters, to the woods, to the sky, to all our gods who live in this place.'

'We have total and complete faith in the one God.'

'That seems to me to be a gamble. But so be it. What puzzles me is why you Christians are so determined that the rest of us must share your faith. Why are you so fierce about it?'

'Because you will die in sin without our faith and we must save you. Otherwise your soul will perish in everlasting fire.'

'How do you know that?'

'Christ taught us that.'

'Erebert told me all about him. Why did this Christ let himself be killed if he is God?'

'He died to save us.'

Reggiani laughed. Not harshly but roundly, merrily even, disbelievingly. Bega, who had been drawn into the web of the woman's weaving looks and spell, was doused back into her own reality.

'You are the enemy!' she said, with surprise but no rancour. 'You are one who works the will of the devil.'

'Oh no!' Reggiani smiled, showing teeth white as any Bega had seen . . . since Maeve. She shuddered at the reminder. 'No need to be afraid of me,' said Reggiani in her even drawl, without any anxiety in her voice. 'I am not your devil. I don't know him any more than I know your God. And to be plain with you, I don't want to know either of them. They don't sound like the gods I would turn to. They don't sound like the gods you need to lead a life through the days of it.'

Once again her sensuous plausibility began to draw Bega into sympathy. But she stopped herself.

'I must make you my prime convert,' she said grimly. 'With God's strength I shall convert you to an understanding of His power and glory.'

'Others have tried,' said Reggiani, laconically. 'I have travelled a little hereabouts and met some Christians, not only Erebert. I was up to Caerel itself once and there are God-ones there too. But no,' she shook her head, 'it's all too much *against*. Look at Erebert – look at the monks and nuns I met up in Caerel. Against any intercourse.' She laughed, clearly enjoying what she thought of as a ridiculous rule. 'They say that God wants them to have no intimacy. The monks must avoid women, the nuns must avoid men. What is the purpose of that?'

'To serve God with all our strength. To be pure for Him alone. To become His perfect vessel on earth. I too am chaste,' said Bega hotly.

'Oh,' said Reggiani, 'Are you now?' And again there was that mocking glance which ruffled Bega's poise.

'Yes,' said Bega, brushing aside what she thought was Reggiani's insulting attitude. 'And I am perfectly happy with that state.'

Reggiani looked at her with an expression which made Bega more and more angrily uncomfortable. Who was this woman who so languidly cast off the power and glory of Christ and the Lord of Hosts?

'By my chastity I show Christ that I am devoted only to Him

and to His cause,' said Bega, much more primly and defensively than she had intended. To Bega's fury, Reggiani began to laugh; Bega all but threw the jug of milk in her face. 'My chastity,' she continued, as Reggiani struggled to compose her features, 'is also a sign for others of the sacrifice I am prepared to make.'

'So it *is* a sacrifice then.'

'In the beginning perhaps. For some,' said Bega, loftily.

'Did your Christ not have a mother?'

'That is not the argument.'

'I see.'

Again there was that gurgle of laughter. Bega turned to leave.

'You will need more than milk,' Reggiani said.

'We were supplied with ample provisions,' said Bega, 'and,' she added, haughtily, 'I am expecting the tributes from the farms to come soon. Cuthbert said they would.'

'They will come eventually,' said Reggiani. 'But people can be slow around here. I am well stocked if there should be a need.'

Bega found her charity the last straw. She nodded, just about courteously, and walked away as rapidly as she could.

Reggiani watched her go with a certain regret. She had liked the bold look in the young woman's face. She liked her intelligent eyes. It would be good to have such a woman as a friend in these dour parts. But the God people were so fanatical . . .

In the next months, Bega discovered the never-ending and exacting demands of work. The great common pestilences of the time – cold and hunger – had been unknown to her in her privileged life in Ireland and at Whitby alike. Here, beside the lake, Bega discovered the lot of the generality. It was cold, often hungry, wet, exhausting, full of fear and rarely far from physical pain. Bega wanted to be part of all this: the more testing, the better.

It took her a while to appreciate the populousness of the valley. Around and about the clumps of oak, hazel, lime and alder were scores of huts and farms almost encircling the lake. Some had a half-wall of stone from the abundant slate stone and rock lying about the valley floor. Others were merely wattle and daub. The simplest were like the temporary dwellings put up for Bega's first days there. She had noted the method carefully for future reference. Sticks were planted in the ground in two rows. The tops were twisted together and tied with ropes of hay. Thin strips of earth, four or five feet in length, would be arranged over the sticks. These would be warm and, more important, waterproof. The better homes were walled with sods and thatched with rushes, grasses, reeds, heather or straw and bound with ropes, weighted down with stones.

The woods held game, there were fish in the lake, the valley bottom was rich earth for crops. In good times.

The first autumn was so wet that she thought that nothing would ever be dry again. It rained, it drizzled, it hailed, it poured, it sleeted, it thunderstormed, it slated down, it mizzled, it cascaded; many times it was as if the air itself had become all water and the earth was to be all flood. The rivers gorged through their courses, brown from the mud they were carrying, fiercely bursting their way to the lake which could not shed its load fast enough to the main river, which thrashed out and down to the sea which loaded up the clouds which swept across the mountain country once more. The meadows became water marshes. The lake on which Erebert had his island and that beside which Bega had her settlement joined into one vast expanse of water. Every day the clouds came in across the sea from Ireland, bellied with water and as the mountains urged them to rise, so they slipped their ballast to meet the challenge.

It was then that Bega began to understand about people's real existence. As she went on her visits to the sick and on the first local missions, she saw a poverty she had seen in Ireland only now and then, and had visited near Whitby only occasionally. But she had never lived with it, nor seen it as part of a life to which she herself was bound.

Some people were stunted in every way imaginable. A child who had been trapped under a storm-struck tree now dragged a crushed leg behind her; a whole family whose bodies were so thin and wasted they scarcely had the strength to do enough work to subsist; half-blind, retarded, face-pocked, variously afflicted.

Sometimes Bega saw the marks of the devil and the punishments of God all about her.

Yet there was much that was sturdy there. The bigger farmers, those who hunted and fished as well as farming, provided a source of Christian reliability. Some had even been able to afford arms. All of them were pleased that Cuthbert's initiative had finally been carried through: it meant a lot to have their own evidence of heavenly industry close to hand.

Yet these, the core of Padric's future army and his future kingdom, were in the minority. Most of the rest waged ceaseless war not with the devil but with their chief foes: hunger and cold. A day was good which saw both of them outwitted. Sometimes Bega felt that a sort of war was broken off when she arrived at the poorer settlements. It was so difficult to engender joy, she understood that. Even the message of Christ was taken not so much for the wonder and delight of the heaven to come but as an added burden on life as lived. There was violence sometimes, which they tried to conceal from her, as they did the bestiality and the incestuous compulsions of some of the families who knew that they were stigmatised for this but did not change their ways.

For most of the people under the rains, life was lived in a welter of mud. The houses, if they did not crumble at the assault of water, became so damp that to be inside was colder and wetter than to be outside. A prime necessity was to keep the fire going. A young member of the family was assigned that as a full-time and cruelly monitored task. But twigs and logs often stored without anticipation of such a sustained soaking made this one of the hardest tasks of all. Bega would find children lying on their bellies, faces grimed with smoke, inhaling and exhaling deeply to keep a feeble flicker alive.

The mud around the less well-sited dwellings became ankle deep and inside it began to swell through the floor, however thickly the heather had been laid under the straw and, in richer cases, the skins. The hovels in which the slaves and servants were kept were as wet as the forest floor itself. Some of the slaves made a huddle for themselves beside a rock or on a flat stone rather than risk the dubious benefit of a saturated roof and sodden walls.

As Bega went about the place she saw how relentless life was for many. A quiet desperation drove the poorer people. From the age of physical competence, the work began, never resting and never ending, dawn to dusk and beyond. Even with this endless endeavour, Bega found the sense of enough never being done remained. Always more: more wool to comb; more fuel to find and cut and gather; more pastures to move the beasts to; more corn to grind; more walls and roofs to repair; more vegetable gardens and small strips of field to tend; more game, more deer, more pheasants, more birds of all kinds to be stalked and, with rare luck, killed; more nuts and berries to be gathered; more clothes to be made. When Bega arrived at a place there was never a let-up in the work. The man, and the more so if he were arms-bearing, might find time to talk. The woman, the bread-kneader to his role as bread-keeper, would find time to welcome the visitor. But their work would go on and Bega would be expected to help.

Soon Bega began to take it for granted. Anything else seemed a curious exception. Just as the stinks of the farmyard, which to a fine nostril might have seemed intolerable, were to her the sweet thick smell of home, so life lived on the dangerous edge of mortality soon became what was. That her own life had been and continued to be more privileged by comparison was something for which she thanked God. She hoped to repay this in her prayers, her care and visits to the sick, and her efforts at converting the heathen. But she accepted that there was a higher and a lower estate. God had created lesser and greater just as he had created men and animals.

In the fastness of small valleys, behind the curve of the huge mountains, were communities which had been occupied in their own strange life, it seemed, uninterrupted for centuries. There were the wild men Padric loved, the Britons who drank deeply and spoke loudly in riddles with harsh voices, were utterly fearless, praised themselves without ceasing and remembered and sang their history and their poetry, disdaining writing as evidence of minds too weak to hold the glorious past. They were a cunning and quick people who loved to see strangers and loved to tease them. As Bega was nimble-minded enough to return the teasing, and sufficiently experienced to unravel some of the riddles – Padric had helped her there – and physically unafraid, she became a trusted stranger. When she went to the remote fastnesses, she thought that she was entering a world so old that Christ Himself would have felt that it was in His past. Yet it endured. And somehow, she thought she remembered Padric saying, it was at the heart of Rheged – the element that would keep it alive.

Over the next three years, Bega began to come into her own. For mass, she sent for a priest from what was now known as Bega's Haven. She returned to Whitby twice. Once to answer a summons from Hilda to whom she made a full report. On that occasion she and Chad and three men of Rheged escorted four nuns back with them. The second time she went to beg for vellum and for information on how to make it, and for the means of writing and anything written that Hilda could spare. On both visits Hilda was rather cool but made none of the objections Bega had anticipated. Yes, Cuthbert and Bishop Colman had convinced her that it was good to have a daughter-cell of the abbey in such a lonely and desolate spot. Yes, Bega could use whatever surplus resources the mother-house could provide.

Bega did not question any of this. She was so wonderfully pleased to make use of the opportunity that she took Hilda's support as proof of the ennobling power of the True Cross.

The abbess was worried that Bega was being turned away from the steep path of fine duty which would surely have led her to eminence in the world of great abbeys and glorious missions. Cuthbert had been most persuasive that she should stay in Rheged deep in the mountains and Hilda saw that Bega herself had embraced the place. Yet Hilda could not quite work out why Cuthbert wanted such a gem (as she still thought Bega to be) tucked so far away from a centre of activity such as Whitby. Nor could she quite fathom Bega's passion for Rheged and for that damp district beside the lake.

She was hurt that Bega had not seen fit to seek her advice. She was worried that the church could be under-using one of its potentially great servants. She was a little doubtful of the wisdom of giving Bega authority so early in life, although she trusted her. During the second winter, Hilda's worry became tinctured with irritation. It was as if she were excluded from some knowledge privy only to Cuthbert, Bega and God, and she did not enjoy that sense of exclusion. Whenever she thought about it she became more frustrated and a desire to blame began to gather up in her, directed against Bega.

CHAPTER FORTY-SIX

In her small settlement Bega was, although she scarcely recognised this, in full imitation of her father. She was lord of what was about her and revelled in ruling and administering her court. Every spring and summer she would add to it.

She organised the day rather differently from that laid down by Hilda. Whitby had enough slaves and freemen to allow the more learned nuns all the time they needed for their spiritual exercises. Here that was out of the question. The four nuns brought from Whitby had been selected by Bega – to Hilda's relief – not from the learned and the wealthy but from the strong of arm. When Hilda later sent a message asking if Bega wanted three more nuns, it was from the same pool that Bega drew her recruits.

First came early morning prayer, then contemplation. Then a meal – milk, eggs, bread, sometimes cheese, nuts or berries. Then a long morning's work on what was, in effect, a farm with no break for formal prayers until the midday service followed by the midday meal of broth, a plate of meat, bread, vegetables and possibly berries. At any time, of course, following the examples of Cathleen and Donal, there could be spontaneous prayers of thanksgiving or pleas for heavenly help. In the afternoon there would again be a long stretch of work with one hour, halfway through, given over to prayer and contemplation. Work once more and then the last gathering before the final meal, which was merely bread and water, and then a few minutes of readings before bed.

Bega led by example. It would have shamed her to admit it, but the organisation of her tiny settlement absorbed her at least as much as her spiritual duties. It was she who bartered with the farmers who brought their rents in kind. She who went to get the seed, to see some of the oats and barley through the primitive water-mill of her neighbouring farmer. The rest was done by herself and the nuns with a quern and grindstone.

For most of the first year they relied on the rent paid in kind. The sheep and goats later ensured the supply of milk and cheese and buttermilk, the two cattle were being fattened up for winter as were the pigs and geese and ducks and hens. Eggs thickened out the diet and there was, in the early years, enough game and fish to ensure they were rarely short of meat, although sometimes it was too high for Bega to eat.

But the basis of the household economy, Bega knew, was bread. Her father had kept the key to the bread larder on his belt. His wife, Una, had to ask him for it each time she wanted to take some loaves and return to him with both key and the loaves she had requested. To hold the key to the bread store was to hold the key to authority. Bega immediately partitioned off a part of the stone-built household for the bread and set about planting for a crop of oats and barley.

One of the older nuns from Whitby was especially efficient at sifting the meal, which would be ground fine and then bolted through various grades of cloth which not only got rid of the bran but also caught the small spiders and the flour moths. The oats fared best but Bega was determined to obtain good loaves. She made both unleavened and leavened bread, finding the yeast for the latter both in the air itself and in the ferment of mead and water.

At Whitby, just before Bega left, Hilda had built a bakehouse. Bega's finances did not run to that and one of the women baked the loaves on a flat pan over the fire. Oaten bread was rarer than Bega would have liked but barley bread with butter or honey was a serviceable substitute.

In these first invigorating years, it seemed that food was plentiful. The weather, though wet, was kind to growth. The harvests were adequate. The goats and ewes and cows gave enough milk; the small surplus was sensibly bartered. Two of the workmen stayed on permanently and formed households with the two women and it was they who milked the animals; their women made the butter, cheese and buttermilk. One of the women turned out to have luck with the cheese. She knew how to introduce the flower of the wild thistle or the seeds of safflower to curdle the

milk. Unknown to Bega, she worked charms on the milk pails
by laying lupins across the top or binding cockle and cress and
saying words which would have troubled Bega's Christian soul.
But it was in her hands that their good fortune lay.

With all the butter she needed for cooking or for adding to
vegetables, and bread enough, Bega had the foundation of her
principality.

She built up a small, balanced farm, sufficient for their modest
needs. The men took care to graze the animals on good grass in
spring and summer. In autumn and winter a proportion would
be slaughtered. Almost nothing was left unused. Bega made sure
that even the bones were split for the marrow extract; the offal
was given to the four Pictish slaves sent by Cuthbert to add their
strength to the community. The bones themselves were used in
soup and every ounce of fat or grease was jealously preserved.
Twice a day she patrolled the stores, measuring everything.

It was convenient to find oak nearby for it provided the best
fuel for smoking the meat. She had learned how to do all this
in her father's house. Some was just hung in the huts about the
perpetual fires and smoked hard and steadily for weeks. Some of
the fish was also smoked and so were the birds brought down with
a slung stone, an arrow or sometimes one of the sharper, lighter,
hunting spears.

When she contemplated her first winter, adequately stocked,
cereal crops and beans and mushrooms dried out, apples and
herbs neatly stored, some cheese and butter well buried, yeast
grown for the ale, Bega gave thanks. The greatest expense had
been the salt but she made an exchange with the itinerant salter.
She was one of the few in the valley who could afford him. He
rubbed the hams with a mixture of common salt, saltpetre and
honey. They were rubbed twice a week – after he had left – for
a month, then soaked for twenty-four hours and hung up to dry.
What she could not afford by this method, she salted down in
the more common way – soaking in brine and then dry-salting
in loose salt before hanging up.

Although Bega managed to buy enough storage jars for fruit,
she had to take the bulk of her grain and peas and beans to the
nearest of the farms. This was where the threshing was done and,
for a reduction in his rent, the farmer stored what belonged to
Bega. She had her own cellarage dug out for the root vegetables.

She solved the long-term problem of the salt by an alliance with that same farm which had its supply brought up every month or so from the coast.

She was particularly proud of the woodshed which she had built and double-thatched. The slaves had children and their ceaseless task – on top of the weeding and helping with the milling and feeding the fire – was to gather up any branch or scrap of wood they could hunt out. Bega had made an earth oven and to heat up the baking stones needed several adult armfuls of wood.

At Whitby they had started the two main meals of the day, on Hilda's insistence, with a soup or broth. Bega copied that habit. Pea soup and bean soup were most common and, less frequently, carrot broth and mint broth or an oats-based pottage. In the slave quarters and even in the huts of the freemen, there would be a stew cauldron on all day, forever added to and subtracted from as advantage and need dictated. With these broths and a sufficiency of eggs, the diet she organised would be adequate even if there were a faltering in the meat and fish. But bread, bread, bread was the mark of the true provider, which Bega never forgot.

Everything was flavoured with herbs, especially wild garlic. To Bega's annoyance, she had to stock her herb garden almost entirely from cuttings given with lazy and amused generosity by Reggiani. Bega had seen Reggiani's priestly 'services' and she was very disappointed that she could not budge this influential woman from her old ways. Reggiani's household – once Bega got to know it – turned out to be more numerous than that of Bega. The crude huddle of buildings near her own well-sited house was wholly dependent on her. Some of the inhabitants were curious and rather frightening. They showed vivid scars and marks, some were twisted in limbs and alarming of face, but all were devoted to Reggiani and prepared to work from sun up to sun down at anything she asked.

From Reggiani at first Bega took some culinary herbs – sage, rosemary, sorrel, thyme – golden, broad-leaved and lemon – lovage, chervil and pennyroyal. Reggiani also insisted on her taking some of the aromatic herbs – fennel, wood sage, marjoram, mint and parsley. At one time, in the first few months, when both Bega's helping women were ill with head-fever and cold, she brought over various medicinal herbs – betony, wormwood, plantain, hyssop, valerian, toadflax and skirret – but Reggiani's attempt to advise on the layout of the herb garden met with no matching generosity in Bega, who could not wish her off the property fast enough. As soon as she had gathered honey from her hives and decided there was some excess, she sent over a slave with the gift by way of payment, and to wash her hands of any obligation. Seductive as Reggiani was, her authority came from sources and gods which were the enemies of the one God. Bega needed to make clear the gulf and the separation between them.

The wood-stockaded herb garden, once it got under way, gave her more pleasure than any other place. When needed, if she was not at prayer or on a specific task she would announce after the morning prayers, she would be in the herb garden, usually on her knees in another sort of devotion.

After about three years she decided to build a proper rampart around what had become a miniature cross between Whitby and her father's household. She would have denied that she was imitating Reggiani in this, but she had observed the rampart around Reggiani's settlement. From the first the men had dragged in long branches and hawthorn and stone to effect a rather makeshift defence against the intrusion of wild animals. Wolves were the greatest danger and some nights the hills rang with their howls and the answering nervous boasts from the dogs on guard. There were also wild cats of a legendary viciousness and the never absent fear of nighttime monsters, raiding strangers, ghosts, loose and evil spirits, imps, devils and indescribable assailants from the dark.

The men brought stones from the lake shore and rocks from the mountain slopes. A deep earth pit dug in soft pasture land provided the body and weight which built up its height until all but the thatched roof of the main building was overtopped. On the outside breast of the wall, thorn branches were scattered and thorn bushes were planted there and on the top itself. There were two small doors – wide enough for an ox, tall enough for a man, but with no extravagance of extra width and height. It was a task done at the end of winter and Cuthbert's four slaves proved invaluable.

Despite Bega's wish to be part of what was around her, she found, like others in religious foundations, that her life was more like that of the better off than the masses. The original endowment had been for a larger monastery, hence the comparative ease with which Bega could afford most of what she wanted. It was now very clear to her, in a way in which it had not quite been before, that men such as Cuthbert and Wilfrid had to get money and resources from the wealthy to construct such monasteries. As she herself went into the world and bargained and bartered, she appreciated that the spiritual life had to be supported. She saw that this could make you hard and seem at odds with a divine mission.

In the case of Erebert, the support was slight and needed few resources but even those had to be found, initially, and replenished by gifts. In the case of a big monastery such as the one currently being built at Ripon, or those at Melrose or Whitby, considerable grants of land, substantial holdings of farms, the rents of which went back into the religious foundation and if possible regular gifts from Christian nobles – all were necessary.

It was even possible for her to understand that the essential piety and humility of Cuthbert and the selfless fearless proselytising and search for a Christian empire on the part of Wilfrid simply had to co-exist with a ruthless, tormented and entrepreneurial life which could distort the character. The price of the double life could be high: hence the strained jealousy and partially thwarted avarice of Cuthbert or the eruptive fantasies of Wilfrid. Now that she herself was having to manage a double life – the one to knit her soul to heavenly perfection, the other to force this small nunnery into a secure and productive existence – Bega found more sympathy for Cuthbert and Wilfrid and more love and admiration for the apparently untroubled Colman than she could express.

There was the cross, too. She understood increasingly why Cuthbert had needed it so desperately. She knew why he needed her to conceal her possession of it. She forgave him. This small fortress of Christ which she looked down on from the little height of the nearby point, this tiny nunnery bulwarked against man and beast and need, her own place, a patch of bare ground now turned into a domestic economy, a holy receptacle, a testament to God, this was Cuthbert's way of repayment. She offered it to God. It was His bounty, His gift through His blessed Cuthbert. Thanks be to God.

For all of this Bega had leaned most heavily on Chad. His physical strength from the years of ceaseless labouring at Whitby was equal to that of anyone. His knowledge of vegetables and herbs, of animals and the chancy art of sowing seed, had saved many a project. He worked as if only the most intensive effort every daylight minute was acceptable to Bega. For it was Bega whom he aimed to please. Just as Cal would pound up to her full of irresponsible affection, so Chad, in his own way, loved her indiscriminately and chose to express it in working for her with such fervour that his passion could not go unnoted. Nor did it. She encouraged him. He worked even harder. She praised him before others. He drove himself to the finger-end limits of his young strength. She wanted to reward him.

Yet when she suggested that he might undertake some elementary training to see if he could become a monk, he would not hear of it. His love for Bega was such that, he thought, he was for ever disqualified from a vocation. It was impure and God would see that. Years of restraint had become habit but at night, that other self of St Augustine drove him into delirious guilt.

Although Bega made strict division between male and female and gave her few nuns schedules and, literally, pathways that kept them clear of the men, it was a small settlement and there was always passing contact. Bega saw the rise of colour in Chad's face when the servant women whispered out a quick tease as they crossed his path. She could see his ardour towards herself. But it was filial, she thought.

Yet she could see there was a sense in which Chad was the most isolated in the community. The nuns had a common purpose and, driven by Bega to whom Hilda had given authority, they maintained themselves in a compact coherent routine of prayer, visiting, and work. The workmen and their wives were again a small community, knowing that the responsibility for the viability of the settlement rested on their skills, however able a leader Bega might be. The slaves were another group forced to be cohesive. Even the local labourers who came for special work on a piecemeal basis were a clan, a clan of strangers. Chad stood alone. As alone as Bega. When she perceived that, she took time to think and pray about what she could do.

One late afternoon in summer, when she was writing on a page of vellum made by Chad and herself, she felt his presence burning behind her shoulder. Often he watched her, but she had never felt him so concentrated. Without looking round, she said, 'What is it you want?'

'I'm sorry.'

'No, Chad. If I sound severe it is because I must not take my eyes off this while I am writing. But I can still talk. What *is* it you want?'

'To watch you.' Chad blurted this out scarlet-faced.

'What about your work?'

'I will go back to it now.'

'No.' Bega was firm. 'Why do you want to watch?'

Chad hesitated. But his experiences with Bega had built up a trust and now he trusted her with what was closest and dearest to his heart.

'I wanted to learn,' he said, 'to write and to read.'

'You can say DEUS,' she said, smiling, 'and one or two others by now.'

'Yes,' said Chad, steadily, 'but not enough. I want to learn so that I can read everything.'

'Why do you want to do this?' she asked.

'Because you do.'

The directness of the response almost stung Bega. How could she have neglected this longing?

She laid aside her goose-quill and turned to him.

'Come with me,' she said.

They went outside and across the compound to the gate which led out to the lakeside. Chad was half a pace behind her as she walked down to the shore. It was a balmy late afternoon. The light was yellow, the sun lazily warm behind a gauze of clouds, the lake still. She looked around for a few moments and then began to gather some reeds.

Chad helped her immediately.

'That's enough,' she said. 'We can leave some for another day.'

Bega found a flat and well-cropped length of grass and began to lay out the reeds, twisting and forming them so that they became the letters of the alphabet.

Then she took Chad down the line, pointing to each letter and pronouncing it.

She did that three times and then asked him to do it.

Soon he was able to recite them. Bega smiled with pleasure at his retentive memory. She then pointed to this and that letter out of order and of course he floundered, but not for long. She made him do it backwards, from the middle, from an arbitrarily called letter, every other letter and so on.

She then picked out four of the letters and asked him to form them from the reeds himself, which he did.

'What do they say?' she asked.

He said the words of the letters.

'Dee. Eee. Yuu. Ess.'

'Good,' said Bega. 'Now say it more rapidly.'

'Dee Eee Yuu Ess!'

'Faster!'

'DeeEeeYuuEss.'

'Faster still! Faster!'

'Deeyuss . . . Deus! DEUS!'

He turned to her with such a wide, irresistibly joyous smile that she felt blessed.

'Deus,' she repeated quietly, 'yes. One day, Chad, you will write on vellum.'

From that afternoon he began to take regular lessons. Eventually, after much persuasion that he would not spoil or damage precious vellum, he drew his first few strokes on the scraps discarded when the pages were finally cut. As he did so, she felt such a sensation of thanks and completeness come from him that she believed God had led her to uncover what could be a true vocation. And Chad felt that Bega had completed his love for her.

Some weeks later, she stood on the rise of ground above her settlement, again in the late-afternoon of a day of showers. Chad pushed out a small boat from the spot where he had first learned from the reeds. It was a good time to look for trout. Her eyes looked with almost sinful affection on the place she had built and which she ruled. Beyond it, down the length of the lake flanked with great mountains were yet more and more heights, some fuming with light, white, vaporous clouds more like mist. In the meadows cattle and sheep lowered their heads, grazing steadily.

Bega felt that she had truly begun work for God. As so often, her fingers sought out the small wrapped fragment of the cross and she thanked God for guiding and helping her.

Her eyes swung over towards the nearby big and fearful mountain. She picked out the clearing below the woods and Reggiani's settlement. From there she saw a man walking towards her abbey. He seemed to float over the water-shimmering meadows. His hair tailed out behind him. The warm wind came off the lake towards him and lifted his cloak. The westering sun caught the metal on his belt and torque and the hilt shine of his sword.

Bega felt her breath coming in shallower and shallower mouthfuls. Her body seemed as if it were suddenly without weight. She wanted to race towards this figure. The nearer he strode, the more she longed to fly to him and yet her feet would not move. They had put down roots of fear. Without looking left or right, without increasing or breaking his pace, he came across the fields towards the lake, towards her household.

Her mouth opened to seek for air to soothe the dryness in her throat. Behind her eyes tears pushed their way forward through memory and denial.

It was him.

It was him.

She began to walk, to hurry, to run, to race, to hurl herself towards him.

CHAPTER FORTY-SEVEN

Before she reached him, Bega had managed to compose herself to walk in a seemly enough manner towards his urgently striding figure. They met beyond her settlement in the open meadow near to the lake and, just as an outside force had seemed to lead her forward to meet him, so a force of equal authority slowed them down to a stop. They stood a few paces apart.

Padric saw the mischievous wild young girl he had left now become a woman striking in her aspect of independence. The dark exciting colour was back in her face. The hair, still black and red streaked in unruly luxuriance, shone as it had done when he had first met her. The sharp face had filled out a little and a settledness, even a serenity relaxed her features into a less singular but even more striking form. The so lightly blue, pale eyes still flickered; with amusement? Delight? A secret? She made him want to smile, which he did, and to hold out his arms and embrace her, which he did not.

Bega saw a harder man. Immediately she noticed the purple and blood-puckered gash on the back of his hand and saw in every detail of his dress the character of a warrior. The sword, the dagger, the shield slung around his back, the loose leather breastplate, all announced a fighting man on permanent alert. He had broadened. His skin too had darkened. His hair was still long and roughly pushed back from his forehead. His smile made her remember so much that had been so patiently buried. She wanted to step forward and hold out her hands to him and feel his flesh on hers. But did not.

'It was Reggiani who told me you were here,' he said, eventually.

'Ah.' Bega nodded.

'We see her,' he continued, 'now and then. When we come to these parts.' He did not mention the weapons hidden in the woods.

Bega nodded and turned towards the lake. Had she always known that this was a place he visited? Or had it been because of the association with Erebert's island on the neighbouring lake? Or was this no more than a coincidence and a temptation? There was a fallen beech near the shore, stripped by now of most of its branches, a suitably isolated seat. She walked towards it and Padric fell in alongside her. Although she was not as tall as he, their steps synchronised. The coincidence of rhythm made her feel a sudden steep dizzying upsweep of happiness.

'Reggiani has been very helpful,' said Bega, rather woodenly, determined to give Reggiani her due.

'She is a remarkable woman,' he replied.

'But not a Christian.'

'She will not see what we see. But a time will come.'

They had reached the fallen trunk and found a length on which both of them could sit. There had been no question but that they would go together and talk together. Those who had seen them had watched the flow of their movements in an inevitable bond. No one would dare approach or interrupt them. Even as the afternoon drew into the evening and Bega was not about her usual work and Padric absent from his war band hidden in the woods, they were left alone. And Bega and Padric noticed nothing but each other, in talk, in silence, knowing somehow that this was a rare, possibly a unique time together.

'I have not been back here for some years,' said Padric. 'But others come and go. Reggiani has been useful to us.' Well rewarded, he did not add. Nor did he mention the hold that Urien had over her and she over him.

'We use these woods,' he said. 'They are a place where we can gather in some numbers and in some secrecy.'

'Reggiani has powers,' Bega admitted, mysteriously relieved of her anxiety by the neutrality of his tone.

'She sees famine,' said Padric, 'in the portents and in the messages from her own gods. She sees a great famine about to arrive.'

'But the land has not been so unkind. In the three years I have been here we have known the blessing of the Lord in crops and fish, milk. It is true that we here are,' she hesitated but only for a moment, 'richer than the others. Cuthbert saw to that.'

'Yes,' Padric nodded. 'And Reggiani told me that you had organised the settlement very cleverly. No doubt her gods are wrong about the famine.'

'Maybe she wants to make her gods seem more important than Our Lord by trying to frighten the people.'

'A famine would do more than frighten the people here,' said Padric. 'My father once told me that the last famine devastated them. Already we are fewer than the invaders. With their several wives and their ceaseless immigration from other tribes across the sea, they grow in numbers every year. Every year it gets more difficult for us and yet we cannot strike until we are ready.'

As he spoke, Bega saw that the idealistic young man had been hardened into a campaigner.

'Oswy is a strong king,' she said. 'And he is not altogether unjust.'

'But he will not live for ever. Ecfrith will somehow become king and Ecfrith wishes to destroy Rheged. He cannot endure the Britons. Not what we are, not the glory that we were nor the hope that we may be great again.'

'Why are you so sure about what he wants to do?'

To Bega, Ecfrith was of the family which supported Whitby and Hilda, and fed the force of expansion represented by Wilfrid. And Ecfrith was not too proud to seek out a blessing from Cuthbert.

'Penraddin, my sister, was his mistress. We rescued her some years ago and now she fights with us. We took her with us over the sea. We know him from her.'

Bega's heart lurched: 'Fights with us'. She saw herself in the war band led by Padric, armed and armoured, sweeping across the country to the field of battle, shoulder to shoulder with warriors she loved as she loved the warrior in her father. What a life that must be. What a fate.

Padric looked at her and she was held firm in the hardness of his glance.

'There will be no mercy from Ecfrith,' he said. 'He wants to wipe us from the earth. I will die to prevent that. We cannot let them win.'

In front of them, across the lake, as if in tune, a full yellow sun began to gather the light into itself as it slid slowly down the wide, scarce-cloud-disturbed sky. Behind them were the thickening woods and the coarse caws of the crows, as if the dark forces of Ecfrith were hidden there. They watched the sun dragging down the light over the earth's edge.

Padric began to talk with a hope and an enthusiasm which captured Bega's imagination.

'We came back from Little Britain in the boat of the king of Mann. From there we went to Ireland where I met a man that I could accept as king of the Northumbrians. God willing. He is the bastard son of Oswy, Ecfrith's half-brother, Aldfrid. His mother was a Celt. He is a man devoted to learning. He made me feel ashamed that I find so little time now to study and copy out the words of Christ.'

'You speak as if you envy him,' said Bega.

'You always knew what I thought.' He smiled sadly. 'I do.' His voice held a sorrow new to her.

'There are times when all of us doubt,' she said. 'Even Christ Himself.'

'Yes.'

'Great doubt can lead to stronger faith,' she said.

But the doubt was still there, lodged in him.

Would it have got through his guard had she been with him?

'Perhaps if we had married,' he said, reading her thoughts, 'these doubts would not be there. Already, speaking with you, I feel less oppressed by them.' He turned to her and met her gaze. He put his wounded hand on hers. For a moment which seemed far longer, they existed in the possibilities they had not realised. 'There is still time,' he said. 'If you want it.'

More than anything she had longed for, Bega wanted to have Padric put his arms around her. How could he not hear the keening of her need? How could she keep it buried in the chill cemetery of chastity? He needed her – he had said that. She could help a cause surely as blessed as any she would ever manage herself. She had very nearly died but God had spared her and Padric had been His messenger. She remembered the way he had lain down beside her and taken her in his arms.

His hand pressed on hers and that gentle pressure pushed down the plunger of memory and her body moved restlessly as it began to feed on the past. She saw them in that gloomy cave, the shadows on the ceiling, the snow blizzard outside, the miracle of warmth after the cold fear of their flight. He had lain beside her and held her and his body had given her the warmth that even the fire's flames could not supply. The grave that threatened her, the earth coffin promised by her father – from this she had been rescued by Padric's warmth, his breath, his hands.

And he had penetrated her.

'Padric,' she whispered. 'I know now.'

He had penetrated her. The knowledge swept through her body like a fast tide over a shore. She had been his. What was her life in God worth now?

He understood but waited. Bega leaned against him. Her body burned. For shame. In memory. A fire of remorse.

'Why did you not tell me?'

'You were ill,' said Padric, 'and I thought your silence meant that you wished to have no talk of what had happened in the cave.'

She wanted to brush her body down with hands first dipped in the coldest depths of the lake. Her lips trembled. Her throat was swollen and the words which came out hurt her.

'The vow I made,' she said, 'to be for ever chaste.' She paused. 'I *knew*,' she said, and swallowed. 'There was *something*. But what it was . . . It was what made me feel different from the others. I must have known, God must have been telling me that although I was chaste I was not whole. He must have been telling me but I would not listen. I was too proud to listen.'

'Or too full of fear,' said Padric.

Bega was grateful for his kindness but disinclined to be easy on herself. She must not cry. She must face this moment like a soldier. She must not cry.

'You were very ill,' said Padric. 'What happened to you in Ireland drove your senses out of you. On the journey you suffered so badly. I could see you wasting away. You were not in your right mind.'

Would Hilda have known? No. She could not have behaved to her in the open, even equal and privileged way that she did had she even suspected as much. And so Wilfrid would not have known either but the fact that her body had known lust made her understand more clearly that twist of passion between them.

'Cuthbert suspected,' she said, abruptly, and she shivered at that thought.

Padric remembered how he had clashed with Cuthbert and wondered again, as he had done before, whether it would have been better to have made peace with him. Aldfrid had gone some way to convincing him of Cuthbert's greatness.

'Cuthbert would tell no one,' he said. 'I am certain of that. He saw devils to be driven out and in the eyes of God he may have been right. There is no doubt of Cuthbert's passion for God. Perhaps he was moved to use you as an example of God's power.'

They fell silent for a while. The sunset was nearing its end. Yellow-orange light played over the lake and the dark hills across the water seemed to come nearer as the sun drew in its final powers.

Why had He let her discover it now?

It could only be to test her. There could be no other explanation.

What if she had stayed with Padric? Her imagination conjured up slender pathways through thick forests, the baying of wolves kept at their distance by the night fire fed constantly, the race into battle and the talking with allies sought in Ireland and the other Celtic redoubts. It was difficult to see her ordered life at Whitby being much more than a shadow of Padric's substance, wafer moon, as the one now rising behind her, to his fierce sun. Bega thought that her chances had passed, irrevocably.

What life could have been like with Padric!

Now, though, she would have to decide. His silence was waiting for her answer. Would she now join him? She was, God knew, his wife in truth. All she had to do was declare it.

If not her, then someone else? The weight of jealousy which she had held off over the years now came to torment her. He was hers! Who else could have him? Who had? If she were to reject him again – who would he find to replace her? This, the saltiest of the onrush of emotions she had experienced in such a short time, disturbed her the most.

'We ride tomorrow morning,' he said. 'We cannot stay here longer.'

'How many men ride with you?' Her mouth was dry. It seemed

to her that the question was almost a rehearsal – to make sure she had a voice to say what she needed to say.

'About fifteen,' he said, rather proudly. It was a good-sized war band. 'And some women.'

She saw the war band scavenging and bartering its way from one battleground to another, carrying the cross of Christ, fighting as His soldiers, dying with His grace, wheeling around the kingdom of the oppressed and the oppressors as Padric gathered and moulded and trained them. Oh that she could be with him there!

'I will have Penraddin bring you a sword,' said Padric, 'whatever you decide. If you stay—' his voice was quite steady, '—then it will be good protection. So few have swords around here and you can use it well. If you will be my wife, then . . .' He looked at her sternly. Suddenly he smiled and Bega's stomach leaped like a salmon.

'I will have to pray,' she said.

'I understand.'

He moved as if to leave her but she tugged his arm, wanting him to stay.

'Please,' she said. 'Not, just, yet.'

The sky was brushed by the first darkness. The lake lapped on the shore. The sound of crows and rooks circling the treetops, a silent kestrel gliding intently on a high current of air. Voices of the fishermen came across the lake. From the forest on the mountainside, the ringing chop of an axe on wood. It was a short time of deep loving peacefulness between them, when even their breathing rose and fell as one.

It was the time when the ghosts came out. Ghosts of soldiers from the Roman army, whom you could see if you knew where to look, marching down their roads which the Northumbrians were afraid to use. Ghosts of the Celts who had fought them and the giants who had wrenched the rocks from the mountains and hurled them down at the goblins who still lived in the reeds and thickets of the valleys. This was a time of bravado fires and scuttling the short distances home. Imps came out of the roots of trees and began to whizz through the dark looking to sting and frighten you and make you cry with alarm. It was the devil's time and all the vile spirits from the woods woke to his call – now like a wolf, now a jackal, now the long hoot of a screech owl. Charms were put out, old bones and other relics were made into circles outside the door. In some huts the God of Bega and Padric was prayed to alongside the others.

In Bega's chapel, the nuns were fearful that night, lonely without their mistress, praying for her safety with this mighty prince who had come to talk to her, wishing she could be with them to lead them through the last prayers of the day. For it was the hour of the ghosts for them too. Even the most pious of the nuns saw ghosts as they hurried from the tiny chapel to their sleeping quarters. Every day most of those who lived by the lake or by a stream or a waterfall would make an offering to the gods of water, those powerful gods of the Celts who would never die. All over this valley, the adjoining valleys, the length and breadth of Rheged, and further across country, to the north and south, as darkness put its grip on the world, the nightly battles began between life and death, between survival and extinction, between dreams and truth, and, for the Christians, between good and evil.

Padric and Bega ignored all the perils of the night and talked until the moon came up, flat bright in a velvet-blue sky. They talked of their past, of the childhood so far away now. They remembered commonplace incidents which were charged with such powerful attraction. She told him about Hilda and Wilfrid and understood both of them more deeply through the observations he made. He told her about Ireland and Cornwall and the Little Britain across the sea.

When, eventually, he rose to go, they seemed the only two people at large on the earth. The biggest of the mountains, massive, forever brooding as if about to stir to life, was finely outlined under the clear light of the moon. Their ears picked up the traffic of the woods, and the water lapping ceaselessly on the tideless shore. She stood and watched him walk away far beyond the point when the blackness captured him. But by straining she could see the occasional wisp of movement which was his cloak, the flutter of an animal which marked his passage, until he must have reached the woods and only then did she turn away.

Dear God, she thought, help this worthless servant. Dear Padric, she thought, I cannot believe you were here. She paced the moonlit shore for some time until, the turbulence of her feelings subdued by the habit of discipline, she was in the right mind to go to the chapel and pray for guidance.

chapter forty-eight

Padric paused as he came to the huddled settlement of huts which made a little principality for Reggiani. The dogs barked and he imagined Urien reaching out for his sword and listening fiercely. He smiled.

The longer they had ridden together, the more affection he felt for his younger brother. Urien's easy carelessness in everything but battle was wonderfully consistent. Nothing at all, it seemed, could put him out of his calm, mocking humour. When women were there and available he took them but he never forced it if they were not willing. He would discuss the details of a battle plan but cared little for the overall strategy – he was content to wander around the kingdoms of the island throughout his life, looking for trouble, living as a nomad. Apart from his weapons, his leather armour and his horse – all of which were well enough though not fanatically tended – he had no interest in wealth.

Urien loved to drink. Riderch could drink as heavily as any warrior was expected to and his big frame soaked it down. Padric had a cut-off point and although he would not back down from the drinking which figured so importantly and testingly in their lives, he usually managed to ease up at the right time and avoid drunkenness. Urien never eased up.

He loved all the declensions of drink. He loved the initiating ease, the first expansion of goodwill to all men, the physical glow of invulnerable well-being, the ever-increasing sense of special friendship and deeper friendship, the stories and the confessions and the boasts, the promises, the affirmation, the revelation of weakness and the hints of glory until the alcohol overcame him and he submitted happily, contentedly, to stupor. Then he was in that lake of unconsciousness but accompanied by friends, men who had fought with him, depended on him and he on them, seen blood spilt and felt fear together, and escaped death into this bliss-filled annihilation. To drink after a battle won, to drink into communal insensibility with men with whom the battle had been won, to be launched on a raft of mead or wine and beer into a sea of stories and heroic hopes, memories of escape and triumph, this to Urien was the completion of life.

Padric, who had controlled his feelings while with Bega, now felt a soaring of hope which called for companionship. While Bega and he had talked and she had rested on his shoulder, he had been as still as he could be. The lust he had felt had been checked. The urge to let her know how much he felt had been resisted. He had not told her of those days of misery when thoughts of her had blocked out the sun; nights when there did not seem space enough on the earth or among the stars to lose her and give him some peace. He was so struck by the fact that she was there, her head on his shoulder, her hair pressed against his cheek, the rise and fall of her breasts matched by his own breathing, this blunt actuality was enough.

But once he had peeled away from her, and walked from the lake towards the mountain, it was as if a blocked spring was suddenly cleared. 'Urien!' he called out softly into the moon-shadowed darkness. The dogs bayed and then stopped when they heard the voice of Reggiani.

Urien was carrying a large leather flask. 'You'll want to drink,' he stated, flatly. 'There'll be a good fire on Owain's patch.'

They walked into the woods in silence. Even in the darker life of the trees, the men walked surely. The years had made them woodsmen as well as warriors and little in the life of a forest took them by surprise. Moreover this was their forest. All over a broad span which ran along the edge of the valley and some way up the mountain was the stealthily camouflaged camp of the war band. There were pin-point pricklings of low fires. The bleat of the goats and sheep they took as stock and sustenance. The unmistakable movement of grouped horses with their short whinnying, the scuffle of their hooves. They would be there for one night and then move on.

The brothers found Owain's fire. Three men were sleeping around it. All of them were alert to the arrival of Padric and Urien but relaxed when they identified the men.

'We'll take some fire over there,' said Urien.

He took two platters of wood and carried some of the fire a comfortable distance away. Padric brought more wood to feed it. Wrapped in their long woollen cloaks they were warm enough as the night cooled down swiftly. They were hardened to cold as they were to periods of hunger.

Urien took a pull and handed it over. 'Strong,' he said. 'And full.'

Padric swallowed deeply. The wine seemed to speak, assuring him that everything was better than it had been possible to imagine.

'So she's well, then,' said Urien and the glow from the crack of birch in flame caught the mischief on his face. It was just the expression the newly-liberated Padric wanted.

'She is,' he agreed, and sucked happily on the stumpy spout of the sack of wine.

'I was wondering when you would meet up with her again,' said Urien, reaching out for the wine.

'Were you?'

Padric was delighted to be so easily diagnosed by his brother. What he wanted — most uncharacteristically — was any excuse to talk at last and at length about someone he had dungeoned for years.

'I told no one about her,' he maintained, weakly.

'There was no need,' said Urien.

Padric's smile broadened. 'If it was so obvious, then why did no one mention it?'

'The way you behaved was always down to a woman. And there was only the one woman who fitted.'

'So what was I like?'

'Oh . . .' Urien was almost as pleased as Padric himself. Rarely if ever had he found his brother in this playful, rather soft, mood. Padric was so aware of being the leader, always aware of the objectives, the dangers, the cause above all that they were fighting for. Now he was clay. Urien loved him for it.

'We would be passing a nunnery and you would look at it with a terrible interest! Or there would be the stories you would tell of Ireland and Cathal and the O'Neills, but never about her, although I always felt that she was the reason for telling the story in the first place.'

'There was all that time of not saying,' Padric began. 'I could not understand why it was so painful. There would be periods in the day, sometimes a whole day, when I would not think about her but then it would come back, with twice the force, as when you are wounded and you know you must fight twice as hard.'

'What came back?'

'Her. Just her. It was sometimes the memory of how she looked, or how she felt or what she had said . . . more often it was just her, like a spirit let loose inside my own. It was as if she haunted me: a spirit or a ghost.'

'And a woman too,' said his brother.

'Yes. When I saw her and touched her just now I knew that I had always wanted her for my wife.'

'Will she accept you?'

'I hope so.' Padric believed that she would and the cautious choice of his words could not keep the elation out of his manner.

'It will not be the first time that a woman has left a nunnery,' said Urien.

'She was only a girl when she was taken in there. She was sick. I should never have left her. Cuthbert saw her as a great soul to conscript into his army. Now I cannot blame him. He takes what he can when it presents itself. He is as ruthless for souls as I must be for this land. He knows that to be a true fisher of men you have to be hard. He is hard on himself. And he is hard on everyone else. I was too young to stand up to him. Of course she can leave.'

Padric's certainty and even brusqueness in reply was partly owing to the steep rise in confidence afforded by the wine and partly, the shrewd Urien sensed, because of uncertainty.

'It's good to see you like this,' he said.

'I am glad no one else sees me like this,' said Padric, taking yet another pull of wine.

'It would do you no harm,' Urien replied.

Padric did not respond. Urien was wrong but he was in no mood to contradict his young brother for whom he felt nothing but love.

'How are the men?' Padric asked, rather as if he had been neglecting them.

'Well enough.' Urien was disappointed that this private talk had switched back to such ordinary matters.

'What do they expect now?'

'Well,' said Urien, pouring in the wine, 'not the great battle. You have warned them often enough that that is years and years away. But they want to get at the Northumbrians somehow. Soon. They don't care how many they face. Ecfrith has been boasting that we dare not face him. He still refuses to accept that we were the warriors who killed his raiding party. He says that two score cowards from Rheged surrounded his men and took away the weapons so that no one should see the blood on the Northumbrian swords and daggers. Our men are impatient to meet his best men.'

'They may have to wait.'

'Then they will have to wait,' said Urien. 'I'll get some more wine.'

'Let's talk no more about battles,' said Padric, when Urien returned.

'Tell me more about this woman, then,' said Urien, obligingly.

'What is a woman for?' said Padric, philosophical in his unaccustomed mellow drunkenness.

'Do I have to tell you?'

Padric nodded, a little ponderously.

'Lust,' said Urien, firmly. Then he thought for a while. 'And one or two can be good in battle,' he added, with a stiff sense of fairness in his tone.

Both of them thought of Penraddin. It had not taken her long to seize the occasion of an unexpected and uneven skirmish to prove that she was fit to be her brothers' sister. From then on she had insisted that, though she would organise the cooking and the domestic repairs, she would ride and fight with the men.

'Bega would have been fine in any battle.'

Urien nodded. He had no opinion either way on women as warriors. It was not as warriors that they interested him.

'And children: boys,' said Urien, eventually. 'Some day we will have children. When we have settled these scum. Will she be good for that?'

'Yes,' he replied, 'she would.'

'And warmth,' said Urien, finally. 'On a night like this. Better than a fire.' He took another gulp of wine and handed it over. 'But *not* better than wine *and* a fire. And not in the same breath as wine and a fire and a comrade.'

Padric drank and then sighed deeply.

'Will she come with you?'

'Oh yes.' Padric's voice seemed to stumble up from somewhere deep in the pit of his lungs. 'Oh yes, now that she knows about the cave, it was, why didn't I, you should, *I* should never have let her go, gone without her.' Urien did not understand a word of what his brother said, but he was delighted by that. Such intimate incoherence was the stuff of true drinking friendship. Padric took an ultimate and mighty pull of wine which, temporarily, shuddered him to a certain clarity. 'With her, Urien, we will win. We have no Merlin. We have no other magician. We do not need them, you say.' Urien was about to protest that he had said nothing but he stopped himself. It was far too much fun watching his utterly admirable, upright and fearless leader of a brother crumple like a leaf in a flame and begin the slump which would end in cramped and toxic unconsciousness. 'We have God. But they think they have God. We know they have God but not in their hearts. But we need. She is, has, something she has, makes her so valuable, without price, to us. She could bring us all the victories we need, Urien.'

To this last sentence, Urien paid his full attention. He was far from drunk and could recognise a deep conviction and separate it from the chaff of pleasantly poisoned rambling.

'Could she?'

'She could.'

'Then you must take her,' said Urien, soberly, seriously. 'You *must* make her come with us.'

'She will,' said Padric, beaming as Urien had not seen him beam since he had been a small boy. 'She will. Don't you see?'

Here Padric waved his right hand upwards, indicating the clear almost full sculpted moon, the harvest of bright silver stars, the inevitability of the divine law. 'Don't you see?' he repeated, murmuring to himself, and crumpled into sleep.

Urien sat over him for a while feeling uniquely protective of his older brother. Though he followed him, he always reserved a little doubt. Now he saw someone riven. He respected that.

He listened to the noises of the night. He loved this time. The spirits that haunted the dreams of men and women and frightened them were enjoyed by this warrior. Urien truly revelled in feeling that there were imps and genies abroad. He picked up the scuffling of a pair of wild cats, luxuriated in the hooting of an owl and heard with delight the whoosh of its wings as it sped towards its prey. Urien felt part of all that.

Should he go back to Reggiani? The recollected sense of her full, smooth flesh and the uninhibited foraging for sex was a strong temptation. But he let it hover as a possibility. To sit and finish the wine, stir up the fire in what was still the dead of night and watch over the unaccustomed contented stupor of his brother was enough.

Urien let his mind wander. All about the populous valley were people and animals asleep while the spirit world took wing. His own Christianity had not wholly conquered the pagan Reggiani's idea of spirits. Sometimes, for instance, he would stand, on a day of rain, well covered in his thick cloak, and be mesmerised by the sight and sound of rain on the water; the rain on the sea; the rain on a lake; the rain on a stream. He would look up and see the clouds untroubled by the deluge they had let loose and his mind and spirit would become numbed in a trance of understanding. Understanding what, he could not hope to explain. But there was a sense of rightness about the way of the water, a sense which he never drew from Christianity.

He sipped the wine at a more moderate pace. He too had somehow slipped into a state of drunkenness. He let his senses stretch like a bat's wings to encompass the movements in the night. He let the restless, unloosed spirits, pagan and Christian alike, come to him out of the darkness. Soon he would be with them, he thought, smiling to himself contentedly, striding soon enough towards a glorious death in battle.

CHAPTER FORTY-NINE

Bega kneeled for some hours before she allowed herself to think about Padric. She called on all the spiritual exercises which she had learned at Whitby. She emptied her mind of everything to allow the will of God to enter in. She murmured the simplest prayers: she concentrated her thoughts on Christ on the cross. When the image of Padric crept in to overlay that of Christ she bent to her task even more determinedly and only began again with her preparations when Padric had faded away.

In time she became satisfyingly uncomfortable. Her legs were shot with pains. The cold which attacked her rigid form was eating into her. A pain across her brow, which she knew to be the working of the devil, blocked her from a clear and Christian address to the crisis she faced. The battle was joined. Not for nothing had Hilda spoken of their heavenly warfare. Cuthbert too maintained that it was fought on the same terms as any earthly warfare.

Bega knew that she could not do this alone. In the pitch black of the windowless chapel where only a little moonlight crept under the door, she called up those who could give her help. Images of Cathleen and Donal attempted to materialise before her but they were like paintings long faded under a hot sun. There was no more strength there, nor any colour to their faces. They came like ghosts who wished her well but their power had gone and when she reached out to grasp them, nothing but a passing scent of their support remained.

She invoked Cuthbert but his presence was so implacable that she took it on herself to discard him and turned to the stories of one he admired, Aidan. Aidan, first abbot of Lindisfarne, a true Celtic monk, humble, indomitable, beloved of God.

Bega brooded on the miracles which had flowed from Aidan.
She did not know why God directed her thoughts this way but
as Aidan was a most holy man, then she must be thankful that
He had chosen to fill her mind with the miracles He had shown
through his agency.

She had been truly alone very little in her life and although she
had felt lonely and heartsick, she had always felt that others, in
the name of a higher force, were looking after her.

Now, in the black night of the chapel, scarcely able to hear a
sound save the sharp sudden cry of a beast or a bird, with only the
few mean rays of moonlight for company, she was on her own.

What was she to do?

She was not whole. In fear and yet with a certain warm
excitement, she knew that she was not a virgin.

But she had thought herself to be a maiden and in that
conviction offered herself to Christ.

Had He known? And if so, why had He welcomed her to the
novitiate and then to the full glory of being a nun?

Was it possible that a devil inside her could have concealed it
from Him as the fact had been concealed from her?

If so, who was that devil? Where was he now? Was it Padric?

The darkness of the chapel was pricked by a sliver of moonlight
which slid through a small hole in the east wall. Bega became
transfixed by it. The closer she looked, the more the light
played, voluptuously twisting itself and eventually assuming a
shape which became defined though never wholly clear. Yet it
was unmistakable. Bega felt her heart shift with glad relief and
her body reached out in hope.

It was the Abbess Hilda, sent as a spirit.

'It was not a betrayal,' said Hilda. Of course. Hilda would
instruct her. Bega turned. The moonray lit up the face and
neck and steeple-pressed hands of the abbess. 'The devil made
you so ill on your journey that you were about to die. He was
full of envy because you had the True Cross. That is why it
was so clever to give part of it to Cuthbert. For Cuthbert
in the power of his virtue can defend the cross against all
the snares of the enemy. By taking it into his own body and
lodging it behind his soul he can ensure that it withstands
all the assaults that the evil one may try to bring against it.'
Hilda spoke solemnly and as if from somewhere further away

than she appeared. But Bega felt her presence as real as her own.

'You are now being tempted once again. Previously the force against you was strong but you were weak in God. You were uncertain. You were a child. You would have died with your work undone – the work of the cross – unless Padric had helped you. But the devil, fearing that he would be defeated, overwhelmed Padric and the warmth became his sex. But God made you once more like a virgin through the intervention of the holy Cuthbert. And it was as such that you came to me.'

'Why did I not know?'

'God must have His reasons.'

'Why was I allowed to deceive others – and you?'

'There has to be a purpose for you. If it is not yet clear to you then that may be because you have not made yourself worthy enough or because the time has not arrived to declare the mystery of the purpose.'

'Is marriage to Padric my purpose? It is to Padric I was wedded before I took my vows to Christ. Those vows now seem false. Padric is doing God's work. Perhaps God was telling me to marry Padric, but then He decided that I needed first to be more fitted for the task ahead and so He led me to your house, to Whitby, to be disciplined and taught as only you can.'

'Is this you talking, Bega, or is it the devil in you?'

'How can I know?'

'You can know by judging the lust in your heart and weighing it against the love in your soul. Do you lust after this man Padric?'

Bega was silent for a while. Her stiff, cramped body, its shooting pains, the singing cut inside her head, the cold nibbling at the flesh, all made a barrier against lust.

'Yes,' she replied, 'I do.'

'You gave vows believing yourself to be a virgin,' said Hilda. 'I too believed that. So did all who received you into our house. Remember that it is not necessary to be a virgin. That is a high state for which not all are fitted. There are those whom God seeks out after they have lost their wholeness in marriage. What you swore was to be a bride of Christ alone and to be chaste and faithful to Him for the rest of your earthly life.'

'I can marry Padric and still be chaste. That is done.'

'It is. But you have confessed to lust.'

'You are saying I should not go with Padric.'

'You are wedded to Christ.'

'Was I not first wedded to Padric?'

'Not in the eyes of God.'

'But God must have known.'

'To know is not to approve.'

'He must have let it happen.'

'The author of all evil can stand between God and ourselves.'

'What if I proclaim my lust?'

'Then we will pray for it to diminish. All of us know lust. To give up the world for God is not to be immune from the vices of the world. On the contrary, it is to make oneself available to be a bigger target for the armies of evil. We who are sworn to practise no vice must feel the onset of the vice, the pressure and temptation of the vice a hundredfold. The enemy comes out into the open. We let him tear at us. We test his appetite with our patience, thanks be to God. But listen, Bega, as your dream of me is ending, listen. God has given you a sign. You must interpret it correctly. I have no doubt that you are a bride of Christ. I have no doubt. Listen to me.' The voice faded. 'Listen to me. Listen . . .'

Slowly the vision began to disappear. Bega felt a chill of loneliness: she reached out for it but it could not be touched. Then it was gone.

Bega was lying flat, face pressed to the cold earth floor. When the swoon had ebbed away, she tried to kneel again but her legs were in too much agony and would not obey her. She rolled on to her back and stared towards the roof beyond which was Heaven.

'Oh Lord, who sent Hilda to this unworthy servant, tell me what I must do. I have been sent a sign – the appearance here of Hilda herself is such a sign. But, God forgive me, I do not want to do what she urges me to do.'

As she said this, a force of giddiness seized her mind and she felt that it swung and spun and swirled around her head, around the chapel, and the valley, the island, the seas and lands of God and a voice shouted, 'Ungrateful! Who are you to deny the gift of God? Wretch! Worse than pagan slave!'

Yet despite Hilda's visitation, despite this spinning as it were under the thumb of an angry God, Bega still clung on to her will to be with Padric, or to be near him if nothing else.

When they came in for lauds, they found her spreadeagled before the altar, stiff. At first they feared that she might be dead. Then the oldest of the nuns, Eafled, kneeled down beside her and began to chafe her hands, commanding all the others to pray. Between chafing the cold stiff hands, Eafled pressed her kindly, warty face on to the unblemished, unusually white, cold face of Bega. She breathed her own hot breath from large sacks of lungs over the immobile leader of their small community. The voices of the nuns filled the chapel with prayer and, Sister Eafled was later to say, it was the sincerity of the prayer and not the poor exercise she herself performed which was to bring back their inspiration.

Bega opened her eyes. She saw the large tremulous face of Eafled and attempted a smile. It hurt her to smile. It hurt her to move. But she forced herself to sit up, helped by Eafled against whom she rested while she looked with some amazement at the weeping and ecstasy of her small band of nuns.

'Why were you afraid?' was what she wanted to say, but no words came out.

But they saw the attempt to speak and redoubled their thanks. Some prostrated themselves, others wrung their hands to heaven. Eafled drew deep breaths to calm the panic she had felt.

Bega attempted to stand but it was as if her legs had no connection with her body. Eafled let her down gently and then put her powerful hands on either side of the solid frozen feet and burned some blood and warmth into them. The tingling and pinpricks which raced up and down Bega's legs were not acknowledged. She had learned how to endure such cramps and aches in silence.

Eventually she stood up.

Alleluias were raised.

She refused to leave for her own quarters but insisted on saying lauds with her community. Only after that did she allow herself to be helped out into an unpromising, truculent dawn and taken over to her hut. They brought her bread and skimmed milk. She took a little milk and only one or two mouthfuls of bread and then asked them all to leave.

She got out of her bed and, ashamed of her weakness, used it as a prop to kneel against. She said nothing. She waited for a voice to make itself known, a voice which would give her the final and true direction. She wanted nothing but to do God's will, which she knew she wanted to direct her to Padric. But to do God's will as He would demand it meant a pure heart and a willing spirit. Did she have those?

The image of Padric came to her, striding across the field just the day before: the way he held himself, the sure thrust of his walk, the deliberate scanning of the landscape for her, her own quick, heart-leaping response, running at first, running until the beating of her own breath told her that she was behaving wholly improperly.

But there was no denying her feeling, there was no denying him. Even though the signs, the words from Hilda, were all against her, there was, surely, no denying where God, it must *be* God, was pointing her.

CHAPTER FIFTY

U rien was disappointed. He had hoped for much more frailty from Padric. But he was, as they all were, immensely strong from the perpetual motion of their hunting, warring lives. Besides, Urien concluded, even if Padric felt the effects of too much wine he would never show it.

Nor did Padric acknowledge that they had spoken intimately. Urien was a little thrown by this and took half a step back from his much warmer assessment of his brother. But only half a step. He could admire the way Padric snapped back so completely into his public role and character.

All about the woods the men were stirring. Women and slaves were making food for the first meal of the day. Stores – bread, dry fruits, eggs, honey – were being secured for the forward journey. There was a sense that this part of the forest was alive and full of deep power. Purposeful activity seemed to be transmitted from the woods, for in the open spaces around the lake, the men and women and children who went about their daily round of work looked over with some apprehension, and some appreciation, to the place which concealed the warriors and thegns and princes, their horses, their weapons, their retinue. All the valley people wanted to be well placed to see the war band move on. The sight of such an armed band, so swaggering, so proud in arms, men of legend, would be the talk for months to come.

'I will go over to see her now,' said Padric, after he had splashed his face and mopped it dry.

'When should we be ready to move?'

Padric considered. He did not want to put himself in an humiliating position. Nor did he want to appear indecisive.

'Riderch caught a wild horse yesterday afternoon,' he said. 'After

he has tamed that – so that we can take him with us – then we
will go.'

Urien nodded and watched as Padric slung himself into the
saddle to cover the few hundred paces to the religious settlement.
Urien noticed that Reggiani was at her gate and he decided
to get some herbs from her. Their game had been tasteless
unseasoned.

Padric was directed to Bega's hut by Eafled, rather flustered
at the return of this tall, red-haired, handsome man, his golden
torque heavy around his neck, several gold and silver armlets up
either arm, the glittering sword handle and the belted daggers
showing off the authority of a noble man of war.

'She is ill,' said Eafled, fearfully. There was something too
determined about him for her taste.

'What is it?'

'We thought she was dead. Perhaps she was. But our prayers
at Lauds brought her back to us. She is sleeping now.'

'I have to see her,' said Padric, gently but with no apology.

He went into her small cell.

Bega had been found crumpled over her bed and put into it
by Eafled and others. Some more skimmed milk had been forced
through her lips. Blankets had been brought from the common
dormitory to give her more warmth.

Already she looked better. Padric sat on a small stool beside
her.

'What is it?' he asked.

'I don't know,' she shook her head. 'It is difficult.' She paused
only for a moment. 'I made a vow to be the bride of Christ
alone.'

'You did not know then what you know now.'

'God knew. He did not stop me.'

'He did not stop me making you my wife in His eyes, Bega.'

'I have thought and better thought about it,' she said. 'I have
prayed and prayed for us.'

Padric began to feel the first warning chill of a defeat.

'You are ill,' he reassured himself. 'It is a great deal I am asking
of you.'

'I would have to consult the Abbess Hilda,' said Bega, dis-
tractedly. 'I cannot just leave this place entrusted to me. Leave
the nuns, those others who work here. Besides, I have built this

place. I have helped to put stone on stone. I have dug for the stockade and worked in the fields and the gardens. It is my own place.'

'You can come back here. It will live on without you.'

'So will you,' said Bega, slipping back into her old role of teasing and contradicting her tutor.

'Yes,' Padric replied and then paused. 'But I have known what it is to live without you.'

Bega waited. But Padric said no more.

She feared he might leave. Yet what could she truthfully say to hold him?

'I want to marry you,' she said, quietly, and as she said it some tension in her relaxed. 'But in the eyes of God I am married to Christ. Do you not see that?'

'You were married to me and in the eyes of God and first.'

Both fell silent.

To herself, Bega wondered why she was so obstinate. So much of her wanted to be with him. It would not be such a terrible act. Many monks were married, many nuns had left husbands and would sometimes return to them. Only a small fraction of that tiny fraction who came into monasteries and nunneries kept virginity or exemplified chastity. Yet tug as she did at the invisible bond, it only tightened. Either the devil was the bond or God was the knot. Who could tell her? How could she be certain, in this extremity of indecision which could affect her immortal soul, that the enemy was not intercepting her prayers to God? It was at such moments – as the gospels taught – that he was at his most cunning and devious.

Padric sat in dumb disappointment. It was a strength and a weakness in him that matters were clear cut. After the overwhelming meeting with Bega the evening before, he had been in no doubt that the die was cast. No one, he thought, could behave with such open and sincere affection and not be ready to follow it through. He knew what she felt. What he himself felt had never been in doubt since he had first identified it. He understood her dilemma but he knew also that there was a solution. And she could find it simply by acting on her strongest instincts.

It was not an angry silence. Nor was it hopeless. It was a waiting silence.

Before Padric had set off to see Bega, Riderch had begun to tackle the wildest horse that had ever come his way.

The previous day they had been out hunting and discovered a small herd of wild upland horses. They were a little smaller than the mounts ridden by the Rheged elite but there was no mistaking their strength and temper. At the very least they would be good for trade. Some might serve as pack horses. One or two, one in particular, could be a true horse of war.

This particular stallion was mud-brown, flaxen-maned, bigger than the rest and, Riderch saw with pleasure, wild as a cat. He went after it.

It took four of them to catch him. Three others had been roped and were shivering in a penned-off area of birch trees. This one stood alone, a tight noose around its neck, lashed to an ash with which for a while it had done such battle that it had all but choked. There was a large knot in the noose which prevented that but the stallion tugged and tugged until the hemp chafed its neck and a burn of blood could be seen.

It was a fearsome sight. It bucked, almost buckled in two as it scented anyone coming anywhere near it. All four legs would kick out. Sometimes it seemed that they flew out at the same time. There was froth on the mouth, the skin was slaked with sweat, the eyes were terrified and frightening, rolling in their sockets, beginning to be bloodshot with the strain.

A small crowd waited to see who would tackle it. It could not be taken along in that unbroken state. It was too much of a prize to leave behind. It was also a killer.

Riderch had a gift with horses. All of the men there had tamed a horse at some time or other. Several were experienced. Almost without exception they followed the same routine: they beat the horse into service. They whipped it, drove it, if necessary starved and beat it, until it was subdued and then they would mount it with a crude switch in their one hand, ready to lash, the other hard pulling on a tight bridle which could bring blood to the mouth.

Riderch, whose size made him tower even among the tallest
of the high bred, enviably well-fed noblemen of Rheged, did
it differently. Some of the men smiled to themselves and even
laughed (when he was not around) at his method. But they could
not question its effectiveness. And no one rode more settled,
malleable and faithful horses than those broken in by Riderch.
This one, though, would be a critical test.

The poor powerful creature was frantic with anger and panic.
Riderch took his own horse towards it, leading it gently, urging
it on now and then as it shivered and hesitated. The killer scent
of the mud-brown stallion was dangerous. But for Riderch's sake,
his own horse walked slowly forward until Riderch bade it stop.
The nearer they had approached, the more frenzied the tethered,
untamed animal had become.

Some of the men bellowed instructions and encouragement.
Some catcalled. Riderch ignored them all. He was already speaking to the terrified beast. The sense of danger between them could
be touched.

He spoke evenly and quietly, explaining what he wanted,
explaining what he would do, telling the beast it would come
to no harm. He seemed to know the location of its fear.

At moments it would seem that the stallion had calmed down
and then, suddenly, the stampede on the spot would begin again.
Even those at a distance flinched. Throughout this, Riderch stood
beside his own safely distanced horse and spoke as if to another
human being.

After a time, when some of the small crowd had drifted away,
he patted his own horse and sent it back to his slave, who stood
with it about twenty paces from Riderch.

The stallion bucked and kicked once again, but the venom
was going out of it. Yet its potential for damage was still
unmistakable.

Riderch began to move forward, directly towards the face of
the horse, staring at it and now — as those who had seen this
before pointed out, some of them laughing — breathing mightily
through his nose, flaring his nostrils. The air from his nose was
sucked up the damp quivering nostril pads of the stallion which
calmed down but still stepped and side-stepped and stamped on
the spot, and looking no less a killer.

Riderch blew his lung air into the face of the unbroken animal with all his force. Then, with steady step, he came forward until his head was beside the animal's head. The velvet lips were bared and the big teeth clashed as if to anticipate the crushing of the bones of his face. Those watching were rapt: most of them anticipated an attack on Riderch.

Riderch simply stood there, making no attempt to touch the nervously trembling beast. Talking, seeking to breathe his breath into the horse. Waiting. There was no attack. There was a sense of disappointment in the crowd which was as strong as the admiration for Riderch's skill and guts.

Others drifted away until no one but Riderch's woman and their two small boys and the slave were watching. They had seen the miracle. They thought the deed was accomplished.

Riderch knew that he had come to the most difficult passage of all. How and when and where did he touch the horse? On its neck, on its forehead, behind its ears, on its back, on the side of its long, alert face? He brooded over the decision while the stallion began to shuffle its feet in a slightly different pattern. Riderch noticed that but did not stop the quiet flow of talk. The horse was asking him to stroke it. That was what he needed to know. But still Riderch waited.

The horse bumped into his face with its own. Riderch smiled and talked a little louder, a little more quickly. The stallion bumped again, and again, and finally it nuzzled its head against the man's head and Riderch's arm came up, not to encircle and entrap the head but to stroke the neck, very lightly, a brush of blossom. The stallion began to butt the man, playfully, demandingly, and Riderch increased the pressure of the stroking and then risked patting the forehead, nuzzling his own head against the foam-flecked face, reaching down to soothe the sweat-saturated back.

He loosed the noose and saw the weal, which he knew how to soothe, but first he had to walk the horse and then mount it.

He gave the slightest tug on the rope, taking care that it did not tug on the red welt, and began to walk forward. After a fraction's hesitation, the stallion followed him.

For some time, Riderch walked with the stallion and stayed very close to him. Then he put an arm around its lower neck. Then he leaned heavily against it, almost pushing it away, and the stallion pushed back, seeming to enjoy it. And then, so quickly that you could blink and miss it, Riderch was lying across the horse's back, slumped across it like a dead man. And after a brief start, the horse kept walking.

Riderch slid off and stopped the horse and talked to it again face to face. He took from his pocket a small leather flask, poured some of the contents into his right hand and rubbed it tenderly on the welt caused by the rope. The stallion shivered strenuously and then went quieter than ever before.

Again he led it around.

Again he nudged against it.

Again he slumped across it.

Then he was on its back, lying up its neck, whispering in its ear, not pressing with his thighs nor giving any but the lightest guidance with his hands.

The stallion moved forwards. Stopped. Seemed set to buck him off. Then began again.

Then trotted; then stretched its legs.

Riderch signalled and his woman brought a basket of the best bran. When the horse had eaten, he led it to the stream and let it drink. Then he dried it down thoroughly and tied it to another tree.

'That will be my horse now,' said Riderch.

'When we were in the far north among the Picts,' said Padric, 'there was a great poet who could sing the epics of his people for many nights. Once I played when he wanted music. We became friends. It was a long campaign, a difficult one in those mountains which are much harsher and fiercer than our own. The rocks threaten the legs of the horses at every step and there are no gradual ascents as there are here in Rheged. We campaigned for many weeks. Along the way, we worked together on a version in my tongue of "The Dream of the Cross".'

He paused, not surprised by the unexpected and sudden tense reaction of Bega. She was unaware that he knew about the cross. Padric waited for her to speak but she said nothing. This famous story of the cross on which Christ had died, a story told by the cross itself, would be well known to her. She must have heard it or referred to it many times.

'Tell me,' she said. 'Tell me what new words you found.'

This was the sign!

There could be no clearer proof, she thought, with tearful gratitude, that God had ordained that they be together. She recollected the words of John, 'Run while you have the light of life, that the darkness of death may not overtake you.' And, in her state of lingering dizziness from the strain of the night and the confusion of the morning, she knew that she did not have to stick to her vows to enter the tent of God. For, as Paul said, it was open always to 'one who walks without blemish and is just in all his dealings; who speaks the truth from his heart and has not practised deceit with his tongue; who has not wronged a fellow man in any way, nor listened to slander against his neighbour'. And Matthew 'Seek ye first the Kingdom of God and His justice and all these things will be given unto you'.

It was as if the apostles were chiming in her head like a peal of bells saying Alleluia! to the signs the Lord had given. Alleluia! Go with Padric. His new Dream of the Cross was God telling her that her vocation would be found with Padric.

It was decided.

'Tell me,' she said, urgently still, though peace was stealing through her, 'tell me what your words are.'

Padric began speaking, slowly, the words spoken by the True Cross, words of a dream which had entranced Christians for centuries. Bega touched the fragment and felt almost unbearably blessed.

'A dream came to me,
    at deep midnight
When humankind
    kept their beds
– the dream of dreams!
    I shall declare it.
It seemed I saw the Tree itself
borne on the air, light wound about it,
– a beam of brightest wood, a beacon clad
in overlapping gold, glancing gems

> fair at its foot, and five stones
> set in a crux flashed from the cross tree.
> Around, angels of God
>   All gazed upon it . . .'

As Padric half-chanted, half-sang the description of the 'glory tree' with its gold and its gems 'spangled with spilling blood', Bega felt herself float into a state very similar to that she now remembered in the snow-fastened cave when first she had landed in Rheged. She herself was bound on that cross. In the deep pocket of her plain woollen dress, the fragment glowed. It was as if she could see the glow and feel it, as if she were being sustained by light as the slow words of the dream came to her from Padric.

> 'Till it seemed that I heard how it broke silence,
>   best of wood, and began to speak:'

To speak!

To speak to her. She felt that she was part of this poem. She could see the cross. It was talking to her.

Words from the cross, part of which, a minuscule fragment, but a true part, was in its folds in her tight fist. What grace had been given her! Through Mary, Mother of Christ.

> 'From my own stem I was struck away'

Bega saw the tree topple. She remembered being with Cathal and her brothers when she was a child. They had ridden into the forest a morning's distance away and the day had been spent chopping down the biggest of the trees. She saw it now in her floating half-dream as clearly as she had seen it then as a young girl kept back by Cathleen from the crashing, the splintering, the whole full-leaf felling of the great trees which beat on to the ground, the sound of the axes in the wood a hard sound, hard as some of the words in Padric's version.

> 'dragged off by strong enemies
> wrought into a roadside scaffold
> they made me a hoist for wrongdoers.'

Her father's slaves had stripped the trees until, Bega now thought, they looked naked, so much less than the trees they really were. Long ropes of hemp had been attached to them and they had been dragged by a line of slaves.

> 'Then I saw, marching towards me,
> Mankind's brave King:
> He came to climb upon me.'

She thought she could smell the woody smell of the cross, deep and fast somewhere in her mind. And Christ coming towards it.

> 'He would set free mankind.
> I shook when his arms embraced me
> but I durst not bow to the ground,
> stoop to Earth's surface.
> Stand fast I must.'

Bega repeated the line to herself.

> 'Stand fast I must.'

The line lay on her mind like a command.

> Stand fast I must.

The True Cross was in her hand. This was the inspiration for Padric's poem, a poem which had endured for centuries, and in her hand was the piece itself.

> 'They drove me through with dark nails
> On me are the deep wounds manifest
> wide-mouthed hate-dents.'

Had a dark nail touched the wood she now rubbed between finger and thumb? A thrill of ecstasy went through her. She caught her breath. Had a dark nail gone through the body and blood of Christ and buried itself in the fragment or even near the fragment she held now in her burning hand? It was too great a gift. What could a poor, flawed, unwhole mortal like herself do with such a gift?

'How they mocked us both!
I was all moist with blood
Sprung from the Man's side
After He sent forth His soul.'

At those words, Bega registered the sweat on her own hand.

The hand that gripped the wrapped cross. In her half-dream, half-swoon, she saw her hand covered in blood. The wrapping was soggy with blood. The blood seeped from the cross itself. Oh God, she prayed, please now give me a true understanding of what I must do.

'They lifted Him down from the leaden pain,
left me, the commanders,
standing in a sweat of blood.
I was all wounded with shaft.'

And she, Bega, became like the cross. For she was wounded with shafts. The deaths of Maeve and Donal were on her hands. Vows undertaken falsely were on her conscience. The decision to leave Whitby and Abbess Hilda had not been taken for pure motives. The building up of her nunnery here by the lake had owed as much to an imitation of Cathal – even the lopping down of the trees, dragging them across uneven ground to form the bulwark – as to any holy inspiration.

And Padric. Padric before her, the words casting a spell on her. Her eyes were closed but she could see him. She knew him so well. He was the wound. He was the truth, also. He could be the earthly commander of the forces of the Lord, who needed the strength of arm of Padric as much as the power of Cuthbert's spiritual resources.

'Set to contrive him a tomb
in the sight of the Tree of Death'

Cuthbert longed for death. The Abbess Hilda and all the nuns of Whitby prayed for their death every day. Bega did not long for death.

She longed to live. This new earthly life.

Bega writhed on her narrow plank of bed. She was not, she

could never be, dedicated wholly in body, mind and spirit only to God. She did not want the tomb. Not yet. This cross. She had to share it once more.

> 'They felled us all,
> We crashed to the ground, cruel Weirds,
> And they delved for us a deep pit.
> The Lord's man learnt of it
> His friends found me . . .
> It was they who girt me with gold and silver . . .'

And then Padric finished.

In the silence the words still seemed to sing on. Both Padric and Bega saw the cross so clearly. Their Lord nailed to it. His moist blood. Saw it crash to earth after He had been taken down. Saw it decked out in glittering jewels.

She turned and took Padric's hand with the hand that had held the cross.

'Your hand is hot,' he said, and covered it with his other hand to cool it.

'I will go to the Abbess Hilda,' said Bega. 'I will tell her everything. I will ask for her blessing to leave this nunnery.'

The happiness which swept across Padric's face brought her close to tears.

'I will give you an escort.'

'No. I can arrange that. I will be safe enough.' She paused. 'God Himself must have inspired you to make the poem sound and sing as it did then.'

Padric looked at her intently. He could see her soul, she thought. She was determined now. Soon they would be together.

'You must go now,' she said. 'I have neglected my duties here.'

She got up from her bed without effort. A little time before she had been clenched in pain. Now she rose like a young girl.

Padric took her in his arms for a few moments and then they stood apart.

'I will go,' he said, awkwardly, not quite knowing how to turn, how to leave, too drawn in by the prospect of such a longed-for future to be able to conduct the present.

'God bless you,' she said.

'And your spirit,' he replied.

They went out together. The sulky dawn had turned into a bright morning – not sunny but clear from the light-grey stretch of cloud which settled across the valley and nudged and concealed the top of the big mountains just in front of them.

He nodded and went for his horse and rode, hard, back to where the men were all but ready, waiting his direction.

Some time later, in mid-morning, when Bega was in the herb garden with Chad, Penraddin bore down on them. She was dressed like a man and looked hardened from the trail.

'Bega?'

Bega looked up and then eased herself upright.

Penraddin slung one leg in front of her and slid off her horse which she left commandingly behind her as she walked to the other woman.

'Padric says you are to have this.'

She handed Bega a sword.

Bega knew that she looked at it greedily.

'I have a faith which is stronger than any sword,' she said, with automatic piety.

'There are few out there with good swords,' Penraddin said, roughly. 'He tells me you are going across country. This will check one or two who might otherwise be tempted. If you can use it.'

Bega looked hard at the younger woman and took it from her. She balanced it. She swung it once or twice. She balanced it again. It was a fine, rather short, beautifully embossed sword, perfect for her reach and strength.

Penraddin watched her closely. Padric had assured her that Bega could handle a sword and in those few definite gestures she saw the truth of it. Otherwise, as she had argued, hotly, it would be a waste of a scarce and valuable resource.

'Padric said that if you don't want to carry it, you can bury it here. Be sure to wrap it in good cloth.'

Bega took one or two paces back and lifted the sword and began to swing it round her head. It spun in the gleaming grey light until it seemed to slice through the very air itself.

Penraddin went back to her horse and slung herself on to it.

'Will you be riding with us one day?'

Bega brought the sword down and stabbed it into the earth. 'Thank you,' she said. 'And thank Padric.'

Penraddin grinned. She liked to meet women as tough as she herself had become. A ruined woman now. Fit to be the wife of none of noble birth. At best a freeman's wife but even he might treat her as a concubine. Yet this road on which she had been cast was one she loved. 'God be with you,' she shouted and urged her horse back to the edge of the forest.

The war party was now ready. Many of the people of the lake came to stare. The warriors lived off their surplus. They came and for mean barter took hard-won food and hides, animals and sometimes chattels. The people of the valley literally looked up to them. High on horseback they were already half-legendary. And they made plain, often enough, the superiority they felt. Arrogance was the required public attitude, reinforced by the knowledge that every day could bring a life or death skirmish and by the need to be ready for that. The people looked up to them as much in fear as in longing.

These were the protectors and the hope of the people. These were the men who would fight to the death. Whether by any cool reckoning this brought commensurate benefits was simply neither here nor there, especially on an occasion of action and pageant such as this. These were their own warriors. These were the soldiers for their cause. Through their victories, the lives of the rest would be secured. And so they stood and stared and felt a thrill of excitement go through them as the dozens of dogs yelped and raced madly between the horses – so many horses! So much wealth in horses! Leather armour shone in the bright grey light, and every warrior held a sword which was no more than a dream to the lake people. They clutched shields studded sometimes with semi-precious stones, daggers at the belt, some wearing helmets, and torques glittering at the throat and rings, the gifts from grateful chiefs and kings, and the pack train already leading on, led by Owain who alone had been told the direction and destination by Padric.

Riderch rode his old horse and led the newly-broken one beside it, the horses head to head, held by a loose rope. He would let him run alongside for a few days, and then switch permanently to him. Urien had his pouch full of Reggiani's herbs and a newly-filled leather bottle of wine bulging across his back. He brought up the rear with two of the best warriors: Padric trusted Urien and Riderch to watch his back.

Now he gave the signal to go. A growl of approval went up from the waiting men. Bega stood up once more and shaded her eyes against the light to see the war band shuffle and appear confused and then straighten out into order with Padric at its head.

Did he look across towards her?

How fine he looked, she thought, tall on his horse, leading. The daughter of Cathal felt a longing to be there with him, setting out for a battlefield where the work of God would be accomplished through their earthly strengths.

Slowly the mass moved along the edge of the forest. The sounds began to die away. The stretched grey sky broke up and long dazzling streamers of white light came through. She stood to catch the last of it, and even when it had gone, she stood and gazed still as if waiting for it to return.

BOOK FIVE

❈❈❈❈

THE SYNOD OF WHITBY
AND THE
HOSTILE SWORD

❈❈❈❈

A.D. 664

CHAPTER FIFTY-ONE

Within the month, Bega was ready to go to Whitby. The nuns were anxious, being left alone without their leader in this remote and rude part of the world, but Bega had promised them her prayers.

Before she went, Bega spent almost two weeks visiting the sick around the wide area of her domain. She wanted to take the word and the blessings of God to all around her. Sometimes she harboured the suspicion that what she really liked was the adventure of travel and her work as a nun gave her licence to do that. This work did enable, or as she would say impel, her to do what scarcely anyone else in the valley, or in any other valley, did. She broke out of narrow boundaries. The warriors swept across the land, from sea to sea and over the sea, but they were a few creatures apart, lords from a different world, rulers of the earth, quite out of reach. Occasionally someone like Reggiani would venture some distance, called by the demand for her skills. Mostly people stayed tight put, bounded by a few acres only. There was much poverty and distress, but Bega had also discovered a complex and largely self-sufficient economy which was able to repair its deficiencies by imports from Ireland, the far Pictish north and the south. She saw it as a place which could become an example of God and His benison. Both had excited her interest and absorbed the energy which sometimes had possessed her like a fire.

Now that fire would go to Padric.

As she left the small lakeside community, although the nuns were weeping, and the workers and slaves standing fearful of their future without Bega, she subversively felt free. This was the start of her own life, under God, but not a life built on a lie to Him.

She had put on her sword which, again, increased the reverence many of her community felt for her. Chad was with her, on foot, and several dogs, including Cal. First they would go north to Caerel where a company would sooner or later be setting out to cross the Wall. It would be safer after Padric's war band's presence in the area to travel across country in a larger group. Once in the kingdom of Northumbria, they would discover other religious folk moving along the dirt roads and it was unlikely they would lack company there.

The day had begun with a steady soft drizzle which she found refreshing. Her prayers that morning had seemed rather stiff to her own ear but she refused to take that as an omen. Chad, who had not been told her purpose, appeared to have divined it which made her feel irritable with him but she controlled her temper. His dolefulness at what he intuited was her intention to leave for Padric hid the fear of a terrible sorrow.

She was determined that Whitby would see her transformation and she kicked the horse along impatiently. At last she would take up her true vocation.

At the court of King Oswy there were also preparations for a journey set to determine destiny. When the preparations were complete, the King called together his sons, his leading eldormen and thegns, his official priest, his poet, and the other monks plus a few mercenary soldiers, who were at the court at that time.

Eanfled, his queen, mother of his two surviving sons, Alchfrid and Ecfrith, sat in the great hall at the opposite end to the King, with Aetheldreda, wife of Ecfrith, and Ada, the new bride of Alchfrid. No reference was ever made to the other woman Oswy had taken, nor to the son of that marriage, Aldfrid, whom Padric had met in Ireland.

Oswy took his seat – a large high-backed chair in oak which was practically black. Eanfled had employed several Celtic artists and they had carved it in highly wrought decorations – plants, the geometric shapes of their culture, and fantasies which turned the ends of the arms into the paws of a mystical beast and the highest part of the back into a crown against which Oswy could lean his own uncrowned mane.

He was a large, even fat man, typifying, the poets said, the best characteristics of his bold Teutonic origins. His hair was almost flaxen and as thick as the long woven shirt he wore. One of his blue eyes, the left, strayed a little, but when he fixed his gaze on anyone he was addressing they felt authority. Perhaps they feared his tyranny, for he had slaughtered his good and faithful brother to take the throne and, when God had granted him a famous victory against the overwhelming force of the pagan Mercians nine years before, he had celebrated in their blood. He was known for the delight he took in divining new tortures and his pleasure in watching his inventions put into practice was itself blood-chilling. He especially enjoyed stripping the skin off those captives on whom no ransom could be raised and from whom no useful future work or slave function could be envisaged. He would have them flogged and mutilated before commanding his main torturers to put their knives just under the skin and peel it off down their backs, down their chests and bellies, down their legs and arms, like the bark of a sapling. Every so often he had a pail of salted water thrown over them to multiply their howls and to wash away the blood so that he could see the detail of the body under the skin. The genitals he left until the end and the final act would be to snuff out their cries with their sex.

Oswy trusted no one. His four bodyguards were mute Picts, men chosen for their height and strength and spared by the King for this role. He had instructed Alchfrid and Ecfrith to brand the brows of these men partly to ensure their hatred for his sons. They were fed as well as the king himself, given slave women and strong weapons. They themselves were watched over, in effect guarded, by the eldormen and thegns who rode closest to the king on all journeys and expeditions and who were no more than two or three strides from him at any feast or event such as this. Oswy, the four Picts and the eldormen lived in the conscious, ancestral fear for their safety both from others and from each other. Oswy found some comfort in everyone fearing someone and all of them fearing him.

When they were gathered, Oswy stood up. To his right hand sat Alchfrid, who looked very like him; on his left, Ecfrith, more like his mother, and nervous, as always, in the presence of a father he hated, a brother he despised and a wife who held his natural carnal appetite in contempt and who perhaps made him a laughing-stock.

Oswy's voice was surprisingly light. It had a reediness at odds with his large, well-barrelled figure. He was also, again unexpectedly for such an uncomplicated and brutal warrior, lavish and expansive with his hand movements. This may have been to flash his rings – every finger and both thumbs were rigid with jewellery. He was proud of the wealth he carried on his body. He wore not one torque but two, of gold, as well as the intricate heavy silver pendants made for him by Eanfled's craftsmen. The armlets, on arms bared for show on an occasion such as this, were the most precious of those yielded by the defeated Mercian household. His sword was the sword of Penda, the king of the Mercians, finely jewelled and enamelled about its hilt and handle. The buckle holding his cloak had been the property of Ecfrith, from the dead body of one of the Irish princes who had come to help the men of Rheged and been killed in a skirmish years before, when Padric himself was still in Ireland. Oswy had taken a liking to it and Ecfrith had no option but to hand it over to him.

His clothes were fresh for the occasion and for the journey. The boots of soft calfskin were new. He had bathed himself in both hot and cold water and the women he had captured in a raid on the Picts had lightly lashed his skin with twigs and leaves and further cleaned him with ointments of highly scented herbs.

It was full noon. The great hall was lit by fat candles which gave the formal assembly the glamour of mysterious shadows.

In his high-pitched voice he began. 'It is time to settle once and for all the questions about our religion which are disturbing so many and threatening the kingdom. I myself am not disturbed. I was given refuge by the Picts and it is the Celtic beliefs that I have followed since. Because of that I won a battle against King Penda and the Mercians, a force thirty times greater than our own forces.' The men, most of them veterans of that astonishing battle, murmured appreciatively.

'My most loved son Alchfrid' (Ecfrith winced but no one saw it: he was well practised) 'believes that the Roman ways are better than the Celtic ways. The argument is about the dating of Easter and it is very, very complicated. I have tried to understand the points made but I confess that I am not certain that I have succeeded. We are simple warriors' (his men liked him for that: his famous victory had made them rich and even more arrogant. The outward pieties of Celtic Christianity were certainly in order, but they did not represent reality for them. Most still held to their older pagan gods from across the sea.) 'We cannot understand the calculations of scholars.

'There are other matters which I can understand – such as the shape of the tonsure, whether it should be the Celtic way, as you see around you, with the head shaved at the front, or the Roman way, which you will have seen elsewhere, where the hair is cut like a crown and the scalp is bare, which I am told represents the crown of thorns on the head of Christ when He was on the cross. And there are even other matters—' his arms waved rather satirically at the endless arcane disputes of these unmartial monks '—which are to do, I am told, with the order of service and the saying of prayers and the line of authority; I am lost but I am determined that we will act.'

He looked fierce. He knew how to impress his authority. He had taken care to receive some instruction from his priest for this speech and he was, he knew, far ahead of all his warriors in this knowledge. It impressed them. His fleshy brows bit deeply into furrows as he spoke on. 'Unresolved disputes cause wars. My own view is clear and fully formed. I will hear both sides but, like most of you, I take my stand on the God of Aidan.' The humble, devoted, miracle-begetting Aidan had become a favourite and their great victory had been due, the Christians among them thought, to his direct intervention in heaven. Though he had died four years before the battle took place, it was Aidan on whom Oswy had called for help when Penda's vastly superior forces had driven him to the extreme north of his kingdom and forced him to what seemed a hopeless confrontation. Aidan's transparent holiness had impressed these warriors. He was someone they were proud of. He was their mascot.

'We all know that in the thirteen years since the death of Aidan, many miracles have happened in his name,' Oswy continued. 'We know that if you take earth from his grave or even nearby, it can effect wonderful cures. The blind have been healed as happened in the gospels. The lame have been made straight. Indeed the miracles of Aidan are to be compared with Matthew, Mark, Luke or John. Imagine that we have a man like that sitting even now on the right hand of God! He is there—' Oswy lifted up both arms in a magnificent gesture and the rings and armlets and torques glittered greedily in the candlelight 'and undoubtedly he will help us, those who deserve it, to enter the kingdom of heaven.' Oswy saw Aidan as his guarantee of eternal life. 'But, there are other arguments and I have called this synod at Whitby to settle them once and for all. This will prove to God that I am a good Christian. This will show Him that I am about His earthly work. They are coming from Canterbury, from the lands of the Angles and the Saxons, from the uttermost parts of the far north, the Picts and the Scots from Ireland. There will be those there from Gaul and those who have been to Rome itself. God will bless this synod and He will bless me for convoking it. Now listen to my son, Prince Alchfrid.'

There was a solemnity in the gathering. The men were rarely solemn about anything other than war or the description of battles, but Oswy had cleverly sensed an unease and they were glad he was acting on it. The arguments from Rome about true Christianity were very insistent and even the most cynical of the elite war band had begun to fear that they might not be on the right track. It was no good worshipping and following this God if you were doing it in the wrong way. When they sacrificed or prayed to their own ancient gods, they followed forms and rules passed down from the immemorial times when the gods themselves had lived here on earth. They wanted the same certainty in outward forms with this new God. It was time to settle the matter. None of them could see how the teachings of Aidan could possibly be challenged.

Alchfrid rather puzzled them. He was a slender, even taller version of his father save that no eye strayed and his love for fine ornament was less obvious. They had all been in wars and skirmishes with him and he had led from the front, fearlessly. Yet he was something of a schemer. He was generous with booty after a victory and suitably merciless to enemies whose further existence would always be a danger. But there were worries. He believed that to free a slave was to do the work of God – provided of course that the slave was a believer. He thought that to give away royal land to the church was to gain favour with God. He had a thorough grasp of the details of the issues involved in this synod which most of them regarded as little more than a splendid excuse for a feast, for pomp and a suitable display of power. Above all he was a close friend – 'as David to Jonathan', Oswy had announced at one feast – of the enigmatic Wilfrid.

Wilfrid worried them most of all. They all had strong opinions about Wilfrid.

Wilfrid came from one of the most powerful families in the kingdom, a family ranked just a little below that of Oswy. His physical prowess as a young man had been remarkable. His skills in speech and scholarship added to his passion for travelling great and untrod distances had only enhanced his reputation. His family was warlike and ambitious. So why, they all asked, had he moved into a world where humility, caring, peace and gentleness – according to Aidan – were the most sought-after virtues? It made no sense unless Wilfrid – whose cunning unnerved them – knew something they did not.

He had been to the court several times, summoned first by Ecfrith's most Christian and chaste wife Aetheldreda, who listened to all he said and obeyed him, and then by Alchfrid, who was entranced by this dashing, eloquent, learned man of God. The warriors who met him were presented with a sincere Christian. He was humble – though they were deeply suspicious of such humility from one so built like a warrior. He praised and seemed to practise gentleness – although many had seen him with sword, in action, and heard the unmistakable grunt of satisfaction as blade bit bone. He extolled peace although he was forever, it seemed, seeking confrontation. He said he despised worldly possessions and yet through Aetheldreda and Alchfrid and the king of Anglia he had already, at an early age, inherited money and land and rents enough to found two monasteries and two churches, all of which were in his power like any earthly estate. They were not surprised that Alchfrid began his speech with Wilfrid.

'You know that I am opposed to my father in this because of my love for Wilfrid, the priest of God, a friend to the best scholars in Rome, spurner of the offer of half a Gaulish kingdom, a man of our tribe and race. It is a measure of the kingliness of my father—' he turned and bowed, something Ecfrith could never have done without his truculence somehow showing through and alerting his father to future contest, but Alchfrid – damn him – did it so gracefully, so easily, 'that he understands that the opposition I have to his religious beliefs does not obstruct the love and service I owe to him as a son and as a subject. We all owe him our lives!'

This, said abruptly, stung the assembled men to closer attention
and Oswy felt elevated on the back of this handsome, brave son's
praise and support. 'We owe him our wealth. We owe him our
safety and the safety of our women and our slaves. But we know,
also, that King Oswy would say – "No! No! You owe it to God".
It is because God so favours him that he has favoured me and
called this synod which will dispel all the rumours of darkness
now threatening to cloud the glorious light of our victory-bringing,
all-conquering Lord of the Hosts.

'It is in Wilfrid and in the experience of Wilfrid that I will put
my trust and before we pray to God to protect us on this journey
to Whitby, I want to put in your minds why I listen to this man
of God whom so many of you know. But you do not know him
as well as I do. I am telling you these things because it is good to
have thoughts in your mind when you are undertaking a journey
of this sort. In those stretches of time when you are riding and
there is no danger and the day seems long between dawn and
sunset, it is good to have something to think over. I want to tell
you just three things so that when you reach Whitby, you will be
prepared.

'First, St Paul says this to Titus: "A bishop" – and Wilfrid, it
is prophesied, will be a bishop – "must be without crime, as the
steward of God; not proud, not subject to anger, not given to
wine, no striker, not greedy of filthy lucre; but given to hospitality,
gentle, sober, just, holy, continent, embracing that faithful word
which is according to doctrine, that he may be able to exhort in
sound doctrine and to convince the gainsayers".

'This is a true description of Wilfrid. St Paul could have been
looking at Wilfrid when he said that to Titus. Wilfrid has
since his childhood been subject to the evil of envy. There are
those who speak of him in the most damning terms and even
dare challenge – although only in whispers – his holy virtues.
They accuse him of lust. But I say to you, ask the wife of
my brother Prince Ecfrith, ask Princess Aetheldreda, who has
spent many hours being taught and inspired by Wilfrid, if she
has experienced from him what in him could be the sign of
lust. It is whispered that he is avaricious – but you yourselves
have seen him give his own food to the hungry and go hungry
himself, fasting as only those chosen by God can fast. What I
give him and others give him he immediately turns into buildings

for the further glory of the Lord. Wilfrid, then, is a man to be listened to.

'He is also a man aided by God in all his battles, spiritual and temporal. This is the second thing I bring to your attention. A messenger has just brought me this story of Wilfrid's latest journey from Rome. On their way back across the sea that separates us from Gaul—' Alchfrid adopted the story-telling posture and slight chant of the court poet: Ecfrith found this an especially irritating affectation, since, in his sour view, Alchfrid could not do it properly. '—Wilfrid and his colleagues who were engaged in singing psalms as the boat carried them home, were suddenly subject to storms just like the disciples on the Sea of Galilee. The boat was thrown around in the high waves and heaved on to the shore by deep and turbulent waters which, when they withdrew, proved to have grounded the boat high on the shore. The sea ebbed, the storm fell as suddenly as it had risen, and Wilfrid and his brothers were thanking God when a horde of pagans appeared above them on the clifftops. These were fearsome men, blue-painted, with all their pagan totems about them, and intent on taking the ship, carrying off Wilfrid and the monks as slaves and slaughtering any who resisted them.

'Wilfrid tried to turn them away from this. He offered them huge sums of money, both then and in the future, but to no purpose. Their chief priest stood on a height – like Balaam – and cursed Wilfrid and all those who held to the true God. He called on his own gods to bind their hands as they stood. The more he cried out to his gods, the more afraid the vastly outnumbered colleagues of Wilfrid grew. Their hands began to fasten on to each other and lock together. It seemed that all was lost.

'But Wilfrid directed a young man in his company called Cedd to pick up a smooth hard stone from the beach. For he remembered the miracle that God showed the world when David slew Goliath. Armed by that knowledge and strong in the prayers of his colleagues, Cedd whirled the sling above his head and the stone flew through the air to strike the pagan priest full on the brow and fell him dead. At once the pagans howled for battle and the followers of Wilfrid, who had begun to feel their hands locking together under the wizard's spell, fell to their knees to give thanks.

'Now Wilfrid knew that there would be a battle and he

commanded his men to pray that God would bring victory to the few as he did to Gideon against the Midianites. The pagans were numbered at two thousand. But Wilfrid had some of his men take the fishing nets and spread them out in front of them while the pagan hordes carried their priest back to the settlement on top of the cliff. Quickly he had holes dug and sand grass laid over them with a sprinkling of sand and cruel spears stuck inside them. Then he addressed them, and all in this hall can guess what he said. For Wilfrid, though a man moulding himself in the perfection of Christ, was and will ever remain true to our own race and a man trained from childhood in arms.

"'We are few," he called out, "and they are many. But we have God on our side and they have only the pagan idols which could not even protect their chief priest from the simple stone of Cedd. You know that while Joshua, son of Nun, fought against Amalek, Moses, Hur and Aaron called on the Lord continually for help. So will we all. While we fight we will chant a psalm of David. And look behind you. The tide is far out but it is on the turn. Perhaps it will reach up again even as far as this, even though the storm has fallen away. Who knows what God will bring us if we can hold out against this mighty host? There is nowhere we can flee to: there is no earthly help at hand. Swear that none will turn tail. Swear that we will stand firm in the glory of the Lord and show His might to the world.'"

Alchfrid had been carried away by his imitation of Wilfrid's eloquence and by the vision he had conjured up of the few against the many, the small band trapped on the high strand, seeking the help of God and each other as the pagan masses moved back from their cliff home and gathered before them.

'They fell on their knees and prayed to God,' Alchfrid continued, 'and Wilfrid gave them the psalm "I will lift up mine eyes unto the hills, from whence cometh my help. My help cometh even from the Lord, who hath made Heaven and Earth. He will not suffer thy foot to be moved". And at the end of the psalm a mighty "Amen!" rang out and the very cliff itself spoke it back to them. "Amen!" they cried and "Amen!" the cliff answered them, and again and again they did it, thus showing how God is everywhere and can speak in the tongues of trees and streams and stones and mountains as well as any of the pagan spirits.

'The pagans were impressed by this call but their own barbarous war cries were also raised up and the clamour alone would have made less resolute men give up all hope.

'After much terrifying shouting, the pagans charged at our small Christian band which Wilfrid had stretched across the sands like a bow. Some of the pagans were naked, some painted, carrying all manner of crude and fearsome weapons; they raced towards Wilfrid vowing to slay all who stood in defiance of them. As they came nearer, Wilfrid called on the men at the end of his bending arc to lift the nets. The pagans became entangled in them and the centre block of Wilfrid's force raced forwards with their striking spears. Meanwhile others had fallen into the hastily dug mantraps and suffered injuries which put them out of the battle. After bloodshed which made all the swords of the Christians drip with the gore from stabbed bodies, the pagans withdrew and took their dead with them. In this first assault, Wilfrid lost only one man.

'The pagans debated what to do next and how to vary the attack, but no difference came of it for once again they hurled themselves forward like a pack of dogs, helter-skelter on each other's heels, their feet drumming the hard, wet sand and their voices promising destruction. All the while Wilfrid kept up the slow chant of the psalm. Once again the nets were employed and the pagans' line was broken and they were thrown back. This time three of Wilfrid's men were lost but scores of the pagans died or were grievously wounded.

'Before the third charge they performed a ceremony and bowed down before some totem they had carried with them and planted in the sand. Another priest rose up and shook his magic staff with all its bones and baubles and the pagan army was excited to a frenzy. Like a command, the frenzy itself made them turn and charge with redoubled strength at the steady few still praising God. More slipped through the nets this time. Fewer fell in the pits. Yet by the grace of God once more they were thrown back and once more they retreated, dragging their dead with them.

But Wilfrid knew that the next attack would be fatal. His men were tired and the pagans had come closer each time. Therefore he turned from the battle and faced the sea. Before that he urged his men to give their fullest voice to the psalm and, while it sounded, he prayed God to speed up the return of the tide.

'Immediately the water began to race across the sands like fire eating through a dry forest. The very waves seemed eager to rush to the aid of God's servants. The sea itself was eager to share in the glory of this day and, while the pagans once more called on their idols and argued their tactics, God made the very tide sweep up and surround the ship. Wilfrid urged his forces back to the vessel and with all their strength and God's help they began to push and haul it down to deeper water.

'When the pagans saw this they cursed and ran towards the small band of Christians who had taken care to put their five – only five – dead on the vessel. The urging and prayers of Wilfrid, however, were stronger than all the idolatrous gods of the pagans and the ship was launched and the wind caught the sail and those pagans whose madness caused them to follow and follow perished in the surging deep.

'What I say to you is this: such a man blessed by God, ought to be listened to and, with respect to all the gentleness of Aidan, ought to be followed for his strength of arm through the power of the Lord.'

'Was it as big a victory as God granted me when I defeated the Mercian hordes – thirty times more in number than we were?' Oswy, his father, enquired.

'Nothing has been revealed more God-triumphant than the battle in which you conquered the Mercians,' said Alchfrid. 'Until then the might of the Mercian force under Penda, enemy as he then was to God, was thought to be invincible. But you brought the whole of his people under the rule of the true Lord of Hosts.'

'And yet you speak of the miracle afforded to Wilfrid,' Oswy continued. Ecfrith went on alert as he noticed a strain of resentment in his attitude towards the favoured son.

'But what of the many miracles afforded to Aidan?' he went on. 'In this very place, here in this palace on a rock where we hold this court.' Oswy now stood, facing Alchfrid. He had no need to remind anyone in the hall that Aidan's prayers had been vital in causing a fire to turn on the Mercians and lead to their defeat.

'No one,' said Alchfrid, rather hoarsely, Ecfrith noted with satisfaction, 'can claim more miracles than Aidan.'

Oswy nodded. Hierarchy was restored.

'I have nevertheless one last thing to add,' Alchfrid said. 'In his talks with me, Wilfrid has convinced me that the Roman way is

the way of the most powerful kingdoms and empires. It is made
to help great empires, father, such as yours.'

Ecfrith listened with close concentration. As his brother expanded
on the theme, Ecfrith saw what the purchase was in this Roman
way. His own religious feelings were not deep but he knew enough
to be able to present and defend the Celtic cause held by the court.
These remarks of Alchfrid made him look at the Roman rule
again. How foolish that he had not thought of it before! Of
course. It could only augment a king's authority. The Pope was
the central power; the bishops were his ambassadors and servants,
beholden to him and utterly obedient to him, sent wherever he
needed to send them; under them the abbots and priests and
nuns, the monks and cenobites and anchorites; under them were
the people they controlled through prayers. And the monks and
bishops and even the Pope would work with the kings. That
was the mere bones of it. The subtlety of the interdependence
of dependence and rule began to excite Ecfrith. Yes, he could
see an attraction there. Moreover, it would unsettle his father,
which could be very helpful. It would be bitter to be on the
side of Wilfrid, whose encouragement of his wife's chastity
made him more of a rival than a man of God, but perhaps
needs must.

At last Alchfrid concluded his oration.

The king stood again and looked most solemn. 'You will all
know that before we became one kingdom we were, though from
the same race, two different kingdoms – Deira and Bernicia. In
that time there were two kings and the tradition continued, as
you know, with my beloved cousin Oswin.'

He paused as if to fight off a challenge, as well he might. For
he had never admitted the murder of Oswin, a man thought of
as holy, and had rooted out, tortured most vilely and executed the
four men he had sent to assassinate his cousin.

'At this time, when we are advancing both in the north and in
the south, when this kingdom is set to become the one which
swallows up all the other rulers in this sea-bounded island, I
intend to reintroduce that custom. I proclaim Alchfrid, my son,
joint king with me. Though he will still give allegiance to my
sword, all here and all else who know him will give to him the
title and all the honours of king.'

Alchfrid stood forward and, from a side door, the abbot of

Ripon, who had come to Bamburgh to help prepare the ground for the synod, appeared in full pomp.

Ecfrith stepped up to be the first to pledge allegiance. He did it without revealing a flicker of his true feeling nor his thoughts, which were focused exclusively and desperately on how he could get rid of these two kings who stood between him and a throne he longed for as he longed for nothing else.

One by one the thegns and eldormen went to Alchfrid, who stood, calm in his new authority but already, Ecfrith could see, imagining himself to be a little above the rest. That superiority could be fed, Ecfrith thought, and it could ultimately do him damage.

Oswy looked on. Ecfrith took in all that he could. Was he seeing Oswy already rather regretting this generous and perhaps potentially dangerous gesture? If so, how could he prise open this feeling in his grim-hearted father and use it against him? It would be difficult to arrange an assassination of Alchfrid in the way in which his father had so successfully murdered Oswin. After that act, more care was now taken. And though Ecfrith had concealed the worst and could be as plausible as any, it had not gone unnoticed that his opinion of Alchfrid was neither warm nor high. He would have to find a better way.

In front of Alchfrid, each man stripped himself of a fine piece of jewellery which he presented to the new young king. The suddenness of it all did not puzzle them: Oswy was well known to be both impulsive and secretive. To have announced this event too far in advance would have been to tempt enemies and allow factions to grow. Declaring the decision on the day before the journey south to this meeting at Whitby gave it a status, while protecting it from the arrows of cultivated envy and opposition. And they liked Alchfrid well enough.

It would have to be a case of setting Oswy and Alchfrid against each other, Ecfrith decided, as the ceremony continued. One task would be to make Oswy's regret harden into a conviction of perilous error. The other would be to make Alchfrid feel so uneasy at the impulsiveness of his father that he would be persuaded to strike first.

Of course, Ecfrith thought, as his face maintained the expression of arrogant neutrality, the mark of that warrior elite, Alchfrid might be convinced on another front. Given that Oswy had blood on his hands, he, Ecfrith, could, with sufficient cunning, make his brother believe that the avenging of that bloody murder would serve him well in the eyes of God. Ecfrith smiled, just a little. There was room for manoeuvre. He would work on Alchfrid so that he murdered the king in the name of Christ and revenge, then he would murder Alchfrid for the same reasons: that would be his course.

'Alleluia! Alleluia! Alleluia!' proclaimed the priest when everyone had sworn allegiance.

'Alleluia,' echoed Ecfrith, grimly.

CHAPTER FIFTY-TWO

Cuthbert and Hilda were in her cell. It was more comfortably furnished now than it had been in Bega's day; woven and painted tapestries on the wall, finely cleaned and combed skins on a neatly patterned rush floor, two ornate candlesticks, chairs carved with scenes from the Gospels.

'I believe,' said Cuthbert, 'that God is about to make a great revelation to us. Something is astir.' He took what Hilda noted was only his third spoonful of gruel. He had decided to give up the serious fast he had engaged in as preparation for the synod because he was becoming dizzy and too lethargic to pursue his basic duties.

'Sometimes,' Cuthbert went on, speaking softly so that Hilda had to lean forward, 'when I close my eyes, Hilda, I see the darkness of the devil with the red of his greedy throat ever open to swallow the innocent and the ignorant alike. Wherever I look he is the ruler. Again and again we go out into the hills and the barbarous places and talk to those who live as animals in dug-out caves and hovels of mud and straw; who breed with each other against the laws, and sacrifice animals and worse as their devils taught them; who have their own wizards on whom they swear more stoutly than we swear on the gospel. But we tell them the true world of the almighty invisible God, all conquering, Lord of heaven and earth.

'For a moment,' Cuthbert's eyes, those eyes which could be so flint in their stare, now softened. 'For a week or even a month, they become the children of God. I or others baptise them and call down the Holy Ghost as He came down to John the Baptist. As I leave the village or the mountainside or the valley, there is much rejoicing and banging of drums and chanting. But then, dearest

Hilda, when I return a year or even half a year later, they are so often back in the swamp of their ignorance. The devil has done his work which is undoing mine.'

'The Lord requires us to be strong in His cause,' said Hilda, rather guiltily finishing her gruel. She took more of the fine wheaten bread. 'He is testing us at all times.'

'We can be tested,' said Cuthbert. 'We wish to be tested. We long to know that He needs to try us. But that is not the chief point I wish to make.' He reached forward, took some bread and then had a sip of water, grimacing a little as if even that were a betrayal. 'When I think of Aidan and Columbanus, of St Patrick in Ireland and St Ninian in Rheged, when I think of the number of saints and evangelists of such holiness in these harsh lands, then sometimes I can even believe that we may be the new Israel. We preach in several tongues in the towns and villages and God gives us the strength to change and baptise whole tribes. We go on as did St Paul, as did St Matthew, St Mark, St Luke, St John and all the disciples save Judas. We persevere because there must be light.'

Cuthbert's eyes hardened now and Hilda swallowed on the last bite of bread. She felt her sympathies distend in anticipation.

'We are now His disciples. It is to us that Christ will be looking to carry the flickering candle through the storms of our savage and indifferent times. I see the darkness all about us.' He paused. She knew that he did indeed see the forces of darkness all about them, always threatening, never resting. 'And what are we—' Cuthbert almost cried out here and this appeal struck to the nerve-soul of Hilda, 'without enlightenment? What are we without learning and enquiry into the knowledge of God? We could be cattle chewing grass all day and at night waiting for no better fate than to chew more grasses. We must be more than that! We are made in the image of God! It is our duty, our joy, to keep the candle alight, to light other candles and those candles to become as fixed as the stars in the sky until one day they form a chain of light which will fill all heaven and bring the perfection of all things known to the whole world.'

'Amen,' said Hilda fervently, 'and again, amen.'

After a short prayer, Cuthbert lay down on the rushes at her feet and was soon asleep. She looked at him fondly. What tormented battles took place in that head which still bore so many traces of the blond curled anglic features of his famous boyhood?

There was a small question in her mind about the sense of strain in Cuthbert. For surely when the great debate began at the synod, Cuthbert would rise up for the Celtic cause and no Roman argument would be able to resist his eloquence and his saintliness? Even Wilfrid, she thought, smiling to herself, would be reconverted! Hilda regarded Wilfrid's liaison with Rome as little more than a sign of his exuberant, embracing nature. She had no doubt that he would either bend the will of Rome to the Celtic cause or abandon Rome altogether if he saw that the Celts needed him. But Cuthbert had always been more complicated. It was the way of those who demanded so much of themselves. She thought of his wasting, of his balked longing for the hermit's life, of his gigantic feats of mass conversion: all of it contained in the huddle of flesh and raggedy clothes at her feet.

As he lay before her, the sweet-strong odour of his unwashed body – another penance – seeping out in the light sweat of sleep, Hilda bent her head in prayer.

The young novice who had been deputed to fetch and carry the meal to the cell of the abbess came in and stopped stone still at the door. Cuthbert, whom she and the others had been instructed to revere, was huddled on the ground, mouth agape. The abbess, of whom the novice was entirely in a state of awe approaching petrification, sat like a statue, head bent in prayer. Perhaps she had interrupted a miracle and God was in the cell. But what if they were dead? Then the devil would be here. She could not move. Was the devil binding her arms with hoops of iron? She could no longer hear the ordinary noises of the abbey. All she could sense in her ears was a muffled stinging of sound which was surely the devil working through her to disrupt this strange but holy communion. She fled.

Hilda had been aware of her presence but she had taken that awareness as a rebuke. To be aware of the presence of a young, innocent novice bent on a trivial task when all her mind and spirit ought to have been concentrated on seeking God was weak. As so frequently happened with Hilda, she found consolation in organisation.

'God forgive me for I have sinned,' she said aloud. 'I know now that I should have prepared myself more carefully for the synod so soon upon us. I have not given importance to that which is the most important. I have wasted time. Let me now devote myself to Your service in full preparation of this great congress.'

Hilda staggered awkwardly to her knees – a painful stiffness was becoming increasingly emphasised in the joints. She liked no one to refer to it, not even herself.

She prayed for a just outcome. She prayed for the Celtic way in which she had been reared and taught by Aidan. She knew that with Cuthbert on the Celtic side and Wilfrid also a pupil of Aidan, theirs would be the victory. She prayed that the victory would be the beginning of the further spreading of that light so movingly described by the good tortured man whose tormented groans – as she had decided they were – in sleep testified that even there he was being lashed and tortured by devils jealous of his strength and closeness to God. What in others were no more than bestial night grunts were, she understood, in Cuthbert the cries of agony from a pure soul resisting all temptation, even in the dark sleep where the devil reigned.

Bishop Colman had wanted to walk from Lindisfarne to Whitby but the small band of followers he took with him were adamant that ponies should be taken. Colman wanted a donkey in tribute to the lowly animal, the joke of animals, the most common beast of burden chosen by Christ for his fabled and fated entrance to Jerusalem. They even refused him that.

This pilgrimage to Whitby was deeply undesired by the proposed spokesman of the Celtic cause. Far better to Colman's honest and simple taste had he been allowed to stay in peace on Lindisfarne, especially at this time of tide when the sea cut it off entirely from the land and it became an island of pure faith, like its beloved mother house, Iona.

'For at this gathering I see myself as the humblest of all the messengers,' said Colman, sincerely, to his monks in the small bare chapel at Lindisfarne. 'I do not wish to debate these matters. They have been self-evident to me as to you and to all of those whose miraculous deeds, thanks be to God, brought us here. Instead of all the preparations that have gone into this journey and this synod we should have been out on our missions converting the pagan, reinforcing the faithful, showing the relics of Aidan to disbelievers.'

'But once this is done, we shall be left in peace to do the work God intends us to do,' said Celland, one of the youngest of the ascetic, dedicated Lindisfarne monks, the warrior elite in the Celtic army of God. Colman smiled at Celland.

They were sitting in a circle in the austere chapel. Celland was almost plumb opposite him, a placing which Colman knew was not entirely accidental. It was he who had winkled out Celland from the edge of Ireland, his homeland, to which he returned regularly. Then a spindly, sickly youth distinguished only by huge eyes and a gift for singing, he had enchanted Colman, who had no trouble in persuading his farmer father that a safer, richer future lay not on the land but in an abbey. Celland had grown into a lean, dirty, ebullient monk, often in petty trouble for laughing in the middle of a service or turning a stint of gardening into an excuse for a water fight or some such mildly disruptive behaviour. But he still sang like an angel – the ancient lengthy songs from his native land which touched Colman and others of his country so tenderly. Colman had been his saviour from the first and he was never far from him and always, when the chance came, in his eyeline. His cheerful willing face would often banish Colman's anxieties. The only time he lost his zest was when Colman left Lindisfarne on his missions and left Celland behind. He had never accompanied him on a single mission until now. He wondered what he had done to offend the man he adored next to Jesus Christ, not understanding that Colman realised the dangers of too much proximity between them and though it pained him, took measures to put Celland in his place – as just another young monk.

Colman had decided to take him to Whitby partly because he thought that Celland might soon be rightly upset that, though all the others had been on missions with the bishop, he was the one who had never once been chosen; partly because Colman was nervous of the whole controversy and wanted the young man's talent for taking his mind off heavy matters.

'Let me rehearse my argument to you all,' said Colman, 'for you are all my friends and brothers in Christ and we have trained our-selves to tell the truth to all men even as we tell the truth to God.'

He began to speak in a rather faltering voice for, though Colman was a man of virtue and good works in the Lord, he had come to leadership with much reluctance. He particularly loathed any call on him to present an argument. A public debate filled him with dismay. For Colman, God was self-evident.

Who had created the earth if it was not an almighty God? And what of the knowledge in the earth? The knowledge that at a certain time when winter had imperceptibly shaded into spring then and only then would a seed grow and begin its struggle to fruition. Who but God? And the beasts including man whose seed was spilled into the womb of a female – who but God could make that seed into new men and women, new cattle and horses and all the beasts of the field? Who but God could hold up creatures in the air without their falling down and let others exist without drowning under the waves? And send in the sun by day and the moon by night? He was everywhere and indispensable, like the air itself. He was the air itself. Only an invisible almighty, all-creating, all-controlling God could explain all things that needed to be explained.

But to argue about matters of organisation!

He stumbled through. It was a long speech.

The criticisms from his brothers were harsh. That which he felt most keenly came from Celland.

'It is clear to all of us that you find this a burdensome task,' said the young monk, standing as he spoke, having waited patiently while his elders had commented on Colman's argument. 'And we all agree that it would have been better had this synod never been called. But called it has been and you have to speak as if you were speaking the word of God. You are speaking for Columbanus and Aidan, for Finan and Cuthbert and all of us here and those abroad on dangerous missions. Therefore I suggest that you make the argument much shorter.' Whereupon in a few neat sentences, Celland stripped Colman's argument to its essential points and represented it to him.

This met with the approval of most of the monks save a few who wished to see their own amendments and suggestions incorporated into such a significant address. The disputation went on for several hours, interrupted only by the required orders of prayers, and it was not until late at night that the monks could finally agree. Celland forbore to point out that their conclusion, arrived at after much stirring debate, was no more than a whisker away from his own initial suggestion. He, too, respected the openness of the Celtic church's means of arriving at a decision and had grown to love and respect it, despite the time it took and the opportunities continually presented for veiled politics and the settling of old scores.

So Colman now, with his new speech, unhappy on a stumpy pony, was heading south by the coast track to take his place at Whitby.

'With respect,' said Wilfrid, with very little respect in his tone, 'I think that I should be the one to put forward the Roman argument.'

Bishop Agilbert braced himself yet again for an onslaught from this formidable young man. Wilfrid was such an obviously sincere Christian, already a proven fighter for God and an outstanding preacher of the gospel, but sometimes he spoke like the very worst of the bullying pagan tyrants. When he would have his way, no one was allowed rest or peace until he obtained it.

It could have been so agreeable, Agilbert thought. They were at the court of the recently converted king of the Mercians who had demonstrated his newly varnished Christianity by showering the leaders of the Roman faction with gifts and hospitality fit for princes. They slept in the palace itself, enjoyed lavish meals and were flatteringly consulted by the king. Did Rome do it like this? Were the courts of Lyon so? At Canterbury was this the custom? Agilbert, sophisticated, Gallic, was quite entranced by this naïvety. And as a scholar he was interested in pagan gods and superstitions which, he soon found out, were still quartered in the Mercian palace. But Wilfrid would not leave him in peace.

Now he had tracked him down to an inconspicuous room into which Agilbert had been directed. Here were the clear remains of a blood sacrifice (a cockerel he guessed) and three small totem figures on what was a pagan altar. He had sat down to study these objects when Wilfrid burst in on him.

'We leave for Whitby in the morning,' said Wilfrid. 'There is never any time to talk when we are on the road.'

'On the contrary,' said Agilbert in his rather mincing tones, 'we talk all the time on the road. I am surprised we keep to the path.'

'Others overhear us and want to join in,' said Wilfrid, 'when it is none of their business.'

'We have two bishops, several priests, and at least four scholars who would be an ornament to any monastery, as well as an escort of eight warriors,' Agilbert replied, drily.

Wilfrid grinned and Agilbert, despite making the effort, failed to be unimpressed by it. Wilfrid's abrupt switches from thunder-brow to laughing face to longing eyes to snapping jaw quite fascinated and in the end mesmerised the elderly bishop.

'It is you and I who will decide what is said,' Wilfrid asserted, not grandly but as an opinion which would countenance no argument. 'Both of us know that.'

Agilbert squirmed with delight. Wilfrid's brutal openness appealed to that subversive voice which always longed to contradict the consensual Latinate exterior.

'It is *my* responsibility from Rome itself,' said Agilbert reprovingly. 'How can I let this grave responsibility loose on a young hound like you?'

I'm almost there, thought Wilfrid. It was the first time Agilbert had teased him in that particularly affectionate way. Press the challenge now.

'There is no doubt,' said Wilfrid, sitting elegantly on the edge of the table, lessening his daunting height but still rather unnerving the hedonistic bishop by his casual and carnal handsomeness, 'no doubt that you are the better man of the two of us: wiser, more learned, more spiritual, more experienced, nearer to God. I bow to you—' he executed a rather perfunctory nod. 'But this is a fight we must win if we are to crush the rising power of the Celts. They are loved by the people. I know them. I was one of them. They are dangerous to our cause and I who have lived among them know how dangerous.

'Moreover,' Wilfrid continued, his arrogance ablaze, Agilbert thought, admiringly, 'it was I who caused this synod to be called. Through the friendship I have with Alchfrid I persuaded him to encourage his father the king to hold a debate which would settle the future. King Oswy did not want it. He is a child of the Celts.

They succoured him when he was in exile. He believes that Aidan will be at the gates of heaven to bring him into God's council. Alchfrid wants it. And Alchfrid wants it because I persuaded him to want it.'

'But now that it is here,' said Agilbert, wilting under the combined bombardment of Wilfrid's physical domination in the small room and his hammer-on-anvil method of talking, 'why can we not express our thanks to you and proceed as we agreed?'

'Because it will not *work*!' Wilfrid slammed the table. 'King Oswy will scarcely listen. He is illiterate. He is a man of no intellectual stamina. But he will be careful to take notice of his son, for whom he has a respect and a fear. Even though the fear might be that he has heard from one of his witches that a son might rise up and murder him. What influences Alchfrid will influence him and I can influence Alchfrid. You, moreover, do not know their language.' Wilfrid and Agilbert spoke in Frankish.

'I will have a translator,' said Agilbert primly. Then added, wickedly 'You could be my translator.'

'I would be unreliable,' said Wilfrid.

Agilbert nodded. Wilfrid grinned mischievously: but it was still a form of blackmail.

'Translators have been good enough for other conferences I have attended,' said the old man.

'But not for this. You have the king against you. You are in the abbey of Hilda – she is against you.'

Agilbert kept his silence.

Wilfrid's mood changed quite suddenly and it seemed all the fight went out of him.

Agilbert gave him no help.

Wilfrid looked away, looked back, considered and finally said: 'You do not know, in your very soul, how dangerous these seeming sweet and often gentle people are. I do. They are fearless, as their brothers are in war. Both are a menace to the world and the order which has to come if Christ is to be triumphant in great kingdoms. You should let me do this, Agilbert.' Wilfrid added a final sentence, spoken as a threat: 'I will now go and pray to God to give you guidance.'

The old man, left alone, looked soulfully at the pagan altar but found that his scholarly peace of mind had gone.

CHAPTER FIFTY-THREE

Bega had known that there would be a synod and a debate at Whitby, but only as she travelled there did she begin to realise the size and importance of the event. They met some Pictish cattle drovers who told them of the royal progress of King Oswy and his court. A soothsayer with the company they had joined at Caerel told them of signs and omens in the east which pointed most certainly to a cataclysm. There were rumours, a monk from Coldingham told them, that from Rome the pope himself had sailed to the island; that there were emissaries from nations where people's skin was black or yellow or orange; that the whole area around Whitby was being plundered by Hilda for meat and bread and eggs, milk, poultry and cheese to feed the vast armies of scholars arriving at the abbey.

Bega understood that her request to Hilda would be a drop in the river if even half of the rumours were true, but she pressed on, even more eagerly.

She saw the stir from the other side of the natural harbour. The abbey, from a distance, seemed dressed for a festival. Temporary huts had been raised around the walls as if a siege were in preparation. In the weak sunlight of the morning on which they approached, she saw the glittering of horses' tackle and the inter-movement of many brilliantly-clad bodies striding about the far hillside.

As she drew nearer the seriousness of the gathering pressed on her. It came first from the seething number of monks and priests, bishops, abbots and clerks and all their ecclesiastical retinue. Bega had some experience of a courtly throng from her father's time and a little experience of churchly pomp from her days with the Abbess Hilda, but this was on an entirely different scale.

As she and Chad walked up the last lap, they went through the spillover, the rude, tented shacks of the slaves and servants of the more splendid visitors. She crested the first brow of the hill on which the abbey stood and was forced to pause, just to look. As always on returning, a shiver of happiness ran through her body. In one rush she remembered the time spent there as a blur of contented achievement: her talks with the stern but loving Hilda, the faces and experiences of other novices and nuns, remembered now as friends and sisters. For some moments she looked on in great happiness, proud of what the abbey stood for and what she herself had acquired there.

She went on and near the gate saw Wilfrid coming towards her. He was speaking in animated fashion to a rather gaunt but distinguished older cleric, a bishop by his clothing, although it was not of this country. Bega felt her heart step up its beat. She was no longer confused about Wilfrid. She chastised herself for misunderstanding his intentions.

How magnificent he looked! she thought. So very tall, his hair tonsured in the Roman manner but somehow suiting the leaner, browner face his latest expedition had left him. His stride an easy even loping rhythm. His intelligence radiating from the eyes, the wit of the face, the gestures, the rapidity of the talk – as they came closer – in a language she did not know. He had not lost his ability to make his ideas sit kingly on him.

She slowed down the closer he came. To pass her he would have to step off the narrow path and surely he would look up and see her. She prepared herself for it. She would smile, though just a little, and drive from her expression all the feelings that marred her opinion of him. She would not stay to talk but should he pause, then she would ask him about the trip to Rome but cheerfully, with no hint of reproach or regret. If he were to ask what she herself was doing she would be modest and imply that she was on a mission among the Rheged. She would not speak of the nunnery, which in any case seemed insignificant now as she mounted towards this new golden Jerusalem of abbeys. Above all she would keep her voice light and traceless of the torments which had driven them apart what seemed at once an age and a few moments ago. How often had she dreamed of that expedition to Rome! How infernal and ensnared those dreams had been!

Wilfrid looked up. He looked at Bega full face – directly. His gaze stayed on her for a few moments and he nodded at her smile. He took the arm of his older companion and ushered him safely off the path and carried on his intense conversation.

It was absolutely clear and without any doubt that he had not recognised her at all.

Bega was crushed.

She wanted to turn and yell out, 'Do you know who I *am*?'

Then she wanted to say, 'How could you treat me as you did? How could *you*, a man of God, be so contrary and so cruel to a bewildered young nun? Have you no guilt?'

Had he *no* memory of her? None?

She moved on, angrily. Could his invitation to her, his – courting of her – have mattered so very little to him? The encounter she had buried with such effort since, could that an emblazoned chapter for her have been no more than a quickly forgotten little stain for him?

Bega bit on it. Yes. It seemed so. In the scheme of Wilfrid she was nothing.

With Chad she entered the gates of the abbey and they were instantly immersed in a gentle pandemonium of languages, colours, faces, dress, a bazaar of sights so rich to Chad's meagrely fed eyes that he could have stood and stared out the day. Bega too felt herself uplifted by this churchly mass but pushed forward towards the parlour of the abbess to declare her arrival.

Hilda was not there but a firm young novice with the thick local accent which made Bega smile with a sweet homecoming recognition, told her to sit and wait. Bega was happy to wait. She let Chad go, and he strode off, his hand firmly on the handle of the sword she had let him bear more, she knew, for fear of its being stolen than from any readiness to draw it in anger. He wanted to be seen with it and went directly to the gardens in which he once worked, searching for old friends.

As Bega sat there, her excitement grew, fed on the sounds and the bustle and the ringing voices in several languages which populated the space just outside the open door.

Hilda came in after Bega had waited for an hour.

'What are you doing here?' The question sounded abrupt but was asked in friendly astonishment.

'May God bless you and keep you from harm,' said Bega, smiling at the flustered greeting. She bowed her head.

'May His blessings fall on you also,' Hilda responded, promptly, a little reprimanded. 'But what *are* you doing here?'

'I came,' said Bega, 'to ask your advice and to get your help on something that matters to me more than anything. But I see that you can have no time for such private and small things at present.'

'I will always be mother to you,' said Hilda, rather stiffly.

'But Abbess,' said Bega, raising her head and smiling fully at the tense, earnest, rather equine, she now thought, face of her dear mother in God, 'I cannot add to the burdens you must be carrying. Let us talk, if we may, when this synod is over.'

'That would be helpful,' said Hilda, and finally she too smiled and held out both hands. 'You look so very *well*, Bega. So very, very well. And all the reports I hear about your work fill me with nothing but pride.'

'All I do is follow the teaching and the practices I learned here.'

'It is true that I know how to teach,' said Hilda, without modesty, 'but we can teach only those who want to learn and you remain still the cleverest novice I ever met. I understand why you think that God needs you to set up a mission to Rheged, but in my prayers I ask God to send you back because we have so few women who are fine scholars. It is so very important that those who can overcome the difficulties of Latin devote themselves to recruiting other women. Our Lord needs the women to serve Him as well as the men and women beget women in the service of God. So you see how valuable I think you could be. When we talk, I warn you,' she shook the index finger of her right hand – a new gesture, Bega thought, or had she forgotten it? – 'I shall try to bring you back under my wing. The library now! Wilfrid brought such manuscripts back from Rome! Once you get yourself in there you will be impossible to prise out. Do you have a servant?'

'The boy – the man, now – who was with me when I was under your roof. Chad.'

'Chad. Yes. He will find his own bed,' said Hilda. 'He knows the place. You will have to join the nuns in the big dormitory. I am afraid there is no room at all elsewhere. As it is we are putting bishops in cells together!' She smiled innocently at what to her was the wonderful outrageousness of such a thing.

How she would have to summon up all her courage to tell Hilda she wanted to cease being a nun. With a comfortingly cowardly shiver, Bega was glad that it had been put off for a while.

'I must go now,' said Hilda. 'The organisation is very demanding and nothing seems to work unless I am there. Do you find that?' And she was gone.

Bega went up to the edge of the cliff to her favourite place. After the tentative lapping on the lakeshore, she welcomed the boom and heave of the great sea and for a while in the sunlight she was quite at peace with herself: unusually so. It would be difficult and sad to let Hilda down, but Hilda was no ogre. She was stern, but no tyrant. And, best of all, most releasing of all, Bega was grateful to know what she had hoped was true: the formidable abbess of Whitby rather liked her. This gave Bega the confidence she needed to sit through the synod, wait, and then, when the time was right, trust in the Lord and ask Hilda to release her from what she saw now had surely been the gentlest of chains.

CHAPTER FIFTY-FOUR

The abbey church was crammed. The door was left wide open
partly to let in the air and the sun and partly so that the
crowd outside the door could catch some of the words about to
be spoken. Wanting to include as many as possible in the event,
Hilda had placed two interpreters at the door, side-by-side with
two of King Oswy's bodyguards. The interpreters would relay the
synod to the crowd which, Hilda had thought as she had made her
way to the church, was rather like that attending on Christ when
He had gone up into a mountain to preach the sermon. They
were spread out from the door of the church down the hillside
like the tail of a monstrous fish, tight at its join to the body, the
door of the church, and then fanning out.

Hilda took her seat opposite Cuthbert. King Oswy sat in
front of the altar flanked by Alchfrid and Ecfrith, all three
in their royal robes. The interpreter inside the abbey, Bishop
Cedd, stood a few paces in front of the king. The supporters
of the Roman cause stood around Agilbert, Wilfrid and Agatho;
those of the Celtic stood around Colman and Celland and the
venerable Bishop Cedd.

Bega had taken the sensible measure of coming early to the
church. She had occupied her time in prayers for the Celtic cause
and special prayers for the safety of Padric and his war band. Her
discreet place against the south wall near the middle of the nave
enabled her to scan everyone.

It was striking how much richer and more confident the
Roman party appeared. Their robes completely outshone the
rather makeshift, plain, careless Celts. Even Colman, though
he had put on the attire of a bishop, looked a poor country
cousin compared with the grandness of Agilbert. Wilfrid, of

course, managed, Bega scarcely knew how, to dress fit to match the king himself.

King Oswy gave a sign: a drum was beaten several times. Silence followed. He stood up.

He took his time. In his heart he had little real gut respect for these men and the sprinkling of women. Could they fight in a battle against overwhelming odds? Could they raise a sword in anger and bring it down in triumph? One or two – Wilfrid, of course, everyone knew about Wilfrid, plus one or two others. But mainly they talked and prayed. He, Oswy, had to do his talking and praying while he was on the march, in foulest weather, under shelter that leaked with boots letting in the snow and a horse that refused to pick up its head and gallop harder that last mile; and then fight.

They depended on him for all their earthly endowment and life. But he, as he knew only too well from the devil dreams which still burned through his new Christian certainty, he utterly depended on them for his eternal life.

'We are here to decide a great matter,' he began in his high voice, and it rang around the high roof giving it, Oswy thought, an even grander importance. He was conscious, on the throne (which he had brought), set on the raised step to the altar, that he stood taller than anyone (save, perhaps, the self-important Wilfrid) in the entire assembly. He savoured that. In a hand-to-hand combat none would stand a chance against him. Why that thought came to mind in such a context did not puzzle him: he often satisfied himself by noting how feared or fearless he was. 'Today we assemble divided. Before this day ends we will part in unity. All of us who serve the One God and have been the recipient of His miracles, as I have, in my great battle against the Mercians, know that He demands one rule of obedience. As I do. All who serve me have to serve me with the same full measure of loyalty.' He paused while this last important sentence was relayed to the crowd beyond the door. Inside, Cedd translated it into Latin for the benefit of the several delegates who did not have Oswy's language.

'All of us long for our place in heaven,' he went on, an unmistakable message in his tone now. 'Thanks to the blessed St Aidan I have a man in heaven who is dedicated to helping me. But all of us want to go to the same kingdom of heaven. There is only one kingdom and we must all observe the same rules and

practices here on earth to ensure that we all go, through the same
rules . . .' Oswy, enamoured of the sound of his voice, was thrown
by the novel double echo, once from the high roof and secondly
from the interpreters at the door. He rather lost his thread. He
felt no anxiety. He stopped and collected his thoughts. It was
understood that the people waited on the king and these matters
were complicated. Alchfrid had given him some help but tried to
be too fussy with his Romanish ways and Oswy had preferred to
think it through for himself.

He continued. 'If we celebrate festivals at different times, then
we may fall into an error and not be true Christians and not enter
the gates of heaven. So we must all do the same thing, not as
we do now, some this day, some another day, so that some are
fasting while others are feasting and some have the Easter on a
Sunday and others any day of the week and so on.' He breathed
more easily. The end was clearly in view. 'Our task today is to
decide which argument holds true. That of the Celts with whom
I was happily turned into a Christian; or that of the Romans who
have many supporters here present. Now I shall sit and listen to
the arguments. I have with me for guidance my sons, my own
priests and scholars and my wife. Should I not be able to see
a clear conclusion – which I doubt – I shall turn to them.' He
paused. He could tell that he had acquitted himself with dignity
and honour.

'I call first the Bishop Colman,' he said and sat down, pleased
but now a little regretful that he had not thought of more to
say. Had he been addressing his thegns he would have been
less discursive and more arrogant. Here he considered himself
untested and, as his own mind was absolutely made up, he had
rather fancied the exercise of his undervalued oratorical powers
in an assembly which, unlike the stop-start exclamations or
epic histories of his own kind, seemed to enjoy long, winding
discussions.

Colman stepped forward with evident reluctance.

Bega felt her heart soften towards this old and, in the tension
of the assembly, rather vulnerable man. But his voice was firm,
and Bega noticed with sympathy the sweet anxiety on the face
of the young cleric standing beside him.

'I observe the date of Easter according to what I was taught
by my superiors and my brothers in Christ who sent me here,'

Colman began. He spoke in the local tongue for the court's sake. He paused, but only to appreciate and take account of the echo in the building and the repeated sentences of the interpreters. It seemed right to Colman that the last echo of his words should be in Latin, the language of the gospel, and he took comfort from a warm surge of memory of the days on Lindisfarne when, as a novice, he had been instructed by Aidan himself and learned his Latin from a saint. Who could deny the truth of such a man as Aidan? Yet this was what the Romans wanted to crush and wholly exterminate. With more vigour, Colman continued. 'All those who came here from Ireland and Iona, those most holy places, observe the customs I keep. They are the same customs long kept by King Oswy and his family before him, including the saintly King Oswald, whose miracles astonish us all to this day.'

He gained confidence as the attentive silence encouraged him. 'We are now told that our customs are wrong and that we must abandon them. Why? Our customs owe their origins to St John, who was especially loved by Our Lord. All the churches presided over by St John observed these customs and so we hold to them. There is no better authority than the blessed evangelist. Our church – following these customs – has nourished missionaries who have been martyred for Christ's sake and been admitted straight to heaven. They are known to everyone. The Lord God has given to the Celts the same blessings He gave to those early Israelites who followed Christ Himself. This too is known. Where there is barbarism, there you will find us with God. Where there is ignorance, there we will bring knowledge. All this is for the glory of God. Our customs, therefore, cannot be anything but correct. Otherwise why would God have manifested Himself to us so often and so effectively?' Oswy nodded vigorously: God had certainly been on his side in battle – the case was proved. Soon afterwards, Colman concluded what had been a crisp, quiet but effective speech. Bega noticed that the young monk grasped the older man's hand in reassurance as he sat down trembling slightly. Oswy, feeling that he was showing considerable fair dealing, called on Bishop Agilbert.

Agilbert looked around him thoughtfully. It would be difficult. A lizard tongue came out and licked the dry lips. The aquiline nose seemed to twitch, just a fraction and, in some distaste, not so much at the sweat-smells and dirty secretions from the pressed mass of bodies as from the necessity to dissect such intellectual and theologically intricate matters in such a vulgar, public way.

'I ask you now to explain the origins and customs of the Roman way,' said Oswy.

Agilbert nodded. He looked at Wilfrid, who stood beside him, arms grimly folded, staring ahead at no fixed point.

'May I request,' said Agilbert, 'that my disciple, the priest Wilfrid, be permitted to speak in my place. We are in agreement with each other and with all those priests who support the Roman cause. Wilfrid will need no interpreter and the full authority and complexity of our case is better explained without intervention.'

Oswy was not pleased. He had been told Agilbert and he wanted Agilbert. Alchfrid had undoubtedly got at this Agilbert. Alchfrid, *King* Alchfrid, was undoubtedly the most brilliant and pious of sons but on this religious dispute he had lost his head. Oswy was about to overrule Agilbert when Alchfrid leaned across to him.

'It was not I who persuaded him, Father. You have my word. It is Wilfrid who has pressed to speak. What they have to say is both complicated and very lengthy. With an interpreter and all the corrections it could last for a very long time indeed.'

Oswy nodded sternly as if some weighty point had been made.

He turned to Ecfrith as if balancing opinion. 'Let Wilfrid speak,' said Ecfrith, 'we've heard a lot about him. Let's see what he can do.'

Again Oswy nodded. He stood up and one raised hand quelled the buzz of chatter. 'I give my permission,' he said.

Alchfrid fought down his sense of exultation. Oswy regained his seat with a touch of the satisfaction of Solomon about him. Ecfrith, for the first time, became fully engaged in what until then had seemed to him a rather tedious ecclesiastical jamboree.

Bega too, already swept up in the pomp and seriousness and the unique grandeur of the occasion, felt a strong lurch of apprehension. Hilda drew an extra breath, worried immediately that his oratorical force would overwhelm Colman. But surely, she thought, refusing to believe the worst, Wilfrid would pay his proper debts to Aidan and the church which had bred him? Surely his Romanism would seek an alliance and not a victory? Cuthbert, Hilda noticed, closed his eyes in prayer.

Agilbert had given Wilfrid a broad hint that he might let the younger man speak, but not until now had Wilfrid been certain. For a few moments the unparalleled opportunity threatened to unbalance him. He chanced a look towards his friend Alchfrid. Alchfrid refused any collusion and Bega saw Wilfrid's gaze turn away, hurt. She watched Wilfrid so intently she felt she breathed with him. He looked around the assembly for a friendly eye which might give him that instant injection of love and belief in himself which seemed to have deserted him. Hilda's head was bent. Cuthbert's lips scarcely moving as his eyes closed in prayer. James, Romanus and Agatho, supporters of Agilbert, were too stunned themselves that the golden chance had been given to this young Northumbrian and their gaze reached inwards, heavenwards. For a moment, Wilfrid's scan crossed the vision of Bega and he hesitated and looked direct and then she knew he *knew* who she was. But she turned her eyes away.

He began over-passionately.

'The Easter customs which I shall prove to be the only true way are observed in Rome itself – I have seen that, I have been there. And Rome is where the blessed apostles, Peter and Paul, lived, taught, suffered and are buried! I can also tell you that the Roman customs are observed, as I have seen on my pilgrimages, in Gaul and Italy. Wherever I have prayed with men of God I consulted them and they all agreed that the Roman customs were the true customs. When I was in Rome I made further enquiry and I discovered that where there are priests in the vast pagan tracts of Africa, Asia, Egypt, Greece,' the heads of most of the assembly were spinning at this mind-stretching view, this dimension of all the earth that Wilfrid straddled and seemed to possess as he raced on imposing his case by his range, undermining it by his nervous boasting, 'throughout the world, I may say as I learned in my conversations with missionaries in Rome and on the way to Rome,' he fumbled for an end to his sentence, 'all of these men practise Easter and follow all the other customs of the heir of Peter on the throne of Rome. The only people who stupidly contend against the whole world are these Celts – British and Irish alike – who inhabit only a portion of these two uttermost islands of the ocean. Why should their stupidity be listened to?'

There was uproar.

Agilbert sunk his head low to avoid the accusing glares of his colleagues. The Celtic monks yelled out their anger. Bega herself felt stung and personally attacked by Wilfrid's contemptuous dismissal. Hilda quivered in indignation at being stained with the word 'stupid'. And from Wilfrid! One of her favourites. What was he doing?

King Oswy leaped to his feet, his hand going for his sword. Alchfrid put a filial but firm hand on his arm and held him back for the moment or two it took to reconsider. The crowd outside began to yell out against Wilfrid. The uproar threatened the synod.

'You are the king,' said Alchfrid to his father. 'Bring the synod back to its business.'

Oswy stood and this time he stood not as the moderator of a synod but as an armed warrior-king ready to do battle. He unsheathed his sword and held it high.

The disorder died down.

In all this, Wilfrid had taken stock. He knew that he had done badly. He knew in what way he had done badly and he knew how to make amends. The uproar stimulated him. The louder they howled outside, the more strident the muttering and accusations inside the church, the colder his supporters, the more heated his enemies, the more certain sure and confident Wilfrid became.

This would be a good battle now.

'I call on Bishop Colman,' said King Oswy and sat down, his hand still on his sword.

Colman replied promptly, stung.

'It is strange that you call us stupid when we hold to customs that rest on the authority of so great an apostle as John. One who was considered worthy to lean on Our Lord's breast! One whose wisdom is acknowledged throughout the world! One who even now sits on the right hand of God Himself!'

The Celts growled loudly and indecorously cheered their champion. Hilda nodded at Wilfrid sharply: honour satisfied. King Oswy beamed and looked around proprietarily as if he himself had voiced those combative words. Bega smiled at Colman's words and then flushed as she felt the full force of recognition from Wilfrid light on her face. Ecfrith nestled down in his large oak chair, his gaze and all his attention fixed on the increasingly calm face of Wilfrid.

'The priest Wilfrid,' said Oswy, without rising from his seat.

Alchfrid noted the insult to his friend but reined in his feelings.

Wilfrid's tone was different. 'Far be it from me to charge St John with stupidity,' he began, spurred on by a ripple of derision from the Celtic contingent who saw a man on the run, 'for he observed the law of Moses. At that time the early Christian church went along with many of the Jewish practices. The apostles were not able at that time – I stress again *at that time* – to go against all the laws given by God to the people of Israel in the Old Testament which contains their specific laws. They could not give offence to all those early believers who were also Jews and who wished to keep some faith with their Judaism. You will remember that St Paul himself followed Jewish practices. He insisted that Timothy be circumcised. He offered sacrifices in the Temple. He shaved his head at Corinth in order not to give offence to the Jews. This is all in the Testament given us by Christ through his apostles. You will remember that St James said to Paul, "Thou seest how many thousands of Jews there are which believe: and they are all zealous of the Law".'

Wilfrid sensed, correctly, that now he had made a start in gathering up the serious attention of the synod. Although there was still passion in his voice it was well controlled, but it gave to his sound a rhythm and sincerity which was impressive. It was the scholarship, though, which was netting the delegates.

'As all of you know,' Wilfrid continued, gently flattering the assembly, 'the early church survived triumphantly, thanks be to God and to His saints and martyrs. There is not time even here to go through the history of the spread of the gospel, although I would willingly clarify any details questioned by those who oppose the true Roman way. The law of the gospel spread. And it changed. Now, unlike the earlier days, it is unlawful for the faithful to be circumcised; it is unlawful for the faithful to offer animals in sacrifice to God as the Jews did and as the early Christians allowed.

John, one of the very earliest of the followers of Christ, followed the custom of the Law. He used to begin the feast of Easter on the evening of the fourteenth day of the month, not caring whether it fell on the Sabbath or any other day. But St *Peter*, later, in Rome where he preached, remembered that it was the day *after* the Sabbath that Our Lord rose from the dead. Therefore he knew that Easter had to be kept on a Sunday. But like John he was dutiful to the old law (as I have explained to you) and therefore he waited for moonrise on the evening of the fourteenth day of the first month.

'If the Lord's day – as the day after the Sabbath began to be called – fell on the following day, he began to observe Easter the same evening as most of the world does today. But if the Lord's day did not fall on the day following the fourteenth day of the moon, but on any day up to the twenty-first, he waited until that day and on the Sabbath evening began his observance of the Easter festival. This method of Peter's fulfils the law which ordained that the Passover must be kept between the eve of the fourteenth and twenty-first days of the moon of that month. This is the custom of all who have succeeded John. This is followed in the church worldwide and has been since Peter made it into an apostolic tradition. The council of Nicaea itself reaffirmed it.' Wilfrid's command of the detail of the argument impressed even those it confused. Now he turned much more gently to Colman. 'It is clear to me, Bishop Colman, that you follow neither the example of John as you imagine, for you have not the scholarship, nor do you follow Peter whose tradition you contradict. John kept Easter according to Moses but not on the first day after the Sabbath – you keep Easter only on the first day after the Sabbath. Peter kept it between the fifteenth and twenty-first days of the moon – you keep it between the fourteenth and the twentieth. You often begin to keep Easter on the evening of the thirteenth day, which is not in the law, nor does it accord with any study of the old Passover or Our Lord's injunction that we should celebrate his Passion on the fourteenth.'

Bega was fully engaged. The quality of the argument could not be denied even though she would never, she knew, succumb to the Roman way – however good the scholarship. Colman, she was confident, would have an equal battery of detail but in the meantime it was Wilfrid's time. She looked again at Cuthbert but his eyes remained closed. He would be the one to set Wilfrid in his place, she thought. In fact, of all those of the Celtic persuasion at this synod, Cuthbert could not only match Wilfrid quotation for quotation but bring to the argument a similar intellectual and moral passion. Bega felt comforted. God would move Cuthbert to speak, she was sure, if the need arose; even now he was calmly rehearsing what he would say. She concentrated on Wilfrid who in emphatic but not inflammatory sentences was hammering the arguments of Colman into the ground.

'I repeat then,' he concluded quietly, 'in the way you keep Easter you follow neither John nor Peter, neither the law nor the gospel.'

Abruptly, to the surprise of Bega and obviously many of the others, he stopped.

There was a buzz of questioning and then silence.

Alchfrid knew that Wilfrid had laid a trap for Colman.

Rather flushed, Oswy stood up – he had been drifting a little helplessly on the edges of Wilfrid's over-intricate argument. To the king it was not a matter of these head-aching dates and calculations but which men you believed in and which side could bring more miracles and victories in battle. He had heard nothing to shift him from the Celtic persuasion. He was however beginning to understand that Wilfrid was a truly clever scholar. The proof was that he had understood very little of what he had said. 'I call on Bishop Colman.'

Colman rose with rather a reproachful look at Celland. At this juncture he would have appreciated more detail. The decision to be brief had not been a good one and he should not have been swayed by the young man. He knew what he wanted to say but he sensed that Wilfrid's relentless scholarship was making a good impression on the synod, filled as it was with those whose lives were utterly governed by the sacred texts. He shook a little as he spoke, but his anger at Wilfrid emboldened him and his tone hardened and rang with accusation.

'Let me ask you this, Wilfrid. Do you maintain that Anatolius was wrong? Anatolius is so highly spoken of in church history that he cannot be contradicted even by you. Did what he teaches go contrary to John and Peter and the law and the gospel? He wrote that Easter should be kept between the fourteenth and the twentieth days of the moon. So how do you answer that? And what would you say to so many other holy men? Are we to believe that St Columba acted contrary to John and Peter and the law and the gospel? Are we to believe that Aidan was permitted by God to celebrate the greatest Festival of Christ His Son on the wrong day?

'Those are men of most exalted holiness. Their piety is confirmed in heavenly signs. Their virtues were manifested by miracles and the miracles continue. They were seen, Columba and

Aidan both, to be collected by the heavenly host and taken up golden paths into heaven itself. All of us long to emulate their lives and their discipline and to follow their customs. Is it conceivable, Wilfrid, in the name of God, that the Lord of all things could have let such servants as those live out their lives on the wrong path, sinning against the God they served so transparently? Are we to believe this?'

The strength of Colman's feeling exhilarated him. No one who knew him had ever seen him so ablaze. Celland squeezed his arm and directed his glance to the throne where Oswy beamed in undisguised approval. Alchfrid made a steeple of his hands before his face and waited on his champion patiently. Hilda – who was thrilled to the marrow by the unexpected force in Colman's words – noticed that Cuthbert had opened his eyes. Was that a small smile tempting the edges of his mouth? Ah! When Cuthbert spoke! Then they would be vanquished. Bega repented her lack of faith in Colman's ability to stand up to the power of Wilfrid. Like all the other Celts she felt the palpable tingle of imminent victory.

'Wilfrid,' called out Oswy laconically, again, pointedly, not standing.

Wilfrid waited until there was complete silence, until in fact the only sounds were those of the eternal gulls out in the shore air under the clear sun.

'I freely and wholeheartedly agree and acknowledge that Anatolius was a holy, learned and virtuous man,' Wilfrid began and Agilbert, who thought the cause utterly lost, nodded rather morosely. 'But although you claim his authority, I fear I must point out, Colman, that you do not act as he acted. You claim him but you do not truly know him. Anatolius followed the Roman rule about Easter. He observed the cycle of nineteen years. Either you do not know that this is the rule of the Roman church followed by Anatolius, or you ignore it. He calculated the fourteenth day of the moon at Easter according to the Egyptian method – of which it seems you are ignorant. The Egyptian method counts it as the evening of the fifteenth day. Again he assigned the twentieth to Easter Sunday, regarding it after sunset as the twenty-first day. But you do not appear to be aware of this distinction.'

Wilfrid paused. He knew that he was far behind but he knew as well that his best argument was still to come.

'Sometimes you keep Easter before the full moon, that is on the thirteenth day which is contrary to all the practice of Anatolius. With regard to Father Columba and Aidan I must reply in the words which will obtain at the Day of Judgment. For when the many say "Have we not prophesied in Thy Name, and cast out devils and done many wonderful works?", the Lord will reply "I never knew you".'

Wilfrid's delivery was now calm, authoritative and unnerving. The intake of breath from the Celts was like a sudden breeze rushing into the church. Was it possible that this young man, a native of the land but now tonsured and dyed in Roman practices, should be saying that their great fathers and saints would be turned aside by God on Judgment Day? It was unthinkable! It was the gravest heresy and wickedness. What devil had hold of the man's tongue?

Wilfrid let the reaction take its course and then overrode the incipient roar of outrage and disapproval. He held his arms wide open and said, loudly, 'I do not apply those words to your fathers. It is better to believe good rather than evil of those one does not know *and*, and,' as the roar threatened once more, 'I do not deny that they were truly His servants, loving God and loved by Him, loving in primitive simplicity but in all sincerity. I too have witnessed miracles near the grave of Aidan; I honour Aidan and all those men. Nor do I think that *their* way of keeping Easter was seriously harmful. For *at that time* they were not shown the Roman way which is the perfect way. They were good men. May they be saints in heaven. But I am sure that had they encountered the arguments of any true Roman they, they above all, would have accepted them and embraced the Roman way as part of their discipline of perfection. What we know of those men is that the word of God and the gospels were the blood of their lives and all due observances had to be preserved. God will pardon them.'

He paused and then he unleashed his final passion, though this time it was well controlled. 'But you, Colman, you and your colleagues are certainly guilty of sin, of sin everlasting which will bar you and all your followers from the glorious life of heaven unless you reject your mistakes and wrong practices and accept the ruling of the Apostolic See. I say again, why should you, the small band of Celts, be so obstinate? Can you, living on the very edge of the known world, can you be right and the whole world be mistaken?'

Oh yes! Bega thought. 'Oh yes!' she heard herself call out with
all her might. That would be glory. Her voice was heard but so
were those of several others who feared this peroration of Wilfrid.
He seemed so very sure of himself and the Celts were suddenly
apprehensive. Was God with him? What would he say next? But
yes, thought Bega, when you are against all the world, as Christ
Himself was, then, if your virtue is secure, then you must at
any cost stand firm, no matter what the threats and forces of
the enemy.

Wilfrid raised his voice and spoke over the rumblings of the
opposition. 'Your fathers were holy men,' he declaimed. 'But
do you imagine that they, a few men in a corner of a remote
island, are to be preferred before the universal church of Christ
throughout the world?' This time Bega's contradiction was kept
to herself but was no less vehement. 'And even if our Columba
– why I do not say *your*, for like me, like us, he was a servant
of Christ – even if he was a saint secure in miracles, can he
take precedence before St Peter, the most blessed prince of the
apostles, to whom Our Lord said—' (and here Wilfrid seemed
to grow. His voice which was quite deep, deepened to a sound,
they said, like the earth moving: there were those who swore
that angels came and hovered over his head and others said they
had seen the face of Peter become for these moments the face of
Wilfrid himself. Like many of those listening, Bega felt goose
pimples.) '—"Thou art Peter," He said, "and upon this rock I
will build my church, and the gates of Hell shall not prevail
against it, and I will give unto thee the keys of the kingdom of
heaven".'

Bega was transfixed. Oswy, who had dallied through the
speeches and already begun to think about what he would like
to eat and drink for the feast to follow, turned pale and glanced
at Alchfrid, who still allowed no expression to colour his face.
Internally, though, he was jubilant at the performance of his
friend. Ecfrith saw the likely outcome and began to construct a
path to meet it more than halfway. Hilda looked to Wilfrid in
disbelief. How could he do this? She would never forgive him.
Immediately her gaze switched to Cuthbert.

Why does Cuthbert not speak? Bega thought. He sits, open-
eyed now, still, so still, the only one who could answer this clap
of thunder. Why does he not speak out for our cause? He is one

of us. His powers come from the Celtic teachers and he is in the line of their holy men.

Wilfrid concluded after relishing the impact of those words – especially on Oswy, now clutching at Alchfrid and pouring questions into his ear. His voice now hammered home his convictions.

'Peter is the rock on which the Roman church stands. He is the rock on which our practices are based. I ask you, King Oswy, king of this mighty land, lord of the great fortress of Bamburgh, owner of mighty herds of cattle and of many estates, victorious in war, to make your judgment in favour of the Roman cause.'

Wilfrid fixed his gaze on Oswy. 'Let us drive wrongdoing out of this country, and out of the Christian world where it has no place. Let us tear it up and banish it and plough over its errors so that soon it will seem as if they have never been. Let your court and you yourself set an example to all your people and particularly to the Celtic clergy themselves that they embrace willingly and happily the true practices. If they fail to do this, if they persist in their wrongdoing now that they can have no excuse whatsoever for not knowing the true way, then the Gates of Hell will be open to them and they will burn in the fire everlasting and the devil will reserve for them the most venomous and relentless of his demons who will torment them day and night, night and day throughout eternity.'

'For the Gates of heaven will be closed to them.' Oswy was now mesmerised by Wilfrid. 'It is only Peter – only St Peter! – who was given the keys to the kingdom of heaven and only Peter can allow a soul to enter there.'

Oswy stood up, tense, with no dalliance or frivolity about him at all.

'Tell me, Wilfrid. Is Aidan in the kingdom of heaven?'

Wilfrid paused for such a fraction that it could have seemed that he was paying homage, executing a bow of silence to his king.

'He is, my Lord. For he did not know the true practice and yet God favoured him most highly as is evidenced to this day.'

'Colman,' said Oswy. 'Is it true that those words – the words about the keys to the kingdom of heaven – were spoken to Peter by Our Lord?'

'It is true, Your Majesty,' Colman replied, seeing the synod, his rule, even his life, suddenly threatened with a complete reversal.

'Was a similar authority,' Oswy continued, urgently, 'about the keys of the gate, was that promise ever given to your Columba or Anatolius or even the blessed Aidan who is in heaven?'

'No,' said Colman, and the word tolled away his followers like the funeral bell.

Cuthbert would now rise up, surely, Bega thought. She bent her head 'Oh Lord God of Hosts who has looked after this Celtic ship of faith, do not, I beg of You, let it be destroyed by Wilfrid.'

Bega's prayer was being echoed in other parts of the Celtic company as they realised that since Oswy had been thunderstruck by this revelation, the favourable judgment they had so surely expected might now not be given to them.

Hilda's eyes were fixed on Cuthbert with a look that was frenzied, even ugly in the effect it had on her face. But Cuthbert's eyes were closed once more and his head inclined towards heaven.

Oswy waved his arms to calm the sounds of fear and excitement which were leaking the air.

'Do you both agree,' he called out, loudly and urgently, 'you, Colman, and you, Wilfrid, that these words were indisputably addressed to Peter in the first place, and that Our Lord gave him the keys to the kingdom of heaven?'

'I do,' said Colman, the ice of fear hardening around his heart.

'I do,' said Wilfrid, fighting down the buck-jump of wild victory he smelled closer with every word Oswy uttered.

'Then,' said Oswy, 'all hear my final judgment. This judgment will not be swayed or challenged and will run from this time, this day, this hour for ever more and which will be obeyed by all who set foot in the lands under my rule and the rule of my son.' He turned to Alchfrid and, for the first time at the synod, smiled lovingly at him.

Oswy pointed to his own priest who struck the rush-laid floor three times with his staff.

'This is my judgment at the end of this synod held at Whitby. I tell you all. I am told that St Peter is the guardian of the gates of heaven. I shall not contradict him. I shall obey his commandments in everything; otherwise, when I come to the gates of heaven there may be no one to open them, because he who holds the keys has turned away. Although,' he nodded at Wilfrid, who returned the nod, 'Aidan is definitely there. There are more discussions to follow on the tonsure and on other practices in the church but these are matters I leave to others. The Roman argument has prevailed. I am now a Christian of the party of Peter.' He raised his hands and his eyes to heaven. 'Praise be to the Lord for making my judgment so clear and to Peter himself for reminding us of his power with the keys at the very gates of heaven.'

The king's party left the church and moved across to where Hilda had prepared a feast fit for them. Reluctantly, still unable to take her eyes off Cuthbert, Hilda followed them.

Once Oswy was gone, the Celts broke into tears, wild prayers and further arguments with their Roman opponents who made no attempt to conceal the pleasure this triumph brought them.

Colman was too stunned to move. He looked as if the whole burden of responsibility lay entirely on him and it was a burden he could never dislodge.

Even though he had feared he might speak below what was expected of him, he had never really thought he would be defeated.

'All is not lost,' said Celland, shaking his arm as if trying to rouse someone from the very grave of sleep.

But it was, Colman thought. It was. In one picture, in one vision, he saw the Celtic church, so fine, so loving to God, so ready to meet any dangers, talk to any man or woman, so devoted to scholarship and learning and the free roam of the holy spirit in man – all that would be tumbled down. All that would go. All.

It was unbearable.

If anything, Cuthbert saw the future more vividly than Colman. But he left the church without addressing his friend and sought out a place of solitude in which to pray and look for guidance.

Bega saw him go and wanted to rush after him and make him speak even at this late stage, speak as she had heard him when he compelled crowds, when he made pagan multitudes bend to the will of his faith. But he was swallowed up by the crowd and then he was gone.

'Bega,' said Colman, smiling wearily, seeing her, putting a hand on hers, unwittingly stopping her pursuit of Cuthbert, 'Why are you here?'

'I'm on a visit to the abbess.'

He looked so very sad, she thought. But what could she say? And he was determined to talk on.

'The best time to come to an abbey,' Colman continued, 'is not at a time like this but on a feast day. Christmas best of all. Or the abbot or the abbess's saint's day. I remember when I was roving these parts I planned my route to be at the few monasteries there were then on a day when I could get a real feed. God be merciful. There were so few houses of God then, you know, Bega, and now . . . they grow, they grow. God's will be done.'

'They grow because of what our missionaries have done!' said Bega, feeling her face hot with the injustice of it all.

'So they do!' Celland looked at Colman urgently. 'Without the work of you and those who went before you, what would there be here?'

Colman held up his hand in a gesture of peace. 'The missions from Rome came to Canterbury and worked for God in the south.'

'There is no comparison!' Celland exclaimed. 'They have secured nothing like – nothing, nothing like the number of souls that you have found for God. And where is their wealth? Look at the wealth that Oswy's royal house has given to the church of the Celts. Why should all this be taken away?'

'And on the word of one trained by us,' said Colman, wryly. 'Wilfrid was the most dashing and brilliant young initiate ever I saw. And then off he journeys to Rome and they capture him.' He sighed. 'But he is not lost to God. He is a fine priest. He has done God's work already in his young age and if spared he will do more. He spoke from beliefs held in virtue and good faith.'

'Do you think he was right?' Bega asked, almost choking on the words.

'Only God is right,' said Colman, 'only He will judge and the judgment will be a true one although to us it may seem mysterious at this time.' He got to his feet. 'Seeing you has given me some heart, Bega.' Celland shot her a jealous glance. 'You and your voice bring that wild beautiful edge of the world with its islands in the final ocean back to me. Maybe that is where I must return.'

'Will you not stay and fight?' Celland asked.

'The battle is lost,' said Colman. 'Did you not hear?' He smiled at Celland as he said the words but they were heavy with certainty and Celland, who had spent all his young energy supporting his mentor and earthly hero, burst into tears. Colman embraced him for a moment and then stood away and spoke to the caucus around him.

'Those of you who want to pay allegiance to the Roman way must do so. To be loyal to the king of this country you must do so. God will not think less of you. He will understand and those who were to be blessed will still be blessed. Those who do not want to go the way of Rome will have a very difficult path to tread. King Oswy is determined. St Peter he now sees as his salvation and he will not let go. Already King Alchfrid is his heir and he has been on the Roman side since the conversion of Wilfrid. Together with Wilfrid he will make a terrible enemy to any who think they can stay in this kingdom and resist. Ecfrith was something of a friend to us but I cannot ask you to count on his support: indeed on the terms of his father's command, it would be an open act of disloyalty for him to give it. The conclusion is very simple. Stay and be Roman; if you would be Celtic, go.

'As I will go. Yes. Already it is decided. But we must go first to Lindisfarne to tell our brothers of the outcome of this momentous synod and to explain to them what their choices are. Bega!' He turned to her and she came and knelt before him. 'I give you my blessing. May God keep you and guard you, free from sin and all harm, this day and for ever more. In the name of the Father and of the Son and of the Holy Ghost. Amen.'

'Amen.'

He helped her to her feet and nodded at the tears filling her eyes, running freely down her cheeks.

'There, there,' he said, 'God's will be done.'

CHAPTER FIFTY-FIVE

Oswy watched carefully as Alchfrid and Wilfrid embraced each other tightly in Hilda's roomy parlour. Had he been in some way manoeuvred by these two whose affection for each other was something he marvelled at? To trust any one human being as completely as that! It was beyond him. But Alchfrid, King Alchfrid now, was as ambitious as any son. Had he devised the whole synod to increase the power of Wilfrid, hence Rome, hence himself at the expense of his father? There was something Ecfrith had said. He only half-remembered it. He must find a way to have him repeat it.

Wilfrid disengaged himself from Alchfrid and came across to Oswy. Wilfrid, dark as Oswy was fair, stood even a little taller than the king himself and every bit as broad, though by no means as heavy. Alchfrid and Ecfrith too, though not of their father's bulk, were tall, big men. The feminine piety of the place seemed to quake at their presence.

Wilfrid looked King Oswy flush in the face, too boldly, and then kneeled in front of him. 'May God bless you and your kin for ever more. I am sure that in heaven there is rejoicing that at last this irregular branch of God's church in the world has joined the main stem of Jesse. Now will come a time – I promise you – when the church in your kingdom will grow to bring you glory not only in Britain but all over the world. I shall bring from Rome and Lyon and elsewhere, from the East and from Africa, painters and sculptors and those who can work in all sorts of metals unknown to us. There will even be singing in the churches and, from your kingdom, soldiers will go out into the wider world extending your fame and the glory of God. All this you have made possible today. The church of Rome will not hesitate to reward you and surely the Lord will, from this moment, number you as one of His select ones.'

Oswy, well used to flattery and not very good at discerning sycophancy, was moved by Wilfrid's kneeled speech of praise. It answered to everything he wanted. At last, he was being told – and by this brilliant young man – he would receive the fame and the rewards he deserved, and in both worlds.

He put out his hands and Wilfrid took the bristly, ringed fingers and allowed himself to be heaved to his feet.

'I will leave you now with your sons,' said Wilfrid. 'This judgment will need all your known cunning and skills to come to pass without too much rebellion.' He bowed and turned to leave.

'So it's St Peter!' said Oswy, smiling. 'St Peter at the gate!'

'Yes,' said Wilfrid, 'with the keys of heaven.' And he left.

Cued by his exit, the deputy guest-master came in with a tray on which was a flagon of wine. Heaped alongside the three polished bone goblets were berries, other fruits, bread delicately shaped with honey thickly pasted on it.

'The Abbess asks me to apologise. She will be here soon.' The young man's broad accent amused Ecfrith, who laughed aloud. The man flinched as if from a blow.

'Your man Wilfrid,' said Oswy, holding out his goblet for Ecfrith to fill, 'I have changed my opinion of him. He has the ear of God, no doubt about that. And of Peter.'

'No doubt at all,' Alchfrid echoed, taking care not to seem too fervent.

'What do you think he meant about rebellion? The monks of Lindisfarne? A few women could see them safely shackled!'

'They can be a very tenacious people,' Alchfrid replied. Ecfrith felt that he was wholly unnecessary to this small gathering but he stood his ground as he had long forced himself to do.

'But they are part of us now,' said Oswy. 'Our eldormen took their women from the beginning. We protect them. We bring peace and riches. And how can monks harm us? They have no swords and no spears and no training in war.' He drank with a flourish.

'They have the loyalty of the people,' Alchfrid replied, thoughtfully, and he held out his goblet to be filled by Ecfrith, who poured as willingly as at some future time he might deal out poison.

'The people obey me.'

'So they do,' said Alchfrid. 'And they fear you. They fear us which is as it should be. But they have always been fickle, especially those in the outlying regions where our rule is most recent and most lightly exercised.'

'Then we must exercise it more heavily,' Ecfrith interrupted. 'We must make sure that their bases of power are aware that to side with the Celtic misdoers will be to incur the wrath of King Oswy.'

'If the monks decide to follow Rome, then there will be no trouble,' said Alchfrid. 'The key to the whole of this may lie in Lindisfarne. Certainly Colman will have influence. If Lindisfarne decides to follow your judgment, then the others will be less restless.'

'Perhaps I should go to Lindisfarne and encourage them?' suggested Ecfrith. 'And from there to those outlying regions to make sure they know the consequences of any attempt to oppose the judgment of the king.'

'Not yet!' Alchfrid spoke sharply. 'You are always too quick to look to prevent trouble which is often the best way to start it. Not yet.'

'But not too late,' said Oswy. 'The judgment has been made at a famous synod. It must be obeyed or where will my authority be?'

'I agree. As always, you are right,' said Alchfrid, soothingly. 'But this is a deep wound. Perhaps they do not yet realise the extent of it. Soon they will. Soon they will see that much of what they have prided themselves on is gone. Like the tribes we have conquered by arms, they will see that they have been conquered. We cannot give them too much time, I agree. But we must have charity for a little while.'

'Not to enemies,' said Oswy, abruptly, a little lightheaded from the heat of the day, the emptiness of his stomach, the heaviness of the wine.

'The best victories are those won with no loss of life,' said Alchfrid.

'They are very few,' said Ecfrith, sure that he was speaking for his father and on his father's side in this, 'sometimes war is essential for peace.'

'See how God let me win a war against massive odds,' said

the king, 'and look at the peace we have all around us now as a consequence.'

'Lindisfarne will tell us what we must do,' said Alchfrid.

'Better, I think, that we tell Lindisfarne what it must do,' said Ecfrith.

Oswy nodded his approval at Ecfrith's contribution and held out his goblet for more of Hilda's wine.

There was one person even more important to Wilfrid's sense of complete conquest of the Celts than his close friend the new King Alchfrid.

He left Oswy's temporary court and stepped out into a crush of people. Big as the abbey grounds were by all neighbouring comparisons, they had never been designed with such a swarm in mind. Horses bumped and jostled against each other; servants and slaves carrying food and beer shouted for passage way; there were cries and threats from some of the Celts while the Roman factions huddled excitedly together. The nuns looked exhilarated as they threaded their knowing way through the crowds but now and then Wilfrid caught an expression of fear: the excitement and bustle was not friendly.

For a moment or two he watched with some distaste. It was all so unnecessarily disordered. Although he had been Celtic-trained and still, though grudgingly, acknowledged the depth of their piety and the strength of their determination to live as they preached and follow in the footsteps of the Lord, he found it hard to conceal his disdain. Their robes were so cheap. The tonsure – the front of the head crudely scalped and the hair falling thick and long down the back – was absurd. Contrast the neat crown tonsure of the Roman party and the care taken to find good cloth, fine leather shoes, leather belts, garments appropriate to those who served the greatest of the kings. And listen to the howling of the Celts! He had heard nothing like it save the funeral wails of dark-skinned Egyptians in the forbidden parts of Rome. They had scholarship but the worst of scholarship

– learning held to with unscholarly fanaticism. They had faith but they gobbled at it every bit as vulgarly as the most naked, skin-painted, bloodshot-eyed pagan. Look even at the way in which it was their clumsy, ill-trained ponies which were getting in the way!

In his new Roman world everything would be organised. There would be none of these impromptu prayers so beloved of the monks of Lindisfarne, none of the sudden summer wandering on a mission leaving the seed unsown, the fields unattended to, the animals gorged with milk, as monks just upped and followed their inner voice to barbarous and wild places seeking comparison with the apostles and the cenobites of the Old Testament. The business of religion would not be this indulgence in the fate of the individual soul but in the future of the whole church, Wilfrid thought. His task was to help build a church as wealthy and powerful and triumphant on earth as was the church of God in heaven.

The more he stared at the disorder of humanity scuffling and barging in front of him, the more convinced Wilfrid was of the strength of his position. All this nonsense that to become a hermit was the highest state, for instance. Who had said that? Where was the authority? What was the point? Devils disappeared when you went about God's work in the real world. Devils were most of all afraid of steady progress. He, Wilfrid, had known his share of devils but the way to deal with them was not to retreat into time-consuming solitude but to go out into the world and preach against them: build churches, found monasteries, convert courts, amass wealth for the church, commission craftsmen, make holy books, do the work of God. No devil could survive that.

As for worshipping someone like Cuthbert and saying that he was at the apex of Christian ambition! What had Cuthbert said or done in the synod? There it was. A meeting of forces - look at them – the Franks, the Gauls, the Picts, the Celts, the Irish, the Saxons, the Romans from Canterbury, the Angles, those from Frisia and even Spain, all gathered to this cliff rock overlooking the sea to settle the central problem of Christian worship – and what had Cuthbert done? Closed his eyes! Mumbled to himself. Said nothing. Yet this man – admittedly a holy man to whom (to Wilfrid's chagrin) God gave miracles – was someone who longed to be 'worthy', to be a hermit, lost to the world, abandoning it in a gesture of selfishness. Had Christ stayed in the wilderness? No. He had gone there for a purpose. Once He had achieved it, He had returned to build the church in the real world.

Well, now I can have my way, Wilfrid thought, with a huge breath of gratification. Now we will see what the real church is made of.

He pushed his path through the congealing mass, modestly acknowledging the praise thrown out by those of his persuasion, forcing a meek countenance despite the burn of ecstatic omnipotence which raged through him. Eventually he cleared the worst and walked towards the quarters of Ecfrith's wife Aetheldreda.

Bega, still sunk in shock, came towards him. Wilfrid now remembered who she was and appreciated the handsome and intelligent face and figure so unlike the ravaged demonic he had rightly skirted away from those years before. He shaped his thoughts for an apposite comment and his face for the telling degree of charm.

She walked clean past him, seeing but ignoring him.

He turned and grinned widely after her. That was better!

Hilda had cleared part of the hospital for Oswy's wife and for Aetheldreda. When Wilfrid arrived, Aetheldreda was alone.

When he came through the door, Aetheldreda prostrated herself before him. Flat on her face on the ground, arms spread wide. He looked down at her and, unseen by her, smiled deeply, wolfishly. She rose up and held out her hands. He bowed and then kneeled before her, eager not to be outdone in the religious theatrical display which Aetheldreda cultivated to an extreme degree.

'It is not for me to bless you,' she said, earnestly, 'All Christendom should thank you and pray for you for what you have done today.'

'Your blessing would be more than enough,' said Wilfrid.

Aetheldreda considered what he had said. She was a sincere, deeply serious woman to whom chastity, religion and her royal duties were all of importance but the greatest of these three was her chastity. It was the governing factor in her character and her life. Its public nature and the imposition under which Ecfrith suffered as a consequence were a source of constant enquiry and gossip. It drove her. She had the white set-faced inflexibility of a fanatic. Sometimes her skin seemed almost translucent from her constant internal battle to purify, purify, purify.

'I will give you my blessing,' Aetheldreda replied, 'but it is not "more than enough".'

Wilfrid's small sigh and further bent head accepted the rebuke. She put her hand over his shaven crown and lifted her eyes upwards to call on the blessing of the Lord. His submission made her feel powerful.

He stood up and Aetheldreda said: 'I will talk to Ecfrith. You must have more land for your work, more farms to support the monasteries.'

'Is Ecfrith still anxious about these gifts?' Wilfrid asked with a face which perfectly suggested that it was all immaterial anyway; that the accumulation of wealth and property was of no serious consequence to a true believer.

'He has an argument,' Aetheldreda replied in earnest fairness. 'He fears that if too much wealth is given to the new monasteries, abbeys and churches, and if too many young men are moved by God to devote their lives to His service, then the kingdom will be weakened. It will not have the reserves to fund its army nor will it have as many men to call on to be warriors. For we know that some of those coming forward for the work of the Lord now are of wealthy and highly born family who previously would have come to our court or found the court of a minor chieftain to train as warriors. Ecfrith fears that you, especially,' Aetheldreda's brows knit hard as she concentrated on being scrupulous, 'are to some degree a bad example. Where you ought to be a warrior, a leader of a war band around your king in the great hall, you are building monasteries and travelling to Rome. Many of the young see you as an example they want to follow.'

'But I am the leader of a war band,' said Wilfrid quietly, 'And I do sit in the hall of my king. Ecfrith's battles are on earth, with the bodies of men; mine are on earth but with the souls of all, converted and unconverted alike.'

'I tell him that of course,' Aetheldreda replied, reassuringly, always a little apprehensive when Wilfrid's voice dipped to a low, friendly whisper, 'but I thought it only right to put his argument before you.'

'I understand,' said Wilfrid. 'But now he need fear less rather than more. With the force of Rome behind us, the greatest throne in Britain will become mightier yet.'

'God is with us,' Aetheldreda nodded emphatically. 'After King Edwin and King Oswald, we now, through our repentant king, have the allegiance of all the chief tribes in the land.'

'We can learn from Rome,' Wilfrid said, dreaming of the conquests of the bearers of the imperial eagle. 'Once Britain was governed on orders coming from Rome. One Roman governor was enough to keep it in order and to build what we have inherited as ruins: walls, roads, towns, cities, forts, shrines all far beyond the capabilities of our people now. That was pagan Rome. Now let us see what we can do with Christian Rome.'

'I wish,' said Aetheldreda, 'that I could stay here at Whitby with Hilda. To lead a life of prayer and service to God with others devoted to nothing else. It would be the height of earthly joy.'

'It is better for the church if you remain at the court,' said Wilfrid immediately. 'You are the true voice of faith in the most powerful court in the land. God must have known this when He caused you to be married to Ecfrith.'

'Must I accept this?' Aetheldreda's plea was heartfelt. 'I hate the court. I hate the eldormen with their servants and slaves, the feasts and drunkenness and the barbarous stories they tell, the jibes. And Ecfrith is . . . Why can I not be given some peace here?'

'When God wishes you to leave the world in which He has put you,' Wilfrid replied, firmly, 'then He will undoubtedly give you a sign. Until then, I am certain that He wants you to be His eyes and ears at court.'

Aetheldreda nodded, sadly. When Wilfrid spoke for God, she had no option but to submit.

'There is a site near a place called Hexham,' said Wilfrid, after due pause, 'which, when cleared, could provide a most excellent location for a house to be raised.'

'Did you know that I have lands near there?' said Aetheldreda, smiling. 'Perhaps your site is on some of my land . . .'

CHAPTER FIFTY-SIX

Later, Bega sought out Colman. He had gone back into the church and was on his knees at the altar when she came in. Celland and three others kneeled nearby. Bega came close to him and she also kneeled in prayer.

The noises and bustle of outside were sloughed off. Bega felt that Colman was in direct communion with God.

Straining her ears, she caught the faint murmur which rose softly from his lips: as if he were so close to God that all he need do was whisper.

He stood and turned and saw her and said: 'I was praying to God to send you to me.'

A thrill shot through Bega and she swallowed hard.

'Leave us,' he said to Celland and the others. 'And if you can stand at the door and kindly beseech anyone who wants to enter to allow Bega and myself a little time to do the Lord's work, I should be happy.'

Celland looked almost reproachfully at Bega but he was still shaken by the defeat and Colman's authority commanded him.

'Come here, Bega. Let us sit together.'

She wanted to burst into tears. He was so painted in misery and yet he appeared even serene.

'Why did the Lord let it happen?' she asked.

'We shall never know all His ways,' said Colman. 'All we can do is to pray and follow His word and look for signs. Some day it will be revealed to us and then the dark glass will be light and we shall rejoice that this has happened on this day.'

'No!'

'You are young,' he touched her arm, 'like Celland. You want all things to come to pass at once. Sometimes the story that God is telling us is a long one with many stops and starts and journeys of digression. All we can know is that this was done for a purpose. Holy men were here. The devil did not dare enter this church.'

'Sometimes the devil can appear as the most holy man of all,' said Bega. 'Look what happened to Anthony when he was tempted in the desert. The most evil words came uttered from the mouths of those he thought his truest friends in Christ.'

'No one today spoke in the words of the devil,' Colman replied, firmly closing that subject down.

Bega felt rebuked: her feelings against Wilfrid were boiling up and, unchecked, she would say the most terrible things. 'What will we do?' she asked.

'We?'

'Our church.'

'Our church is now a defunct church.'

'No! I hate their church! I hate all their rules and organisation and wealth and all the ordering of you about. We are on earth to prove our souls, not to behave like little emperors!'

'Beware that you neither say nor think that which you will regret before the Lord.'

'But what *is* to become of our church?' Bega reined herself in but her plaintive note was unmistakable.

'It is the church of God,' said Colman steadily, 'and belongs to no one. And it is not so simple. Bishop Agilbert, for instance, who prepared the case with Wilfrid and then passed on the burden of speech to him, trained with me in Ireland. He came there from Gaul. We studied together and he was a true man of God. Is he now my enemy? Wilfrid himself began with the Celtic teaching. Conversely, at Lindisfarne I have not only monks out of Ireland and the far north and the other Celtic regions but those German-English, some from good families in Northumbria, who prefer our way. There are Celts in the southern lands of Britain and both Celts and English in the mountains of Northumbria. And again, in Ireland itself there are those, like the revered Ronan, who are of the Roman persuasion.'

'Yes,' said Bega, her self-possession recovered to some degree, but still obstinate. 'Yet the truth is that this announces the end of the Celtic church. Doesn't it?'

'It does,' answered Colman, after a while, and the two words tolled so unhappily that Bega wanted to reach out and touch his arm in comfort. But her training forbade it.

'We have followed our own way for so long!' said Bega, almost bitterly. 'As you said, how could God give us so many saints if we were all so wrong all of the time? I know that the exact date is important and Wilfrid argued cleverly,' she said this loudly as if to tell God that she was weighing all things fairly in the balance, 'but how much more important is prayer, and good practice?'

'I was not given the tongues of angels,' said Colman.

'Everything you said was true.'

'God moved King Oswy to decide against us.'

Bega bit her tongue on her impression of the big, sprawling, reedy-voiced Oswy. She had heard widely how he perpetually boasted of his God-given victory and held lavish public baptisms for visiting or for submissive chieftains beside the remains of the great wall which overlooked the site of that battle. Yet he had been unseated so easily and by a common quotation any Irish Christian would have absorbed with their mother's milk.

'Why did Oswy not know that Peter kept the keys to heaven?'

'Perhaps he had never been told. Perhaps he had not fully understood the meaning of it.'

'He looked to me as if he had never heard it.'

'The king is not a scholar. But he is a Christian.'

'Is he a Christian as we – we in our church' asked Bega defiantly, 'would consider? Padric,' she flinched but the name had come out, 'always told me that he suspected that these invaders now calling themselves English simply added Christ to their list of pagan gods. He said that they did it for nothing more than advantage. They had not nor would they ever understand the beauty and the truth of the way of the Lord.'

'King Oswald has many miracles to his name,' said Colman, of Oswy's most saintly ancestor.

'He could have been an exception,' Bega replied, grimly. And then, all but blurted out 'What will you do?'

Colman did not hesitate. 'First I will go back to Lindisfarne and report my failure to my brothers in the community.' He lowered his voice. 'And then I will go back to Ireland where I will continue to practise the old ways. If I am misguided, then God will punish me. But I cannot change. Wilfrid is indeed a clever man but he did not convince me. God forgive me but that is so. Oswy is king of the Christian land of Northumbria and lord of many other lands of Britain whose kings do him homage, but his judgment did not change me. God have mercy on his soul and on my soul.'

He looked at her closely and she felt drawn into a great confidence. 'I shall go back to Ireland soon. It is a place favoured by God and I put my trust in that. I cannot suddenly be turned into a Roman. I will find a place near where your father had his court. There is an island out to sea called Inishboffin: the island of the white cow. The stories are of a dark people coming there near the beginning of time but I know that now it is all but empty. Once rid of its spells and the witchcraft, which must overlie it, Inishboffin will be a place where myself and other free souls will make our stand and live until we are told to die.'

For a wild moment Bega wanted to beg to come with him. She thought she had never admired anyone as much as she admired the defeated Irish bishop at this moment.

'That is where you can help,' said Colman and once again he looked around, but the church was theirs alone. 'That is why I prayed to see you. You live in a place ideal for those, for I will not be alone, who will be on the move to Ireland. Resistance will be offered against today's judgment and that resistance will provoke a pursuit. Our people will need help along the way to escape to Ireland. Your nunnery on the lake is perfectly placed. Rheged is small but it is a kingdom they still prefer to leave alone. You are all but hidden there in those savage mountains where no one who does not know them likes to enter. Near you is the sea to Ireland, the best route, one that passes by the Mann Island, which always provides a refuge. All I ask you now, Bega, is that you promise me that you will be there to help us. That when I myself come or send others, they can know that you will be there to help them on their way.'

'I promise,' said Bega, instantly, proud to be asked, longing to serve this resolute old man who would not surrender.

'Thank you,' said Colman. As he levered himself to his feet she noticed the deep lines of anxiety and exhaustion on his thin brown cheeks. Around his eyes the skin was blue-black with fatigue. Now she did reach out and help him. He held her hand warmly.

'God bless you, Bega,' he said, 'and bring you safe to His kingdom.'

She watched him go, knowing that she could never let him down. Yet the terrible consequences of her promise had already begun to creep into her mind.

CHAPTER FIFTY-SEVEN

Later, when Hilda found the time, she tracked down Cuthbert. He had left the synod and gone immediately to the edge of the cliff. There he had found a narrow goat track and slithered down until he found an overhanging rock to afford him the concealment he searched for. In this place, rock above him, sea to the right and the left and before him, grey-lead sea, lead-grey sky, he prayed that Oswy's judgment would be proved to be good.

Like all the others who knew the king's sympathies and background, he had been thrown by the dramatic twist at the end of the synod. He had been unsurprised at Oswy's ignorance. But unlike the rest of the Celtic party, Cuthbert had found Wilfrid's arguments sound. He had not expected to be swayed by them and still wished that Colman had been able to counter them with evidence as scholarly, but either the evidence was not there or God had counselled Colman not to seek it. But whose side God was on was not the question. What was the meaning of God's decision through King Oswy? It was that alone which had to be understood.

In a world of zealots Cuthbert's zeal was outstanding. At a time when there were those prepared to go to any lengths to torment and torture their bodies for the good of their souls, he was unparalleled for the ferocity with which he attacked what he contemptuously called 'the weak vessel' of his body. Among learned men he was known for great learning: among preachers his preaching was held as a model. His bouts of strange, contorted spasms where he seemed possessed by devils or imps were forgiven as evidence of the forces the enemy had to bring to bear against such a champion of God.

In all that he did he aimed to be in the elect company of

saints. He wanted it so much he dared not think about it. He cursed his own presumption when the thought crossed his mind and punished himself as harshly as he possibly could for thinking that one day he might join in perpetual happiness in heaven with Paul, Matthew, Mark, Peter, John, all the apostles, and be near the light of Christ Himself. He would arrive there only if he followed the true path.

But what was the true path?

Like others educated in the Celtic way, he had venerated its open and simple and effective traditions. He had also taken on some of the Roman ways. This was common. But he had been faithful to the Celtic cause.

Now God, through Oswy, had thrown it all over.

Was Oswy the true voice of God or was the ancient foe using Oswy to mislead the church?

Why should Oswy, saved as a boy by the Celts in the far north, proud to speak their language, ever boastful of the love he bore for Aidan, so unexpectedly turn against all that had nourished him and sustained him and primed him? Was his ignorance real?

Was Oswy being instructed by God or by the Devil?

Cuthbert got on to his knees which were scraped by the sharp rocks. The knife east wind hit him full on but the cold sweat still stood on his brow as he struggled to discover the will of God. There could be no compromise. Either Oswy was to be obeyed or he was to be disobeyed, in which case exile would be the only answer.

The wind rose and cut into his smarting face as if to lash him into a solution. Below him the sea crashed on the shore, the spray splitting the roll of waves into a thousand protests against the rule of rock.

Eventually, with no revelation granted him and feeling very weak, he clambered back up the slippery cliff in the entombing dusk. As he walked rather stiffly back down to the abbey, he was spotted by Hilda.

'You look like a ghost,' she said.

Cuthbert started. Had he been turned into a spirit? Was this the punishment for doubt? He swayed and would have fallen had not Hilda been there to hold him.

She was a strong woman and frequent fasting had left Cuthbert lean. She had no trouble in helping him back into the abbey. She took him to her quarters. Hot gruel and wheaten bread was sent for. Cuthbert ate gratefully, shivering all the time. A second bowl of gruel and some honeyed cakes calmed him down a little but still he would shake uncontrollably for a few minutes before declaring that he was in no difficulties.

When he had recovered enough to talk coherently, he began in the middle: 'Where does it leave us, Mother? What are we to do?'

Hilda had come to Cuthbert to ask him precisely that question. Was he not the wise one, revered by all? But, obediently, she took on his question and tried to answer it.

'We must obey,' she said, dully.

'With whose tongue was the king speaking?'

'We are not to know now. If it was not God, then God will reveal it later. For now we must accept that it was God and we must obey.'

'I looked out to the sea,' said Cuthbert. 'The vastness of it, the clouds and the sky under the heavens – so massive and so incomprehensible. I have not enough faith. The water, I thought, it comes down on to us from the clouds and rolls into the sea. The clouds bring us water but not the water of the sea. Where does the new water come from if not from God? Yet the salt water is His also. If we drink the one we are refreshed: if we drink the other we are maddened and eventually we will die. Yet both have the same source in God. How are we to tell, Hilda, whether in the mouths of mere men, whether kings or not, we hear the Almighty or the black angel foe? Can we drink it or not?'

'Why did you not speak these things? At the synod.'

Cuthbert shook his head.

'You would have spoken in the Lord's voice.'

'Would I?' Cuthbert looked at her, directly, and the hardness which could quell a crowd intimidated her. 'Would I?'

'Yes,' she managed, decisively. 'Most definitely.'

'Are you certain? Are you convinced that we must abandon all our loved and proven ways?'

'We must obey the king. God was with him in the synod. When such a number of holy men are gathered together – as the apostles knew – then what comes to all of them must be the voice of law.'

'The men and women who nurtured us were pure in heart,'

said Cuthbert, sadly. 'Wilfrid, whom I love in God, is a different soul. With him the church comes more and more into the world. It needs to command and to organise. Our simple Celtic church wanted to go more and more out of the world. It wanted to convert and to liberate. A time is passing, Hilda. I see it. A time is going. One age is about to give way to another. If this is the will of God, then so be it. But who but us will be so wholly concerned with the souls of the pagan?' he said, jealously. 'Who but us will take such care to learn and read and teach and copy and take through the dangerous world the very words of God? The Romans have none of our passion.'

Cuthbert fell silent and Hilda waited, feeling that she was watching over him. His body rocked slightly as if he were seeking a conduit to God. These two holy people, long friends, sat and attempted to understand the divine will.

'We must obey,' he muttered, sadly, finally.

'Perhaps it will be all for the best,' she said, 'there is always so much that we cannot see or know.'

'There are things that I can see,' said Cuthbert, firmly.

'Can you tell me?'

'Are you one who can be told?'

Hilda was offended. She bowed her head, silent and out-wardly meek, and struggled with her anger at Cuthbert's casual questioning.

'For what I see,' Cuthbert continued, in a voice of strained passion, looking beyond Hilda, at some distant point, 'is a most terrible storm. It comes up out of a calm and even sea. At first the storm seems composed of clouds as most storms are, but as these black twisting billowing shapes grow larger and come closer, I see that they are not clouds but devils disguised as black skeletons, their tattered black garments twisting in the wind, the skeletons spirited into all manner of horrible contortions, grinning. The bare black skull-mouths are agape and there is a terrible howl of joy coming from their dead mouths as they sweep towards us and I can see now that they have swords under their tattered rags, swords glistening with fresh blood. They are hungry for more as this monster of destruction comes closer and closer to us and will surely overwhelm us all.'

He had stretched out his arms during the trance of his prophecy. Abruptly the energy left him and he fell back. Hilda looked at him in alarm. There could be no doubting the truth of Cuthbert's prophecies. Though she herself had not, until now, been present when such a forewarning was uttered, she knew that Cuthbert had foretold deaths, illnesses, loss, famine, restoration of health. It was one of his apostolic gifts.

'What does it mean?' she asked, in a whispering, fearful voice.

'The devil is let loose and will come to strike, and he will strike hard.'

'Where?' Hilda rushed on 'Here? Here because of the synod? I have seen storm clouds like that coming across the sea and sometimes they have been so black and evil that I too have thought them devils. But our prayers averted the arrival of devils in that way. Will it be aimed at the abbey? How can we repel it?'

As soon as she found herself talking about going on to the offensive, Hilda felt more secure. 'We *must* repel them,' she said with that boundless enthusiasm which drove on her scholars.

'When we know more,' Cuthbert replied, 'only when we know more.'

He went back to his food and gobbled at it with wholly uncharacteristic greed. In some way, Hilda regarded this as a sign more ominous than the prophetic storm of devils. Prayer, she decided, briskly, a barrage of prayer would be laid up against that invader. But how to understand the ascetic, self-punishing, self-neglectful Cuthbert scraping his long fingernails around the bowl to get the last of the gruel?

'Are you still hungry, Cuthbert?'

'Yes. Yes.' He handed his bowl to her. 'We must all be strong,' he said.

❧❧❧❧

Agilbert saw Colman and his party going towards the horses and he broke away from his company to go across to him.

Celland saw him coming, scowled and put an arm around Colman's shoulders to keep his gaze firmly averted and hurry him away.

'Colman!' Agilbert's accent was unmistakable. Colman turned

immediately, paused for no more than a single heart beat and walked towards him, shrugging off the restraining hand of Celland, who followed him with the intensity of a bodyguard.

The two men, old by the years of the time, distinguished in their bishop's robes, so different in feature – the round-faced Celtic-tonsured Colman, the hawk-profiled Roman-tonsured Agilbert in much more considerable sartorial majesty, came together with unaffected pleasure.

'May God bless you.'

'And His blessings on you.'

Agilbert spoke Hisperic Latin and Roman Latin as well as his own native tongue. Colman too had good Latin.

'Are you setting out on your journey now?' Agilbert asked, kindly.

'I must tell my brothers before someone else does and alarms them with the presentation of the judgment.'

'That is thoughtful of you, Colman.' Agilbert's face expressed a sorrow through which he tried to smile encouragingly. 'It need not be so very bad, you know,' he said. Colman merely smiled.

'And you?' he asked, with genuine warmth. 'Will you be going back into Gaul soon?'

'I'll stay a while,' Agilbert replied. 'To make sure that the details are all worked through properly. These young men can be in too much of a hurry. No stamina.'

'I've left two of my best monks to work with yours,' said Colman. 'They are true men of God and will be honest.'

'I've no doubt of it, Colman. If you brought them along then that is a guarantee.' He smiled. A sweet smile, Celland had to admit. He was surprised by it. 'I didn't imagine, all those years ago,' Agilbert continued, sadly, 'when we were so happy in Ireland as students, that we would be face to face in this way.'

'Nor I,' Colman responded. 'You know, I still find it difficult to absorb the gravity of it. Is all my church and all it has been and all it has done to be hobbled and pushed aside in this way?'

'Not "pushed aside".'

'Not in your scheme of things, Agilbert. But I fear that your young Wilfrid has a less lenient view.'

'He will find that the rock of truth will break the wave of his fanaticism.'

'He thinks of himself and of his argument *as* the rock of truth *and* the wave of fanaticism or, as he would undoubtedly put it, the will of God.' Colman's tone hardened. 'Why can we not co-exist? Surely, Agilbert, mere men cannot say that there is only one right path to the throne of God? Is it not wise to allow many in case the one we all choose turns out to be mistaken?'

'That is not how things can be any more,' said Agilbert, firmly. 'Everywhere the church is in danger – just a few places keep it alive, often thanks to the monks and scholars who come from Ireland and your other strongholds, yes, Colman. But to survive, the Word of God must go through the pope himself. He declares that now we must come together and stand side-by-side and fight the enemy.'

'We Celts were never reluctant to fight the enemy, Agilbert, as you know.'

'I do know. And many things that we have said annoy me because I have been in your beautiful and pious country, blessed by God Himself when so many were in total darkness. I am annoyed, for instance, even at times by the very Christian enthusiasm of Wilfrid when he speaks of what Rome will bring to you in your kingdom. It is you who have so much to bring to us. Your arts, your crafts, your books and your evangelism, above all your living as you preach. We need that, Colman. Would it help you to know that I, and others, long for the virtues of your church to be on our side?'

'But we are,' said Colman, simply, 'are we not? We are on your side. You, like me, like all your brothers and all mine, are on the side of the Lord of heaven. What more is there to say about "sides"? What other "side" matters to Christ?'

Agilbert sighed and this time his smile was not percolated through any regret. 'I always knew that there would be some who would not come with us,' he said, 'and I ought to have known you would have been one of them, Colman, bishop and friend in Christ though you are.'

'And friend in Christ I will remain,' Colman replied.

'So you will defy the judgment?'

'First I must talk to my other friends in Christ, at Lindisfarne.'

'But you will, I can see it, go against the judgment.'

'I trust,' said Colman, with quiet passion, 'that never in my earthly life will I go against the judgment and the will and the love of Him who rules my heart. I will pray for you, Agilbert. God bless you.'

Agilbert made the sign of the cross as the Celts moved away to be on their return journey. He stayed in the fast-cooling dusk until they had mounted and turned their horses down the path which led to the safe harbour, leaving Whitby, Bay of the Beacon, behind them.

For ever, Agilbert saw that. Colman would not come back to Whitby nor would he come to all that Whitby had stood for.

The east wind whipped at the thin cheeks of the old man and the salty specks of water felt like the tears he wanted to shed for the loss of Colman, who had been such a helpful, cheerful, innocent scholar with him when they were young and in love with the words and the meanings of Christ; who had never been anything but a true example of piety and faithful working; who most likely had never strayed from the straight path although as beset by the devil as any man, perhaps more than most, for the soul of Colman would be a fine prize to secure.

A lift in the wind set off a shiver. He had been standing too still in the cold for too long. The shivering brought a foreboding. Agilbert shook the fear out of his mind: they were all men of God.

The last of the Lindisfarne travellers disappeared from view and Agilbert's heart sank.

'God bless you, Colman,' he said, aloud, into the wind, 'God bless you and keep you safe all the days of your life.'

CHAPTER FIFTY-EIGHT

Bega had come to a tremendous decision.

She waited outside Hilda's parlour until she could bear it no longer. Finally she gathered all her courage and went in from the cold dark to a room, fire-warmed and glowingly lit by fat tallow candles.

'Bega!' Hilda whispered in fierce reproach at this unappointed visit.

'I'm sorry, Mother Abbess,' Bega began.

'Shhhh!'

Hilda, proprietorially, directed Bega's glance towards Cuthbert, fast asleep, curled up beside the fire, knees high upon his chest, breathing so lightly now that a feather would scarcely have been stirred by it.

'I do not want to leave him,' Hilda whispered. 'He has had a vision and he may have more. I want to be with him if they should become too violent. In his sleep and dreams he is too open to the devil. I am praying for him and keeping them at bay. What is it you want?'

'I must,' Bega took a deep breath, 'talk to Cuthbert.'

'He must sleep. The Lord needs his strength.'

'It is important for the Lord that I speak to him.'

'You will say twice your prayers every day for three weeks for assuming that you know the mind of the Lord above His wish that Cuthbert, His most faithful servant, benefit from sleep.'

'I am sorry, Mother Abbess, but I *must* talk to him.'

'What is to be gained by this urgency?'

'While so many of them are still here. Colman is already gone but he has left some of his party so that's better than nothing. Others will be off at dawn. Cuthbert and I must do something while they are here.'

'Cuthbert and you?' This was not whispered. Cuthbert stirred. Hilda shot an angry glare at Bega who had provoked her into normal speech.

'He will understand when I wake him.'

Possessed as she was by the mightiness of her idea, thinking indeed that it may well have come directly from God Himself, Bega, quite to Hilda's astonishment, walked the few paces forward, bent down and shook Cuthbert by the shoulder, at first rather gingerly and then with some muscle.

He woke with a querulous whimper and sat up rubbing his eyes like a child.

'Whatever did you do that for?' said Hilda. 'What have you learned in Rheged? You have been out of my care for too long, Bega. This will not do.'

'Bega?' Cuthbert peered out, seeing her and sensing that her zealous look engaged him alone.

'I have thought of something – perhaps the thought was put in my head – but I have thought of something which can utterly change this day and restore our church to where it was before the synod.'

Cuthbert caught the dangerous certainty in her tone and was fully awake. He stood up. Hilda too. The three of them looked at each other with Hilda the most in ignorance.

'Do you know what you are talking about, child?' she asked Bega, coldly. 'Or has the excitement of the day curdled your mind?'

'For a while it made my mind as black as a devil,' Bega confessed, 'but now the burden is lifted. I can see a way.'

'Let us talk about this in the morning,' said Cuthbert. 'It has been a momentous day. It needs prayer and meditation before we can discuss it with profit.'

'The morning will be too late!' Bega's urgency increased. 'Most of them will be gone. We must talk now.'

'I beg of you, Bega,' Cuthbert offered a faint smile, 'let a more experienced Christian advise you. All that has happened needs careful thought.'

'No. It needs action,' said Bega. 'It needs to be reversed. And I know how that can be done. And so do you, Cuthbert.'

Cuthbert glanced at Hilda who took the cue firmly. 'Bega, I

command you to leave this place. Cuthbert will talk in the morning if you have anything to say. I shall decide that when we two talk – as we will – after Lauds. God go with you, Bega.'

Bega had forgotten how Hilda's clear and fair-speaking imperiousness could shake her. She all but made to leave but the stakes were far too high. She stood her ground.

'May I be forgiven, Mother Abbess, and may you give me all the punishment you think I can bear, and more, if what I have to say seems to you to be less than essential for the blessed future of the church that you and I and Cuthbert and Colman and all the others heard today was to be no more. Cuthbert—'

'I think, Mother,' said Cuthbert, holding up an effective hand to silence Bega, 'that despite all your proper reservations, I must speak with Bega. To spare you any further trouble at the end of such a day, I will walk with her and she will have her say. God's will be done.'

Hilda drew in a powerful lung full of breath and squared her shoulders as if to offer defiance to this man who had turned to her and now pushed her aside. But Cuthbert's understanding glance did something to reassure her.

It was hardly tolerable that she was not to be included. Yet Cuthbert's attitude allowed for no dissent.

'I will go to the chapel,' she said. 'I had intended to do so when you fell asleep, Cuthbert. I too need to come to terms with this "momentous day". God be with you.'

'And with you.'

'And may He keep your soul in its perfect charity,' said Cuthbert, smiling warmly at her.

Hardly mollified, Hilda left them together.

An embarrassing silence descended on them. Cuthbert stared down rather moodily at the low, spluttering fire. Bega was disinclined to speak first.

'Now, Bega, tell me what it is you have to say.'

'I think you know.'

'Nevertheless. Tell me.'

Now, for a moment, she was uncertain.

'It is the cross,' she said.

'I thought we had agreed not to discuss that,' said Cuthbert, amiably enough.

'Did we?'

'Perhaps I misremember. What I do remember,' he turned to full face her, the flow of the fire further gentling the comforting expression on his face, 'is that when you came to the new monastery – at Bega's Haven, as we call it now! – I was exhausted from a bitter, venomous struggle with one of the most vicious of our enemy's army. I thought he had broken my faith.' He paused. 'You gave me the strength I needed in the Lord, Bega. I still feel that I asked you for what no earthly creature had the right to ask. Forgive me.' He steadied himself for what he knew would be an assault from this bold, attractive young woman now as utterly dedicated and fearless as any warrior.

'I have already forgiven you,' said Bega with some resentment.

'We must repeatedly be forgiven for sins which we repeatedly remember, especially those gross and irremovable sins for which at the gates of heaven we will need to offer up an explanation.'

'The cross would help us all at the gates of heaven,' said Bega, suddenly seeing a way forward. 'That is why I want to see you and talk to you. You most of all can judge what a revelation of the power of God it would be if I were to show the king the fragment of the True Cross. Don't you see? If I were to show – to King Oswy, to Wilfrid, to Bishop Agilbert, to all of them – that the True Cross had been revealed through the humblest handmaiden of God *and in Ireland* which is the home of the Celtic Church, do you not think that would make them think again about crushing our church? Do you not think that this evidence would convince King Oswy even more than the keys of St Peter? He cannot be seen by God to reject the True Cross, can he?'

She stopped and waited for an answer. Cuthbert had turned away and was once more staring down at the fire. He made no response. The silence became strangulating. Bega forced herself on.

'And then there is the cross which is in the living body of a Celtic monk. How that will strike them! How will Wilfrid talk his way out of *that*? It will be seen as a sign. So it is. It *is* a sign. Is it not? Is it not a sign?'

Again she ran against the wall of his silence. It made her falter – for what was it she was doing that was wrong? Into the silences of God she had been trained to read many answers. Into the silence of Cuthbert, all she read was a reproach.

The silence said that she was not speaking true.

The silence said she was on a wrong course: so wrong that for Cuthbert even to join her would endanger his far more purified soul.

The silence said: I am the silence of Cuthbert and what I bid you is to add to it the silence of Bega; and then we will part in peace.

'But don't you see?' she cried. 'This is why it was given to me. This is its meaning. God alone knows how unworthy I am. How vile I have been. How weak and scheming. But He gave it to this feeble vessel precisely to show the careless glory of His benison. Let me show the cross to those remaining here; let me try, I beg you. Otherwise,' her voice began to break and tears filled her eyes, 'otherwise it is over for us! All that we have done. All that so many have fought for with pure hearts and the understanding of the Lord, all the tortured and the martyred and the lost and lonely and desperate who gave their lives and their souls in our free simple way which can touch the people so. All that will be over. How can you bear it?'

And still he made no reply.

Bega sank to her knees and grappled her hands tightly before her in prayer.

'Dear Cuthbert, I beg you in the name of the Father of all things, let me do this. Let me show to the world what grace and eternal bounty God has given us.'

His silence was implacable.

Even when she sank to the floor and prostrated herself before him, he did not turn from the fire.

Only in the tension of his face did he reveal the effect of her cry. It was one of the greatest of temptations, he was sure of that. To use the cross for such an advantage, such a merely earthly advantage, a political advantage, to display it and have it questioned and then worshipped throughout Christendom and the whole of his further life to be lashed to this fragment of wood. No. He knew. That was not why God had commanded his soul. That was not why the cross had been given.

When Bega had cried herself out and reached silence, Cuthbert turned and prayed 'In the name of the Father, and of the Son, and of the Holy Ghost, Amen. God rest you and keep you safe this night and for ever more.'

'Amen,' said Bega, choking back a final sob.

When she stood up and looked around, he was gone.

CHAPTER FIFTY-NINE

The time came for a crucial decision to be taken and Ecfrith did not balk at it. He had no love for Wilfrid, fearing the handsome and brilliant young priest's influence over his wife. He was suspicious of his territorial ambitions. He was even so bold as to have doubted whether Wilfrid's religion – which seemed to entail constant travel, bequests from king and pope, trappings beyond the reach of all but the most powerful princes – was an allegiance to God or Mammon.

But the synod had convinced him of one big matter. Wilfrid was a force, and it was better to go with him than against him. Wilfrid had left him in no doubt that he was at the front of an army which would not be denied. It was time to strike a truce. From now on, he would need Wilfrid. In the mêlée of triumph, a reconciliation could be made without any loss of honour.

Ecfrith, therefore, rather to Alchfrid's dismay, stuck beside him when he left their father. Alchfrid would have preferred to be alone. The new young king's intention was to indulge in an informal stately progress as the night drew in and the candles and flares and rushes lit up the cliff side so that, from afar, families crept out of low huts and forest lairs to gaze at the sight as if stars had fallen from heaven on to the earth. In truth, Alchfrid simply wanted to seek out and return congratulations. It had been a fine victory and, though it was not wholly Christian to exult, it was wholly impossible not to.

He found all he wanted. As the day had gone on after the dramatic ending of Wilfrid's speech, the excitement had increased. How huge a reversal! How much change would follow! What of those who disobeyed? Would there be spoils for the victors and how would they be divided out? Was Colman . . . ? Would Wilfrid

. . . ? And the king himself . . . ? Unashamedly, Alchfrid breathed
in the seething atmosphere of jubilation and deep anxiety, the
murmurs of prayer and conspiratorial speculation. Half a pace
behind him, Ecfrith expertly directed all praise to his handsome
brother whose hair gleamed in daylight and, later, rushlight, whose
fine Germanic face was flushed by the flames from the torches and
the fires sprinkled around the abbey.

Eventually, in the evening, Alchfrid met up again with Wilfrid.
Ecfrith was still alongside him. Wilfrid, also, was far too excited
for sleep. He wanted to keep moving, seeking the applause, the
touch, the compliment, the tribute.

'I have not been able to tell you directly how magnificent you
were,' Ecfrith began, even before he had greeted Wilfrid. 'Alchfrid
and my father know how much I have been speaking out in your
praise. Such scholarship! And St Peter's keys! That completely
finished them.'

Wilfrid looked a little warily but there seemed no doubting
Ecfrith's sincerity, and praise from the normally truculent Ecfrith
was worth savouring.

'I was merely the messenger,' said Wilfrid.

'But without a messenger, how will the word be delivered?'
Ecfrith countered.

'We always thought you were too absorbed in your war bands to
be moved by such matters!' Alchfrid spoke of Ecfrith but ignored
him and smiled at Wilfrid. Ecfrith made an effort and decided
not to be offended at their attempt to cut him out.

'I am not as devout as you, Alchfrid, nor will I ever be. As for
Wilfrid, today he has proved to me as to many others that not
only is he a true Christian, a man through whom God Himself
speaks, but he is one who can lead us into new times which will
make our kingdom even stronger.'

'Ah!' said Alchfrid, 'You see military advantage here, Ecfrith.
That's it, is it?'

Ecfrith controlled himself with difficulty. Alchfrid was treating
him like a buffoon. 'I see that my eyes have been opened by
Wilfrid.' He knew that flattery demanded all the exaggeration it
could command and he laid it on. 'I think – Wilfrid must guide
me here – that the church and the court will march together.
This church of Rome, Wilfrid, is itself a court – it has its pope
who is king on earth and through his authority its thegns and

eldormen. Its priests and bishops go out to conquer the world but always hold on to their oath to the pope. So we send out war bands and warriors to conquer and we too demand that the oath of allegiance brings all they do back to our court – the court of my father and my brother.'

He had Wilfrid's full attention now and he ignored Alchfrid's impatient gestures. 'But you spoke of a more powerful empire, Wilfrid: concerned with the kingdom of God, of course, but determined to reinstate the warrior force of the Roman legions. This is far different from the Celts. This is news you have brought us, Wilfrid, news which will change and encourage us and strengthen us if we seize it as we should. For this I am grateful. I wish to count myself as your true friend. You will find me your strong right arm in upholding this new order: quick to defend it and ruthless in putting down its enemies, in scorching the fields of tares.'

Ecfrith embraced Wilfrid, powerfully, letting the full square strength of his body impress itself on the taller man.

'God bless you,' said Wilfrid, grateful that a thorn had been removed. 'I too will be your ally and as you work for the victory of our church, so shall I.'

Ecfrith held Wilfrid's gaze for a moment, his blazingly sincere eyes confirming this healing gesture. Wilfrid experienced a genuine release of tension. Ecfrith as an enemy had not been comfortable. His reputation as a killer was already well established and Wilfrid had sensed real danger over his religious friendship with Aetheldreda. Ecfrith knew it was time to go.

'To bring over Ecfrith,' said Alchfrid, when his brother was barely out of earshot, 'is like changing the lives of the Philistines, and all the inhabitants of Sodom and Gomorrah in one blow.'

'He has shown he can be saved,' said Wilfrid, concealing his satisfaction under pat piety.

'He has shown,' said Alchfrid, glancing around carelessly to see his brother striding through knots of people who gave his imperious stride full space, 'that he knows when he needs to forget a grievance.'

'Not a fault, surely?'

'Perhaps not.' Alchfrid was about to go on when Wilfrid interrupted: 'Agilbert must be rewarded.'

'I have spoken to him. He wants to go to Paris where he will take up the bishopric.'

'Ah. He has decided.' Wilfrid was a little piqued that Agilbert had informed Alchfrid of his decision before telling him. Indeed, the only wrinkle in the smooth roll of that day's fame had been the rather masked, even grudging attitude of Agilbert. Jealousy, Wilfrid concluded, though he would never say this out loud, was a most poisonous devil: almost as wicked as material envy.

'There will be bishoprics here to fill if Colman, as I guess, and one or two others – Cedd? – decide that they cannot live with my father's judgment.'

Wilfrid bowed his head.

Alchfrid reached forward, put an arm across his neck and pulled him towards him, playfully.

'Can we think of any young, able priest of the Roman persuasion who could be offered one of these bishoprics without bringing disgrace on the office?'

Wilfrid had a humble moment and then he looked boldly into Alchfrid's eyes.

'It was a good day!'

'It was a good day!'

The two young men smiled at each other in silent triumph.

They had won! They had changed the world and now it was theirs! They had *won*!

'Praise God,' said Wilfrid. 'Praise God!' And both of them laughed loudly and challengingly in the shadowy flickering light.

⟡⟡⟡⟡

It was not until two days later that Bega found an opportunity to speak to Hilda with the prospect of some undivided attention.

By then the crowds had drained away. A few of the temporary camp-homes remained: Hilda thought that they would be useful for the servants and the workers who came in to help with the gardens and the farming in summer. Otherwise the cliff top which had fructified with life and the clash of colours, the noise and rich stench of animals and the sounds of strange voices, was as it had been.

Hilda felt relieved. The organisation had worked. The abbey had served the synod well. The king, bishops, priests and scholars all had thanked her and no one had complained. It was a mundane part of God's work – to provide hospitality – but at such a vital confluence of minds and at what had resulted in such an historically important outcome, the mundane rose up the scale of values. She had cause to be satisfied and she allowed herself to enjoy that.

Now that all but a handful of clergy and scholars had gone there was some trepidation. Some of the monks, a few but unfortunately one or two of the brighter ones, had already refused to be tonsured in the Roman fashion. This visible defiance worried her. She was prepared to let it pass for a few days until the deep sense of order, which she had tried to introduce into the abbey as, she put it, her poor attempt to imitate life in heaven itself, was fully resumed. But it would have to be tackled. It was not much help that one or two of the monks she had always suspected of frivolity were prancing about with their new tonsures like children with their first dagger.

There was also confusion. The offices of the day had to be changed and she found in herself a reluctance which all but threatened disobedience. The offices and daily order she had brought into Whitby had been honed in Lindisfarne. Though no woman had ever been allowed on to that holy place, the rule had been given her by Finan, who had learned it from Aidan, whose authority stretched back through Iona to the distant sanctity of Ireland itself. Hilda knew its ways. It had come to fit her so well that it was her life. Before he had left, Wilfrid had explained the superiority of the Roman offices and pointed out how little they were different in many cases from those from Lindisfarne: but they were different enough and she had to pray hard to melt her reluctance.

Most of all there was a feeling of sadness. Something had gone. Not just from her life. Not just from Whitby. Not just from the kingdom itself. Something which had been part of the earth and the air had been exiled and part of her own spirit felt exiled too. Although she scarcely dared to admit it, she felt that Wilfrid had betrayed her and Cuthbert had failed her. Yet how could she criticise such proven men of God?

It was in this reflective mood that she met Bega who appeared at her door just after dawn in a state of distress.

Hilda's thoughts about her had been fair but severe. She had not enjoyed being usurped in the presence of Cuthbert. The young woman's apparently very close relationship with someone who stood so alone had always puzzled Hilda. Now it amazed her as well. Moreover Bega had arrived at Whitby, uninvited, at the most inopportune moment imaginable. Bega looked in need of serious help just when Hilda herself was in need of restoration after the demands of the synod. Yet she was fond of Bega. Even now, as the wretched figure came so unhappily to her, there was so much she liked about this zealous but elusive, waif-like woman.

'I am busy,' she began. 'This cannot be a long meeting. You must come to the point.'

Bega nodded and swallowed the misery of not being allowed to ease herself in. But she was used to obedience, especially before the Abbess Hilda and most especially after the way in which she had behaved when Hilda had left her with Cuthbert.

'I have sinned greatly.'

'Then you must confess. But not to me. I am not prepared to take confessions. I am too agitated.'

'I must talk to you.'

'Very well then: talk.'

Hilda indicated that Bega could sit down. She leaned forward in her own chair and exuded a forbidding briskness. Bega, as often, took strength from the strength of the opposition.

'I fear that when I made my vows they were made under false pretences.'

She paused, distressed as she had been increasingly over the last two days, at the way her life had been shackled to this fate because of her own ignorance and the diffidence of Padric.

'Go on.'

'When I made my vows I thought I was a virgin.'

Hilda's brisk manner became harder, almost menacing. 'Would you explain that remark more fully?'

'I truly believed I was. A few days ago, I discovered that this was not true.' Briefly she outlined what Padric had told her. Hilda's menace softened to an earnest interest.

'Did you have any recollection at all of the – fact, the – act?'

'None.'

'None?'

'None.'

'Then God must have spared you that memory with some purpose in mind.'

'God has spared me for a purpose,' Bega said, surprising herself both by the words themselves and the even tone in which she delivered them.

'What, may I ask, is that?'

'I am not allowed to say.' She decided on a course of action. 'Cuthbert can tell you. I may not.'

Hilda nodded slowly as if she understood everything but in truth to conceal the new rush of annoyance and jealousy. She had been right . . . there was a link between the two of them. But what it was she could not begin to guess.

'There is another matter,' said Bega, more confident in having confounded the abbess.

'Well?'

'I wish to renounce my vows.'

'There is perhaps no real need for that. In fact,' Hilda continued, thoughtfully, 'unless you are given express and authoritative permission to quit your vows then you are still bound by them. And nothing you have said makes me want to grant you that permission.'

'But I must,' said Bega. 'I must be allowed.'

'Why?'

'Because I have promised Padric that I will go with him and be his wife.'

'You were not free to make such a promise.'

'You must release me.' Bega felt panic beginning to swarm up inside her. 'You must!'

'What about yet another promise?' Hilda asked. 'Are you not going to tell me about that?'

Bega's head jerked back as if the question had been a fist to the jaw.

'Bishop Colman is a very old friend,' said Hilda, lowering her voice. 'He told me of the escape route he was planning in case anyone I knew should need it. Of course,' said Hilda, 'only in the most extreme cases would I allow anyone under my charge to go into exile in defiance of the king's judgment. But Colman knows how sympathetic I was – and I am – to his missionaries. And you are the key to his plan. You gave him your promise.'

'I did.'

'How then can you go off with Padric and also remain at your nunnery to help those whose aid you promised Colman?'

'I could arrange it.'

'How?'

'It need not have been me at the nunnery. As long as someone was there who was trusted.'

'It was you who promised. And in the disturbed times ahead, who can be trusted?'

'Very well, I could stay there until the storm blows over and then I could go with Padric.'

'In which case you will remain in orders and under my authority until the storm has truly blown over.'

'Please let me go. I am unworthy of this calling.'

'According to yourself and, you say, Cuthbert, you have been especially selected by God.' Hilda's tone was hard.

'That could be to help Padric to protect our church. That is clearly much more important now than when I arrived here. He will want to defend it.'

'But I am now under obedience to suppress and change some of the teachings of our old church,' said Hilda, 'and, Bega, so are you.'

'I was brought into a church different from the one described by Wilfrid and accepted by King Oswy.' Bega did not add 'and so, Hilda, so were you', but the unsaid sentence hung uneasily in the air between them.

'Why did you not speak at the synod?' Bega asked, surprising herself as well as Hilda.

Hilda blushed angrily. It was a question she had not quite had the courage to ask herself and she greatly resented it coming from her inferior.

'Everybody would have listened to you,' Bega persisted. 'Even Wilfrid. You often told me how you knew him as a young man. You made him sound like a younger brother. He would have listened.'

'Wilfrid . . .' Hilda could not trust herself.

'We should *all* have spoken,' said Bega. 'We should still be speaking. We should not have stopped until we had defeated them.' And once more she said 'Why did you not speak?' and the repetition sliced through Hilda's friendship for the young woman, however brilliant, however close to Cuthbert. She could not be challenged and impaled in this way.

'We will pray,' said Hilda.

'What am I praying for?'

'Guidance.'

'Guidance? For what?'

'For the salvation of your soul, Bega, which now stands in danger. Let us pray.'

Bega clenched her eyes tight and longed for a sign. In the deep pocket of her habit, the fragment of the fragment of the True Cross lay; when would it reveal its final purpose? Would she understand when it did?

Hilda moved steadily from one prayer to the next.

Bega felt that for the first time she was in a position to decide on her life for herself. Until now she had been shifted by others, whether Cathal or Padric or Hilda or Cuthbert. She had not been blessed with that inner certainty she saw in others; until now she had seen that as a failing, almost a sin. Her excessive fasting, her over-determined learning, were her attempts to show to God that she could serve Him. This was despite the awful admission that somewhere in her heart there was still the continuation of that first doubt over her vocation and her reason for choosing the vocation. Had she always betrayed Him? And always failed Padric? And was she now to fail Colman? Would there always be this battle in her soul?

As Bega found that she could think more clearly about herself and her own needs and choices than ever before so, simultaneously, she felt almost crushed by the weight of a desperate unhappiness. Even the prayers of Hilda gave no comfort.

Perhaps this was being a lost soul, she thought; perhaps she had been abandoned by God.

CHAPTER SIXTY

She stayed on at Whitby, hoping that in such a highly trained community of prayer she would find her way. It was a relief to enter once more into the routines which were a rich substitute for individual thought.

It was only in the dead of night that Bega could face the truth about herself, perhaps because it was a time which belonged to the spirits and in that other world other rules applied. She embraced it. It set her free.

In the silence, folded up in her narrow cot, with only the occasional moan of the wind for company and the distant smack and rush of the sea, a dog's faraway lonely howl underlining the blank dark silence, she probed for the source of this remorseless unease in mind and body. What was the true cause of it?

It was a longing as keen as the most bitter of the east winds that would cut through her on the cliff top. It was an agitation, a heat, a skin-crawling, vein-itching infection. Sometimes wildly she thought that she might be harbouring a plague. And there were those who had come to the synod at Whitby from the south who had murmured about another plague which would soon beset them.

She did not pray for help or guidance. She feared that what lay inside her was too dark to bring to God's light.

What did she seek? The question was so simple. Why could she not answer it?

The answer was in her instincts. It was in her longing to be the individual she was. Yet how could she learn to think in this way, selfishly, personally, when her training had taught her to submerge herself totally, then drown in the ocean of God's will.

The sense of delinquency grew intolerable. Still she would not turn to God. She left her bed and went outside.

It was midsummer and the northern light was up. From her black cell she moved into moon shadows and a rim of dusk-dawn light which encircled the rising land like a glowing white band. She walked until she came to her place. She sat now and imagined Padric there.

Yes.

That was what she sought.

Not to be denied any more. She wanted to touch Padric and to be touched by him. She burned for it, even in the coolness of the night. She wanted to have his breath on her face and see him so closely that he became blurred. She wanted to be held by him and to hold him so that he knew of her longing as much as she of his.

She felt her breasts tingling, even hurting a little and her sex, that terrible black unknowable part of her foresworn life, craved . . . Padric.

She stood and walked a few paces quickly as if to shake off this perversion. For that was her first thought. That while she was proudly pretending to herself, the devil had slid inside her body and now possessed it.

How could she get rid of such a devil?

The devil had become her.

She had been told of such devils as this. When the Christian was not fully alert at all times, the devil would slide in at first so gently, go in so very, very smoothly that the Christian would not know. She would feel it, if at all, only as a silky completion to herself, a loving gesture which made her feel – free? Free. Light? Lightness itself. Bold? But then the devil would begin to stir in such a trusting soul and twist and push now here, now gone, until the soul became confused, but excited. For the devil had now joined her and the soul was opening wider and wider to him and letting all its defences down because, proud soul, it believed that no harm would come of it.

Then the devil knew he had seduced the soul and he began to cry out in triumph and stab – she had felt the stabbing – stab and stab again at her until she cried out in agitation and writhed in pain which she misthought to be ecstasy, the false ecstasy of selfishness. When, with horror, she realised that it was not herself but the devil, it was too late, the devil had penetrated every part of her. The devil rode inside her. The devil remade her. The devil changed her shape at his will. The devil became her and she was no longer, never would or could be the Christian soul she had been before she had so proudly opened the gate to self. It was unbearable.

'No!' Bega cried – but wrapped the cry inside her head. 'No!' 'No!' 'No!' – the denial ricocheted in her head as if it were an object lodged inside the skull desperately banging at the walls to get out.

'No' was true.

Bega stopped and stood stock still.

The sea was lapping the shore so calmly tonight: that was God's real world.

The light cool breeze now soothing her rushed warm face: that was God's wind.

The all-present rustles and noises of the night which she could pick out note after sound, across the fields, in the woods: all that was God's real world.

So was her body. So was what her body meant.

She had to fight to live.

Bega spoke aloud: 'I am not possessed by you or any devil,' she said. 'This is me, Bega. I am in God's real world. I am possessed by longings of memory and desire. For Padric. I want his arms around me as I now wrap my arms around myself. His body against mine which is not whole without him. And that is also God's real world.'

With this simple admission, dug so deeply out of her – so against all her training – she felt as if a huge sting had been suddenly removed from her body. Even her bones felt slack with relief. She knew now that what she felt was not for the devil but for Padric. She had denied the womanly and the animal part of that feeling for too long. Never again could she do that. She would always want him and always be afflicted or enriched by this want.

Now that she had admitted it, and the early dawn began to rise up as if in salute, and the whistles and chirps of the birds advanced into the silence, she could admit the next concern: that although it was real, her vows of chastity were also real; that to lust even in the mind was a sin; that eternal salvation was a reward worth all earthly sacrifice; that God had given her the strength for chastity in order to use that chaste strength for His purpose and His glory.

Unless she could unlock her vows she could not let her desire for Padric be consummated.

Only God could tell her if she could cast off those vows.

She would pray. There was no other way to resolve it. Those prayers would decide what she must do. Never had she been so calm and certain and full of truth. God would surely guide her now that she herself knew what she wanted.

The next day she left for her own place.

It was many weeks before Padric heard of the judgment of the synod. This, accompanied by alarming rumours of its savage consequences, drew him back to Rheged. He had been on islands far out to sea at the edge of the known world. With six of his men and Urien, Riderch and Penraddin, he had been sent on a hazardous mission which none of the Pictish chieftains' own followers would support – to clear the outlying islands of occupying warriors from the furthest north. Nothing had come of it. The invaders were much more skilful at sea. Four of his men had been lost. It was when Padric returned to the Picts to confess to failure, that he learned the news of the Roman victory.

Immediately he asked the chieftain to be released from his task. With ill grace and using the excuse to pare down the payment to a pittance, it was agreed.

Padric drove hard on the journey south. Even Riderch complained. But it was with ever-increasing foreboding that he made for the heart of his kingdom. This, he knew, could be the excuse for which Ecfrith had been looking and waiting.

CHAPTER SIXTY-ONE

The tide was on the turn. Ecfrith and his war band of twenty thegns hobbled their horses and sat among the spiky, marram-grassed dunes, looking over at Lindisfarne. The island was so peaceful under the hazy summer sun that it took the keenest eyes to see any signs of habitation at all. The monks had tucked their buildings behind the headland. If there were any smoke from the fire it was too thin to catch the eye or it melted into the haze. It seemed an empty, barren place. None of those waiting for the tide to ebb would have wanted to live there. To these warriors it was a source of both amusement and wonder, more often the former, that such barbarous places were the preferred habitat of the wild monks. To these thegns and eldormen, it was a bleak, defenceless spot, in danger from the lashes of a cold and sometimes violent sea, unprotectable and unnecessarily remote.

Ecfrith looked south and saw, in the haze, the huge rock of Bamburgh where his father ruled. There was the bastion and stronghold of kings who had come across this cold and inhospitable sea and clamped themselves to the rock.

Some of his men had begun a loud and makeshift game, with an inflated pig's bladder which they had brought along. They rushed in a pack, swarming around the bladder like bees around a queen, then suddenly breaking away as it flew loose, and once more they chased it. Ecfrith normally enjoyed the game and was a keen player, but now he wanted a little peace to settle his plans and scheme for his future.

Out there, at sea, was the island of Lindisfarne which had given his father and his ancestors the God who had turned certain defeat into the most fertile and far-reaching of victories. But He was a strange, distant, ungraspable God, who had not made Ecfrith or any of his thegns abandon their prayers to their forested, familiar, ancient, Teutonic warrior gods, to spirits of the springs and the rivers. Nor had this new God prevented Ecfrith from holding on to the small, carved idols, the small, flat-nosed, large-headed phallus which was slotted into his belt, the amulet dedicated to the goddess Fre. Yet with this God, Aidan had snared the blood-stained, brute-thinking Oswy.

That holy island, Ecfrith now thought, had become like a worm in the fruit of the kingdom. It had its own purpose which was only occasionally coincident with that of a military power. Wilfrid's Roman church would be much more useful: it knew about conquest; it knew about organisation; it knew about property and possessions. It knew about the authority of earthly kings and respected them in a way the Celts never had done. Ecfrith had now converted to the Roman way and, very soon, as the tide drew out, that seeming-innocent, sea-land, the most obvious internal enemy, would be Roman too.

The Northumbrian reaction to the judgment at Whitby had been more hostile than anyone could have anticipated. There were already proven stories of slaughter and torture. Intransigent, rebellious Celts were hunted down. Ecfrith wanted to reassure those on Lindisfarne who, like many others, were simply dragging their feet, he thought, that there was no real danger. When, eventually, the tide swilled out and the bare sand glistened, he began to move, relaxed in the saddle in his slowest sauntering mode. So, slouching, they came to Lindisfarne.

The horses, who did not like the giving sand under their hooves, were glad to heave themselves on to more solid land even though the long spiky grasses scratched their flanks. Soon the party came over the natural rampart and looked down on the abbey of Lindisfarne.

For those who had never before been to this centre of legend and miraculous power, breeder of saints and school of fearless evangelists and martyrs, it was a disappointment. They were always convinced that what they saw were the hovels of the servants. The abbey, the grandeur of Lindisfarne, would surely heave into view over the next low ridge. But the beehive hovels *were* the abbey. Oak and thatch and strict modesty of scale prevailed everywhere. Even the church was no outstanding size.

The library and the scriptorium were only a little bigger than
the huts which slept four or six monks. The refectory, too, and
the buttery, were of the same modest proportion. Here, said the
place, we who teach simplicity of faith live in simplicity sheltered
by faith. We who call on Him who blessed the meek and the poor
live meekly and possess nothing for ourselves. Any wealth we have
is shared with the poor or given to the glory of God in the purchase
of fine jewels to ornament the books which carry His word.

Only a few looked up as Ecfrith's war band came into the
middle of the settlement where Colman and Celland and a few
of the older monks waited to greet them. The others continued
with their business in the garden, or further away in the farming
fields, in the pursuit of that circuit of industry which gave them
their bedrock of self-sufficiency.

'You sent us no messenger, my Lord,' said Colman, smiling, although his heart was icy in anticipation, 'otherwise we
would have been prepared with hospitality which would match
your rank.'

'We need no hospitality,' said Ecfrith. 'We will be gone before
the tide returns.'

Ecfrith looked around at his men, one or two of whom had
dismounted.

'Why do you not have the Roman tonsure?' Ecfrith asked,
before Colman could construct another line. He put one leg in
front of him and slid off his horse. A servant reached out and
took the reins.

'We are still discussing the arguments raised at the synod,' said
Colman.

'There have been more than two full months since then,' Ecfrith
replied, easily. 'The king requires his commands to be followed
sooner than that.'

'Our heavenly king has commands too.'

'And He, through my father, declared against you.' Ecfrith
spoke softly. The low wind in the long grass seemed a sin-
ister accompaniment. The men who had dismounted walked
steadily towards the beehive cells. Three of the riders turned
the horses towards the fields where the monks were working.

'And the date of Easter?' Ecfrith asked. 'Is that still being
discussed on Lindisfarne?'

'It is!' Celland interrupted, easily triggered to a youthful out-burst. 'We were not satisfied with the arguments.'

'Ah,' said Ecfrith, 'when the master falls silent, the little dog barks.'

'He speaks for me,' said Colman, firmly. 'Although perhaps he speaks with too much heat.'

Ecfrith folded his arms and looked directly at Colman. 'We are here to give you the Roman tonsure. After that I want your oath that you will, from today, follow all the practices judged lawful and godly at Whitby.' Ecfrith raised his voice. 'Leave Colman. Take the others.'

These were monks hardened to sudden violence. But when it was directed against them it was usually well anticipated.

This bloody exercise on their own sacred and hitherto inviolate island took them by surprise. Their spears and swords were stored away.

Ecfrith's men grabbed the weaponless monks and began to hack them around the head with their sharp daggers. The struggle put up by some of the monks and the slide on the part of Ecfrith's thegns from easy sport to savagery brought blood. The sight and smell of blood bred more blood. Even when the monks agreed to be docile, they were slashed around the skull and a handful of hair would rarely be shaven off without its mat of blood. They were dragged from their work in the huts, they were pursued across the fields; but few of them ran or resisted being caught. It was only when the daggers came to slash them into the Roman way that their struggles began. Even so, the cries were singular and separate: there was no attempt at massing a resistance, verbal or physical. It was as if they refused to believe what was happening until the blade-edge cut into the skin.

Celland stood beside Colman, ready to defend him.

When Ecfrith indicated that Celland too should have the whole top of his head shaved and the hair which hung down his neck chopped off so that the beginning for a crown of thorns tonsure was in place, Colman put out a protective arm.

'Only you will be spared, Bishop,' said Ecfrith.

'I will *not* do it!' said Celland and turned on his attacker with his fists raised. The thegn grabbed him roughly and threw him to the ground. Celland was much slighter, but wiry, and the thegn found Celland's sharp fists pummelling his face. He slammed the feisty young monk down even harder. Colman stepped forward to intervene but Ecfrith set himself between the bishop and what had now become an unruly and desperate fight.

'Order this man to obey us,' Ecfrith said, rapidly, 'or he will be hurt.'

'Celland,' Colman saw how fast the temper of the thegn had risen, 'Celland, struggle no more.'

It was doubtful that Celland heard. The humiliation and frustration of weeks burst out as he fought as if to preserve all that he had ever believed in. The thegn, so much bigger and stronger, was attempting to pin down this fierce monk, half-laughing at the youth's spirit, half-angry at his resistance.

Celland reached out and grabbed a sharp stone and brought it hard to his assailant's forehead, drawing blood. The man recoiled, drew back, and then drove his dagger deep into Celland's throat. He twisted it in and held the young man down despite Colman's frantic clawing at him.

When he rolled away from the warm, dead body, the blood welling down the plain habit, the thegn looked to Ecfrith and saw no disapproval. He stood and walked across to a stream in which he could dowse his hands and clean the blade.

Colman kneeled beside Celland. When he knew that he was dead he began to pray in a loud, keening tone. The prince was uneasy at the sound and at the authoritative fervour of the praying. Colman's wailing rang across the settlement: its high note reached the fields and what had been the distinguishable individual cries of alarm and pain became a general lament. As Colman's Celtic dirge passed from monk to monk, the clamour intensified.

It became not only a lament of sorrow over the death of Celland, nor just a lament for their individual wounds or for the coercion which would make them what they were not: the sound was a dying call, the last song of a dying church. This was the cry of the Israelites taken into captivity. This was the visceral and deep spiritual recognition that a whole life and way of being and serving God was now passing. Something had gone from the earth and Colman's lament over Celland's slaughtered body symbolised that passing. It rose up of its own accord; it uttered its remote melancholy message across the sea and then, as naturally, it died away leaving behind a ringing accusing silence.

At length, Colman rose and turned to Ecfrith. He was dazed.

'I will pray for the soul of your warrior,' he said, 'and he too must pray.'

'Your friend ought not to have resisted in that way.'

'"Thou shalt not commit murder",' said Colman severely. 'Now you will leave us while we prepare our brother for burial.'

'I will leave you,' said Ecfrith, unrepentant now that the unnerving sound had ceased, the sound that so nearly had threatened to move him to yielding sentiments, 'but we will be back in seven days. By then you will in every way be practising the offices of the Roman church, as commanded. If you are not we will not be so merciful.'

Colman took the unspoken meaning. He was being given seven days to flee. His face had lost all vivacity: the blood of Celland was on his hands. He made himself speak out. 'Our churches can coexist,' he said, 'if you give them the time. There is much in common. But by forcing us in this way you are causing a schism. If even half of what I have heard is true, you are using this judgment as an excuse for butchery and for stealing estates which belong neither to us nor to you but to the God who will judge you.'

'Say nothing to me of judgment!' Ecfrith's full-voiced authority rang out. 'I came armed with the judgment of my father who spoke the judgment of God. It is all of you—' his voice commanded the field and the bloodied monks and swaggering warriors '—all of you here on this unchanged and unrepentant island who will suffer in hell. Not we who came to help you on the true way. We came to save you. You resisted us. We came as friends. You treated us as enemies. We came to give you a life. You fought us and we took a life. Is he with God?'

By now many of the monks were gathered around Colman who was still standing – as if on guard – by the body of Celland. Of Ecfrith's warriors, some listened, others went to their horses or moved across to the stream to drink the water. But their leader's challenging questions engaged them all. 'For if the soul of this monk is not with God, then you are the damned ones. Not us. Unless you follow the true way you will be damned by God. And until you follow the true way you will be pursued by us with a hostile sword. Bury your brother. Pray for him. But remember – your prayers will not pass through the ears of heaven if you are not cleansed of these Celtic heresies. It is my duty to cleanse you of them and, as God is my judge, and as He is yours, I will do that. Today is a warning. We will be back and when we come back we will expect total obedience or we will see it as our duty to rid this holy place of its corrupt souls.'

How, thought Colman, how could this bullying, half-believing, half-pagan pretend to speak for God while he was standing on ground which had supported the bodies and souls of some of the purest saints in all Christendom? How could he use such threats and show of force to a pacific defenceless, God-loving, evangelical community which existed to do nothing but uncover God's virtues and exemplify them? What enormous sin had they all committed that they should be so punished?

To discover that would be his task. That would be his burden when he went into exile.

CHAPTER SIXTY-TWO

Bega was shaken at the sight of him. Colman looked as if he had seen the devil, she thought.

He had come alone, ahead of the others, he said, to test the ground.

Bega, who had hurried from the garden where she had been digging up parsnips, looked at him in some anguish as his once calm and benign expression flickered in agitation as if seeing the devil's messengers flying past like pollen in the air, everywhere and inescapable.

'What is it you need to know?' she asked.

'I thought they might have ridden on ahead of us,' Colman said. 'All the way across here I knew that we were being followed but they were very foxy. I never saw them. But I knew they were there.'

He stood anxiously close to his horse, holding the bridle, as if he were ready to hurl himself on to the animal and gallop away at a scent of trouble.

Bega had never seen anyone so transformed: he was haggard and utterly without warmth in his expression.

'Would you like some milk?' she said. 'It is hot standing out here and you must be tired after such a journey.'

'I am only beginning my journey,' he replied, rather sharply, she thought. 'Is it safe here?'

'I have seen no one who might harm you.'

'They can hide so cunningly,' said Colman, glancing over his shoulder and back at the woods that swept up the lower flanks of the mountain which today soared clearly towards a heaven without cloud.

'I have seen no one who would harm you.'

'They will come,' said Colman, 'they will come.'

'Please,' Bega held out her hands, 'let me take you to a cool place. There is goat's milk, and we have some oatcakes and cheese, fish . . .'

'Milk is all I need. Or water. Water.'

'Come then.'

Colman was still uncertain but, when Bega reached forward and took the bridle and led the horse towards the nunnery's mounded wall, he followed.

In the small cell which was also the parlour, he sipped at the water in silence. Bega waited.

He had drunk less than half the cup when he put it down and looked at her as if seeing her for the first time. 'It's so quiet here,' he said, and Bega quickened at the more normal tone in his voice. 'Perhaps when we chose this place, we chose a holy place. Lindisfarne is a holy place. God was waiting for him when Aidan reached it.'

'There is peace here,' Bega agreed.

'There is something more here,' said Colman. His head almost pecked the air as if he were seeking to discover a sound or a signal, all but out of reach. Bega watched him closely, impressed that through his own religious instinct he should have sensed the power which came from the cross. Perhaps the favour shown by Hilda and the interest taken in her by the younger, impulsive Wilfrid had been connected with their appreciation of the radiance of holy power which belonged to her through the possession of that fragment. But Colman, more than all the rest, Colman in his distraught state, knew certain sure that a holiness was there. 'Something,' he said, eventually, and smiled at her. With that smile his face lost all its frantic lines and tics of fear and anxiety. 'Something,' he repeated. 'God has chosen this place, Bega, for a special purpose.'

'Perhaps,' she rushed in, to prevent vanity loosening her into a revelation of the cross, 'that purpose is to be a refuge for you and the others.'

Colman nodded, took up the cup of water and drank deeply. Then he spoke with more vigour. 'There will be many others.'

'What has happened?'

Colman told her of Ecfrith's ultimatum. He did not mention the death of Celland. The killing of his young friend and disciple grieved him too much for him to speak of it. Every hour, it seemed, he reconstructed the scene with a simple intervention from himself or an appropriate prayer to God saving the life of the passionate young monk he had loved. Every day he blamed himself for being supine and passive. If . . . if . . . if . . . For God had wanted him to intervene, he knew that now. Why had he not known then? Had Ecfrith become the serpent and hypnotised him?

'You are tired,' she said. 'Tell me where you have left the others and I will go and bring them here myself. Some of them will recognise me.'

Colman nodded. His directions were clear. Before she left she led him to her bed and encouraged him to sleep. He fell asleep so suddenly and deeply that she stayed for a while to be sure that he was safe . . .

The monks were huddled behind the oak trees he had mentioned, a mile back, a few score paces off the track. She was shocked. There were far more than she had anticipated – about sixteen – and every single one of them had been wounded about the head. They had scabs, gashes and some fresh bleeding from scratching an itching sore spot. The tonsure had not had time to take any shape and all of them, once quit of Lindisfarne, had allowed their hair to begin to grow back into its original style. But this uniform affliction, and the nervousness which pervaded the large party struck her with pity.

'Bishop Colman has asked me to take you to the nunnery where you can rest,' she said.

'Is it safe?'

'Have any of the Northumbrians been here?'

'Is Ecfrith or his men familiar with this place?'

'Are there any warriors from Rheged to protect us?'

'There will be,' said Bega, hoping that Padric would return soon. 'Meanwhile, Bishop Colman is sleeping in my cell. He feels safe enough to do that.'

They conferred by quick glances and a few muttered words.

'You were at the synod, were you not?'

'Yes, I was.'

'Did you want to cry out against Wilfrid?'

'I did.' Bega blushed, hotly remembering the rage she had felt.

'He will take Bishop Colman's bishoprics and abbeys and churches now.'

'He is a friend of King Alchfrid,' said another, 'and he wants an earthly kingdom to equal that of his friend.'

'You know Cuthbert also, don't you? I have heard that it was he who brought you to Whitby.'

'Yes. I know Cuthbert.'

'Why did he not speak?'

Bega did not answer. Like all of them she was still devastated and perplexed by Cuthbert's silence.

'All things will be explained to us,' said Bega, heavily, 'in God's good time. Come. Come with me.'

She turned, knowing they would follow, and went back to where Chad stood with her horse. Cal, alert and obedient, was at his feet. Chad had insisted on bringing the sword.

With heads bowed as if in shame, the monks came out on to the track and followed Bega and Chad down into the broad mouth of the valley. It was an abject caravan.

As the monks were used to making overnight camps, the nunnery suddenly appeared to have grown an extra wall. Against the turf-topped rampart were propped simple refuge tents and once settled, the monks immediately returned to their monastic discipline. They would not use the church at the same time as the nuns but either waited or held their prayers in the open beside the lake.

Around the lake all this was noticed. Reggiani in particular kept the rival settlement under observation, trying to read the true meaning into this sudden and strange influx of Christian holy men.

They had planned to continue their journey the next morning but Colman, who had slept deeply, woke up more clearheaded than he had been for some days but also much weaker. His limbs felt waxy. Even the few steps to the door of Bega's cell left him breathless. After their usual disputatious meeting, the monks agreed that the best policy would be to wait until Colman recovered fully. Meanwhile they would help Bega and her nuns in anything that was asked and stock up on the provisions needed for the rest of their trip.

Colman took a little soup and bread and some berries, though he ate seemingly without appetite or enjoyment; then, once more, after some simple prayers, he fell into an exhausted sleep.

It was on that day Bega learned of Celland's death. The details were not spared. Then she knew that here Colman had found a time and a place in which to mourn.

Several things satisfied Bega over the next few days. Colman grew stronger and the strained, dazed expression on his face began to fade; the monks were happy to obey her admittedly light commands, but as Bega had never before organised men who were her equals – as distinct from servants and slaves – this gave her an unpredicted confidence.

A group of three monks who had gone to the village beyond the southern tip of the lake brought back reports of an impending plague but such reports were not infrequent and the evidence was slight.

On the third morning, Colman woke up and ate a little meat, an egg, some oat cakes and berries and took two cups of cow's milk. He summoned Bega. Without ceremony or introduction, he began speaking with an urgent solemnity.

'I was not sleeping, Bega. I was summoned on a journey by the Lord. The angel who led me on the journey told me to tell this to you but to no one else. When you saw me the other day, I was sick to the root of my soul. The death of my beloved young brother in God, Celland, lay on me like a rock on my chest, like the tortures our brothers have suffered in some of the wilder hills where they load rock after rock on to them until at length all life is pressed out. So did I have pressing on me the responsibility for the death of Celland. I thought I was to die as just punishment for my lack of courage in not defending Celland, one of the purest of God's creatures.

'I was in despair, Bega, because my soul for which I have striven through prayer and fasting and works all my life was soiled by the death of Celland. He died in anger. What were his last thoughts? That was another torment. How could he gain entrance to God's heavenly kingdom if his last thoughts were of murder? Perhaps, in the divine balance of these things, I was to die so that the soul of Celland could be purged. For this I was ready.

'I remember your leading me to your bed and then, over the next days, though once or twice I woke to take a little earthly food, I was taken by an angel and shown part of the domain of the Lord of all.

'Oh Bega, Bega! How right we are to worship Him! How all powerful and majestic is His kingdom! How beautiful His purpose!' Colman's eyes shone with the memory of it all and Bega felt his joy irradiate her own spirit. He went on, his tone warm, reverential, intimate.

'From your small bed I was lifted up and taken by the hand of the angel, up above the lake, up to where the clouds travel with their watery benediction and there I was told to look down on what I had left. What a plenitude there is here, Bega, when you see the lakes and mountains, the rivers and forests, the animals and the settlements of men all, to God's eye, so small and insignificant and yet so intricately going about so many different purposes of the Lord. He took me even higher and once more bid me look down and I saw all from sea to sea. I saw clouds beneath me and even the eagles were not as high as I. Once again, Bega, I marvelled. The earth looked like the most intricately wrought page in the *Book of Durrow*.

'The wonders I saw would almost equal those of the most blessed St Brendan himself. I met creatures of all sizes, all white-skinned, white-feathered, with silver tongues singing praises from golden lips to the glory of the Lord. I saw the haloes of the saints and though the sight almost blinded me, my good angel pointed out which saint was which and deep in the heart of the mystery of crystal colour was the pure light of Christ. On I was led through orchards filled with golden fruit and heavenly fields where white cattle, sheep and goats grazed on the whitest clouds.

'Near us, was a high cliff. There, I saw my beloved Celland.

'Then I understood the purpose of this journey. I was to change places with him. He was to be brought back to earth and I was to be left there, on the cliff of uncertainty, for ever, or until the Last Judgment, duly punished for my cowardice. Praise God!

'But in His infinite wisdom the Lord knew better. After Celland and I had embraced, the angel explained that Celland had to forgive me. It was Celland who had summoned me from earth and thanks be to God the call was heard and obeyed. He had to release my soul from its anguish and enable me once more to fight for the souls of others and capture them for our Lord. Until he had done that his own way was not clear to join the joyful throng moving up through the verdant and dew-sparkling pastures to the celestial certainty of heaven. How ingenious is the Lord! How wise in His complexity! Celland and I embraced once more and then he descended from the cliff, eager to be gone and claim his heavenly reward. Alleluia! My soul doth glorify the Lord!' Colman looked, to Bega, in that moment, as if he were still with the angel and in sight of heaven. How powerful the Lord must be, she thought, to take a man and show him such amazing things!

'"And now," said the angel, "you must pay for such a privilege. And whatever you see you must say nothing."

'He took me by the hand and down we sped to those fatal and smoking dark devilish kingdoms of hell where the devil moves in a thousand disguises.

'Down we plunged and I saw sights which would have made me weep, save that my eyes were wide open in horror. Oh, never let me, never let yourself, never let anyone you meet be under any doubt as to the torments of hell! We know of tortures by the living: imagine how much more terrible are the tortures by devils.

'It was then that I saw the beloved St Aidan as clear before me as you are. As I watched, a huge and vile devil, three-headed with teeth like daggers and a countenance blacker than charcoal, came behind him with a net made of vipers. He was about to cast the net over our beloved Aidan who was, as you would expect, kneeling in prayer even in this pit of hell, praying, I had no doubt, for the souls of others as much as for his own soul. My voice leaped to my tongue to warn him, I was about to cry out, when suddenly I remembered what the angel had said. Though my mouth opened and the word formed on my tongue, no sound was uttered and, as we passed by the saint, he changed from the beloved Aidan into a monster as vile as that which had seemed about to ensnare him. I had been deceived!

'It was only there that I understood the full deception and power of the devil. He can change himself into anyone, into any form. He is not constant like Christ. He is not the one and indivisible like the Lord. The devil is the evil spirit which can pretend to be so many different spirits. The devil has the power to look like the saints themselves. That is why we need to keep our souls pure: at last I understood. It is because only a soul pure in Christ can defy the devil.

'And so I was shown the downfall of man.

'But my ordeal was not over. For the angel said that in order to return I had to be taken through the future, through the times immediately to come.

'What I saw were frightening portents, Bega. I saw plagues and famines and wars.

'After the three portents – those afflicted with sores, those dying of starvation, those butchered in war – all lying out in open fields, naked and moaning piteously, I saw one last thing.

'I saw a shadow sweep across the earth like a hand reaching out to snuff a candle. Slowly at first the light was taken away from us and I heard all the people of the earth wailing and calling on God to help them see. I heard them declare all their sins and then the angel said – "Only those of true faith can drive away this shadow which shall surely come and soon. Stay on this holy soil. Meet the shadow with prayer. Stay until you have sent it back to the devil who will bring it." So you see, I must stay with you.' Colman paused.

'But if you do stay here,' said Bega, as the pause lengthened, 'won't you be in danger?'

'What is the greater danger? The wrath of Ecfrith or the wrath of God?'

Bega bowed her head.

'I see the true hand of God in this,' said Colman. 'When He wished to set the Israelites free from Egypt, he sent the ten plagues. Only after the tenth of these, which took all the first born, did the Pharaohs agree to let their captives go. Then the true faith was released back to seek and find a place where it could flourish. So with us now. God will send signs and portents and plagues to this kingdom so that His people will be let go. But we must show our strength and prove to the people that we are worthy to be saved. Therefore we will stay here in this spot and wait for a sign before we go on our journey.'

CHAPTER SIXTY-THREE

Reggiani's followers would walk down to the lakeside to laugh at the scared, stubble-headed monks who came out of the nunnery seven times a day and prayed to their God to avert a catastrophe.

'What catastrophe?' they asked.

'It will come.'

'Where is it?'

'It will be in the sky.'

'That is where your God lives. The invisible one. Is he the catastrophe?'

'We beg you, for your own sakes, abandon your idols and give your souls to God.'

'What do we want with your God? Look at how he locks up the women and has them pray and pray. Why is one prayer not enough? Is he deaf?'

'May God forgive you. You must be warned. Join us or you will be damned for ever.'

'Who are you to say that we will be damned?'

Sticks were thrown by some of the youths and stones by some of the children, but Colman and his monks ignored them and prayed intently.

Bega watched over the monks anxiously. They had not invited her or her nuns to join in their prayers but she supported them with prayers of her own inside the church. The weather was exceptionally warm and, as the evenings were so long, there was the rare phenomenon of some free time. One evening Reggiani, growing plump now, came to walk into the cooling shallows of the lake. Ignoring the monks, she took off most of her clothes and lay down so that the warm water lapped all over her flesh.

Her followers, especially the young, followed this practice and some of the younger monks were disturbingly tempted.

There was never more unlikely weather for disaster. The sky was clear day after day. The sun was huge and beat down on the land. Though the food was nothing like as plentiful as in other years – and there were stories of severe shortages in the high settlements – the promise of ripe berries and nuts, of cherries and other fruits and the fast ripening of the grain assuaged most fears.

Yet day after day Colman led out his small band. Resolutely they kneeled on ground hardened further under the relentless sun and, lifting their eyes to heaven, they prayed for the sins of the world.

Bega's fears for their safety grew. She knew that Padric would be trying to reach her; she knew too that Ecfrith would sooner or later send out war bands to harass and hunt down those seeking exile. But no words from her could shift Colman from his set purpose which was to be in this holy place when God needed him.

The pagans soon grew tired of throwing sticks but still they would come to jeer and ape the pious, earnest kneeling attitude of the monks and look into the clear sky crying out 'Look at the catastrophe!'

When the shadow, in the second week of Colman's vigil, and just after the noon time of the day, did indeed move between the earth and the sun, Colman and his monks felt the general terror but also a thrill of self-justification. Their prayers were redoubled. Bega watched in mesmerised horror. She knew this was to be the end of the world. It was God's judgment on Whitby. The bell which the farmer had given them pealed out its message and all the nuns and the workers ran into the settlement. Bega would not let them go inside the church. What is right for Colman to do, she said, we must do. Outside the rampart the monks kneeled and looked up as the dark shadow edged relentlessly across the burning, unblemished face of the sun. Bega joined them and soon the nuns and Chad joined her.

From all around the lake there were cries of distress: howls of men and women and dogs; screams of children. Some said that they heard sounds so loud that they thought the earth was splitting open as the heavens were going into darkness. Others saw the lake drained away and an army of the dead rising up through the mud. Phantoms, spirits and devils were released from all the graves and burial grounds and they flew and screeched through the air looking for their kin to be with them as the Last Judgement finally arrived.

Oh God, Bega prayed, keep Padric safe from here. Make him be somewhere this is not happening. And if it is happening all over the earth, then forgive his soul the blood of slaughter, oh Lord, for it was Your earthly battles that he fought.

When half the sun was covered, Reggiani and her followers could be heard raising their pagan spells. Colman and his monks, like a small disciplined army, kept on their knees and in their faith, praying as one body, their murmuring unbroken, steady in the cohesion of the group.

It was then, when the sun was more than half blacked out and the shadow of extinction appeared inescapable, that many of the pagans hurried across the fields to be near the force of Colman and Bega and share in whatever power they had. In these moments of the most tremendous slow drama when the whole of a blue sky was darkening to cobalt and the sun's flames appeared to be on the way to extinction, taking all light and warmth away, the activity in the valley was divided between frantic rushing and jostling like the horses and cattle which caught the prevailing fear and sought wildly for somewhere to run, and the magnetic solidity of Colman and his monks and Bega and her nuns.

As the shadow drew yet further across the sun and the sky darkened more, all the birds of the forests lifted off their branches and filled the skies with their terrified sounds as they swung and spun in circles, not knowing where to go to find the light. Some said the wolves raced down to the fields to be with the lambs and all the vile and cruel creatures ran crazily to be with the most innocent of creatures, which were seen to have power just as Colman and Bega and their innocent followers had power.

But as the sun was almost completely blotted out, all sense of direction and safety fled and the air was full of wailing and lamentation and pleas for help from whatever God. The noon-time darkness compounded the pressure.

It was then that Bega knew what she must do with the cross. For this must be the time when its meaning was truly revealed.

She took the fragment from her pocket and, with a sharp-edged stone, she dug a hole in front of her. When she had finished digging, the sun was gone.

She held up the cross in front of her and said quietly:

'This is the True Cross on which Christ your dearly beloved son died for us and for our sins.'

Her voice was heard by no one but God. Colman was now urging on the trembling and fearful and yet still disciplined monks – 'As our Saviour commanded and taught us to say "Our Father, which art in Heaven, hallowed be Thy name: Thy Kingdom come, Thy will be done . . ."'

In the powerful darkness with the merest flickering of light around the edges of the black disc which had taken away the sun, the wailing dropped low as everyone waited for the terrible thing that would now follow. Would the horsemen appear in their chariots to slay them all? Would the gods lean down and pluck them out and eat them? Would the earth open and swallow them up? Would they hear the last trump?

'I now plant this fragment,' said Bega. 'From this spot let Your light grow again, refreshed through the terror of this sign of Your fearsome might.'

Like so many of the others, Bega was shivering from fright and from the sudden coolness. It took much of her courage to repress the longings to prostrate herself in sobs or simply to run and run and hope that in another place she might survive.

She unwrapped the fragment and, in the darkness, dug it into the hard ground and shovelled back earth with her hand, patting it down, praying ceaselessly during this dead and apocalyptic suspense of light.

'Into Thy hands, Oh Lord,' she said, shaking now that the fragment was planted, 'I commend our spirits. To the Blessed Virgin Mary, all hail. Thanks be to God . . .' She found it difficult to breathe.

The darkness hung over the earth and Bega could feel it begin to press down on them.

Already kneeling, she bent down until her forehead touched the patch of earth underneath which the fragment of the True Cross now lay. She drove every thought from her mind but the image of that fragment. Only the divine power of such a relic could stir the earth to shake off such a darkness. Bega's prayers disappeared into silence: she seemed to become no more than an object, a stone, bereft of life, giving everything to this hope in God that the light would be returned. So much time appeared to pass.

Her eyes were as tight clenched as her body but eventually she felt on her head a flickering and then, gradually, a slow growth of heat. Still she dare not open her eyes but the murmurs all around and the low 'Alleluia!' from Colman and from the nuns convinced her that the cross was indeed revealing its force and throwing off the force of darkness. Bega's mind and body did not yet stir and, even when the murmurs of relief and wonder and gratitude swelled up, she stayed, her head pressed hard to the earth, willing on the powers of God which had flowed so mercifully from the dedication of His cross.

Who could doubt His power? And how could she now doubt that a purpose had been ordained for her? Surely it was to be God's servant for ever more.

As the shouting grew louder, Bega kneeled upright and looked up and there was the sun, reappearing as slowly as it had disappeared.

'God be praised,' she said, quietly, and then, more loudly, 'God be praised!'

She stood and looked down and found some stones to mark the spot with a simple cross. She would not move from it until it was securely identified. 'Thanks be to God.'

The nuns were all around her, weeping and hugging her and hugging each other. Colman called out 'Alleluia!' 'Alleluia!' and the jubilant monks took this as a signal to break from their concentrated prayer.

'On this spot,' said Bega, 'we will build a cross in stone which will tell the story of the power of Our Lord on this day. Now, bring some stones from the lakeside, so that we can find the place again.' Bega felt as if she herself had sunk roots in the place and could not move until God's will had been fully done.

None of them questioned why it should be that particular spot. They were glad to be released into activity. They ran to the lakeside. 'Alleluias!' and praises and thanks to God and the Virgin Mary and Christ and all the saints skimmed across the water and the joyful high voices of the women bounced on the surface and reached the banks on the other side. Those pagans who had once scoffed looked on rather forlornly as the Christians continued their praise and thanksgiving. But even in that immeasurable relief, Colman knew what his responsibility

was and some of the monks were sent off immediately to tell
unbelievers that God had brought back the light.

Wearily but with a smile which could not disguise a sense of
triumph, Colman came up to Bega who was building a small cairn
on the earth under which the cross was buried.

'Your prophecy was fulfilled,' she said. 'The shadow came, as
you foresaw. Must we now wait for the plagues and the torments
or can we turn them aside with our prayers?'

Colman nodded.

'Our prayers won us back the light.'

Again Colman nodded and then he looked at her directly, his
sweet, cornflower-blue eyes misting slightly as he did.

'But I know that it is to you we owe the victory, Bega. God
worked this wonder through you. You are now for ever bound to
this most holy spot.' He looked at the cairn and then back at her.
And then, to her embarrassment, he kneeled before her.

'We will leave now,' he said. 'We will cross the mountains and
the sea and then cross the land of Ireland and over another sea
until we come to the island at the edge of the world. There we
can practise our old ways, our own ways. But before I go, I need
your blessing, Bega. For today you have brought us a miracle.
Even though only you and I know this, the truth of it will one
day be revealed to all when God is ready, and this will become
a place of pilgrimage.' The nuns who had carried more stones
stood off in surprise as Colman first took Bega's blessing and
then prostrated himself over the simple pile of stones they had
laid as the basis for their cairn.

'Blessed art thou,' said Colman. 'Amen.'

CHAPTER SIXTY-FOUR

Padric rode into the valley with Riderch and Urien. He had left the servants with Owain some miles behind camped in a deep sandstone dell. They had travelled light and with only bare provisions, but the coin they had earned was sufficient to buy what they needed in Caerel. Now food was scarce and Owain was glad to be left behind for what promised to be a couple of days of fishing and hunting.

After some time of apparent invincibility, Padric's small war band had slid into a run of bad luck and failure. They had forged south through the dangerous and arduous country of the Picts and ridden into an ambush set by one of their old enemies, a chieftain whose lands straddled the main route down to Dumbarton Rock. The skirmish had forced them back to seek a much more difficult route and they had suffered two fatal casualties. It could have been avoided, thought Urien and Riderch, if Padric had taken his usual care instead of being so hot to reach Rheged.

As the three brothers rode towards the lake, they split. Urien made for the settlement of Reggiani, Riderch rode across to the house of a farmer who had become a friend. The peeling away of both of them also had the courteous advantage of leaving Padric free and alone to meet Bega.

She was not there.

With one of the older nuns, Saethryd, she had gone on a mission from which she was already overdue. Padric was given a meal by the young nun who acted as guest mistress and then, rather aimlessly, he looked around.

The place was in good order. There were signs that the buildings had recently been refaced. The turf had bitten into the ramparts and they looked solid now. The church which he looked into was cool despite the heat of the day. The furniture was simple but adequate. In the tiny scriptorium a nun was working on some letters which Bega had let her copy and Chad was mixing the colours and watching every stroke of the quill. The smells from the bakery were tantalising and Padric was touched to see that the small queue of beggars at the gate were being given milk and bread despite – as he had already picked up – the shortages in the nunnery itself. All in all, he concluded, Bega had made a fine settlement.

He walked out of the gate which pointed to the mountain. There he found two workmen carving on a long stone pillar slung across two large logs.

'What is this?'

'This is to mark where Bega brought back the sun, my Lord, through the intervention of God.'

Padric too had been stunned by the shadowing of the sun. They had been high in the mountains, on the wearying detour, nursing one badly wounded, all of them carrying deep cuts and bruises and the exhaustion that follows defeat. Unlike at the lakeside, the air had been cold and the chill of the darkening sun had struck into their hearts. Padric had sunk to his knees, his sword planted before him, and commended his spirit into the hands of God. The others had followed his example. All that was heard was the frightened whinnying of the horses, tugging at the reins tied around a rock, the shrill, frantic caw-caw of crows, and their own quiet breathed prayers, murmuring tonelessly in the desolate mountain region in which they had been wandering like a lost tribe.

'They do say it was Bega who brought us back the sun.'

'Bishop Colman swore it was her, my Lord.'

'Are you from Ireland? That is the accent, I think.'

'We were, my Lord. Then we were sent for to work on Lindisfarne. After that we were passed on to Melrose. After that it was Coldingham.' He grinned. 'Back they said to Lindisfarne, not that they want much stone work on the island. Still, we did what they wanted. Then after Ecfrith says "go", we decided to go along with Bishop Colman. But here, after the miracle, the nun Bega asks us to stay on and carve this pillar and seeing as we are not monks and have nothing to fear from Prince Ecfrith, here we stayed.'

Padric questioned them more about Ecfrith, but they merely

confirmed what he had already learned from various sources on the way south, especially in Caerel, where the Celtic community had practically vanished, leaving only a few who were rather pathetically declaring themselves Romans without quite knowing what to do about it.

Padric spent some of the day sitting by the stone carvers, simply watching the swift and skilful way in which with their chisels and mallets, they drew the shape of a leaf or a donkey out of the hard shank of rock.

'Getting the stone is the hard part,' the talkative one said. He had long black hair and was dressed in a wonderful mixture of rags picked up, it would seem, from every stop along the way. 'But they're lucky around here. It's good rock, a bit hard on the implements but that's no great hindrance.'

Padric saw that up two sides of the pillar they were wreathing the curvaceous Celtic leaves and flowers which marked the best of the work he had seen in Ireland. The two other sides were different. One showed the Virgin Mary and the Angel Gabriel, then the Virgin and Child, then the Virgin beneath the cross in three tableaux. The man told him that Bega had chosen this. On the other side there was a representation of the shadowing, with the familiar Celtic spirals and circles bordering the frieze which showed men and women, an ox and a horse, all with heads bowed while one woman stood, holding a cross before her. This represented Bega herself, the man explained, and it was there at the insistence of Colman who had lent his experience to the design just before his departure. At the top, Padric knew, there would be a decorated circle inside which lay the cross itself.

As Padric sat in the strong sun watching the men about their business, he felt a longing for rest. He would like to live in his own household with Bega as his wife. But what a waste it would be to marry Bega only to throw her into the saddle like Penraddin, who was back in the camp with Owain and living like a man. What the nunnery told him about her was rootedness, the great temptation. He could never rest. So what could he offer her? Why should she leave all this, especially now when, it seemed, she had been blessed with miraculous powers? His awe at the great gift which she had received was reinforced. How could he tempt such a chosen one?

Less resolved, then, and more tentative than he had been when

he arrived, Padric was relieved when Bega came back tired and
late and asked him if she could put off their discussion until the
morning.

⊗⊗⊗⊗

Padric had slept deeply in the guest house. The unnatural idleness
of the previous day and the heat of it beating into his lethargic
body had exhausted him. Even though, as he always did, he put
his sword by his side in readiness, a stealthy assassin could have
killed him without waking him. When eventually he rolled out of
the bed, he was still heavy-headed and he drank the milk and ate
the oatcakes and honey which had been left for him slowly and
almost painfully, as if he had drunk heavily the night before.

It was another hot day. There was something almost ominous,
Padric thought, in the naked sun in the blank sky and the haze
rising up from the lake like an offering. In Caerel and two of the
other port towns through which he had passed, they had feared
the heat and blamed it for the symptoms which were beginning
to spread.

He spoke to the men working on the cross. Two others were
massing up an earth mound on the spot marked by the cairn. This,
they explained, was what Bega wanted. First the earth mound,
then turf laid over it. Then large stones set around it and finally
the cross dug in, not into the ground itself – she had been emphatic
about that – but into this earth put above the ground. This was the
exact spot, they told him, where she had prayed for the sun to be
brought back to them and her prayers had been answered. All the
people had seen it and, although Reggiani claimed that it was her
spells and sacrifices which had sent away the darkness, most of
the people believed in Bega.

At length she came over to him and he noticed a nervous
briskness about her which alerted him. She did not want to
go to the fallen tree trunk against which they had leaned and
talked. Instead she took him the other way, in the direction
of the farm which stored some of their resources. She asked
him to look out for wood. They could make little heaps and

collect them on the way back. It did not do to be idle, she said.

For a while they walked in silence. The noises around the lake and the patterning that she recognised in the fields had the effect of soothing her and soon enough her pace slowed.

'Will Colman be safe, do you think?'

'In Ireland he will be as safe as anywhere in the world,' replied Padric. 'The place he has in mind is far away and will bother no one. It will be a haven.'

'You sound as if you yourself would like to be there.'

'I would,' said Padric, simply. 'I did not realise when I was there how much I loved the place. It has its quarrelsome chiefs but that is nothing like the oppressive invading force which we suffer here. Your land has always been saved by God. We are told Arthur went there for sustenance in the long period of his preparation and I can believe it. St Patrick, too, from the kingdom that came before Arthur, loved the place even though he was taken there as a slave. Perhaps there is something about those of us who are born in Rheged that joins us to your land.'

The implication was plain. She glanced at him, softened and then strode ahead of him.

'The exiles will keep coming here,' she said. 'Colman said that Ecfrith is determined to hound out all who do not follow the Roman rule and take all their lands and titles. Do you believe that he will?'

'I do. This is the opportunity he has been waiting for. Because of this he can turn his war bands on the British here who sympathise with the other Celts. The synod gives him the perfect excuse.'

'Both Hilda and Colman asked me to promise to help them.'

'How can you do that?'

'I can give them shelter. I can find guides who will take them through the mountains where Ecfrith's men will never find them. I can be the one who links the messages to and from Ireland. Even Ecfrith would not dare attack a woman of God in a house of God. Even if he suspected he would not dare.'

'But you will not be here,' said Padric. He stopped now and, finally, Bega turned to face him. What was this pain she felt, this arrow tip twisting in her heart?

They were near the tip of a small headland. Behind Bega was the lake, a shield of silver light. A few boats pocked the serene surface. Bega was clutching a bunch of twigs as if it were a bouquet. Padric stood on slightly higher ground, taller anyway, and his strength and size were framed by the mountain which soared up to heaven behind him, its top as clear as the face of the man himself, the heather a scorching rash of purple across the bared flanks which reared up from the woods. Bega had begun by being somewhat comforted by the mountain as it had reminded her of her home; now she was a little afraid of it. On too many nights the clouds and mists, the thunder and the roars from within and beyond it had scared her and tempted her to think that Reggiani's powers were inspired by the devil. It made Padric even more majestic.

Although Bega knew that she ought to reply she was not yet composed.

'You are to come with me,' he said. 'That was your word.'

'It was.'

'Someone else can be here for those who need refuge.'

'I am sorry,' said Bega, finding her mouth so dry, her throat tight.

'What has happened that you have had to break your word to me?' He forced himself to put aside his knowledge of the cross: its power would not leave her, he thought, although still he could not find the courage to mention it.

'I have to stay here, until God releases me from this place. I can go on a mission to do God's work but this must be my home. I must stay here now.'

'Why can you not do His work and be with me?'

'It is not possible.'

'What has changed?'

'Forgive me.'

'What has changed?'

Bega knew that the only explanation which would satisfy Padric would be the true explanation. Yet how could she explain the binding power of the cross when she was utterly sworn not to?

Padric understood that this was the determining moment. He would not let go. She would have to throw him off. He wanted her. He had loved her. He had waited. She had promised.

Later, when they thought of this short time when so little was said in words and so much that was unsaid changed their lives, they configured each other in images.

To Padric, Bega became the lady of the lake and then the lake itself. This long slit of water, oval-shaped with the bush of reed and sedge fringing its jagged edges; this place of magic and legend where, as Padric saw in his dreams, the arms of a woman, always, to him, Bega, appeared from the depths to deliver to him the sword of Arthur. This holy lake, its floor strewn with sacrifices of blood and the gifts of gold and jewels cast upon the waters to appease the gods who ruled it; this deep, sensuous skin of surface, skin of lake with plunged depths and holy powers: this was Bega. Bega, who stood there, slight bodied, dark red hair still a wild entanglement, face seized with intelligence and individuality, robed as soberly as the other nuns but wearing the long gown with a careless loose shrug. Bega, whom he had loved in her ignorance of his love and of whom he had dreamt under the stars, in a stench-filled thicket with hail pelting, on ice-banked fields of battle, in danger and in rare solitude. Bega became like the lake, this shimmering, heat-smacked, glittering lake.

To Bega, Padric was the mountain which seemed to spring out of him. The massy force of it, the incredible height where only eagles nested, the soaring power of it so big and thrusting and present. He was fearless in war, she knew. His constant love for her was part of her love for him. Her fearful watch over him in her prayers mirrored the times when in fear she watched the mountain as it gathered clouds and mists and thunder about it. After this time, as her life went further and further into a chaste and solitary future, the mountain was to become her mainstay, even her friend. Each morning she woke and looked towards the mountain rather than to the lake. For Padric was that living colossal dominating force.

'Nothing has truly changed,' she said.

'Nothing?'

'Do not ask me,' she said. 'God forgive me but I can tell you only this, that in this spot I am rooted. And I cannot go.'

Padric knew that she had told him all that she ever would tell him. 'What am I to do?'

'Find your land.'

'I will go, Bega. But I will never leave you.'

'I know.'

'Some day I will come back.'

'Yes.' Her heart lurched but she held back her tears.

'You will always be here.'

'Always.'

She looked at him now, at last, directly. His acceptance had given her the courage she needed. She saw the eyes that she loved clouding a little; the face which made her hands want to stroke its skin tense itself in resolution; the man hold to his restraint, respecting the truth in her.

'Let me stay,' she said. And then, widening her eyes to prevent the sudden access of tears and repressing the gasp of loss, she managed to murmur: 'let me break my word to you.'

There was a terrible silence between them.

'I will.'

He looked at her with a final deep, even hard look as if he were branding the image of her on to his mind: as if he were taking her image to carry it for ever.

'God be with you.'

'God be with you.'

She watched him go: watched him until he had crossed the fields and disappeared into the woods. She clutched the bundle of twigs. When, finally, he had gone, she could bear it no longer and wept and wept until she was exhausted.

'God forgive me,' she said and then, 'Praise Him.'

BOOK SIX

❈❈❈

A TIME OF PLAGUES

❈❈❈

A.D. 664–683

chapter sixty-five

the first plague

After Padric had gone, Bega had violent dreams. The devil sent his most seductive and dangerous messengers to enter her while she slept. She would wake in a spasm of sweat and sweet, forbidden pain fending off the hellish being. Prayer. Prayer. Prayer on cold earth before dawn until thighs stiffened and knees numbed; prayer at the beginning of the day: prayer with her nuns whom she begged to pray for her. They were unused to seeing Bega weak and during these days the small settlement grew subdued. The effort of her prayers to remove the great shadow on the sun, they whispered, had taken all her strength away. The depth of her anger and sadness at the defeat of the Celts at Whitby had prepared her weakness. They prayed with her and for her and watched her carefully. Her lean whip figure seemed frail, her slightness small: they closed about her.

She dared not tell them that the figure which disturbed her waking and dreaming was Padric. Although God knew of this betrayal, she was ashamed but did little more than murmur a shamed confession to Him. She had not anticipated the impact of the loss. For now Padric was finally gone and she would not have him back. She felt something amputated. She walked a little hunched, her small fine body huddled around its centre for comfort. But there was no respite. Voices which could not be silenced would taunt her with what might have been: had she married Padric; had she taken to his bed; had she ridden with him across the land; had she borne his children and fought with him for the kingdom they would rule. She felt sickly from the loss of it, faint as if she had fasted too long, and shamefully near to tears at every moment.

The first news of the plague came to Bega as a relief, for which she begged forgiveness.

'Who can doubt it any more,' she said to the oldest of the nuns, Saethfryd, 'that God is on our side? The Romans won at Whitby but what a false victory it is. First He threatens to extinguish the whole earth. Now He sends a plague. The Romans will know better now. He will not rest until His Will is done.'

Saethfryd nodded but the workings of God and the politics of Whitby were both part of that great unknowable of which she stood in awe. Bega, her poor, starved-looking Bega, seemed to take heart from these signs. Saethfryd was terrified by them. She had wholly expected the world had come to an end in that darkness. For days afterwards she had caught herself looking up anxiously. Like others in the valley, she credited Bega's power of prayer with the retreat of darkness. Since then, the little church had been full. The people were sufficiently Christianised to believe in the power of the invisible God at a time of such unique crisis even though they would often defer to Reggiani or whisper over their old pagan totems.

'Let us pray for the triumph of the Celtic church,' said Bega, and the two women kneeled beside Bega's stone bed.

To her shame, as she thought, and certainly to a loss of favour in heaven, Saethfryd could not concentrate on the triumph of the Celtic church. Her mind reached back to the last outbreak of plague when she was a child here in Rheged. She saw again the pustules, the convulsions among the children, the vomiting and delirium and the inflamed eyes and yellowing skin, adults staggering around as if they had drunk beer all day and all night, the rigor mortis which seized them ... a series of vivid and distressing pictures came into her mind as she screwed up her eyes and twisted her hands together and tried unsuccessfully to pray for the conquest of Rome by the one true church.

Bega herself was surprised by her exhilaration. God had sent a warning. He wanted the Celts to be left in peace. Perhaps (and here her heart lifted, she could almost feel it rise inside the small birdcage of her chest), He wanted them to roll back the Roman occupation just as Padric wanted to roll back the Northumbrian occupation.

So Padric's mission was part of her own and it was now part of God's wish. They were entwined. She blessed God for restoring Padric to her, not through lust or desire but through the faith. She would express it. He would defend it.

They were reunited!

'Alleluia!' she exclaimed, loudly, and Saethfryd mumbled an echo. 'Alleluia.'

Bega got quickly to her feet, the older woman with her touch of arthritis followed more wearily.

'We must visit the sick today,' said Bega, and Saethfryd could only wonder at the sudden stream of cheerfulness, of joy even, and confidence. 'But first we must break our fast and gather strength.'

The other nuns – there were now seven of them – were also impressed by Bega's dramatic change of mood. Saethfryd told them that she had prayed not for the victims of the plague and not for strength in the Lord to fight it, but for the Celtic church. Saethfryd was lost for further explanation, but somehow that had refreshed Bega and appeared to have removed all the silt which had been choking and oppressing her.

Bega made her plans. She spent the next three days securing as much information as she could. The plague had come in through the ports, it was thought. Tradition pointed that way. It was strongest, therefore, along the coast, and people were beginning to move inland, despite the upheaval of dislocation. She decided that the small dormitory which housed the nuns would be the hospital and their beds were moved into the church.

Food supplies were not high – that was the problem in many of the adjoining districts: people had been weakened by a number of poor harvests. But the nuns had stored skilfully and Bega had been frugal. And they had always been over-provided for their numbers. Moreover her herb garden and their vegetable garden had struggled through in that gentle and well-protected location. Where others had failed, Chad, and across the field Reggiani, had nursed their gardens and, following Reggiani's example, Chad had cut out little channels to assist the irrigation. The lake people still fished hard if unskilfully in the lake and the game in the forests gave them a little sustenance, though it was thinning out. Yet they too had been enfeebled by the thinness of the crops, they and their cattle and goats, sheep, poultry and other stock.

Now the sun blazed when rain was urgently needed. Just as months of unceasing rain and hail and bitter cold had nipped and strewn and destroyed the early seedings and the young growing, so the unusual heat of this big sun scorched the chance of a second seeding. They knew that God and the gods were angry. They could see that the sun had grown since it had disappeared behind the blackness. And the news of the plague was around the valley fast as the wind.

Late on a hot morning a messenger came for Bega: a boy, who reminded her of Chad when she had first encountered him. He told what was already becoming a regular story: he had been sent in advance by some monks to make sure all was safe for them to use Bega's nunnery as a resting place and stopover in their flight from Ecfrith and his men. Like the others, they were bound for the coast and Ireland. Bega saw that the boy was fed and watered and sent him back with reassurances. She offered Chad as a guide but the boy insisted that he could remember the way.

She walked along the path that Chad had laid out along the lakeside. He had shored it up with driftwood and rock-boundaried it so that the walk had a slight and formal elevation. It was here that the nuns were to be seen, especially of an evening in their few minutes of leisure. Here that some of the local young men, in late summer, came to watch or tease them. Bega preferred it when no one else was there. She knew that this seeking for solitude in one whose duty it was to mother a house, however small, was a dereliction of her duty. But being alone was essential for her very life, she thought.

On this quiet walkway, under God's immense sky, in the interstices of calm she could look on her little principality and be pleased. The church was neat and a little mellowed now. Before it the cross stood like the champion of God, a sign throughout the valley of the supreme sacrifice and a totem for many people to the power of Bega's prayers. The dormitory was small but again a sturdy building. The outhouses were wood and thatch but no less secured against the weather. There was even a small wooden guesthouse and a minute parlour for Bega, after the manner of Hilda. The outer wall was bedded and had a look of defiance about it, though there was no well within, which was a drawback. Despite several explorations, no spring had been discovered, but the nearby stream gave them crystal water. The nuns were conscientious, well chosen by Hilda, and though some might have resented being delegated to such a remote spot they accepted it as a challenge from on high and saw added virtue in their isolation.

As she walked in this midday, still too hot for her taste, she felt she could almost breathe in the smell of quiet, purposeful, industrious self-containment which the fear of the plague had not yet tainted.

The mountain's mass of height had grown into a comfort since she had seen it as part of Padric. It seemed to shelter her. It watched over her. It was a protector. She had the beginnings of an impulse to climb it: to be like Donal and seek to approach nearer to heaven. For surely the peak of such a mountain must be near penetrating heaven itself. Her excitement was stirred at the dangerous but growing certainty that one day she would ascend it. The prospect brought an unaccustomed tremor to her body so used now to sensual denial. So she looked at the bare, sun-baked, wrinkled hide of the monster, clear cut out against the sharp blue sky and made a pact: soon, soon she would dare. But now, sharply coming out of her reverie, she must put all her energy into fighting the plague.

The jolt which had broken the unaccustomed luxuriance of calm reflection was provided by Cal, who was suddenly a couple of yards in front of her in his favourite greeting pose: standing, feet planted wide forward, head pulling back and full throat displayed, tail swishing the air, barking happy.

Chad was some paces behind. 'Reggiani wishes to see you,' he said. 'She is asking all the leading men in the valley to see her tomorrow just after dawn.'

Bega pretended to be only mildly interested. Her association with Reggiani was still a little distant and she preferred it that way. So, she thought, did the woman herself, variously known as the healer, the medicine woman, the mother, the priestess, the loose and bawdy one, the magician.

'What does she want?'

'I have no news of that.' Chad had become a rather earnest young man and even the casual question thrown at him while Bega was playing with the dog was taken on most seriously. He had found refuge in this seriousness. It was his mask. And he thought, rightly, that it pleased Bega. 'But from her tone I think that you most of all should be there.'

'Most of all?'

'That was what I gathered.'

'Most of all?'

Chad looked a little flustered and thought hard.

'It's true that I cannot think of any words addressed to you. It was just that when she spoke of the plague, she made me understand that you, of all people here, would be wise to attend.'

'Did she?' The words were skittish.

Chad nodded sombrely. His opinion of Reggiani was much higher than that held by Bega. Yet if Bega had told him to change his opinion, he would have done.

'I think we should be there,' he continued, rather gloomily.

'We . . . ?'

Chad turned away to shield the sudden hotness on his cheeks.

'Well then, Chad, *we* shall go.'

The gangling youth nodded and turned away, longing to find logs to chop or stones to whistle out of the earth or any hard physical thing which would hammer away the confusions in his blood.

CHAPTER SIXTY-SIX

Reggiani had dressed in all her magnificence. Though the steel dawn was only just raising itself, her jewels and polished ceramics glittered. She was as blond as Bega was dark, as lush as Bega was lean, as open as Bega was secretive. She had acted all her adult life in the knowledge that no one could afford to be without her skills in medicine and no man would resist her wish to take him. Legends were woven about her powers, her life and reputation in that valley and even beyond, and she was aware of this. She glowed as if she herself had brought up the dawn.

Bega affected to have a tolerant amusement at her. The medicines and the herbs impressed her and she was grateful both for herself and for others for the work that Reggiani did. The open lasciviousness disturbed her but she was determined not to admit it. Bega would have been outraged at an accusation of envy. Pagans must live while they may, Bega thought. Their life was short and for them it would be the only life.

For the priestess in Reggiani, the sticks rattling with bones and amulets, the teeth around her neck, the idols perched on little pedestals behind the perpetual burn of the fire in the shrine, Bega had little patience. When Reggiani began by shaking the stick and rattling the bones and chanting and stamping rhythmically on the ground, which hypnotised Chad, Bega turned to Saethryd and smiled. But Saethryd, like Chad, was impressed.

'The plague is coming to us again,' Reggiani began. 'We must be prepared.'

A murmur of apprehension came from the dozen or so elders of the valley who had come, each one with a henchman or servant, to listen to this woman. Bega was aware of the power of Reggiani to bring to her camp such a gathering. Each man there would have claimed precedence over her. Three had short swords, many had daggers, all had spears and knives and any one of them would have favoured himself in direct contest with her – the basic measure of judgment – but they had come at her command and her simple first sentence drew their attention immediately.

'It has come because we have forgotten how to take guard against it.'

'It has come as God's judgment on the Romans and as punishment on us for letting them persecute the old church,' interrupted Bega, speaking without a quaver in her voice.

'You have your way and I have mine,' said Reggiani, conciliatingly.

'I have no way,' said Bega. 'I follow God's way.'

'The plague is approaching,' said Reggiani, ignoring the argument, 'what will we do?'

'Pray,' said Bega, briskly, 'and look after the sick.'

'We will all pray to our own gods,' said Reggiani.

'Only my God can answer prayers,' said Bega.

Reggiani paused. She nodded. She was a wise woman. 'The plague is not yet in this valley,' she said. 'It is not yet here.'

Again she paused. She now had the attention she needed.

'I know how to protect us from it,' she said. 'In my dreams and through my own gods, I have been told how all of us can be spared this plague.'

Saethryd nudged Bega hard and Bega did not interrupt.

'This is a valley,' said Reggiani. 'There is only one road through the valley. There is a lake which can also be a barrier. There is our sacred mountain which no one can cross. We are defended. We have no more than the single path.'

'Our sacred mountain': it was the first time that Bega had heard Reggiani speak in these terms and she felt a twist of jealousy. It was foolish but it was undeniable. How could this pagan shaking sticks and bones lay claim to such a monumental work of God? Saethfryd again felt her young mistress rising to exclamation and again she elbowed her down.

'I say that we block off the road and all the valley until the plague has passed,' said Reggiani. 'It will mean that we turn away some friends and some traders and some who need to travel here – but it will bring us safety.'

The immediate, assenting sigh indicated that Reggiani had

found the spot and, already sure of herself, now doubly sure, she carried on.

'The few things we need – like salt – we can ask to be brought across the lake and thrown on to the shore. Only our own valley people will be allowed to land there. We will be shut off and, without touching people, without their breath coming into our air, we shall be safe. I know this. My mother told me this when I was very young and she had kept alive all those in the high valley we lived in. She did it as I have said and we must do it too.'

'Who would guard the roads?' someone asked.

'We would. We would have men at both ends of the road. You would have to take turns. It would not be easy but I tell you that we will know no plague if we do this.'

'What if the people insist that they must come through the valley?'

'They can go around the lake, across to the side where the sun sleeps and pass by that way. Or they can take a boat at the head of the lake and sail down the water and thus pass us by also.'

'What if they resist our plan?'

'Then we must resist them.'

Reggiani shook her charm-laden sticks in the air and the rattling sound seemed to give heart to the men. A leading man of the valley, a thegn, and friend of Bega, stood up.

'We can make many enemies by doing what Reggiani says. When there is a plague it is a time when we must help each other. I am of the One God of Bega and He tells us to pray and to comfort the sick. I have heard this from the mouths of holy men and women. We will make many enemies if we follow Reggiani and we will defy the will of the almighty conqueror on high.'

Reggiani was about to reply but another man stood, a younger man, holding his sword high.

'I too have become a worshipper of the God of Gods in the sky. I do not know whether it was the prayers of Bega who brought back the sun or whether it was the spells of Reggiani. My view is that it is better to offend no one. Therefore I worship still the gods of Reggiani and the God of Bega. But I say there is something else. What use are we to any of the gods if we are dead? The great God wants us when our souls are ready. I have not been a worshipper very long. My soul is not ready. I do not want to die until it is and then I will go gladly. I say that we follow the plan of Reggiani.'

Another stood up as that one sat down on his thick-skinned coat which kept out the dew. He was an old man, with only three long yellow teeth in his mouth. His skin was exceptionally pallid and stretched over his face tightly as if the bones kept threatening to pierce it. His sheep and cow skins were grimy and shiny with an age that seemed to outreach his own and he leaned on a staff as he talked, but his intensity and the respect given him compelled the fullest attention yet from an increasingly restless Bega.

'I know about the plague,' he began. 'I saw a plague and I lived through it and perhaps I lived through it to be here today to tell you the tale. I gave sacrifices to all the gods at that time. I had a most beautiful lamb. You have never seen a prettier creature. It was my pet and it followed me everywhere. But as the plague deepened and nothing could be done I was urged to sacrifice my lamb. I had protected her against thieves for many days. There were those who were hungry but somehow I held on to the life of this creature. Then they took her from me at dawn one day, and the bigger men held me while they slit its throat and offered its blood.'

He paused as if revisiting that moment. Then he continued. 'But the plague did not stop. In numbers we were more than the days of half a year in our valley when the plague began. When it ended there were fewer than four score of us. It will be the same here. Most will go. Gods cannot help you. It is gods themselves who have sent the plague for who else has the power or the wish to torture us poor creatures save the gods? It is a horrible, horrible thing.'

Here the old man's skull-like head seemed to stretch its skin even further until it was indeed an intimation of death. 'You will never have seen sores like that. Nor people behaving crazily and helpless. Nor vomiting and howling in anguish like that. You will never have seen children writhing in such pain and old people staggering around in a madness. In the church of Bega there was a man who talked about hell. I wanted to stand up and say to the man – "You do not know about hell. I have seen hell. It is the plague. You are wrong to tell me that hell is after I am dead. After I am dead I go back into the dark. Hell is what I have lived through!"'

He looked around him, surveying them all. 'Let me tell you now: most of you will not live through a plague. Most of you will be white bones by the lakeside by midwinter if we let in this plague. The priestess is right. We must keep it out of the valley.'

There was silence for a few moments after he sat down and then Bega's neighbouring farmer got up. He was the most robust man there and respected for his strength of arm as much as for his mill and the wealth it brought him.

'If we turn people away,' he said, 'why should they come back? If we send people across the lake or down the lake, why should they ever follow the path through our valley again? And if they do not, how should we survive without the goods they bring us and the goods we exchange with them? There is another thing. We are a small valley. Already our food is low. Less has gone through my mill in the last months than at any time I can remember. Everybody is hungry and some are beginning to starve. I see one or two animals already being slaughtered when everybody knows that you must not kill them until deep into winter and yet summer is not over. If we turn everyone back from here, will we not be cutting ourselves off from help that might be brought us or food that could come and we could barter for it? I say no to the plan of Reggiani.'

Reggiani braced herself. Until this intervention she had been sure of them. It would not do to leap in immediately and cross such a powerful man.

No one else was moved to speak. They sat dumbly, all, as if waiting for a sign. The farmer had swayed several of them, especially with his hopes of relief and aid from other quarters. That glint of hope was worth a weight of Reggiani's arguments.

Eventually, Bega stood up and Reggiani, for a moment, felt a glow of anticipation. She had always sensed something kindred behind Bega's obvious difference from her. Now she felt herself reaching out to this slight, dark, intense woman who waited until all were aware that she intended to speak.

'I agree with Reggiani,' she began, and the pagan priestess held her breath. 'We must do all we can to keep the plague from this valley. Padric, your prince, when he was here, told me that a previous plague had caused more deaths among his people than among the children and youth of the invaders. We must help him.'

It was strange, she thought, how the public utterance of Padric's name gave her such pleasure. It was such a luxury just to hear herself say the name. Instead of being the memory locked on the very floor of her mind where it stirred ancient pains and fears, it flew, like a prayer to heaven, and it was as if for a moment he were alive and standing there beside her. In her heightening state of chastity, the name alone uttered in front of others, dispelled her perpetual sense of loneliness.

'But while I agree with what she says, I have a different answer. The only way to avoid the plague is through prayer. If we are strong in our prayers, if we have in truth prepared our souls for His eternal reward, then we will be spared to do battle yet longer against the enemies who rise up to test His will on earth.' Her passionate tone in the distinctive foreign accent and the reputation she had gained, principally after the darkening of the earth but also in her zeal, commanded their respect. Besides, they knew she could read and write. Many had seen her do this. These gifts were to be prized. Few valleys had anyone as accomplished as Bega and she was regarded as a charm.

'Whether or not your God sends the plague I do not know,' said Reggiani, loudly, rather desperately claiming back the attention of a company she had so recently thought she had won over. 'If He does then He is a very cruel God. But the plague is coming here. And all who know about the plague have told me that it passes from man to man, woman to woman, child to child. If you do not have the plague near you, then you will not be with the plague. Yes, pray. Pray to keep those with the plague out of our valley. When they come here, we will be marked like them. If prayer can keep our valley without those who have been in contact with the plague, then I too will pray.'

'There are monks arriving here who will pray for us all,' said Bega. She chose her next words with political care. She did not want to admit to her place on the escape route. Some of them undoubtedly guessed it, but no one had mentioned it. But she did want to impress on this company which was still reluctant to commit fully to either argument, that help was at hand. 'These men are the holiest monks. They have devoted their whole lives to the service of God. Their souls are as clear as the stream. When they speak to God, there is nothing between their lips and His ear. When they arrive, which will be today, there will be a special service at which we shall pray and show the power of our prayer and see this plague never reaches us.'

'Where are these men come from?' asked Reggiani.

'From the lands of the Northumbrians.'

'If they are from the sea then we must avoid them,' said Reggiani. 'Are they from the sea? Were they living near the sea?'

'I do not know,' said Bega.

'The plague comes from the sea,' the priestess said. She spread out her arms. 'We must close the valley! They cannot be let in! We are clean. There is no plague here. These monks will have walked for many days and they must have passed through plague villages. How could they not? And how could one of them not be given it? They beg for food – you have seen them. All the time they go to people to talk to them and touch them. You have seen them. You have seen Bega visiting the sick. She holds people to drive out their devils. How many have these monks held who have the plague? And while holding them, did not the plague leap across to them? How can we let them come into this valley?'

Reggiani's voice had risen, almost into a panic. Her arms opened to reveal the magnificent heft of her full body.

'Will you let them in?' she asked. She pointed one of her two totems at the nearest man and shook it near his face. 'Will you? Will you go and embrace these men?' To another. 'Will you? Will you go to this service and stand beside men who have walked through the plague? Will you ignore the sores on the neck and the vomiting?' And another, the sticks shaking to shiver the bones of the feeble-hearted. 'Do you want to invite plague here to meet your women and your children?' She stopped and then turned in a full circle, slowly, dramatically, arms outstretched, totem sticks silent. When she faced them again she said 'I have told you what to do. I have told you what to fear. I will tell you one thing more. When you leave here none of you will return until the plague is over. You see my wall. I will live behind my wall until the plague is gone. I have my well. I have what I need. My household will stay with me and we will not move beyond the wall. If you decide to do as I have said then come at noon and shout it to me. If not, I know that I will never see most of you again.'

Reggiani walked away from them and stood in front of her small altar. The men left, hurrying across the fields or cutting through the woods to be back to the security of their houses and their work.

Bega wanted to go and talk further with Reggiani and moved forward. Once again Saethfryd took her arm.

'Let her be,' she said. 'She is with her own gods now.'

'She must be saved,' said Bega. 'Imagine how God would rejoice if a soul like hers were to be saved!'

'We must go now,' said the older woman, who was troubled at the amount of credence she had found herself giving to Reggiani's arguments. 'We have work to do if the monks are coming.'

'They will not be here until the evening,' said Bega. 'He told me where they had rested. We have until sunset.'

'Still leave her,' Saethfryd urged. 'Look.'

Reggiani had now bent double over her altar and been joined by three women and two men from her household. One was carrying a white cock.

'I cannot allow this pagan rite to be performed in front of Christians,' said Bega.

'It is the way they are,' said Saethfryd, always worried by the impetuosity of Bega. She tried to tease her away, but Bega was in pursuit of a soul. She saw a great prize for the Lord before her and she would have walked through a circle of fire to reach it.

'Reggiani!' she called, imperiously but not loudly.

Reggiani was not a woman of pretence and she turned to face Bega.

The others stood aside, humbly in train to her.

Bega began to walk towards her.

'I will walk to you,' said Reggiani. 'This is my sacred ground.'

Bega stopped and Reggiani came up to her. There, in unconscious agreement, the two women moved away from all the others over to the edge of the clearing where they stood beside the fallen trunk of a felled beech. The sky was now much brighter and behind the mountain the sun was already visible.

Reggiani had brought her totem sticks with her and she leaned them against the trunk.

'Why do you need those?' Bega asked, her voice almost drained of criticism.

'Why did you build your cross?'

'To honour Our Lord who died for all our sins,' said Bega, promptly, 'and to be a reminder to us all of His suffering and our path to glory.'

Reggiani smiled. Sometimes Bega seemed so young that she

was endeared to her even though she feared the woman's fanaticism. She picked up one of her well-carved staffs.

'Perhaps these could be called my gods,' she said. 'These tell me that my gods rule all the waters from the springs to the great lake; my gods rule the sun and the moon, the day and the night, and these are tokens of their power. When I have these and honour these, the gods know that I am serious.'

'How can you be? How can you make a god from stone or from wood or from shells which could be used for anything at all? My cross is not my God. Yet over there, on your altar, I see an idol carved in wood, and you were worshipping the idol.'

'That is the god of fertile land,' said Reggiani, solemnly. 'She will help us if we can placate her. She has held back her nourishment from our land, first with the cold and the rain and now with the drought and the sun. We have made her angry.'

'But how can you believe that! A piece of wood! It could be carved for any other purpose and then what would it be? A God, to be a God, has to be unseen. We cannot describe Him. We can know Him only through prayer and through our worthiness.'

'How do you know that what he wants is "worthiness"?' Reggiani asked, rather severely. 'How can you know if he is invisible and nowhere?'

'His Son came to earth to teach us,' said Bega. 'If we conduct our lives as He has taught us, then we will join our glorious Lord in the life to come. And then we will know.'

'What is this life to come? When I first saw Erebert on his island (where I first met you, and a sickly thing you were) he talked of nothing but "the life to come". He prayed for his life here to end so that he could enjoy this "life to come". But what is it?'

'Our Saviour Christ has taught us that it is life everlasting in the company of the heavenly host,' said Bega. 'For that we dedicate all the short years of our brief earthly existence, so that we can enjoy eternal happiness.'

'That means that this life doesn't matter for anything else,' said Reggiani and smiled. The smile annoyed Bega.

'It means we have to use it to prepare our souls.'

'What if you fail?'

'Then we are damned, equally for eternity.'

'What if you have to choose between an earthly benefit and something that helps improve your soul?'

'We must choose the soul.'

'So rather than take measures to stop the arrival of the plague you will concentrate on improving your soul?'

'No! The plague can only be prevented by prayer. Prayers are best heard from purest souls. Therefore the work we do on ourselves can also help others.'

'How are you so sure of this eternal life?'

'Because Jesus Christ Our Lord died and was buried and then on the third day He rose again thus proving that earthly death has no dominion. After that He ascended into heaven as recorded in the gospels.'

'You believe all this?'

'Of course.' Bega paused and then added: 'I would like you to believe it too, Reggiani. You have such a power in the valley. Many are Christians here but there are many who are not. More would come to Christ were you to give them a lead.' Bega took one of Reggiani's larger, stronger hands in her own. 'Let me convert you, Reggiani. Let me take you away from these sticks and stones and sacrifices of cockerels. If you believe, your soul will begin to strengthen. Soon it will grow and exult in Christ Our Lord and soon you will be with Him in paradise.'

Reggiani smiled and with her free hand she reached out and stroked the earnest cheek of the slighter woman. Bega resisted flinching. Even though the hand was coarse, there was in the caress that which tightened not only her flesh but some other hidden source.

'Do you have to be a virgin to reach paradise?' Reggiani asked, and that mocking look appeared in her eyes, not for the first time, the look that Bega could not abide.

'No.'

'Then why are you?' Or *are* you? the eyes seemed to add.

Bega blushed. 'I wish to serve with all my might,' she said, in a flustered manner. 'But there are many women, many holy women who have husbands and I am sure that God is as open to them as He is to anyone else.'

'But how can you endure it?' Reggiani persisted. 'Urien tells me that Padric wants to marry you. He thought that he was going to marry you.' Reggiani paused and the twinkle in the eyes made

Bega shift nervously on the uneven seat. Reggiani would not let go of her hand. 'If God does not object to husbands, why do you?'

The question was such a simple one. It cut through all the torments she had endured like a sharp knife through rope which had bound her up. If God did not object to husbands, why should she? Why indeed? She could not reply.

'I think I want this life too much to believe in your God,' said Reggiani, seeing that nothing would come from Bega. And this, though an open remark, further exacerbated the agitation which Reggiani's blunt enquiry had caused. Was she, Bega, lacking in want, in desire for this life? Was that in itself perhaps a sin? God had given her this life. Were her original doubts as to the strength of her calling now seen, too late, to be justified? Suddenly she wanted to go. But Reggiani, feeling the tremor of movement, strengthened her grip.

'You must not let strangers come into the valley,' she said. 'It is the only way to stop the plague. Believe me. Please.'

'Believe someone who believes in killing an innocent cockerel!' Bega found leverage in this for a riposte and to initiate her departure from what had become far too uncomfortable an encounter. 'Why should I believe you? I will not turn away those who are coming to me for refuge. I have made my promise.' She stood up, all but flinging off Reggiani's hand. 'Just as I have made my promise to God that I will be faithful to Him and betray Him with no man.'

Reggiani stood, sorrowful but equally resolute. 'I have my gods too,' she said. 'And they have not let me down. I will live with them.'

Bega nodded, it was almost a bow, and turned and walked away. Chad, who had come and posted himself nearby, walked with her. Saethfryd joined them, relieved that they were at last on their way out of what she thought of as the devil's kitchen. Bega felt on fire. Her palm still tingled from Reggiani's strong grip. She interpreted that as a sign of victory even though she had failed to breach her pagan faith.

The further they walked, the more the sun warmed their backs. They heard the cock cackle, screech out and then gutter to silence and Bega imagined the blood spurting over Reggiani's strong hands.

✂✂✂✂

Reggiani returned at noon but she had already read the signs in the stones she had cast after the sacrifice. No one came. She accepted it. Then she set two plans in motion, one for the valley, one for herself and her followers.

For the valley she employed her charms against unfruitful land. She had tried it without success twice already in the year and she was allowed to try it thrice.

She instructed her servants to go with all speed to the four corners of the valley. She specified where. Before sunset, four sods were to be collected, as well as oil, honey, yeast and milk and a part of every tree that grew on the land and of every well-known herb except burdock.

The sods and all the other materials would be placed on the altar and a bowl of blood would be taken from a pig. This would be spilled three times on the bottom of the sods with the chanting of the words 'Grow' and then 'Fill' and then 'The earth'. The four who had cut the sods and brought the branches and herbs would each come and dip the four fingers of their right hand in the bowl of blood and touch all the sods in turn, uttering the same words.

Then Reggiani would utter a prayer to the goddess of the valley and the goddess of the earth and, as the sun began to go to the dark region, she would turn seven times and repeat 'Grow', 'Fill', 'The earth'. Before dawn the sods had to be returned to the spot from which they had been cut, and replaced. The milk, honey, oil and leaves from the trees and the herbs would be mulched up with the blood sprinkled on them and these would be daubed on the ploughshares so that when they struck the soil they would carry the power of the gods.

While this was being done, through the day, Reggiani gathered herbs for the nine-herb charm, the most powerful of all her charms. This would be her surest stay against the plague, this and isolation. As she gathered the herbs in the proper measures, she murmured some of the verses to herself:

'Remember Mugwort what thou didst reveal,
What thou didst arrange at Regenmeld,
Thou wert called Una, the oldest of herbs,
And power against three and thirty,
Thou power against poison and against infection,
Thou power against the foe who fares through the land.
And then plantain, mother of herbs,
Open from the east, mighty within;
Over thee chariots creaked, over thee queens rode,
Over thee brides made outcry, over thee bulls gnashed their
    teeth.
All these thou didst withstand and resist;
And so mayst thee withstand poison and infection . . .'

Reggiani stored her herbs with great care. Year in, year out she
added to them and dried them and every day she checked that
they were ready for use. She kept them in a small dry cave which
led off from her own house and it was these, she believed, and
her skill in them, which would see her through.

So she took mugwort, plantain, lambs' cress, cockspur grass,
camomile, nettle, crabapple, chervil and fennel. With some old
soap and juice of the apple she pounded them to a powder. She
prepared a paste of water and ashes. She took the fennel and
boiled it in the paste and bathed it with a beaten egg. Now she
had the salve.

She sealed it and put it in a cool place. Should the plague break
through all the barriers, then this was her last line. That was for
the valley.

For herself, she closed up the gate finally that night, ready to
see out the plague.

CHAPTER SIXTY-SEVEN

Reggiani did not see the monks who arrived just before sunset. There were seven of them. Four carried a litter on which a fifth lay, the two others walking ahead, one of them reciting aloud from an early psalm. 'Oh Lord, rebuke me not in thine indignation, neither chasten me in Thy displeasure. Have mercy upon me, Oh Lord, for I am weak. Oh Lord, heal me for my bones are weak, my soul also is sore troubled. But Lord how long will thou pursue me? Turn thee, Oh Lord, and deliver my soul: Oh save me for Thy mercy's sake.'

The boy had once again come ahead and as Bega stood beside him watching the small procession cross the last field, her uneasiness subsided. This was her true work. This was what God had sent her to earth for. Her soul was strengthened as the lulling voice drew nearer over the parched earth with the large naked sun circling the lake like prey and making for the sea to the west.

The sick man was put into the newly arranged hospital, with no little pride on the part of the nuns who vied with each other to serve him.

Bega herself washed the feet of Caelin, who had led the group, speaking the gospels along the way. His scalp was wounded and bruised, the wound's dark blood clotted where a forced tonsure had taken place. Three of the nails of his right hand had been torn out. All the monks had been whipped. It was only through the eccentric sympathy of a laconic eldorman that they had not been flayed alive. Their journey across the land, clinging to the great wall for guidance, had been slow and painful.

'But we are sustained by our love for God,' said Caelin, whose thin face looked misleadingly well thanks to its exposure to the fierce sun of the past few days. 'And we knew that once we arrived here, with Bega, then we would be safe.' He smiled, showing a mouth utterly devoid of teeth, but the smile was so warm that Bega returned it happily.

Caelin insisted that once they had rested and washed, they must thank God before taking any food, near-starved though they were.

It was an evening as light as the day. The sun seemed engorged with gold and copper, still vibrating with its own victorious power after that escape from darkness. The few clouds were being drawn into its progress and crimsons, blood-red and purples were beginning to edge and shoot through them.

'Let us give thanks to God in His good air,' said Caelin.

He began the prayers and the monks and, at first apprehensively, the nuns gathered around him. Bega quite soon steered it to a good enough approximation to vespers and the nuns were reassured.

Bega felt refreshed by the service.

Hard as the monks tried to restrain themselves, the sight of bread – however thinly baked for the sake of economy – and cold herb soups and some berries, together with a little milk, was too much for most of them. They blessed the house, the hosts, the company, the maker of all good things, and then they fell to ravenously. So intense was their assault on the food that several of the nuns, who had been taught by Bega to learn the techniques and the joys of abstinence as a way to survival, willingly gave up their portions and offered them to the men.

Afterwards, Caelin brought Bega the latest news. 'Ecfrith is becoming more and more determined to force us to change,' he said. 'He fears only the holy Cuthbert, they say, and he has made up his quarrel with Wilfrid. But Cuthbert, it seems, has agreed with the decision taken at Whitby. He came to Lindisfarne and though he was questioned and some of the monks were very angry with him and spoke most boldly and critically, even to one who will be a saint, he said it was of little importance, God's will be done.'

Caelin spoke with deep regret. Bega repressed her ready anger at what she still saw as Cuthbert's betrayal.

'Yet he still leads the life of a monk like us. He prays to be a hermit. He groans under the yoke of office. He says openly that he wants to go to one of those minute islands beyond Lindisfarne and compose himself there for a final battle against the author of all evil. Ecfrith cleaves to him and Cuthbert's complaisance gives Ecfrith strength.

'Wilfrid, of course, is jubilant. He never thought to have two such powerful princes on his side. Though Ecfrith's wife continues to practise chastity, she seeks out Wilfrid for her private confessions and confers lands on him, and yet Ecfrith holds out the hand of alliance to him.' Caelin had some difficulty in uttering Wilfrid's name without an accompanying spit of bitterness. 'Wilfrid too is determined to destroy us. He thinks we are too wild, we are not lovers of buildings, we do not like to form part of an empire. Where we have a huddle of beehive huts, enough for our needs, he wants to raise great churches. He sends to Rome for craftsmen as if we had not craftsmen here who could not outcraft them all. But no, they must come from Rome. Even when we try,' continued Caelin, ruefully, clearly regretting that he had indeed tried to conform to Ecfrith's rules, 'his men will come and find new faults.'

'He is determined to drive you out.'

'He is mad to do it,' said Caelin, in a puzzled manner. 'I have heard that even Wilfrid has intervened. Even Wilfrid thought that Ecfrith was mad.'

'Does anyone know why it is?'

'Some say it is to impress his father. Some say that he has been driven mad by his wife and that since Prince Padric's sister was stolen from him he has hated her and all the house of Rheged even more and regarded them as guardians of the Celts. Others, like our Bishop Colman, think that the devil has possessed him and he is never in his own true senses.'

'Tell me what he has done.'

It was still light outside and still throughout the valley the people were scavenging and working for every last purchase of food and nourishment. Not a berry-carrying bush was unknown to the children. The men were out on the over-fished lake for the fifth or sixth time of the day. The women were garnering what they could from roots and herbs and the diminishing stores to make gruel which would last many days. The poorer families who lived in the meanest turf-covered hovels or under overhanging rocks high in the woods were at the beginning of the road to starvation.

Bega had put on her best display for the monks, knowing that on their journey they would have eaten little besides that which they could gather. But she too was anxiously aware of the slow-growing terror of famine. And plague, she knew, fed on famine. Not one of the men at the dawn meeting had come to the service with the monks.

Caelin described the tortures perfected by those he, like Padric and Bega, called the invaders. He was in a way proud of the extremes to which the Celtic resistance had forced this strange cruel alliance of the Northumbrians and Romans. He also wanted to be able to call on Bega as a witness to the suffering and perhaps martyrdom of those who could one day seek sainthood. He described tortures which forced her to ask him to stop.

'Will they keep coming here?'

This was asked almost anxiously. Her position as link in the chain was essential to her.

'They will all be driven away, finally,' Caelin replied. 'Even those who seek glory by enduring all that the enemy can do. And it is to you that they will come.'

Bega took her customary last walk along the lakeside path, glancing now and then towards Reggiani's encampment. She was still uneasy, yet unafraid to admit it, about the encounter with the woman. Surely God would not have visited the plague on such holy men?

Bega walked longer than usual and when she left the lake, the moon was high above the mountain, sharp and bright in a cobalt blue sky, and reflected on the lapping lake waters in a thousand silver glints and ripples.

Caelin and his monks left at dawn with Chad as their guide, but their sick brother could not accompany them. He had vomited and been delirious through the night. Bega in her deep sleep had not heard him. Some of the nuns had. Saethfryd had not slept all night, she said, looking at Bega imploringly. Bega took Chad aside.

'Were you in the hospital last night?'

'No.'

'And yesterday, when they came?'

'I was with the children at the farmer's home.'

Chad had taken up with enthusiasm one of the fundamental roles of the Celtic church – teaching the young. 'Suffer little children to come unto me,' Christ had said and the Celts took this seriously. Chad, himself a new learner, was full of the passion of the converted and had seized on this as a chance to prove himself outside the mundane chopping and planting and building and other heavy work he still performed. When he taught, he felt that he might be within hailing distance of the learned monks.

'Keep well to the front of the monks,' said Bega, struggling to find a way to tell him to keep clear of those who might be plague-carriers without actually being caught instructing him to be less than helpful and friendly to those in need. 'And when you have delivered them over the mountain, come back here but do not cross the wall until I have spoken with you.'

Chad only half understood but he accepted her instructions. Saethfryd clarified the communication, just before he left.

So it was that the first plague came to the valley. The monk soon died and was buried in the grounds of the tiny nunnery. Soon afterwards a nun came out with the symptoms and then another and both of them died. Bega's prayers and self-lacerating fasts and the penalties she imposed on her weakening body were to no avail.

Chad returned to be their exiled messenger. He built himself a hut outside the wall. Bega had decided to confine her company as Reggiani was doing. Even old neighbours made Chad stand his distance, and a pail of milk would be brought out and poured into a pail brought by Chad while he stood apart. No one spoke openly of blame.

A savage winter came and famine set in. The plague had not taken a grip on the valley as it was reported to have done elsewhere and Bega lost no more nuns, but now she was forced to go outside her own walls to scavenge and scour with everyone else, looking for roots and berries and herbs. Chad fished half the day and the other half he would be in the woods taking more and more risks, going higher and higher up the mountain to see if he could land game. When he had a lucky day, Bega insisted on half their bounty going to the poorest of their neighbours and this charity, combined with her fearlessness in visiting anyone thought to have the plague took the sting of blame away from her. A few monks still came through and Chad still took them over the mountain but they were not harassed, as Bega had feared they might be.

Reggiani was true to her vow. It was claimed by some that her servants could fly out of her settlement at night and catch the sleeping birds on the bough or fetch in a deer to be meat for a month. Bega looked at her settlement with such contradictory feelings that she could scarcely bear it. Sometimes she wanted to go and ask forgiveness of Reggiani; at others she wanted to assail her for her selfishness. Mostly she wanted contact with her – just to talk to her about the crisis in a valley which seemed in a clenched and tightening fist.

The spring of the following year was mild and fresh. Seed was scattered. The summer was warm and only beneficially wet. The crops flourished as did the fruit and berries. The roots were succulent, the woods became fuller of birds, even the lake seemed to give up more fish. The first plague retreated.

Reggiani emerged, thin, even gaunt, but with her household intact. No word of reproach came to Bega's ears. Indeed, despite the knowledge that it was a monk who had first contracted the plague in the valley, the general fatalism together with Bega's selfless nursing left the nun with a warmer reputation than the priestess whose clever isolated survival drew no admiration.

Over the next few years the valley built back its strength. Bega's nunnery did not grow: she had no wish to aggrandise the settlement. Already she could feel yearnings to be more isolated, more alone. If God could see her worthy to be a hermit then, she prayed, in years to come she would joyfully embrace that fate. The two nuns were replaced by two novices. Bega made one journey only to the mother house at Whitby and Hilda, still remembering how unworthy the young woman had made her feel, encouraged her to stay where she was. Chad accompanied Bega on that trip and so impressed the monks with his great interest in learning that they gave him paper and writing implements and some pages of manuscript to copy.

Bega escaped without a spot of the plague on her flesh, yet she had been scarred. She told herself that her God had been victorious. How could Reggiani's spirits of rivers and trees and stones possibly claim credit? Reggiani had said that the infection was spread by contact with the plague and yet she, Saethryd and some of her nuns, even Chad, were whole. So what could Reggiani say to that? God gave and God took away. Life and death were in His gift. Alleluia, she ended her prayers of thanksgiving. Alleluia!

Yet the devil kept assuring her that Reggiani had been right and she had been wrong: that Reggiani's gods had told her ways which, if followed, would have saved all the valley. It was something she did not want to consider but, even as the good years grew and confidence in the valley grew, she could not cast off the shadow made worse by the amiable and open and uncritical manner of Reggiani who seemed to welcome her whenever their paths crossed.

⚜⚜⚜

Six years after the first plague, Ecfrith became king.

Dark and contradictory stories circulated about how he had succeeded to the throne when Alchfrid, his brother, had been so clearly the favourite both of Oswy and of the other lords who were apprehensive of Ecfrith's excesses. There were those who pointed to the influence of his wife Aetheldreda. This was the wildest of the rumours, but no one was above suspicion in that court. The rumour which implicated her was that, jealous of the love between Alchfrid and Wilfrid, she arranged for Alchfrid to be killed in what appeared to be an accident on a hunting expedition. Aetheldreda's power of determination was certainly terrible. As soon as Ecfrith took the throne after Oswy's death, she began to distance herself from him. A year later she left to become abbess of Ely from where she continued to help Wilfrid in the vicissitudes of his volatile fortunes.

The greater, more plausible, voice, though, cited Ecfrith as the author of his own triumphant ascent to this wealthy and powerful throne, now the most commanding court in all the land. This story involved the teasing out of Oswy's fear of death and his jealousy of Alchfrid's open wish to succeed. Ecfrith, so this version went, had convinced his father that Alchfrid would assassinate him and laid a plot which was misunderstood by Alchfrid, convincing to Oswy and perfect for Ecfrith: Alchfrid was killed in defence of the rightful king.

That Oswy's next two years were spent in a mysteriously accelerating enfeeblement was not thought suspicious. Neither medicine nor the women brought in from their lonely retreats could find a cure for the poison that seemed to consume him. Ecfrith appeared to be in a frenzy to discover the cause and he shook the kingdom with threats until the very day of his father's agonising death. Yet rumours now suggested that Ecfrith had been seen visiting the cave of a most vile and evil soothsayer, a mistress of deadly herbs.

One of the last of the monks to take the escape route as the persecution reached a peak, told Bega that the coronation had been the most splendid event anyone had ever witnessed. Bishops had come from far and near with princes and thegns, gold was given out as freely as wine was poured, the feast went on for seven days. There were sports and epic sagas detailing the victories of the heroic house of Ecfrith. It cried out splendour, the exiled monk said, as if to defy God Himself.

CHAPTER SIXTY-EIGHT

THE SECOND PLAGUE

When Penraddin, Urien and their servant rode into the valley it was near midsummer. It had not been a good year for crops and vegetables but once again the nature of the place had kept it somewhat above the level of desperation already being reported elsewhere.

Bega was not there when they arrived. She had gone with Chad to visit Erebert.

When she returned they had been there a day. The nuns were glowing. Penraddin's pregnancy thrilled them. Urien's open, mischievous sexuality tweaked them. And their handsome young servant had been ill, which gave them the fullest opportunity to exercise their hospital skills.

Bega cried when she saw Penraddin. She had not realised that she had become so weak. Perhaps it was the fasting or the disappointment at Erebert's meagre and unhelpful words. More likely it was the resemblance that Penraddin had to her brother Padric and the sunny beam which lit up the young woman's face when she saw Bega, who had so nearly been her sister.

'Padric sent me here,' were her first words as she advanced, rather slowly, to Bega, her arms outstretched, her face wider and more lovely with the advancing pregnancy, her manner overwhelmingly warm and friendly.

She took the weeping, thin Bega to her bosom as mother to child. She looked so much older, Penraddin thought, and so unwell. 'He said it was you I should stay with until the child is born.'

Bega, snuggled in the rough cloak and leather breastplate of the younger woman, nodded vigorously but did not yet trust herself to speak.

'He said I could not be safer or in better hands anywhere on earth.'

Bega pulled herself back from Penraddin and at last had the strength to return the smile without a wash of tears.

'You *will* be safe here,' she said; but allowed herself to say no more.

'The child's father is dead,' said Penraddin with obvious control.

'God rest his soul.'

'Amen.'

'We shall pray for him at vespers.'

'God be with you.'

Penraddin, who had walked out along the lakeside to meet Bega, linked arms with her in a comradely fashion and fell into step. At each stride, Bega felt replenished. The life in Penraddin! The stories! The touch of strong flesh on Bega who had begun to shrink away from all fleshly contacts. The excitement of battle and the scent of Padric!

Urien had gone to see Reggiani, which might have unsettled Bega at another time but now she welcomed it as a chance to have Penraddin to herself.

'We will have a feast,' she said impulsively, when the two women were alone in the parlour. 'I am expecting some monks tomorrow and they will be starving, they always are. We have some geese which are as fat as they will ever be this year.' Bega's face lit up at her own plan. 'We have never had a feast. My father loved feasts. Hilda too would have feasts. We shall have a feast!'

Penraddin, near her time and having space to reflect a little, saw her own life as a marvellous adventure compared with the local drudgery of Bega's round. She was sure that Bega envied her. Very likely, she thought, it was the envy which explained why Bega seemed to find it such a nervous strain to look on her, attentively scrutinising her and then flicking her gaze away with a desperate gesture as if suddenly pulling at the head of a running horse. 'These monks,' asked Penraddin, 'where are they from?'

'Melrose,' Bega replied. 'The messenger came yesterday. I

thought that all of those who had defied Oswy had got out but it seems lately that there are still a few more.'

'Ecfrith,' said Penraddin grimly, but with a certain bitter, proprietorial pride. 'Since he took the crown he has become even more angry with the Celts. If they do not do all that he commands in the way he commands then he sends in his war bands. In one monastery, it might have *been* Melrose, his men made all those who believed in the Celtic tonsure – not Easter, no one dare murmur a word about the Easter date – to put their hands in a cauldron of boiling water. This was stood over a great roaring fire. Fat was poured into the cauldron. Five monks stood around, praying, their arms up to the elbow, being melted by the scalding water and fat. They could not withdraw their hands until they said that they would accept the Roman tonsure! Ecfrith and his men laughed at them.

'I was told that although two of the monks withdrew, one collapsed face down into the water and would have drowned had he not been hauled free, but with a face which will never know skin again. But the two others raised their voices to God and prayed and then welcomed the excruciating pain as an opportunity to show to the world the strength of their God. The louder they prayed the more restless the war band grew, the more the other monks began to join in the prayers, the more the triumph of the Celtic church seemed to be imminent. And so these brave warriors of Ecfrith finally took these unarmed, innocent creatures of God, strapped them to poles and dowsed them, one at a time, dowsed them in the cauldron until the pain overcame their senses. They were then tossed outside.

'Everyone was forbidden to help them. All of them died of their burns. I'm sure that Ecfrith thought that it was a good day's work. He would think that. I know.'

'Was he always such a monster?'

'He has become one,' replied Penraddin, with the slight complacency of one who had superior knowledge of the subject. 'When I was with him he was already an evil man but he had to check himself if he wanted the crown. Now that he has it, he thinks that he is the strongest king in all the land and I fear that his evil will know no limits. He is plotting against Wilfrid now that his wife has gone to Ely. He clings to Cuthbert but no one knows how long Cuthbert will support him. Perhaps he does not really care. His war bands bully the countryside.'

Bega tried unsuccessfully to repress her pleasure at the news of victorious Wilfrid's fall from grace. 'They might come here,' she said. 'I have heard that there have been war bands seen nearby throughout the winter.'

'Padric gave you a sword. Didn't he? I remember. I brought it over.'

Bega nodded.

'Are you the only one here who could fight?'

'I think so. Chad would try but he was never trained. And besides, we have only the one sword.'

'I'll give him a short sword I have when I leave.' Penraddin looked down at the bulky belly with a certain frustration.

'There will be plenty of time before then, won't there?'

'Never done this before,' said Penraddin, in her gruff and soldierly mood. 'We shall see.'

Bega left her to set about organising the feast for the next day. She summoned memories of the two or three feasts given by Hilda as a reassurance. Because of her limited resources it would be on a dramatically smaller scale: but it would be a feast.

She instructed Chad to kill two geese which, she knew, was over-extravagant. But Penraddin had excited her generosity and unearthed buried affections.

Saethryd would help Chad to use every part of the geese. Bega felt that this helped justify the uncharacteristic gesture. The feathers would be used by the nuns to stuff mattresses for the hospital. Saethryd would collect the goose fat and store it for winter, when it would be rubbed on the chests of those with coughs or painted on and not removed until Easter. Saethryd instructed Chad on the multiple properties of this fat. Mixed with the flowers of broom and gorse or the leaves or watercress, it became a skin rub which revived the whole body of the palsied or the very old. Mixed with horseradish juice and emulsified with egg yolk it was the best balm for that stiffness in the joints which was so common in the damp climates. Nothing would be lost. Saethryd would take the skin and carcass and giblets and flavour them into a form of potted meat. Chad could take the beaks and carve them as spoon ends.

Bega's excitement at being so close to Padric through his sister was transferred into the preparations for the feast. When the seven

weary monks came from Melrose they walked into a little paradise
of smells and preparations which reminded them of the luck that
had befallen St Brendan and his followers. Bega insisted that this
time it was she alone who washed their feet.

Urien wanted to bring Reggiani, but she had not allowed his
whim to rule. She loved his audacity and the generosity with which
he treated her: coins, gifts, stories. And there was protection in
his sword. She accepted his unannounced visits as easily as she
relinquished him at the end of them. Perhaps, this time, when
they made love so noisily and often, when they drank too much
and she rubbed oils in his body and brought him to her again, when
he produced a magnificent armlet which he slid caressingly over
her hand and up to near her shoulder and then let his hand drift
across to her breasts, when in the heat and joy of it she looked at
him in firelight, she wished he would never go. Or should she go
with him as he asked? She was older now and increasingly aware
of her mortality.

Like everyone else, she had heard of the cruelty of Ecfrith and
wondered how long Rheged itself and even this unobtrusive valley
would be fully immune from his virulent outbursts. If she went
with Urien, he would protect her. Besides, if she loved any man
above others, and the concept was not an easy one for her to grapple
with, all men, all people, being equally spirit driven, then Urien was
that man. Yet she refused to accompany him to his wars and would
not even go across the fields to the feast. She felt in no mood so to
face the Christian woman. Perhaps the spirit of the lake which had
protected her so far would continue to watch over her. She would
make even more sacrifices to the lake goddess.

Urien came alone and, with very public ceremony, left his swords
and his dagger at the door. He demanded in a loud voice that
all the nuns and monks do the same. The giggling of the nuns
fluttered to the roof-beams. Two of the monks shamefacedly
produced short swords and two more, after some urging, disclosed
daggers. Penraddin took some persuading to lay down her arms.
She could feel the child moving in her and knew that its time was
very near and tried to ignore the anxiety that the lack of weapons
inspired in her.

Urien was soon drinking the beer which a slave girl lugged
around.

Some of the monks, half-starved both by choice and necessity, were swaying after their first pull of the beer. Only Laistranus, the leader, was strong headed and it was he who began to recite and to sing, after the fish and the geese had been rapidly devoured. Bega had memories of poetry and song, of sagas and vying drunkenness. Her small gathering could not aspire to that. Nevertheless, she wanted something of the smack of those far-off feasts. Laistranus, an Irish monk who had gone straight into Northumbria from Ireland itself, became her poet and her musician. He was older than the others and had come into the monastery late, after a famine which had carried off his family. It was the famine that he sung about: a dirge but beautifully chanted, tipping the listeners into an agreeable melancholy and drawing tears from Saethryd and others.

Chad served the meat. This was the first feast he had ever attended. He worked as quietly as he could, fearing that the slightest presumption would result in his expulsion. He accepted every scrap of food and beer and was soon in a wholly foreign state of stupor, grinning like a skull. He slid back into boyhood as swiftly as if he had skidded down a wet mud bank. Plop! Splash! He was a child again, wide-eyed as he had been those first days with Padric and Bega, amazed that the world could contain such beings. The song of Laistranus brought tears to his eyes, and a sob which he neither could nor would repress.

To Bega, Laistranus' chanted tale brought back the very smell of Connachta and indolently, sinfully, she knew, her senses seemed to detach themselves from the terrible disciplines of her mind and body and take wing home.

'That was very fine,' said Urien, banging the table until it shook. He sank more beer – the monk had been worth listening to. Now there were stories to be told and it was his duty to lead.

'Let me tell you about your King Ecfrith. Last spring, a message came that the Picts wanted our help against the man. Prince Padric has often been suspicious of the Picts but he needs them. We rode north.

'We were well into the land of the Picts when a messenger met us and invited us to the fortress of his chieftain, a man known to us to be a friend and one of those we counted on. We were very happy at this. Mostly we sleep in the forests or in caves, so we were grateful to go to this great hall. We handed in our armour at the door and without suspicion we unbuckled our swords but, on

Padric's nod, placed them inside the great doors and not outside. He pleaded that the rain would rust them and the shed showed us for storing them was open to the sky.

'Never, not in all their travels, can men of Rheged have been plied with better food and drink than we were on that night. As the rain pelted on the thatch and the smoke danced up to the dark cross beams, the women brought flagon on flagon of mead, cask on cask of beer, and enough pork to choke us. There were poets and music from the pipes they have which first screech your ears and then, by some magic, slither to your heart and make you rosy with melancholy.

'It was Penraddin there who first noticed that, with multiple excuses and well organised casualness, one by one our hosts began to desert us.' Penraddin smiled at the compliment. 'Padric was soon aware of it and, being the leader he is, he reacted immediately by seeming to throw himself yet further into the feast. He began to pretend to be drunk although he never takes more than he can hold.' Urien grinned. 'But by now they were as aware as we were: it was like chess,' he said, 'but while all of *their* pieces were alert, some of ours were completely unaware: three of our men, swollen with the hospitality, had flung their arms across the table and fallen on them in deepest sleep.' He shook his head at this recollection and drank again.

'There is a time on these occasions when a fight is brewing, and that is a time to watch. You watch like you watch a cauldron slowing simmering when you need it to bubble. It happens suddenly: even if you are watching constantly. How to describe it? Like a bird darting up in front of you from a covert, startling you though you had known it was there. Like a wildcat dropping down on to the rock beside you and ready to spring. There was a shout. Riderch had edged across to our weapon pile. He bellowed and picked up a sword and charged. Padric leaped on to a table and raced towards the weapons. Penraddin was with him. Those who had so deceitfully given us their poisoned hospitality somehow wriggled out and slammed the door shut on us and slotted in the cross beam that held it, but one was dead through Riderch, another stunned (the son of the king, which was useful, we thought) and we had most of our weapons.

'They said that they would starve us out. We tried to barter our noble young hostage but they outside were as defiant as he himself, to his credit. He urged us to kill him as boldly as he urged his father to ignore us.

'For two days and nights we waited. We were comfortable. There was food enough and drink enough. We were content to let it unfold as it would. The boy, our hostage, refused to speak to us and would take food from none of us, though the little thief was quick to pinch it when he thought we were not looking. He could not have been more than thirteen but a fine brave youth, insolent and feisty as they come, full of lip and fearless as a banty cock.

'Padric organised us and we waited. "Let them be worried about *us*," he said. "The worst they can do is burn down the building and the Picts would not do that, not with such a fine building. Anyway we have the rain pelting down harder by the minute. Burn the chairs and benches to keep up the fire and let them see thick smoke coming out of the roof. Let them hear quiet mild talk or singing – perhaps, Urien," he says to me, "you can persuade the servant girls to sing – if they come from the outer islands as I believe they do then they have the sweetest voices on earth and songs that go straight into the ear of God. And tell them," he says,' Urien grinned, '"tell them that they will come to no harm – not even from you! *And*," he finishes off, "imagine the Picts outside in this foul upland rain or huddled in their insignificant outbuildings with the leftovers of the feast while we have this bounty to feed on and the warmest, grandest shelter to the north of the great wall."

'It was just what we wanted to hear! Some of the men began to cheer and then we all cheered and cheered and cheered ourselves silly so that the Picts must have thought the Britons had all got drunk or been driven out of their wits. Believe it or not, they were two good days. "What I cannot understand," Padric would say time and again until I thought I would hit him for it, "is why they turned against us. These men have been our friends. We fought with them. We gave our lives into their hands and theirs into ours. Why is this the way we are received?"

'What I did not then understand was that Padric's endless repetition of the question was a snare in which to trap the Pict boy. He would have the answer, Padric thought. Eventually I saw that Padric was playing a clever game with him: he would ignore him though sitting next to him, and then he would turn away having left something dainty within reach of our loosely tied young prisoner who would wolf it down and think he had gained one on all of us. Then Padric would come very close to him, face to face, so that you could not put a spanned hand between them, and he would say, "What is it, boy?" We did not know his name then. "What is it that has turned your tribe against us?" The boy would look away or glower back: once I saw him gather spittle in his mouth but Padric would have seen it too and he would have noted that glint in Padric's eye and he did not spit.

'But as the second day went on, you could see he was troubled. Padric made no effort to conceal our plans from him and you could sense the boy's admiration for the various tricks and stratagems which the twelve or so of us were going to employ against the superior enemy. And when some of those who had been with us on the trail for many years told their stories then you could see his eyes straining with excitement. He was a little warrior of a boy!

'Riderch was especially good at playing him along and told, as sometimes he does, the most wonderful tales about giants in Cornwall and goblins in Wales and dragons in Mercia and flying serpents shooting out of the sea into the land of Wessex and wizards flying in clouds towards Brittany and sorcerers in the mists of the Fenlands where the earth itself is mostly water. "What turned them against us, boy?" Padric would utter, gently, and though he is older and more worn since you last saw him, with a scar on his forehead,' Urien smiled a little cruelly at Bega when he said this, 'he is still a fine man, will ever be, and the boy could sense it.

'It was in the middle of the second night that we made the discovery. It was still roaring with wind and rain and we knew that our enemies outside were beginning to give in to their frustration. Padric talked more earnestly to the boy than he had ever talked before. I think the boy had expected to have had his throat slit or to be tortured. Padric's kindliness baffled him. But still he would not talk and Padric let him sleep.

'About the middle of the night the boy began to shout. It was "Mother!" It was "Don't kill her!" It was "Not the girls!" He was thrashing like a landed trout and when he woke up with Padric kneeling beside him a torch in his hand, he flew at him as far as his loose bonds would allow and, before Padric could defend himself, his nails ripped into his cheek, drawing blood, and his sharp little teeth were going for the throat when Padric took him by the scruff of the neck and pulled him back and held him up and just shook him. And even that not as hard as I would have done.

'"What is your name?" Padric asked after he had set the boy down. "Finan," the boy muttered but we caught it. "Finan," Padric repeated. "Now then, Finan, tell me why it is that I came to your land in peace and was met with a sword. Tell me now. It is time." And there's that iron comes into Padric's voice when he will have his way. The boy picked up the scent. "You are good enough now," the boy said in that broad brogue of theirs, "you are all fine and easy now that my father has you trapped. But what about seven days ago? What about that?"

'Padric stood back and considered. I was completely puzzled. The boy could have told me a brand new riddle and I would have had a clearer view. But Padric of course is an expert in riddles.

'"So it was him," he said. "Now I understand." But I did not and neither did the boy and neither, I suspect, did anyone else who heard this exchange except one.' Urien nodded at Penraddin, who took up the story.

'Ecfrith had impersonated him and murdered and raped and looted in the name of Padric and the men of Rheged. Padric knew that he had to clear his name or infamy would remain, and the house of Rheged would be stained.'

'Ecfrith,' Urien explained to those who did not know, 'looks so like Padric – the face, the hair, the manner, to those who don't know, they could be two peas.

'Ecfrith had heard that Padric had been asked to help the Picts. While we journeyed there, he had led a war band into the heart of the land and slaughtered children, women, cattle – but no men; burned farms and households but spared this hall. Shouted everywhere the name of Padric and the power of the kingdom of Rheged. He then let it be known that Padric was still circulating in the district.

'Revenge prompted the idea that Padric should be invited to the hall to be feasted as the victor. It was in this false spirit that the invitation was given. Padric's bold acceptance fitted in perfectly with those who thought he saw himself as the new ruler of this domain. The feast pretended to be a tribute to Padric and his valorous men. But behind the hospitality burned the fires of vengeance. The Picts had intended to slip out and covertly bring back their weapons and rise against us as we fell unarmed into drunkenness. We foiled them in that but how were we to convince them that we were not those whom they wanted to kill?

'That *was* a riddle.' Urien took a long draught of beer and looked around him to savour the attention. 'You see,' he spelled it out, 'we had to convince the Picts that it was not he, Padric, but Ecfrith the king who had ravaged their families and their property in order to bring about the destruction of Padric. How were we to do that?'

'The wicked man!' said Bega, violently. 'May God forgive me for my judgment but such a man is the devil. The *wicked* man!'

Her nuns looked at Bega with concern. She was not known for such abrupt and vehement outbursts. She ignored them, looking so fierce that no one dared comment.

'"There is one single way," says Padric, "and that is to use the boy." He turns to him and says: "Finan. We will put you on the roof in the morning and your father and his men can throw you up a rope. There will be a log jutting out at the front, above the doors. Tie it there and slide down. Then tell what I will tell you. It is simply this. Your father or some of his men, have to go to see Ecfrith. They can say that they came to complain about the terrible raids of Padric and want Ecfrith to help them take revenge on Rheged. Let them look on Ecfrith closely. Let them look at his forehead. Then let them return. They must say nothing about those of us here."

'He repeated this to the boy who was quick and had understood it all without the second telling. And we were as good as our word. Whatever the boy said it must have been convincing because we were told – it was shouted through the door – that the men were on their way, it would take up to six days. We settled down to lean pickings, but by then we were ready for a fast. Another factor that might have helped was the information the boy gave them about the plans he had heard Padric make. But this was a trick on Padric's part. He had always intended that the boy would be a messenger and had deliberately let him overhear plans that were misleading and referred to all sorts of allies available who were nowhere on earth! That too would make them hesitate.

'By the time the men came back our food was finished. The king came to the door and said that his men had done as directed (taking the credit for himself) and Ecfrith had promised that in spring he would ally himself with him and march on Rheged but it would be better, he said, if Padric were dead before any invasion. "All I want to know," Padric said, through the cracks in the door, "is, did any one of you see the so-called Padric plain in the raids on your people?" There were two who did, the king said. Two who say they will never forget his face as long as they live.

"'Then," said Padric, "open the door, put those two men in front of me, and I shall walk out, alone, to prove that I am not he whom they saw. I will be without arms and my brothers will swear to me that they will take no action until your men have made their judgment."

'After some conferring, this was agreed.

'You can imagine,' said Urien, 'how fast we buckled on our leather chest plates and put on our swords to be ready to rush out after him. I tried to dissuade him, but of course it was no good.

'The door beam was lifted up. Slowly the doors creaked open. The first body I saw was the boy Finan gazing at the door as if transfixed. A floating angel on a golden horse would not have surprised him at that moment.

'Padric walked out into the endless rain, some paces clear of the door, and halted. For a moment which I can still enter,' said Urien, 'for a moment which stretches from that time to this, I felt the earth pause. They had such good cause as they thought for revenge which alone heals humiliation. He stood still and straight like the stone cross outside your church. Then,' Urien glanced at Bega, 'the two men came near and sniffed around him like dogs about meat they do not quite trust.' He looked to Penraddin. 'It was then that Penraddin walked out. She simply started to walk and she was out of the hall before any of us could catch her, letting her sword fall, taking off her helmet so that her hair fell about her shoulders and even down to her waist, clearly a woman and, when she stood at Padric's side, clearly this man's kin.' He nodded to Penraddin who eased herself yet again into a more comfortable position and said:

'I said "Look at us. We are brother and sister. Look hard and you can see that? Does Ecfrith have a sister? He does not. Yet I am sister to this man who is not Ecfrith and this man is not the man who slaughtered your women and children. He is the Christian prince of Rheged, he is the one you have heard of who roams all lands seeking to restore his kingdom. I knew King Ecfrith when he was a prince. You will have heard that he took a sister of Padric for his other wife. I was that woman. Consider this – why were you men spared as the boy Finan told us? Which army spares its chief foes? I will tell you. Ecfrith spared you so that you would do what he is afraid to do himself – to fight my brothers. But God has intervened. This man is not the man you saw, is he?"

'I said this directly to the two men and they shook their heads. Then Padric spoke. "I am Padric of Rheged," he said. "The man who did this to you is my cousin, King Ecfrith. He is evil as my sister tells you. At some time I will come to you to help me put an end to him."

'He went to the king and said, "You have a brave son. One day we three will ride together, God willing. I would like to have him near me in a fight." The boy ceased to scowl for once and almost smiled. "Ecfrith will pay, I vow to God, for what he has done to you and to others but also for fouling my name and that of my family and my country." In those words,' said Penraddin, 'I saw his anger.'

'I never saw his anger,' said Bega.

'We walked out,' said Urien, 'fully armed to meet the Picts, also fully armed, four times our number and until minutes before ready to cut out our hearts and slice off our heads. It was still uneasy. There were many on both sides who would have fought for the sake of fighting and some of the Picts were convinced that they had been tricked. At his own pace Padric made himself ready and picked up that fine long sword which has around it tales which begin to rival the sword the priest Merlin gave to Arthur. He sliced the air with it a few times as he always does before putting it in the scabbard and as he did so he caught the eye of the boy.

'"You try," he said to the boy.' As Urien said this, a thrill of connection elated Chad, who was suddenly overcome by his love for this noble warrior. It was himself he saw with the sword, years ago now when the world was such a dark painful ignorant place to him. That sword, he realised, by that sword he had been cut free. 'The boy took it up instantly,' said Urien, 'and whirled and whirled it around his head like the old warriors still do and it was that, I will swear,' Urien concluded, 'that above all which finally persuaded the Picts to stand back and open their ranks and let us pass on unharmed.'

'We must give thanks to God,' said Bega.

'And then get on with the feast,' said Urien.

Penraddin felt a little lurch of fear in her throat and felt faint. But she would not surrender to it.

CHAPTER SIXTY-NINE

The six soldiers had slouched into the valley on that mid-afternoon. They were saddle sore, a little drunk and very pleased with themselves. They had been down beyond all the lakes to the lands given, unaccountably in their view, to Cuthbert by King Ecfrith and there they had collected the rents. On the way back they had taken tributes. The rumoured imminence of another plague and years of coarsening service in Ecfrith's army had loosened the already ample boundaries of their morality. They were on the lookout for a comfortable billet for the night and they would not hesitate to seize the best and expect other favours. Failing a settlement big enough to absorb themselves and their train (about as many again, servants and a monk), they would seek out a religious house where at least food and shelter would be provided. They knew about Bega's nunnery.

'Why is it that Cuthbert looks the way he does?' asked the youngest of the soldiers.

Cuthbert had been down in Cartmel to greet them and rather fretfully usher them around the land and the farms.

'Did you see his toenails? That young novice took off his shoes to wash his feet and – the nails! – I've seen shorter talons on an eagle. Great big yellow things curving round – how does he *walk*? The same with his fingernails, although some of them's broken off. And his hair is longer than my woman's. The bones stick out of his chest like a starved partridge. Yet he'll pace around his new lands even though he is telling us how unworthy he is to have them, he'll pace around every bit as gimlet-eyed as any nobleman I know.'

'It's to show his contempt for the earthly world,' said the monk. He was a jolly man and determined to remain so. He had joined the warriors for protection on his way to Hexham. 'Cuthbert is telling us that outward show is of no importance. Let the body be a sacrifice. The more vile it appears to the world the more it shows the world that it shuns the world and attends only to the soul. Perhaps,' the monk continued – he was a Celt who had converted but he had not lost the love of hearing a good argument even if it were one put by himself, 'there is another meaning. He looks vile, as you say. He looks like a beggar, the least and poorest among us. So when the devil and all his malign forces are flying about the world to seek whom they can pervert and bring down, how much easier to pass by one who looks so unprepossessing. Why waste time with a filthy looking beggarman? One whose hair is matted, whose nails are all yellow, whose clothes are held together by holes, as my old teacher said, who limps along and seems to take no heed of open sores on his legs. How can such an object be worth our trouble, they say? Off! And so on they fly and for a few hours maybe a few days more he is undisturbed until the weaver of all lies himself calls the roll and notices that Cuthbert has not been visited and seeks him out. But by then, Cuthbert's soul has become more crystalline. He is nearer the saints. The devil has harder work. It is a disguise!' the monk concluded affectionately. 'Just as one of you will disguise yourself to go among the enemy. So Cuthbert who knows all the arts of man disguises himself to deceive the arch deceiver.'

'He's very keen on his land.'

'He measured out every bit and gave that farmer who objected a devil of a time, I thought.'

'His estates are not as big as Wilfrid's—'

'Wilfrid's just a prince in a monk's clothing!'

'Wilfrid is a man of sublime holiness and worldly godliness,' said the monk with instant piety, hoping to be reported on this correct stance.

'King Ecfrith's blowing cold on him. He's too greedy!' He laughed. 'They all are.'

'They were allies once and by the grace of God they will again be allies,' said the monk quickly, covering his back. He was only too aware of the fate waiting for those who crossed the line at the bloody court of Ecfrith.

'The king is devoted to Cuthbert. He can't do enough for him. Now he wants him to be a bishop.'

'Cuthbert dreads that,' said the monk, happy to be an authority on this important figure. 'Again, you see, things of the world in the base sense – not that a bishopric is base—,' he was a little confused for a moment. The soldiers enjoyed that, 'but it all comes back to his soul. He is willing to submit his soul to the fiercest duel with the devil himself and what is more important than that?' There was a touch of defiance there, and the soldiers let it rest. There was a limit to their interest in teasing the talkative monk or discussing the nature of Cuthbert's soul. And apart from hard tack and a few berries, they had eaten nothing substantial since the previous midday: the night before had been an unfortunate bivouac in a damp forest beside an empty and gloomy lake.

It was approaching twilight of the late-summer, shortening day as the six men and their baggage train sauntered towards Bega's settlement.

Penraddin had come out of the refectory for air. The feast was in that contented state of bloated tiredness.

The life of the child kicked inside her and she thought with only a little sentimentality of the father and hoped the child would be more forceful than he. The man had been the mildest of Padric's warriors, happier to talk to Padric about the lives of the apostles than to join in the continuous commentaries on battle and war. Not that he was afraid in war, none of the men was, but he had not relished it the way the others had. There was, as she remembered fondly, a tender, almost womanly quality about him, very rare, a love of words, an instinct of understanding. When she thought of him she found herself smiling and a calmness came over her. Then she would see him in that final battle, fighting off one man when another came behind him and, before anyone could cut him down, rammed his sword deep, so deep that he had to pull with both arms to extract it. And her lover had stumbled, half turned . . . and did he smile at her before he fell?

She looked across the valley and, with a lurch of sickness to her throat, she saw the war party and knew its menace. In case the war party had also spotted her, Penraddin zig-zagged back into the refectory with apparent unconcern. She was determined to make them think she had not seen them – they were still some hundreds of yards away – and sure she had succeeded.

When he heard the news, Urien shook his head, angrily chasing away the fumes which were clouding inside it. A smile settled on his face. Six!

'I will hide,' Urien said. 'Bega, tell them that Penraddin is a noble
lady from the north whose servants – the one in hospital, Chad, you
are the other – brought her here because her time is due. Laistranus:
it will be hardest for you. Say you are visiting the abbey on the
instructions of your superior at Melrose with a view to making
this a joint community.' As he spoke, Urien was collecting not
only his weapons but all the weapons. 'It's not entirely convincing
but I can't think of anything better. If you can, use it. I'll take all
the weapons.' He was at the door. 'Penraddin, have I time?'

'Just.'

'If we *do* have to fight,' he said, 'then we will form up around
the cross: all facing outwards.'

He was gone.

Bega was at a loss. The monks whose swords had disappeared understood that their weapons would have been provocative
to King Ecfrith's men but still they felt exposed. Penraddin
shed her armour and, with the help of Saethryd, was almost
indistinguishable, save for her pregnancy, from the nuns.

'A feast!' said the leader of the war party when they pushed into
the refectory. 'God bless this house.'

'And all who enter,' said Bega, hot, flushed, looking daringly
and guiltily at this large, grizzled man clanking with armour and
weapons. 'You are welcome to share what remains,' she continued,
'but I would be obliged if you respected this house and left your
swords at the door.'

He did not answer but walked around, taking a half-eaten goose
leg from the platter of a monk and stuffing some vegetables into
his mouth. The others joined him and behaved in just the same
way, invading the place. They neither acknowledged nor spoke
to anyone. Round and round they went, scavenging, picking at
everything until there was not a tasty mouthful left. Their servants
nibbled on the margin. Laistranus shifted around uneasily, his
posture unapologetic but unable to bring himself to break the
bullying silence.

They turned to the beer and took the casks and poured their
contents down their throats. They belched as loudly as they could
and then waited while the leader looked around.

'Who is abbess here, if such a miserable little settlement has such
a fine figure?'

'I am not abbess,' said Bega, firmly, well under control, 'but

I am she whom the Abbess Hilda of Whitby has made responsible.'

'Do you have more food?'

'A little.'

'And beer?'

'Yes.'

'Well! Bring it out then!'

Bega bowed slightly, turned to her servants, gave them instructions and turned back to stand her ground. The rush of anger earthed her. She had not felt as fully alive for some time. She was being called to act, not to pray or nurse or writhe over her unredeemable sins but to *act*. 'We will go,' said Laistranus, 'so that you may sit. The room is too small for us all.'

He spoke obvious truth. The war band and their servants crowded it to claustrophobia.

'Who says it's too small?'

'I thought,' said Laistranus, 'that perhaps you might like—'

'Who are you to decide what I might like?'

'We have finished,' said Laistranus, firmly, and stood up. He was immediately pressed down by the soldier nearest to him.

'We like you! We want you to stay. Ah!' This acknowledged the scurried entrance of the servants with a large jug of beer and some bread and goats' cheese. 'We want some fresh conversation while we eat, don't we?'

His men were only minimally interested in this mild tormenting of the monks. They launched themselves at the food and drink like the hungry animals they were.

'Is there no more meat?'

'Why do these holy fools get meat – goose! – and we none?'

'There is no more,' said Bega steadily.

'Why are you so wealthy when so many around you are so poor?' asked the young soldier. Bega grimaced in guilt. 'I am not so wealthy. I pray that God will replenish what we have spent today but—'

'—you wanted a feast. Why?'

'My noble sister,' said Bega, beckoning Penraddin, who came forward. She was almost unrecognisable having knotted her hair in an unaccustomed way and strained her face to give it an altogether different look in case any of the soldiers could remember her from her time with Ecfrith, 'is about to deliver a child into the world.

And,' this time she beckoned Laistranus, who took his cue, got up and with difficulty made his way across to her, 'my friends from Whitby who had arrived to discuss whether we should make this a double house, I thought that we should mark the double event with a feast.'

'What were you Celts doing at Whitby?'

'We are not from Whitby,' said the truthful Laistranus, with a wounded look at Bega, 'we are from Melrose.'

The gap of silence was precipitous.

'So, little no-abbess, you lied.'

Bega nodded: her shame was visible.

'God forgive me,' she said.

'*Is* this your noble sister?'

'No. She is not. But she *is* a woman I have known over many years. Like a sister and she is, as you see, in need of a secure lodging at this time.'

'What other lies has God to forgive you for, hmm?'

'None, I trust.' Her exhilaration was gone as quickly as it had come. The physical crowding seemed to break through her skin and into her body. Her thoughts, her feelings, her soul itself felt pushed, pressed and menaced.

'That,' said the warrior with a triumphant leer, 'could be the next lie!'

His men knew when they had to laugh and one or two of them did.

'So you're a Celt on the run from Melrose.'

'"On the run" – no.'

'Why are you here, then?'

'We are going to Ireland,' said Laistranus. 'As King Ecfrith encourages us to do.'

'Did you get the express permission of the court?'

'Do we need it?'

Laistranus winced at the force of the blow which hit his face.

'Don't question me, heretic!'

'I am no heretic.'

'We can find that out.' He drank some more beer. 'Can't we? While our lying little not-an-abbess and her not-a-sister and the other whatever they ares get us more food – we'll go and find out if you are a heretic.'

Laistranus found himself between two of the soldiers and

hustled to the door despite the pleas of Bega's nuns, the futile flailing of his monks and the beseeching eyes of the warriors' companion monk who seemed to be miming to Laistranus: "do whatever they say and they won't really hurt you". But Laistranus resisted his tormentors violently all the way to the lakeside. The others spun out after him, trailing behind like the wayward but fixed tail of a kite. Laistranus was dragged to the water's edge.

'Do you accept the true date of Easter?' one of the soldiers yelled. All of them were getting drunk now, from the drinking on the journey, and from swallowing beer as fast as it filled the goblets. He could have been asking if Laistranus accepted that a tree was made of wood: the question was no more than a taunt.

'What about his hair?'

Like many others, Laistranus had temporised about the tonsure. He had made a half-hearted attempt to follow the Roman way but the clearer pattern was Celtic. One of the men drew his dagger and moved towards him with plain intent.

'No!' Bega heard herself shout out. 'No! God have mercy on him!'

The leader saw her face and a faint memory of her importance brushed across his mind. But he did not make the effort to trap it: in any case, it was not the little non-abbess he was harassing but these Celts, still stubborn on the run and deserving all the harassment they got.

Ignoring her he joined his henchmen and the three of them led the still struggling Laistranus deeper into the lake. One of the monks sprang forward to help his brother but he was tripped and felled before he had covered half-a-dozen paces. Then he was booted. The nuns who were already cold with fear closed their eyes, raised their faces and prayed to a louring sky. The other monks too addressed heaven for help while Laistranus was ducked and held under the water seemingly beyond endurance.

'Penraddin!' Her name was very softly fluted just above audibility. She stepped back a few paces without drawing any attention to herself. Urien had hidden nearby, fearing this might happen. Now, with the soldiers getting more and more drunk and eyeing the nuns and daring the monks to resist so that they could chop them down, he saw that it would only get worse the longer he left it.

'The swords are around the cross,' he said.

'Bega has a sword,' she said, without turning around.

'She must get it.' Her back was still to him. 'You must keep away,' he said.

'I shall see you at the cross.'

He knew that argument with her would be time wasted. 'Tell Bega,' he said. 'And tell the big monk there on the left. Let the others run for it when I strike.'

Bega was now being held by one of the soldiers. He enjoyed having his arms around her and cupping her breasts as she tried to wriggle free and go to help Laistranus, whose breath surely could not hold out much longer.

Penraddin whispered the message to the monk and indicated to Chad that he ought to follow. She was not sure that Chad understood but at least he registered that something was about to happen which he should be ready for. He held Cal tightly by a collar. The dog, old now but still sharp-toothed, was bristling against what was being done to Bega but Chad knew that should he let him loose, the men would have no compunction at all about striking him dead.

Quite suddenly, Urien was there and he stabbed one of the soldiers deeply, fatally, in the neck and slashed open the arm of a second as he turned round to help. In a single moment, it seemed to Chad, the warriors simply dropped Laistranus and ran through the water as well as they could back to the shore. The soldier threw Bega aside, drew his sword and raced towards Urien. The one whose arm had been slashed nevertheless had found his sword and was engaging Urien. The nuns and monks fled in all directions. Chad followed the call of Penraddin and let go of Cal who leaped forward to hurl himself at the man who had been harming his mistress, balking him and giving Urien a few seconds to turn and flit back towards the settlement.

Urien, who knew its layout better than the others, went in over the top of the mound wall thus, he hoped, giving the monk and Bega, Chad, perhaps, and no doubt Penraddin, time to collect their wits and their weapons and regroup where he had ordered them to. He did not know that Chad had waited for a few moments and then, greatly daring, had taken the sword and the shield from the dead man. Cal was racing about furiously, the scent disturbed everywhere he turned.

The cross was a well-chosen site. It was so placed that there was one wide and obvious front of attack and it was there that Urien pitched himself as if he had all the time in the world. He planted a spear and a short sword behind him, brought his dagger to the front of his belt, fastened his shield and helmet tight and balanced the long sword in his hand. When Penraddin appeared he gestured her to the least vulnerable position. The monk he put to his left and when Bega reached them he smiled. He had a comrade in arms. Padric had told him about her skill with a sword and he could see it even in the way she held it and set herself. Chad came and Urien told him to give the shield to Bega, hold the sword and stand beside Penraddin. Cal crouched close beside Bega.

The Northumbrians swept around the southern wall of the church and stopped.

The leader gestured to his men to spread out and prepare themselves. The wounded man stood apart and tried unsuccessfully to staunch the blood from the deep cut in his upper arm. The limb hung, dangling, held by a thin cord of sinew. He would take little part in the fighting.

Before the leader spoke, Urien said, mockingly, 'We have the advantage. Five against four. Why don't you lay down your arms now?'

'It is you we want. The others can stand aside.'

'Tell them.'

'We do not want to harm the women,' the man said, 'but we will have you. We know you, don't we? We know you.'

'You know nothing,' said Urien. 'Your heads are full of boasts, you mouth words you don't understand, and it takes three of you cowards to hold a half-starved monk under the water. Once, long ago, my two brothers and I and an old man now dead sent eleven of you to hell. You boast, but you dare do nothing alone. Stand forward, any of you, in single combat. I challenge you.'

'We have no need for that.' The reply was swift. 'And it is rich to hear talk of cowardice from one who needs women to protect him.'

'It is he who protects us,' said Penraddin. 'But our women can fight.'

'Look at the little non-abbess. Her sword is too heavy for her to lift.'

'Why does no one take up my challenge?' said Urien. 'Could they be true, these stories of the bluster of you Northumbrians who are full of wind and piss? You move in war bands and burn down the farms of poorly armed Picts, I hear, and spear their children and mutilate their wives but leave the men alone. Are these the true stories? Look at you. Fat oafs let loose with sharp instruments – afraid to stand toe to toe.'

'Come here, big mouth. Come over here on your own and we will stand toe to toe.'

Urien made as if to move forward. The four Northumbrians arrowed in on him. He stepped back and they stopped.

'Four to one is what you want,' he said. 'Well then. You have it. I'm waiting for you.'

'For the last time, tell the women to go.'

'They will go if they choose,' said Urien, whose eyes had never once left the eyes of the Northumbrians, who were subtly jockeying for position.

The monk cried out and all of them followed the direction of his voice. Laistranus had appeared beyond the war party with the spear and the dagger of the dead man. So quickly that Chad never knew who threw it, a spear from one of the four was flung at Laistranus. He stood stiff, then tottered backwards, the deadly shaft sticking gruesomely out of his chest. The monk screamed and rushed across to the fatally struck figure, despite Urien's urgent order 'No! No!', and Chad watched in horror as a sword thudded against his neck and split it from the shoulders: the monk staggered, his legs splaying more and more wildly, his hands reaching up to his half-severed head seeking to reposition it. The blood poured out and, when the soldier smote him again, higher, splitting the skull, the brains which flew in the air and then tumbled slowly down the disconnected head made Chad vomit.

Penraddin moved away from Chad. She stepped forward and took the reckless monk's position.

'As I expected,' said Urien, still calm but much quieter, 'very good at slaughtering the innocent and helpless. But faced with a warrior from Rheged, one who rides with his brother Prince Padric – yes, look pale you filthy weaklings – faced by one man only, you stand and barter and haggle like old women at market. What old women's guts you have. Look at you. Strike down a poor fool of a monk and then strike down his more foolish, faithful brother. What stories you will have to tell! How you will be admired when the cup is passed around! What nobility!

What cunning of brain and strength of arm! What heroes! What heroes! What epics will be written! You shame your race. You shame us all!'

Urien's tongue whipped and whipped them and now they came forward. Two came directly for Urien; one each faced the women, believing that a few parries would wound them – perhaps at the beginning they meant no more – and then they too could turn on Urien. Chad they had utterly discounted.

Urien waited until they were so close he could feel their breath on his face. Then he struck out and whirled and yelled with such ferocity that the valley rang with his cries and Chad found strength to swing his sword and the men fell back. Bega's opponent had slid his eyes over to Urien at the terrible sound and she slid in her sword to pierce, though not deeply, his right thigh. He raised his sword and would have slashed it down on Bega's head but Cal leaped up to take his wrist, bit and only let it go when the edge of the sword caught his neck fatally. The dog fell between them. Bega used the moment to cut again, this time square across his face, slicing across the cheek and into the nose. The man screamed in pain and for a moment he pulled back.

Penraddin was not faring so well. Her opponent saw as soon as he was close that she was a serious fighter. He came at her with all his force. From the start she was on the back foot and in difficulty. Seeing this, Chad, waving the sword before him, rushed across to help but one forceful parry of the iron shield sent him bloody faced and badly dazed to the ground.

Penraddin backed up the mound which supported the cross and for a few moments the height gave her strength. Bega held her ground against her wounded enemy's desperation. Urien also waited: he knew precisely what he would do as the two who were attacking him attempted a pincer movement. His left leg pushed against the reassuring short sword planted behind him; he loosened his grip on the shield, ready to smash it into the face of the man on his left. He sensed that Penraddin was struggling and called out to her to hold on and shouted to Chad to get up and help her.

The fighting was heard all over the valley. People dropped their work and rushed towards it, scarcely believing that it could be in their nunnery. The summer evening which had been proceeding on its placid and weary way under a low, quietening sky was suddenly

activated and the energy of the clanging conflict stirred blood and
nerves on all sides.

Chad got to his feet but as he tried to move forwards he was
again violently sick. When his head reached up for air he saw –
again it seemed all at once, that the shield flew out of Urien's hand,
a sword appeared in it, a long stabbing wound left the other sword
in the man's body but, most terrible of all, Penraddin was slashed
on the thigh and fell forward. As she collapsed, so the sword dug
deep into her throat and her body sagged towards death. In that
same instant Urien leaped with an unearthly cry over the mound
and rammed his short sword straight into the man's throat and then
– Chad had never seen or imagined anything like it – still howling
as if in pain, he turned and jumped down on Bega's tormentor,
simply parrying the sword thrust with his thickly leather-bound
right arm and stabbed him with a dagger. Finally – still, it seemed
to Chad, in the one uninterrupted flowing movement – he flew at
the leader of the war band and threw himself on him, clubbing
him with his sword, forcing him down, whereupon, hoisting his
sword high, he severed his head. Then he turned. The man Bega
had wounded was pleading for mercy. Urien showed none. For
those few seconds, Chad was for ever convinced that Urien had
become Satan: he saw the flames, he smelled the burn of fire and
other-worldly power, he felt the terror the man provoked.

'Get sheets,' said Bega. 'Get water. Bring Saethryd.'

Chad rushed to obey.

Urien kneeled and lifted Penraddin's head. The blood was
oozing from her wounds and there was another pain. She looked
down at the swollen belly and moaned and then her eyes closed.
Urien bent over her face.

'She is not yet gone,' he said.

Saethryd and the other nuns came, as did the monks.

'Here!' said Bega. They had moved towards their fallen brothers.
'Here! Give her your prayers! All of you!'

Those not helping Saethryd and Bega directly knew where
their duty lay and began to pray in sober and steady terms for
the ascension of the soul of this valiant woman who had fought
for the kingdom of God with her sword.

'She has no strength to push,' said Saethryd. 'She is ready but
she has no strength to push.'

'Then I must do it,' said Bega. 'Hold open her legs, stretch them as far as you can.' She clambered over Penraddin's body and began to squeeze at either side of the enormous belly, simulating, as she thought, the rhythm of contractions.

'No.' Saethryd's voice was strained but authoritative. 'You must stop. That will harm her.'

She looked up. Reggiani was there. She nodded approvingly to the old woman.

'Give me your dagger,' she said to Urien, 'the long one.' To Bega, 'I agree with the old woman. You must not do that. Talk to her.'

Urien handed the dagger to her and she went swiftly into the refectory where she drew it through the fire. She had sent Chad for water from the stream and when she returned she plunged the hot blade into the cool water and held it there.

'Make sure all the sheets are secure about her,' she said. 'Bega and Saethryd, hold her legs. Urien, hold her two arms.' Reggiani bent down. 'Penraddin!' she called. 'Penraddin, do you hear?'

By the merest flicker of her eyes, the dying woman acknowledged the question.

'I am going to cut your child free. It will mean that I cut into your body. You must tell me . . .'

For a few moments there was no expression on Penraddin's face. Then, slowly, her eyes opened a little and seemed to find focus; and then she smiled. Chad never had and he knew he never would again see such infinite, deep and quiet joy in such a smile.

Reggiani brought the dagger, still in the water, close to the body, studied it, dipped her hands in the water and rinsed them, then took out the dagger and made the cut from high between the breasts down the bloodied body to the vagina. The cut was steady, sure and clean. Chad watched frozen in time and wonder as Reggiani made six smaller lateral cuts and then opened up the body, reached in and, with some effort, pulled out a bloodsoaked child. She took the cord between her teeth and bit it, tied the knot at the navel, held the child upside down and slapped it gently until its wheezing coughing gurgling cleared into a little bleat, a sharp little cry and, swiftly wrapping it in the sheet held ready by Saethryd, she held it out to Penraddin, hoping that once again her eyes would open.

But they did not and they would never open again.

CHAPTER SEVENTY

Beside the cross there appeared what Bega had often prayed for: a spring. It was Saethryd who noticed it first and she summoned Bega. There it bubbled slightly but steadily on the very spot on which Penraddin had died giving birth to the boy. Bega ordered special prayers and Chad built a little stone basin to collect the water which was, they all said, the sweetest they had ever tasted. Just a few yards away, Penraddin lay and next to her grave were those of Laistranus and the faithful but foolish monk who had called out to him.

Even before his sister had been prepared for her burial, Urien was gone. He bought a sled from the miller and put on it the bodies of the Northumbrians, covered them with straw and harnessed two horses to pull it. Their servants were now his slaves. The monk, after seeing the outcome of the battle, and fearing that he would somehow be held in part responsible, decided to take up his old ways, become a Celtic believer once more and journey with the surviving four monks from Melrose to join Bishop Colman in Inishboffin.

Urien's plan was to bury the bodies somewhere in the forest on the way to Caerel. When he left, Chad took the bloodied body of Cal and went along the shore to bury it. He was joined by Bega and the two of them put stones on the grave of one who had seen them through so much and in the end perhaps saved Bega's life.

Reggiani had offered to find a woman to suckle the child but the woman who had agreed to do it had so little milk that within two or three days the child was continually crying. Reggiani explained that the reduced diet of the valley people made it harder to find women and besides, with rumours of the plague growing, they were less and less inclined to leave their own homes and settlements. Even the hill women who had always done this to supplement their straitened resources, were refusing to come down from the upland settlements in which they thought themselves safe.

Then Bega, when the child was crying bitterly, took him to her breasts and began to suckle him. The pleasure this gave her was overpowering. For some moments, once the scramble for a hold and the hard sucking and her own squeezings had passed, she felt a sweetness which tingled her entire body in a way which she had never before experienced. It was difficult, it hurt, yet slowly a little milk came. There was eventually almost enough milk in her for one feed, and so she also gave the baby goat's milk. Between her comforting breast and the milk, the child would be fed nursed and nourished.

The following spring, Bega was on the lower slopes of the great mountain to which she was increasingly attracted, in a small settlement where the plague had struck. The woman of the house was blamed for it – she and her son had gone out of the valley towards Caerel to sell skins; on the way they had fallen in with a group of exiled unfortunates who were being driven away everywhere they turned. Soon the woman's son had been affected by the staggering, vomiting giddiness. His mother had managed to get him back to their poor settlement only to see him die.

Word had spread quickly and the place was avoided. When any of that family or its household went anywhere else, the valley people shouted them away, threw stones and even threatened them with weapons. It had been a very severe winter once again and food stores had gone fast. The people were weak and in no condition to fight the plague.

Bega went to see them, taking such food as she could spare. Like many other dwellings in the valley, those of the poorer sort, it was a pitiful cluster of hovels. The earth had been dug into and the crude structures barely lifted above it, heavily piled with large cuts of turf. When Bega lowered her head and all but crawled

into the main hut, the stench and the smoke, the rank sense of
poverty and neglect made her fearful before it moved her to pity.
She had been in such places before, though rarely as denuded of
means as this. Beasts lived better.

Such people, she found, cowered away from those who approached
them even in good times. She had visited them regularly and yet
they still suspected her and complained that the food she brought
was not enough. It seemed to her that their souls were so very
far from God that to convert them would be a renowned victory
over the devil. It was he, the destroyer of good, who kept them
in such terror and ignorance; it was the devil who made them
so slow-witted and careless that they were always misreading
the signs of the clouds, always planting too early or too late,
butchering their few beasts when others were still fattening them,
invading their stores at will rather than husbanding them for the
lean months ahead.

Yet despite their hopelessness, the more she dealt with them,
the more Bega's heart went out to them. There was nothing, she
thought, that true prayer and sound practice could not cure.

It was late in the morning and Bega was fretting to be back in
the nunnery, but that very fretting was a warning, she thought,
that she must stick to her task. Penraddin's child was drinking
goat's milk all the time now and taking soft food and there were
quite enough people willing to help him. He had, God knew,
more than the children of those bare upper woods would ever
have. So she bent her will to her work and crawled into the hut
and let the smoke sting her eyes without complaint and let her
lungs inhale the fetid stench and endure it.

'Over here.' The woman, whom Bega knew, pock-faced, small,
bone-thin but with fine anxious blue eyes, tugged her across the
stinking straw into the corner. A child lay restless, naked, clearly,
Bega thought, suffering from the first effects of the plague.

'Is it?' the woman asked.

'I think so,' Bega said. Knowing it was most likely too late, she
added, 'Is there a separate building you could take her to?'

'Just the shed for the beasts,' she said, 'but she can't go there.
My man says no to that. He wants the beasts protected.'

'Then we must pray,' said Bega. 'What have you that she
could eat?'

The woman went away stooped in the hut even though it

was no height and came back with a small bowl of congealed
vegetable gruel.

'Warm it up.'

While the woman did that, Bega made the girl as comfortable
as she could. She took off the filthy garment that was wrapped
around her and wiped her down.

Bega had seen this family several times before. Though feckless
they were more victims of ignorance than pagans through choice.
She knew that she had all but converted the mother and now she
called her in for help in the prayer. Two of the three children had
died in the previous year and soon the father, his brother and sister
and the two others who crawled in with them were also praying
for the body and soul of the girl. Bega spooned some of the warm
soup into the sick girl's mouth, having bodied it with some of the
herbs she carried with her.

The small, damp, smelly hovel on the breast of the massive
mountain seemed held in a spell of prayer. Bega found that she
was locked into this battle for the girl's life and could draw on deep
resources of energy to keep praying beyond any normal limit. The
others stayed with her, themselves drawn more and more deeply
into this community of hope.

The little girl coughed some sick and moaned. When Bega
reached out to touch her brow she felt a cold profuse sweat. She
redoubled her prayers. The girl's restlessness increased. Outside,
it was past midday and it would be warm, Bega thought. The soft
airs of spring might help relieve the congestion which was making
the child's breathing so arduous. She took her in her arms – to an
intake of breath from the others, none of whom had dared touch
her – and went outside.

The sun sparkled through the budding trees. The air which
Bega gulped in was as fresh as spring water. The woods rustled
with growing, energising, hopeful life. Timidly, the others followed as Bega walked with her burden up the steepening side of
the mountain, through the last straggle of wood to the bare flank
which could look so daunting from the valley floor. Above her,
white, insubstantial clouds seemed to dance like lambs, a sudden
frisk of movement, a dart here, a playful run. Bega turned and sat
on an outcrop of rock to rest, but though the weight was numbing,
she did not set down the child.

She looked over the woods down to the lake. She could see the cross. It was as if the sunlight singled it out and struck it. The cross which had yielded a spring on the birth of one child could surely, to show God's infinite mercy, intercede for her for this poorest of the poor. She stood up.

'To the cross and the cross beneath the cross, I offer my body as a sacrifice for all my life. I pray to Our Almighty God to show His all-powerful mercy and cure this poor sick child.'

She held the girl out before her. Every pore of her body yearned for a resolution.

She stood for as long as her arms could endure it and then sank to the ground, still holding the child.

The miracle occurred the next day. The child's plague began to ebb and the rest of the house was saved.

This was accounted to be Bega's first miracle and although the plague had come to the valley for a second time there were those who were saved and many of them praised the holy woman in their midst, the woman of God who could bring about miracles.

CHAPTER SEVENTY-ONE

THE THIRD PLAGUE

The valley recovered slowly from the second plague and many believed Bega that there were more to follow. It was, she was convinced, the equivalent of the seven plagues which God visited on Egypt. She had suspected it from the first; now she had no doubt. The difference now, she thought, was that the end of the world was being signalled. The third plague came and went much more lightly than the other two, but there would be more.

Bega became even more active in the valley. She was settled now. Padric was stored deep and habit helped her ignore him. Her only value to God was on this earth, she thought. Her soul, though she could and she did pray for it and fight for it, would never be the pure sacrifice needed by Him. Her task was not to spare herself in saving souls while there was yet time.

'Why do you travel around so much?' Reggiani asked her. 'I thought you could move your God to actions best by prayer. Surely you have no need to visit people so often. Does your God not do it for you?'

There was no mockery here. Reggiani was puzzled by this vivid woman who seemed about to burst open with energy or, Reggiani could see, with pain.

'I can pray to God,' Bega replied, 'and I do for the salvation of myself and of you,' she smiled, 'and everyone in the valley but I must also show them that God's servants are not afraid to visit even those who will bring about their earthly death.'

Reggiani probed a little, as she was more inclined to do latterly. Bega was bartering for herbs which she would distribute among the poor. Reggiani sensed that the nun was not impatient to go out into the drizzling autumn morning. The fire was cleverly positioned and well fuelled so that there was little of the smoke-fug which choked many huts. Bega had ordered that there should be a fire only in the hospital and the refectory – she enjoyed this unaccustomed warmth.

'Why do you want to tempt death when it is natural to avoid it?'

'Death has no sting,' said Bega, unwilling to engage herself in such a conversation where Reggiani's argument could often make her feel uncomfortable.

'But everything in us wants to live,' said Reggiani, persistently. She wished the woman would sit and talk at some length, but Bega always stood in the doorway, always indicating that she was merely passing through. Yet, Reggiani sensed, there was a terrible loneliness there. 'It is as if you want to deny everything that might please you,' she continued, taking up her thought. 'When you scrape the skin off your arm or leg, the skin wants to live and will grow again. When you break a bone, the bone wants to live and will mend. Some things won't – or perhaps we do not know yet how to make them grow again. You cannot grow another eye, you cannot grow a hand that has been chopped off. But perhaps we will find medicines to do that. Yet you want to deny all this. Why do you go so near to death and care so little?'

'What is my own life compared with the glory of God?'

'This life is all you know that you have,' said Reggiani.

This, Bega knew, was true in her case. But, conscientiously, she argued the orthodox case.

'No,' Bega replied, firmly. 'A Christian has the hope of ever-lasting life. This visit to the earth is only a short trial.'

'Why did you defend yourself with a sword, then, against Ecfrith's men?'

'That was to defend God's creatures against the pagan.'

'Why do you eat or drink at all? Why not go now to this everlasting life?'

'You go when you are called,' said Bega, rather wearily. 'It is not for you to decide. It is a sin and a crime against Our Lord for anyone but Him to decide when you must go.'

'Why do you want to be so helpless?' asked Reggiani. 'You obey orders but you are never sure what they are and so you make them as hard as you possibly can. When you visit those families which may have the plague, why do you not cover your face with cloth, as I do, to avoid the spirits of the plague which must come in through our mouths or noses?'

'The plague is sent by God. It is He who decides when to send it and who will live, who will die.'

'No.' Reggiani shook her head emphatically. 'It is part of the world that we can see. We see the rain showering its seed on the earth like a man showers his seed in a woman. The earth grows fat with life as a woman does. We see what is born and what dies, what grows and what fails, the manure that follows the food, the spring that follows the winter and it is these matters we have to know and to worship. I know the spirits who have disappeared into the great mountain, whose hair is now the tresses of the waterfalls and these I can talk to, as I can seek out the great gods of the earth who fell from the sky. But how can we speak to one we never see? Whose work we never know? Whose work is so cruel – if he does send the plague? How can we know?'

'Through prayer,' said Bega firmly, 'and through the intervention of the saints and martyrs, we can know something of His purpose and His glory. But yes, much is hidden from us. Only when we are worthy of Him, will it be revealed.'

And, tired in a way she did not understand from such a conversation, Bega said farewell and went out to visit some settlements at the southern end of the valley. This weariness: of course she was older now, with, now and then, a stiffness in her joints, especially the wrists and the knees. It had not yet manacled her – she was nothing like as stricken and limb-twisted as Saethryd – but the intimations were there. While there was another loss which she would soon have to face up to – the boy.

Bega did not let herself think about it. She was well trained in suppressing and compartmentalising her feelings; well able to impose a timetable on her mind. The matter of the boy was removed from her superficial attention but in the waiting zone it would, Bega knew from her experience, fester and be increasingly difficult to address.

So she battled on against the gentle prevailing veil of drizzle which soaked into her heavy woollen cloak, a slight, unstoppable figure, always, it seemed, bent into a wind, observed wherever in the valley she went. She thought about her meeting with Reggiani.

The priestess attracted her even though she was doing the devil's work. It was as if she cast a spell on her. She remembered how deeply her father had believed in the spells of the woman he had exiled to the woods. Bega knew examples of Reggiani's arts.

Some months before, a woman had come down from the hills seeking Bega's help. Since her first miracle with the plague-ridden child, several other miracles had been attributed to Bega, much to her disquiet. She was embarrassed and even annoyed that she should become a person known to conduct miracles. Could people not see how unworthy and earth-limited she was? But perhaps God needed to use her in this way in order to distract the envy of the devils from others more worthy who were working out His will in secret. On these terms, Bega submitted to her increasing reputation as a miracle-worker.

The old woman suffered badly from warts – not at all uncommon in the valley, but hers were exceptionally big, and two, in the corners of her eyes, threatened her sight. She wanted Bega to remove them.

She showed her right arm which was an unsightly mess of scars and warts and bruises. Her local medicine woman had tried to cut out the warts and used the arm as a testing ground. But however deeply she had dug – as the woman pointed, rather proudly – the warts had sprouted up again. She showed off one particularly large wart which was surrounded by a crater of a scar. This, she said, had been dug out deep to the root: she had seen the root. There was nothing in the resultant hole but blood. She had put in her finger and stirred it around and there was no trace of the wart. But no sooner had the skin healed over than the wart came back! A bigger and nastier wart!

That was why she had come to Bega. She wanted a miracle. The holy woman, she had been told, was a daughter of the invisible God that so many worshipped. All her life she too had worshipped this invisible God. And she had come to get her warts removed. Or, if not all, those which threatened to force shut her eyes. She had brought food and could stay at least seven days.

Bega was distressed at this complete trust. It was true that at least three times since the last plague, she had nursed or in some way aided people back to health. In one case, which she did not understand, a little boy's sight, which had been lost after he had been struck by lightning, had been restored after a single prayer and her gentle massaging of his face while getting him to repeat the Lord's Prayer after her. These were accidents of God, she decided, marginal to a greater purpose she would never understand. But when people approached her directly as this woman with the warts did, she was genuinely upset. She felt powerless. Yet to deny the woman any assistance would be to deny her own belief in the ultimate ability of her God to cure all sins of the flesh as of the spirit. There was desperation in her but she had to bear witness to God's power.

Every day for seven days there were special prayers. Every morning the woman examined the warts on her face by tracing her fingers over them. In the first three days she rejoiced. The warts, she was convinced, were subsiding, driven back by the power of God. After seven days, though, she had to admit that not only were they still there, they were as big as ever they had been. She was not generous. She paid no respect to Bega's obvious and taxing efforts nor to those of the other nuns. She stopped short of cursing, but only just.

It was from the farmer that Bega found out what had happened next. The woman always had conceived of a reserve plan. She had brought a small bangle and this she offered to Reggiani.

By whatever arts, black or simply unknown to those who had not studied as she had with her mother and other priestesses, Reggiani caused some of the warts on the upper face to go. The woman's skin was not unblemished but the threatening warts and three or four others nearby receded.

Bega was amazed and yet she did not want to be. This, though she did not dare to articulate it aloud, seemed a true miracle.

She reckoned it was near noon and found a boulder by a narrow fast stream which glanced lightly off the mountain as it splashed down to the lake. She said her prayers and then cupped her hands to take a few mouthfuls of the cold, sharp water. Saethryd had insisted she take a hunk of bread even though Bega had resisted the notion, though it was not a calendar fasting day nor was it one of her own penitential fasts, and now she was glad of it. She softened the bread a little by dunking it in the water and sat looking down on the lake.

After a few mouthfuls of the bread, a rare sense of utter peace overcame her. It was as if she were deeply asleep and could enjoy and be aware of every particle of it. It seemed to her that there was some great harmony in the arrangement of life. She saw the tiny boats drifting on the lake, fishermen as Peter and his brothers had been on the Sea of Galilee, and she thought that Christ Himself could have walked here. Slowly down the lake there crept one of the barges with the tree trunks and other goods making their way from the heart of this wild district to the rich capital of Caerel for merchants to buy. Everywhere smoke rose freely for the drizzle had stopped and though there were still clouds there was bright light and the day had calmed. She could pick off by name almost all the wreaths of smoke and imagine those who inhabited the buildings. It had been a bad winter and a bad summer, the signs were not fair, but in this mood of wholeness, God-sealed-ness, Bega could hope that somehow there would not be a fourth visitation of the plague: somehow the prayers of all those who were interceding with the ruler of all would change the course of that fate this time.

Meanwhile, she worked for the immediate relief of those she knew. They could be so strong in the Lord. They just lived. Work was all of life. Subsistence was a daily ambition, survival a daily achievement. Yet she was constantly surprised. For there were many as pious and inwardly optimistic as any of her nuns. They would press gifts on *her*. They would shame her expectant gloom.

Now, secure, overlooking what was becoming 'her' valley, seeing in the distance the smudges of the settlement small as a pebble on the shore, and feeling as contented as she had felt for many years, Bega allowed herself to think of the child.

'If there were a temple we could take him to,' Chad had said solemnly when she had engaged him about the boy's future, 'then without doubt he would astound his elders.'

Chad was invariably solemn about the boy these days, who had siphoned off much of the love he felt for Bega. He had taken to him so fast that his whole existence was organised around watching over, then playing with and soon instructing him, who now at six years old was about to sail past Chad in his accomplishment at reading and writing.

'You must not say that, Chad,' said Bega. She would rebuke him from time to time, even though she shared his pride.

'I can teach him no more,' Chad said, proudly.

'You can go on and learn more together.'

'He will outstrip me before the next Christ's day comes.'

'Perhaps you should stop teaching him for a while and let him go on the lake with the fishermen or into the woods with the carpenters or stay some weeks with the farmer.'

'He sees all that,' said Chad, too obviously jealous that anyone else should have the child's time. 'Besides, I have taken him fishing and hunting. He can do that as well as any other boy. But he is passionate about learning.'

'Are you sure that it isn't just that he is trying to please you? That he admires you so much?'

Chad puzzled away with poorly concealed pleasure at this very rare compliment. 'I don't think so,' he concluded. 'He may have been to begin with. But now – you see it for yourself – he needs no asking or telling to read and copy the words and when men and women of learning come here – you have seen how attentive he is. He has such a memory! He knows all the services by heart. He can quote from the gospels without stumbling.'

'He is indeed fine,' was all that Bega would allow herself to say.

Chad did not notice that he had lost most of her attention. Nor did it occur to him that talking passionately about the boy could upset Bega.

Chad had tried for some years with only a little success to persuade families to let him teach their children to read. They resisted it. They needed the children at work, they said. But more than that, they resisted the idea in itself. It would fit the children for nothing, they said, it would spoil them, it was not for them, not for valley people.

'But they don't see,' he would say to the child to whom he talked adult-to-adult, 'once people learn to read God's word then the gospel will be spread and there will be no more evil in the world. Just imagine,' Chad lowered his voice here and confessed to this child what he confessed to no one else, his wild dream, 'if *everyone* could read. God would be on earth. His word would be heard in all the laws. All the dark places would be lit up. That is what you must do.' He would look so hard and dearly at the boy that the lad's eyes would flinch away from the undisguised loving intensity of it. 'You must be a teacher and bring the word to the world. That is what will save it from plagues and shadows on the sun and all wars and all pain. You must do it,' he said, urgently,

seeing in the boy a saviour, a light to lighten the world, a soldier
of learning who would cut open the blinds of darkness, 'because
once people know the word of God – there will be no more pain
and no more sorrow.'

The boy had a look of Penraddin and so of Padric, Bega
thought. He also had a gentleness which came perhaps from
what Penraddin had told her about his father. He was, in
any case, a charming and affectionate child and Bega feared
for herself when she was near him. It would be so satisfying
to embrace him: she forbade herself that after he had ceased
to be a baby. She longed to spend time with him, as Chad
(whom she envied) did, simply walking by the shore of the
lake, holding his hand, listening to his precocious prattle, but
she did not. When he fell she wanted to be the one who
ran to help him, but she did not. She denied herself him.
He was, she had known very early on, a temptation she must
resist.

God was trying to help her to help herself. The child was a
test. God knew that she was for ever flawed in her devotion to
His Son but He loved her enough to try her once more. Perhaps
if this test could be passed, then there would be some chance of
a glimpse at last of the glory that was reserved for the pure souls
He called to His eternal feast.

It was in this spirit that, to his initial dismay, she withdrew
herself from any close contact with him and would sometimes be
seen to go out of her way to avoid him. She saw his puzzlement
and his sadness but there was nothing she could do to help
that, she decided, without confusing him more and breaking
her pact with God. Yet when the boy, in his turn, pulled
away from her and sought out Chad and Saethryd more readily
and laughed with them but not with her, Bega felt a twist in
her heart.

At times, when he was within arm's reach and she caught a
look of young-Padric hope in his eyes, she could scarcely bear it.
He would have to be sent away. She had decided on that early
on. He would be sent to a monastery when he was seven, and
dedicated to the church. His love of learning was a good omen
but even without that she would have pursued the same course.
For she could only foresee increasing pain for both of them should
he stay into adolescence.

All this was decided. But in moments alone such as this interlude on the rock, she dreamed a little of what the boy might have been to her, in other times, in other circumstances.

The wind grew a little and whispered around her ears. Reggiani had once told her that such whisperings were the voices of spirits and with true knowledge they could be understood. Bega loved the sound and the sensation it bred inside her and again the contentment swelled up. She must remember and protect good times like these, and others now came to mind. It was good to recognise the gift of happiness and the deep, too-often unacknowledged joy of her vocation.

The drizzle began again, and she got up from the rock rather stiffly. She had sat too long and her slight frame had to be forced on up the curve of the hill and over into the remote hollow where this settlement lay.

⁂

The moment she came over the lip of the brow she sensed something untoward. There were no dogs to signal her arrival and no animals abroad that she could see – no geese, hens, no movement save for the inevitable plume of thin grey smoke from the three related homes. In the poorly tilled fields, a broken plough lay on its side.

She came towards the poor buildings with an increasing sense of dread. It was as if the evil one had encircled the place with his bands and she had to press with all her might to penetrate his invisible barrier. She found that she was reciting the *Magnificat*. 'My soul doth magnify the Lord and my spirit doth rejoice in God my Saviour.'

Bega was almost up on the houses when a man suddenly appeared. Gaunt, even skeletal, red-eyed, savage in his manner and his tone. 'We do not want you here!'

Bega stopped. He was unquestionably in a mood to do her harm.

'I have visited you before.'

'Go away!'

He stood with one foot set inside the door as if he was fastened to the house and dared not relinquish it.

'I have come to help you to pray,' said Bega.

'We can pray without you! We don't need prayer! We don't pray any more! We can't pray! Why do you want us to pray?'

Bega tried, without any success, to find a way through these abrupt sentences. 'The boy?' she said, 'the little boy who hurt his foot – it was swollen – it was very painful – how is he now?'

The man bent down, picked up a stone and threw it at her. It hit her on the shoulder. She stood her ground. 'Go away! Go away or I will . . .' He looked around at the desolate upland landscape, trying to find a suitable threat. But found none.

'Let me at least see him. If you do not want me to go in then bring him out here.'

'He is dead! He is dead!'

Bega took a deep breath and then kneeled and prayed fervently for his soul.

'Where is he buried?' she asked, 'I must pray over his grave.'

'He has just died. Just now.'

'And where . . . ?' Bega indicated the emptiness all around her.

'Just after you went away, enemies came and took everything we had and told us that they would kill us all if we moved from this place. They said that there was the plague everywhere else, so we have not moved.'

The man was in agony. The longer he stood there, the more agitated he became, his head twitching to look inside the hut, then glaring wide-eyed back at Bega. His cloak was a ripped and tattered thing, no use in that weather: his trews were filthy and ripped. He had no shoes and his feet were mud-caked. His hair was long, down way beyond his neck, greasy, heavy, dull. It was his expression, though, which was most striking of all. It was full of horror. As if that moment he had just come from seeing the most terrifying thing and was too shocked fully to think about it. As if, Bega thought, at any moment he would burst into tears or begin to scream.

'We must pray together,' said Bega and, without emphasis, she began to move forward.

'No prayers – no prayers!'

Once again he picked up a stone and flung it at her. This time it struck her on the forehead and she stopped. She touched the place with her fingers and felt the blood. Now she was calm and utterly resolute and walked on.

'Go away! Go!'

The man picked up a handful of smaller pebbles and sprayed them over her. This time she did not even break step. To herself she murmured the *Magnificat* once more. 'For behold, from henceforth, all generations shall call me blessed. For He that is mighty hath magnified me; and holy is His name. And His mercy on them that fear Him, throughout all generations . . .'

She was near him now. The man was frantic. He reached out for a larger rock but it was just out of reach. He could not gather it without taking his foot from out of the doorway which seemed impossible for him to do. Bega let that fact inform her without attempting to understand it. He glanced wildly at her, she was very near him now, and looked longingly at the rock. She was all but on him when he flung himself full length and grabbed the rock and scrabbled back upright, desperately seeking the doorway. He stood above her, taller by a head than Bega, and raised the rock ready to smash it down on her.

It was a long, still moment. There was a deep sense of acceptance in Bega and so for a moment she stood without defiance as he was poised to smash down the rock on to her head.

Then she caught, from the door, a stench of meat which somehow threatened to curdle her guts. She looked into the wild man's eyes with something approaching comprehension of why he was so barbarous. Her embryonic understanding transferred to him and he shouted, loud, howlingly, letting out an intolerable pain, and he readied himself to bring down the rock on her unprotected skull. But Bega's mood of languor had been snapped by the meat-stench and she snatched a small dagger from her belt and thrust it into his upper arm at the same time swaying out of the line of the rock.

She stood back and waited. The man looked at his wound and then, more sanely, at Bega.

'I must see inside your house,' she said.

He nodded. Holding on to the wounded arm, he turned, ducked into the low doorway and went in. Still bearing her dagger, Bega followed.

The sight silenced her soul.

There were four adults crowded in the far dark corner of the hut. Four, she thought, there could have been more. In the gloom of the place made more dense by the thick coughing smoke from the turf-laden fire, they were little more than shapes, or even one shape, a cowering, huddled, massy form seeking a hiding space.

Bega saw the bones. Her stomach clenched. She forced herself not to vomit. The bones were slender: some still had a little gristle on them. They were, she knew, from the atmosphere and the evil pall in the place as much as from the bones themselves, human: children.

It was difficult to begin. The more deeply she breathed, to steady herself, the more giddy she became. She did not know what to say. She took one more deep breath, but it was too much. The lurch in her stomach was unmistakable. The nausea permeated her and she rushed for the door.

The vomiting exhausted her. All her stomach felt pinched to dryness. The compulsive heaving would not stop even though there was less and less and then nothing at all to bring up. Her brow was wet with cold sweat. Some of the sick had splattered her gown and her sandals. To compose herself, she went some paces off and tore at the short wet turf and used it to wipe her sandals and wipe her gown.

No one came out of the hovel.

Bega stood and breathed deeply once again, but this time it was clean air which cleared her lungs.

Now she was resolute.

She walked to the door.

'Come out!' she commanded, 'All of you. Come out.'

After some snivellings and one or two whispered words, they came out. Three of them crawled. They were bone-sacks. The others walked, the man with his arm now bound, a young woman – the mother – bold in the way shameless but guilty people are, and a very small man who looked everywhere save into anyone's face.

'You have committed a terrible crime,' said Bega, 'against the laws of your heavenly king and against the laws of Rheged. I want you to take the utensils you have, take those things you need and then come with me.'

'Why should we?' said the woman. 'Why should we obey you?'

'If you do not, then others will come for you,' said Bega sternly.
'And when they discover the horrible thing you have done, they
will be much crueller than I am.'

'Why should they discover it?'

'I will tell them.'

'And if you don't return?' said the young mother, far the boldest
of them all.

'You will have to kill me to prevent that,' said Bega, trying
to curb the excitement she, this daughter of Cathal, felt at the
prospect of what might be to come.

'She has a dagger,' the man said. 'And besides . . . who . . .
what are we . . . to do . . . else?'

'I'll not go,' said the woman. 'The little nun can take you but
she won't take me.'

'Do you know what you have done?' said Bega, unable any
longer to quell her outrage. 'Do you realise what you have
done?'

There was silence. Even the bold woman was not prepared to
answer.

'This is a most terrible, terrible sin. Even God in all His infinite
mercy will find it difficult to forgive you after the thousand years
you will surely spend in hell where fire and tortures will torment
you every day and night until you scream in your agony and beg
for a respite, but there will be none. You will – all of you – be
condemned to tortures you cannot imagine. You have eaten the
flesh created by God Himself. Only by prayer *now* and for the
rest of your short, miserable lives can you hope for any mercy.
Kneel now! Kneel! And beg forgiveness. *Beg* it! Kneel or by all
the saints in heaven, a thunderbolt will come down on to you and
fire you into that eternal damnation this moment!'

The weaker of them had already collapsed in moans of fear.
The wounded man kneeled, awkwardly. The woman stared at
Bega and tried to outstare her but whatever she saw subdued
her. Finally, truculently, politically, she too kneeled.

'Oh Lord, forgive us! Say it.'

'Oh Lord, forgive us.' The voices were weak, almost whispers.
Bega drove them through the prayers.

'But,' said the man, 'what were we to do? We are told not to
take our own lives. That is God's law. There was no food. We
could not move. We were so hungry. We wanted to take our

own lives. But God says it is a sin. Which is the bigger sin? Tell us.'

'You should have prayed,' said Bega. 'Had you prayed long enough and strongly enough, God would have heard you.'

'We did pray,' the bold woman had surrendered to fear and her tone was piteous, 'we *did* pray. We prayed until our throats were dry. But we were so hungry.'

'We . . .' the man began an explanation and then stopped.

'We did pray,' the woman sobbed. Then she looked at Bega straight. 'They were *my* children.'

Bega paused. But only for a moment. 'Get their bones,' she said harshly, 'and bring them here. You,' she pointed to the others, 'dig graves.'

They obeyed her in everything now, even eagerly, even pleased to be asked to do things.

The graves were dug, shallow on that thin turf, but mounded with stones. Bega went through the service for the dead while the drizzle fell steadily and the light began to close down.

'I want these houses burned down,' she said, when the few utensils had been removed.

They tried, but unsuccessfully. The roofs and walls were too sodden.

'Then break them down,' said Bega. But she was the only one with the strength to make any impact.

'I'll send someone later to destroy them,' she said. 'Now we must go down into the valley where you will meet the lawgiver.'

Dejectedly, but with a certain resigned compliance, they followed in her footsteps down the mountain.

꠸꠸꠸

The lawgiver decided to take the matter to Caerel. Its importance was, he thought, too great to limit to the valley.

Bega had not thought through the reaction in the valley. It was powerful and made itself felt the morning after the captives had arrived at the nunnery. Bega made the hospital available. Ill and crippled as she was, Saethryd elected herself as the one who brought them their food, thus excusing the three other nuns and all the servants of the disgrace and complication of succouring such deeply stained sinners and criminals.

There was a mob at the door soon after dawn. Some carrying sticks, some with stones, one or two with knives, some, Bega noted, almost as gaunt and ill-looking as those who had so feebly come down the valley with her. Bega talked to them and eventually they went away, but not before the offenders were fully aware of the danger they were in. This increased their dependency on Bega which had begun the moment she had left their settlement.

The bold-faced woman, the mother, particularly put herself in Bega's hands as if she had found her saviour. 'The little nun will see us through this,' she would repeat, 'we'll get a miracle. My own children – that's what makes the difference. Who wants to be a Judas, hanging from the tree and off into damnation for ever and more? That was what I'd come to? The little nun understands all this. She'll give us the miracle. God listens to her.'

Bega feared that she was beginning to hate this woman.

They sent four guards from Caerel and the captives were put on to a wooden sled and hauled away at dawn. Nevertheless there were enough about to be by the roadside throwing stones. Was their fury, Bega wondered, to do with their own fear? For another plague – a fourth plague – was on the wind and everyone knew it. With the plague would come famine and with the famine madness.

The news had travelled before them and at intervals along the route there were people lined up to shout and curse those who had done such a dark and irredeemable thing. Bega was constantly aware that most of them were people who had experienced hunger on many, perhaps most days of their lives. Rarely did they eat enough; their basic experience was that of schooling the pangs between meals geared to sustenance. This most terrible crime was also a frightening temptation.

As the procession which had the air of a cortege wended its way slowly out of the valley and down the undulating hills to the plain, Bega tried to keep in her mind the three children. What must have been their last moments? What did the others think when the first one was sacrificed? Who plunged in the knife? Who severed the limbs? Which of those in front of her prepared the child-meat? They would have known such terror that it hurt her to think of it. No one would have heard their confession. No one could possibly have blessed them. Where were their souls? God was all merciful. She prayed now obsessively for the souls of the children and saw her 'own' boy's face in her mind as she did so.

Bega rode behind the sled and tried as best she could to beg the people not to throw stones at the helpless captives. Saving from harm those she wished to see punished with death!

'She'll give us a miracle.' A sharp stone had cut the woman's cheek and she let the blood flow down freely as if it were some mark of honour.

They stayed at an inn a few miles from Caerel. It was considered too dangerous to go in when the town was full. They crept in before first light, unobserved.

It took the lawgiver only a little time to hear the evidence. The woman loudly admitted to everything. The man repeated his point about the choice between two of the blackest sins: suicide or murder. Murder, though, was only part of the story. There might have been more sympathy had it been the whole of it. But the cannibalism was beyond all endurance.

They were sentenced to be thrown from the city walls beside the river and then stoned to death.

The woman smiled when the sentence was pronounced. She pointed at Bega and yet again chanted 'the little nun will save us. She'll bring us a miracle'. In some way, Bega knew that this mad accusation contaminated her but she could do nothing about it. Her reputation for miracles was known in the city and since her arrival several cripples had been brought to her. There had already been one cure: a boy seized by uncontrollable fits and spasms had been calmed utterly after he had drunk from the same cup that Bega had used and been held by her as she asked him to repeat the Lord's Prayer with her.

She went to the city wall with the guards and the lawgiver and the other officials of the city. Bega stood aside while a monk from the double house which had been founded by Cuthbert heard the last confessions and gave the last rites.

The confidential smirks of the bold woman were intolerable to Bega, but she concentrated on her prayers. Save for the woman who still clearly anticipated a miracle, and the gaunt man who showed signs of resistance – soon and brutally quashed

– they seemed more than reconciled, even a little impatient to have it over.

One by one they were hurled from the walls.

'A miracle, little nun!' The woman's voice was frightened now as she stood and waited her turn. 'A miracle, little nun! They were my children.' Why did she repeat that? And why did it gouge so deeply into Bega's anger? She cried out as two guards took hold of her. Her hands were bound behind her back. Her feet were hobbled. 'A miracle!' she screamed now, looking desperately at Bega who prayed for her end. 'They were my children.'

Then she too thudded on to the rocky ground beneath where the mob was waiting to club and stone her to death alongside the others.

CHAPTER SEVENTY-TWO

When she heard that Cuthbert would come and visit her, Bega made up her mind about the boy. She called Chad to her and spoke about him. 'Put him in his warmest clothes,' she said, 'and he must wear his leather sandals. I want to walk with him up the great mountain. We will be away the whole day,' she announced with relief. The mountain, she thought, had been waiting for her for many years and she had been longing for it but avoiding it. It needed courage. The stories about what lived and happened on the summit of the mountain were frightening.

The thought of missing a whole day of the child's company upset Chad. The boy trusted him so much. Who else had done that? And looked up to him. Who else had ever done that? His eyes shone whenever Chad appeared.

'May I come some of the way?' It was not a question but an entreaty.

Bega included him.

They set out before dawn and said their first prayers while they were still in the woods. It was a wet autumn day and their shoes and lower clothes were soon soaked from the dampness of the undergrowth.

Bega led. She had no real idea what to do except to keep going up. She had quizzed the mountain so many times from the valley and thought that she had worked out a route but now that she was on the mountain she had no sense of it.

It was a clouded, undramatic dawn as they toiled up the steep flank. Bega took frequent stops for the boy. In truth, she herself found the going hard. She was used to physical effort and hardened to walking. The steepness of this, however, was new and her increasing fear was also a pressure. For what would be at the top? She had seen it fuming with clouds as if the devil himself were astride it, using it as a massive cauldron. Perhaps it was hollowed out inside, certainly there were caves. At other times the top would be completely hidden as if what was happening there was so wicked that a cloak of cloud had to be wrapped around it. Then there were days of clarity and sunshine inducing the feeling that it would be so easy to float to the top of this innocent monster: those days, Bega thought, were the most dangerous of all. She was too well educated in the disguises of temptation to be taken in.

She wanted to climb, to see, perhaps hoping that she would meet with a fate not dissimilar to that of Donal: a fate, that is – for she knew there could be no question of the True Cross again – which would take her life in a different direction. She longed for that. Even as her feet hauled her up the mountain she rejoiced that she was doing something different. The small boundaries of what, after so many years, had become her parish, sometimes threatened to crush her. She prayed for forgiveness but she could not deny it. Perhaps if she had truly confined herself to the nunnery, then she would have found satisfaction in the one spot as true hermits did. She still longed to be a hermit, especially now when the loneliness of this high place seeped into her like soothing ointment. She was always full of the contraries, she thought, always the oppositions. That was her sin. God needed certainty.

She stopped and turned and the others stopped obediently. Chad was already sweating badly, as much in fear as from exertion. The boy looked around him with calm curiosity: his light step carried his slim frame without seeming effort. She smiled at his coolness and the boy, caught by surprise at this unusual token of affection, smiled back broadly in return. Bega turned away. His smile was too much. She had to harden herself. The smile would slip through all her defences.

Up they went, without knowing it taking the hardest way until they came to a ridge. Here they paused and prayers were again said and some bread and cakes were eaten. Bega had assumed that there would be streams everywhere but the only one in sight was a long way below and none of them had the energy to clamber down to it. Why was there no water?

A quick pain flashed through her. Was it truly because the devil came here and his inconceivable heat dried up the land? But the turf under foot was still wet. In fact, Chad and the boy were stroking water off the stumpy grass and sucking it from their hands. Bega followed suit.

Further up, the clouds thinned and the autumn sunlight changed everything so radiantly that Bega had a premonition. Was this a magical mountain where shapes could change so fast and views come and go so fast and the very mountain itself seem to shift about?

Firmly on the ridge now, Bega looked down at the valley and felt a surge of extreme dizziness. She dropped to her knees and found that she was shaking: the vertigo appeared to have blanked out of her mind everything but itself.

'Are you ill?'

Chad's words coincided with a gentle touch to her arm. She turned around. It was the boy, standing as confident and easy as a young hound, eager to help.

'I'll be, I am, fine,' said Bega and levered herself to her feet in stages.

What was it that could, out of nowhere, hit her so violently? Her legs shook. She reached out, all but unconsciously, to take the boy's hand. He grasped her fingers tightly. But what could it be? She glanced down; the side of the mountain under the ridge seemed sheer, as if one careless step would plunge you into a free fall until you hit the ground so far below, where the people seemed to move like insects and even the bigger settlements looked as if you could lean down, pick them up and crunch them in one hand. Again she fell.

This time, because she was holding the boy's hand, he too was pulled down and he slithered dangerously. Bega held on to him and soon he was once again beside her. She must not look down. The devil had tempted her to look down so that she could ape God. So that she could see His creatures as the devil saw them – mean, small, feeble, of no account. She would not be tempted by the devil. 'All this will I offer thee,' the devil had said to Jesus Christ after taking him up a high mountain.

Now Bega knew why God had pointed her here. It was another test. She took strength from that. She was battle-hardened in tests for God. She let go the boy's hand, not letting his disappointment impinge on her.

They went up yet further, very, very slowly, and clouds, white, wraith-like, which could have been the mantles of archangels or the veils of the devil, began to dance and swirl around them. Sooner than they could make provision, they were inside the clouds. Bega was terrified. Even the boy's voice was subdued.

'We must hold each other's hand,' said Chad. 'And we must sit and wait until God takes this away from us.' His voice was hollow and sombre, ghostly through the cloud.

They sat in a strange and tingling silence. A slight wind blew. There were noises as if someone or something were sliding on the scree. Bega listened hard but there was no sound of water.

The cloud lifted.

'Shall we go on?' Chad asked.

'A little way at least,' said Bega, 'but first, let us give thanks.'

After the prayers they followed the curve of the top and everything was clear. But when they came to what they thought was the summit, they saw that some way further on there was yet another height. Bega's spirits fell.

'It looks easier,' said the boy, helpfully.

'Look at the sun,' Chad said, hoarsely, and repeated 'Look at the sun.'

The sun was clear and clean cut above a snowdrift of cloud. A magnificent rainbow circled the golden orb perfectly.

'What does it mean?' Bega asked.

'Thanks be to God,' said Chad. 'Praise be to His great glory.'

'Is that where heaven begins?' the boy asked.

Bega nodded. That seemed the best explanation. She could not take her eyes off the wonder and beauty of it. A rainbow wrapped around the sun!

'It is the heavenly choir,' she said. 'They are so dazzling that all we can see are the colours of their garments. They are bearing the sun towards God and singing His praises as they go. That is what it is.'

'Thanks be to God,' Chad mumbled, longing, longing to be back on the flat ground and away from such disturbing wonders.

'Shall we go on?' the child asked.

'A little,' said Bega, 'if you wish.'

The journey was easier now and they made good progress to the next peak.

'There is even one more,' said Chad, rather mournfully. 'But I am afraid that by the time we reach it and then rest and plan our return it will begin to be dark.'

Bega welcomed this cowardly but sensible suggestion. She took out the remaining food and the three of them shared it. Chad tried not to betray his nervousness by eating too quickly.

'Have you noticed that there is no water?' he asked.

Bega nodded but did not answer. She looked around her at the rocks and stones: everywhere a barren landscape. Yet she felt it could not be without some life. Two hawks hovered above but she realised they did not seem to land on this high place. Yet she could sense a presence there. Not a presence with which she could empathise. Something beyond, and with a mystery she would never pierce.

It was not, as she had hoped, nearer to God. But why not? It was demonstrably nearer to heaven. The clouds themselves had touched her. Bega was subdued. The journey up the mountain had brought too many questions, no answers; none of the sure touch of reaffirmation she had so long expected over the years with every comforting look up at this awesome mass. The stones and the bleakness made a landscape of desolation. This surely was God's work undone. Perhaps the old storytellers were right that the mountain was hollow and inside it lay a devil's forge which shaped a terrible hell and cast out on to the upper earth the rocks they saw as unfit for their building.

Bega looked in amazement to the lake of Erebert's island and beyond, to the intricacies of peaks and clouds, valleys and looming receding shapes. That God could have created such might! What force He must have, what power. Bega's heart swelled with a sort of pride in it. But there was still the intimation of fear. Something here on the barren mountain was disturbing; something threatened to unnerve her.

As the three of them went down, the curtain of vaporous white cloud which had trailed around the mountain throughout the day, settled below them. The sun was now behind them. They walked down into what appeared a white downy goose-backed silence of unearthly mass.

It was the youngest who faltered first. Then he stopped. Chad followed his example instantly. Bega walked a few paces on but then came back on Chad's word.

'Look!'

Below them, on the white cloud, were three enormous shadows. Bega moved from left to right and knew that the shadows were theirs. It was both terrifying and exhilarating. They marvelled at them, not daring to look at each other. What did it mean, those three vast black figures going before them? Were they to be turned into black devils? Was it their new bodies out on the clouds waiting to receive them? Bega was about to kneel and pray when as it were an extra lift of light put a halo around the head of the boy on his shadow below. She gazed at it, humbled.

'Look,' the boy said, 'around the head of Mother Bega. Look, there is a halo.'

Bega started. She could not see it. It was his, surely, his halo. How could it be?

'I see it,' Chad said. 'I see it on Bega and . . .' he moved a little way to one side, away from the boy, 'and I see the same on you,' he said.

Bega shook her head and the monumental shadow moved across the clouds.

'There is no halo,' she said.

'I see it,' said the child, almost sharply, his high voice crystal on the mountainside.

'I see yours.' She frowned. 'We must never talk of these things,' she said, 'never. This mountain is too mysterious for us. Let us hurry back down.'

Rather than tease out any answers, Bega put all her mind, as she had to, on the steep descent.

She held the boy's hand and stopped while Chad pulled ahead. Then he stopped, turned and looked up and she saw that he wanted to wait for them. But she waved him on.

Most reluctantly, but well trained at hiding his real feelings, Chad continued to step his way gingerly down the steep flank, feeling forlorn. He knew that she was about to send the boy away. How could he possibly live without him? He dared not face the prospect and simply hoped that time would somehow intervene and put it off for ever.

Bega had no niceties with which to cushion him. She feared that if she adopted the path of tenderness, she would fail in her plan.

'I brought you with me up this mountain,' she said to the boy as they sat side by side on a rock, looking down at the lake and their valley, 'because I want you to remember what I will tell you. I have told you about your father and mother. That is all you need to know of them. What you must do now is go to a monastery where you will be educated in the gospels and the commentaries and in everything that makes a scholar. I wish to make God a gift of your life and your talents.'

'Will I have to go from here?'

'Yes,' said Bega, firmly. 'The monastery I have in mind is many miles away. In a day or two a man of God, Cuthbert, will visit us. I will ask him to take you with him to that place. There,' she continued, quickly, avoiding the tears which threatened her eyes, 'you will meet men who will be wise and learned and you will learn from them. I want you to obey them in all things. I want you to remember your prayers at all times. To be humble before God and obedient before those in authority over you. To avoid vainglory and the vanity of earthly riches. To remember that I and even Cuthbert once, belong to a church of Christ which believes in the power of the word of God above everything else.'

She paused and breathed deeply. He was staring hard at her. She could sense it, but she would not meet his gaze. Way below them, Chad grew smaller and smaller. 'It will be your duty, in these perilous times, to carry that word forward. You must never betray the true church. The church I have told you about. You must promise me that you will do all this.'

The boy looked at her, almost tugging her with his gaze, but her eyes remained straight in front of her, avoiding all contact with his tear-glistened face. To his young mind she looked very calm, severe and not at all unhappy that he was to go far away from the warmth of Saethryd and the daily comforts of the other nuns, from the loving friendship of Chad and the comforting though remote presence of herself; from his world.

He pursed his lips and took a breath to check the tears.

'Do you,' she asked, 'do you promise?'

He nodded, suddenly unable to speak because of the lump which had risen into his trembling throat. He took her hand and squeezed it very hard and for a moment she allowed him to do so and felt a spring of warmth and love race through her body and her nerves like a benediction.

'Chad is waiting for us,' she said, swallowing the words. 'We must go.'

She set off so quickly that she almost tumbled down the mountain.

‌⚬⚬⚬⚬⚬

At first Bega had thought she would send him into Ireland, to Inishboffin, where Bishop Colman would keep him secure and uncorrupted by the Roman way.

She had decided against that for two reasons. The first, which she was loath to admit, was that it was just too far away. Once he had gone over the sea and then across the whole of Ireland and yet another stretch of sea, he would be as lost to her as if he had gone to Rome. Despite her powers of denial, she had not the final strength to do this. At least where he was going now could be reached in a few days and word could be brought of any severe illness.

Secondly, she had made herself reconciled to Cuthbert. This was partly because of the endless stream of miracles and astounding signs coming from him – the latest was that he had stood up to his neck in the sea throughout the night in penance and then collapsed when he came out to the shore, only to be revived and brought back to life by two otters. And the healing continued. He was a true man of God and although she would never forget what she saw as his failure at Whitby, she had to forgive it. She wanted the best for this child, and Cuthbert would undoubtedly give him better direction than she could. Even if it meant his going into a monastery which had made its compromise with Rome? Even that, Bega had decided in her hard, unblinking way. She herself would never accept what the Romans were trying to do. But her prayers had told her that her duty to this boy was to bring him to God and Cuthbert was nearer to God than anyone on earth. Therefore she would send him to Cuthbert.

CHAPTER SEVENTY-THREE

The boy did not meet Cuthbert. Chad, knowing now that he would soon be gone and as yet unable to work out a plan to be with him, was determined to spend as much time with him as possible. Bega understood this and was inclined to be co-operative. When, therefore, Chad, the morning after the adventure on the mountain which had left all of them rather confused, asked if he could take the boy for a day's fishing, Bega agreed. She knew that he loved to be in the little coracle with Chad, loved to fish, loved to bring back any catch and chatter on about everyone he had encountered. Such treats were few.

They left after prime and Bega watched them paddle out on the calm grey sheen of water which matched the skin of morning in the sky. She heard the child's high voice, a good singing voice, bell-clear, echoing across the water. And Chad's warm happy laughter; not a sound, she thought sadly, much heard in the valley. She could have watched and waited all day. She remembered the fisherwomen when she was at Whitby, bringing their work to the shore and watching and waiting all the while for the boats and their men to come back.

The routine of the day was the comfort. Habit could anaesthetise anxiety. The primary order of the services and duties could rub out many fears. The sense of serving God, of adding to good through prayer and devotion was a steady help. Bega was now, in what many saw as her greying, ageing years, more reliant on this routine than she would ever have imagined.

She let the wonders and questions which she had seen and apprehended on the mountain trickle slowly into her mind. She percolated them through prayers, purifying them. The ascent had not brought her the satisfaction she had wanted and there was disquiet in her soul at the memory of that bleak and stony wilderness. But there had been the signs.

Cuthbert arrived in the middle of the day. He had two monks with him and a youth. It was his custom, as with other monks, to take a novice with them on some missions and break him in early to the harsher aspects of the work.

Bega brought a bowl to wash his feet. To the surprise of his monks, for he would always forgo this ceremony in order to exercise greater discipline on himself, Bega exercised authority over him and he obeyed her. She drove out of her mind all memories of Whitby and she could see that he understood that.

She forbore to comment when she took off his battered, badly scuffed leather boots. The feet were calloused and bruised everywhere.

Bega knew better than to reproach him. She bathed the feet very carefully and, without any permission, she took her small dagger and sawed through the nails. To the calluses she applied ointment and bandages. Saethryd was given the boots to clean.

When his feet were done, she offered to do the same for his long fingernails and his hair, but he smiled sweetly and said, 'My feet you may wash because that service was done to Our Lord. Therefore I follow His example. For the rest, I must take my own way which is to ignore the world and let it do its worst.' She understood. 'Now I must sleep, but only for a short while,' he said. 'We have walked hard since dawn and there is far to go before dusk.'

Bega knew that Cuthbert would have been awake most of the night and in prayer. She could see the exhaustion on his thin, lined face. Yet there was, about the fine skin as about the long flowing greying hair which time and weather had cleansed, an even more powerful aura of holiness. There was the knowledge, Bega thought, that his was a soul whose heavenly reward was assured.

While he was asleep – and the youth, too, slept, having been spoiled a little by the nuns – the monks told Bega of some of their master's miracles.

'He fulfilled his ambition and became a hermit for a while. He chose a rock near Lindisfarne, one of those known as the Farne Islands . . .' The monk continually shifted his gaze as he talked, searching out the eyes of his listeners, part-hypnotising them into his story. '. . . I went with him and we found that there was no fresh water. The cold sea blew across the rock which had little vegetation. It was a nesting ground for many seabirds. But Cuthbert prayed for a while and then pointed to a spot near the centre of the little island. We dug and struggled with the ground where he pointed and – a spring of fresh water appeared!' He did not catch the way the nuns looked slyly first at each other and then at Bega. They too had a miracle woman who had brought forth a spring! Bega's look commanded them to say nothing.

'Glory be to God,' said Bega. The nuns echoed her.

'And after he had planted wheat which did not grow, he planted barley,' said the second monk. 'He told us – for he knows it strengthens our faith to hear what God has done for him – that the birds began to devour it as soon as it started to ripen. So he addressed them – this he told us himself! – and said 'Why do you reap what you have not sown? If God gave His permission for you to eat this barley then so be it. If not, I forbid you to eat of this barley again.' And the birds were ashamed and left the island rock and his crop was saved.'

'Glory be to God,' all of them murmured. They were entranced now. This was a true soul of God. This was their Almighty God showing His power. They were with someone who would be in paradise.

'The demons would throw rocks at him when he was tending his crops or feeding the geese and hens. But though they struck him and bruised him, still they never succeeded, he said, in harming his soul.'

'Thanks be to God! Glory be to God! Alleluia!' The voices of the women quickened with excitement.

'He spoke often of the brevity of life and quoted Solomon. "If a man live many years and rejoice in them all, yet let him remember the days of darkness for they shall be many."

'But after two years of pious bliss on the island, King Ecfrith insisted that he come back into the world. That too he had prophesied and he could not demur. But he knew it was only for a time. Then he would be released to pursue his final hermitage. So now he visits lands given to him by King Ecfrith – for the last time.'

When Cuthbert woke up he heard the tail end of yet more wonders and miracles surrounding his name and presence. He silenced the monks with a sincere firmness which impressed

Bega. 'Let us take some air, Bega,' he said. 'My feet are so sweetly repaired that I feel they have wings.'

When they went out, he paused and kneeled by the spring under the cross to scoop up some water.

'This is convenient,' he said. Noting Bega's reluctant expression, he persisted. 'Was it a gift from heaven?'

'It was,' said Bega, glad that he had avoided the use of the word 'miracle' which always made her flinch.

'Thanks be to God.'

'It is beneath the cross,' said Bega, pointing, and explaining no further save to add 'I buried it there the day after the devil threatened to snatch the sun out of the sky.' Cuthbert nodded and genuflected deeply to the cross.

'I knew that your prayers had been powerful,' said Cuthbert. 'Word of your work has travelled from this difficult and remote spot. We know of the ways in which God has favoured you.'

They moved on to the little path alongside the shore. The monks and nuns saw them but none dared approach this holy couple so earnestly in discussion as, for some time, they paced slowly backwards and forwards against the lake, the sky a bright light shimmering grey with occasional flashes of silver as angels, so one of the monks swore, came to earth to eavesdrop on what was being said between two such holy people.

'These miracles,' said Cuthbert, at ease with the word, 'that are attributed to me. They are of course the work of God but also they came through the intercession of the Virgin herself and the cross and for that I am for ever in your debt.'

Bega said nothing.

'I tell no one about the cross,' he continued, 'and I know that you have not spoken to anyone.' He paused and waited until she shook her head. 'The uproar would not be helpful,' he said, 'but believe me, in a dream I have seen that the fragment of the True Cross which you gave me will be a blessing for all Christian men and women and will help them even after my death.'

'But will there be time for that?' asked Bega. 'The sun was threatened. Another plague, we hear, is on the way. There are stories of King Ecfrith's cruelty and barbarity everywhere and yet he claims to be a Christian king. Others say he is the devil's own. Are these not signs that we are near the end of the world?'

'We are not ready,' said Cuthbert, solemnly.

'We never shall be.'

'I have seen more pain to come. I have seen terrible battles and many deaths,' said Cuthbert, and she looked and saw his eyes strained as if indeed he were seeing into the future at that moment. 'But God, I pray, is too merciful to bring His Last Judgment to bear on such a wicked and imperfect world as this.'

'This is the final time of God. For how else can we interpret all these calamities? And,' she hesitated only for a moment, 'how else can we account for the persecutions of the Celtic monks? There have been no truer believers since Matthew, Mark, Luke and John – why are they persecuted in this way? Why are all our ways thrown over?'

Cuthbert was silent for a while. Then he spoke, wearily.

'Much of my time at Lindisfarne is spent in these quarrels. Fifteen years have passed and still there are those who will never accept the synod nor go away to where their views are acceptable.'

'Why should they go away?' Cuthbert smiled at her temper. Very few talked to him as angrily as Bega did. But she had fed him the cross and she had the right to say whatever she wanted. 'Why should they leave the place they have been sent by God?'

'Many have gone away. Were they wrong?' Cuthbert knew that Bega had sheltered them. He knew that Ecfrith saw him as the one who would lead him into heaven and this gave him some power. His hold over Ecfrith had spared her any direct assault on her nunnery.

'They have left because they have been tormented into leaving,' said Bega, bitterly. 'I have seen them. And I have seen the warlords of Ecfrith at work.'

'It is not a big matter,' said Cuthbert, patiently, 'in the age of God and under the canopy of eternity, the synod itself was no grave matter.'

'Then why are we persecuted so violently?'

'We? Who has persecuted you?'

'I have been left alone,' Bega conceded. 'At times I am ashamed of my immunity and I cannot understand it. Save for . . .' She was reluctant to employ the True Cross in this context. Cuthbert kept his counsel.

'Do you seek martyrdom?'

'No. No.' Bega shook her head. 'But I do seek justice for those who truly serve their God.'

'Do I not seek the same?'

Bega hesitated fractionally.

'*Do I not?*' His voice hardened rather than rose and she felt the saw of it, viscerally. Cuthbert had authority.

'Yes . . . yes. But why does your King Ecfrith wish so much harm on us?'

'Why can your people not accept the ruling of the holy synod?'

'How can you?'

'Because there are far greater matters than any dispute over outward forms. It is the soul, the inward life, the life seriously lived, the life we dedicate to God, the holy and beautiful life in all of us, which is important. For this is in all people, in kings and in the least of your servants, not outward show. How can we speak of that? How can we allow that to be part of God's purpose when there is so much inequality in outward show? Those few who are overladen with riches, those many who hunger and thirst in poverty. Who but God Himself knows why that is? But the inner man or woman or child of God, that is equal to all, that is the soul given by the Divinity itself to prove itself on earth. Bega! End this barren argument. There is so little time for us to prepare ourselves for a heavenly existence.'

Bega was impressed by his command and fell silent for a while.

'This boy,' said Cuthbert, eventually, 'will he be a monk?'

'Yes,' Bega replied, grasping the chance to talk about him. 'He will most likely be a scholar. His birth was difficult and he was not well as a child. Even now he can look fragile. But he is gifted and will be of use and perhaps of benefit to any monastery. I do not want to tell you more about him.' Bega sensed that it would do the child no good to be known as a son of the House of Rheged.

'I will see that he is well placed.' Cuthbert looked around at the hills. 'How sweet and perfect it would be to walk into those hills and walk on until a spot were found where no human foot had trodden before. And to stay there. To feed on whatever the Lord provided. To wrestle for Him with all the temptations sent by that author of all lies.'

'Surely,' said Bega, 'you have conquered many of the temptations by now?'

Cuthbert took her arm. 'I can talk to you as a confessor, Bega,
because we share a secret with God which is so jewelled and unique
that God must have intended us to be utterly free in our talk with
each other. You have been free in your talk about Whitby. I know
that I have not answered your criticism, but between us that will
not prove disastrous.' He stopped and the pressure of his hand
on her arm brought her to a halt. They were looking across the
lake deep into the hills, clearly etched now and perfectly reflected
as the grey had been slowly dissolved by the sun. Bega found that
her eyes were seeking for the little boat which carried Chad and
the boy.

'I am still beset by temptation by day and by night,' said
Cuthbert, quietly. 'Sometimes I think that the Lord has chosen
me for His work because of the many temptations I am so prey
to. If I can show that they can be overcome, then there is hope
for all. On many nights I dream of wealth, Bega.'

Bega turned to stare at him. How could a man as holy and
gifted lust so strongly for perishable earthly things? He nodded.
He went on. 'I have the means to buy display. I have been given
estates. There is no bar in this Roman church to public pomp.
The Archbishop Theodore at my confirmation into the bishopric
vied even with Ecfrith himself in the dazzle and grandeur of his
coat and jewels. Wilfrid is as lavishly adorned as any prince of
Northumbria. Even Ecfrith draws envious breath when Wilfrid
comes back from one of his missions to Rome with garments of
rare texture and jewels of curious design not known here. Indeed,
I think that it is largely because of Wilfrid's wealth that Ecfrith
continually persecutes him. But I want it too. I long for it in my
dreams. That is why I have to reject it so totally.'

They recommenced their walk. 'And there are other temptations. The reason I try to avoid sleep is because it is there the devil
works most seductively on my body. The night emissions which
I cannot seem to control are evidence of his victory and I wake
myself and sleep as uncomfortably bedded as I can at all times
to win the battle with him. But he is terribly cunning. He will
let me drowse and then send into my dreams thoughts, images
delightful, profane, aimed to make me show weakness. When he
finds a fault he returns to it again and again. You see why I want

to be isolated in some extreme spot. Where I will never see the glitter and glisten of gold and wrought jewels and courtly earthly riches; where the daily, nightly round will be so severe that sleep will merely be a snatched thing and the lure of sweet sensuous flesh will not trap me.

'But now I must obey the prophecy made of me that I will be a bishop. That is why I have come here. I will show the devil my truest colours. I am divesting myself of the properties given to me. I have been south beyond the mountains to where I own farms and lands and I have given them over to some monks who will build a monastery there and be secure from the rents of those lands. This I will do all over the kingdom so that when my day at Lindisfarne is done I shall be equal with a beggar and truly fit to be a hermit.'

How could a humble, sin-flawed nun such as she was, one not worthy to gather up the crumbs from under Cuthbert's table, resist the strength of purpose of this man of God, so clearly destined to be one of the eternal saints?

They walked a little further and talked about the plagues and other matters until Cuthbert said 'I must go now. One last thing. Abbess Hilda has been suffering for several years with an illness so painful few others could bear it. Through weakness she shows strength. It may be good for you to visit her soon. I fear that God might need her and take her even though she rejoices in her pain and everyone who knows of it wonders at the strength of our faith when such agony can result in such happiness.'

'I will go.'

The monks were waiting for him. The youth had gone to the lake shore and was skimming stones across the water but a light word from Cuthbert brought him racing back. The monks were impatient to be on their way and, unless Bega was mistaken, a little jealous at the close attention Cuthbert had paid to Bega.

Saethryd, so crippled now that she hobbled with a rocking motion rather than walked, had given them fresh bread and all of them had drunk from the spring.

'I have been told,' said Cuthbert, finally, 'that there is a pagan temple near this abbey.'

'There is,' said Bega.

'Can you not make it a temple of the Lord?'

'The priestess,' said Bega, 'is strong and many in this valley, even if they follow us rather than her, would be fearful if the temple were to be destroyed against her wishes.'

'People's opinions can be changed very quickly if the will of God is seen to prevail.' Cuthbert spoke as the bishop of Lindisfarne, an authority to be obeyed. 'I hope that you will bend your efforts to see that such a canker is removed from this valley. Will that be your task?'

'I will do my best.'

'I will pray for you and expect that your strength in the Lord will prevail over whatever idolatries the priestess follows.'

Bega bowed her head to him. She watched as they walked away and then looked over to the temple and settlement of Reggiani.

It was long past dusk when Chad and the boy returned. The boy raced from the boat to where Bega and Saethryd were waiting, Saethryd holding up a flaring rushlight as a steer for Chad. While he tied up the small craft, the boy hurtled towards Bega, all his trained composure gone completely.

'I saw the elves and the imps!' he cried. 'Down at the end of the lake where it is all marshy and Chad says no one dares go in. You should have seen them! They looked like fire! They darted here and there and everywhere on the marshes and Chad said, "Keep very quiet so they don't know we're here and come and get us." They didn't! We back-paddled with our hands so's they wouldn't hear us go. But the further we went away the angrier they seemed to get. Maybe they could smell us. They whizzed about! They whizzed and whizzed and whizzed about – fire, it was like stabs of fire or lightning on the ground but smaller and lots of it and they didn't catch us! They didn't catch us!'

He flung himself at Bega with triumphant sobs of excitement, relief, exhilaration and thrilling fear. The weight of him, the palpitating, overwhelming life and warmth and love of him, all but made her groan. Must he go? Must he go?

CHAPCER SEVENTY-FOUR

On the way to Caerel to join up with a caravan which would be going across the wall, Bega and her party met up with two monks they had sheltered some years before on their way to Inishboffin.

'Why did you not come by way of our valley?' Bega asked.

'Bishop Colman has told us to avoid you,' one of them said. 'He had heard the trouble you had gone through and he said to give you a rest. Besides, it is almost as safe if you take the coast road some of the way and then cut across.'

'And easier,' the other said, 'on the legs. The mountains here are . . .' He shook his greying head.

They were, they said, taking messages to Melrose and Lindisfarne, encouraging the final few who dissented to come across to Ireland.

'You should come yourself,' said the grey-haired one. 'Inishboffin is the haven of God Himself. We've a fine little monastery next to a freshwater lake and near to the shore with little islands reaching out from it towards the end of the world. You've never seen such a place for growing things, although the rain can be ruinous but we pray against that as you do, I expect.'

'Things are easy there,' said the other. 'Some of the Northumbrians came with us and complained when we went off on missions in the summer while they stayed and worked the land. Why should you have the food it's taken us so long to work for, they asked, and they had a point. But we were off saving souls and there's no comparison. However. We didn't need a synod. Bishop Colman led them to land which can be their own on the big island. Now they go their way, we go ours without a harsh word.'

'It's the place for scholars,' said the older one, 'a place that breeds a man like Aldfrid. He should be king of Northumbria by rights –

his father was the King Oswy, but his mother was British, a Celt of some sort, so he's been driven out. But there's no envy in the man. He follows our ways. He uses the wealth and the lands he has to encourage the craftsmen to write out the gospel books and bind them with sacred jewels. They flock to him from all the kingdoms on God's earth.'

On they talked as they journeyed down to Caerel, along the twisting but well-worn forest path, through safe, thinned woods and past friendly settlements. Bega reflected that Ireland might be a good final home for her and quite soon. The word 'home' could still stir her heart to a most uncomfortable love: there would be the grave of her father; the nunnery by the sea where Padric had taught her to sail and where they had skimmed the surface of the water like the stones Cuthbert's boy had skimmed across the lake. She could retreat there. It was a happy, luxurious daydream and Bega was comforted by it for many miles.

The journey along the wall was without incident, though Bega noticed the population appeared to increase and fatten the further east they went. If so, did that mean the plague was less ravaging here? There was no one to ask. But there was no shortage of doomsayers. Her fear about the imminent end of the world was mirrored and echoed by two wandering groups they met along the way. They had cut themselves off from everything, they said, to tell everyone to prepare for the Last Judgment.

The further they rode, the more aware Bega became of a weight pressing against her heart. She felt like Abraham taking Isaac to the mountain as a sacrifice. She dare not look at the boy and still less at Chad. Chad had tried all his life to imitate the chastity and dedication of the monks and scholars he admired so much. The boy had been his one object of reciprocated, warm, physical, daily, sinless, heart-bonding love. And now he was being taken away.

Eventually they came to the new monastery of St Peter's at Wearmouth held then by Bishop Benedict. They had diverted their journey to see the newly arisen magnificence of Hexham, set in train by Wilfrid, now once again in Rome seeking justice against what he claimed to be his illegal persecution by Ecfrith. Once Ecfrith had become king, his need for any alliance with Wilfrid was over. Moreover, like other nobles, but more savagely, he feared the territorial power of the dashing, apparently unstoppable young bishop, whose lands all but equalled those of the king himself.

Noble women all over the country contributed to Christ through the coffers of Wilfrid.

Ecfrith had begun to fight back by the crude method of seizing Wilfrid's estates and stripping him of his titles. Wilfrid, though, was not easily crushed. Year after year he took his case to Rome and proved that injustices had been done against him, returning in legal triumph to Northumbria only to find that, with scarcely a pause, Ecfrith would do the same again. Despite all this, Wilfrid continued to build and to furnish lavish monasteries, in Northumbria and elsewhere, awesome monuments to all who looked on them.

Wearmouth was not so impressive, to Bega's relief. Hexham had raised all her instinctive objection to Romanish authority and show. What need was there for such a towering pile of stones? Wearmouth was modest and acceptable.

Cuthbert had sent word that Bega would be bringing the boy to the monks there. Bishop Benedict himself was absent, having set off on one of his expeditions to Rome which he undertook as frequently as Wilfrid, though he went solely for relics and paintings, for gorgeous tapestries and church ornaments and finely skilled craftsmen.

The novice master accepted the boy immediately. Too immediately, too briskly for Bega and certainly for Chad. The boy had become stoic about his fate and Bega was not one to unbutton emotions closed up at some cost. Chad was literally lost for words and simply stood there, staring at the boy, until the ascetic and rather testy monk ushered him away.

Outside, the two of them rejoined their servants and set out south for Whitby. Neither spoke for a long time. Bega was waiting to feel the full pain. The cut had been made; it had to be made. The boy would be a fine gift for God and in a place such as that, his learning would flourish. But the pain would come.

Chad was too numbed to speak. He clenched himself around his feelings like a bitch protecting her young. The only hope which kept him from turning and racing back to that bleak abbey at the mouth of the wide and dangerous river was the thought that when their journey was completed he would ask Bega to let him go and be a servant at Wearmouth.

After three days they came to Whitby and both of them stood still for a while to take in its splendour, its organised turmoil, its greatness, a city of God crowning the cliff.

The late-afternoon sun illuminated the stone and wooden buildings, lit up the thatch, showed off the regular gardens and all the neat arrangements of the abbey. It had about it an air of enchantment. They climbed up towards it, as if they were indeed about to reach the kingdom of heaven.

Chad and the servants saw to their own arrangements while Bega took her place in the line of those awaiting an audience with the fast ailing Abbess Hilda.

She waited through that day, spent the night in the dormitory and then, save for the services, waited on until late the following afternoon. The abbess was weak and could not see visitors for long, nor more than two or three in a day. Bega was well disciplined in patience and there was much to absorb in the many comings and goings about this so much ampler place.

Bega picked up what news she could and found that here, too, there was the fear that a fourth plague would come. But the place was so stocked with holy people, with prayers and riches of all kinds that it appeared to her and, she suspected, to its inhabitants to be an impregnable fortress, an exception chosen by God.

At last she was admitted to Hilda's parlour. It was even more lavishly and warmly furnished than the last time she had seen it. There were hanging tapestries depicting Christ's life, from His blessed birth to His cruel death, and on the floor lay matting overlaid with yet more colourfully woven tapestries: too precious, Bega thought, to walk on, but there was no alternative.

Hilda was so thin, her face such a document of suffering, her body bent and curled, her hands gripped in the malady, her skin whiter than vellum.

'My dear.' The voice! The voice was exactly the same and Bega flushed with joy, knowing that she was ready to obey whatever command would issue from it. 'Come nearer. It is dark in here. I do not like too much light now. Come near. There.' Bega obeyed. 'Well,' said Hilda, after a penetrating appraisal, 'you have worn quite well but your face shows signs of unhappiness.'

'It is an open record.'

'I hear good things about you,' said Hilda, rather distantly, almost, Bega suspected, a touch resentfully. 'One is always disinclined to believe all this chatter about miracles unless someone of the calibre of Cuthbert is involved but what I hear is, decidedly, more good than bad.'

Bega smiled a smile of relief. That would do. She was distressed by the wasting of Hilda. Despite the unshakeable voice, evidence of a mind still as clear and untroubled by any doubts, there was a fever about the eyes, an involuntary shivering which accompanied it. The plainly beautiful, long stern face was set against any show of pain, but Bega could sense the burden of it. This, she knew, was God's way, with favoured ones, of making strength perfect in weakness.

'Are you in great pain?' The unnecessary question was tentatively expressed.

'Yes, thanks be to God.'

'Can I read to you?'

'No thank you, my dear. As I remember you were very clever but your reading voice was a little too harsh for my ears.'

Again Bega smiled. How she loved her! 'Shall I tell you what we do over in Rheged?'

'Would that interest me?'

'I could try.'

'Very well; but if I fall asleep, you must not be offended. Sometimes I am given that blessed release and I must accept it.'

'I understand,' said Bega, gravely.

'You know,' said Hilda, 'I had hopes that you might stay here. At one time I thought that you might succeed me. That is still not impossible. Would you like to come back here?'

'Praise be to God for your words but I am, I believe, doing His work in Rheged.'

'Yes, yes. But this is a much bigger, much, much bigger task altogether.' She was firmer now and very sure of herself. Her spirit delighted Bega so much that she wanted to smile although it would be inappropriate. 'From what I hear you can be firm. You were always sharp and so the clever girls now coming here in such droves from the noble houses won't unsettle you. And you had some sort of background yourself, didn't you?'

Bega assented, still managing to keep grave, but why did she feel like smiling and even laughing aloud in the presence of someone so plainly near death?

'Well, think about it. We need a strong woman here. It's all very well having a double house but it must be run by the women or we shall become just another appendage of a monastery and I will not abide that.'

'I will pray for guidance.'

'And so shall I. Now. If you have something to say, say it clearly.'

Could she say 'Mother, I thank you and love you for letting me be your daughter'? She could not. So Bega began to entertain her about the valley. She spoke openly about the movement of the Celtic monks – information she knew that Hilda would possess in any case. She spoke of the little nunnery and of Bishop Colman; of Cuthbert's visits and the plagues. She did not touch on the desperate case of the murder and cannibalism of the children, knowing that Hilda would have heard of it.

Gradually the older woman's eyes flickered, started open, flickered once more, her head rolled to one side, her crippled tensed body seemed to find a touch of ease, and soon she slept with a light almost melodious snore.

For a while Bega simply sat with her. This would be the last time. She got on her knees in front of the ailing, old abbess and thanked God that such a life, such an example, such a soul had been sent to earth to be the inspiration of so many. She took the hem of Hilda's robe and kissed it. Then, feeling the prickle of the tears she had left unshed for the boy, she walked quickly from the room and up the cliff to the spot where she had so often stood or sat and called her own. She looked at the gulls swerving and listing; at the dark grey sea stretching out and on until it met the darkening sky.

Less than a month later, Bega was praying beside the lake, just before dawn. The particular clarity and disturbance of the noises towards the end of the night seemed to orchestrate her mood. It was the long Easter fast and, to make it harder on herself, Bega had fasted for ten days before Ash Wednesday, and now she was purifying herself further with an all-night vigil.

Clouds swanned massively across the dark sky, now and then revealing a sharp, bright, all but full moon, crisp and shining. The lapping of the lake water on the shore and the lilt of the stream across its final pebbles merged into the sweetest sounds, she thought, the sounds of water: the endless, infinite, incalculable stresses and pitches and rhythms. They seemed to possess the body.

For every lap, ripple, break, push, fall, trill, muffle of water there was a corresponding note in her.

Her knees felt as hard as the pebbles into which they were pressed and cramp threatened her cold, stiffened thighs. Occasionally, she looked up, not hoping for a sign but simply to observe the greatness and majesty of a God who could command all those miraculous sights: a fleet of stately grey clouds, not one the same, as different each from each as children are; the polished face of the moon which, when revealed, sprinkled silver on the dark surface of the lake. Beyond all that was the house of God, to which she prayed. Especially for Hilda, her mother. A trader had told her that Hilda was now entering the last phase of her struggle.

Was it a wolf's howl or the pitiful cry of a tethered dog which set the village beasts in a commotion? Commands from the voices of men whipped through the night and the dogs were hushed, though a trail of bleats and lowing still came from the compounds. Not a bird. Not a note.

The wind which shifted the clouds and picked up the waves circulated through the trees, distinguishing alder from spruce from lime to ears long trained to discriminate.

To concentrate on Hilda was not difficult although the twinges of cramp and the pains in the joints of her hands were distracting. Her spiritual exercises and great love for the abbess took her far into the meditation. What really disturbed it was the subversive longing for the bath of warm water and a little gruel which the aged and hobbling Saethryd would bring to her after Lauds.

Bega struggled. Cuthbert fought mighty demons who hurled rocks and threatened him with mountainous forces. Her struggle was against the too-salivating anticipation of a warm bath and a bowl of gruel.

Bega concentrated on the last time she had seen Hilda. She conjured up the face she had looked on so often. She could remember the sweet smell of pine wood on the embering fire. But the warmth led her directly back to the gruel and the devil pranced before her eyes, gobbling up her piety and spitting it out.

Bega felt the strength slowly going out of her. A bowl of gruel. Why this test? Why this trivial test? Why now? A weariness threatened to extinguish what spark of fight she had left. Was the soul of Hilda in her prayers not capable of being more powerful than the image of the ancient Saethryd holding out a warm bowl of soup?

The devil seemed to have sent imps to prickle her. She began to feel twitches or pinches of pain everywhere on her body. She tried to isolate the sound of water from the stream and see Hilda's soul as a pure source running to complete its natural course and entering a new vastness, becoming part of a wholly different mass, still the water from the stream but wholly and irrevocably changed by this entrance into the lake. Just so, she prayed, would Hilda's soul run effortlessly out of her body and into the vastness of those other souls who had been saved.

The warmth of the thought drew a quiet cry of longing from her lips. For the soul of Hilda? For the intervention of divine mercy? For the gruel?

Bega clenched shut her eyes and her hands and drove down into her reserves of devotion. Hilda and Hilda alone must be her prayer, her thought, her being, her existence.

Hilda, summoned, appeared in Bega's mind, not as she had last seen her, nor at any dramatic time in their relationship but simply in the garden of the abbey, loping along at high speed, undoubtedly on some errand of reprimand. She had the eager positive look Bega knew well which signified that someone had fallen short and was going to be set straight! The memory made Bega smile in her mind and the smile came to her lips and it was as if the smile were a sign which the devil could not bear for he darted and prickled in vain and slowly his wicked temptation was expunged. This picture of the brimmingly virtuous Hilda, in that garden, racing towards her victim.

Bega opened her eyes and looked up. The clouds had broken in such a way that the moon's rays shone down to earth in a number of broad silver pathways. The clouds themselves were silvered from behind. The brilliance of these pathways to heaven was of an order that Bega had never before seen.

She heard sighing, the susurration of voices, angels' voices murmuring, then growing a little louder as these pathways became the welcoming route to heaven of some great soul now being taken into that eternal kingdom. Her eyes strained and she was sure she saw the pure white of angelic gowns, the glitter of golden horns, the singing of alleluias as the soul was gathered in. And then the clouds moved on and the rays were gathered up.

Some weeks later, she learned that on that very night, and at that time, Abbess Hilda had died and ascended into heaven.

CHAPTER SEVENTY-FIVE

THE FOURTH PLAGUE

Saethryd was bedridden and Bega spent as much time as she could reading the Gospel of St John to her. She interpreted it according to the commentaries she had learned both in Whitby and from the monks who had rested at her nunnery. She owned some plainly copied pages from the commentaries as well as a set of the gospels which she had worked at over the years.

Bega knew the gospels by heart and had many of the long passages of commentary similarly stored. The Old Testament was at her fingertips and although she declined to lace her every sentence with verses from a psalm or a minatory reference to Jeremiah or Solomon, David, Jacob or Baalam, Nebuchadnezzar, Esther or Ruth, Noah, Abraham, Moses or Joab, nevertheless it was known that she knew. The valley people thought that she knew everything there was to know. There were those who had talked to her not only about the gospels but about medicine or herbs, about plants, animal husbandry or the old stories and always this slight, dark-faced, dark-haired, holy woman with the palest bright eyes and swift manner, seemed to know more than the questioner. The fact that she tried to hold her silence and speak, for the most part, only when asked, was held to be an indication of her saintliness. Everything she did reinforced this saintliness.

When the sun shone they would say she brought fine weather with her. When overdue rain came that was her doing too. And the hail and the snow was God's punishment sent through Bega to shrive them once and for all.

Her boldness was another source of evidence. Often she walked alone in the fearsome high woods and into the lonely settlements of obstinate paganism. Alone she went where wolves preyed, where wild cats hunted and wild dogs ran loose, and where the undergrowth shook with the terrifying presence of a wild boar, and yet she was never harmed.

'God loves her.'

'The Lord protects her.'

'There was a wolf mad with hunger about to launch himself on her when she turned and looked at him. She said: "I serve the Lamb of God who is yet far fiercer than you." The wolf just bowed its head and walked away, crying to be forgiven.'

'In the forests there were the white cattle, the bulls that come some summers. They left three of the finest young bulls behind many years ago and these now escort her and see her safe when she moves . . . they are invisible to anybody but her.'

'She can pray night and day without a pause for forty days. There's not a soul goes to heaven that is not helped by the prayers of Bega.'

This and suchlike talk grew and was reported and added to and believed. The tiny settlement by the lake became a place of pilgrimage. It was not on the scale of Cuthbert, whose life had become a sort of holy progress, a procession of piety. Princes, nobles, scholars, warriors, women of great rank and most of all King Ecfrith himself all wanted to be in the holy presence of Cuthbert. When Cuthbert had become a hermit on one of the Farne Islands, he had to forbid the boatmen on the mainland from bringing over supplicants more than once a month. Yet in her local way, Bega's fame extended. And, however much she strove to suppress it, the rumour of her miraculous powers grew. Even Saethryd could seem affected by it.

'You will pray for my soul, won't you?' she would ask again and again, however often she was reassured. 'I want to know that your prayers are lifting me up. There's nobody else can do what you do.'

Calmly, suppressing embarrassment, Bega reassured the old woman and there and then prayed alongside her.

Saethryd was now very ill. Her body, always large, had become bloated and sometimes the pain in her stomach made her cry out loud, honking cries which set off half the valley.

'It's the goblins in there,' she said, pushing her fingers into the mass of her stomach, 'they can't wait until I'm dead before they eat me up. They have to be doing it now. Dirty little beasts.' She would look at her hump of stomach and curse them and Bega waited until she had exhausted herself before once again offering up her prayers.

Prayer, she knew, was the answer to everything on earth. To be pure enough in spirit for your words to reach God was the only way to bring about betterment, healing, fertility, victory, plenty, all that was desirable on earth.

Chad wrestled hard with his prayers. He prayed to all the apostles and many of the Celtic saints ever increasingly loved and revered by Bega. None would give him the sign he needed to prove to Bega that he had to go to Wearmouth. What was it he was failing to do which severed his prayers from reaching a sympathetic ear?

After their return he had waited for the right moment. He was unable to tease it out. Bega seemed as preoccupied and tense as he himself. Finally he broke into her evening walk some weeks after their return. He would follow her back and forth, he vowed to himself, until she gave in.

He explained that he wanted to join the boy in Wearmouth.

'It is impossible,' said Bega, flatly.

'There is nothing I do here that could not be done by others.'

'That is not true,' said Bega. 'You teach. You keep the garden in good order. You are our main man with the cattle and the sheep and goats. You can repair a wall or a roof. You help with the scholarly work to be done.' Her words had softened the longer the list went on. 'We would all be at a loss without you, Chad.'

For some moments, he was silenced. Chad was unused to praise. Long stretches of his life had been accompanied by not the remotest sound of applause. Nor had he expected it. Bega's commendation winded him. But only for a moment.

'In the monastery at Wearmouth,' he went on, doggedly, repeating a speech he had learned by heart and delivered aloud to the goats and sheep and cattle many a dozen times, 'I could be useful to him. He's just a little lad. He wasn't well at first – remember? That never goes away. I could make things easier for him. And I'm sure I could make myself useful enough around the place for them to let me live there. They might even let me help them at their work on the manuscripts: I

could grind the colours – you taught me that. I could prepare
the vellum—'

'You are not to go.' Bega continued her walk uninterruptedly
and no temper showed in her voice. Struggling by her side, Chad's
agitation increased.

'May I ask why not?'

'First because you are needed here.'

'Others could do what I do.'

'Second because you are under my rule and will obey me.'

'Yes. But why? He's such a little boy.'

'He needs to be transplanted whole and without you. And
without me.' Even on those words her voice did not falter and
Chad sinned to think, as sometimes he had done in the past,
that Bega's saintliness took all her feelings and strength leaving
nothing for the ordinary earthly emotions experienced by others.
Why, otherwise, had she been so distant from the boy towards
the end, when he had looked on her as a mother?

What if I just went? Chad thought, wildly. If I just walked away.
I know the route. If I offered to be a servant and worked there and
watched him grow. The boy was his own idealised childhood, the
son he would never have, someone loving and loved who could
never be replaced.

'I think,' said Chad, desperate, almost crab-like at her side,
pleading as she measured out her evening walk beside the glassy
lake, 'that he needs me. I dreamed that he needed me.'

'He must be left alone. They will teach him well. Your presence
would be a distraction.'

Bega could both see and understand Chad's distress. Was she
ignoring it entirely for good reasons? As she walked, beside the
glassy lake, she turned on herself. Had she always been a little
jealous of the easy friendship between Chad and the boy and was
she now being so very firm because she did not want Chad to
enjoy a friendship, a parenthood from which she had debarred
herself?

In one of those peculiar leaps of comprehension, Chad saw
what Bega was thinking. He blushed for her weakness.

'We could both go,' he said, as the only way he could cope
with this knowledge.

'Why should I want to leave here?'

'I could leave here and go alone,' he said, defiantly at last. She looked tenderly on his raw, simple, honest face, coarsened by work and weather but still keeping that sweetness of the boy Chad.

'But you will not,' she said, firmly and finally. She was used, as she had been since the first moment of their meeting, to commanding his absolute obedience.

'I could just go,' he repeated hopelessly, swallowing hard, braving this new territory.

'No.' Bega turned to him not unsympathetically and smiled a little. 'No,' she repeated, 'you could not.' She paused and nodded and made it clear that the conversation was over.

Chad stopped in his tracks and watched her walk away from him. Instead of peeling off the preserved walk, he waited. She would turn and walk back and towards him and he waited.

He had no plan. He had no words. There was nothing he could identify about his attitude save a feeling that he had to remain standing there. To move would have required energy he simply did not have. Suddenly there was no future on earth that he could contemplate with any sense that he would be there to be part of it. What was there for him to do?

Bega turned and began to walk towards him at her steady pace.

What would he say?

Chad tried to stir himself to words as she drew nearer. But none came. He longed to be with the boy. He was grieving from the loss of him. How could she not let him go?

The nearer she came, the calm step, the strong presence so relied on now in the valley and still adored and feared by Chad, the more and more impossible it became for him to say anything at all.

He began to sob. Bega came up to him and stopped. His head was lowered, his hands simply dangling by his sides. She put out her hand and touched his shoulder. As if given an order, Chad fell to his knees and huddled in the smallest shape of himself.

Bega kneeled down beside him.

'We must pray,' she said.

Chad gave no indication that he had heard her words. His broad, strong frame shook as if someone imprisoned inside it were rattling the bones.

'We must pray,' Bega repeated.

'No.' The single syllable tore itself from Chad's mouth. 'Oh no! No! No!'

Bega ignored him and continued her prayer.

'I must go!' he said, still crouched in a ball of himself. 'Let me go.'

'I will pray for you, my friend. And you must pray for your own salvation.'

'No!' His sobbing was heart-wracked but Bega hardened her own heart against it. It would not be the best for the boy, she thought, that was certain. Chad would bring too many questions with him which the boy would be happier without. Let him drop all the baggage of his brief boyish past and, lightened, be better able to scale whatever heights were set for him by God. Chad, she knew for certain, would pull him back, perturb him, cloud his purpose.

'Oh no,' whispered Chad.

'God in Thy great wisdom,' Bega prayed, 'give balm to the soul of Thy poor servant Chad.'

When the next plague came, four years later, Bega almost committed the sin of wishing it would take her with it.

The cutting off from the boy had left her bereft although she fought against admitting it. She feared that yet again, as with Padric, the devil was making her prefer love on earth to love for heaven. Her strong earthly feelings would for ever bar her from any heavenly reward. Chad, simply in his sad presence, reminded her continually of her loss. But if she sinned in even allowing the thought of her death for inglorious reasons, she also rejoiced that the new plague gave her a task worthy of the apostles.

As before the valley had begun to recover but this fourth wave caught them in despair as well as physical weakness. No one doubted now that these plagues would never cease. Such wrong had been done, such was the anger of God, that they were to be punished, the innocent and the guilty alike, while the wrath of God prepared itself to call the Last Trump.

A large part of Bega's task was to make them want to live at all. Why should they struggle when the result would be to put them under sentence of another plague?

Prayer, said Bega, prayer and the purification of the soul through devotion to the precepts of Christ.

Chad was terrified that the plague might reach the boy. One moment he would thank God that he had been removed from this infested valley, the next he would torture himself with fears that the plague might be raging much worse in the land of the half-heathen Northumbrians. If God's severity were such against the largely Christian people of Rheged, how much more violent would He be against the invaders? In the middle of the night, he would wake up in a spasm of anxiety. Whenever there was a death, he would make two calculations: one, that God had slain another here and therefore He might be near the total for His harvest figure and not need many more and therefore the boy's chances were improved; the second, that this course was irresistible and it could be only a matter of time before it cut down everyone. If only he could see him just once more before that fate.

Saethryd died, her stomach by the end grotesquely swollen. Two weeks later, one of the three younger nuns caught the plague after a mission out of the valley and into the lands around Erebert's island. For two days, Bega thought that Chad was afflicted but their prayers and the grace of God intervened and he was spared.

Once again Reggiani made an island of herself, almost as effective as the natural island which spared Erebert.

The work took all the hours they had. When it was over, both Chad and Bega ached with exhaustion. Once more the nunnery had become a hospital and when they were not out in the fields and hills visiting the sick and attempting to treat them with herbs and poultices as well as prayer, they were working in the hospital. Chad would clean it, a never-ending task; Bega and three remaining nuns attempted to save souls as well as lives.

The tiny cemetery in a corner of the herb garden was outgrown and another had to be established on the north side of the buildings. The shallow graves were overlaid with narrow flat pieces of slate. One upright piece marked the head.

It was more than three months since the last fresh case of the plague had been recorded and, from her previous experience, Bega

could reasonably assume that this meant that the present plague
was in retreat or over.

It had not been the worst. Slowly, over the months, the valley
came back to life; tentatively, people began to mingle again and
move around. The autumn and winter were mild, the spring warm
and balmy and just sufficiently wet, there was a good harvest. Bega
held a special service of thanksgiving.

Afterwards Chad came up to her. This plague had worn him
down much more than all the others. He looked old and tired,
his face was wasted, his manner all but crushed.

'May I go and see the boy, Bede?' he said simply. He had wanted
for so long to restate this request. 'I will not talk to him. I will not
even approach him. He will not know that I was there. But, God
willing, I will know that he is safe. And if he is, then God's word
will live on for another generation.'

'I have been cruel to you,' said Bega, briskly. She was as moved
by Chad's honesty as by his great faith in the gospels. 'Yes. You
must go across to the monastery in which we left him and bring
me word.'

Chad looked at her intently. 'You, too, want to know . . . ?'

'Oh yes,' said Bega, finally, showing no emotion. 'Yes, I too
want to know.'

These were early spring days and by rising at first light and
walking hard, sometimes hurrying into a run, Chad completed
the journey in four days.

When Chad discovered that Bede was not at Wearmouth but
had been sent to Jarrow, he had to kneel and try to pray to calm
his panic. What dreadful circumstances had forced this? What
calamity? Had the plague struck? Had he been sent to Jarrow to
be safe or to be cured or to be buried?

A monk who had come only recently to the monastery pointed
out the way.

It was late afternoon. At first Chad ran; ran until a stitch slowed
and stopped him. He sucked in the air and went on even though
dusk seemed rapidly to merge into twilight, then into a darkness
which forced a halt.

He was too late, he thought, to find shelter in a settlement. He
ought to have gone into one of those he had passed but the urge
to find out about Bede had made him careless. In the evening
gloom, unvisited by a moon which had not yet risen, he found

a fine big oak. In its lower branches, after some manoeuvring, he established himself safely enough.

Valuable time was lost on the following morning. He had strayed off the path and when finally he found someone who could put him back on it, the sun was well up.

Jarrow at first appeared as an island. Then he saw it was on an elevated promontory, surely cut off by an unusual high tide, but clearly part of the land. It kept touch with the earthly kingdom more definitely than Lindisfarne and yet the ancient preference for an islanded retreat was still recognised.

Chad approached cautiously. He made no attempt to enter but pretended that he was searching for reeds. He collected them as he moved towards the place and waited until someone would appear and help him. When two monks did come out, he had to screw up all his courage to ask them – was there the plague in Jarrow? And was there a boy there called Bede? The answer to the first question was no and to the second, after a little consideration about Chad's purpose but thinking that he was a simple man, was yes.

Chad's heart leaped. He could scarcely bear the presence of the helpful monks. He wanted to fall to his knees and give thanks. Then they told him how Bede had been saved in Wearmouth and how the boy and the only other survivor had kept the services going. They spoke reverently of his scholarship and high calling. They boasted to Chad of their association with so gifted a spirit. The more they said, the more Chad grew hot with pride. But, also, the more chillingly sure he was that it was not for him to make any claim on the boy he had once known. He had been given the news he had hoped for. God had granted his prayer.

Now he should return.

But he could not.

He gathered reeds and his stomach ached with hunger but he could not go.

As the afternoon drew on, he came closer and closer to the gate and then, as if absent-mindedly, he slipped in and was welcomed, was given food in the guest house and invited to vespers.

He sat at the back of that portion of the church set apart from those who served in the monastery.

He recognised Bede instantly. The boy had grown and become more angular. His face was pale but not wasted, Chad noted, anxiously. He walked with humility and dignity and when the service began, Chad could distinguish his voice and listened to him only. He swayed on his feet, transported with tearful happiness at what the boy had become and moved to dream of even greater things from that slight, devoted, fine-faced youth so consummately a monk, so clearly a scholar, so profoundly where he should be in God's scheme. It was enough that he, Chad, had known him and perhaps helped him a little in his early years. For that, thanks be to God.

The service was so short, the pleasure was so intense. Chad's gratitude was so strong he could feel his heart open like a leaf in spring.

Once he thought that Bede's gaze scanned the church as if looking for someone but Chad was in the candle-glimmering shadows. He turned his head away.

In the morning he left as soon as the gate was opened and hurried back to Bega, so full of what he had seen and heard that the journey was as light as a snowflake. Bede was safe. He was doing God's work. He was home.

BOOK SEVEN

✦✦✦✦

THE LAST BATTLE

✦✦✦✦

CHAPTER SEVENTY-SIX

Padric, in his forty-eighth year, was now thought by many of the princes to be the greatest warrior in the known lands. In Brittany and beyond in the land of the Gauls, in Wessex and Anglia, in Wales and in Dumnonia, some of his battles were already legendary. In epics at feasts he was compared now to a fox, now to a wild boar, now to the lion of Judah, now to Gideon, to the great emperors of vanished Rome. There were those who saw him as the very reincarnation of Arthur.

His long-tongued sword, though not endowed with the magic of Excalibur, was feared on battlefields hundreds of miles apart, now seen as a silver serpent, as a stab of lightning, as the flashing arm of God, as the symbol of vengeance. Stories were told of the sword floating freely in the air and fighting on its own, defending Padric who lay wounded on the ground, giving him the time to staunch the wound and regain his feet before taking the sword from the invisible hand that guided it and once more laying to.

His brothers followed close behind, Urien for his wildness and audacity in war and peace and Riderch for his tremendous strength and his gift with animals. Out of the three of them were spun tales to match the sagas of the old heroes.

The larger Ecfrith's ambition grew – to subdue or to eliminate all other tribes but his own – the more obsessed Padric became that it had to be thwarted. After his final rejection by Bega, the obsession hardened and even his brothers would at times find its increasingly dour, fixed, unyielding character draining, even uncomfortable. He seemed to lose so much of his amiable nature on the rack of this idea.

So many years had passed with so little to show. True, there were alliances waiting to be called; and some men were trained and the epic of his own small forces on their long journey to the great battle was sung at many feasts. But when would God grant him the final battle? What had he yet to do?

Padric spoke openly of his long-delayed ambition to Aldfrid, Ecfrith's half-brother. Aldfrid, a scholar-prince, had founded a monastery in the centre of Ireland, where Padric went whenever there was an opportunity. He had grown close to Aldfrid. When Padric and his men came to the sprawling monastery which included so many young noblemen and scholars from other lands, he would be pleased to take up again the studies he had no time for on the road. There was a subtlety in Aldfrid's manner, a playfulness, a larger sense of the possibilities in life, which Padric fell on with gratitude. The life of a nomadic soldier, especially one so painstakingly and in such a fragmented, uneven way building up a network, allowed little time for Aldfrid's arts of leisure. 'I am just a blunt soldier now,' he would say to Aldfrid, half-proud, half-regretful. 'Just a sword arm and a shield. One year I make an alliance. The next it is gone.'

Yet, like all noblemen, Aldfrid had been trained in war. And he still practised the martial arts. He also followed every move made by Ecfrith, whose natural successor he was.

Ecfrith still had no children. 'It is because of that,' said Aldfrid, as Padric and he rested between sword fighting practice, 'that he hates me so much. He cannot conceive that I am not about to raise an army to cross the sea and march on him.' Aldfrid smiled – he had a handsome, open face, Padric thought, ascetic but not strained, and always that amused smile ready to be released. 'From here?' He looked around. 'From Ireland? From this land of monks and scholars! Who would be a soldier when there is so much better to do!'

'You have good fighting men here,' said Padric, thinking of the O'Neills.

'We have. A few,' said Aldfrid. 'But it has changed a lot since you first came here. The warrior-families are still here. But the island has become much more peaceful. The monasteries and nunneries, the abbeys and the works of our craftsmen are what absorbs most of us now. Men and women come from all over the world to enjoy the peace and scholarship of Ireland. It is a safe place. There is nothing here for an invader. Even the plague touches us less than elsewhere.'

'It is true that Ecfrith will never come here,' said Padric, thinking himself into Ecfrith's strategy as he did so often, 'there is nothing for him to gain. But now that he has made dominating alliances with almost all the other royal houses, he is turning his full attention to the Celts and, above all, the Britons.'

'But he has not treated Rheged with his greatest cruelty.'

'He is held back,' Padric agreed. 'There are many reasons. It is a place special to God. But now . . .'

'We must wait for God's good time,' said Aldfrid. 'Then Ecfrith will fall.'

'Amen.' Padric stood up and picked up one of the wooden swords they used for exercise. 'Or we must kill him before he kills us.'

Aldfrid smiled and took up his mock-sword and prepared himself. 'So.'

As the wooden swords hollow hit each other in the meandering late afternoon, Padric was sufficiently in control to be able to sense what lay about him. He envied it.

It was his ideal. Here were sound, unpretentious buildings, cultivated pasture lands, fat cattle and well-fleeced sheep; goats and geese accompanied by their young shepherds and both men and women and monks and nuns alongside each other in field and garden, church, study and the many places which underpinned and ornamented this fine life: kitchens, craftsmen's workshops, blacksmiths, metalworks, laundries, storehouses . . . It was as if Aldfrid and not himself were the real incarnation of Arthur. After all, Aldfrid's mother was British. For it was here in Ireland that the real kingdom of Arthur survived, he thought. All it needed now was the grace of God and his own constant struggle to bring it back home.

His thoughts strayed – a home. Was one never to be his?

'A kill,' said Aldfrid, jubilantly, lunging forward with his sword and tapping Padric across the neck.

'A kill,' Padric acknowledged, 'I must take more care.'

⊗⊗⊗⊗

Ecfrith was now an awesome king. The fury in his head had not been sated but merely whetted by his treacherous accession twelve years before. His brilliant and cruel raids and tortures had subdued even the Mercians; as far south as Wessex allegiance was given to him. Only once since the departure of the Romans had the land acknowledged one ruler south of the great wall effectively to be the leader: that was in the time of Arthur.

Ecfrith was hated whereas Arthur had been loved. He knew this. Though at first he had writhed, now he exulted in it. His conquests became crueller. He dipped his arms in the ripped-open stomachs of victims and held up his bloodied hands in triumph, just as he did after killing a particularly brave stag. His tortures became more elaborate.

His queen had not let him divorce and she still lived in a state of chaste holiness. No women he had bedded had ever become fertile. Therefore God did not want him to have sons. This God he cursed, but secretly. Openly, publicly, he bowed down low before Him. The queen was not only tolerated but applauded because she had now made herself a benefactor and confidante of Cuthbert, which had given Ecfrith access to that most holy of men and thereby to the Almighty God Himself. He took his revenge on Wilfrid and her desperate and repeated objections to that were crushingly ignored. He was sycophantic to Cuthbert. Yet he could see that the more powerful and the more savage he became, the less Cuthbert seemed to respect him.

Ecfrith's wealth was prodigious. His tributes were meticulously collected and ruthlessly increased. His conquests had brought the rents of hundreds of farms and estates into his coffers. The loot he had claimed after his victories in war was unparalleled.

The court at Bamburgh could now out-shine, out-glitter any court in the known world. Golden torques and armlets, ornamented swords, jewelled shields, silver helmets and bracelets. Both women and men had rings and clasps, belts and brooches of extraordinary designs – worked by the craftsmen Ecfrith had enslaved or bribed to come to the fortress. From Rome, Lyon and Paris merchants came bringing tapestries, pictures, relics and rare manuscripts, fine velvets, ancient curios, glass of many colours, rare stones and golden daggers.

Ecfrith loved ceremony. The necessary and regular feasts were turned into events of unimagined grandeur. All the most gorgeous jewellery and clothes would be displayed in competitive vying before the superlatively attired king. Players, jugglers and poets were sought throughout the conquered lands to come and perform at these events. In the sports, prizes of great value were offered to the bravest and the most skilful. His house warriors preened themselves in the fame of their master, seeing their own grow with it. His enemies were cowed by the cliff of awesome wealth which confronted them in the rock-strong fortress-palace. Though Ecfrith was of a temperament never to be satisfied, he found deep pleasure in his tyranny on such envied occasions.

Nothing remained to him but the final push: to the far north, the Picts, always a threat, never at ease with him, never conquered by the Romans; to the west, Rheged at last, despite Cuthbert's insistence that there was in that kingdom something which must never be violated. His credit with Cuthbert was deep, he thought: he could afford to risk his wrath one time. Rheged must be destroyed. And with it, Padric, too much admired, too dangerously, for too long.

First he would do what no one expected him to do. He would turn his fury on the most loved of places, the place where the Celts defied him with impunity, the land of milk and honey, the second Israel, the protector of his only rival, Aldfrid, his bastard brother. The most unsuspecting place on earth. A place on which an attack would raise him to the very throne of villainy in the eyes of some, while to others it would show that his determination to serve the forces of the pope, Peter's successor, the rock, Christ's chosen, knew no limits.

As he stood, posed on the ramparts of wind-blown Bamburgh in the full fig of his regalia, looked on by fearful slaves, guarded by his thegns and envied by all, he worked out his plan.

It was here, looking over the cold, leaden sea, skinned by white waves and brooded on by heavy clouds, fast moving, here where the wind whipped his face and ruffled the heavy cloak and made him feel so alive, that he most felt his power. Beyond this island, over that sea, was the source of his dark strength, a land infinitely strong which would send and send again men, warriors whose force would subdue the world. His ancestral tribes would now have their day and he, Ecfrith of Northumbria, would lead them. Who could prevail against him? Which army could match the might and force of his mass of men?

Yet to conquer men and kingdoms was not enough. He wanted to shout in the face of God who had cursed him with a chaste and

contemptuous wife, subjected him to imprisonment as a despised
hostage, humiliation before a preferred brother and, he feared,
derision as a ruler without heirs. All he had achieved he had
earned alone. Now, standing alone, to himself, he could get his
greatest revenge.

He would take up arms against God's most favoured land. And
do it with the blessing of God's most favoured priest. He smiled
and then he shouted into the wind at the exhilaration of the
idea. His cries shrivelled the hearts even of those hardened to
his cruelty.

He would raze all Ireland. He would crush it and destroy it and
do it in the name of the God of Rome.

ᏭᏭᏭᏭ

The dream had troubled Bega for some months but she ignored it
until that night. Then, with the wind swirling across the lake and
curling around the small buildings, whistling through the stones
and threatening all manner of devils unleashed in the storm, it
became too vivid to ignore.

In the dream she went once again up the mountain. She felt
its firmness under her feet. In front of her it rose up seemingly
endlessly, louring, a mass of rock. She clambered to be up it. She
stumbled and fell as the wind pushed her to the ground. She felt
its hardness on her palms, the splintering slate edges cut into her
rough hands.

She wanted to embrace this great thing, she did not know why.
Her body tightened with the desire to command and absorb it. It
was itself a force, pushing her, driving and demanding, exhausting
her. But she felt free, though in danger. She wanted to be in
danger. She did not know why the mountain was so threatening
and exciting to her but it was. In the dream, she crawled up its
steepest side. Danger became freedom. No one could feel this free.
No one should. It was a sin against the Holy Ghost but still she
climbed.

Below her, when she turned, she saw the valley which was her
home. But she saw it as hell. Fumes of cloud rose from it like

smoke from fire. She saw the scarred and ruined faces of young men and women, plague-pocked, sufferers from hunger, prey to incurable diseases, shivering in mysterious illness and fear all the days of their life. She looked harder and saw mouths agape with longing and in pain, a landscape of open mouths, empty gullets, thin cheeks, wide frantic eyes, the mouths moving the air crying agony for food, for drink, for any sustenance.

You must go on, said the dream. You must find out what this means. She would always wake up with this command.

After the dream had visited her seven times on seven nights, she decided to go up the mountain and seek out its meaning. She went alone, screwing up all her courage.

It was a dull day in early summer but as she toiled up the mountain so the clouds rose up and the sky cleared until there were only trails of veiled haze on the hard blue sky.

Strangely, as soon as she had left the woods and come on to the bare side of the mountain, her fears and the dark troubles of the nightmare began to slide away. When she looked back on the valley, she saw a peaceful settlement: from here, on high, it had the look of prosperity and harmony and the order of long-enjoyed peace. When she looked up the mountain it seemed neither threatening nor troubling but a friendly beast. Soon she came to a little rocky outcrop made for sitting down.

This was far enough, she decided. The dream had clearly been a device of the author of all deceit. Now that she had faced the mountain, God had simply vanquished the devil. She felt at peace and wished that she had had the good sense to do this before. She stroked her right cheek: it had become an habitual gesture and it soothed her.

As she sat, an awful stillness developed. Sound stopped. It was as if the whole earth had been silenced and the air itself was holding its breath. The moment seemed so long, so extended, as if it were all time, as if it were the end of time.

With a cry of fear, Bega slid to her knees and clasped her hands in prayer and looked to heaven. She heard the voice of Donal, who said: 'Bega you have done well. The Lord is pleased with you. As your prayers grow in strength, there need be no more plagues. Tell that to your people. And for a sign, tell them that the Lord your God has said that you, Bega, will be given for His church all the land covered white next Midsummer's Day. Tell all the people of this promise. Return here on Midsummer's Day.' The voice ended and the sounds of the earth slowly reassembled around her.

Bega was deeply disturbed by the message but did as she had been bid.

On Midsummer's Day she went to the mountain leading over two hundred souls. Only a few shepherds had been even half way up the mountain before. The rest stoked up their courage with singing and holding each other's hands and offering prayers through Bega to God.

The word had spread and the sick and the lame from miles around came in hope of one of Bega's miracles. The route took them past the settlement of Reggiani who recently had fallen ill. She stood at the gate of her household smiling, frail but resolute that she would not join the throng. Two of her own followers looked so imploringly at her that she encouraged them to join in. Midsummer Day for Reggiani did not begin until the sun had finally set.

The procession was a spectacular sight. Those who had not joined but stayed at their work in the fields looked up and envied the vast crowd steadily progressing over the heather up the mountain side.

It was a cold day with low, unbroken, dark-grey clouds. When they came to the rock outcrop where Bega had heard the voice from heaven, she stopped and kneeled to pray. Everyone followed her example. Then they waited.

Bega had now reconciled herself. Either it had been the voice of the tempter and her vanity had led her astray in which case God would surely strike her dead, or it could be the purest sign of all. They waited.

It began to hail. With no warning, no gentle introduction, hard pellets of hail spewed down from the sky. A dense curtain of the white, glittering shards. More and more heavily it came and then it stopped.

Bega stood and turned and held out her arms triumphantly. All the valley and all the hills around her were white, white, white.

'Let us praise our God,' she said, ecstatically, 'the Lord of All Creation. The prophecy has been fulfilled!'

Now she could be saved. This pure sign from God clearly meant that at last her soul was freed from its bondage of sin. She would be allowed to think that there might be a place for her in the company of the saved.

Bega felt a power of violent happiness. She could be saved! God had forgiven her. He had seen the sacrifice of Padric and then of Bede and knew that she followed Jesus Christ before all earthly lust and love. The arrow of her desire for Padric slid out of her heart and she put her hand to her breast. Yes! It was whole. The arrow was gone. She had come to God.

'Praise Him!' she said, loudly, the voice a clear bell of sound across the Midsummer whiteness: and the crowd below said 'Amen.'

chapter seventy-seven

Despite the ferocity of the waves, heaved high by the bitter wind which came from the north, Ecfrith's crew reached the island on which Cuthbert had once again established his life as a hermit. It was small and from the mainland appeared little more than a wave-lashed rock. It was not easy to land and Ecfrith and his men had to leap for their lives in order to get on to it. There was a tiny settlement built in stone: a place of worship and a place in which Cuthbert lived and studied and received those fewer and fewer guests allowed to visit.

For the first time in his life Ecfrith felt unsure of Cuthbert. He attributed that to the dream in which he had seen himself pitched from the rock of his castle at Bamburgh, into the boiling, ice-cold sea, there to be dragged down by his riches and jewels and ripped to pieces by wild-fanged sea beasts waiting under the waves. As before, he was fleeing to Cuthbert for reassurance.

He noticed the reluctance in Cuthbert's greeting but decided to ignore it. 'I have brought you food,' he said. 'Food which will last and some wine. And skins to keep you warm. I heard that you were fasting and praying outside in cold so severe that you could have been turned to stone.'

As Ecfrith laid out one present after another, he grew increasingly uneasy. Cuthbert's response was usually much warmer.

Ecfrith and Cuthbert were alone inside the high embankment which surrounded the small buildings. An embankment so high that all that could be seen, Cuthbert would explain, was the face of heaven. It was a place of such intense holiness that Ecfrith quickly became uncomfortable: the silence of the place and Cuthbert's unaccustomed willingness to let silence develop between the two of them disconcerted him. Perhaps Cuthbert had divined his impious

thoughts and plans about invading Ireland or heard rumours of his
latest evil – the raping of young Pictish virgins captured in a border
skirmish. Perhaps Cuthbert could see into his soul.

Eventually, out of deferential custom, Cuthbert yielded and
began to talk and, at Ecfrith's request, showed him around his
tiny kingdom: the small field where he grew his barley; the quern
and grindstone with which he ground it; the spring which God
had given the island; the minute church where prayers were offered
so many times a day and where the devil was fought in battles
sometimes lasting weeks on end.

Cuthbert, lapsing, despite his will, into his usual habit of
wanting to please the king, sought for something to entertain
him and began to talk to him about the marvellous poetry of
Caedmon.

'I have heard of him,' said Ecfrith, gratefully. 'He is in the
monastery which used to be ruled by Hilda. She found him.'

'Yes. He is a swineherd who had never been taught. He could
neither read nor write. But he began to compose verses. He slept
in the cowshed with the beasts and it was there that the inspiration
of God visited him. The words came to him in a dream. He
remembered them. And he would sing what had never been heard
before. He is a glory of God. And so you, my lord, as God's high
king on earth, must be careful to cherish the weakest and the most
defenceless for fear that by accident or neglect, you stamp out His
glorious work.'

Ecfrith pulled his thick robes more tightly about him. They
were standing on the edge of the island which looked out to what
seemed a limitless leaden sea and sky, the two merging into a fast
wall of severe majesty.

'Look what He can do,' said Cuthbert, pointing to the waves
which split into ten thousand particles as they launched themselves against the rock. 'This rock is the faith of our God;
the sea is the force of the devil which for all its fury cannot
prevail.'

'Cuthbert,' said Ecfrith, suddenly kneeling before him, 'I came
here to ask you two things. The first, that you become a bishop as
was prophesied.'

'Must I?' Cuthbert's cry of dismay was unfeigned. 'See what the
Lord has allowed me to do here. Here I am His naked soul in
unremitting contact with His great enemy, showing him day by

day that even a lowly servant of the Lord our God can withstand all Satan's deceits and lies and punishments.'

Ecfrith looked around in awe that such a bare, near barren, rain-lashed, exposed and isolated spot could yield such passion. But he did not waver.

'It was prophesied,' he said, 'that you should become a bishop and soon there will be a see vacant and worthy of you. I have come ahead of that time, as your friend, to prepare you. Next time, I shall come with other bishops and monks, with a host of holy and learned men and women whose prayers will surely prise you from this sacred rock.'

Cuthbert lowered his head. He knew the prophesy. It had been made long before by a bishop who had favoured him greatly. The prophesy was not to be denied and it was that alone which made him fear that he would some day have to leave the island.

'But do you not see that it will plunge me back into the temptations I have come here to resist? All the splendours of the earth are there and I am weak enough to lust for them. When I am away from them I despise them. When I am near them I am disturbed by them. Why do you want me to engage in such a small struggle when the greater battle and the greater glory lies here?'

'Who knows where glory lies?' Ecfrith asked smoothly and, with hardly a pause, 'If I were to take my army and enforce the will of God in parts which have not fully accepted His proper ways – would that not be glory even though on the way there would be blood spilt?'

'Some innocent blood?'

'Yes,' said Ecfrith, braving it out, 'some innocent blood.' Would Cuthbert see what he was about to do?

'There have been battles in which the innocent perished but the greater glory was to the Lord,' Cuthbert said finally.

'And the truly innocent,' Ecfrith rushed in, 'those who were truly Christian would surely be received into heaven.'

Cuthbert did not deny this.

Ecfrith was elated.

'Then there is God's blessing on such a thing as a holy war,' he concluded, all but giving everything away, for Cuthbert looked at him closely – but finally he assented.

Ecfrith then told Cuthbert his troubling dream.

'The rock,' said Cuthbert, 'is the rock of faith. The riches and jewels and heavy cloak – these are the luxuries of the world. You fear that these will drag you down into the teeth of hell. God is telling you to give Him some of your earthly riches – to lighten yourself for the greatest battle and journey of all.'

'And if I do this – if I give more estates and money to the church – will I be let into heaven? Remember what was said: "It is easier for a camel to pass through the eye of a needle than a rich man to enter the heavenly kingdom".'

'Our Lord was issuing a warning,' said Cuthbert. 'Learn from it and you will be saved.'

'So I need not fear the dream?'

Ecfrith looked intently at Cuthbert. The dream had frightened him. It was simple but relentless and he had woken up in fear far too often. But Cuthbert – he was certain of this – could exorcise it.

'Will it go away?'

Cuthbert was well aware of Ecfrith's anxiety and his endless aching for reassurance. He knew that he could relieve it now as he had done in the past. But the longer the king stared at him, the more sensitive Cuthbert grew to a stench of foulness. He knew the evil of this man. He knew the dream could be interpreted in a completely different way – as a revelation of the man's understandable fear of retribution for his horrifying sins. He knew that Ecfrith saw him, Cuthbert, as his passage to the heavenly life. Sometimes Cuthbert wondered if Ecfrith believed in heaven at all. Whatever the cause, Cuthbert's blessing was absolutely essential to him.

Was it better to take him for a good man and bless him and keep him on the side of God? Or condemn him and cast him out and thereby lose him and all his court and wealth and influence to the earthly kingdom? Which was of the greater benefit?

Ecfrith would not break this silence.

'I give you my blessing,' said Cuthbert, and wondered why a feeling of nausea swept through him.

To conceal his triumph, Ecfrith stayed longer and joined the hermit in prayers and talked to him about the monasteries he would endow in his kingdom. Finally he was rowed away carrying with him Cuthbert's blessing like the rarest battle honour.

⚜⚜⚜

'Although you have lived in my valley for many years,' said Reggiani, 'you know little about me and my ways.'

'I know enough to want you to change them,' Bega replied.

'But that is not enough.' Reggiani smiled and Bega was touched by it. Sitting opposite Bega in her little parlour which had become somewhat less spartan over the years, was a frail woman, Bega thought, suddenly so much older, hardly connected with the powerful and vivacious she-priest of the recent past. But then she, too, was much older, stiff-jointed, greying – although her face was still wonderfully full of energy.

'Even now,' said Reggiani, speaking with some difficulty, feeling the weight of cold and stiffness and pain in her chest, 'when there is something I want to tell you, to help you, you will not come to me, I must walk to you.'

Bega flushed but said nothing.

'I have listened to you and talk of your God,' said Reggiani, wanting to waste no more time. She had, she knew, little of it left. 'I have often puzzled over it. I have questioned many in the valley about it and many have left my ways for yours.' She smiled and once again Bega was weakened by the sweetness of the smile. 'After all, someone who can turn the earth white on Midsummer's Day . . .'

'It was God, not I.'

'But it was you, not God, that people saw.'

'I am glad that the power of the Lord brought converts to His way,' said Bega, stoutly. 'Miracles are necessary for those of us who struggle in His cause. They prove His greatness.'

'You have become a miracle woman,' said Reggiani, without irony. 'Perhaps that is why you were spared the dangers of childbirth.'

Bega swayed a little. It was as if the mocking demon of longing and memory had suddenly entered the room.

So much passed through her mind that she had to breathe deeply.

Reggiani, who had not made the remark to wound Bega, saw that she had unsettled her and waited for it to pass. 'There was another like you,' she continued. 'The mother of my mother who lived here in this same valley but further along the lake. She too was known for miracles. But she followed our gods not your sole God. So I think that perhaps there are miracles waiting to happen and the gods choose whoever is most deserving. Do you think that?'

Bega made no comment.

'You are very like us,' said Reggiani, thoughtfully. 'I have studied you. Your father, from what Urien tells me, and all of your past, is full of the history and spirits which we in these valleys and you in Ireland have in common.' Reggiani held out her hand. 'I feel that we are cousins. Yet your great God insists on dividing us.'

'He comes to unite,' said Bega, slowly re-establishing her balance. 'It is others who divide.'

Reggiani let her arm drop down. 'You must see what we have on our side.' Reggiani gathered her diminished forces. 'You have no curiosity. Can your God really know everything about all there is to know and to know in the future? Do you know what powers have been handed down to me? Do you know of our Druid priests – many of them women like myself and my mother and her mother – whom the previous conquerors feared so much? Do you know of the women among us who were great warriors and teachers – equal on all counts with men? Do you know that like other tribes we take our inheritance alongside our brothers? When we marry we can divorce in a year if we are not satisfied, and the law does not punish us. Those are some of the traditions which are ours and which I see being driven out with so much else by your church. Not by you. But, as Urien tells me, you are a small voice. The real church, which persecutes the monks who used to flee for their lives through this valley, wants to cut down all our traditions. I am here, probably for the last time, because I am curious to know answers to questions. Your God makes you all obey so much. So many rules. So many "nots" – that is what Urien calls them. "Thou shalt *not*" he says, "and thou shalt not and not and not!"' She smiled to think of him. 'Do you want to be the sort of woman who becomes a slave?'

'If by slave you mean servant,' said Bega steadily and then, flaring up, 'or even slave. The slave of God I am proud to be.'

'I am amazed,' said Reggiani. 'Did no one tell you of the women who have been your ancestors? Women who led in battle. Women who turned into fish. Women who brought kings into their bodies to make more kings. Women who beguiled sailors for hundreds of years and then turned them into ashes.' Reggiani coughed a little, a short, hard spasm. She waved away Bega's move to help. 'I want you to know that I am from a religion more ancient than yours and more astonishing.'

'The Lord of all creation is unequalled in His miracles,' said Bega, gently.

'That is not true,' said Reggiani, flushed now and insistent, 'I see you taking over the valley and I fear for what will happen to my ways which have done so much good.'

'The Lord of Hosts will overcome all on the face of the earth.'

'No!' Reggiani cried. 'No! He must allow a place for others. He cannot simply be such a cruel tyrant to murder anyone who stands in his way.'

'His kingdom come,' said Bega implacably, 'His will be done. On earth as it is in heaven.'

'I cannot accept that,' said Reggiani, 'nor, I prophesy, will it be accepted. Even your story – I have heard Chad recite it many times – about how life was made is not as true as ours . . . Life began,' said Reggiani, softly, drawing in Bega's closest attention, 'when the virgin of the air came down from the sky and entered into the airless sea. The sea and the winds breathed life into her and after swimming in that sea for seven centuries she gave birth to the first being.'

'I will hear no more,' said Bega.

'There is so much more,' Reggiani begged. 'So much I want you to know about *our* heroes and our heroines – like the saints I learn of from Chad . . . as I know yours, you must know mine because they have brought so much good to the earth, Bega, and now their spirits are all around us, in the winds and the trees, sometimes locked in a stone or passing in a cloud, everywhere in the water, and they will cry out if they are ignored and made mute by this cruel one God of yours. You must let them have life, Bega. You must speak for them in this world or they will burst their bonds and come back from the spirit world to destroy all that is good. You cannot expel them from life!'

Reggiani was glistening with perspiration now. Bega felt the force of her plea but prayed for the power to resist it.

'I will pray for you, Reggiani,' she said, after a pause. It was said humbly but it was decisive.

Reggiani made as if to go and then said, 'One last thing. Urien tells me a little about his brother Padric. He is a hero for us as well as for you. He will be like Arthur was – though he will not replace Arthur for it is ordained in *our* songs that no one will equal him – but he is for all the people and all their beliefs because his belief is in a people. A people is many. Your God is too much one. But I ask you this, Bega. Again, it is no more than curiosity. Urien tells me of their life, the harshness, the perils, the despair as well as the victories. Urien also tells me that Padric grieves for you.' Bega put her hand on her heart as if to hold it from leaping. Reggiani smiled faintly and saw it all. 'And, Bega, you grieve for him.' She shook her head as Bega rose to protest. 'Tell me, tell me from your heart, Bega, why is it that your God will not allow you to be together with him? Why is it that you will not bear children from this man? Why is it that your God denies you the pleasure that I have had so often, of a man's body beside yours and all that follows? Why does your God torment you, Bega? Please tell me. I want to understand.'

Bega looked at the frail, sick, old woman, the lineaments of her great beauty still to be seen, her hair still thick though grey now, her eyes, so often amused, now searching for an answer.

'Why is He so cruel to you, Bega? Why will He not let you be with Padric?'

Bega's throat tightened as a fierce access of tears threatened to sweep over her. Why? Yes, why did He demand this?

'So that I can prove my greater love for Him,' she murmured, falteringly, and turned her face to the wall and eventually composed her feelings.

When she turned back, Reggiani was gone.

chapter seventy-eight

K ing Ecfrith was triumphant but shrewd. Cuthbert had not specifically sanctioned the invasion of Ireland although he would have to admit that he had, in effect, blessed it. But Ecfrith knew enough about the reverence in which Ireland and the Irish were held, even by hard Romanists, to be afraid of soiling his own hands. At his council of war, therefore, he excused himself, saying to his ten leading eldormen that 'it is a land undefended, unprepared for any attack, with few military households and those small and scattered. It has no great king, no single army. It is dedicated to the arts of peace and not the rigours of war, in brief it is the easiest of conquests. Save for one thing: Prince Padric of Rheged, his brothers and their men. They have spent an increasing amount of time in Ireland recently at the court of Aldfrid who pretends he has a claim on this throne. Some of you have seen Rheged's men in battle. They are neither as valiant nor as skilful as our warriors but by cunning and magic and deceit of all kinds, they have caused us some harm. It is better that Padric is out of Ireland when you get there.'

'Why not leave him there? He will never be easier to kill.'

'I have other plans,' said Ecfrith. 'He will be dead very soon.'

The company, who had met together in the new vast hall built at Bamburgh to show off Ecfrith's ever-expanding wealth, were satisfied enough with that. Padric was, to most of them, a feared but ever elusive figure: someone who came out of the woods, raided swiftly and retreated. Known for tricks such as dressing up his men as monks thereby gaining entrance to courts which he would then attack from within. The legend of Padric and his men as the hooded and cowled men of justice from the forests had bitten deeply into the popular imagination. He took from the rich, they said, only to give to the poor. The legend irritated Ecfrith. It included him as the villainous tyrant. He saw it as yet another trick of Padric's. Those few who had met him and lived were disinclined to say much save that he was indeed a man of legend.

'He is now a force,' said Ecfrith, gauging the mood of his men with his usual foxiness. It was his policy never to let them settle into an opinion, always to present alternatives which gave him the certainty of claiming clairvoyance. 'He can rally his own small band and inspire even the monkish Irish, perhaps, to inflict more wounds than we need for such an adventure as this. This raid is a chance to build up your wealth. I have told your commander what things I want and he will bring them to me. But they are few. The plunder of this war is yours. And you are going to a country with the richest jewels on earth, with tapestries and golden bowls, with manuscripts of silver and emeralds and rubies, with fine strong horses and, we are told, beautiful women to bring back as your slaves. All that you can carry is yours. I will not be there to take my half.'

This prospect made them restless: why could they not go immediately.

'What I will do,' continued Ecfrith, 'is to say that we are march-ing north against the Picts. I will proclaim this tomorrow morning and make sure that the message is carried far, even into Ireland. We will wait for some days, maybe seven, maybe ten, maybe more. Then we will set off to the northlands – at leisure – with as much noise as we can make. This will draw Padric from Ireland. It is in the land of the Picts that he thinks he can conquer me.

'You remember the spy we captured? Well, when he had lost his ears he agreed to tell us what he knew of his former master's plans. It is in the far northlands that Padric has drawn up his plan. And I laugh. Because they are so weak. Whatever his plan, it cannot succeed there. But he will go there – he will race there to be ready for us. And we will never arrive, for bit by bit our army will slip away and ride to the other sea, take the boats and reassemble where there is no one at all to hinder your rich and wealthy progress.'

Ecfrith's plan worked out precisely as he had proposed. What he had not told his men were the two things that he had told to his chief eldorman. The first, that the head of Aldfrid be brought back as a trophy. Second, that the devastation of Ireland be merciless.

It was reported that there had never been slaughter and rape and brutality on such a scale. News came back from Ireland of a whole convent of nuns attacked and mutilated, their sex abused, their breasts severed, their tapestries and manuscripts torn away and crumpled into saddlebags; of monks whose bellies had been ripped open and live rats put in before the belly was roughly stitched up again; of the few men with arms, surrounded and given no quarter so that even the mighty O'Neills were cut down and only the boys escaped to race into the hills and brood over their hatred for another day; of graceful and beautiful monasteries put to fire; of those cattle and horses which were not herded back towards the boats, slaughtered; of men and women and children brought back as slaves and sold on into the lands where the Germanic tribes had come from; of the cries and prayers unanswered and the search for the source of a sin so big that such a punishment was the reckoning. Why God's wrath on His new chosen people?

Aldfrid escaped. Padric, who had indeed made his way to the northlands, came back with all speed when the news reached him: but too late. The harassment, the murder and pillage, was over, and the English, as the Northumbrians were now called, returned on their crowded boats back to their fortresses. They left behind an island once thought of as especially favoured by God, devastated.

In the monasteries of Northumbria, many monks were angrily ashamed – Coelfrith, Abbot of Wearmouth and greatly dependent on the patronage of the royal household, was bold enough publicly to lament and deplore the unnecessary invasion. It was, he told all his followers, including Bede, an act against God who would surely have justice. Bede had never heard his master preach such a passionate sermon.

Cuthbert, now translated to his episcopal see, cringed at the very thought of it and knew now, in his heart, that Ecfrith had come to him for a blessing for the slaughter – and he had given it. He felt his body go hot and cold as the guilt and shame of it skewered his soul. Surely God would understand? Surely he had done what was God's will? He led the monastery in prayers for the souls of their Irish brothers, prayers which, for him, lasted until he fainted from hunger and cramp.

At first, Bega could not believe it. The traveller from Caerel who brought the news was so inflamed with stories of torture and courage that he was incoherent. Chad was despatched to the city and came back after two days with a report which made her weep. Now indeed Armageddon was near.

Cheated of the head of Aldfrid, Ecfrith stripped the man who had led the expedition and had him flogged, his immense plunder divided between the other leaders. This, announced Ecfrith to a large assembly ranged in the courtyard on the rock, this punishment and shame – for the man would be cast out – was because his order to gain the allegiance of the Irish had been so grossly misinterpreted. He, King Ecfrith, loved the learning and piety of the Irish monks and nuns. It was well known. At his own court were craftsmen from Ireland – welcomed – and many monks from Ireland had chosen to stay in his kingdom despite God's judgment at Whitby. He was no Herod and this public flogging of the villain who had destroyed too much in Ireland would show the world and high heaven that he repented the sins of those who had so wickedly used his name to scorch the earth of that fair garden of God.

When Padric and Aldfrid finally met they were too numb for some time to say much. Then Aldfrid gave Padric details which shook both him who told and him who listened.

'It is the time,' said Padric, 'for the final battle.'

'You are so greatly outnumbered,' said Aldfrid.

They were in the burnt-out monastery where Padric and Aldfrid had over several years built up a friendship. Aldfrid had come back to it as soon as he had been told that the invaders had left.

'We will always be outnumbered,' said Padric. 'I watch the invaders grow. I see Ecfrith now circling for the kill. What is left of Arthur's ancient kingdom are a few isolated territories and an idea which becomes more lustrous as it grows less attainable. I have tried to bring together the remains of Britain. It is near impossible. When Dumnonia is with us, Wales is not; when the

Picts are in battle formation, neither Wales nor Dumnonia nor the New Britons overseas nor Rheged itself is ready. I have failed.' It took effort to admit that and he waved away Aldfrid's consoling objection. 'We are not only too few, we have been divided out of power.'

The butchery and the despoliation all about him had finally decided him. There could be no more waiting. The time was now. There was certainty in his tone.

'What we will do now is take our stand and trust in God. I have spent my life trying to put together an alliance which would gradually build up to challenge the might of the invaders. Again and again I have seen it within my grasp but it has always slipped away. Now I am sure. I will go back to the northlands and tell Ecfrith that I am there and waiting for him there. The Picts say they will join me. I will send messengers to Wales and Dumnonia and Little Britain over the sea but put no trust in them. This is for the kingdom of Arthur to settle: it is right that it should be enacted by those who come from his estate and from his house. If we die, we will die well. Ecfrith will come north. He will be so puffed up with pride that he will not be able to resist. He will see this as the last conquest, the battle which will make him emperor of the whole island. I will feed him stories to draw him into battle.'

'I will come with you,' said Aldfrid.

'No.' Padric was quietly emphatic. 'You must stay alive. I will kill Ecfrith. I may be killed. You have to be alive to take his throne.' Padric looked at him and smiled. 'Our kingdom could be in worse hands. Maybe I was never destined to rule but only to prepare the way. Maybe that is why the alliances eluded me. I am not Arthur. Perhaps he will live on in you. You are a Christian. You are a scholar. You will respect the kingdom of Rheged and all the other British kingdoms and let them grow. You will pursue the life of worship and carry forward the word of God just as you did here. But,' the smile went away, 'make sure this time that you have an army to protect you.'

Aldfrid argued against the decision but Padric was not to be persuaded and Aldfrid knew better than to ride where he was not wanted.

'Give me your blessing,' said Padric and bent his head.

'God will give you the victory,' said Aldfrid. 'We will pray for that.' He looked around at the wreckage left by Ecfrith's men. The scholar slipped off and the warrior prince came through. 'I want vengeance. That man is the devil's captain. "Vengeance is mine," said the Lord. And you, Padric, are now His right arm.'

'If you move north,' said Cuthbert, 'you will be in danger.'

'From a few Picts and one British prince? They will run away when they see the size of our armies.'

'It is a time for prayer not for war,' said Cuthbert. 'I fear for you on another expedition. It is tempting the favour of God.'

For once, Ecfrith was inclined to feel superior to Cuthbert. Here in his fortress he felt at the summit of his powers. His strategy of publicly criticising the Irish raid followed by an ostentatious display of repentance and the showering of many gifts on monasteries and nunneries throughout all regions with Celtic communities, had worked rather well. The people either blamed his eldormen or were confused. Ecfrith had escaped the brunt of the blame. Cuthbert now, in his bishop's robes, completed his sense of superiority. He had outwitted and outmanoeuvred them all – even Cuthbert and Cuthbert's God! And he had kept the best until the last.

With one strike he would conquer the fractious Picts and eliminate his troublesome cousin Padric. This would enable him finally to lay waste and utterly destroy the obstinate last redoubt of the kingdom of Britain which, however fragmented, had for so long haunted his days. Britain, it was always prophesied, would never be conquered. No matter how pinned down and seeming enslaved, no matter how ruined and pummelled, yet it would rise up again and fight for its own particular rights and laws and traditions.

He, King Ecfrith, would end all that. A mighty kingdom would fall at last, people whose ancestry and powers stretched back beyond any Roman conqueror, would finally be wiped out utterly and the world would know that Ecfrith, in early days so humiliated, King Ecfrith alone had done this.

'I want you to go to Rheged,' he said to Cuthbert, 'to Caerel. Take my wife with you. Say you are there to look at the working of my laws and the laws of your church – which is true. But be in Caerel for several days and tell me, Cuthbert, when I return, tell me what they said when their kingdom was lost.'

chapter seventy-nine

Reggiani believed that it was her powers which brought Urien to see her for the last time. He had in truth come to Rheged to cull the final crop of recruits for the battle which lay ahead. It was convenient to see Reggiani. She lay on his journey along the Celtic escape route in from the west coast.

'I am very sick,' she said simply, seeing the undisguised shock on his face.

Urien kneeled beside the bed and attempted no sentimental deceit. Reggiani even felt that he was rather impatient with her – he had not come to nurse her. Or perhaps, like all warriors, he was deeply superstitious of being with the dying.

'What ails you?'

'I have diverted so many evil spirits from others. They caught me when I was sleeping and now they have their revenge.'

'Are you dying?'

'Yes. I am dying.'

Urien nodded. He recognised courage and he took her hand. Now he could face her for she had faced the finality.

'You would have been a fine warrior, Reggiani.'

'I would have liked that,' she said. Her voice was soft now but, in response to his affection, it warmed and grew a little stronger.

'You are going to a great battle,' she said.

Urien registered no surprise. Her power of foresight was one of her fascinations for him. He looked with unaccustomed tenderness on this once flaxen-haired woman, so bold, so sure of her medicines and her spiritual powers, so generous in her healing, her wisdom and her sex. He realised how deeply he cared for her. He had a son, not by her, and he had felt once or twice a similar brief vertigo of love, but soon passed it by. As if exploring his own mind, he reached out and touched her face, an unusual, gentle touch.

'It will be a terrible battle, this one,' said Reggiani.

'It is the one Padric has waited for all his life.'

'And you? Have you waited for it?'

Urien smiled again and stroked her forehead, surprised by the dry heat of it. 'Whatever comes along,' he said, 'Padric is the one with the dreams.'

'We need the dream of Padric. Our dreams become our lives. You must dream now, of victory.'

'We'll see,' said Urien. 'They're good fighters. There'll be many more of them than us.'

'You will have to use cunning,' Reggiani whispered. 'Where force will not conquer, cunning will.'

'Ecfrith himself is a fox.'

'But he will be unaware of what you have.'

'He has good scouts.'

'But he is not a desperate man. For Padric this has become his sole purpose on earth. This battle is why he was born.'

'Sometimes,' Urien grinned widely and Reggiani smiled in response to that craggy, tooth-broken, lip-scarred grin, 'sometimes he talks like that.' He laughed. 'Truth is – he's always talked like that!'

'What do you think?'

'I want to beat them,' said Urien, steadily, 'I want them driven out of here.'

'Listen to me then,' said Reggiani. She sat up, unable quite to suppress the groan of pain which this simple action released. Urien put his arm around her back and was surprised once again: how bony her shoulders were, how thin and fragile she was. She took some deeper breaths and said: 'To win this battle you must seem to lose it. To advance you will have to flee. To be heroes you must first seem cowards. He who gains the victory will lose all. Tell this to Padric and say that the raven spoke it.'

Urien nodded.

'You must go now,' she said, 'and do your work.' He lowered her back on to the bed. 'When you return I shall be gone from this body. They will burn me and cast me on the lake so that I can join all the others. This place will always be sweet to me. My spirit will be in these woods and when you call me, I shall be there.'

The soldier stroked her brow once more and watched until she fell asleep.

He ate some food, made his way over to Bega's chapel for a short time and then went to find soldiers.

❧❧❧❧

Bega and Chad were now alone in the settlement. The two old friends, for that is what they had become, went their ways almost without words to each other.

Chad now understood or at least accepted Bega's reasons for not letting him stay with Bede. He buried his pain in work. Chad had always worked hard but now he allowed no gap of time which could let in the destructive forces of regret and lost hope. He farmed, he fed the animals, he kept the buildings clean and he redoubled his efforts to teach children to read and write. Just as Bega had done to him, he would try to tempt them to the lake shore, with twigs of ash to draw in the mud, or twigs and pebbles to shape the letters. Besides all this he was attentive to Bega, watching her health and her moods daily, hourly, living by her.

Bega had cut down the servants. Two men helped Chad outside and a girl from a settlement nearby came at dawn and left at sunset six days of the week.

This still left much for her to do. She followed the same routine of services which she had inherited from Hilda even when only Chad and herself were there, although others put in an appearance on Sundays and fast days. When they had guests, the little chapel would regain some of the small intimacy of a real congregation. And on festival days the numbers were greater. Sometimes there were crowds. Year by year Bega's fame grew. The armlet Padric had given her became the object they all wanted to touch. Drinking the water from the spring under the cross was increasingly reputed to have healing powers. And that water, mixed with a little earth on which Bega had trod could be used to salve wounds and fever.

Bega regretted that the place was not more isolated. She also regretted that this fame interfered with her evangelical work. On the one hand she longed to be allowed a hermit's life but knew that she would never deserve it. On the other she still dreamed of vast journeys to dark places on the earth and the opportunity to bring pagan souls to God. On her best days she saw that God had given her something of both and she praised Him for His wisdom.

And there were times just after dawn, under the awesome canopy of the dark sky slowly lightening to day, or just after sunset when lingering streaks of light made a last play before the darkness, when she walked beside the lake and glanced up to the mountain and felt a sense of bliss, a deep calm, a spring of peace. This was why she had been born. God had blessed her. Finally she lived for the faith and the life was good.

Urien's hurried visit, his brief indirect talk, ended the calm. Padric was putting himself into the greatest danger.

Now she could pray for him and in those prayers be serving God. For Padric was fighting for the ancient true Christian kingdom and God would be well served by a victory. Therefore to pray for him was to please God. And to pray for him meant that, legitimately, she could once more luxuriate in the thought of him, the image of him, his name on her lips to be loud on the air which formed it and she felt blessed even though she feared for him. She could be with him without sin.

Erebert had been sent word that Cuthbert was to visit Caerel and despite his savage rheumatism and previous resolution never again to leave the island, he had set out to walk through the twisting valleys and down to the plain.

The years had been quite kind to him save for these bodily aches which he welcomed as evidence that he was worthy of a severe trial. His gaunt, ascetic face looked younger than his years under the billowing, snow-white hair. Time had eroded his awkwardness of gesture although he was still fussy. His life on the island had survived so much that even those who had ignored or resented him came to regard him as a talisman. There were those who were persuaded that he was a truly holy man and although no miracles attended him, he was a presence much valued. When sick or troubled souls had rowed over to see him, he had rarely been found wanting in sympathy and sound advice. Moreover he was not a tax on the community. Often those who came to give left with more than they brought.

Most of all, it was known that around the lake there had been less suffering from the plague than in many other areas and there were several who attributed this to the steadfast presence of Erebert.

Cuthbert had arrived with Ecfrith's queen – now returned from the abbey of Ely. She had brought with her a score of courtiers and twenty-four soldiers as guards. The purpose of the visit was for Cuthbert, as bishop of Lindisfarne, to assess whether Caerel should have its own bishopric. Ecfrith had been particularly keen that his wife travel across country with Cuthbert and sent them off in rare style. As they went along the road beside the wall, there were those who thought it was the king himself.

Many reached out to touch the magnificent gold cross set with garnets recently given to Cuthbert by the queen and worn around his neck, at her request, day and night, a symbol, she said, of the communion of earthly beauty and his heavenly spirit. This cross had become a thing of power and fame: just to touch it was to be favoured by God. Cuthbert tried not to flinch as the hands of the poor and, often, the afflicted, reached up, clawed up towards his neck.

Cuthbert suffered at the extravagance of it all. Even though his bishop's cope was little less splendid than the queen's own fine embroidered coat, he still thought of himself as a mendicant and it was poverty of pocket and appearance which gave him comfort. This show was to offer a temptation to the devil.

Yet this ambling mission to Caerel had so far proved to be beneficial. The road they took was safe. They were met by pious people. They were going to a town which had been a Christian place for centuries and was strengthened every day in its Christianity.

Cuthbert was welcomed like a potentate, which indeed he seemed. All the dignitaries of Caerel had ridden out to meet himself and the queen and escort them into the city, where a feast had been prepared in their honour. Cuthbert had to be persuaded to attend the feast and it was only after a strong plea from the queen that he agreed to go.

First, having heard that Erebert was in the city, he sought him out and, when they met, which was soon after Erebert had arrived and sunk exhausted on to his cot in the guest house, he insisted on washing the feet of the hermit and bringing him food for his dinner before he himself touched a morsel. Erebert's fame, already well established in the city, soared.

Word of Cuthbert's act of humility hummed around the monastery.

Cuthbert rubbed ointment into the old man's joints and gave him some rare oil, a present to him from the queen. Oil which had powers to ease the pain that troubled Erebert so much.

'I still have my prayer of our death,' said Erebert.

'You do me too much honour.'

'No, God willing, you will guide me into heaven.'

'It is you who will guide souls there,' said Cuthbert, firmly. 'Your long fight against the forces of darkness, your solitude on that island, resisting so many enticements, stepping over the slyly laid snares and traps of the devil, that is true grace. I bow to you, Erebert. I ask your blessing. It is you who will be my guide.'

The monks were amazed to see Cuthbert prostrate himself before the hermit. Several resolved on the spot to make a pilgrimage to Erebert's island as soon as Cuthbert and the queen had left the city.

'There are still many wonders to come from you,' said Erebert, overwhelmed by the attention being paid to him by one whose life he revered. 'You will be the rock of our church here in this kingdom. On you and your saintliness the church will be founded and it will never fail.'

'Thanks be to God,' said the monks who heard all this. 'Alleluia.'

'Let us all pray,' said Cuthbert.

The city of Caerel had put on its best for the queen. Nothing in Northumbria had its ancient stone grandeur. If Ecfrith were beginning to think in imperial terms then here, in massive buildings, in the forum, however depleted, and the amphitheatre, however overgrown, and in the great houses, was a standard for him. There were those who hoped that Caerel could become Ecfrith's capital and once more the centre of the whole land.

When Cuthbert was being shown around the Roman remains in the city, he stopped dramatically beside a Roman well and looked up into the sky and suddenly fell on his knees. There was a turbulence in the air, a wildness about the clouds, a twisting, turning wind, a sense of disorder.

'There is a battle on this day,' said Cuthbert, his eyes closed, his hands tight clasped. He said no more for a while but thought – this is why Ecfrith sent us away; this is why he wanted his peace-loving queen who had so criticised him for the Irish massacres, and myself, to be on the other side of the country. Ecfrith was going to slaughter the Picts and the British in a final battle. An unnecessary battle. A battle unprovoked and unworthy of a king of so vast a kingdom and with so many other kingdoms giving him tribute.

Cuthbert stood and looked at the queen.

'We must go back,' he said. 'What is to happen will judge us all. This is a battle foretold.'

❦❦❦❦

Bega stood on the shore until the boat had burned itself out. About two dozen of Reggiani's followers and friends had taken her body to the lake. More might have come had there not been a fear that to support Reggiani was to oppose Bega.

It was true. Although Bega had been attracted to Reggiani, and admired her, she saw her more and more as one who prevented souls from preparing for heaven. As such she was an enemy of God and no amount of understanding and attention could weaken Bega's determination to prove herself and her God superior. But she did not interfere.

She had watched them put the body in the coracle and set it about with dry rushes. She had not interfered when they had laden the boat with gifts and the jewels of Reggiani to prepare her well for her journey to the next world. She had stood back when the old man from a nearby farming valley who was also a pagan priest had prayed aloud in his fashion and invited the flowing wave, the soothing wind, the warming sun, the guiding moon, the nourishing earth, the consoling stars, the growing rain, and all the spirits of their ancestors to come and escort the boat to the new land. When he had done, he and others towed out the laden bier and, in the middle of this lake which was to them holy, he had set fire to it and praised the god of fire for taking Reggiani into the next world.

Bega had listened to all this with hostility but still she did not interfere.

She watched until the boat burnt itself out and the embers in the dusk were reflected in the calm mirror of the blackening lake. Only when the last glow was gone did she kneel and pray that God would give her the strength to convert those whose paths were so far from the true way; and pray especially, even at this late hour, for the soul of Reggiani.

CHAPTER EIGHTY

As Ecfrith rode north he thought that the earth trembled under the power and the majesty of his army. In all the years of his kingship he had never ridden at the head of such forces. The army of Arthur had been a gang of thieves by comparison. His favourite poet had told him that only when the Romans had ruled all the world and terrorised the land with their might, only then had there been anything to compare. And the Romans, said the poet, had never conquered the Picts. It would be given to Ecfrith to do that and be called more than any Roman emperor.

He moved up the coastal strip at his leisure. The weather favoured him – hard summer sun, warm on the face through the day and easy on the body when they camped out through the night. To the east the sea twinkled and sparkled, flicked by a light breeze. At some stages they rode along the firm white shore. When the tide was out they could be thirty or forty abreast and Ecfrith felt that no army on earth could match this one.

He swivelled around to gaze at what was his glory. Thousands, thousands of men had come for this easy victory. They wore their finest armour, dressed more for feasting than fighting. Helmets shone back the hard sun, polished shields glittered in the jostle of the horses and ponies, the tips of spears and the blades of swords flashed and winked as if delighted to be on this romp of a war. The wealth of the Picts, so remote, so long unconquered because of their mountain fortresses and the hitherto accepted impossibility of holding what you might overcome, had become mythical. No one thought that death was possible: all believed that enormous booty as in Ireland would fall into their hands.

Never had there been such wealth on the hoof in this island, Ecfrith thought. The increased power of his kingdom, the many tributes, the recent plunder from Ireland, the money engendered from the farms, the woodlands and the sea had made him mighty. London itself, becoming again as active and metropolitan a market as it had been under the Romans, and drawing in peoples from all the known world, now quailed at reports of Ecfrith's northern army but happily sold its skills or its products at his lavish orders.

Most of all Ecfrith prized his sword. The buckle was of gold and garnets; the wooden scabbard was lined with a wood chosen for its oily texture; the blade had been made from eight bundles of iron rods hammered together to form a patterned core to which the cutting edge of high carbon steel was forged. Between the gold and garnet guards on the hilt was a wooden handgrip while the pommel was made up of five separate units, each carved with different animal motifs. There were bosses on the scabbard, decorated with a petalled design containing an equal-armed cross. Exquisite tiny pyramidical mounts made of gold and set with cloisonné garnets were the wonder of a sword of wonders: one which would remain the king's sword, Ecfrith had decided, long after his day.

The sword had been made in London. Ecfrith had brought the craftsmen into his kingdom. Even the leather belt was fitted with gold and garnet buckles and other fittings. Ecfrith knew of only one sword in any way comparable – that of Padric. But though Padric's long sword was renowned for the blood it had shed and the lives it had ended, no one dared claim that its lustre even began to compare with the sword of Ecfrith.

Ecfrith's iron helmet had been made by the same craftsmen. The cap was formed from a single piece of iron, the ear-flaps and the broad neck-guard, also of iron, were cleverly hinged to it, as was the mask which covered the upper half of his face. The surface of the iron was covered in bronze and panelled and decorated with scenes from his triumphs – a boar's head, a dragon which curled down the neck-guard.

His shield, made in his own workshops, was no less magnificent. It was made of limewood and covered with hide which had been glued on to it. The rim had been clamped by a gilt-bronze strap. For the shield bowl itself, the craftsmen had exercised their highest arts without weakening the effectiveness of the weapon. At the centre was a fantastical iron boss decorated in bronze with a frieze of animals; a bird of prey and a dragon, both cast in bronze, flanked the boss and all around the rim, bronze clips both reinforced the shield and served as yet another surface for decoration. The shield was held by an iron handgrip with bronze embellishments.

His spear carrier had six spears; his horse was fitted with glittering tackle, bronze shimmering on the bridle; his own cloak, dark-red fur combed and refined to a sheen, was held with silver and bronze shoulder clasps. Thus prepared, armed and distinguished was King Ecfrith. He saw many from his kingdom whose accoutrements caught all eyes, but none approached his own. Ecfrith felt himself the Lord's anointed in war and had his poet sing some of the Psalms of David as they rode relentlessly north.

All the noble families of his kingdom were represented. Despite the plagues, this big, breeding, healthy tribe ever enriched by more coming across the sea, was swelling in number. They were the dominating people now. Such a conquest, Ecfrith thought! In less than one hundred years, his tribe had landed, fought, been knocked back but fought again, until now it owned this rich, enviable, infinitely various island, the most fertile in the world. He thanked God for it in his public voice; but privately, he saw himself as invincible, the product of the most powerful, heir to the spoils gained by the strongest.

On their journey north they were met with nothing but submission. Those who wanted to fight against them had long ago retreated further north into the hills with the small army of the Picts and their allies. Of the rest, some had fled with whatever possessions they could accumulate, and in caves and in the heart of dense woodlands or unfrequented moors, they waited for it all to pass. Others welcomed the invader and offered to help, to join, to deal in betrayal and seek out pacts. Ecfrith made a show of being merciful to this group and even welcomed them: but where settlements had been abandoned or there was suspicion of opposition he was brutal, and his road to battle was marked with funeral pyres.

On the first night they made camp just up from the shore and the feasting, the songs and the music, the dancing of thousands of flames were like a drug to Ecfrith whose eyes raked restlessly over this vast order of men, fearless, eager for battle, obeying his will.

When, on the second morning, a peacemaker came from Nechta, king of the Picts, Ecfrith had no hesitation in rejecting all he said and advising him to prepare for the wrath of God's greatest army.

'We will not go away,' the boy said. 'If you will not take us, then we will stand apart from you. But we will not go away.'

Padric looked at the boy tenderly. He was an O'Neill from the black crinkle of his hair to the high cheekbones and lanky young form.

'How old are you?'

'Nearly fourteen,' the boy said and stared boldly up at this questioner.

Probably twelve, Padric guessed; and yet the head of a gang of boys – more than a score, who had somehow got themselves out of Ireland and across to this meeting place for the allies of the Pictish king. They were a wild, even vicious lot: ragged, hard, pinch-faced. Padric felt a desperate boldness coming off them which, he thought, could be put to good use.

'You should be back in Ireland helping to rebuild the place,' said Padric, 'and comforting those who lost so much.'

'The only comfort in the world,' said the boy, steadily, 'will be the head of King Ecfrith.' His eyes were those of a killer.

Padric nodded. He had seen boys fight, boys as young as this, expert on their barebacked ponies, able to squirm through and often strike a useful blow before the stronger force of a man cut them down.

'Very well. You can fight with me,' said Padric, 'but I want you to keep on your horses.'

'Why can't we stand and fight like you?'

'Because you'll be more useful to me on horseback.'

The boy turned to his gang and addressed them in a dialect he thought that Padric could not understand. Padric smiled, but only a little: he could not have them think that he was in any way taking them lightly.

'The man wants us to do the dirty work for him,' the boy said. 'He says we're not to get off our horses. If we don't agree he'll not have us. We know that no one else will. I've heard my father talk about this one, Padric of Rheged. We'll do well to stick here. Let's agree then, and when the battle starts, we'll do what we want.'

After some dispute and comments from the others, he turned to Padric and, in the Irish tongue, said 'I've got them to agree.'

'Yes,' said Padric, in their dialect, 'I heard you. And them. If you disobey my orders, I will tell my own men to cut you down.'

The boy did not blink.

'Will we be at the front?' he asked.

'Only if, on your oath, on the memory of your father and all the O'Neills slaughtered by this man, you do as I say. Then, yes, you can be at the front.'

Once more the boy turned to his friends and this time the discussion was shorter and warmer. They were impressed that Padric knew their dialect. They wanted to be at the front. And whatever private and individual decisions they were making about the battle, the promise of being at the front of it sealed their loyalty.

Padric called one of Riderch's sons to take them to be fed and placed in the camp. He watched them go: not a fraction of them that would not fight to the death, be as fearless as only savage and ignorant boys can be. But an army? Underfed, some of them still carrying unhealed wounds from the barbarities visited on them by Ecfrith's invasion; their horses as scraggy as they were; their clothes, rags; their weapons, the merest armoury of begged or stolen spears and swords.

He rode across to Nechta, king of the Picts. Riderch and Urien were already there. Nechta and his chief lords came out of a makeshift hut and it was about a dozen men who sat down on the spread fur skins to talk about the imminent battle.

Nechta was a small man with merry blue eyes. He had fought alongside Padric several times and neither was in doubt about the other's courage and cunning. He ruled his kingdom fairly, though harshly when he thought it was demanded. With such a place of wilderness and desolation, unmapped territories giving way to fertile valleys, the narrow land between the two firths abundant in pasture and wood and game, he needed skills of diplomacy as much as the reputation of cruelty.

'I still can't fathom why he wants this battle,' he said, after the servants had taken around the cups of mead.

'He wants to be known as the man who conquered all,' replied Padric. It was taken for granted, and not resented, that at the war councils it was these two men who talked. Nechta always spoke beforehand to his own leaders and none of them resented Padric. On the contrary, they were more than happy with him, bringing as he did about seventy hardened men and twice as many again in recruits drummed up for this battle.

'We have an alliance,' said Nechta, 'it gives us both what we want. It has worked well.'

'He's back!'

One of Nechta's men pointed and they picked up the messenger and his escort moving swiftly through the small groups of men towards the council.

'Tell us all,' said Nechta when the man had dismounted, 'and,' he smiled at Padric, 'tell all of us.'

'He wants war,' said the messenger, 'he will consider no terms of peace. He would consider no increase in tribute, no increase in cattle, no promise of horses nor gold nor precious stones and no number of slaves. I was sure that even if I had said that we would submit to him and let him take the whole of our lands, he would have rejected that.'

'His forces?'

The messenger's escort had compared notes afterwards. It was their task not only to represent the forces of King Nechta and provide some sort of token in case of trouble, they were to report on the strength of the enemy.

'We think,' the messenger hesitated a little and looked across at where the escort stood, 'we think well more than five thousand. Perhaps even ten. And well armed. With spear carriers and their chariots by the hundred and—'

'Ten thousand?' Nechta looked for a denial.

'Yes.'

Nechta looked around in amazement. These were terrible odds, far bigger than he had feared. 'So they have all come. Well armed? Each would you say with their servants and slaves?'

'We thought so.'

He paused again. 'So they have all come, Padric. They think they smell a fat carcase.'

'The fewer we are, the greater the victory,' said Padric, quietly.

'We strain to be two thousand men, Padric. Some of those are raw. Some are boys. The tribes from the far north have not come, pretending on some old quarrel and hoping that distance and the mists and the mountains will keep them safe. From Ireland we have no one.' Padric thought of the boys but stayed silent. 'You have done what you can, Padric, and without you . . . but ten thousand!'

'What was the feeling?' Padric asked.

'They jeered at us,' the messenger said, fiercely. 'When we rode through the camps towards the king, they laughed and called us dead men and said they would slaughter us all within an hour and then take all that we had, our wealth, our women and children as slaves, our cattle and horses, and burn the land so that no one would be able to live there again. Nor would there be any British – only them, only their tribes would rule the land.'

'How were they dressed?'

'As if for a wedding,' the messenger replied, bitterly. 'I have never seen as many jewelled swords and embossed shields, never looked on cloaks as magnificently clasped or horses more splendidly dressed nor helmets better fashioned and decorated.'

'As if for a wedding . . .' Padric nodded. 'Were they drinking much beer?'

'Some of them seemed to have done little else since the start of the expedition.'

'They are still fighting men,' said Nechta, 'half of ours . . . ten thousand!' The number seemed to have hypnotised him.

Padric looked at Urien who had told him, in his characteristically offhand way, about the advice and prophecy of Reggiani.

'We must have a new strategy to fight this battle,' Padric said. The messenger took this as his cue to leave. 'Where were you thinking of fighting it?'

Nechta stood and indicated some low hills a mile or so away. 'I thought we could take our stand there.'

Padric nodded approvingly. 'And beyond those rises of land?'

'You're quickly into the twisting narrow mountain passes.'

'Let us go and see them,' said Padric.

Nechta took his measure for a moment only and nodded. He knew that Padric would ride with Riderch and Urien and their sons. He took his three sons and his two most powerful chiefs.

It was a few minutes ride to the foothills and then they were swept into the passes. Padric rode close to Nechta and although he never let his horse be in front of the king, it was his quietly requested directions that were followed. Soon they were on a height which commanded the passes and looked down on the hills and beyond that to the plain where their army was scattered in attendance. From that vantage, as Nechta said, it looked peaceful.

'Who would think that tomorrow so many will be dead?'

Padric nodded. He liked the musing tone of the older warrior's mind. There was little doubt that he was now steeling himself against likely defeat and possible death. Padric let him have his sad-eyed moment and then he said – 'We must draw Ecfrith and his men into these passes. From what we know, they are too many for us to risk meeting them on open ground even if we have the slight advantage of these low hills. Had we been more evenly matched,' he reassured Nechta, whose plan it had been, 'the hills would have been perfect. But let us put some men there and spread them out and make a big noise with drums so that they think we are all of us there.' He worked from Reggiani's prophecy, which fitted uncannily to his own thinking.

'Then we must seem to run away. With God's help, they will be so full of the swagger of their own strength that they will give chase. If our men split and some run up that valley,' he pointed, 'and others go up that and yet others go there, we could draw in his whole army. Other parts of our forces will be waiting behind those hills there and we could come at them not only from behind but from both sides in that valley over there. They would be hemmed in against each other, tight-packed and unable to use the width of their army, unable to have more than a small number fighting at any one time. And if we could spring some surprises . . . you and your men know these hills better than any of us; many of my warriors are hill-bred. If we have a plan and concentrate it in these narrow and rocky passes – then we could win.'

'But who,' said Nechta, 'will stand on the low hills over there and run away?'

Padric braced himself. When this idea had first dawned on him he had seen this as one of the principal objections. For which of Nechta's chieftains, let alone the king himself, would consent to seem the coward and run away at the Northumbrian charge.

'I will,' said Padric, softly. Even though he had prepared for this battle since his return from Ireland with Bega so many misty years ago. Even though he knew that this was to be the last real battle that the British could fight to prolong their existence. 'I will do it,' he repeated.

'There will be no shame in it,' said Nechta, relieved.

'No,' said Padric. 'But one thing. I will draw them in. I will pretend to be – in retreat. But at the head of that,' he pointed to the easiest of the passes, 'I will turn and we will make our stand.'

Nechta agreed. They called together their chief men and worked out the strategy in detail. By the time they had finished, it was still a simple plan, easy to transmit to every warrior, but it had developed subtleties which could harass and baffle the army of Ecfrith.

'It is a good plan,' pronounced Nechta, rather morosely. 'It could work.' But in his head the words went on and on – 'ten thousand!'

'We must get it ready now,' said Padric, 'we may have only one more day.'

Within a few hours, the army was in the passes, prising away boulders and rocks, felling trees, setting traps, building hiding places, preparing to meet force with cunning.

Padric took Urien and his son with Riderch and his two sons to the place where they would make their final stand. 'We prepare here,' he said. 'Before that, all we have to do is retreat. We can take the horses, put them behind us, draw them to us and then—'

'Run like hell!' concluded Riderch. 'Well, that will be new for us.' He paused. 'Except – twice!' He laughed. 'When we had to.'

'I'll wait for you up here,' said Urien. 'I'll not run.'

Padric had expected this. No one save himself was more respected for his fighting than Urien and for him to refuse would send restlessness throughout Padric's men. Padric had decided to ignore it.

'We must make some traps for them to slow them down,' he said, 'and then dig in here so that when we finally turn, they have no chance. First, we must get to know this valley as if we had lived here all our lives.'

The young Irish boys had attached themselves to Padric and he accepted them largely because no one else would. Their eagerness for battle he already regarded as good fortune. He had made them swear on his sword that they would obey him and with that surety he encouraged them to become part of his army. They flew to carry out his orders like starving pups pouncing on food.

The summer day was long this far north and by the time night finally came, the heavily outnumbered army had given itself the certainty that it would make Ecfrith fight.

The next day was a reprieve. Though reports had come that the vast army was near enough to strike, it held off and enjoyed the tributes of minor chieftains who came to swell its already engorged ranks. On that day, Nechta and Padric drove their men even harder until those few narrow passes were laced like a net.

Yet much of the sense of impregnability simply vanished when, at the end of that day, Ecfrith and his army appeared on the plain below and came across towards the low hills. Thousands and thousands of men. Drums beating. Threats yelled out. Horsemen galloping ahead and taunting the Picts and the British.

They set up camp and the vast plain heaved with the weight and power of them. The sunset raked across them seemingly miles deep. The dark showed up the hundreds of small fires. The threats and boasts and songs of war went on most of the night.

On the orders of Nechta and Padric, the Picts and Britons lit only a few fires and those on the lower slopes. No songs were sung. No defiance returned.

The talk was serious.

'Be careful that acting the coward doesn't turn us all into cowards,' said Urien. 'I can feel the blood running out of our feet while those over there swell themselves up and feel they will conquer the world.'

Padric looked around the circle of his own men. They were sitting around a small fire, listening carefully to Urien. Padric had never disallowed anyone from talking: just as in the Celtic church a prayer could be said anywhere by anyone and be as valid as the prayer spoken by a priest in a church, so Padric always let his warriors speak out. In the end he made the decision. And so far they had followed him.

'We have never faced an army of this size,' Urien said, 'I doubt if anyone has. They may be merry tonight but tomorrow they will fight like true warriors. See their numbers and the quality of their

arms. The like of it has never been seen on a battlefield. And they
know us. They know the men of Rheged. If we flee, will they not
smell a plot? We have always stood firm. The world knows that
we have never yielded. When we turn and run away as if we are
afraid – why should they believe it?'

He was listened to very closely. He went on, 'And fear breeds
fear. As triumph breeds triumph. If we act fear will it not grow
and settle in our minds and hearts? If they feel triumph, will it not
give them the strength of victory? My brother is a clever man. I
have not fought with a man cleverer than he is. But in this I am
against him. I say that we should stand.'

The evening was mild. Many of the men had not yet bothered
to wrap themselves in their heavy woollen cloaks. Several were
sharpening their swords and daggers or greasing them with pigs'
lard or simply rubbing them for luck and comfort. Of about two
hundred, half could be described as hardened soldiers who for some
or much of the time had ridden with the brothers. The rest were
willing enough, men and boys, but only recently brought in by
Urien and not as experienced as Padric would have wished. He
would place them in the second and third ranks when the time
came for fighting. As for the Rheged boys, he planned to deploy
them alongside the Irish boys who sat in a close group near the
low fire, some sleeping as they sat, all but two or three bleary-eyed
and rather overcome by the food and the welcome and the sudden
arrival at their goal.

'It is because they are so strong that we must use cunning,'
said Riderch. His sons, who flanked him, looked to the ground.
Padric smiled. It was clear that they were much more in favour of
Urien's argument than that of their father. Urien's wild-looking
son, called Wolf as a nickname, all but laughed at the moderating
voice of Riderch whom he liked to tease. 'When an enemy is as
big and as well armed as this,' said Riderch, 'then the pressure
of the men alone, the mass of them, can force you back and if
you have no plan you will find yourself crushed. You will be
forced back by the weight before you while those behind you
with stout hearts will press forward. You will not be able to
swing your sword arm or loose your spear and that is when the
battle's lost.'

'Who says we fall back?' asked Wolf. 'I know of battles that you
yourself have been in, with my father and my uncle when only three

of you took on odds as great as those we face tomorrow and you never thought of running away.'

'I do not think of running away now,' said Riderch evenly, easily able to ride the implied jibe of the nephew he liked, 'I am thinking of winning a great battle.'

'It is different,' said Padric, thoughtfully, 'I do not know why. But to have four men against twelve is possible: to have three hundred against twelve hundred is different; to have our two thousand against ten thousand – that is wholly different. Because there is so much which you cannot control. When your father and Riderch and myself fight alongside each other, when six or twelve or even fifty of the men around you fight together each of us knows the other; each of us knows his strength – perhaps it is that. But we cannot know the strengths of our own two thousand tomorrow and such heavy odds demand cunning. Riderch is right.'

'What will the Irish boys do?' Urien asked, playing for time, Padric thought, unwilling to let his brother down but as yet unable to go back on his vow.

'I have promised them that they can fight,' said Padric, noticing the sudden alert among some of the boys. 'And I will hold to that promise. But first, like us, they have a task. I have called a number of boys from Rheged and made two groups. Those two groups will ride along the ridges of the valley into which we will have drawn the major part of Ecfrith's army. When we reach the top of the valley, our fastest horses will take Nechta's best men around behind the ridges where they will join others and cut off the rear of Ecfrith's force and follow them in. We shall then turn and stand at a place I have chosen.

'The boys will command the ridges with boulders and stones which they can sling, and as many spears as we can afford to give them. They will drag branches to kick up dust and give an impression of a large force. All this will make Ecfrith's men reluctant to scale the steep sides. Therefore with Nechta and his men behind, and the boys harrying above, when we move forward we should press them against each other, they will not have space: that is our chance. And when the boys see that they are truly hemmed in, then they can ride down and join the battle on equal terms.'

'It is a good plan,' said Riderch. 'And with the traps and pits we have made for them, we should disrupt them so much that they might panic. Without space a man cannot fight.'

'We will appear first as fewer than we are, then as more than we are,' said Padric. He paused. 'If anyone has a better plan I am ready to hear it.'

'Do you promise that we can fight alongside you?' the Irish boy-leader, whose name was Donal, asked.

'I promise.'

'I think it is a good plan,' he said, 'because it will let us kill a lot of them win or lose.'

Padric listened as several others had their say and though he sensed that many were waiting for him to argue with Urien, he did not take that path.

'I have heard you all,' he said eventually, 'and while some of you propose other plans and there are those who dislike the plan I offer, I bind myself to it and ask you to be bound with me in it.' No one spoke against him. He looked at Urien.

'How about some sport?' Urien asked. 'Who will come with me and cause some harm in their night camp?'

There was a murmur of consent.

'We need all the men we can muster for tomorrow,' said Riderch.

'Let him go,' Padric said. 'Were I not to see Nechta I'd go myself. We've often enjoyed it before. But no more than half a dozen men, Urien, and a couple of boys to blood them. Take Donal for one.'

Urien saw that his night-attack had been absorbed and instantly shaped into the pattern Padric required. He would not be so curmudgeonly as to argue.

'That'll be enough,' he said. 'How many heads do you want?'

Padric did not reply. He too knew that the compulsion to bring back the severed head of the enemy was ancient and powerful. It was one to which he himself had yielded more than once. But he could not help his fear that it was against the greater laws of God.

'As long as you bring back your own,' said Padric, 'and that of Donal.'

The boy, hearing his name mentioned a second time and with a tinge of affection, looked at Padric with a mixture of awe and gratitude. Had Padric schemed to lash him to obedience on the next day's battlefield, he could not have done anything more effective than utter that kind word.

'I will not take you and your sons, Riderch,' Urien said. 'It would not do if so many from the royal house were to be at risk. Nor you,' he said to his own son. Wolf kept his fury to himself.

Padric left them, confident that a sufficient number would come back, that Urien would certainly be one and that the Northumbrian army would be reduced and part of it badly harassed by the harm and disruption those bone-hard guerrilla fighters would inflict in their glad, confident, night raid.

After Padric had talked with Nechta and one final time rehearsed the strategy, he wandered among the Picts before returning to his own men. Everywhere he found the same mood: quiet, even thoughtful. Among these fighters were men who had run risks as high as could be run, but who had calculated the odds. This time they had been jumped into a battle of which they had little warning and they knew that the motive of Ecfrith was nothing less than their extermination or enslavement. All of them had heard the epic poems of miraculous victories against odds and some had taken part in battles which approximated that. But these were big odds.

Yet Padric was curiously reassured. To him, the jubilation on the plain and the occasional cry of havoc indicating most likely the thrusts of Urien and others, were far less impressive than the uncommon self-absorption of these northern warriors. He believed that this nonchalantly-worn apprehension masked a deeper digging into that final will which made the indefinable difference on a field of battle.

So he moved among the few fires calmly and did not try to rouse them up. When he was recognised and greeted he stayed only for a moment and passed on. Finally he arrived at the mouth of the valley, at the point where he would stand in front of his forces; and then, at a moment which could not possibly be suspected by the enemy, he would turn tail. Not so soon as to alert them nor so late as to give them a genuine military advantage.

He had always dreamed of being so much better prepared for this final battle. His life had been the preparation. At this moment he thought of his father and regretted his impatience with one whom experience had now taught him had been a wisely brave man. There was his murder to be avenged. He smiled as if he had caught sight of his father giving him a blessing.

His brothers had been so loyal. He knew how much they had given to his ambition. He saw them and their growing sons, men now, who had known nothing but the questing trail which led from court to kingdom, battle to war, uneasy peace and pause and then back to the saddle. It had become a faith. With Riderch and Urien he felt as intertwined as three trunks of the same tree. Their sons he had taught as if they had been his own.

Bega would be sleeping or perhaps – again he smiled to himself, remembering reports of her challenging spiritual exercises – she would be praying. Who could say? If word had reached her she would be praying for his victory. And she would be one of many secured by it. Ecfrith meant to exterminate the British and the Celts with this one mighty hammer blow. Woden was being invoked by some of Ecfrith's followers. They called up their old gods more boldly now even though Ecfrith would plant a cross on the battlefield.

Padric knew that Christ would surely be on the side of the true believers. He would be on the side of his faithful servants. Not those who used Him for empires robed in church gowns or kingly furs, not those who wanted to kill all who disagreed, but those who stood up for Him in their souls.

'Into Thy hands, Oh Lord,' Padric prayed, 'we commend our spirits and our swords. Thy will be done.'

Suddenly, he was impatient for the dawn and impatient for blood.

CHAPTER EIGHTY-ONE

When they came to tell the story of the battle of Nechtansmere, the poets could choose from many versions. Never had such a battle been witnessed: never such victories and valour, such stabbings and woundings, such cunning and boldness, so many bloody deaths, such violent surprise.

Some concentrated on the story of Ecfrith, his mighty army, burnished and glittering in the early sun, drawn up in so many ranks that the fields seemed a harvest of shields and swords.

Some spoke of the appearances and disappearances and reappearances of King Nechta who with his lean bands now commanded and now abandoned the steep sided valleys here now and then gone faster than a gust of mist.

Some told of the boys on their ponies, dragging the brushwood, raising the dust, faking the form of many more than they were.

Some sang the dirges of the Northumbrians and exalted their story and let the songs of their future ring through incredulous ears.

Some of this individual warrior. Some of another. Some of the mountains of the dead. Others of the booty beyond measure of the armour and spears, daggers, swords, helmets, cloaks, torques and rings which fell on that bleak upland place like a waterfall of wonder.

All spoke and with awe of Urien and his son, of Riderch and his two sons, and of Padric who gave the battle its undying honour.

As he saw Padric and Riderch and their men racing back towards him, Urien remembered the prophecy of Reggiani. The

Northumbrians were falling into the trap.

Urien had stuck to his word and he was entrenched, alone, at the head of the valley on the spot chosen by Padric for the final stand they would make.

He itched to be down in the valley but knew that he had made the right decision because he would not have been able to run away, as those he could see down the valley were being so convincingly led to do. He would have turned and fought and others would have followed him, ruining Padric's plan.

Urien saw that Riderch led the retreat, partly to guide the men around the traps but also to give them confidence so that they believed it was not a retreat at all. Padric, he made out, with Riderch's two sons and with Wolf, was at the back, nearest the enemy. He was the tease. He was the target, he was their greatest trophy.

Ecfrith had waited to start the battle longer than Padric had anticipated. Standing at the very arrowhead of the battle force, Padric could see far to his left and to his right the wild displays of a few of the madder Celtic warriors, drink- and war-crazed, naked but for their shields and swords, strutting between the two lines, daring the Northumbrians to single combat. When a Northumbrian warrior came through to take up the challenge, the one-to-one conflict would be strictly observed. The cries of the Celts along the whole front were furious and non-stop, like a rolling scream, bubbling into a rhythm as shields were struck to emphasise and syncopate the sounds. The Northumbrian-Teutonic response was a slower roar, a deep ripple of growl, an enormous animal in its cave content to wait until it was good and ready.

The mass opposing him brought a thrill of pleasure to Padric. He looked at Riderch and saw his mood reflected. This was a most magnificent enemy. They could have hoped for nothing better than to face such splendour. The massive odds against gave Padric the very deepest satisfaction.

Now was the ultimate test.

'Praise God,' said Riderch aloud.

'Praise God,' Padric echoed.

The reports brought back from Ecfrith's morning scouts confirmed those of the previous day. That the Picts were few, the men of Rheged fewer, that there were ragtaggle boys and no great display of weaponry, that the factions seemed to have quarrelled, so queerly were they set out.

Still Ecfrith waited a while. He had no small opinion of Nechta's cunning and a loathed admiration for Padric and his brothers. He wanted to feel sure. His priests and the soothsayers had both said it was good to attack, but he bided his own time. Perhaps he waited to draw out the enjoyment. For there could be no doubt of victory and then the greatest authority in all the lands would be, uniquely, him.

He looked at the stock still British, the dancing Celts and Picts, the scatter of horses on far ridges. The sun had been up a good hour and his men were now impatient to set to and chop down this last resistance to their power.

Ecfrith looked around him. His men had dismounted and they stood stretched in lines, line on line, way across the plain. It would take only a signal from him and they would roar and walk forward and on and on and raze this pitiful opposition, let their blood into the earth.

He had never in his life felt so strong and so sure.

He raised his sword high and held it there until the roar from his men gathered behind him like a wind, like a great storm, ready to propel him by its elemental force. He slashed the air with that glittering jewel of a sword and the sound behind him broke into thousands of cheers.

The army moved forward.

Padric braced himself with exhilaration and then he forced that feeling away. It was not the time. Yet as this mass moved across the plain towards them, a tidal wave of armour and noise, of swords flicking the air like white waves on a surging ocean, of seemingly limitless men as far as the horizon, there was something in him that longed to stand and fight. It was good that Urien had not stayed with them.

He waited, waited. The noise, the presence, the size were all awesome.

He saw Ecfrith's shining helmet and wanted to rush forward and hack at the head it covered. The nearer the vast yelling roaring sword forested army came, the more mesmerised Padric grew. He wanted to challenge and fight Ecfrith there, now, now, man to man like the Celts. 'Ecfrith!' he shouted. 'Ecfrith!' But his voice was lost in the boom and rush of sound. He felt himself lean forward to step

into battle when Riderch laid a hand on him and, after a
second's wrenching indecision, he turned his back on Ecfrith
and his men.

With degrees of reluctant obedience, his men turned with him.
They began to run.

For a few moments, Ecfrith was suspicious.

Now that Padric was actually doing something, he felt a release
even if it was only the activity. He shouted and steered the men
in front of him, urging them back as skilfully as he longed to urge
them forwards.

Ecfrith's pause transmitted itself to his chief eldormen but the
push to pursue was so strong behind them that they, like their
doubts, were simply rushed away.

The larger part of this vast army funnelled its way into the
deceptively wide mouth of the valley.

In the valley, large potholes had been strewn with branches and
some of Ecfrith's men stumbled and fell; few were at all badly
injured but these and other traps disrupted the progress of the army
which gradually found itself narrowed to a more columnar shape.
The valley began to twist and from the hill tops, large boulders
were heaved down, causing more bruising and frustration to the
Northumbrians.

Padric turned and saw below him an uncomfortably compacted
mass not yet aware of the trap which would close on them. He saw
in the distance the full power of Nechta's best horsemen turn into
the mouth of the valley and begin to engage instantly, pressing
the Northumbrians further into the funnelling mass of their army
further up the narrow valley.

Above him, on the pinnacle they had chosen, stood Urien.
Around him, three planted spears each one of which carried a
head which he personally had severed in his night raid. Behind
that, as Padric had ordered, a wooden cross. Urien was grinning
hugely and his blackened teeth gave him the look of a devil in
full spate.

Eventually, all the men of Rheged regrouped. None had been
lost.

Padric rejoined them and stood between Urien and Riderch and
their sons. Padric was slightly to the fore, as was his right, and
he waited with a feeling of final joy for that full army to come
upon him and his men. Along the ridges the boys rode back and

forth like demons whirling their spears and pelting the seething Northumbrians with whatever they could lay their hands on.

Ecfrith rounded the corner and saw the men of Rheged. He held back for a few minutes until his men reformed and then, the cauldron of bodies once more restored to a frighteningly large order of warriors, he moved towards his last enemy, the man who looked so like himself.

Padric fastened his hand more tightly on his sword and held up the big shield. He knew that he would yield only to die. He had never felt more at peace or more relaxedly tense: as if he had been sculpted hard over long years for this one moment.

❧❧❧❧

Padric and his men stood for some small time – although time was collapsed and extended so often and so confusingly in battle that morning there could be no telling for how long it was that with their broad shields, the superiority of the ground and their swords they pushed back the attacks of the Northumbrians.

With every glance over the heads of the immediate warriors, Padric saw that more and more Northumbrians were crowding into the bottleneck. He sensed Ecfrith's frustration at so big a force not being able to sweep aside such a small number. For Padric's men stood at a sort of pass on a high ridge and all of Ecfrith's advantage was lost as only a few could approach.

He saw Ecfrith attempting to make a space and consult and turn this way and that, but the sides of the valley were steep and the boys were now grouped on the ridges creating whatever mayhem they could, giving an impression of strength in depth. Padric breathed easily for a few moments as the Northumbrians dragged away their dead and wounded.

Then he noticed a ripple of panic towards the back of that part of Ecfrith's army visible to him. Nechta must be pressing up from the mouth of the valley and those who had hidden behind the ridges must be racing down to crowd the enemy together immobilising and neutralising most of the men impotently locked inside their own forces.

It was the moment Padric had longed for.

The enemy was now in full view. He saw that the years of trial and disappointment had been years of testing. Now finally he had been given his reward. What had seemed to be failure was the long hardening of preparation. At last God thought him worthy of the task. His right arm was, this day, the arm of the Lord.

He turned to Urien and Riderch and nodded at them.

He moved forward.

At first Ecfrith thought that Padric had gone mad and was playing into his hands. It was then that he discovered that so many of his men were blocked in, unable to fight at all. And, when the Northumbrians attempted to retreat to find more favourable ground, they found it impossible because of the pressure from those still panting to join what they hoped was the front line.

The compact British forces began to scythe their way through, bringing about a terrible slaughter. The advantage of height was not so marked after a while but panic was beginning to grip the imprisoned Northumbrians and Padric and his men were relentless. Donal, from his hill, waited impatiently until Padric reached the agreed marker which would allow him and his band to charge down; and he and all the boys marvelled at the sight of this hardened, focused, cohesive force, forged into fighting shape over years, never for a moment letting the pressure ease as they moved forward and forward, felling the retreating Northumbrians, butting them down with their massive shields, which Padric had always insisted they have, simply trampling over the dead and wounded bodies, ignoring the carnage and somehow calmly exercising a blood-lust.

Sometimes they were checked, but once they began their move they never retreated. Although the three princes of Rheged were always in the front line, it was constantly refreshed – as Padric had instructed – by men falling back for a few minutes while others took their place. The enemy, though far more numerous, was for ever being forced down the valley and had not bargained for this mountain warfare. The mid-morning sun burned in their faces.

The Northumbrians found themselves, with relief, on a small plateau and here Ecfrith managed to restore some semblance of order and put himself, like Padric, in the centre and at the forefront. Even now, with the dead carpeted up the mountain, the Northumbrians were a daunting army and Ecfrith's call to order had steadied them somewhat.

Padric felt the excitement beat off Urien as strongly as he felt Riderch simply breathe more deeply and brace himself.

Padric singled out Ecfrith, who was no coward and knew that to kill this man Padric would be to maim his army.

It was said afterwards that when the two men met it was like two suns colliding and exploding in the heavens or two beasts of the earth shaking it with their wrath or two giants and heroes from the past born again and inhabiting these bodies. So alike as they moved around each other, swords glistening with blood, neither yielding, a space somehow kept inviolate for them though the stream and fracas of battle continued around them without pause.

Ecfrith was strong and a cunning fighter. His sword was subtler than Padric's and his shield lighter and more flexible. When Padric stumbled he thought it was his victory and lunged for the kill and wounded him in the body, but Padric rolled away and came back at him with a fury that Ecfrith could not match. Padric felt that his life, his past, his sacrifice, his ambition, his lonely journeys and long waiting and his prayers were all soldered into his sword and sword arm. As the blood seeped from his wound so he seemed to grow more and more savage.

Ecfrith began a retreat from which he had no escape. However hard he struck, the blow was taken on the shield or the sword and a violent return struck him back yet another step. No man who lived, they said, even those who slew dragons and killed sea monsters, could have withstood the power of Padric who grew into a sacred rage of implacable iron until Ecfrith was battered to the ground, where Padric showed him no mercy. When he turned he saw Donal, and the boy's eyes shone as if with the divine light of thanks. Then the boy ran across and with his short sword he hacked and hacked off the head of the fallen King.

It was the fall of Ecfrith that turned it. Harried and leaderless, outwitted and outfought, the Northumbrians began to run, to be picked off as they clambered up the ridges and fell into the traps in the lower valley. Some fighting went on until the evening, but the battle had been won before noon. Thousands surrendered and were enslaved to be sold into the southern kingdom or across the sea. The haul of arms and jewellery was beyond any imagination or reckoning.

In his monastery, Bede was told that the Picts and the British had won a victory which proved that God was on their side and they ought never to be underestimated again, for to attempt to exterminate them would surely fail.

Cuthbert, who had prophesied the outcome, led prayers at Lindisfarne and looked out from the rock at its southern tip to those remoter rocks far off where he wanted to end his days, for now, with Ecfrith gone, he felt that he had served whatever temporal purpose God had intended by their alliance.

Bega had a vision and it proved true. For in the fight with Ecfrith, Padric had been wounded and the wound proved obstinate. Padric had the energy to make Urien responsible for the settlement and division of spoils with Nechta, and then Riderch and his sons hurried him back towards Caerel.

It was there that Riderch would become king of Rheged and from there that his sons took an ever-weakening Padric to the northernmost lake where Bega, who had dreamed that he would soon be with her, waited for him.

CHAPTER EIGHTY-TWO

The wound and the journey had weakened Padric further but Bega's skills and her care returned some strength to him.

The small hospital had been empty for some months. The last victims of the plague had died and Chad had cleared and washed it down as if in unconscious preparation for the arrival of Padric.

Riderch's sons went back to Caerel. They wanted to leave behind a servant who would ride to the city immediately were there any news but Bega pointed out, firmly, that she had her own servants whenever necessary. She wanted as few people as possible to be there while she devoted herself to Padric. Even Chad felt in some way banished, but he accepted it. Bega gave her armlet to him and the few visitors were allowed to hold it and pray over it. Its powers were growing and it stood in for her; even Chad himself felt blessed simply holding the simply-spiralled artefact.

All was done to quieten the nunnery and isolate Padric and Bega. After a few days the intensity of the concentration between the two became so marked that Chad felt embarrassed even to cross her path. Rumour spread that the prince was dead but not yet released to heaven because of the power of Bega's prayer. More pilgrims came to experience this phenomenon but when Chad told them that a divine spell was being worked which it would be sinful to break, they kept their distance. So an encampment developed, about a quarter of a mile from the settlement, and people waited to see what would be the outcome of this rare and wonderful death.

For it was said in the valley that in truth Prince Padric had died on the battlefield of Nechtansmere. He himself had slain more than a hundred of the false and tyrannical Christians from Northumbria who had invaded the island from heathen parts. Then he had singled out his like-faced cousin Ecfrith and after a duel which shook the mountain and caused rocks to tremble, he had slaughtered him and sunk to his knees to praise God and been treacherously run through the side by cowardly retainers of the cruel Ecfrith. As he was about to die, his soul was arrested by a prayer from Bega that he be taken back to Rheged and back to her whose prayers had sealed this miraculous victory, they said. God was so pleased with Padric's victory that he had granted her prayer. Bega was now putting his soul on to the path of perfection and allowing Padric to give to Rheged the presence of his body which would fix truth to the victory and, in the marvel of his own life in death, show that Rheged and the British would never die.

As the days passed the encampment grew and so did the superstition that to infringe the two most holy people at the nunnery condemned one to hell. Even the water from the holy spring at the root of the cross was fetched and carried by the servant of the nunnery who was regarded as safe and unlikely to incur wrath or rouse the devils which hovered so jealously around what had become a sacred place to the British, as sacred as Reggiani's druidical grove had once been, a few hundred yards away.

The devils came like the locusts descending on Egypt. Disguising themselves as furious clouds, scudding and spinning across the lake and up the great mountain, swirling down with their wet misty bodies, crackling – some saw – above the settlement with envy and fury at the inviolable redoubt of God. Those most sensitive to the spirit wars described daily battles in the sky as devils and imps sped towards the ark of God only to be beaten away time and time again, driven off by the force of immortal love within. It was a battle watched over by God Himself, they said, when fulminous clouds parted and chutes of light brought angels down to dazzle and bewilder the devils and sudden sun was the smile on God's face as He saw His will being done.

Eventually they were vanquished and day after day a white sun sat in heaven. The earth was calmed by it. The white sun, they said, was the triumph of the prayers of Bega.

Over these few weeks, the fact of victory settled into truth and went into legend. With every day the role of Padric grew: he had been the fox, the eagle, the lion. His sword had dripped with blood and shone with the light of Christ. Those few who had scythed down the most powerful and well-armed force in history were all men to be named in heroic halls for ever more. Never to be forgotten as long as tongue laid claim to tradition, and tradition lay at the heart of the present as it had to be in every great race. Urien was given praise, Riderch and his sons and Nechta were lauded by the Picts and the wild children from Ireland became as avenging cherubs. But Padric had taken the palm. He was the one through whom God had shown His power and, as in Israel itself, marked out a chosen people.

To be there at his final death would be to share in that godly greatness and day by day the reverent crowd grew.

Bega did not think she would survive the sweetness and the torment, the pleasure at being so often alone with Padric and the knowledge that soon he would leave her. As Erebert prayed to die at the same time as Cuthbert, so Bega prayed that she might be taken with Padric.

But she knew that the prayer was selfish. She was not worthy even to trail behind him in his triumphant entry to a place in which her own status was not secure. For her love for Padric had not been conquered. In all the years of her grown life she had been divided, now for Padric, now without him. Again and again it had seemed resolved one way or the other, only to swing back again, so fierce and deep were the opposing forces. Now, it was finally resolved.

She had suspected and feared it for many years. Now she knew it as only something is known when indisputably it forms part of daily life. She felt an overwhelming love for him and the days and hours were not long enough to sit beside him, to feed him, to arrange, on one rare warm and calm day, that he be carried out and look across the lake, bathing his eyes on land he had freed. It was on that day that he gave to her and the nunnery all the land around that he could see and so her dream and the prophecy and the miraculous midsummer hail which had followed it became true.

When he became a little stronger, she wanted him to talk and in talking to her he too seemed to find peace. He drew out the characters of Urien and Riderch and others he had ridden with. He brought her tales of their victories and some defeats, of the curious peoples in this land and over the sea, their differences, their customs, their magic and their creeds. When she asked him about his early years, he would talk about his mother and about the politic flexibility of his father which he had too often impatiently mistaken for weakness. But all of this was merely a preliminary to two topics: their time together in Ireland which consumed Bega's real interest; and the future of the new kingdom under the over-arching kingship of Aldfrid.

Of their time in Ireland, Bega could never hear enough. She drew on her memory with loving tenacity. She was determined that nothing would be unexamined. Not only the high points of excitement and rarity such as the adventure on the boat; nor the scarring and inflaming end to their life there; in fact, those easy recollections were the least cherished. What Bega wanted to remember – and to have Padric remember – were tiny, mundane moments. Fleeting, meaningless, but just between the two of them. Those were what she sifted for, glad on any day to find one glistening particle of what that past life had been like. Padric indulged her and knew, as she did, that there was a life together they had both wanted but accident and circumstance and misunderstanding had taken it away from them. And God?

Yet was not God wise? he thought. Had Bega been with him, would she have become the source of miracles, the inspiration to so many that she was? And had he married her and had the children he had never known, would he have been as free and independent to go on the long, often fruitless quest which had led, in the end, through God's infinite mercy, to victory?

Yet her loving eagerness beguiled him and it was that, he thought, that kept the shallow draughts of breath coming into his body. The dark skin, the eager, clever, too-thin face, the tremulous touch and the shimmer of her body near his nourished him with pleasure. In those few weeks they had a life together.

He would talk about the future, especially about Aldfrid.

'Aldfrid will be a fine king,' Padric said. 'He sees that God's work can be done on earth through craftsmen and scholars as well as through monks and nuns. He will take on the reduced kingdom of Northumbria and invade no one with arms but everyone with words and jewelled gospels made in honour of God. There will be such a peace as we have not known since Edwin, while Riderch and his sons will be free to reign in British

Caerel. Aldfrid will enlarge the name of his kingdom through the work of eye and hand.'

'It is you who have paved the way,' said Bega, loyally, 'like John the Baptist.'

'We must not elevate ourselves,' Padric smiled and held out his hand. 'But,' he laughed, a gentle low sweet laugh, 'that *is* what I feel!' He paused and then, 'He will be a good man, Bega. You can tell all those who ask you that he will be a fine king bringing scholarship not a sword, seeking heavenly fame and not earthly glory.' Bega felt the regret – that it would be Aldfrid and not himself who would inherit the victory. He admitted it. But such dreams were over. Now she devoted herself to keeping him alive day by day.

She fed him on a soup enriched with many herbs; that and a little bread was all that he would eat, but it seemed to satisfy him and there were days when Bega almost deluded herself that he might never leave her.

On such days, she moved between the kitchen and the church and the hospital in a trance of happiness and hope. Just to have him so near. And so open to her. The scarred and grey-bearded warrior, hair thinned, face lined as if the skin had been putty and the crevices dug in with a knife, and his complexion, raw once under all weathers, quite slowly softening.

She made no secret now, neither to God, nor to Christ nor to Padric nor to herself that she loved him. She would sit for hours reading to him and holding his hand while they talked, or simply holding his hand. As the days went on and he ebbed so steadily, serenely but relentlessly away, she would say her prayers with him, from lauds to compline, praying also that God would forgive her for not going into the church but taking heart from what Donal had taught her so many years ago: that prayer was good wherever the need or the inspiration struck. And so the time that she most feared came on them: Padric began a marked and unmistakable decline.

Bega's strengths of denial which had helped her refuse Padric for so many years now at last worked in his favour. For she could force herself to stay awake and concentrate every atom of her attention on the wounded, dying man and ease him through the last going. When he grew cold, she lay beside him as he had done once for her, and she held him for warmth and her hands brushed across his cold face and her mouth kissed its sleeping skin again and again. When he stirred and woke, she left the narrow bed and brought some gruel which was always warm in the iron pot on the low fire. He would take one or two sips and nod his thanks.

The day came which she knew would be the final day of Padric on earth. The white sun had gone and the morning sky was brooding with jagged grey-black clouds massing over the hills. Something of Bega's growing fear and concern over the last few days had transferred itself to those who had come to witness the passing of their earthly saviour. When Bega glanced across the fields she saw the glittering of fine cloth and fine arms and jewellery. Some of the noblemen in Rheged had arrived and requested that they might come and bid farewell to Padric.

Bega struggled between the jealousy of her own proprietorial love and what was right. She knew that King Aldfrid had come, on his way to Bamburgh to be crowned king of Northumbria, but even he would wait. She told Padric that Aldfrid was in the encampment beyond.

'Let him come,' said Padric, 'and some others. Let them come now and be gone by the middle of the day.'

Bega called for Chad and the king led over those who had made the journey. He, Urien and Riderch, who had been made ruler in Caerel, went into the small hospital and took their blessing from Padric. Some others, those who had fought near him at Nechtansmere, and those who had ridden with him for many years, were shown in too. Bega kneeled at the foot of his bed and the bond between the two was so very strong that none, not even Aldfrid, stayed more than the few moments. Bega prayed for patience as these men came one after another to acknowledge Padric's greatness and ask him to bless them. When they had all seen him, all he had the strength to see, they pulled back and, under the guidance of King Aldfrid, they kept a vigil. They would wait until it was time and, with full pageant, bear his body back to Caerel where more and bigger crowds were gathering daily to see him buried in the grounds of the monastery just inside the west wall.

Now she was alone and would be until he left her. The murmur of prayers came from across the fields. The lapping of the lakeside water was loud as the wind which carried the prayers slapped the water. Many swore that they saw the clouds part and a shaft of moonlight set down a stair flanked by angels ready to escort the warrior on his last triumphant walk to join the greater army of God in His heavenly kingdom.

Bega sat beside him and held his hand which now and then clutched at hers, clutched convulsively, reminding her of his life, of their life. All sounds save his softening and slowing breath dissolved and again and again she bent to kiss his cold brow and murmur his name. Inside her breast, her heart felt as if it were being squeezed and dilated both until it seemed to swell into her throat, all but choking her with the strain of it. Oh that she could be taken in the same hour and be joined with him at last in that!

He opened his eyes. In the rushlight she saw his gaze blank at first, as if puzzled. Finally the gaze, a faint tender look, found her own eyes and held her for a few moments. And then he gave her the most serene and loving smile.

It was that which brought her to tears for the first time since he had been brought to her from the battlefield, and she wept uncontrollably as his eyes closed, his last breath was drawn and his soul was seen to ascend to its eternal reward and rejoin its maker.

CHAPTER EIGHTY-THREE

As a just punishment, Bega thought, she was made to live on for many years. She did not complain to God in her prayers or blame anyone but herself in her heart. She went about her business as she had done before, more powerful now because all the lands in the valley belonged to her, but no different in her demeanour or in the work that she did. There were suggestions that the nunnery should be enlarged and other nuns come and join Bega but she was reluctant for that to happen and somehow, at the last moment, she always avoided it. The place was now so rich in memories of Padric that she did not want it invaded by the lives of others. Nor did she want anyone to hear the sobbing which followed her last prayers night after night. She pronounced herself content with the role of near-hermit and because of her spiritual status, she was allowed to have her own way.

She left the valley on three occasions only. The first was two years after the death of Padric. Erebert had died on the same night and, it was thought, at the same time as Cuthbert. Cuthbert's death on his outpost island had been signalled by beacons across the sea to Lindisfarne and thence to Bamburgh. No one could recall the passing of a soul so great and tales of the miracles which had increased around this holy man multiplied from after his death.

Bega herself still continued as a fount of miracles and holiness. In the re-established kingdom of Rheged, her fame was sure and both the armlet and the holy water continued to be a source of healing and blessing.

She helped to bury Erebert on his island. Chad dug the grave and Bega read the service over it. Around the island there were those who feared to join such a distinguished congregation. For Aldfrid had sent over courtiers and Riderch had supplemented them with his own. Those who lived nearby came in their coracles and made a second boundary around the island, their boats scarcely moving on the calm lake as the hermit's body became part of the island on which it had fought against temptation for so long.

It was eleven years later that she left the valley again and this time it was in response to a summons. During those years she had done what she thought the Lord wished her to do, knowing that He neither would nor should forgive her for putting Padric before His only begotten Son. She had seen Padric's prediction come true: Aldfrid was indeed a new Arthur. There was peace. Scholars and craftsmen in stone and manuscript and illumination came from Ireland and all over the world to be at the court of this scholar king and the kingdom of Northumbria became the place where learning was most cherished and the arts most cultivated. From here it would spread back out into the darkest places. The word of God was safe. The summons took her to the magnificent court at Bamburgh.

'It was because of Padric that all this was saved,' said Aldfrid who had called her to his court. 'Without him and without Cuthbert who took the word to where it had never been; without those two soldiers of God, you would not now be surrounded by so many young monks and teachers whose aim and success is to gather from the past the truths and wisdom of God and ensure that it will be passed on to the future.' Aldfrid took Bega's arm. 'Now you must see a miracle.'

Without saying more, Aldfrid took Bega out of Bamburgh and set off for Lindisfarne, with no more than half-a-dozen men in his guard and even they were more for ceremony than protection. The tide-table had been consulted and they passed over the causeway immediately to what had become part of the mainland. Aldfrid took Bega straight to the monastery.

As they came through the gate, Bega saw that there was great excitement among the monks. She looked around eagerly at this sacred Lindisfarne. She saw that it was wholly organised for prayer and scholarship and sustenance. All she had heard of its austerity and simplicity appeared to be true. Some of the buildings were less impressive than the cluster which made up her own settlement. Chad, who had scarcely left her side since the outset of their journey, was rather disappointed that Lindisfarne, of such fame, should seem so workaday. But Aldfrid told them that in one of

those small buildings the Gospels were being illuminated in rare
and brilliant colours in honour of Cuthbert. He himself would give
gold, silver and jewels for the cover of the Gospels.

They came to the place where Cuthbert was buried.

Bishop Eadbert was waiting for them.

'Has she been told?' he asked.

'No,' said Aldfrid, 'it is right that you should tell her.'

'We have kept the news to this island,' said the bishop, 'save of
course for the king. But rumours are spreading and we must tell
the people soon.'

They went into a church, much larger than Bega's own church
but no less plain. Here, she thought, Aidan, Colman, Cuthbert
and even the bestriding Wilfrid had preached. From here God
had been taken out into the wilderness which was now sown with
His words.

They walked towards the altar and stopped just below the
chancel step.

'We decided to exhume the body of Cuthbert,' Eadbert
explained, 'in order to rebury him in a more conspicuous place.
His fame is so great that pilgrims are coming from everywhere.
There are shrines throughout the kingdom. When this decision
was made, I was approached by an old monk who had visited
Cuthbert on his island just some weeks before his death. He said
that the saintly Cuthbert had told him that one day he would be
exhumed and reburied. Then, he had prophesied, a miracle would
be seen. The monk was to tell no one until this took place. Then
he must go to the bishop and say that this had been foretold by
Cuthbert and he had said that Bega from Rheged must be sent for
to witness the miracle. If she did not witness it and bless it then
its power would quickly fade. She alone would have the truth of
it and after she had blessed it, God would make use of the miracle
and the relics and saintliness of Cuthbert for hundreds, thousands
of years until the Last Judgment.'

Both king and bishop looked at Bega with undisguised curiosity.
What was it about this woman – the first woman ever to be
allowed on Lindisfarne – that could cause Cuthbert to put her
in the position of arbitrator of his future state? Aldfrid, who had
last seen her with Padric and understood the secular love she had
for him, was doubly intrigued that this old, slight, quick-featured
woman should command two such different and influential men.

'We opened the stone coffin,' said the bishop, indicating to the waiting servants that this action be repeated. They grasped the thick heavy slab of stone which formed the lid and shuffled themselves into position for the effort of lifting it. 'And we expected the flesh to be dust and the clothes rotted. But look!' He gave the sign and the men drew back the great stone lid.

Cuthbert's body was incorrupt. He looked not dead but sleeping. The limbs were soft to the touch. The clothes in which he had been buried were fresh.

Around her, king, bishop, followers and servants fell to their knees, some in terror.

Bega leaned over the body and smiled to herself. The nails were still long and curled. And had his hair even grown? She reached out and pressed her hand through the cloak until her hand gently printed itself on his heart. There she rested it and prayed. In a few moments she felt the sliver of the True Cross pressing inside Cuthbert's flesh towards her hand.

'When Cuthbert is seen like that,' said Aldfrid, quietly, 'he will convert all the heathen in the world. Just as Padric gave us the earthly power so Cuthbert, blessed in this way that no one has ever seen, will show the people the power of God and the word of God will never be defeated.'

So this, Bega knew, was the final purpose of that fragment of the cross given to Donal more than fifty years ago. This had been the true fulfilment of God's plan. 'Praise Him,' she murmured. 'Praise Him.'

Yet Bega had the sense of a most terrible loss. Life seemed to drain out of her and she lifted away her hand. She had served Cuthbert's purpose and the greater purpose of God through Cuthbert. Her own life had been destined for this only.

'What have you to tell us?' asked Bishop Eadbert.

Bega shook her head.

'What did he mean by insisting that you should see him and how did he know you would live and what is it that you have seen that we have not seen?'

'I see what everyone will see,' said Bega eventually, and speaking very slowly as if in pain. 'I see a man who was tormented by the forces of the devil and tormented himself in response. I see one who was frightened at times of the hard way he had chosen. He was a single light in darkness for so long and at times he seemed possessed because he did not know what was being demanded of him but he knew that he must go on. I saw the best and the worst of him. What he wanted me to tell you was to show him to the people. I know that he will never perish. Churches will be built around him until the Day of Judgment and miracles will flow from him. He needed a messenger and I was chosen. Cuthbert will never die. Nor will his church. Nor will the word of God and the teachings of his saints.'

Bega then walked back to the west door and out into the gust of fine, rain-sprayed wind and looked on the sea which was beginning to race in once more to shut off Lindisfarne as an island.

It was more than a year later that Bega left her settlement for the last time. With Chad she had taken a long route back after Lindisfarne. Chad had gone to Jarrow, again without revealing who he was. He had discovered that Bede was considered already to be an exemplary monk and an unusually brilliant scholar. Chad's pride was almost unbearable but the report made him even more determined not to confront Bede. He saw the young man's profile. He had changed, Chad thought, become quite solemn and contained in his movements and completely absorbed in a world from which Chad was excluded. The old man's love for the boy had never faltered but he knew that this was the last time he would seek to go to the monastery at Jarrow.

At Hexham they had stopped and heard the singing of the Gregorian chant which Wilfrid and Benedict had recently introduced into Northumbria. Chad thought that the sound was that which must fill heaven. Even Bega, who was dismayed by the grand constructions at Hexham just as she was distressed by the endless power struggles and lawsuits and land seizures of Wilfrid, was touched by the ancient thread of song which came from such distant lands and different cultures, like so much else in Aldfrid's new kingdom, to enrich what once were such plain lines.

In Caerel they stayed in the small monastery and here Bega was loath to leave. She went to Padric's grave many times a day and stood there in silent prayer until her attendance became a small wonder in the city and people would stand off and watch this example of pure devotion.

Finally they returned to their nunnery and on that very night Bega told Chad that she intended to go back to Ireland.

'When I have sorted out everything here,' she said, 'I want to go back the way I came and go to Inishboffin and . . .' she did not complete the sentence. Chad thought she would have said 'and die there'. But that was not so. Bega stopped herself from saying 'and look out at the sea and back across to the place where I was born and once had such great happiness without knowing it was so.'

As the year went on, her urgency grew. She still had some fears that the world might end soon and she wanted to be in Ireland for that. The cessation of plagues and the peace brought about by Aldfrid had lessened her anxiety greatly, but Bega's fear had been hard forged during the four plagues and, despite her prayers and her belief in the ultimate goodness of God, she did not see why the world deserved to last much longer. Although the piety and good works of Aldfrid and many of his men, of the bishops and monks, nuns and scholars, were beyond question, the world of men and women, as she saw this even from her enclosed and protected space, was not a worthy creation to offer to such an Almighty God.

In the last year of the century, in the early summer, when she was about to set off, Bega contracted a violent cold which punished her body and all but sealed up her lungs. It was, she thought, a bitter but deserved trick of the devil. She had dared to imagine that the world would end, without any authority in the Bible or any true indication from God. She was leaving her parish to go back to the west of Ireland, not for religious motives but for a secular emotion and because she was also drawn in a pagan and animal way to return to her beginnings. This was not doing the work of God as she had vowed. Therefore, seizing on her weakness, the devil had entered in and now he squatted on her heart.

A mild and comfortable summer helped her recover, though she put down her restoration to the prayers of Chad and the many other voices in the valley which had been raised to heaven on her behalf. It was all the more painful, then, to leave such loyal people when she decided in the autumn that she would stick to her plan and still go to Ireland, despite the threatened turn in the weather.

Everything was arranged as it should be. Six nuns came over from Whitby. A final service was held. Those who had known her a long time, some who had known her all their lives, came down to the lakeside the morning that she left and shivered in the raw air as Chad loaded the pack horse and Bega, stiffly, carefully, mounted the other. She rode around the settlement and stopped and dismounted in front of the cross. There she lay on the ground and kissed the earth.

Their journey of departure was watched all along the valley floor, and stories were told of the years of her time there, the healing, the miracles, the death of Padric, the plagues, the sweep of war, the wonder of her learning, the brilliant boy, the fearlessness and tirelessness of the slight, fierce Irishwoman who would go into the heart of forbidden woods or climb the big mountain itself in her quest to serve God.

Soon they were turning up into one of the high passes and the wind from the north east which had been biting but bearable turned harsher and cold. It was as if the air tightened. Chad wanted to turn back but Bega had taken good advice and knew that there was time to get over the worst of the pass and find refuge well before nightfall. It was not yet midday.

The first snow fell in large soft flakes innocently, stroking the face, lying lightly. They went on. The snow fell more thickly and more rapidly. In an instant they were in the middle of the clouds themselves. Chad called a halt but to stand still was to become a column of snow which began to freeze. Bega had seen the path ahead, empty of any refuge, bare of any large rocks which would have provided cover, but looking safe enough, a slow, upward-wending road trodden into the side of a steeply uprising mountain. To the other side was a deep gulley. Higher up, Bega thought, they might encounter rocks which would give them shelter.

They went on, cautiously but determinedly, the snow now so thick that Bega felt dressed in it. Chad led with the packhorse; to Bega he gave the end of a rope fastened to the horse's load.

Soon the snow was so heavy, and the weight of it so impenetrable, that Bega called Chad to stop. He was touching her before she saw his outline.

'We must stand between the horses,' Chad shouted, 'and wait.'

Bega saw some sense in it. Chad swung the packhorse around

and the two horses stood head to tail, with Bega and Chad between them, getting some degree of protection from the wind and snow and some warmth from the horses.

'Let us pray,' said Bega, even as she knew that this was the last and just punishment. Cold had been sent to her, cold on cold to show how far she was from the warm love of God.

'Our Father . . .' she began, and Chad joined in. But after three more prayers, they fell silent. The snow was beginning to rise up around them, threatening to bury them as it was burying everything else on the high mountain.

'We must walk on,' Chad shouted and he took the bridle of his packhorse and turned it around into the snow and where he remembered the path had been.

But he had lost it.

After no more than two score paces, Chad found that he had wandered far out to the edge of the verge marking the plunge into the deep gulley. He was knee-deep in the snow, forcing a path through it for himself and his horse which would make it easier for Bega. Then the ground seemed to give way under him. He held on to the horse to save himself but the horse too began to slide on what was suddenly a thinner thatch of snow already iced over, down into the steep and treacherous gulley.

Bega had stopped as soon as she had heard Chad's first shouts. Now his cries and the panic noises of the horse disappeared into the bitter snowy gloom. She called his name again and again but there was no answer.

She crossed herself and prayed for his soul.

She turned her horse back but knew herself to be lost and she let the beast itself take her where it would.

When the horse stopped through weariness, Bega dismounted. The only way, she thought, was to keep walking.

Sometimes the clouds lifted a little and she saw the rise of the mountain, white as goosedown, immense as the sea. Then they would settle once more and she was in a blanket of cloud and snow, with the wind whipping at her face and even the heavy wool of her cloak unable to withstand the force of the cold.

She did not know whether she was growing tired or being borne up by invisible hands but her head which had ached from the bitter, icy blast began to lighten and sing in its own strange way and she looked for somewhere she could sleep. Just for a few moments, just until the snow passed by and she was a little rested.

Never more, she knew now, would she be able to think of Padric. Thinking itself and remembering, though full of pain, had kept him alive. Now no more. She lay down. 'Into Thy hands, oh Lord,' she whispered, 'I commend my spirit.' It was so comfortable in this deep bed of snow. 'Glory be to the Father and to the Son and to the Holy Ghost.' Just for a few moments. Oh Padric!

She slept.

She woke up at the touch of his hand. There, standing above her, lit by a shaft of sun which pierced the still swirling snow, was Padric. He was young as he had been on the sea and smiling as he had in their very last moments together. He held out his hand. Without any pain now, she reached up and clasped it. Gently, he pulled her to her feet and turned into the sun.

'As it was in the beginning, is now and ever shall be, world without end. Amen.'

AFTERWORD

The following characters are freely based on historical fig-
ures: Erebert, Prince Ecfrith, King Oswy, Prince Alchfrid,
Cuthbert, Princess Aetheldreda, Queen Eanfled, Abbess Hilda,
Tuda, Wilfrid, Bishop Colman, Cuddha, Prince Aldfrid, Bishop
Agilbert, Bishop Cedd, Agatho, Abbot Coelfrid, Bishop Eadbert.
(I have used the titles which obtain on our first meeting the charac-
ters. Cuthbert, Wilfrid and Hilda, for instance, all became saints.)

Bede arrived at the new monastery of St Peter at Wearmouth
in 680, when he was seven. His background is unknown although
it has been assumed that he came from well-born or well-educated
people within the Northumbrian rule. Two years later he transferred to St Paul's at Jarrow, where he remained for the rest of
his life and produced his magnificent history, his biographies, his
commentaries and his poetry.

There is still only the sparsest historical evidence for the existence of King Arthur. But the latest and most scrupulous contem-
porary research, N.J. Higham's, for instance, tentatively suggests
that if he lived at all then he was born in the Solway area in
the kingdom of Rheged which embraced the extreme north-west
of present-day England and the south-western part of Scotland.
Carlisle (Caerel in the novel), an ancient Roman town of some
significance near the western end of Hadrian's Wall, would have
been his capital city. Padric, though an invented character, is a
plausible prince in that period and could have had a fair claim to
Arthur as one of his ancestors.

The O'Neills were a kingly and powerful clan in Ireland.

Cathal and his household, like the immediate family of
Dunmael, is an invention, though I have worked to give them
historical underpinning.

Like so very many from centuries where records are so fragmented and tantalising, Bega hovers between the historical and
the mythic. Some scholars have no doubt of her existence and
point to place names and the great local strength of her miraculous
powers. Others see her as more of a legend, even though the
few facts to hand are more substantial in her case than in many
other cases. Bega's flight from Ireland has been variously dated
– the middle of the seventh century is one of the contenders.
There are place names – most notably St Bees, the harbour
where she landed – in West Cumbria. Her armlet or brace-
let continued to inspire miracles until about 1300. Her story
was first written down – as were many others – in the twelfth
century.

My use of place names is wholly idiosyncratic. When writing
the novel I went along with what was convenient to me at the
time. Connachta sounded fine and so I used that; I thought the
seventh-century names for Carlisle were uncomfortable and so I
used Caerel, a local dialect name for the city; sometimes I used the
name of the time, as with Nechtansmere, and on other occasions I
used the present name, as with Jarrow and Hexham. Having done
that for my own convenience I decided that it would be equally
convenient for others.

Many of the historical events of the second half of the seventh
century are used in the book. These include the territorial, even
imperial, ambitions of King Oswy and his son Ecfrith; the desperate resistance of the Celts, the British and the Picts to the invading
Teutonic forces; the missions of the Celts throughout Europe and
into Northumbria and south through Lindisfarne; the Synod of

Whitby in 664 and the pursuit of the Celts thereafter with 'a hostile sword' (Bede); the eclipse which followed the Synod in the same year and the four plagues which arrived over the next two decades. Ecfrith did invade Ireland against all advice in 684 and in the next year at Nechtansmere in Forfar he experienced a wholly unexpected defeat by forces greatly outnumbered by his own army. He was killed in that battle, after which, Bede reports, 'a portion of the British themselves recovered their freedom which they have now preserved for about forty-six years'. (He was referring to the year in which he wrote the book.) The kingdom of Northumbria was reduced but ruled by the scholarly King Aldfrid, who had been brought up in Ireland. The melding of the mongrel race which became 'the English' was under way.

In the lives of Hilda, Cuthbert and Wilfrid in particular, the characterisations are my own, but I have used Bede's account as a source for many of their actions and achievements, their miracles and their struggles. The translations of J.F. Webb and D.H. Farmer in the Penguin edition were used for the *Life of Cuthbert* by Bede, of *Wilfrid* by Ennius Stephanus, and for the outline of the *Voyage of St Brendan*. I drew strongly on Bede for the central debate in the Synod of Whitby.

It was claimed – in Bede's lifetime, and he talked to those who had seen it – that Cuthbert's body was discovered 'incorrupt' about ten years after his death. This, together with his miracles, made him one of the greatest and most inspirational saints in the European Early Middle Ages. His remains are now in Durham Cathedral which was built to honour and celebrate him. The Lindisfarne Gospels were also created in his name.

The great debt for the largest part of the historical access to this elusive, largely unknown but, in my view, most dramatic period in our history is to the Venerable Bede's *A History of the English Church and People*. I used the Penguin edition, translated by Leo Sherley-Price and revised by R.E. Latham, for whose work I am immensely grateful.

This book is a work of fiction. While I enjoyed both using and following the history, I 'made' the characters – even the historical figures – as I wanted them to be. I tried not to misrepresent the history but I always put the fiction first.

✠✠✠✠

I would like to list some of the books which I found most helpful.

F.M. Stenton: *Anglo Saxon England*
Peter Hunter Blair: *The World of Bede* and *An Introduction to Anglo-Saxon England*
N.J. Higham: *The Kingdom of Northumbria A.D. 350–1100* and *The Northern Counties to A.D. 1000* and, with Barri Jones, *The Carvetii*
Charles Thomas: *Celtic Britain*
Dorothy Whitelock: *The Beginnings of English Society*
Angela Cave Evans: *The Sutton Hoo Burial*
Janet Backhouse: *The Lindisfarne Gospels*
Barry Cunliffe: *The Celtic World*
Ann Hagen: *A Handbook of Anglo-Saxon Food*
Michael Richter: *Mediaeval Ireland*
M.B. Salu (translator): *The Ancrene Riwle*
Charles Arundel Palmer: *The Ancient Crosses at Gosforth, Cumberland*
Timothy Fry O.S.B. (ed): *The Rule of St. Benedict in English*
Louis J. Rodrigues: *Anglo-Saxon Verse Charms, Maxims and Heroic Legends*
Kathleen Herbert: *Spellcraft, Old English Heroic Legends*
Joy Chant: *The High Kings – Arthur's Celtic Ancestors*
The Transactions of the Cumberland and Westmoreland Antiquarian and Archaeological Society especially those on Bega, by L.A.S. Butler and John M. Todd.

Peter Hunter Blair and N.J. Higham's books were the ones I returned to most frequently, next to Bede himself. I owe a particular debt to Michael Alexander of St Andrew's University, whose translations of *Old English Riddles from the Exeter Book*, *Beowulf* and *The Earliest English Poems* (including *The Dream of the Rood*) were of considerable interest and value. On Lindisfarne, in Durham Cathedral, in Inishboffin and Carlisle there were several local pamphlets, most often anonymous, which were useful.

I was lucky to be helped along the way by many people, including Frank Delaney, who covered some of the same territory for his *Walk Through the Dark Ages*. The Benedictine Community at Douai Abbey where I stayed for a few days welcomed me warmly.

My thanks go to Dr Lesley Young for her advice, especially on Bega's state of mind and memory during and after the sequence in the cave. I am indebted to my good friend Julia Matheson for her help throughout. I want to thank Dr Alan Crosby, historian, of Liverpool University, for his reading list, his help on the Irish side and his reading of the final version, and Dr William Rollinson, author and historical geographer, whose own work on Cumberland and Westmoreland I have read and admired for years. Finally, gratitude to Professor Lawrence Stone, who introduced me to this period in some inspiring autumnal tutorials in his rooms in Wadham College.

When I was at school, I used to cycle with friends into the Lake District, usually to the most northerly of the lakes, Bassenthwaite. There we would hire a boat and row across to a small, dramatically isolated church on the western edge of the lake. I did not realise then that such lonely churches had often been built on the site of a hermit's dwelling or the settlement of a holy man or woman.

I grew interested in the Dark Ages in 1958, when I was nineteen and in my first term at university, reading History. We had more or less skipped the years 410–1066 at school and certainly none of the riches and power of the Early Middle Ages was known to me before that autumn in Oxford.

At that particular age and time I was eagerly open to it. I was a fully committed and practising Christian of a Church of England variety which would nowadays be thought of as Roman Catholic. I was interested in scholarship and I had come south from the Celtic fringe of the north-west of England which I now discovered had been the land of saints, scholars, miracles, abbeys, gospels, crosses and the survival of the British.

Over the years I tried to write about the period and set about reading for it seriously in the early eighties. The central subject was obvious – although I did not recognise it as such until ten years ago. It was St Bega.

The tiny lakeside church I visited as a boy, which may be built on an older foundation, dates from the pre-Norman period. Parts show evidence of Saxon or Norse construction. It was, and is, dedicated to St Bega and, incidentally, the lake is that which is said to have inspired Tennyson (who stayed nearby) for several of the key passages in *Morte d'Arthur*.

It has become one of my favourite haunts in the whole of the Lake District. Even today it is not at all difficult to spend hours around and about the church in virtual isolation. Certain places do have an undeniable spirit – life in such a place seems to reach into the past, to be mysterious and yet, somehow, quite open and accessible. St Bega's by Bassenthwaite has that for me.